3 COMPLETE NOVELS

A

Lloyd Alexander

COLLECTION

◆

The Arkadians

◆

The Remarkable Journey of Prince Jen

◆

The Iron Ring

DUTTON CHILDREN'S BOOKS ◆ NEW YORK

The Arkadians
Copyright © 1995, 2001 by Lloyd Alexander

The Remarkable Journey of Prince Jen
Copyright © 1991, 2001 by Lloyd Alexander

The Iron Ring
Copyright © 1997, 2001 by Lloyd Alexander

This collection copyright © 2001 by Dutton Children's Books

CIP Data is available.

Published in the United States by Dutton Children's Books,
a division of Penguin Putnam Books for Young Readers
345 Hudson Street, New York, New York 10014
www.penguinputnam.com

Printed in USA
ISBN 0-525-46777-7
1 3 5 7 9 10 8 6 4 2

The ARKADIANS

1

BOOKS BY LLOYD ALEXANDER

The Prydain Chronicles
The Book of Three
The Black Cauldron
The Castle of Llyr
Taran Wanderer
The High King
The Foundling

The Westmark Trilogy
Westmark
The Kestrel
The Beggar Queen

The Vesper Holly Adventures
The Illyrian Adventure
The El Dorado Adventure
The Drackenberg Adventure
The Jedera Adventure
The Philadelphia Adventure

Other Books for Young People
The Fortune-tellers
The Remarkable Journey of Prince Jen
The First Two Lives of Lukas-Kasha
The Town Cats and Other Tales
The Wizard in the Tree
The Cat Who Wished to Be a Man
The Four Donkeys

The King's Fountain
The Marvelous Misadventures of Sebastian
The Truthful Harp
Coll and His White Pig
Time Cat
The Flagship Hope: Aaron Lopez
Border Hawk: August Bondi
My Five Tigers

Books for Adults
Fifty Years in the Doghouse
Park Avenue Vet (with Dr. Louis J. Camuti)
My Love Affair with Music
Janine Is French
And Let the Credit Go

Translations
Nausea, by Jean-Paul Sartre
The Wall, by Jean-Paul Sartre
The Sea Rose, by Paul Vialar
Uninterrupted Poetry, by Paul Eluard

The ARKADIANS
Lloyd Alexander

DUTTON CHILDREN'S BOOKS / NEW YORK

Library of Congress Cataloging-in-Publication Data
Alexander, Lloyd.
The Arkadians / by Lloyd Alexander.—1st ed.
p. cm.
Summary: To escape the wrath of the king and his
wicked soothsayers, an honest young man joins with a
poet-turned-jackass and a young girl with mystical powers on a
series of epic adventures.
ISBN 0–525–45415–2
[1. Fantasy.] I. Title.
PZ7.A3774Ar 1995
[Fic]—dc20 94–35025
CIP AC

Published in the United States by Dutton Children's Books,
a division of Penguin Books USA Inc.
375 Hudson Street, New York, New York 10014

Editor: Ann Durell
Designed by Claudia Carlson
Printed in USA

5 7 9 10 8 6

For *hopeful storytellers*
and *fond listeners*

Contents

The ARKADIANS

MT. PANTHEA

Sanctuary of the
Lady of Wild Things

Land of
the Horse Clan

Village of the Goat Folk

N

MT. LERNA

Cave of
Woman-Who-
Talks-to-Snakes

Metara

TAUROS

NAXOS

ARKADIA

CALLISTA

Map by Claudia Carlson

I

King Bromios and Woman-Who-Talks-to-Snakes

This is the tale of a jackass and a young bean counter, a girl of marvels and mysteries, horsemen swift as wind, Goat Folk, Daughters of Morning, voyages, tempests, terrors, disasters. And the occasional rainbow.

But all this is yet to come, and our tale begins with King Bromios and Woman-Who-Talks-to-Snakes.

So: When Bromios was chosen king of Arkadia, long custom obliged him to seek a prophecy from the oracle pythoness, Woman-Who-Talks-to-Snakes, in her cave at Mount Lerna. Bromios, for his part, would have gladly avoided the whole squirmy business. He was a heavy-fisted, barrel-chested man with a big voice and a hard head; no coward, certainly, but any thought of snakes made his flesh creep.

His royal soothsayers, Calchas and Phobos, insisted.

"Allow me to remind Your Majesty," said Calchas, "when our Bear tribe forefathers came to Arkadia, they found a shocking state of affairs: a country governed by councils of women, all devoted to that figment of female imagination, the Lady of Wild Things. Knowing it only proper for men to command and women to obey—a simple truth that women seem incapable of grasping—our heroic warriors overthrew the councils and made themselves lords of the land. Since then, your subjects have enjoyed the rule of kings—guided, naturally, by the unerring advice of their soothsayers."

"The women, however, cling foolishly to their old ways," added Phobos. "They still believe in the Lady of Wild Things; and the pythoness is venerated as highly as the Lady herself."

"Seeking your prophecy is a mere formality," said Calchas, waving a plump, bejeweled hand, "observed only because the women expect it. Otherwise, they would be most unsettled."

"They're women," said Bromios, "so what does it matter?"

"An alarming number of men also revere the Lady." Phobos pressed his thin lips and shook his head. "Which is absurd, since she does not exist. Has any of us ever seen her? Received the slightest sign from her? Of course not."

"What better proof?" said Calchas. "If she existed, I and my dear colleague would, surely, be the first to know."

Calchas and Phobos were authorities in such matters. They were skilled at finding signs and portents in stars, clouds, flights of birds, and chicken gizzards. On the death of the old king, the pair consulted one of the oracular chickens, nicely roasted, understood that Bromios was to be monarch, and so proclaimed him.

"As for the Lady's followers," Calchas went on, "their devotion to her lessens their devotion to Your Majesty. They should be encouraged—vigorously encouraged— to see the error of their ways. This, I foretell, will happen when the time is ripe. At the moment, it would be imprudent to rub them the wrong way."

"Your Majesty must visit the pythoness," said Phobos. "A question of state policy."

"Policy, policy, whatever that is," grumbled Bromios. As the old king's war leader, he preferred yelling and smacking heads to sitting on a throne. More comfortable using his fists instead of his brains, he had been tempted to decline the honor. Calchas and Phobos promised that he would seldom, if ever, have to think at all. Few kings did. It was not required.

"I won't have to touch any snakes?" said Bromios.

"No, no, no." Calchas brushed aside the notion.

"Nothing like that. You go, you listen to some nonsensical babbling, and you come back. Goodwill all around, and everyone satisfied."

"You're sure about the snakes?" said Bromios.

Next morning, Bromios rode the half-day's journey from his palace in Metara to Mount Lerna, his bodyguard galloping with him, Calchas and Phobos carried in litters at the rear. As the soothsayers advised, Bromios wore full regalia: the bearskin cloak, the necklace of bear teeth and claws, the bear's head helmet. His leather leggings were bound with thongs, his thick-soled boots made him look even taller than he was. At his side hung the great two-handed sword. Bromios himself had cheered up and felt royally scornful of any stupid old hag of a snake-woman.

When the road ended, he had to climb off his horse and go tramping down an overgrown, winding path. Calchas and Phobos, on either side, guided him deeper into the woods. The weather had turned mild, though streaks of snow still whitened the upper slopes of Mount Lerna. The Sky Bear had rolled the sun high into the cloudless blue, golden shafts of light bathed the clearing and danced over the pool at the mountain's foot. Even so, Bromios suddenly shivered. He had the nasty impression that many beady little eyes watched him from the bushes.

Near the edge of the pool stood a ring of stone columns and broken archways. Taking his arms, Calchas
and Phobos led him past these old ruins to a tumble of
huge boulders. The entry to the cave was a narrow, jagged cleft in the rock. What with his heavy cloak, he could
barely squeeze through. No sooner had he stepped inside
than flames sprang up and ghostly white shapes floated
toward him.

He stumbled back, flung one hand to his eyes, the
other to his sword hilt. Then he blew out his breath in
relief. The ghosts were two small girls wearing white tunics and holding torches. The chamber in which he
found himself was large, reaching some distance into the
shadows.

"Bromios?" A high, clear voice echoed all around him.

Bromios answered with an angry growl. A king should
not be startled like that.

Calchas spoke up. "Yes. Here is the Bear King, Lord
of Arkadia. He will see the pythoness."

A third, taller girl dressed in a blue robe had appeared as if from nowhere. In each hand, she carried a
clay cup. With a graceful gesture, she offered one of the
vessels to Bromios.

"Drink, O Bear King. This is the Water of Forgetting."

Bromios shifted uneasily and scowled at Calchas. "You didn't tell me about this part," he muttered. "What's the brew? Poison, for all I know."

"To cleanse your mind of all concerns for the world outside," said the girl. "Think only of this moment, here and now."

"Drink it, drink it," whispered Calchas. "It's plain water."

"Not thirsty," snapped Bromios.

"Drink it anyway," said Phobos. "Let them get on with their rigmarole."

Bromios made a face and gulped down the contents. He licked his teeth. Water it was, and icy.

The girl handed him the other cup. "The Water of Remembering, so that you may forever recall what you will see and hear."

Bromios swallowed hastily and wiped his mouth on the back of his hand. The two little girls raised their torches and beckoned him to follow. With Calchas and Phobos nudging him from behind, Bromios trod warily to the rear of the cave, where stone steps led downward. The girls descended easily and lightly, but Bromios nearly lost his footing on the stones worn smooth and slippery. He must have drunk the water too quickly, for his head pounded and his stomach gurgled. He clenched his jaw to keep his teeth from chattering. Even under the heavy fur cloak, Bromios felt so cold, so cold.

The steps ended on the earthen floor of a long, domed chamber. Flames from iron braziers made the walls seem awash in blood. A sickly sweet smell of incense choked his nostrils and made his eyes water. He stopped in his tracks. No one had told him to, he simply did. A dozen paces ahead was a deep recess hewn into the living rock. Hunched on a high, three-legged stool sat the pythoness.

Moldering black robes shrouded the frail, stoop-shouldered figure; covering her face was a mask of polished silver crowned with a tangle of silver serpents. In the shadows behind her, Bromios thought he glimpsed the rolling coils of some horrid reptile.

The pythoness straightened and shook her head, as if rousing from a long dream. The gleaming mask turned full upon Bromios: a woman's features, a calm expression frozen in the metal. When at last she spoke, the voice rang hollow.

"Bear King, do you truly desire your prophecy?"

"That's why I'm here, isn't it?" grumbled Bromios, adding under his breath, "Why else would I come into this foul den?"

"So be it, then." The pythoness paused. When she spoke again, her tone was thin and faint, the words seeming to come from some great distance:

> *"O Bromios, Bromios,*
> *Your life-threads are spun.*
> *A city in ashes, a king in rags,*
> *And then your course is run."*

The pythoness bowed her head and folded her arms. Bromios waited, but she remained silent.

"Let's have the rest of it," Bromios demanded impatiently.

"There is nothing more."

"What?" cried Bromios. "That's all? Ashes? Rags?"

"As you heard."

Bromios was no quick thinker, but it took hardly any time for him to grasp that he had been given something unpleasant.

"Take it back," he ordered. "Give me a better one."

"I cannot do so."

"You will!" shouted Bromios. "Don't tell me ashes and rags. I won't stomach that."

"I fear you must."

"Change it!" roared Bromios. "Right now! Do as I command, you scruffy old hag." He stepped forward, hand on sword.

"Silence!" The pythoness slid from her perch to stand straight and tall. She pointed at Bromios. "No closer. I am Woman-Who-Talks-to-Snakes!"

Bromios felt his words shrivel in his throat and his fingers freeze on the hilt. With all his might, he tried to draw the weapon. In vain.

"Take your prophecy and leave." The voice of the pythoness filled the grotto and thundered in the king's ears. Her eyes blazed through the slits in the mask. The crown of serpents seemed to writhe and hiss. "Go. Before I lose my temper and set the snakes on you."

Bromios had been standing with one foot rooted to the ground, the other poised in midstride. Now he spun around and plunged headlong up the steps, Calchas and Phobos scrambling behind. He burst from the cave, went crashing through the undergrowth as if a dozen serpents were at his heels, and galloped for Metara as fast as his horse's legs could carry him.

Safe inside his palace, behind the bolted doors of his inner chambers, Bromios vented his wrath. He roared, ground his teeth, shook his fists, kicked over tables, smashed bowls and goblets, all the while cursing and threatening Woman-Who-Talks-to-Snakes.

"If I could get my hands around her skinny neck!" he shouted. "I want her rooted out! Put down, cut off, done away with!"

While Bromios ranted on, Calchas and Phobos exchanged glances.

"I wonder," Calchas murmured, raising an eyebrow,

"if this might indeed be the moment? Has the time turned ripe sooner than we hoped?"

"To end the pernicious influence of the Lady of Wild Things?" said Phobos. "Yes, dear colleague, I believe the perfect opportunity has just been presented to us."

With the enthusiastic approval of his soothsayers, Bromios sent warriors to Mount Lerna. They filled the pool to the brim with dirt and gravel, stopped up the spring that fed it, and toppled the circle of columns. The cave was empty. They piled boulders to block the entrance.

They could not find the pythoness. Woman-Who-Talks-to-Snakes and her maidens had vanished as completely as if they had never been there. The only trace of her, which the warriors carried back to Bromios, was the silver mask.

It appeared to be smiling.

2

Lucian and the Jackass

During the weeks that followed, Bromios turned more gloomy than wrathful. Worn out by roaring curses and breaking furniture, he spent most of the days chewing his nails and pacing his chambers, demanding to know why his warriors, presently scouring the countryside, had not yet laid hold of Woman-Who-Talks-to-Snakes.

Also he sent heralds to towns and villages, proclaiming it forbidden under pain of death to observe practices or customs having anything to do with the Lady of Wild Things: a heavy blow to wise-women, healers, midwives, water-finders, and such, for they were all followers of the Lady. This was declared in the king's name but actually was done at the urging of Calchas and Phobos, who commended Bromios for his wisdom and strength of character.

"That," Calchas remarked confidentially to Phobos, "should put these women in their place and keep them in it once and for all. High time, too."

"Indeed so, dear colleague," replied Phobos. "Further, since we are the ones who decide what is lawful and what is not, in practical terms we have as much power as Bromios himself."

"And considerably greater opportunities," said Calchas. "On the whole, things have fallen out more profitably than we could have foretold."

Meantime, while Bromios gloomed and glowered and the soothsayers congratulated each other, a clerk named Lucian went about his duties in the royal counting house.

Now, this Lucian was a large-framed, long-legged young man, mostly knees and elbows, and more by way of ear size than he really needed. His mother had been a palace cook; his father, a harness maker. Orphaned in earliest childhood, he had grown up in the kitchens and stables. Sturdy enough to be a palace guard, he was judged too nimble-witted for a military future. He could read and write, was quick at numbers, and showed so much promise that he had risen from sweeper to pot scraper; later, to archive copier. This very week, when the post fell suddenly vacant, he had been put in charge of inventories and accounts.

Lucian told himself he should be grateful; all the more since he had no prospect for any different occupation. If he applied himself, worked hard, did as he was told, and kept out of trouble, he could look forward to a long life doing exactly what he was doing. Which he hated, when he stopped to think about it; and so he thought about it rarely. He loved hearing every kind of tale or story, but that was the only serious flaw in his character.

Late on this particular afternoon, Lucian was in his cubbyhole, rummaging through boxes of scrolls and records of past accounts. At that moment, Calchas himself happened to pass by. He cast a cold fish eye on Lucian and the jumble of documents and demanded to know the reason for such disorder.

"Lord Calchas," Lucian said, getting to his feet, "my accounts don't balance. Something's wrong, but if I've made a mistake I can't find it."

"Mistake?" snapped Calchas. "It does not please me to hear of mistakes. They signify slackness and weak moral fiber, which I do not tolerate."

"But my sums are correct, as you can see." Lucian held out a slate covered with figures. "Only they don't tally with the provisions in the storehouse."

"Indeed?" Calchas had been about to turn away but now he stepped closer to Lucian. "Exactly how did you arrive at that conclusion?"

"My Lord, I've gone myself and counted every bean, every drop of oil, everything. I don't find what's supposed to be there. But it's been recorded as bought, and a great deal of money paid out.

"So much goods can't disappear into thin air," Lucian pressed on. "Rats couldn't have eaten them all. Were they stolen? Or even bought in the first place? Lord Phobos and your honorable self authorized the purchases, but I can't find who got the money—"

Lucian choked off his words. The soothsayer's pink cheeks had gone dead white, glistening with little beads of sweat, and his mouth seemed to be chewing on air. Lucian's blood froze as he suddenly understood that the answer to who got the money was standing in front of him. The realization took his breath away. He dared say no more. He felt as if a very large pit had opened at his feet and he had nearly blundered over the edge.

Calchas regained his composure and smiled. "What a painstaking young man you are. Now, my good fellow, tell me what you propose doing about it."

"I—I don't know. First, I thought I'd take it up with the chief steward, but—"

"That would be quite proper," Calchas said smoothly. "Only consider: Would it be prudent? The chief steward might see this business in a different and unfavorable light, reflecting your own incompetence. You yourself could be blamed, with painful consequences.

"No, you will not report this mysterious state of affairs. Lord Phobos and I shall do it for you. We can explain your difficulties more lucidly and sympathetically. With you, there might be some doubt as to your honesty. Whereas, our veracity is beyond question."

Lucian did not answer. Calchas, beaming, clamped a hand on Lucian's shoulder.

"Our pleasant little conversation has proved most fortunate," remarked the soothsayer. "It has made me realize that you are far too intelligent and enterprising to waste your talents counting beans and scribbling numbers.

"It just so happens that Lord Phobos and I require an assistant, a young apprentice to learn our sacrificial procedures. The question: Where to find a suitable individual? The answer: Here he stands. Namely, yourself. Yes, my dear young man, the very position for you."

Lucian bowed his head; not out of respectful gratitude but to keep the soothsayer from reading the expression on his face. He could imagine all too clearly the sacrificial procedures Calchas had in mind.

"Come to our chambers," ordered the soothsayer, giving Lucian an affectionate tug on the ear. "By sundown, no later. Ah—yes, I shall take those obviously erroneous documents with me."

At that, Calchas snatched the papers, gathered up his robes, and went down the passageway as fast as he could waddle. The instant the soothsayer was out of sight, Lucian took to his heels in the opposite direction, running to find his closest friend in the palace, Menyas, the old stableman.

He was in a cold sweat when he reached the yard in front of the storehouses. There, one of the royal provisioners, a rough-bearded merchant called Cerdo, had just arrived and was bustling about, shouting at porters to haul away sacks and baskets of goods. Menyas was tethering Cerdo's pack animals to a railing. Lucian pressed through the huddle of mules and donkeys.

"Menyas, listen to me." He seized the stableman's arm. "I'm in trouble. I have to get away from them. They're going to kill me—" He blurted out a hasty account of his encounter with Calchas.

"Whoa, there, whoa." Menyas shook his grizzled head. "Let me get a saddle on this business. Goods missing, money paid, nothing to show for it? Eh, there's a mucky smell to all that. As for you being done away with—I wouldn't put anything past those royal chicken pluckers. They won't be skittish about cutting your throat to save their necks. If you're sure that's what they mean to do—"

"You should have seen the look on Calchas's face. He knows I'm onto the scheme. He and Phobos are waiting for me. If I don't go to their chambers, they'll come looking for me. If I try to hide, they'll turn the palace upside down until they find me. I have to get out. What else can I do?"

Menyas chewed his lips and thought for a moment. "I don't see anything better. Yes, lad, I'm afraid you'll have to clear out. Fast and far. Before those two get their hooks into you. All right, you stay quiet and wait here. I'll collect a few things you'll need."

Menyas hurried into the stables. Lucian sat down and put his head in his hands. One of the donkeys nuzzled him. He glanced up. The animal was scruffy, with patches of hair missing from his back and haunches; his ribs stood out, his long ears were notched and ragged; all in all, the most wretched-looking jackass that Lucian had ever seen.

"You're a sorry sight, poor beast," Lucian murmured, "but you've less to worry about than I do."

"I doubt it," said the jackass. "I overheard your plans for an immediate departure. A wise decision. Furthermore, I beg you in the name of mercy: Set me free of this terrible merchant, Cerdo. Take me with you."

3

Unfortunate Fronto

I 'm sorry," Lucian began. "I don't think I could—" He stopped short. "What am I doing? Talking to a jackass! And he's talking to me?"

"Indeed, I am," said the jackass. "I believe I expressed myself in the clearest possible terms, but let me try again. My dear young man, I need help. Require assistance. Implore your aid. Now, if I have your full attention—"

Lucian stared. Head spinning, he tried to scrape together as much sanity as he could. Common sense told him he was not holding a conversation with a donkey. The voice, he decided, came from someone crouching among the pack animals. He bent down to find whoever was hiding. He saw no one.

"You? You spoke?" Lucian stammered. "How? You can't. You're a jackass."

"My name is Fronto," the beast replied in a tone of wounded dignity. "I'm not a jackass. I'm a poet, though some might call that one and the same."

"I'm dreaming this," Lucian murmured. "Or lost my wits. Whatever, something's gone wrong with me."

"Gone wrong with *me* would more accurately describe the situation," said Fronto. "Horrible, monstrous. Never mind the details, I'll discuss them later. Right now, all I want is to be out of Cerdo's clutches. A matter of life and death. Mine. If you call it a life in this humiliating carapace, this asinine shell."

"Shell?" said Lucian, relieved by this peculiar but at least plausible explanation. "Someone stitched you into a donkey skin? Here, I'll peel it off."

He began tugging at Fronto's ears and mane, trying to strip away the shaggy hide.

"Stop, stop!" Fronto tossed his head and reared on his hind legs. "This is all me. I've been transformed, transmogrified. I'm jackass through and through."

"That's—terrible," said Lucian, at a loss for a better way to put it. Though still bewildered, he was growing a little more used to the idea of a talking jackass. "Uncomfortable, too."

"Understatement," said Fronto. "*Litotes*, to use the rhetorical term. Now that you seem to have grasped my predicament, I entreat you to do something about it. And about your own, as well.

"And you're quite right," Fronto added. "Those larcenous soothsayers, those sanctimonious frauds, are stealing money hand over fist. And I'll tell you something else: Cerdo's in the scheme with them. He gets a fat share to line his own purse. I know. I heard him bragging to his cronies. They're all as crooked as a ram's horns, and murderous into the bargain. Unless you get moving as fast as you can, you won't live out this day. Unless I get free of that brute, I won't last much longer."

"Menyas can help you better than I can," said Lucian. "He's good with horses—donkeys, too, I'm sure. You'll explain to him—"

"No." Fronto stamped his hooves. "When I see the effect my deplorable state had on you, no telling what it may do to him. Least said, soonest mended—as I wrote in one of my more successful odes. Unlike poets, most people get upset over apparent impossibility. The question is: Will you take me along? Since you're departing anyway—"

Fronto broke off. Menyas was there, with a bundle on his shoulder.

"Best I could do at short notice, but it should tide you over a while. A little money, too," he added, slipping coins into Lucian's hand. "Quick, now. Out the back gate. The guard's not on duty yet."

As the stableman began hustling Lucian from the yard, Fronto flicked his tail and made sounds of clearing his throat. Lucian held back. "One thing more. This jackass. I want him."

"Steal one of Cerdo's pack animals? For a bean counter, you're turning into a bold rogue. Well, why not? You're in such trouble now, a little extra won't matter. But snaffle a good mount, at least. Don't bother with this miserable beast."

"Him," said Lucian. "No other."

"He's a rawboned wreck, two steps from the boneyard. For heaven's sake, lad, why?"

"He asked me—I mean, look at him. He wants to go with me as clearly as if he spoke the words."

"All right, all right, whatever you say. We can't lose time wrangling over this piece of crow bait." Menyas hoisted the bundle and roped it onto Fronto's back. "There. Let him make himself useful, anyway."

That moment, Cerdo came out of the grain shed. Seeing Lucian and Fronto hurrying from the yard, he began bawling at the top of his voice: "Thief! Donkey robber!"

"Giddyap," cried Menyas, giving Lucian a shove and Fronto a smack to speed them on their way. "I'll deal with him."

Leaving the stableman doing all he could to hinder the furious merchant, Lucian darted through the alley behind the storehouse, Fronto after him, and clattered along the wooden walkways, past the fenced-in run for the oracular chickens. Like most of the palace, the back gate was made of timber; it was so seldom used, however, that the bolt had frozen in its socket. Lucian, despite his efforts, could not draw it free. He flung himself against it, hammering with his fists, battering with his shoulders.

"Allow me," said Fronto. He turned and kicked out with his hind legs. The door sagged; and as the assault continued, it broke loose and fell open.

Fronto plunged out. Lucian, having not the slightest idea where they were going, could only seize the poet's tail and let himself be pulled along. Only after they had crossed the public square did Fronto slow his pace. He trotted briskly down winding lanes, through back alleys, clambering over rubbish heaps, and nipping around corners. Lucian, who had never set foot beyond the palace walls, asked how he knew his way in such a maze.

"I've had some previous experience," said Fronto, "eluding tiresome creditors, tavern keepers, magistrates, not to mention physically aggressive critics. For poets, that's an essential skill, an art as necessary as turning a rhyme. Sometimes more so."

No sooner had Fronto finished speaking than Lucian cried out. He was spun around and a lantern thrust up to his face.

"Here, now, let's have a look at you." A city watch-man was peering at him. "What are you up to, eh?"

"Ah—sir, we—that is, I—" Lucian choked, then went on quickly. "Yes, glad I found you. At the palace —a terrible commotion. The oracular chickens got loose. They're flapping all over the streets. I was ordered to summon every watchman to go after them."

"Then, fool, don't waste time yammering." The man set off with all haste toward the palace.

"You have a glib tongue," said Fronto as they hurried on. "A nice bit of invention, those chickens."

"I had to think of something. I couldn't let him arrest us." Lucian grinned with wry satisfaction. "I never had to tell a lie before."

"It gets easier with practice," said Fronto.

They reached the outskirts of Metara without further challenge, but it was well after nightfall by the time they passed the outlying farms and made their way into the woodlands.

"Calchas and Phobos," Lucian said anxiously, "they'll be looking all over the place for me."

"Better to have them looking for you than finding you," said Fronto. "Don't worry. We're well away and safe here for the time being. I'd be much obliged if you'd remove this bundle your friend imposed on me."

As soon as Lucian did so, Fronto threw himself on the turf, rolling about and kicking his knobby legs in the air. Fearing the poet had gone into some kind of fit, Lucian started toward him.

"Sheer exuberance," Fronto assured him. "Animal spirits, literally and figuratively. At last free of Cerdo's clutches! What a relief, you can't imagine." After a few more rolls, the poet heaved himself upright. "I feel better already. This would be the crucial time—"

"To tell what happened to you," Lucian put in.

"—to explore the contents of that bundle. I suspect it holds edibles. I hope so, for my belly's empty as a drum."

Lucian hurried to untie the pack. Wrapped in a cloak were figs, cheese, some olives, a hunch of bread, and a large jar of wine. "I'm sorry. There's not much that you —a donkey, that is—would like."

"Not much?" cried Fronto. "A feast! One of the few advantages of my condition is that not only can I eat grass, thistles, hay, and all such disgusting vegetation, but human nourishment as well. My digestion is universally excellent. So, too, my appetite, growing keener with every fleeting moment."

Lucian spread out the provisions. Fronto munched away, bolting down his share, then helping Lucian to finish his own.

"That wine jar presents a small difficulty," said Fronto, chomping and belching at the same time. "Would you be kind enough to tip it into my mouth? On these occasions, hooves can be inconvenient."

He squatted on his haunches and stretched out his neck. Lucian held up the jar and poured some of the liquid down the poet's gullet. Fronto extended a long tongue and licked his lips.

"Pure nectar! I've had nothing like it since my regrettable accident."

"That's what I want to hear about," said Lucian.

"Just another taste," said Fronto. "It will clarify my mind. I've been treated like a donkey for such a while, sometimes I fear I've begun thinking like one."

Lucian did as requested, and with one gulp after the other, Fronto drained the jar. He nosed around to make sure nothing remained of the food, then settled back on his hindquarters.

"My dear Lucian, no human being is more miserable than a poet who has lost his inspiration. That was the situation in which I found myself a few weeks ago. My head was empty, my spirits leaden. What should have been winged words barely crept along, earthbound. The poetic spark had flickered out, the divine afflatus had blown away, creative rapture had fled; and my landlord, insensitive oaf, kept bringing up the question of rent. In short, a glorious career had come to an inglorious conclusion. What, I ask you, did I do?"

"I suppose," Lucian said, "you took up some other line of work."

"Abandon literature?" Fronto gave him a horrified look. "Impossible, unthinkable. Once a poet, always a poet. No, dear boy, I did what poets have always done in such a predicament. I flung myself to my knees and implored the Lady of Wild Things to send me inspiration."

"Fronto—" asked Lucian, shocked, "are you telling me you actually believe in—her?"

"Of course," replied Fronto. "All poets do. The Lady, as we well know, is the fountainhead of artistic intuition, eloquence, imagination. You don't suppose I'd direct my entreaties to some hairy, toothy ancestral bear. I was seeking inspiration, not hibernation.

"My continued supplications, alas, brought no result. My poetic spirit lay as lively as a dead mackerel. Then a thought came to me. I understood what must be done."

Here Fronto sighed and broke off. Lucian waited some long moments and finally asked, "What was it?"

Fronto did not reply. Rattling noises came from his open mouth. Lucian at first believed Fronto was sobbing, heartbroken by his own unhappy tale, until he realized the poet was snoring.

Impatient for the rest of the story, Lucian nudged him and prodded his flanks. Fronto stayed motionless, his long ears and shaggy head in stark outline against the moon. The poet had fallen unwakeably asleep.

Lucian, disappointed, could only curl up on the turf, pull the cloak over his shoulders, and try to do likewise.

4

Transformations

For a moment, on the ragged edge of wakefulness, Lucian believed a nightmare had ended, that he was on the straw pallet in his cubbyhole, his life was not in danger, and there had never been such a creature as a talking jackass. With a sigh of relief, he opened his eyes, blinked at the dawn light, and there he was, shivering on the turf, his cloak dew-drenched. With the truth of his situation like a cold lump in his stomach, he sat up and tried to rub away the chill in his bones and the crick in his neck.

Fronto was hunkered on the ground, still fast asleep. Lucian stepped over to him and prodded his flank, warning him it was daybreak.

"Really?" The poet opened one eye. "Yes, well, thank

you for that fascinating information. Wake me closer to noon, there's a good fellow."

Without Lucian's continued prodding, Fronto would have drowsed off. At last, with much yawning and head shaking, he got himself up on all four legs. "It's been some while since I've enjoyed a civilized morning's repose. With Cerdo, it was always the crack of the whip at the crack of dawn. In happier times—ah, how long ago they seem—I found it difficult to take anything seriously until midafternoon. However, if you insist. Did you mention breakfast?"

"The food's gone," said Lucian. "I should have put some aside."

"No matter," said Fronto. "Seize the day, whatever's in it to seize, before something comes along and seizes you. Had I known I'd end up a jackass, I'd have seized a lot more."

"Speaking of that," said Lucian, "you never told me what happened to you."

"I didn't?" said Fronto. "Ah—yes, you're right. I only meant to pause for dramatic effect, and here it's tomorrow already. Now, where was I?"

"You knew what you had to do."

"Exactly so." Fronto nodded and resumed his interrupted tale.

"At Mount Lerna, near the oracle's cave, there's a pool

dedicated to the Lady of Wild Things and strictly forbidden to men. It's said to have mysterious powers. The oracle, so I'd heard, drinks from it and receives her inspiration. I resolved to go to that pool—surely the Lady wouldn't begrudge me a few sips from it, all in a good cause.

"And so I did. Late one night, I stole into the grove. Not a soul in sight. I tiptoed to the edge of the pool, knelt, cupped a little water in my hands, drank it down, and waited eagerly for the glorious moment.

"Inspiration?" Fronto glumly went on. "Not a flicker. And yet, conditions should have been perfect: gnarled trees, whispering wind, moonshine so bright I could see my reflection in the limpid pool—the kind of atmosphere that's stock-in-trade for us poets. Had I been even halfway at the top of my bent, I'd have dashed off a dozen rhapsodies on the spot. But no, my only thought was I'd likely catch cold in such a damp and chilly spot.

"The difficulty was clear. I had not sufficiently imbibed the magical waters. I gulped down more and more. With no result. Did I say no result? Ah, my dear Lucian, there was a result, a most horrendous one. As I bent over the pool, I observed my reflection. Believe me, I make no claim to being in any way a handsome fellow—modesty has always been one of my endearing qualities—but I saw a blunt, hairy nose, certainly not mine, the end as white as if dipped in flour; ears long and shaggy. In short, the face of a jackass stared back at me.

"Aghast, I bent closer; so close I lost my balance and tumbled in headlong. I went floundering to the bottom, gasping for breath, suddenly so heavy I feared I'd never rise to the surface.

"But the pool was shallow and, at last, I managed to clamber out. On all fours! My hands and feet were hooves! My neck, elongated—and I had the distinct impression I had grown a tail. Terrified, I peered back into the pool. One glance confirmed it: I had become a complete ass."

"Horrible!" burst out Lucian, who had been hanging on Fronto's every word. "Enough to drive you mad!"

"Almost, but not quite," said Fronto. "We poets are used to finding ourselves in odd states, and I tried to keep my wits about me. I would go to the oracle, confess what I'd done, beg her forgiveness and help. She'd know how to deal with this kind of thing.

"I started toward the cave. That instant, a troop of palace warriors, brandishing swords and torches, came whooping into the glade. I bolted in panic. The last place in the world I wanted to be was in the midst of those rampaging ruffians.

"I galloped into the underbrush and hid until things quieted and it seemed safe to venture back. What devastation! The pool, a mud hole; the grove, a shambles; the cave, blocked. The oracle—I had no idea whether she was alive or dead, walled up in her cave. In any case, I could not enter to find out.

"There shattered my first and best hope," said Fronto. "I confess, my dear Lucian, I sank down and wept as never jackass wept before."

Fronto shuddered and sighed miserably at the recollection. Lucian put a comforting arm around the poet's neck. "There must be some way of getting you back to yourself again."

"An idea uppermost in my mind," said Fronto. "I might go so far as to call it a preoccupation on the verge of obsession. The prospect of remaining forever a jackass is enough to take up one's undivided attention.

"Since the oracle herself was unavailable, I decided on the next best thing: to seek out a wise-woman, a healer who might have knowledge of such matters.

"Accordingly, I set off across country, hoping for a road that would lead me to some nearby village. I had not gone far when I glimpsed three rough-looking fellows squatting around a cook fire. They were as villainous a lot as I'd ever seen, all my instincts warned me to keep clear of them.

"Regrettably, they caught sight of me at the same time I caught sight of them. Before I could turn aside, they jumped to their feet and raced after me. One seized me by the mane, another by the tail; and, no matter how I kicked and struggled, they held me fast.

" 'Oho, what's this?' cried the third. 'A wandering jackass! Just what we need.'

"Next thing I knew, I was tethered to a tree. At first, I considered speaking up and explaining that I was no jackass at all; but I thought better of it, fearing these ruffians would take me for some freak of nature, and no telling what they might do.

"So, I held my tongue until I could take stock of my situation. They did not hold theirs, talking openly among themselves as if I were a dumb beast. I listened in growing dismay, for they were plotting no less than robbery and murder.

"There was, I gathered, a corn dealer, Kroton, living on his country estate not far from here. It was whispered about that he kept sacks of gold squirreled away under his floorboards. These villains intended burglarizing him. After dispatching him and his servants, they would require means of carrying off the heavy sacks and any other valuables. My accidental arrival resolved this difficulty, for it was I who would bear the burden of their ill-gotten gains.

"They, and I with them, kept hidden until deepest dark of night. Goading me along, whacking me whenever

I tried to hold back, they stopped in the forecourt of the house. The vile scheme they were about to undertake outraged my every moral fiber, conscience, and scruples—furthermore, the despicable criminals had neither fed nor watered me—and I formed a plan I hoped would defeat them, at possible risk to myself, though with possible gain, as well.

"While one stood guard outside, holding me at a rope's end, his disgusting companions cleverly and silently sprung open the door. Now, for me, came the crucial moment. As soon as the pair disappeared inside the house, I suddenly reared up, kicking and bucking, shouting at the top of my voice: 'Help, ho! Murder! Robbery! Come, friends, all ten of you. Trap them within. Don't let them escape, strike them down without mercy!'

"The first result of my outburst was to startle and terrify the robber beside me, and he dashed off with never a thought for his comrades. The second result was to rouse Kroton and his household and to alarm the robbers, who believed themselves ambushed. They raced from the house, the servants at their heels.

"Kroton himself now appeared, wrapped in his night linen and brandishing a butcher knife. Having urged his servants to pursue the robbers, he turned to me.

" 'Those villains may escape,' he raged, 'but not you,

their accomplice. I'll have my revenge if not on them at least on you.'

"Eager to vent his wrath even on an innocent animal, he started toward me with every intention of cutting my throat.

" 'Stop, stop!' I exclaimed. 'It was I who gave the outcry that saved your life and your gold.'

"Indeed, he halted in his tracks, dumbfounded. Confident of his gratitude and assistance, I hastened to assure him I was the harmless victim of a great misfortune and implored his help. He gradually calmed, and when I finished, he scratched his head, studied me shrewdly, and declared: 'A remarkable, incredible tale. If I didn't know I was awake, I'd think I was asleep. Have no fear, let me consider what best to do for you.'

"Before the servants came back, he warned me against speaking to anyone but himself and led me to an empty grain shed where I impatiently spent the rest of the night looking forward to what he would do to help me.

"In the morning, Kroton returned. He put a halter around my neck and instructed me to come with him to the village adjoining his property. My heart leaped, for I assumed he would take me to the local wise-woman; but, when I told him this, he laughed and said: 'I'll have no dealings with those frightful crones. No, my fine fellow, you're going to make a fortune. For me, that is.'

"When we arrived at the little marketplace, the meaning of Kroton's unsettling words became all too clear.

" 'Gather round,' he called out to the local idlers and passersby. 'Come and hear the amazing talking jackass, the only one of his kind in the world. With utmost patience, I've taught the brute to speak, which he does with greatest eloquence. Do you doubt it?' Kroton continued while the crowd burst out in cries of disbelief. 'I'll wager money on the truth of what I claim.'

" 'And I'll wager all in my purse that you're hoaxing us,' retorted a bystander, flinging down a number of silver coins. The others followed his example, eager to wager that Kroton was trying to trick them.

" 'Don't you contradict me,' Kroton muttered in my ear. 'Do as you're told or so much the worse for you. Now, go on. Say something. Recite one of your verses, lacking anything better.'

"Outraged by Kroton's treachery and ingratitude, determined to have my revenge, I only wheezed and hee-hawed like any common ass.

"At this, the crowd began hooting and jeering, accusing Kroton of being a liar or out of his wits. They picked up their money and demanded that he pay off his part of the wager.

" 'He can speak, he can speak as well as any of

you,' protested Kroton. 'I had a talk with him only this morning.'

"While the crowd threatened bodily harm if he reneged, Kroton pummeled and kicked me, shaking his fist, ordering me to prove him right. I, however, stood mute as a stone.

" 'I warned you,' shouted Kroton. 'Treacherous poet! To the knacker's yard, to the slaughterhouse with you! I'll have the hide off your back for a rug and boil your hooves into glue, and get that much from you, in any case.'

" 'Hold on there,' put in a rough-bearded man— Cerdo, as I later learned. 'That's wasting a perfectly serviceable jackass. I need a pack beast, and I'll give you enough to make good on what you owe these folk before they take you yourself to the knacker.'

" 'Done and done!' returned Kroton, snatching Cerdo's cash with one hand and giving him my halter with the other. 'Take him away. Beat him within an inch of his life and beyond, for all I care. Never again will I trust a poet.'

"So it was," concluded Fronto, "that I fell into the clutches of Cerdo. He subjected me to the painful indignity of branding his mark on my rump with a red hot iron, setting the seal of my slavery to him. From then on, my life at the hands of that brute was nothing but cudgeling, starvation, endless toil—a donkey's a sturdy creature, but with such mistreatment my days were surely numbered. Until you, my dear Lucian, set me free; for which I am eternally grateful.

"But here," Fronto added, "our ways must part: I, to keep on with my search; you, wherever your own road leads. I'm too sentimental a fellow for long good-byes, so let us simply take brief but fond leave of each other. I wish you the best of good fortune. Should you ever meet another donkey, I trust you'll do as well for him as you've done for me. You never know who he might be."

5

Joy-in-the-Dance

W ait," Lucian called as Fronto started from the clearing. "You can't roam around by yourself. You'll be grabbed again. I'll stay with you until we find a healer."

"A generous offer," said Fronto, "but you have your own troubles. You're not the most popular fellow in Arkadia. If those soothsayers lay hold of you, they'll carve you like one of their chickens. Also, you made off with Cerdo's property and he's a vengeful sort. You'd best find some backwater hamlet and quietly hole up there. I'll manage. As a poet, I'm accustomed to the seamy side of life."

"You're a donkey now," said Lucian.

"You have a point," said Fronto, "and even a poet must occasionally bow to logic. Yes, I'll be grateful for your company. Come, then. I suggest we find whatever poor excuse for a road they have in these parts."

Fronto picked his way through the undergrowth and struck on a path leading away from Metara. Lucian, at first, kept glancing over his shoulder, as if Calchas, Phobos, and Cerdo were about to pounce on him at any moment. As the morning wore on, however, he began striding more lightheartedly. He laughed at a gray squirrel sitting on its haunches, forepaws folded, looking like one of the old palace archivists. He glimpsed a hard-shelled beetle armored like a warrior. He had never heard such chirping and whistling as he heard from the many different birds in the woods. But what fascinated him most was his companion trotting along beside him.

At last he ventured to ask, "Fronto, tell me. How did you get to be a poet?"

"I haven't the least notion," replied Fronto. "I didn't get to be; I always was. As I wrote in one of my elegies: 'Poets are born, not made.' It isn't something you acquire like a skin rash."

"That's all there is to it?"

"Certainly not. One should learn the nature of odes, anthems, apostrophes, and so on. And, of course, the proper use of metaphor, simile, metathesis, just to begin.

"Then, epithets, your nice little ready-made phrases: rosy-fingered dawn, sandy shores, wine-dark seas.

They've been stock-in-trade for time out of mind."

"You don't have to think them up?"

"Originality?" Fronto shuddered. "Heavens, no. Why risk upsetting anyone? These are tried and true, sure to please. You can cobble up whole epics from them. Next, the matter of rhyme schemes, rhythmics, dactyls, anapests, spondees—"

"You know all that?"

"Of course not. I only mean one should. If I ever escape this ridiculous carcass, I might devote a little time to studying them. They do come in handy. Prose, however, is a different piece of business. Tales, anecdotes, narratives. All quite simple. Any fool can tell a story. Take a few odds and ends of things that happen to you, dress them up, shuffle them about, add a dash of excitement, a little color, and there you have it."

"You could tell the story of your turning into a jackass," Lucian said. "That's an amazing tale just as it is."

"No," said Fronto. "Too bizarre, grotesque, unpleasant. But, to give you an example, I could build a tale from, say, the moment I looked into the pool. Instead of me, it would be a handsome fellow, a conceited young fop who gazes so closely at his own reflection that he falls in and drowns. Instead of an ass, he's transformed into—oh, some kind of beautiful flower. That's more charming than a donkey and would go down better with the audience. And—ah, yes, he has a sweetheart who pines away until she's a mere shadow of herself. I'd have to work it out, but you grasp the method."

"Here's a good idea for you," said Lucian. "How I found a mistake in my inventories and had to run off before Calchas and Phobos got hold of me."

"Boring," said Fronto. "Forgive me, I'm yawning already. Conflict, struggle, suspense—that's what's needed to make a tale move along. You don't just run off. They seize you. You fight them with all your strength, almost win; but they bind you hand and foot, get ready to chop you up with meat cleavers. You escape in the nick of time. I don't know how. That's a technical detail."

"It didn't happen that way," Lucian protested.

"My point exactly," said Fronto. "All the more reason to spice it up. The meat cleavers are an especially nice touch."

"But it wouldn't be true."

"Not important," said Fronto. "If a storyteller worried about the facts—my dear Lucian, how could he ever get at the truth?"

❧

Over the next several days, Lucian began to despair of finding a wise-woman. In some hamlets, the folk were devoted to the Lady; they would have helped him, but the local healers had fled, no one knew where. In other villages, the dwellers belonged to the Bear tribe; the men scorned anything to do with the Lady and drove him off with curses, plus a few rocks to speed him on his way.

One afternoon, he stopped in a village to buy food with the last of his coins. Smarting from previous welcomes, he was cautious and roundabout in asking information. Prepared for yet another disappointment, he was happily surprised when the shopkeeper drew him aside and whispered that an old wise-woman lived on a patch of farmland only a league down the road.

Needing to hear no more, Lucian ran from the shop. So far, he had walked beside Fronto, feeling it was somehow disrespectful to ride on a poet. Now, while the shopkeeper kept waving and shouting after him, he jumped on Fronto's back and they set off at a gallop.

He found the place easily enough and smelled it before he saw it. Smoke billowed from the windows. The farmhouse roof blazed. Warriors were thrusting torches into sheds and outbuildings. Fronto reared in alarm. Lucian tumbled off. By the time he scrambled to his feet, the troop captain had ridden up to him.

"You." The officer pointed a short-bladed sword. He was a burly man, sweating in a leather breastplate, his helmet tilted on the back of his head. "What's your business here?"

Lucian stared. The buildings were past saving, along with anyone inside. The shopkeeper, he realized, had tried to warn him.

"Who are you?" The captain leaned from the saddle and squinted at Lucian. "Let's have a better look." He climbed down and gripped Lucian's shirtfront. "I've seen that face before. Where? Metara? The palace?"

"Me? In a palace? Don't I wish it." Lucian smiled innocently, trying to keep himself from shaking with fright at the same time. "I'm going to visit my Uncle Dimitrios. He's laid up with rheumatism something terrible. The dampness, you see, when the roof started leaking. He needs someone—"

"Leave off all that. You tell me quick: What do you want with the old hag that lived here?"

"Sir, I lost my way. I turned off to ask directions. I don't know anything about hags."

"Good thing you don't," said the officer, shoving him aside. "All right, clear out. On foot, my lad. One of my pack mules pulled up lame. I need a fresh one. This jackass is officially commandeered. He's a royal ass now.

"Throw a rope on the beast," the captain ordered two of his warriors. "Take him to the village. We're done here."

"Get your hands off him." Lucian flung himself against the nearest warrior and sent him stumbling back;

then spun around to grapple with the other. Fronto bucked and shied away. Lucian flailed wildly with his fists, pummeling so furiously that his bewildered opponent lost his balance and dropped to one knee. Darting to Fronto's side, Lucian swung a leg over the poet's haunches.

The troop captain, shrugging as if obliged to deal with a tiresome hindrance, brought up his sword and launched a sweeping, backhanded blow. Struck with the flat of the blade, Lucian pitched to the ground, stunned out of his wits.

By the time he remembered how to operate his arms and legs, the warriors were already far down the road. He lurched after them, shaking his fists and hurling threats. He managed only half a dozen floundering steps before tumbling down again.

"I saw them take your donkey," remarked a light voice behind him. "Let's see what damage they did to you."

Lucian turned to stare into the gray eyes of a slender, long-legged girl, her braided hair the color of ripe wheat. She stood, hands on hips, observing him with concern, curiosity, and a little glint of wry amusement. At sight of her, Lucian felt some difficulty catching his breath. Despite a sudden giddiness, he straightened up, squared his shoulders, and hoped to give the impression that he was sitting on the turf only because he wanted to.

"I was watching from the bushes," the girl went on. "That officer gave you quite a whack."

"I'd have given him worse," Lucian retorted. "Sneaking coward. He hit me when I wasn't looking."

"The most sensible time to do it, from his viewpoint. Just be glad you're not missing a head. Here, swallow this. You'll feel better."

From the cloak slung around her shoulders, the girl produced a small phial and poured the contents into Lucian's mouth, then knelt to examine the result of the sword blow.

"I was looking for the wise-woman." Lucian grimaced at the bitter taste of the liquid. "Someone told me she lives here."

"Not anymore. She was warned in time. She's safe away. As I'll be, once I'm done with you."

"Are you a healer?"

"That depends on what needs healing. In your case, not much. I'm called Joy-in-the-Dance. And you?"

"Aiee! Ouch!" cried Lucian as her fingers probed a tender spot behind his ear.

"Odd name." The girl gave a teasing grin. "Well, then, Aiee-Ouch, you'll mend. Put cold water on that lump. Nothing more to be done."

"The healer's not for me. For my donkey."

"Your donkey's gone. Or don't you remember?"

"I'll get him back. No matter what I have to do. They took him to the village. I'm going after him."

"And then? Knock down the whole troop? Not likely. You'd do better to find another. There's no shortage of donkeys."

"He's not a donkey," Lucian snapped. "He's my friend. I mean, my friend's a donkey now. But he's not himself. He used to be himself—"

"I think I gave you too much of that willow extract," the girl said.

"He needs a wise-woman, a healer, anyone who can help him."

"He's sick? What with?"

"Not sick. He's fine. No, he isn't. He's a poet. Was a poet."

"So far," said Joy-in-the-Dance, "you're making no sense at all. Start with this: Who are you? That shouldn't be too difficult. Once you've managed that, you might get around to telling me how your poetic donkey comes into it."

"My name's Lucian. When I was in the palace, in Metara—"

"What?" burst out Joy-in-the-Dance. "You're one of

the king's people? Spying for Bromios? Hunting down wise-women? I should have left you to mend your own head."

"No, no," Lucian broke in. "I ran away. I had to. They'd have murdered me."

"I'll do worse than that if you don't give me some better answers."

"I'm trying to explain," Lucian flung back. "You keep mixing me up. We're here because Fronto—the donkey —had an accident when he was a poet."

"Aiee-Ouch, I'm running out of patience."

"How it began, you see, before I met Fronto—" Lucian hesitated. Something peculiar was happening to him. Facing this wheat-haired, gray-eyed girl, he suddenly felt, among other sensations, that he was a very dull fellow, with his dull beans and dull inventories. It became urgently important to put himself in a more interesting light, as any young man in his position would have done.

So, recalling Fronto's advice about storytelling, he cleared his throat and offered the following account.

6

The Invisible Dinner

I was chief scribe in the king's great palace high above the sandy shores of the wine-dark sea," said Lucian. "One day, at rosy-fingered dawn, my duties took me into a storeroom to count—to inspect, that is—tall jars of oil. I was just coming from behind a row of these jars when the royal soothsayers, Calchas and Phobos, entered, and, with them, one of the provisioners to the royal household, a merchant named Cerdo.

"Unaware of my presence, they were talking intently among themselves. I could not help overhearing their conversation, and I was shocked and horrified; for I quickly understood that they were scheming to steal huge sums of money from the palace treasury.

"Not daring to move, I listened with mounting in-

dignation at such dishonesty and treachery; and grew so
agitated that my foot scraped against one of the jars. At
this, Cerdo broke off and scowled villainously.

" 'Hark,' he whispered, furtively glancing around.
'What's that noise? Are you sure we're alone?'

" 'Only a rat,' replied Calchas. 'The place is crawling
with them.'

" 'Yes,' I thought, 'and I see three of them right there.'
I pressed closer behind the jars; but, amid the dust and
spiderwebs, I began sneezing violently.

" 'A rat?' burst out Cerdo. 'Next, you'll tell me he'll
blow his nose.'

"Seeing no other course, I boldly sprang from my
hiding place. 'Your vile conspiracy is exposed!' I exclaimed. 'You are no better than common thieves and
deserve to be treated as such.'

"At first, they cringed in terror, knowing their criminal wrongdoing would cost their lives. They begged me
to keep their secret, promising a share of their ill-gotten
gains in exchange for my silence. This offer, naturally, I
refused.

"Overcoming their alarm, they realized that they were
three against one, and they all set upon me. As much as
I fought and struggled, they overpowered and bound me
hand and foot with ropes. Next, they lifted me up and
put me into one of the jars.

" 'There you stay, my fine fellow,' said Calchas, 'until we come back and decide how best to dispose of you.'

"What was I to do? Imprisoned in an oil jar, my life hanging in the balance, I nevertheless remained calm and sought a way to release myself. I quickly discovered the means. Some oil was still in the bottom of the jar. I soaked the ropes in it, covering hands and feet with the substance. This lubrication allowed me to slip free of my bonds.

"However, no sooner had I climbed out of the jar than Calchas and Phobos returned; in their hands were sharp, glittering meat cleavers.

"Seeing me about to escape, the villains pursued me all around the storeroom, brandishing their murderous cleavers and vowing to chop me into a hundred pieces. Dodging Calchas, I was nearly overtaken by Phobos; spinning away from Phobos, I strove to elude Calchas. Step by step, inch by inch, they pressed me closer and closer. Another instant and I would be hopelessly trapped. Calchas raised his cleaver, about to bring it down on my head.

"The gleaming blade whistled through the air. In the nick of time, even as the fearsome weapon was no more than a hair's breadth away, I sprang through a window, raced across the courtyard, scaled the wall, and dropped to the other side.

"By good fortune, a donkey happened to be standing at that very spot. I landed astride—"

"Stop," Joy-in-the-Dance broke in. "Enough."

"It's a terrifying scene," said Lucian. "I'm sorry if it upset you."

"It didn't," said Joy-in-the-Dance. "It's ridiculous. The most preposterous tissue of nonsense I've ever heard."

"It's true," protested Lucian. "Almost. Some of it. The facts—yes, all right, a little different. They're not important. Fronto himself told me so."

"You take advice from a jackass?"

"He's a poet. I'm trying to explain—"

"Save your breath," said Joy-in-the-Dance. "First, you claim you need help, then you come out with some absurd fabrication. I don't know what you're up to and I don't think I want to. I certainly don't want to be fobbed off with meat cleavers and oil jars and jumping out of windows. If you're going to lie, at least be convincing. Good-bye. I have things to do."

"I thought you were a healer," Lucian burst out as the girl turned away. "You're supposed to help people, aren't you? Never mind, then. Go on, walk off. Good-bye yourself. I don't care if you believe it or not, but my friend got changed into a donkey and that's a fact."

Joy-in-the-Dance turned and strode back to him.

"What did you say? Changed into—is that more of your nonsense?"

"It's exactly what happened," Lucian retorted. The girl's eyes were fixed on his own, as if she were trying to peer through them into the nooks and crannies of his brain. He had the uncomfortable impression that she might be succeeding.

Joy-in-the-Dance said nothing for a few moments, then stretched out a finger to prod Lucian's chest. "Listen to me, Aiee-Ouch—"

"My name's Lucian."

"Yes. Well, listen to me, Aiee-Ouch. If you're spinning out another tale, I'll be very unhappy with you. But I'm going to assume there's a grain of truth in all this."

"A grain? Thank you for believing that much. Do you mind telling me how you'll make sure?"

"Simple. I'll go and ask your friend."

"Oh? As easy as that?" Lucian said wryly. "If you didn't think I could get to him, I don't see how you will. You? A girl?"

"You noticed? That was clever of you." Joy-in-the-Dance smiled. "Yes, Aiee-Ouch, I'll be interested in having a few words with your jackass."

Joy-in-the-Dance beckoned him to a sheltered spot away from the smoldering farmhouse. There, she sat cross-legged, folded her hands, and lowered her eyes.

"What are you doing?" cried Lucian. "You said we were going after Fronto."

"We are. At the right time. Meanwhile, I'm sleeping. Or was, until you interrupted."

"You sleep sitting up? Like a chicken? I never heard of such a thing."

"You Bear people wouldn't know how. It's a little knack we learn when we're children; and it's more comfortable than sprawling on the ground—like a stunned ox. You'd be wise to get some rest, too, instead of flapping around."

The girl took a deep breath and again shut her eyes. Lucian paced back and forth, chafing at the delay, impatient to reach Fronto. At last, he gave in to weariness and sank down with his knees drawn up and his head resting on them. Long after moonrise, Joy-in-the-Dance leisurely climbed to her feet and motioned for Lucian to follow.

Stepping quickly and quietly, they reached the village just before dawn. The little marketplace was empty, nothing stirred. Lucian would have clung cautiously to the shadows, but the girl walked straight to the inn and glanced through a window.

"Good," she whispered. "The captain and his louts have stuffed themselves and swilled everything they could find. An earthquake wouldn't rouse them. That's why I waited."

"They'll have sentries on watch."

The girl shrugged. She beckoned Lucian to the rear of the inn, where an open-fronted shed served as a stable. Amid the tethered pack animals, a guard squatted, head nodding, a guttering lantern beside him. Lucian glimpsed Fronto, ears woefully drooping.

"Stay here," said Joy-in-the-Dance as Lucian started forward. She went boldly to the guard, who roused and reached for his sword.

"Put that away. You don't need it," Joy-in-the-Dance said reassuringly. "I brought you something. Just what you've been wanting. See here. Look. Look close."

The girl made a few quick motions at the sentry. "A roasted partridge. It smells delicious. Done to a turn. Your mouth's watering for it, you're so hungry. Go on, eat your fill."

Lucian saw nothing whatever in the girl's out-stretched hands. Yet the sentry's face lit up, he licked his lips, and put his fingers to his mouth as if he were cramming in morsels of food.

"It tastes so good." Joy-in-the-Dance nodded approval while the man chewed and gulped empty air. "You'll want something to wash it down."

Again, she held out her hands. "A big pitcher of what

you like best. Drink up, don't stint yourself. You deserve a little refreshment, sitting here all night.

"It's strong," she went on as the guard made a show of swigging from an invisible vessel. "Oh, I'm afraid it's gone to your head. Spinning round and round. Tipsy, are you? Yes. Very tipsy. No matter, you'll sleep it off. Now."

At this, the guard swayed on his feet and sat down heavily, belching and snoring, lost to the world.

"What did you do?" Lucian gasped. "There's no partridge. No pitcher of drink. How——?"

"Don't babble, Aiee-Ouch. Go fetch your donkey."

Lucian darted into the shed, warned the poet to be silent, and hastily untethered him.

"Let's get out of here," said Joy-in-the-Dance. "That sentry's going to wake up soon—with a pounding head and a bad case of indigestion."

The girl moved quietly and calmly across the marketplace, Lucian and Fronto behind her. Once out of the village, she headed into the woodlands, setting such a brisk pace that Lucian wondered if she could see in the dark as well as conjure up roasted fowl. It was sunrise by the time she halted.

"Very well," she said. "Here's your donkey. What does he have to say for himself?"

"Who are you? What are you?" murmured Lucian.

"You cast some kind of spell back there. I've heard tales of that." He drew back uneasily. "Are you a girl at all?"

"I should hope so. And I didn't cast a spell. I only suggested what the guard wanted and he did the rest himself. You might thank me for saving your jackass instead of gaping like an idiot; but, never mind, I want to hear him talk."

"It's all right," Lucian said to Fronto. "Joy-in-the-Dance is—claims—she's a healer."

"Blessings on you, my dear young woman." Fronto tossed his head. "I'm delighted beyond words to make your acquaintance."

"He does talk," the girl said to Lucian. "That much is true."

"You're not surprised?" said Fronto.

"Why should I be? Every animal talks. I admit you're the first jackass I've met who uses human speech, but being able to talk is less important than being able to talk sense. Your friend has difficulty along those lines. So, you tell me straight out what happened."

"Once you hear my sad history," said Fronto, "I have no doubt that you'll be moved by those emotions I conveyed in one of my finest odes: pity and terror."

"In that case," said Joy-in-the-Dance, "keep it mercifully short."

Fronto quickly repeated his account, concluding with

his misadventure in the pool. Instead of pity and terror, the girl displayed what Lucian had to judge as fury. She seized Fronto by the ears and began shaking him until his teeth rattled.

"You drank? You swam?" she burst out. "How dare you—"

"Let him be!" Lucian sprang to protect the belabored poet. "You're supposed to cure him, not batter him to pieces." He tussled with Joy-in-the-Dance, who was much stronger than he expected; at last he pulled her away. She and Lucian fell back, out of breath and glaring at each other.

"He meant no harm," declared Lucian. "He wanted to go to the pythoness and beg forgiveness. It's not his fault if the warriors attacked the sanctuary and walled her up.

"As for that," Lucian hurried on, "the pythoness herself started all the trouble. If she hadn't given Bromios that prophecy to begin with, there'd have been no attack. Or farmhouses burned, wise-women hunted down, or anything else. Fronto might have made a little mistake, but it's the pythoness who's responsible for the trouble he's in now."

"Oh, yes, twist everything around," Joy-in-the-Dance snapped back. "To be expected from a man, and one of the Bear tribe into the bargain."

"Bear tribe or not, that's how I see it," Lucian re-torted. "I'm sorry for what happened to her, but I wish she could know what a mess she began."

"She does." The girl's eyes flashed. "I'm Woman-Who-Talks-to-Snakes."

7

Mysteries of Women

M y dear girl," Fronto said as Lucian's jaw dropped, "the oracle has resided in her cave from time immemorial. In which case, you'd be as ancient as Mount Lerna itself. Clearly—and charmingly, I hasten to add—you are noticeably younger. I'm grateful for whatever assistance you gave my friend here, but you can hardly expect us to believe—"

"Fronto, I don't know who she is or what she is," Lucian murmured, "but she's the one who rescued you. She did it all. That business with the partridge—"

"Was a bird involved?" said Fronto. "Did I miss something? I was deep in unhappy thoughts, paying no attention until the moment you untied me. How did a partridge come into it?"

"Never mind, I'll explain later." Lucian paused and shook his head. "I don't see how it's possible, but is there any way she could be telling the truth? She can do amazing things. I've seen that for myself."

"I quite understand," replied Fronto, "that any lad would be eager to believe whatever an attractive young woman chooses to tell him. Only apply a little reason and common sense. The oracle was walled up in the cave. We must presume she perished there."

"When the two of you decide whether I'm old as the hills or dead as a mackerel," said Joy-in-the-Dance, "I'll be interested in your conclusions. As for you, Aiee-Ouch, I'm delighted to hear one of you Bear men admit that a girl can do anything at all. It must have felt like having your skin peeled off.

"As for you," she added to Fronto, "you're a poet, so apply a little imagination. Did it ever cross your mind that there could be another way out of the cave? Or more than one pythoness? Oracles don't live forever. There were dozens before me.

"I served the last one. She taught me her lore and learning. When she died this winter, I was chosen to take her place. I'm not used to having my word questioned; but, for the sake of ending the discussion—"

From beneath her tunic she drew out a medallion on a silver chain: the figure of a woman crowned with a tall headdress and holding a serpent in each hand. "Here. The emblem of Woman-Who-Talks-to-Snakes. Only a pythoness may wear it."

Fronto stared a moment, then burst out: "Revered oracle! Venerated pythoness! I humbly apologize for doubting. And let me add that I wholeheartedly deplore the disaster that's come upon you."

"Disaster, yes, it's every bit of that," Joy-in-the-Dance said, her features tightening. "The Lady's devotees are hunted down, their lives at stake. I've seen to it that my maidens are safe in hiding, and as many others as I could reach. I sent away the healer at the farm. Right now, that's the best I can do. Which isn't much in the way of settling things.

"Aiee-Ouch was right," she added bitterly. "My prophecy started the whole mess—as he was very quick to point out."

"I didn't mean to put it quite that way," said Lucian.

"It's true, no matter how you put it," Joy-in-the-Dance said. "I knew there'd be trouble for sure, but it turned out worse than I foresaw."

"Couldn't you have changed the prophecy?" asked Lucian. "Made it a little easier for Bromios to swallow? Or thought up something different?"

"You don't think up a prophecy. It comes to you. First, it isn't there; then, there it is. The same way, I suppose, that a poem comes to mind. I can't explain it. Fronto should know what I mean."

"Indeed I do," said Fronto, "though it hasn't happened to me lately."

"But—yes, I thought of changing it." The girl's face fell. "I wanted to. It was my first prophecy. It frightened me. I couldn't understand what it meant. I didn't want to be the one who pronounced it. I was tempted a dozen times to put it aside. Who'd have known? Not Bromios. I could have told him any sort of harmless nonsense and that would have been the end of it.

"I even wondered if it was false, or if I'd misunderstood. Until the moment Bromios set foot in the cave, I still wasn't sure what to do."

The girl's chin went up, in pride and defiance; but Lucian saw tears glinting in her eyes. "Then I decided I couldn't turn away from what I had to tell him. I spoke the prophecy as it had come to me. Now that I see what it brought on us"—she glanced down and shook her head—"I'm not sure if I did right or wrong."

"I'm not the one to say," Lucian admitted. "I don't know about such mysteries. I just count beans. What I do know—what I didn't realize before—you risked your life rescuing Fronto in the midst of the king's warriors. They're hunting the pythoness everywhere."

"They think she's an old hag," said Joy-in-the-Dance.

"Do I fit that description? But you and Fronto shouldn't linger. I'll miss my guess if the captain doesn't send his men out searching."

"They won't go to that much trouble for a missing donkey."

"Not for a donkey. For me. The guard's bound to report what happened. The captain isn't altogether stupid. Even a Bear warrior has brains enough to reckon that anyone who makes a roasted partridge appear out of thin air is worth some close questioning.

"Let them look for me. They won't find me. I'll set so many false trails they won't know which way they're going. It will keep them off your track, too. They'll be so busy they won't think about following you."

"You're not leaving—"

"Yes, I'm afraid I have to. Good-bye—Lucian." She grinned at him. "No. Aiee-Ouch suits you better."

"Stop! Stop!" burst out Fronto. "You're forgetting something most important: changing me back to myself."

"Fronto, I'm truly sorry for you," the girl said. "I wish I could do as you ask."

"But surely you can," said Lucian. "You speak prophecies, conjure up partridges and who knows what else; you can sleep like a chicken—"

"Adorable pythoness!" exclaimed Fronto, in growing alarm and dismay. "Turning an ass into a man—what effort would it take, with all those powers? Hardly enough to raise a sweat."

"It doesn't work that way," the girl said patiently. "Let me explain. No one, these days, has magical powers. Not even I."

"Oh?" Fronto snorted. "Then what happened to me?"

"I'm trying to tell you. We don't have magical powers. The powers we do have are useful, but they aren't magical. All of us devoted to the Lady learn about healing herbs, the movement of the stars telling when to plant and reap. How to find water underground. We understand the speech of animals—but only because we watch and listen and know their ways. And a lot more, besides. All perfectly natural. You men call them 'women's mysteries' because we keep them to ourselves. We don't share them with men, Bear men least of all."

"How can you not?" interrupted Lucian. "These are marvelous things for everybody."

"We don't trust you men with them," said Joy-in-the-Dance. "Thickheaded oafs like Bromios? Worse yet, that pair of greedy soothsayers? They're vicious and ruthless, beneath all their oiliness. They'd twist that knowledge to their own purposes. They'd use it to kill and destroy. We women won't let that happen."

"If you don't mind my saying," put in Fronto, "you're straying from the point."

"No, I'm explaining the point," said Joy-in-the-Dance. "The pool at Mount Lerna was truly magical. There used to be other magical places—groves of trees, rings of standing stones, fountains. That was long ago, when real enchanters lived here. The Bear tribe destroyed most of those places to build towns and villages. The magic simply faded away from the others. The pool was the last. Now it's gone, too. As for you, Fronto, magic changed you into a jackass. Only magic can change you back."

"You just told me it's all gone," wailed Fronto. "I'm a jackass forever. Send me to the knacker! Fling me into a river! Anything to end this asinine existence!"

Joy-in-the-Dance laid a calming hand on Fronto's neck. "There's still a chance. One person might help you: the Lady of Wild Things."

"How can she?" put in Lucian. "She isn't real, she's just an old wives' tale."

"That's what you Bear men think. Believe me, she's very real. She lives on the north coast, in her sanctuary at Mount Panthea."

"If that's true—all right, yes, I'll believe you," said Lucian. "I'll take Fronto there. Can you tell me how to find the sanctuary?"

"I can," said the girl. "I can also tell you it's forbidden to men of the Bear tribe. And that, I'm sure, includes jackasses. You couldn't set foot anywhere close to the place."

Fronto, having brightened for a moment, looked more dismal than ever. "No use, then. My dear Lucian, do me one last good turn."

"Wait a minute. Let me think," said Joy-in-the-Dance. "There might be a way around that rule. I can speak on your behalf. I'm going to Mount Panthea. I have to see the Lady of Wild Things."

8

Forbidden Enchantments

Y ou have my undying gratitude!" exclaimed Fronto. "I'll dedicate a hymn of thanksgiving to you—once I'm in a position to do so."

"Don't thank me yet," said Joy-in-the-Dance. "Even the Lady might not be able to help. Whether she can— that's one thing. Whether she will—that's another. You committed a serious offense, Fronto. She could decide it served you right and leave you as you are; or lay on a worse punishment."

"I hadn't thought of that," said Fronto, "but my considered opinion is: Anything's better than what I am."

"And I—" Lucian began, "I wonder if the Lady might help me, too? If Calchas and Phobos get their hands on me, they'll kill me. I don't dare go back to the palace or anywhere they could find me. What can I do? Hide away in some hole and corner for the rest of my life? Count beans forever? No, that's over and done with. Fronto was a poet. He'll be one again, if the Lady transforms him. But I? What could I be? I haven't been anything much in the first place. Would the Lady tell me?"

"Aiee-Ouch, you do astonish me," Joy-in-the-Dance said. "People have implored her for riches, fame, magical secrets, and whatever else you could imagine—without getting them, naturally. But wanting to know what to do with your life? I've never heard of such a request. If she's willing to see you, you'll have to ask her yourself.

"I hadn't bargained on traveling companions," she added, "least of all a donkey and an Aiee-Ouch; but I dread to think of you two blundering about on your own. Yes, I'll take you to Mount Panthea. You have to keep pace, though. No wandering off, poking into things that aren't your business, making a nuisance—"

"Agreed most happily!" exclaimed Fronto.

"You're the pythoness." Lucian turned away and grumbled under his breath to Fronto, "Pythoness or not, she doesn't have to give me lessons in common sense. I'm no child. I'm a man, after all."

"Yes, exactly," said Joy-in-the-Dance, whose ears were keener than Lucian supposed. "Now, let's be away from here or we'll have a pack of warriors on our heels."

The girl set off, with Lucian and Fronto scrambling after her. For the rest of the morning, however, Lucian saw little of their guide. She was continually leaving them to wait while she disappeared into the brush, reappearing later from a different direction; or circling, or doubling back on her own footsteps. Once, she popped up without her cloak, explaining she had dropped it where the troop would surely find it; another time, her cheeks and knees were crisscrossed with bramble scratches, her braid had come undone, and she looked thoroughly pleased.

"That," she remarked, brushing twigs from her hair, "will do nicely. They'll end up chasing one another."

If Lucian had been nettled by the girl taking her authority for granted, over the next few days he grudgingly admitted to himself that he would have been lost, famished, bone sore, and parched without her. Joy-in-the-Dance was always able to pick the easiest pathways and most comfortable sleeping spots. She found hidden springs of clear water, unearthed odd-shaped edible roots, dug out nuts the squirrels had buried: meager fare, but it staved off hunger and thirst.

One day, she found a honey tree. While Lucian and Fronto kept a safe distance, the girl calmly walked straight to it and began a high-pitched, wordless singing. The bees swarmed from the hollow trunk and formed a starlike crown on her head. Still singing, she reached into the hive and broke off a portion of honeycomb. As she stepped away, the bees streamed back into their tree.

"How—? What did you do?" stammered Lucian. "Or is that a woman's mystery?"

"Only a small one."

"No use, then, asking you to teach me," Lucian said wryly. "All right, I can understand why you don't share your secrets with Bear people like Bromios, or soothsayers like Calchas and Phobos. But I'm not the Bear tribe, I'm only me. Besides, I've heard that a lot of Bear men are devoted to the Lady. They won't turn your mysteries against you."

"How do we know?" said Joy-in-the-Dance. "We can't be sure what they'd do once they had that kind of knowledge. We won't take the risk. We decided that long ago. We have a tale about it, handed down from mother to daughter—"

"A story?" broke in Lucian, pricking up his ears. "Would you tell that to me, at least? I've never heard anything but Bear lore."

"Not surprising. No wonder you're an Aiee-Ouch."

Though Lucian pressed her to tell him, she said no more on the subject, leaving him disappointed and more than a little vexed.

"My boy," Fronto later remarked to him, "I've been observing. I do believe our admirable pythoness has a bit of a soft spot for you. I'm a poet, I detect such things."

Lucian snorted. "Well, I'm not a poet, but what I detect is: Half the time, she doesn't make sense; the other half, she makes me feel like an idiot."

"Precisely," said Fronto. "That's another of those women's mysteries."

That same day, Joy-in-the-Dance halted in a dense corner of the forest and beckoned Lucian and Fronto past the tangled undergrowth.

"It's summer here!" Lucian hardly believed his eyes. A ring of ancient oaks stood in full, rich foliage. Flowering vines clung to the gnarled trunks. Crimson and white blossoms covered the bushes. He took a deep breath of the warm, fragrant air. Only a few paces behind him, the trees had just begun to put out new leaves. "Why here and nowhere else?"

"It stays like this all year-round." Joy-in-the-Dance took his hand and led him to a pool glittering in the sunlight. A ledge of polished marble rimmed the water. Nearby rose a little pavilion; ivy twined to the top of its slender columns. "This used to be one of the magical places I told you about. Most of the magic's gone, but there's still a little bit left. From the days when the Great Ones lived in Arkadia."

"Where are they now? What happened?" Lucian asked. "Can you tell me?"

"Yes. It's something you ought to know. You, too, Fronto. It's about a man meddling with things that didn't concern him." The girl settled cross-legged at the pool's rim. Lucian drew closer to her as she began: "Long ago, before the Bear tribe came to Arkadia, there was a man called Think-Too-Late.

"He had everything he needed. His vines gave him the heaviest bunches of the sweetest grapes. In his orchard, ripe fruits fell into his hands without his climbing to pluck them. When his wife, Giving-All-Gifts, sat at her loom, the cloth wove itself with never a knot or broken thread. Clear water filled his well to the brim, his crops sprang up in abundance, his livestock never sickened, nor did he. For all that, he was restless and unsatisfied."

"How could he be?" put in Lucian. "I don't understand that."

"You will," said Joy-in-the-Dance. "In those days, mighty enchanters lived in Arkadia: the Great Ones. They were tall and graceful, fair of face and generous in spirit, with powers past mortal understanding. One, for instance, Arbikanos, knew the secret of transforming himself into any animal, bird, or sea creature, and back again. Another, Stephanos, knew the opposite art: how to change animals into human beings. Of yet another, Dalbenos, it was said that he could, whenever he chose, start his life afresh as a newborn infant. And there were many more, all gifted with magical skills and knowledge.

"But the most powerful was called Woman-Three-Women, who could take the form of a beautiful maiden, a kindly mother, or a frightful hag. She could spin life-threads, measure, and shear them off. She knew how all things began and ended, and the shape of mortal destinies. The other Great Ones honored her in their sanctuary and council hall at the foot of Mount Panthea.

"It was thanks to these Great Ones that Think-Too-Late, like his fellow mortals, was showered with so many blessings. The enchanters provided for all his needs. They caused his fields to flourish, his animals to thrive, his household to prosper without toil or trouble. Out of their loving kindness, they kept Arkadia a land of peaceful happiness."

"She's setting the scene very nicely for us," remarked Fronto. "Building up the atmosphere. It's no doubt one of those tales of sentiment and tender feelings. The ladies enjoy that sort of thing."

"As for Think-Too-Late," Joy-in-the-Dance went on, ignoring Fronto, "having nothing better to occupy his mind, he began to think about his condition; and, the more he thought about it, the more fault he found.

" 'The Great Ones have given us good things,' he said to his wife. 'All very nice, I admit. But no one with any sense or wisdom gives away everything. So, if the Great Ones have given us this much, they could surely give us more if they chose. Since they haven't given us everything, they're holding something back. And if they're holding something back, it must be most precious. And if it's most precious, I find it mean-spirited and tightfisted of them not to share it.'

"Giving-All-Gifts told him to put that notion out of his mind and be glad for all he had. But Think-Too-Late kept gnawing at it so much that soon it began gnawing at him.

"It had long been rumored that the Great Ones had buried an iron-bound chest at the peak of Mount Panthea. Some whispered that the coffer held a vast treasure; others, that it was filled with magical objects, even the secret of eternal life. Think-Too-Late had never given much credit to this gossip. Now, he believed the rumors must be true.

" 'Whatever's in that box,' he told himself, 'has to be more precious than anyone can imagine, or it wouldn't be hidden. Yes, the Great Ones are holding something back. Since they won't share it freely, I have every reason to go and take it.'

"When Giving-All-Gifts warned that it was not only dangerous but also downright stealing, Think-Too-Late brushed aside her objections. 'Stealing?' he cried. 'How so, when they've given me everything else, why not this? Why should the Great Ones lord it over me, and run my life as they see fit, as if I were a child?'

"Though Giving-All-Gifts pleaded, wept, and wrung her hands, nothing would change his mind. 'Woman,' he said, 'you don't understand manly matters. If I turned away from what must be done, I'd be a sorry specimen of manhood.'

"Then and there, with his wife wailing and begging him to stay home and mind his business, Think-Too-Late set out for Mount Panthea.

"His journey was long and harsh. He soon ran out of what food he had taken with him; instead of fruits falling into his hands he had to scrape for roots and acorns. Nights, he shivered on the cold ground; days, he went hungry and thirsty. Nevertheless, he kept on his way. When, at last, he came to Mount Panthea, his path only grew more difficult. The higher he climbed, the sharper blew the icy gales, freezing him to the marrow. Sleet and snow blinded him, jagged rocks bloodied his hands and feet. Still, he climbed until he reached the peak.

"There, his eyes lit up as he saw a tall heap of white stones. He clawed and scrabbled away at them, and when he flung aside the last one, he cried out in both triumph and dismay. Indeed, a chest lay exposed, but hardly bigger than the palm of his hand.

" 'How can a little box hold great value?' he exclaimed. 'I've been cheated again!'

"Then he saw the coffer was sealed with the emblem of Woman-Three-Women. 'Aha,' he said to himself, 'if it belongs to her, it must be worth something, at least. Whatever it holds, I'll have it for all my pains.'

"He snatched it up. That same instant, before he could break the seal, the ground rumbled and shuddered beneath his feet. The hollow where the chest had lain gaped open. From the jaws of this pit, flames and molten rock shot upward in a crimson column reaching to the sky. The roar deafened him, the fire scorched his face. The mountain writhed and convulsed. Think-Too-Late hung on for dear life, but the mountain shrugged him off like a horse twitching away a fly. Down he tumbled, still clutching the chest, swept along on a torrent of stones and gravel.

"The earth split, a river welled up; and, next thing he knew, he was being borne farther and farther, spinning and tossing like a leaf. Behind him, a barrier of high crags jutted where once had stretched a flat plain. Springs gushed to form lakes, waterfalls poured from newly risen cliffs. Bruised and battered, Think-Too-Late was at last pitched ashore, astonished to find himself alive and his bones unbroken.

" 'That,' he said, 'was a bit more than I bargained for.'

"Picking himself up, he set about making his long way home. This journey proved easier than his first, for he taught himself to build shelters from leaves and branches, to find forage in even the roughest country; and so, when at last he trudged into his dooryard, he was not in much worse condition than when he left.

"Giving-All-Gifts ran to embrace him, weeping with joy, and in the same breath, scolding him furiously for having risked his life to gain only a little box.

" 'Better than empty-handed,' said Think-Too-Late, casting around for a means of breaking the seal, which had not yielded to any of his efforts along the way. However, no sooner had he set the chest on the ground than the lid flew open by itself.

"Giving-All-Gifts cried out and covered her face with her hands, Think-Too-Late fell back in terror as a huge black cloud swirled out of the chest. From it strode a giant figure bearing a flaming torch; and, wherever he passed, trees were blighted, fruits withered, and fields lay barren. While Think-Too-Late stared, too frozen in horror to turn away, another giant shape appeared, gripping a lash with a dozen knotted thongs; and, wherever he swung this scourge, all living things sickened, racked with plagues and pestilence. Before the cloud melted away, yet another giant sprang from it, brandishing a bloody sword; and, wherever he passed, men fought and slew each other without mercy.

"Then, as if from nowhere, crowned with a crescent moon, there stood a tall figure in a cloak shining with stars. Think-Too-Late and Giving-All-Gifts fell to their knees. Though a shimmering veil hid her face from them, they knew this was Woman-Three-Women.

" 'Think-Too-Late,' she said, in a voice that chilled his heart, 'do you know what you have done? That is what we wished to keep from you. Now you have set these monsters at large, and never again can they be called back.'

"Think-Too-Late bowed his head. 'Take my life. I pay it for the ills I unloosed.'

" 'Wretched little man,' replied Woman-Three-Women, 'do you suppose your death can make up for your deed? No. Your punishment will be far greater.'

" 'So be it,' said Think-Too-Late. 'It can be no worse than what I deserve. And yet—and yet'—here, he raised his face and a spark brightened his eyes—'despite all else, wrong or not, I did what I did. I climbed to the very top of Mount Panthea, I rode the avalanche, I was burned, frozen, nearly drowned, and lived to come back; and this, no man has ever done.'

" 'You are a fool,' said Woman-Three-Women, 'but, I

admit, you are, after a fashion, also a hero: a combination typical among mortals.'

" 'Whatever his punishment,' said Giving-All-Gifts, 'I, too, wish to suffer it with him. He is a foolish creature, as I know better than anyone; and, thus, all the more need for me to help him bear it.'

" 'So you shall,' said Woman-Three-Women, 'and give him more comfort than he merits, and show better sense than he will ever have. Now, farewell to you.'

" 'You banish us?' cried Think-Too-Late, his heart torn. 'Cast us out into some terrible wilderness? Spare my wife this fate. She has done no wrong.'

" 'You stay,' said Woman-Three-Women. 'I and the Great Ones must go from here. I have long known this would be the shape of our destinies, and a day such as this would come. It is in the grain and nature of things. You were right, Think-Too-Late. We treated you as children. As children grow up and lead their own lives, so must you.'

"Woman-Three-Women turned to Giving-All-Gifts. 'To you, I entrust the arts of planting and harvesting, of healing and consolation, and all secret knowledge you will share with all women. As for you, Think-Too-Late, your punishment is so harsh I dread to speak it. You are a hero, and you are welcome to that cold glory. But you, and all men after you, shall be forever cursed with discontent, with a spirit never at peace, curiosity never satisfied, seeking that never finds, questioning never answered. You shall be driven by a goad you sharpen yourself, and go blundering and stumbling, misjudging and misunderstanding to the end of your days. In sum, you are condemned to be human. I can inflict nothing more painful. Too much so, perhaps. Therefore, I leave you one last thing.'

"As she spoke, out of the chest flew a small white bird, so graceful and beautiful that Giving-All-Gifts caught her breath in wonder and reached out to it. And, indeed, the bird came to perch a moment on her finger before it spread its wings and fluttered away.

" 'Cherish and treat it kindly,' said Woman-Three-Women. 'It is a fragile creature, easily frightened. But, always you will find it when you need it most. Its name is Hope-Never-Lost.'

"With those words, Woman-Three-Women vanished as quickly as she had come, never to be seen again by mortal eyes."

9

The Pharmakos

And that," said Joy-in-the-Dance, folding her hands, "is how the Great Ones left us and women became keepers of wisdom, because of Think-Too-Late."

"A terrible punishment," said Fronto, with a wheezing sigh. "Being a human, let alone a poet, is difficult enough. However, compared with being an ass, I rather envy him."

Lucian had been so caught up in the girl's story, as if he himself had climbed mountains and ridden avalanches, that it took him some moments to realize he was back at the pool's side. Hoping to hear more, he asked, "Is that the end?"

"Of that story," said Joy-in-the-Dance. "After Woman-

Three-Women vanished, a mortal woman was chosen to take her place. She, and those who came after, held the title Lady of Wild Things.

"Mount Panthea and all the old sanctuaries are now places of study, where lore is handed down, as the story says, from Giving-All-Gifts. The Lady of Wild Things is first among our teachers, our guide and counselor who knows more than any of us. She teaches us to remember."

"Who needs to be taught? Everybody can remember. You just do it."

"Not the way you think. We learn by word of mouth. We memorize our lore and know it by heart. It isn't written down."

"You have all this wisdom, all these secrets," said Lucian, "and you don't even know how to write?"

"Of course we do. Mother Tongue's our first language. We certainly know how to speak it. And read it, and write it. But when it comes to lore and learning—no, Aiee-Ouch, we don't write it down. That's too dangerous.

"Don't you understand? Think about it," Joy-in-the-Dance went on. "If something's written down, it can be stolen. Or destroyed. Or copied wrong. Or changed all around so it doesn't mean what it was supposed to mean. Memory's the safest place to keep it."

"I don't see that," Lucian said. "Everything's gone forever if you happen to forget."

"We don't forget."

"That's true, my boy," put in Fronto. "It's been my experience that women never forget anything. There have been times when I wish they did."

"And all this came about because of what one man did long ago?" said Lucian.

"Not exactly," said Joy-in-the-Dance. "Once, our lore was written down. Not anymore. Not since the Bear tribe came to Arkadia. But that's a different story."

Joy-in-the-Dance closed her eyes, leaving Lucian all the more curious but none the wiser.

&

Next day, the wolves found them.

For much of that morning, Joy-in-the-Dance led Lucian and Fronto along a smooth forest track. After a time, however, Fronto began turning skittish, uneasily sniffing the air. Lucian glimpsed ash gray streaks flickering through the brush.

"Only wolves," Joy-in-the-Dance said, unperturbed. "We're in their territory."

"Then let's get out of it," urged Fronto. "I'll be turned into meat before I'm turned into a man."

The pack broke from cover that same instant. Half a dozen of the lean, rough-coated animals stationed themselves to block the path. A huge, yellow-eyed she wolf, tongue lolling and ears laid back, loped forward.

Lucian stepped quickly ahead of Joy-in-the-Dance. He snatched up a fallen branch. The gray wolf halted and crouched. Her hackles went up and she bared her fangs. Lucian's hands shook so violently he could scarcely keep a grip on the makeshift weapon. Nevertheless, he dug in his heels and braced for her attack. The wolf fixed her eyes on him and pointed her long muzzle.

"Run, you two," Lucian ordered. "I'll hold her off."

"Don't be such an Aiee-Ouch." Joy-in-the-Dance strode next to him, pulled the branch from his hand, and tossed it aside. "She won't bite."

"What's she showing me, then? I'd call them—teeth."

"I'd show mine, too, if somebody was shaking a stick at me."

The wolf trotted up, wagging her tail. She hunkered down in front of Lucian, snuffling and nuzzling his ankles. Lucian swallowed hard. "Good doggie," he said.

"Interesting," said Joy-in-the-Dance. "She likes you. She has something in mind."

"So do I," muttered Fronto. "Galloping in the opposite direction."

"Best go with her," advised Joy-in-the-Dance as the wolf took the hem of Lucian's tunic between her teeth and tugged him toward the waiting animals.

The pack closed around him. Next thing, he was willy-nilly bounding along with them. The wolves quickened their pace, urging him on with an occasional nip at his heels. As Lucian, to his surprise, found himself able to keep up, racing faster and faster, legs at full stretch and heart pounding, he began to relish the wild excitement of it. Joy-in-the-Dance and Fronto followed well behind him.

They halted at last, where several other wolves sat on their haunches at the foot of a tall beech tree. While Fronto eyed the pack uneasily, Joy-in-the-Dance came to Lucian's side. The wolves were looking at something high above. Lucian shaded his eyes and peered upward.

There was a man at the top of the tree.

"What are you doing?" called Joy-in-the-Dance.

"Nothing," the man shouted back. "I'm stuck. I can't climb down."

"Why are you there at all?" the girl demanded. "Oh, never mind. I'll come up and get you loose."

"I'll do that," said Lucian, stepping in front of the girl. He felt marvelously sweaty after his run with the wolves, his muscles stretched and limber, and he decided that climbing a tree was exactly the challenge he wanted.

"Yes, it's man's work, of course," Joy-in-the-Dance said caustically. "I suppose you've done it a hundred times. Please, Aiee-Ouch, just keep out of the way and let me—"

"I think even a Bear man can figure it out." Calling Fronto, Lucian sprang to the poet's back and wrapped his arms around the lowest branch. He swung up and reached for one limb after the other, finding it easier than he expected.

Glancing down, however, made his head spin. The upper limbs grew thinner and bent under his weight. Swaying back and forth, trying to keep his heart from escaping by way of his mouth, he began wishing Joy-in-the-Dance had made more of an effort to keep him on the ground. Nevertheless, gritting his teeth, he clutched another branch and swung upward. What came to view was a foot, bare and mud-caked, tightly wedged in a fork of the tree.

"Good of you to stop by," said the owner of the foot. "I don't know when I'd have untangled myself, if ever. Sorry to inconvenience you."

The speaker, though a man no more than a dozen years older than Lucian, was in a terrible state of disrepair; for the most part, he was a collection of rags and tatters. Long yellow hair hung about his bruised forehead; his short beard had been plucked half away. Lucian turned his attention to the immediate matter of the foot, struggling until he pulled it free.

"Thank you. Excellent." The ragged figure set about unwinding his arms and legs. "I can manage quite well now."

The man began climbing down with surprising agility. Following his example, Lucian discovered it to be as difficult as climbing up, and far more unnerving. By accident, he adopted a quick method of reaching the ground: sliding, tumbling, bouncing off one branch after another to land sprawled in what he hoped was a triumphant posture.

"That was wonderful, Aiee-Ouch," the girl said. "I take it all back. You did perfectly, except for the one little moment when your skull hit the ground. Now, this fellow—he didn't get those stab wounds and bruises being caught up a tree."

The stranger, meantime, brushed himself off, looked around, and bobbed his head.

"Ops," he said.

"What's that?" said Lucian.

"Ops," the stranger repeated. "My name. Argeus Ops. Feel free to call me Argeus. Or Ops. Either will do. Forgive me for troubling you. I stopped to put a fledgling crow back in its nest. The parents thought I was stealing it. Understandably, they set upon me. Vigorously, too.

The little one, as it turned out, didn't need my assistance. It flew off with its parents. Then I clumsily got my foot caught. Luckily, the wolves happened along. I asked them to find help."

"You talked to them?" said Joy-in-the-Dance.

"Why, I suppose I did," said Ops. "I wonder how? Sheer necessity, no doubt. Now, how may I be of service to you? Or your donkey? He doesn't look in very good state. Is something troubling him?"

"You don't know the half of it," muttered Fronto.

"He speaks?" said Ops. "How interesting." He bowed courteously to Fronto. "No offense. I'm sure you're an excellent donkey."

"Poet," corrected Fronto. "What happened to me— never mind, I'm tired of explaining."

"As you wish." Ops turned to Lucian and Joy-in-the-Dance. "Have you two any miseries you'd like me to take on for you? Bad luck to get rid of? A loathsome disease?"

"You seem to have enough miseries of your own," said Lucian.

"It's my occupation," said Ops. "But, since I was cast out of my village, I've had little to do. I'm a pharmakos."

"Oh, no!" Joy-in-the-Dance cried in dismay. "When did this happen? Where?"

"What's a pharmakos?" asked Lucian.

"In Mother Tongue, that's the word for a scapegoat,"

said Joy-in-the-Dance. "A blame-taker. An old custom no one's followed for years. The country folk used to believe they could wish all their misfortunes onto someone else, blame him for whatever went wrong, throw him out into the wilds, and that would set everything right."

"Exactly so," said Ops. "Things went badly in my village after King Bromios made it a crime to deal with wise-women. We had no healer for ailing animals; no water-finder when two of our wells went dry; and, worst of all, no medicine woman for the infants who sickened for lack of good water. The village council decided a pharmakos could carry off their troubles. Oh, it was quite a celebration when they cast me out."

"I was afraid something like that might happen," Joy-in-the-Dance said, her eyes darkening. "They're slipping back into ways best forgotten. What next? Human sacrifice?"

"That was discussed," said Ops. "Luckily for me, they decided against it. They thought it best to lay their woes on a scapegoat.

"I'm sure they felt better, blaming me for everything," he went on, "and I was glad to do them a service. But when they got carried away, pulling my hair, hitting me with rakes and hoes—it seemed a little too much."

"No one stopped them?" demanded Joy-in-the-Dance. "No one spoke out against such a thing?"

"A few," said Ops. "Finally, most approved."

"What about the village chief?" said Joy-in-the-Dance. "He, at least, should have known better. He's supposed to have enough common sense and authority to forbid such doings."

"True," Ops agreed. "But, you see—I was the village chief."

10

Hidden Treasures

Their chief?" exclaimed Lucian. "They turned against you?"

"Not exactly," said Ops. "There's a little more to it. The treasure under the stone, for one thing. And the old shepherd. And my parents, of course."

"Please, please," Fronto put in. "Go at it a step at a time. No one can follow a tale that bolts off in all directions at once."

"Very well," said Ops. "To begin: My father-name is Argeus Ops. My mother-name is Bright-Face."

"Your parents each gave you a name?" said Lucian. "That's an unusual thing to do, isn't it?"

"I think I know why," said Joy-in-the-Dance. "In the

Bear tribe, it's the father who names his child; among my people, it's the mother."

"Yes," said Ops, "my father was a Bear man. My mother was a sanctuary maiden assigned to tend the local woods and fields."

"That's what I supposed," said Joy-in-the-Dance. Seeing a questioning look on Lucian's face, she added, "Our sanctuary maidens have always been free to marry with men of the Bear tribe or whoever they please. It doesn't happen too often these days." She turned back to Ops. "What about your parents?"

"My father died when I was a small boy; my mother, not long after," said Ops. "I was too young to remember them clearly, but the shepherd who raised me told me their story time and time again. How my father, hunting, had come upon a stag caught in a thicket. Just as he drew his bow, the most beautiful maiden he had ever seen sprang up and flung her arms around the stag's neck. She warned him if he tried to kill the creature he would have to kill her first.

"Naturally, he let the stag go free. He and the maiden fell in love at first sight. They dwelt happily together in the forest, and he never hunted again.

"When my mother knew that her life-thread had spun to its end, she gave me into the care of an old shepherd and his wife. They fostered and raised me as lovingly as if I had been their own. I helped tend the sheep and do other little tasks.

"When I was old enough to understand, the couple told me that my parents had hidden my birthright under a certain stone. The shepherd led me to a glade near the pasture and pointed out a boulder taller than I was. I begged him to move it for me so that I might possess what was underneath.

" 'That is forbidden to me,' he said. 'Your dear mother told me that only when you yourself move the stone shall you have what lies below.'

"Impatiently, I tried to wrestle it loose. But, of course, I was too small and weak. Even so, time after time, I would go and test my strength against it. Through each passing year, I struggled to raise the boulder, always failing. Often, I would sit on it, playing my shepherd's pipe, dreaming of what could have been treasured up for me, while the sheep, gently bleating—"

"Oh, get on with it!" cried Fronto. "No need to string it out, we understand the situation. There, Lucian, is an example of bad storytelling. Ops, for the sake of mercy and my patience, come to the point."

"Oh—yes, well, after I reached the strength of young manhood, a day arrived when I did shift the stone a little. I sweated and strained, and at last I rolled it away. Under it, I found a pair of sandals and a silver amulet and chain. Puzzled as much as excited, I picked them up and ran to the cottage.

"Instead of joy and pride at my accomplishment, the shepherd and his wife gazed at me with sadness.

" 'Alas, the day has come when you must leave us,' the shepherd said. 'The amulet is for your protection; the sandals for you to walk your own road. When the sandals wear out, there will you stop and stay.'

"They hung the amulet around my neck and put the sandals on my feet. With loving farewells, I set out from the cottage. My sandals were stout and well crafted; but, in time, the bindings broke, the soles came loose. Just as they fell from my feet, I found myself nearing a small village. I entered it, though hardly believing I would wish to stay there.

"The folk heartily welcomed me and showed me all the hospitality due a stranger—less than they would have liked, for their provisions were scant. The reason, they told me, was the constant raiding of their stores and granaries.

"A band of wanderers prowled the fringes of the village, darting in to pilfer whatever came to hand. 'Worse than mice,' one man complained, 'and too quick to catch.' 'A nuisance growing into a pest into a plague,' another added, 'gnawing away a little here, a little there.

If it keeps on, there won't be enough for us; or them, either.'

"The villagers had found no way to stop this raiding. As I listened, a plan took shape in my mind. I offered to help them, warning them to do as I instructed, without question. At their wits' end, they eagerly agreed.

"Next, I went alone to where this rootless band crouched in their makeshift camp. A ragtag lot of starvelings they were; men, women, and children, unkempt, round-eyed with hunger, for even what they stole was barely enough to serve them.

" 'Friends,' I declared, 'why waste your time and strength being sneak thieves? Walk with me straight into the village. You shall have all you ask and more.' However, I insisted on their following my orders and doing whatever I required.

"That they vowed and followed me—to the dismay of the villagers, who nevertheless kept silent, as they had promised.

" 'Take what you please,' I told the wretched band, pointing to the granaries. 'Take all, if that suits you. But—the grain must be threshed and winnowed first, and you must lend a hand in doing it.'

"Scowling, glaring, villagers and strangers nevertheless joined in the work. I kept them so busy they forgot to distrust one another, and there was even some good-natured jesting back and forth. That night, I called for a festival with dancing on the threshing room floor; and there, high spirits and laughter softened hard feelings.

" 'Before the grain is shared out,' I now told them, 'part must be set aside for the animals and for brewing, and the rest ground into flour. This is a long, hard task, so all must join in.'

"For days, the strangers labored at grinding the grain, receiving food enough to satisfy their hunger. When they finished, I declared, 'This is well and good, but the flour must be baked into bread. You must help to knead and shape the loaves before you claim anything more.'

"And so it went," Ops continued, "one common task after another until planting season came round and I required the wanderers to help in plowing and sowing. By this time, they were no longer wanderers. They had found occupations among the villagers, some were even betrothed or married, with little ones on the way, and few remembered when there had been ill will.

"I was chosen by all to be village chieftain and leader of the council. It was then, at last, I told the former strangers they were free, if they chose, to take everything they wanted and depart.

" 'Go from here?' retorted a lad who had apprenticed himself to a potter. 'Live hand-to-mouth in the woods? I'm no such fool.'

" 'We can't spare them,' added the winemaker. 'How did we get along without them? Here they all stay, as friends and kindred.'

"The village prospered," said Ops, "until, as I told you, we were forbidden to deal with wise-women. As things turned worse, the villagers grew desperate. Their fearful thoughts went back to a grim and ancient custom. They demanded a scapegoat.

"By no amount of reasoning, pleading, or angry protest could I change their minds. The council, among themselves, had already settled on the victim: an old woman, half-blind and so feeble she could barely put one foot in front of the other. 'Who better?' they declared. 'Her life-thread is at its end. As she is no use to herself, she can be of use to our village.'

"This I straightway refused. 'If she is so close to death, she will have no strength to carry the burden of blame.'

"They passed over the old woman but next chose a poor, half-witted boy. 'What difference can it make to him?' they said. 'His brain is addled, he will neither know nor care what becomes of him.'

"Again, I refused. 'Your victim must accept his fate of his own will and full understanding. Otherwise, as well sacrifice a dumb beast or a lump of clay.'

" 'You have only one choice,' I told them. 'I am your pharmakos.'

"They shouted against this, protesting that I had saved their village, guided them wisely, and they honored and valued me above all others.

" 'All the more reason,' I answered. 'A sacrifice that costs nothing is no sacrifice. Accept me or no one.'

"I confess I hoped this would bring them to their senses, but their desperation was too great. So, I became their scapegoat.

"And that," Ops concluded, "is how it came about. They drove me from the village, pursued me into the woods, where I outdistanced them. You know the rest."

"What a story!" exclaimed Lucian. "But it's not a tale, it happened to you. It's your own life."

"Very touching," admitted Fronto. "But, Ops, if you tell it again, go at it more briskly. Forget that business about tootling on your pipe and sheep bleating. Who cares? Now, as for my own story—"

"I want to know about the amulet," Joy-in-the-Dance broke in. "Ops, what became of it?"

"I still have it." Ops dipped into the wreckage of his shirt and fished out a silver disk at the end of a chain. The girl nodded in recognition. Lucian, peering over her shoulder, saw the figures of three women clasping hands.

"This means your mother put you under the protection of the Lady of Wild Things," said Joy-in-the-Dance. "Which also means, at the moment, you're under my protection. Fronto, you explain it to him. I want a word with Aiee-Ouch."

"My account won't take as long as his," said Fronto. "Then, Ops, my good fellow, perhaps you'd like a chance to provide your scapegoat services? I have a number of personal complaints and grievances from long before I was given my present shape. I'll be happy to lay them on you."

"I'd appreciate that," said Ops.

Leaving the wolves sitting in a circle around Fronto and Ops, Joy-in-the-Dance drew Lucian apart. She glanced back toward the pharmakos. "He'll have to come with us. He's entitled to the Lady's protection and I'll see that he gets it.

"Another thing—" She paused, looking away for some moments. Then, turning her eyes squarely on him, she added, with much effort, "Thank you for defending me against the wolves."

"Oh, yes, those ferocious wolves," retorted Lucian. "Those slavering jaws and sharp teeth, ready to tear you to pieces. All I did was make a fool of myself. You knew perfectly well they were friendly."

"But you didn't know it," said Joy-in-the-Dance. "So, thank you."

The unemployed scapegoat was delighted to accompany them. The wolves, reaching the limit of their territory, vanished as quickly and silently as they had appeared. The forest had begun to thin out, Lucian glimpsed high crags in the distance, and Joy-in-the-Dance headed straight toward them. With Ops in tow, however, progress was not as rapid. He continually halted for one reason or another. If he found a beetle struggling on its back, he would stop to set it on its legs. Crossing a stream, he noticed a beaver lodge in disrepair and insisted on delaying long enough for him to gather twigs to mend it.

To Lucian's surprise, and without his asking, Joy-in-the-Dance began pointing out patterns of stars as they rose glittering in the evening sky. He watched and listened, fascinated, as she explained how to find directions and calculate time.

"I didn't think you were supposed to tell men about such things," Lucian said.

"I've been wondering if you were right about sharing our secrets. Well, it won't do any harm to share these. They aren't the truly big mysteries. Those, you men couldn't even begin to understand."

"You've never taken the chance to find out."

"And, dear Aiee-Ouch, we don't intend to."

"My name's Lucian. I told you that when we first met. For somebody who remembers everything, you seem to keep forgetting it."

"Don't be surly. You aren't good at it," said Joy-in-the-Dance. "As for when we first met"—she gave him a sidelong smile—"I haven't forgotten."

In addition to star patterns, the girl willingly pointed out plants he never would have noticed—fever-begone, wound-balm, quicken-the-heart—as she named them and explained their use. In the course of the days, she was obliged, with some reluctance, to admit that he had grown clever enough to find these herbs without her guidance.

In his eagerness to collect the best medicinal plants, Lucian took to roaming farther afield on his own. One afternoon, outdistancing Joy-in-the-Dance, he clambered up through the scrub-covered foothills. He halted, his eyes wide in amazement as he looked down into a green cup of pastureland. The rarest and most valuable of herbs, wound-balm, covered the lower slope in unbelievable abundance.

Excitedly calling Joy-in-the-Dance to see what he had discovered, he scrambled down. Almost at the bottom, he heard something buzz past his ear. A stone rattled into the undergrowth, then another.

Warning the girl to stay away, Lucian hastily turned back toward the crest. That same instant, a hard object connected with his skull and he lost interest in the outside world.

11

Catch-a-Tick

There must be something about your head," Joy-in-the-Dance remarked, "that makes people want to hit it."

The girl, sitting on the floor beside him, held an earthen bowl of some sharp-smelling concoction. Fronto was there; and Ops, smiling in relief. As best Lucian could judge, he was on a straw pallet in a chamber domed like a beehive. Shaggy figures with dark, leathery faces peered down curiously. Stubby horns jutted from their brows, curly beards covered their chins.

"Goats?" Lucian blinked and looked again. They were, he realized, men in goatskin jackets. Their horns were twisted locks of hair stiffened with clay. He started up. "Who—or what are they?"

"Gently, gently," Joy-in-the-Dance whispered. "Don't worry. They're friends."

Exploring the landscape of his head, Lucian discovered a lump the size of a goose egg behind his ear. "What do you call this?" he muttered. "A token of goodwill?"

"Awake, are you?" boomed a voice. "By the beard of the Great Goat, it's about time."

The speaker was bandy-legged, stocky, with grizzled hair falling in ringlets around his pointed ears. His disposition struck Lucian as being as rough as his garments.

"Buckthorn Goat King," Joy-in-the-Dance said under her breath. "I've told him all about us. He can be helpful—if he wants to."

"Here's the little wretch who cracked your noggin," declared Buckthorn. He kept a tight grip on the ear of a snub-nosed boy dressed like his elders but with a stumpier set of clay horns. "Catch-a-Tick. I could call him a few other names, too. He's had a good hiding. Yes, and by the Great Goat's left hind foot, it's one he won't forget."

So saying, Buckthorn shoved Catch-a-Tick in front of Lucian. The boy dropped to his knees. Despite the humble posture, his bright, black eyes stared boldly and a grin played around his lips.

"I was punished for missing you," said Catch-a-Tick,

"not for hitting you. We Goat Folk are supposed to hit our target with the first shot."

Being ambushed and brought down by a small boy did not raise Lucian's self-esteem; especially as he had, once again, looked like a fool in the eyes of Joy-in-the-Dance. He frowned sternly. Catch-a-Tick, in trying to keep himself from laughing, seemed so close to bursting, choking, and making such faces that Lucian finally chuckled despite himself. "All right, kidling. No hard feelings except for the lump you gave me. If you've had the tanning you deserve, that's the end of it."

"Oh, no, it isn't," said Buckthorn. "He's here for the rest of his punishment. He broke a sacred law of the Goat Folk. You came unarmed, a stranger. We owe you hospitality, not a crack on the noggin."

"I only wanted to test my new sling," protested Catch-a-Tick. He held up a leather pouch dangling from rawhide thongs.

"Hold your tongue," cried Buckthorn. "You know our law." He turned to Lucian. "He's in your hands. Do whatever you want with him." Buckthorn hesitated a moment, then went on firmly. "By rule, if you choose, you can claim his life."

The chamber was silent, the onlookers held their breath. Catch-a-Tick's grin faded.

"His life? For a knock on the head?" replied Lucian. "Surely not. Let him go. That's that, over and done with."

The watching Goat Folk breathed again. Buckthorn, though clearly relieved, held up a gnarled hand. "Not done with. Demand something of him, no matter what. That's our law. We obey it. So will you."

"There's nothing I want from him."

"You think of something." Buckthorn glowered. "Speak out now, or it won't sit well with me or any Goat Folk."

Lucian pondered for a few moments then folded his arms and addressed Catch-a-Tick.

"I won't claim your life. I already have one of my own and trouble enough with it. However, you don't look very repentant. In fact, I've never seen anybody who looked less repentant. I intend, therefore, to pronounce a harsh sentence on you. I condemn you—to teach me how to use that sling."

"Acceptable!" Buckthorn clapped his hands. "Honorably judged, by the horns of the Great Goat! His mother will be glad you let him off so easily. She dotes on him." The king's face softened. "So do I, for that matter. The little goat-scut is my son."

Catch-a-Tick winked. "Next time, I'll aim better."

"Please," said Lucian, "don't."

For a king, Buckthorn's house was modest. Though somewhat roomier than the other dozen or so dwellings, it had the same beehive shape, a hole in its dome that vented smoke from the fire pit, and, like the rest, it was built close against the hillside. Goats and chickens wandered in as they pleased. May-Apple, plump wife of Buckthorn, bustled about, stuffing goat cheese into Lucian's mouth, pouring goat's milk down his throat, adding fresh straw to his pallet, and every way showing gratitude for his dealing so kindly with the irrepressible Catch-a-Tick.

Buckthorn, also pleased by Lucian's judgment, had agreed to help them all he could. He and a few of his kinsmen had gone with Joy-in-the-Dance to see the state of the mountain passes; for she intended crossing the barrier of snowy crags and reaching the grasslands beyond.

To Lucian's surprise and discomfort, the girl's absence made him feel as if he had a toothache in his chest. Since Fronto was absorbed in long talks with Ops, and Lucian was too restless to sit waiting for her to come back, he decided this was the best moment to execute his sentence on Catch-a-Tick.

"You Goat Folk live very nicely here," said Lucian as the boy led him through the pasture. "Snug and peaceful," he added, half wistfully. "The goats should be pleasant company."

"They don't do much of anything. It gets boring after a while," said Catch-a-Tick, with a shrug. He stopped beside a stream and knelt to collect a handful of smooth stones. "Here, watch this."

He set a pebble into the leather pouch. Then he whirled the sling over his head, let loose a thong, and the missile shot across the pasture. "Your turn, now."

Lucian, taking the sling, followed the boy's example. Instead of flying straight, the pebble nearly hit his own ear. Catch-a-Tick burst out laughing, rolling about on the grass and kicking his heels in the air.

"Do you want me to brain myself?" cried Lucian. "I think I'll claim your life, after all. I'll have you boiled in your own sauce."

Chuckling, Catch-a-Tick repeated his demonstration and Lucian began again. It took half the morning, but at last he caught the knack and could send a stone almost as far as his teacher and hit his target more often than not.

Delighted with himself, Lucian squatted by the edge of the stream and splashed water on his face. Next moment, sputtering and flapping his arms, he was boosted head over heels into the current. If he had envied a herd boy's peaceful life among the goats, that prospect vanished as he glimpsed a burly, long-bearded billy goat observing him with wicked amusement. Catch-a-Tick, capering on the bank, looked enormously entertained.

"Stand up on those long legs of yours," called the boy. "It isn't deep. Climb out."

Despite this advice, Lucian could not keep his feet from slipping. Catch-a-Tick shrugged out of his jacket and dove into the water. He set Lucian upright, then paddled around him, cavorting like an otter.

"Can't you swim?" The boy bobbed up and down. "Look—take a breath. You won't sink. Move your arms, kick your heels."

Lucian awkwardly imitated Catch-a-Tick and, to his astonishment, found himself actually moving across the surface. At the boy's urging, he soon dared to swim underwater. Suddenly, he was in a world where fish darted through the water like birds through the air; and Lucian himself soared up and down as if weightless, skimming over the greenery rising from the stream bed. Reveling in his new skill, he bobbed up only long enough to fill his lungs, then plunged down again. For the rest of the afternoon, he divided his time between slinging stones and jumping in and out of the stream.

"Catch-a-Tick," said Lucian as they rested on the bank, "you're a good fellow. I won't have you boiled."

"You're not a bad sort, either," said the boy, chewing a blade of grass. "For an outlander. My father says you came all the way from Metara. It must be a great city."

"It is. They say the port alone is a city in itself. Docks, taverns, ships with masts as tall as trees and sails big enough to cover this pasture. The palace, where I lived. The public square, the shops, eating houses—"

Catch-a-Tick whistled. "You've seen all that?"

"Just some of it, passing through. Fronto and I had to get out as fast as we could. Otherwise, a couple of thieving soothsayers would have chopped me to bits."

"Marvelous!" burst out Catch-a-Tick.

"With huge meat cleavers—" A glint came to Lucian's eyes; then he glanced over his shoulder, as if Joy-in-the-Dance were listening from somewhere. "Ah—not exactly. But it was a narrow escape."

"Then what?" demanded Catch-a-Tick.

"Not much. We came up against a troop of warriors, but—"

"You call that not much? Did you fight them hand to hand? Did you have a sword?"

"A sword was definitely involved," said Lucian. "Then Fronto got stolen, I had to risk my neck getting him back. After that, we fell in with a pack of wolves—"

"And they made you leader of the pack?"

"Well—I did run with them awhile," said Lucian. "That was before I rescued Ops from the highest tree I'd ever seen."

Catch-a-Tick's eyes lit up with awe and admiration. "Then?"

"Nothing, really. Until you cracked my skull with a rock." However, as Catch-a-Tick insisted, Lucian went over his account again, warming to his tale as Catch-a-Tick excitedly urged him on. By the time he finished telling and retelling, Lucian was uncertain what was fact and what was preposterous invention; and he was glad that Joy-in-the-Dance, at the moment, was elsewhere. Dusk had gathered when they returned to the beehive palace, Catch-a-Tick still demanding more.

Lucian's face was red and smarting from sunburn and his arms ached. When May-Apple scolded the boy for tiring their guest, Catch-a-Tick waved away her reproach. "He's not tired, he's a hero. You should have heard. They tried to chop him up with meat cleavers. He fought an army of warriors single-handedly. He led a pack of wolves—"

"Great Goat!" cried May-Apple, throwing up her hands. "And him only a lad!"

"Nothing out of the ordinary," said Lucian, with the modesty he thought befitting a hero. "Anyone would have done the same."

12

The Great Goat
and Never-Filled

Joy-in-the-Dance, Buckthorn, and the others came back that evening. They had found the nearest passes blocked by deep snow and rockfalls. "Buckthorn knows another way, a couple of days east of here," the girl told Lucian, shucking off her borrowed goatskin cape and leggings. "He'll guide us. It should be open enough to get through. We'll start at first light tomorrow—your nose is blistered, Aiee-Ouch—so, best get a good night's sleep."

"Why does she call you Aiee-Ouch?" Catch-a-Tick asked Lucian. "It's a silly name for a hero."

"Because—well, because she does," said Lucian.

Catch-a-Tick nodded sagely. "She's a girl, and who knows why they do anything. I still think it's silly."

"So do I," said Lucian. To his own surprise, he added, "But I'm getting to like it."

May-Apple had found capes and leggings for Lucian and Ops, as well as for Joy-in-the-Dance. In the dawn chill, they gratefully put on these garments. Fronto, eager to start, hardly complained at all about being laden with provisions. Catch-a-Tick, however, complained loudly and lengthily, pleading, cajoling, and demanding to be taken along. Buckthorn seemed tempted to let the boy have his way, but May-Apple would hear none of it. So, as the journeyers made ready to leave, the downcast Catch-a-Tick went to Lucian.

"Here." The boy held out his sling. "For you."

"But that's your best one," said Lucian. "It's too valuable to give away."

"You might need it," said Catch-a-Tick, pressing it into Lucian's hands. "This, too," he added, offering a pouch full of smooth stones. He wiped his nose on his sleeve, then regained his usual grin. "Good-bye—Aiee-Ouch."

"Good-bye, kidling," said Lucian, before hurrying to join the impatient Fronto. "Next time, we'll see who hits who."

That day, and most of the following, Buckthorn led them along the lower, gentler slopes. As they drew closer to the high pass, the Goat King, with a couple of his kinsmen bringing up the rear, nimbly picked his way over steeper and rougher trails. Lucian was glad for his warm cape; the air had turned crisp, sharply scented with pine and fir. These mountains, Joy-in-the-Dance told him, were part of the range that sprang up when Think-Too-Late had been swept from the crest of Mount Panthea. "Or so," she added, "that's how the story goes."

"Well, now," put in Buckthorn, overhearing the girl's comment, "if that's what you've heard—no, those crags were here long before any such tale. They're from the time of the Great Goat himself. Just as we've been here long before Woman-Three-Women and anyone else."

"Your people were first in Arkadia?" said Lucian, his curiosity, as always, aroused.

"Born and bred in these very hills," said Buckthorn. "Until then, there was nobody here at all."

"My dear Buckthorn," said Fronto, who had been listening to this exchange, "I wouldn't dream of denying that your ancestors are as ancient as any in the country, but they had to come from somewhere to get here in the first place."

"No, they didn't," declared Buckthorn. "As for lowlanders, bog trotters, you citified folk, and such, all you lot are newcomers compared with us." The Goat King, during this, had taken a couple of stones from his jacket.

Lucian watched, fascinated, as Buckthorn struck one against the other. Sparks flew to the dry moss and twigs that one of Buckthorn's fellows had gathered in a pile; up sprang a flame, which the Goat King fed with larger branches until a good-size fire blazed and crackled.

"I'd like to hear more about that," said Lucian.

"I can only tell you what's been told to me," said Buckthorn, squatting on his heels while the other Goat Folk drifted over to join him. "So, one day, as it happened, the Great Goat was out and about, walking in his pasture—"

"One moment," broke in Fronto. "As a poet, I don't like to niggle and nitpick over small details. But for the sake of accuracy, when you say 'walking,' was he strolling around on his hind legs? Or all fours? In which case, you might have said 'trotting.' "

"By a billy goat's beard, it makes no difference," retorted Buckthorn. "He could do anything he pleased. He was walking. Or trotting. Or both."

"Were there other animals in those days?" Lucian ventured to ask.

"Of course," Buckthorn answered. "They were here before anybody, but that's naught to do with this tale. Now, as I'm trying to tell you, one day the Great Goat was out and about, walking in his pasture, when he came to the edge of a pond. And there sat a little creature with a bald head big and round as a pumpkin, a mouth like a frog's, a pair of skinny arms and legs, and eyes googling and goggling in two directions at the same time.

" 'Good morning,' said the Great Goat. 'I haven't had the pleasure of meeting you.'

" 'I live at the bottom of this pond,' said the creature, 'and eat whatever bits and pieces come my way. But these are lean days and I'm perishing with hunger.'

" 'I'll see what I can do about that,' said the Great Goat, taking pity on the creature, who was sighing and groaning and holding his empty little belly. So the Great Goat led him to his house and sat him down at the table.

"Then the Great Goat brought out a wheel of cheese and cut a wedge from it. Instead of the wedge, the creature took hold of the wheel and swallowed it down in one gulp.

" 'You've an appetite bigger than yourself,' said the Great Goat, 'and the inside of your paunch must be larger than the outside.'

"The Great Goat then cut a slice from a loaf of bread; but the creature gobbled up the loaf instead of the slice; and, instead of the cup of milk that the Great Goat set out for him, he poured the whole pitcherful down his gullet. Then he licked clean all the jars of honey, ate all the sacks of wheat and barley, chomped up all the stores of fruit and vegetables, and looked around for more. Yet his belly was shrunken as ever, despite what he had crammed into it.

" 'My name is Never-Filled!' the creature cried in a terrible voice. 'I've eaten everything in your house, now I'll eat you, horns, hooves, and all. After that, I'll eat up the whole world.'

" 'An ambitious undertaking,' said the Great Goat, who understood that he had to deal with something more than a feeble, googly-eyed pond creature, 'but I think not.'

"And so, when Never-Filled opened a mouth gaping like a cavern and sprang at him, the Great Goat changed himself into a grain of wheat and hid in a crack in the floor."

"Amazing!" Lucian said aside to Fronto. "Who'd have ever expected anything like that?"

"A slight weakness in storytelling," said Fronto. "Buckthorn should have hinted right at the start that the Great Goat had such a power. This way, it comes at you all of a sudden. But, I suppose you might accept it as an element of surprise. Yet, if I were doing it—"

"Hush, you two," whispered Joy-in-the-Dance. "Let Buckthorn tell it his own way."

"I already said the Great Goat could do anything he

pleased." Buckthorn cocked a severe eye at Fronto. "And you might notice that of all the things he could have chosen, he didn't turn himself into a jackass.

"Now, where was I? Yes, he turned himself into a grain of wheat, but Never-Filled turned into a hen, scratched him out of the crack, and swallowed him down.

"But the Great Goat turned into an egg, and when the hen laid that egg, out hatched the Great Goat as a fuzzy little chick and scurried away.

"But Never-Filled turned into a weasel and darted to snap him up. Then the Great Goat jumped into the pond and became a fish; and Never-Filled changed into an otter and swam to seize him. Then the Great Goat changed into a bird and flew off; but Never-Filled changed into a hawk, with wings so wide they made the sky dark as night.

" 'A good trick,' the Great Goat said to himself, 'but I have a few of my own.'

"The Great Goat turned himself into a mountain valley, but Never-Filled turned into a rainstorm and flooded it. Then the Great Goat turned into a rainbow; but Never-Filled turned into a north wind and blew it away.

" 'This is beginning to get serious,' said the Great Goat and turned into a summer day; but Never-Filled turned into a winter night and snowed all over him.

" 'I need a little more elbow room,' said the Great Goat, and he turned into the full moon; but Never-Filled turned into a giant rat and began gnawing it.

" 'Enough toying with him,' said the Great Goat. 'Now I'll have the game go my way.'

"And so, just when Never-Filled had gnawed the moon down to a sliver, the Great Goat turned into a comet and circled around so fast that he flew behind the giant rat and set his tail on fire. Squeaking and squealing, Never-Filled shot across the sky; and now things were the other way round, for it was the Great Goat who went chasing after him.

"They streaked through the sky, through all four houses of the seasons, until Never-Filled spied a black hole and darted into it. 'Let him dare come out,' said the Great Goat, 'and I'll be waiting to give him a good butt in his ratty rear end.'

"The Great Goat's been standing guard, protecting us ever since," Buckthorn said, pointing at the night sky. "There, you can see him. Those stars—they're his horns; those others, his legs; and those three little ones, his beard."

"That's very interesting," said Joy-in-the-Dance. "We call those stars Amaltheia, 'Tender Nurse,' but she's a nanny goat, not a billy goat."

"Ah, well, I'm afraid you women have it wrong way

round," said Buckthorn. "It's a billy goat, no question."

Joy-in-the-Dance smiled knowingly. "You men like to think so."

"But, Buckthorn," Lucian put in, "you were going to tell about the Goat Folk."

"So I was," Buckthorn said. "Yes, what happened, you see, was this: While the Great Goat was running after Never-Filled, he kicked loose a herd of stars. They fell on these very mountains so hard they buried themselves into the ground; but then they sprouted up as men and women—us, the Goat Folk."

"Come now, Buckthorn," said Fronto, "do you mean to tell us your ancestors grew out of the ground—like so many cabbages?"

"We're here, aren't we?" said Buckthorn. "That's proof enough. And I don't take kindly to having my ancestors likened to cabbages." He went back to poking the fire.

"A wild tale," Lucian said later to Fronto. "I don't know what to make of it."

"A bit rough in spots, but it does have its moments," said Fronto. "A professional storyteller should be able to polish it up."

Lucian's last glimpse, before he shut his eyes to sleep, was of Buckthorn sitting by the fire. In the flickering light, he looked half-man, half-goat, and ancient as the hills themselves. As Lucian's dreams went spinning in his head, he saw Buckthorn as the Great Goat, with Joy-in-the-Dance riding on his back across an ocean of stars, her shining hair streaming like a comet's tail as she vanished behind the moon; and Never-Filled had turned into a dragon, snapping its jaws so ferociously that its teeth came loose and fell to earth; and there was Catch-a-Tick, May-Apple, and the Goat Folk popping up where the dragon's teeth had fallen; while Lucian swam through the stars as fast as he could after Joy-in-the-Dance.

She was nudging him. Still dream-fuddled, Lucian blinked at her. "I found you, after all."

"Aiee-Ouch, what in the world are you mumbling about?" said Joy-in-the-Dance. "I've been here all the time."

13

Lord See-Far-Ahead

Buckthorn's judgment proved to be right. As he expected, the pass was clear, with only a few stretches of snow, and there the journeyers took leave of their guides.

"Here, lad," said Buckthorn, handing Lucian a pair of firestones. "You may have use for them. And you, little pythoness, your way should be easy now." After clasping hands with Ops, he gave Fronto a good-natured whack on the rump. "Poet, I forgive you for talking about my ancestors as if they were cabbages. I hope you'll soon be walking on two legs instead of four."

They soon gained the rolling plains beyond the pass. Lucian had never imagined such a sea of green, where grass often reached higher than his waist. It shimmered and rippled in the sunlight, and he plunged through it as if he were swimming. Joy-in-the-Dance, pressing ahead of him, constantly scanned the crests and ridges.

"There—yes, there they are." She pointed to the high ground rising just ahead. "I knew they'd find us."

Across the brow of the hill, a loose string of a dozen mounted figures had suddenly sprung up. It could have been the dazzling sunlight, or his eyes playing tricks on him; but, for a moment, Lucian thought they were half-horse, half-human. They sat their steeds so closely they seemed to grow from the forequarters of their animals. They bore long, slender lances topped with horsetail streamers; short, oddly curved bows and quivers of arrows were slung about their backs. Sighting Joy-in-the-Dance, they sped down the slope.

As they galloped closer, Lucian saw them to be men and women dressed alike in fringed tunics and trousers of soft leather, yellow hair tumbling below their shoulders, their faces sunburnt to dark gold, cheeks and brows painted with bands of crimson and white streaks of gypsum.

Before Lucian knew what was happening to him, one of the riders bore down at full tilt. Hardly slowing his gait, he leaned over to seize Lucian by the jacket, hauled him up in one powerful motion, and set him in front of himself. The bewildered Lucian groped for reins or harness, but there were none. So he could only wrap his arms around the horse's neck and cling for dear life as the rider wheeled and galloped after his companions.

What had become of Ops, Lucian had no idea; but he glimpsed Fronto being swept along amid the horsemen. Joy-in-the-Dance was out of sight. After that, Lucian gave all his attention to hanging on as best he could while horse and rider flew over the ground without seeming to touch it.

At last, they halted at a circle of bell-shaped tents of horsehide, lashed with leather thongs. Here, the rider sprang down easily, and though he spoke in a language Lucian could not understand, Lucian was clearly being ordered to dismount—which he did by more or less falling off the steed's back.

Joy-in-the-Dance had already jumped down. By the time Lucian picked himself up, she had run to a tall man who had come out of the largest tent and flung herself into his outstretched arms.

Ops slid off his own mount and went to fetch Fronto from the midst of the horses. Wheezing, puffing, rolling his eyes, the poet muttered to Lucian, "They galloped me so fast I thought I'd sprout wings at any moment. Yes, and a couple of the mares took quite a fancy to me. I tried to explain my condition, but they didn't understand a word I said."

Joy-in-the-Dance was beckoning urgently. Lucian, still collecting his wits, elbowed through the crowd gathering at the tent.

"Hurry along, Aiee-Ouch," Joy-in-the-Dance called. "And you, Ops. Fronto, you needn't worry; I've told about your difficulty. Here, Aiee-Ouch, this is the *basileus*—oh, I'm sorry, I forgot you don't speak Mother Tongue—chieftain of the Horse Clan, Lord See-Far-Ahead."

The man so named stood head and shoulders taller than Lucian. A thin circlet of gold held a long mane of tawny, gray-streaked hair; a sun disk of beaten gold hung at his throat. His craggy face had been sunburnt to the same color as his leather garments, bands of yellow ochre and white gypsum barred his high cheekbones and arching bridge of his nose. For a moment, he looked Lucian up and down through lightning-blue eyes, then nodded with an air of easy authority and amused tolerance. Lucian shifted uncomfortably, suspecting that Lord See-Far-Ahead was perfectly capable of taking him apart limb from limb if he had any interest in doing so.

"*Khaire.* Hail and greetings." The chieftain, in a flowing gesture, raised one hand palm outward and laid the other on his heart. "Aiee-Ouch? What tribe is that?"

"Not a tribe, it's just what I call him," put in Joy-in-the-Dance. "He's Lucian."

"Why, then, do you call him by a name not his own?" See-Far-Ahead raised an eyebrow. "What is its meaning? Surely, it has one. All things have meaning."

The girl did not answer. For some reason, to Lucian's surprise, she actually blushed. The chieftain continued, "Be welcome, Lucian Aiee-Ouch. And you, little *parthenope*, it gladdens my heart to see you. I am told you are a pythoness in Arkadia Beyond-the-Mountains. A high honor, Terpsichore, but one that keeps you too long apart from us."

"Terpsichore?" Lucian whispered to her as the chieftain turned his gaze on Fronto and Ops.

"My clan name, that's all."

"Are these people your kindred?"

"Yes, but I'm only partly of the Horse Clan," said Joy-in-the-Dance. "See-Far-Ahead's my father. My mother—well, my mother's the Lady of Wild Things."

14

Yellow-Mane and Cloud-Rising

L ucian stared at the girl as if he had never seen her before. "And you said nothing?" he burst out. "Nothing? All this time?"

"It was better you didn't know. I was wrong even telling you I was the pythoness. I certainly wasn't going to tell you who my mother is."

"Why? Another secret you kept to yourself? Because you couldn't trust a Bear man? Is that it? Because you were afraid—"

"Yes, I was afraid." The girl's chin shot up. "Suppose we'd been caught. They'd have made you tell everything you knew about me, they'd have beaten it out of you. Bromios would have won more than he hoped: the pythoness—and the Lady's daughter, as well."

"I don't believe that. You were never afraid we'd be caught."

"Yes, I was," Joy-in-the-Dance said in a low voice. "More than I let on. And something else." She paused a long moment, then added, all in one breath, "I didn't tell you because I didn't want you to think of me as anyone's daughter, no matter whose. Only as me. As I am."

"How could I, when I never knew who you were in the first place? I don't understand what you're talking about."

"Of course you don't." She turned and strode from the tent, joining the maidens beckoning to her.

"Let be." See-Far-Ahead put a hand on Lucian's shoulder as he was about to follow. "She has given you something of value: the truth in her heart."

"Oh?" Lucian said angrily. "How do I know that?"

"You have yet to learn the ways of women." See-Far-Ahead smiled at him. "It is an endless study."

&

That evening, See-Far-Ahead ordered a feast, with music and dancing. The sides of the tent had been unlaced to make a sort of pavilion. Still angry and confused, Lucian sat silently with Ops and Fronto, who the chieftain chose to rank as a poet and only a temporary jackass.

Lucian had seen nothing of Joy-in-the-Dance until

See-Far-Ahead signaled the Dance of Colts to begin. Then he caught sight of her among the young men and women forming a ring around a blazing fire. Like the other maidens, she was now ceremonially dressed in a long, fringed skirt, with beads, bracelets, and flat slippers bound with colored ribbons, her hair in one thick braid.

"I'd be tempted to try a few steps," said Fronto, "if I had two feet instead of four. No matter, I'll investigate this basin of—what is it? Fermented mare's milk? A delightfully heady brew."

As the musicians plucked stringed instruments, tapped drums, and shook rods fitted with jingling metal disks, the dancers joined, broke away, and joined again. Laughing and smiling, her head flung back, her arms shaping graceful movements, the girl sprang lightly in and out of the swirling patterns. Lucian preferred to ignore the glances cast on her by the tall, loose-limbed youths of the camp.

"She dances well," said See-Far-Ahead. "Her feet tread the measure, but I think her heart turns toward you. And what of yours, young man with a name not his own?"

Lucian did not answer. See-Far-Ahead gave him a look half-warning, half-pitying, and did not pursue the question.

Joy-in-the-Dance, cheeks flushed and eyes shining,

came back to the tent with a handsome young warrior, Swift-Arrow, the chieftain's second in command. He was the rider who, earlier, had so easily snatched up Lucian, who now felt singularly ungrateful.

See-Far-Ahead clapped his hands and summoned the *lyrikos*, a bent-backed elder with white hair falling below his shoulders. The chieftain addressed him most respectfully, inviting him to entertain the guests with song or story.

Fronto raised his nose from the basin. "What did See-Far-Ahead call him?" he asked Lucian. "Gold-Horse? Something equine, whatever. I've heard of these minstrels. They're a good many cuts above the sort of local bard you find slouching in some backwater tavern. A shade too barbaric for most of my colleagues; but, I've always thought that a touch of splendid barbarity livens up a tale."

Lucian's dour spirits lifted as the *lyrikos* hobbled forward. Cradling an instrument whose sidepieces curved like warriors' bows, he brushed his fingers across the strings, and silvery notes rippled through the tent. Gold-Horse raised his head. His back straightened, his eyes brightened, and his voice rang as if he were still in the strength of his young manhood.

"This is a story of Lord Yellow-Mane, mightiest warrior of all the Horse Clans," he began. "The tale of his last and greatest battle."

"These old geezers do quite well at this sort of thing," Fronto remarked to Lucian. "It should be marvelously gory, swords clashing, fellows cloven to the chine— whatever a *chine* may be."

"There are battles of many kinds," said Gold-Horse, silencing Fronto with a glance, "some calling for more courage than others. Be you the judge of this one.

"In that time, Mother Earth was but a half-grown girl," Gold-Horse continued. "There were few meadows of sweet grass, few streams of water, and the stony fields yielded barely enough to keep men and animals from hunger. Tribes fought each other to the death over a scrap of pasture and shed more blood than the water they gained from the shallowest brook.

"Now, Lord Yellow-Mane was the strongest and wisest of chieftains, vigilant to defend the lives and well-being of his clan and kindred. With his great bow that he alone could draw, his arrows that flew true to their mark, his sword that never lost its edge, and his unbreakable shield, he and his war band withstood every foe.

"Yet, on a certain day, his old enemy, Lord Quick-to-Strike, armed himself and his warriors and challenged Yellow-Mane to mortal combat. Though such rashness puzzled him, for the sake of honor Yellow-Mane could not refuse. Nevertheless, on the eve of battle, his spirit was troubled; and, sleepless, he sat before his tent, pondering deeply.

" 'Why does Quick-to-Strike seek combat?' he wondered. 'My warriors far outnumber his, our victory is assured. What drives him to such folly? Has he gained some secret power unknown to me?'

"As Yellow-Mane sat alone with his thoughts, his beloved steed, Cloud-Rising, white as snowcapped Mount Panthea, beautiful as sunlight on morning grass, trotted up, laid her head on his shoulder, and spoke softly to him.

" 'Even you, Lord, in your wisdom,' she said, 'have not seen to the heart of the matter. Quick-to-Strike does have a secret power: the strength of desperation. What drives him is not folly but starvation. He must risk all or his people will surely perish of hunger and thirst. Would you, Lord, not do likewise?'

" 'Yes,' replied Yellow-Mane, 'and his despair makes him all the more dangerous. Therefore, I must fight him fiercely lest he destroy my people. This is my obligation and first duty to my clan. Even so, my heart aches; for this will not be battle but slaughter. I see no other course.'

" 'Always have I done your bidding,' said Cloud-Rising, 'and always have you trusted me to do so. Now I ask you to do my bidding in all things, exactly as I shall tell you.'

"Yellow-Mane gave his word. But when Cloud-Rising bade him follow her, he hesitated a moment. 'The morning of battle draws near,' he said. 'I must be at the head of my war band.'

" 'So you shall,' said Cloud-Rising. 'Where we go there is neither time nor space. When the moment comes, you shall be at the forefront of the fray.' "

"Now we're getting down to it," whispered Fronto. "We'll soon have heads rolling, chines cloven—strong stuff, but don't let it upset you. It's only a story."

"Yes, and I want to listen," replied Lucian. "I've never heard one like it before. So, please, Fronto, if you don't mind—"

"Yellow-Mane then mounted his faithful steed," Gold-Horse went on, "and instantly she soared through the air as if she had grown wings. When she touched earth again, Yellow-Mane found himself in a land he had never seen before. In front of him rose a wall of fire blazing so fiercely that Yellow-Mane, brave though he was, drew back from it.

" 'Pass through it without fear,' said Cloud-Rising. 'But

what you must know is this: As fire eats all it touches, so it will consume all your joy of battle and of setting your strength against others.'

" 'I am a warrior,' said Yellow-Mane, 'and have always gone eagerly and happily to the fray. Such has been my nature. To lose that is to lose the very warp and weft of my being.'

" 'Turn back if you choose,' said Cloud-Rising, 'but what you will gain will be greater than what you lose.'

"And Yellow-Mane passed through the flames. As he felt his pride as a warrior burn away, he understood it had been only ashes to begin with.

"Next, Cloud-Rising led him to a great waterfall, a roaring cataract so high that Yellow-Mane could not glimpse the source of it. Again, he hesitated and drew back from the thundering waters.

" 'Pass through it without fear,' said Cloud-Rising, 'but what you must know is this: As a flood sweeps away all in its path, so will this torrent sweep away all striving for power and predominance.'

" 'I am a chieftain,' said Yellow-Mane. 'My striving is for my people above all. Without that, how shall I lead them?'

" 'Turn back if you choose,' said Cloud-Rising, 'but what you will gain will be greater than what you lose.'

"And Yellow-Mane passed through the rushing waters. As they swept away the power he had so striven for, he understood it had been no more than a bubble borne away on the tide."

"Where's the gore?" said Fronto under his breath. "Not a drop, so far."

"Cloud-Rising then led Yellow-Mane across a field to a high tent, where sat a man wrapped in robes and blankets. A mask of painted wood covered his face. With artistry such as Yellow-Mane had never seen, the man was carving dolls in the shapes of men and women. Yet as soon as he finished one, he would break it and cast it aside.

"When Yellow-Mane cried out at seeing marvelous handiwork so treated, the doll maker replied: 'As they are mine to make, so are they mine to break.'

"Then, with his knife, the doll maker drew a circle in the dust and within it set many tiny figures on horseback. He beckoned Yellow-Mane to look closely at them.

" 'They are warriors arrayed for battle,' said Yellow-Mane. 'I see the faces of my war band, and myself leading them. There, too, is Quick-to-Strike and his men.'

"The doll maker, in one movement of his hand, swept all these figures together in a heap. 'Now, Yellow-Mane,' he said, 'sort them out, one from the other, friend from foe.'

" 'Easily done,' said Yellow-Mane. Yet try as he may,

they all appeared alike to him. 'I cannot,' he said at last. 'How can they be sorted when among them is no difference?'

" 'Go from here,' said the doll maker. 'If you have understood what you have seen, you will know what you must do.'

"Yellow-Mane mounted his steed again and, that instant, found himself at the head of his war band. Now came Quick-to-Strike with his own men ready to battle. But Yellow-Mane galloped forward and halted between the two lines of warriors.

" 'I will raise no hand against you,' Yellow-Mane called out as Quick-to-Strike rode up, sword unsheathed, to join combat. 'To slay you is to slay myself as well. Your warriors and mine are not two tribes, but one people of one body. Does a man cut off his own limbs or plunge a blade into his own heart? Let us join together in peace.'

" 'I have no thirst for blood,' replied Quick-to-Strike. 'But it is easy for you to cry peace when your weapons are greater than mine, and with them, you may turn upon us whenever you please.'

" 'Behold, then, what I do,' said Yellow-Mane, 'in token of good faith. My warriors shall do likewise, and so shall yours.'

"With that, Yellow-Mane flung his great bow high into the air, drew his arrows from their quiver and scattered them to the wind. He plunged his sword into the ground up to its hilt, and cast aside his shield.

"Seeing this, his warriors cried out in dismay. But Quick-to-Strike nodded agreement, saying, 'I and my warriors will do the same, but on this condition: Your sacrifice must be complete. One last thing must be added: your war horse, Cloud-Rising.'

" 'No,' retorted Yellow-Mane. 'This I will not.'

" 'Yellow-Mane,' said Cloud-Rising, 'you promised to do my bidding. Now I bid you: Take my life, or all else goes for naught.'

"Yellow-Mane's heart shattered in his breast. Yet he had given his word. So he took the sword from the hands of Quick-to-Strike. Turning his face away, in a single sweep of the blade he slew Cloud-Rising.

"No sooner had a drop of her blood touched the earth than a fountain of clear water gushed from the spot. His sword rose up as a tree laden with white blossoms. Where Yellow-Mane's arrows had fallen sprang shoots of tender grass. Where his shield lay, there spread a lake sparkling like crystal; and, where he had flung his bow into the sky, now arched a rainbow.

"And, that same instant, Cloud-Rising became a

winged maiden garbed in shining white robes. Smiling with love, she took the hand of Yellow-Mane and bore him upward with her, higher and higher, until they vanished from sight.

"Some say that Cloud-Rising was Woman-Three-Women in maidenly guise; others, that she was a sun-daughter and took Yellow-Mane to dwell in a golden tent, and they ride Father Sun's horses each day from dawn to dusk; still others give different accounts. Who can tell? All truth is one truth. And so it is that the Horse Clan follows the path of peace."

Gold-Horse set aside his instrument and bowed his head, and his years once again cloaked him. Fronto was loudly snuffling and blubbering as huge teardrops poured from his eyes and streamed down his nose.

"Too much, too much!" he wailed. "I couldn't bear it when Yellow-Mane slew Cloud-Rising. I know it's only a story; but, in my present state, I don't want to hear of such things happening, as it were, to my kinfolk. Dear Lucian, be so kind as to fetch me another basin of mare's milk."

"Thank you for the tale," said Lucian as Gold-Horse approached to offer courtesies. "It was beautiful, and more than that. A gift I'll never forget."

"I am grateful," said Gold-Horse. "As for you," he

added, taking Fronto's head between his hands and looking deeply into his eyes, "yes, I do see a poet in there. I
hope for your successful transformation. I fear, however,
that you may always remain something of an ass."

15

The Game of Warriors

The feasting, with more dancing and music, kept on well past daybreak. Fronto, having investigated several basins of mare's milk, snuffled about for yet another. Lucian would have gladly crawled under a blanket to sleep; but Swift-Arrow, still fresh-eyed, jumped up, stripped off his shirt, and called for his comrades to fetch their horses.

"My young hotheads will play the Game of Warriors," See-Far-Ahead explained. "Their blood stirs, and better for them to sport than quarrel."

"Local custom?" said Fronto, belching luxuriously. "Always interested in local customs. Because, you see, they're so interesting."

"What kind of game?" asked Lucian.

"A simple one," replied Swift-Arrow, smiling. "Horse-men gather within a circle. A leather ball stuffed with grass is put in play. Each rider strives to seize and carry it past the boundary."

"That's all?"

"No rider may dismount," said Swift-Arrow. "If he leaves his horse's back for any reason, he forfeits the game. That is the one and only rule. A harmless amuse-ment, but it demands a small measure of strength and skill. It might please you to observe our sport—from a comfortable distance."

"It might please me even more," said Lucian, return-ing Swift-Arrow's glance, "to try this harmless amuse-ment. I'd enjoy it."

"Your presence would honor us," replied Swift-Arrow as Lucian began peeling off his shirt. "We shall find a gentle old nag that will suit you best."

"Here, here, no need for that," put in Fronto. "I'll be delighted to serve. I'd enjoy a little romp. This delicious beverage has made me feel marvelously light-footed."

Swift-Arrow burst out laughing. "A jackass? In the noble game?"

"You told me there was only one rule," said Lucian. "I'll ride Fronto."

"A jackass, then. Perhaps two." Swift-Arrow strode from the tent and whistled for his horse. Joy-in-the-

Dance seemed about to speak; but Lucian turned on his heel and hurried after the warrior. Licking up the last few drops from the basin, Fronto trotted eagerly to join them.

The dance ground had been cleared, and a circle had been marked out. The folk of the camp made way for the riders. Lucian, perched on Fronto, entered the ring, and the onlookers closed ranks. A young boy ran up with a ball several times larger than Lucian's head and, at a signal from Swift-Arrow, tossed it into the ring.

The warriors all seemed to go mad at that same instant, whooping and yip-yipping, yelling and screaming until Lucian feared his ears would split. Fronto burst into raucous hee-haws and went lurching toward the wheeling, rearing horses. One rider had already leaned from his mount and snatched up the ball, which was attached to long, rawhide loops. As he made for the boundary, the whole band galloped straight for him, jostling their steeds against his, jabbing him with elbows and fists, and, by sheer force, knocking the ball from his grasp. When a second rider scooped it up, he, too, was kicked and pummeled until he dropped it.

"All against all, every man for himself?" Lucian felt his blood rising. "Well, then: Yip-yip-yip!"

Fronto needed no urging. His eyes lit up, he laid back

his ears and, braying wildly, plunged into the fray. Shorter and closer to the ground than the horses, the poet darted in and out among them, dodging and wheeling with joyous abandon.

Deafened by the endless whooping and pounding hooves, Lucian's head spun as he found himself buffeted from all sides. The flank of one horse crashed broadside against him; an elbow jabbed him in the face, he choked and snorted at the blood streaming from his nose. A couple of riders had been knocked off their mounts and, in penalty, were sent from the ring. Though infuriated at being so belabored, Lucian was afraid of losing his own seat. Seeking a moment to get back his breath and his balance, he pulled away from the press of warriors. The ball, at the same time, rolled clear of the struggling riders.

"I have it!" cried Lucian, about to seize the rawhide loop.

"First, a little poetic license," said Fronto as the warriors, losing sight of the ball, milled around in all directions. Straddling the object as if he were hatching an oversized egg, Fronto trapped it between his hind legs and waddled toward the edge of the ring.

"They can't find it. Pick it up now," ordered Fronto. "We'll make a run for it."

Lucian snatched the ball from under Fronto's belly. The other players, by this time, had seen him do so. All bore down on him in full whoop, Swift-Arrow grinning in the lead.

Bracing himself for the assault, Lucian clapped his heels against Fronto's flanks. The poet stood motionless.

"Go! Go!" shouted Lucian.

Fronto did not budge, his eyes set on Swift-Arrow's mount. "Why, that's one of the mares that took such a fancy to me. And there's another. Good morning, ladies."

Swift-Arrow's steed gave a flirtatious whinny as she plunged toward Fronto. When she reached him, she stopped so abruptly that Swift-Arrow sailed head over heels to land heavily on the turf; likewise, the riders behind him.

"Later, perhaps, my dear," said Fronto as she fondly nuzzled him. He made for the boundary at a wobbling gallop, with Lucian still clutching the ball. The spectators laughed and cheered. Swift-Arrow, climbing to his feet, looked as if he had swallowed a porcupine.

"Well done, my boy," said Fronto. "What an exhilarating sport! Brightens the eye, sets the pulse racing and the blood coursing."

"It certainly does," Lucian agreed, "and I don't ever want to play it again."

"I hope those mares won't come looking for me," said Fronto.

That night, at a special feast to celebrate the occasion,

See-Far-Ahead declared Lucian and Fronto honorary members of the Horse Clan.

"Never have I seen our game won in so unusual a fashion," the chieftain said. "I congratulate you. And I thank you. It is good for my hotheads to have their pride cooled a little."

See-Far-Ahead called for pots of color and daubed clan markings on Lucian's forehead and cheeks, and on the nose and brow of Fronto.

"Does this make me an honorary horse?" said the poet. "That's a step up from jackass."

"Aiee-Ouch," said Joy-in-the-Dance, drawing Lucian aside, "I have a couple of things I want to tell you."

"Oh?" Lucian, beaming with happy satisfaction, had decided to accept her humble apology, generously forgive her, and bask in her adoration at his triumph.

"Aiee-Ouch, what you did," Joy-in-the-Dance began, "I can only say—well, it was the most foolhardy, dangerous, silliest, stupidest—"

"Was it?" Lucian abruptly stopped basking. Instead, he bristled. "I'd call it a matter of honor. Besides," he added under his breath, "I won."

"Aside from pointing out that you could have broken your neck," she went on, "what I mainly wanted to say —I hope you managed to see why I didn't tell you who I was."

"I don't know—All right, I suppose I did."

Joy-in-the-Dance took his hand. "I thought you would."

"So the two of you are on fond terms again," Fronto remarked later. "That's gratifying."

"Yes," said Lucian, "but I really hate it when she's right."

⚬

See-Far-Ahead decided that he would go with his daughter to Mount Panthea. Leaving the camp in charge of Swift-Arrow, he picked half a dozen of his warriors to journey with him, ordered his tent struck and provisions loaded onto pack animals. Joy-in-the-Dance, lightly astride a slender white mare, rode beside her father's black stallion. Swift-Arrow, having made a sour sort of peace with Lucian, offered him a sturdy chestnut-and-white pony and provided Ops with a similar mount.

Lucian was not sure how thankful he should be to Swift-Arrow. For the first few days, he was too sore to sit down and no less so when he stood up. He never acquired a taste for being bounced and battered and having his teeth rattled at every jolt. Even when he could gallop over the grasslands, yip-yipping as well as any of the warriors, he would not have chosen to be a permanent member of the Horse Clan.

"You're a long way from bean counting," said Fronto, observing the daubs of color still vivid on Lucian's face, and his skin broiled nearly black from the unclouded sun. "My boy, you're turning into quite the picturesque barbarian—and, as a poet, I've found that a touch of wildness never goes amiss, especially with the ladies."

"Picturesque barbarian?" Lucian shook his head. "I don't know what I am. Or what I'll be." He turned to Ops, who was looking thoughtfully at the snowcapped peak of Mount Panthea rising just ahead. "And you, Ops? What will you ask the Lady? Is there something she could grant you?"

"I doubt it," said the scapegoat. "Oh, perhaps more opportunity to be of service. Not so much wandering at random. It's hit or miss, finding people to blame something on you. Yes, I would like a steadier occupation."

"That's a modest request," said Joy-in-the-Dance, joining them in time to hear this remark by Ops. "I hope my mother will be able to grant it."

The girl, throughout these days, had stayed a little apart, withdrawn into her own thoughts. Now Lucian ventured to go and sit beside her.

"You'll soon see your mother. You'll be glad of that, won't you?"

"Yes. But I still wonder if I did right, not changing the prophecy. She's the only one who can tell me. If I did wrong, I'll have a lot to answer for." She smiled at him. "I can't guess what she'll say to my bringing along an Aiee-Ouch."

"Does it matter?"

"No. Not anymore. Did you think it would?"

"I hoped not," said Lucian.

Next day, they came to the sanctuary of the Lady of Wild Things.

16

The Lady of Wild Things

All that morning, See-Far-Ahead had borne westward over gently rising foothills, and across the shallowest ford of a wide river. Soon the ground fell sharply away, and at the foot of Mount Panthea, Lucian glimpsed clustered buildings of white stone, colonnades and walkways, groves and gardens in full blossom. What held his eyes and astonished him all the more was an enclosure of tall columns, some broken and lying on the expanse of rutted stone steps. Of what had been a roof, only the high-peaked forefront remained. Even from these ruins, he could imagine what the building once had been; the grace of its design and proportions made him catch his breath in wonder. Massive though they were, the columns seemed light enough to soar into the air and float away.

"This must be the work of the Great Ones," he murmured. "Who else? They truly lived here once, just as Joy-in-the-Dance told us."

"No doubt," said Fronto. "No one today could build anything like it. In comparison, the palace of Bromios comes off like an oversized rabbit warren."

As the travelers entered a grove of poplars, a number of young women in white tunics greeted them, happily embracing Joy-in-the-Dance and leading her and the warriors down a wide avenue. When Lucian, Fronto, and Ops attempted to follow, one of the maidens stepped in front of them.

"The Lady will send word when she wishes to see you," said the girl, who gave her name as Laurel-Crown. Auburn-haired, with a narrow band of gold at her brow, she nodded courteously to Lucian and Fronto; her full gaze lingered, however, on Ops, and she looked him up and down with unconcealed interest. For his part, Ops did something Lucian had never seen him do: He blushed crimson to the roots of his hair and the tips of his ears.

"I'm to stay with you until you're called for," said Laurel-Crown, her hazel eyes still on the scapegoat. "It may be a little while. I can show you some of the sanctuary, if you'd like. It's quite lovely."

"What I've seen is most attractive," replied Ops, giving the maiden a few sidelong glances of his own.

"You're speaking of the ruins?" said Laurel-Crown. "There are other things, as well."

"Indeed there are," said Ops. "I hope to grow better acquainted with them."

"That," Laurel-Crown said primly, "would depend on what you have in mind."

"I don't think they're talking about ruins and sightseeing," Lucian said under his breath to Fronto.

"That rascal Ops," Fronto chuckled as Laurel-Crown led the way to a fountain and pool. "Who'd have thought it of him? He no sooner sets foot here than a young lady takes a shine to him, and he to her. At first sight!"

"It happened to his parents," Lucian said. "Maybe it runs in the family."

While Ops watered the horses, Lucian noticed women of every age strolling along walkways or talking together on marble benches. "Do they all serve the Lady?" he asked Laurel-Crown.

"No," she said, momentarily turning her glance away from Ops, "they've come to take refuge since Bromios began persecuting them. Only the Daughters of Morning, like me, and the Moon Maidens serve the Lady as her chosen companions."

"But men and boys are forbidden here?"

"Of course not, if they're followers of the Lady. We have infants, too, though only a few right now. All women are free to bring their children to be raised among us. Their sons often become village chiefs when they're grown. Their daughters, if they choose, study our mysteries, then return home to teach them to other women; or, if they show promise, stay to become Moon Maidens or Daughters of Morning. At least, that's how it was until Bromios took power. Now it may be that our sisterhood is broken. Of that, even the Lady isn't certain."

Other Daughters of Morning, carrying baskets of food and drink, had come, trailed by a crowd of younger girls eager to see a talking donkey. Giggling and nudging one another, they pressed around Fronto, patting his head and urging him to speak. Some had woven wildflower garlands to hang around his neck or drape over his ears.

Lucian and Ops, likewise, were objects of curiosity. Taken at first for one of the Horse Clan, Lucian explained that he was only an honorary member, then wished he had said nothing, for the girls drew back, round-eyed and fearful.

"They have never seen a man of the Bear people,"

said Laurel-Crown, "but they know what happened here long ago."

"Which is more than I do," said Lucian.

"Haven't you been told your own history?"

"Not that part of it," said Lucian, "but I'd like to find out. Would you tell me?"

Laurel-Crown hesitated. "It's a story that won't please you."

"Even so," Lucian insisted, "I still want to hear it."

"As you wish," said Laurel-Crown.

"Generations ago," she continued, "when your first Bear King conquered Arkadia Beyond-the-Mountains, he journeyed here to seek audience with the Lady of Wild Things.

"With gentle speech and honeyed words, he paid homage to her beauty and wisdom and claimed that he desired to learn her peaceable ways.

" 'Your purpose is commendable,' said the Lady. 'Only tell me this: Why have you brought your war band with you?'

" 'Lady, these are my close companions. I wish them, as well as I, to benefit from your teachings.'

" 'So be it,' said the Lady. 'I will not deny knowledge to any who truly seek it. Only tell me this: Why come you armed with sword and spear, and your companions likewise?'

" 'Lady, to defend ourselves against peril on our way.'

" 'So be it,' said the Lady. 'Then let us begin your instruction. As you have studied the arts of war, now shall you study the arts of peace.'

"With that, she led him to her spinning chamber, bade him to take up wool and distaff, teasel and spindle, and to sit at her wheel and spin thread.

" 'You ask this of me?' cried the Bear King. 'Lady, I am a warrior and do not turn my hand to women's work. If my men were to see me like some handmaiden at a spinning wheel, they would laugh me to scorn.'

"The Lady did not insist but next led him to her stables, bidding him to sweep them clean, to feed and groom her horses.

" 'You ask this of me?' he cried. 'Lady, I am a king and this is labor for baseborn servants. Set me a task worthy of my rank, my strength of arm, and my fleetness of foot.'

" 'So be it,' said the Lady. 'Will you run a race against me? If you win, all my wisdom and secret knowledge will be granted to you.'

" 'That is a suitable challenge,' said the Bear King, for he knew that none was swifter than himself. 'I gladly accept.'

"So saying, he stripped off helmet and breastplate and laid down spear and sword. The Lady, having girt up her tunic, marked out the course, the Daughters of Morning lining one side, the king's war band on the other. And so began the race.

"Quick as wind ran the Lady of Wild Things and, at first, outpaced the Bear King. But he, bending all his strength, drew ever closer, closing the distance between them, gaining on her stride by stride.

"Now, the Lady of Wild Things had seen into the Bear King's heart and well knew that his purpose was not the gaining of wisdom but the conquest of her domain. Therefore, from the folds of her garment she drew an apple fashioned of purest gold and dropped it on the ground behind her.

"At sight of the precious object glittering in his path, the Bear King broke stride and eagerly snatched it up. In that instant of his delay, the Lady of Wild Things pressed ahead, speeding first to the finish of the course. The Bear King shook his fist and roared in fury.

" 'Woman's treachery and deception! Victory should have been mine. You have cheated me.'

" 'You have cheated yourself,' replied the Lady. 'Your own greed blinded you, and you chose to seize what lay nearest at hand, heedless of the farther goal. You dare cry treachery and deception? No, it was you who came with a man's fair speech and false heart.'

" 'Here, let this be your prize,' cried the Bear King,

and he picked up his spear and flung it straight at her breast. But it struck the amulet she wore around her neck, the spearhead shattered, and the shaft fell to the ground.

"In rage, the Bear King and his warriors drew their swords and would have slain the Lady and her maidens had they not sought refuge amid the crags of Mount Panthea. Unable to attack them in their mountain fastness, the king and his war band pillaged the great sanctuary, seizing all volumes of lore and learning, intending to possess these secrets. But the mysteries had been written in Mother Tongue, which the Bear men could not read. And so they spitefully burned every book, every scroll, then toppled the columns, shattered the roof, and wrought all destruction they could.

"The Lady sent an eagle bearing word to her beloved friend, Lord Yellow-Mane, who led his Horse Clan against the Bear King and his men and put them to flight.

"Although the books had been burned past recovery, the Lady and her maidens remembered all their contents. However, the Lady vowed that none of the lore should be written down again but kept only in memory and handed down by word of mouth. Thus, it could never be stolen or destroyed, or turned to evil ends."

"Joy-in-the-Dance told us that your knowledge was no longer put in writing," said Lucian. "So that's how it came about." He had listened to the tale with fascination; at the same time, it had made his heart heavy with grief and shame for what the Bear men had done. "I see why you don't write down your mysteries, but why was the sanctuary never rebuilt?"

"It cannot be," said Laurel-Crown. "Its marble came from one place only: the cliffs near Metara. That's the finest in Arkadia, no other is worthy to be used. But we don't venture into the realm of our enemies. So the ruins remain as you see them, a symbol of Bear men's perfidy."

"I very dimly recall my mother telling me that story," said Ops to Laurel-Crown. "In Mother Tongue, at the time—Ah, it's been so long since I've heard or spoken the language that I've forgotten it—but I well remember my mother's voice. She was a sanctuary maiden, you see, and what happened—"

"Please, Ops," said Fronto, "don't go into all that tootling and bleating again."

"I'd love to hear more," said Laurel-Crown, glancing at Ops with even warmer interest. "Let's sit over there while your friends do something to occupy themselves and leave us—"

Laurel-Crown broke off, for one of the Daughters of Morning had come to say that the Lady of Wild Things waited to receive them. With the moment upon him, Lucian's uneasiness sprang up to entangle itself with his hopes as he followed the maiden through a colonnade and into a sunny courtyard. In the center of it a fountain played; nearby, on a marble bench sat a woman draped in a pale blue robe. At her feet stretched two sleek leopards lazily observing the new arrivals.

Joy-in-the-Dance, garbed in a fresh white tunic, sat beside her mother. See-Far-Ahead, arms folded, stood behind them. The Lady of Wild Things beckoned with an easy gesture. She wore no rings on her slender fingers, nor bracelets on her bare arms. Her only jewels were the brooch of amethyst at her shoulder knot and the silver diadem, set with a single gem, holding her long, golden hair. Joy-in-the-Dance gave Lucian a quick smile, and he thought, "She has her mother's eyes."

The Lady's glance lingered a moment on Lucian, then she looked past him at Ops, who had hung back a little.

"*Khaire*, Argeus Bright-Face," she said in a kindly voice. "You are under my protection and welcome here. By mother-right, you may count this place your home."

She now set a stern gaze on Fronto, whose four legs began to quake. "I know what has befallen you, by your own doing. Come to me, poet. Only at my daughter's entreaty have I agreed to see you."

"Honored Lady, my deepest gratitude, heartfelt thanks," Fronto stammered, bending his trembling forelegs in an attempt to kneel, "and may I say that for one so youthful to have a grown daughter as charmingly beautiful as yourself, dear Lady, you are most amazingly—ah, unexpectedly—"

"Well preserved?" said the Lady of Wild Things. "Fronto, of all the creatures you might have become, an ass befits you most."

Fronto bowed his head. "I have been punished as I deserved. But I meant no disrespect. I sought only inspiration."

"As a poet, you should have known better than anyone," replied the Lady, "that inspiration is not found in a gulp of water or anything else. Not even I can bestow it. If it sustains you and gives you courage to imagine that I can, well and good. It is a harmless, perhaps useful, fantasy. But at the end, your inspiration must come from yourself. I can do no more than wish you well."

"I'll let my inspiration do as it pleases," said Fronto. "At the moment, I only beg your mercy and forgiveness."

"You are a poet," said the Lady, "and much foolishness is to be expected. Your intentions were good, you have always honored me, and I look kindly on your devotion. Yes, I forgive you, as I always forgive those I cherish, however asinine they may be."

"Gracious benefactress!" cried Fronto. "Thank you.

My hopes are fulfilled. Will you change me here and now? Or is some formality to be observed? A small ritual, perhaps? In any case, the sooner the better."

"What happened to you was not my doing," the Lady said, "and is not mine to undo. I cannot transform you to what you were. The first service I can offer is plain truth.

"Your time is short. You have the power of speech, but soon it must leave you. Then will you become less and less a poet and more and more a donkey, until, at last, you will be truly a dumb beast, and so remain as long as you draw breath."

17

The Shipmaster

The Lady of Wild Things fell silent. In the sun-washed courtyard, the only sound was the splashing water of the fountain. The leopards licked their paws. Fronto lowered his head and turned away.

"All for naught," he murmured. "My last hope gone."

"There is always hope, however slight," the Lady said. "I have told you the worst, so that you may truly know the gravity of your situation.

"I have thought carefully on this," she went on. "Ancient lore tells of other means of restoration, seldom used, if ever; for, most often, they destroy instead of cure. You would not like them, Fronto, and I counsel you against them."

"I'll take any risk," said Fronto. "I could hardly be worse off."

"Yes, you could," said the Lady. "Would you accept, for example, to be set on a blazing pyre, with no assurance of surviving that ordeal? Or, if you did, with the likelihood of emerging in a shape more unbearable than your present one? I assure you, compared with other methods, that is the least painful. Or would you choose to have all the blood drained from your body, and then—"

"Please, please, say no more," wailed Fronto. "I catch your drift."

"One possibility remains," the Lady continued. "It is the most promising. An island named Callista lies off the southern coast, unspoiled by the coming of the Bear folk. Some of the Great Ones' magic still flourishes there. A water-maiden guards a pool much like the one at Mount Lerna. Journey to Callista. In my name, ask her help. She will, on my authority, permit you to bathe in the waters. The chances are excellent that they will transform you."

"Bless you, dear Lady!" cried Fronto, his spirits lifting. "That is, thank you for blessing me with your kindness."

"Be warned," said the Lady of Wild Things. "I told you that your time is short. By my reckoning, you have until the first full moon of the Harvest Festival. However, you should reach Callista before that if you sail without delay."

"How can we find it?" put in Lucian. "How can we even get there? Without a boat—"

"I shall take up that matter once I have dealt with you, Lucian, who my daughter, for reasons of her own, prefers to call Aiee-Ouch.

"I permitted you to come here because of your care and affection for this wretched poet. Now you must leave and never set foot here again. I offer no welcome to my enemies."

"I'm not your enemy," Lucian replied heatedly, despite his attempt to hold back his anger and resentment. "Do you judge every Bear man alike? That's not much different from Bromios, only the other way round." He stopped short and bit his lips, fearing he had dared to go too far.

"He speaks truth," See-Far-Ahead said quietly. "My heart aches when I think of the long hatred between you and the Bear tribe."

"With good cause," said the Lady of Wild Things. "Once, there might have been friendship. That is no longer possible."

"I know it's possible," said Joy-in-the-Dance, to Lucian's astonishment. "Aiee-Ouch and I—" She halted as color rose to her cheeks. "I mean, it's a beginning—"

"Which must end when he departs," said the Lady. She turned again to Lucian. "My daughter has told me that you seek to know what shape your life should take. It is beyond even my knowledge to answer such a question. You alone must learn that for yourself."

"Then we've come here in vain," Lucian said bitterly. "If you have no help for me, so be it. As for Fronto, all you've done is tell him about an island we don't know how to find, and can't reach in the first place. You give him hope and take it away. That's cruel—"

"You speak with more haste than judgment," said the Lady. "For the sake of this poet, I will grant a favor larger than you might expect from one you call cruel. In the harbor, at the foot of the cliffs, there is a fishing village. Its folk have dwelt in our care from long before the days of the Bear kings. Among them lives a shipmaster, Oude-is. A seafarer of great skill, he knows the waters from here to Callista and can set the swiftest course."

The Lady took an amulet and chain from the folds of her robe and set it around Lucian's neck. "Show him this. He will do all you ask."

"I'll gladly go along," said Ops before Lucian could reply. "If the wind dies or the boat leaks, they'll need someone to blame. A wonderful opportunity for me."

"No, Argeus Bright-Face," the Lady said. "Your place is here. My daughter has told me of your request. I must give it long and careful thought. Be patient and stay among us until I see what is best for you."

"I've brought Aiee-Ouch and Fronto this far," declared Joy-in-the-Dance. "I'll certainly go the rest of the way with them."

"No, you shall not," replied the Lady, as Lucian's heart sank. "It is not fitting. Now leave us, child," the Lady went on. "Take Argeus Bright-Face to his chambers, then remain in your own."

The girl's chin shot up. Her eyes and the Lady's met and locked. "I do not speak as a mother to a beloved daughter," the Lady said in a low voice, "but as the Lady of Wild Things to her pythoness. Do as I say. You know that you must."

Joy-in-the-Dance stood, as if she would step toward Lucian, then turned abruptly, head high, and strode from the courtyard. Ops followed. Lucian started after her. The Lady rose to stand in front of him. The leopards, alert, twitched their tails.

Lucian faced the Lady of Wild Things. "Let me say farewell to her. That much, at least."

"No," the Lady said. "Do you think me heartless? I am not. I am doing you a kindness. It would be too painful for both of you.

"I will tell you this," she added. "My daughter was torn in spirit when she came here and questioned whether she should have changed the prophecy she gave your king. I have made it clear to her. By speaking the true prophecy she proved herself worthy of her rank. She is a pythoness. That is her life. You can have no part in it."

❦

He was filled with her absence and might as well have been sleepwalking for all the heed he paid to where he was being led. Laurel-Crown had been instructed to guide him and Fronto down the cliffs to the fishing village, where she pointed out the shipmaster's hut, and left them there.

"Hurry along, my boy," urged the poet. "Glooming never mended a broken heart, as I've discovered a thousand times. Think of something else. Anything. Go alphabetically. Anthills. Beetles. Callista—Ah, that's a happy prospect.

"We'll go in style, too." Fronto tossed his head toward a little cove and a sleek, high-masted ship. "This what's his name—Oudeis—let's get him stirring, reef the anchor, hoist the rudder, whatever these nautical fellows do."

Fronto eagerly trotted across the threshold of the hut. Lucian, at his heels, was surprised to find that the hut was more spacious on the inside than it appeared from the outside. The reason, he understood, was that the chamber had been so cleverly laid out. Tables and benches of polished wood had been set into the walls; what looked like a fishnet was slung between two beams of a ceiling crafted of wooden ribs. Storage bins nested one on top of the other; an oil lamp hung from a chain. Only one thing seemed to be missing: the occupant.

"I hope he's not gone far," said Fronto. "We've no time to lose. Seek him out, lad, at the piers; perhaps the local tavern, or whatever sort of place might attract the seafaring trade."

The words had barely passed his lips when a voice boomed from the doorway: "A jackass! Away with you, lumbering lummox!"

A figure as high and wide as the doorway itself dropped the wineskin he carried on his shoulder. With hardly a glance at Lucian, he seized Fronto by the ears and would have hauled him bodily from the hut if Lucian had not brandished the amulet. At sight of it, the man stopped and drew back a pace.

"What are you up to with that?"

"Are you the shipmaster?" Lucian stepped between him and Fronto. "Oudeis?"

"Who else?" The man loomed bulkier than Bromios, with a salt-and-pepper beard in tight curls, hair closely cropped, a jutting hawk's beak of a nose, and shrewd black eyes flecked with gold. "And you? Is that your jack-ass? Yes, well, take that sorry bone bag away before he makes a mess on my floor."

"My good shipmaster," said Fronto, tossing his head and looking down his nose, "credit me with at least a measure of refinement. I'm not what I appear to be. Has it not occurred to you that I can speak?"

"I don't care a fig if you can whistle out your ears," retorted Oudeis. "Make a mess, you clean it up. What do you want? The quicker you tell me, the quicker you're gone."

Fearing the testy Oudeis would throw him out the door despite the amulet, Lucian hurried to explain their circumstances. The shipmaster's weather-beaten face fell, he scratched his beard, puffed his cheeks, and muttered to himself.

"The Lady told us you'd do as we ask," Lucian insisted.

"I will," grumbled Oudeis. "I owe her more service than I can repay. There's been times when she's held my life in the palm of her hand. Aye, her spirit bore me up, else I'd have drowned a dozen times over. I'll take you where you want to go. That doesn't mean I have to like it. I've shipped many a strange cargo in my day, but never a jackass, let alone a talking one."

"I assure you," said Fronto, "on our return voyage,

when I'm back to myself, you'll find me most entertaining. Once my difficulty is resolved and my mind can concentrate on my profession, I'll compose a few rhymes to amuse a seafaring fellow like yourself—though unsuitable for the ears of your lady wife. On that subject, we have not had the pleasure of her acquaintance."

"For good reason," Oudeis replied. "There isn't one. I lost my best chance these long years past." He sighed, his eyes wandered an instant. Then, with a shrug, he went to fetch a smooth, flat board.

"I regret to hear that," said Fronto, "and I'm astonished, as well. Your snug abode betokens a feminine hand."

"Only mine. I keep my little haven shipshape. I'm the one who built what you see here. Aye, and devised it all myself." This while, the shipmaster had been unfolding wooden poles neatly joined and hinged into the board; within the moment, there stood a table.

"Remarkable!" exclaimed Lucian, intrigued and delighted.

The shipmaster beamed proudly. "I wasn't called Clever Oudeis for nothing. You won't find a better mariner, if I say so myself. Besides that, there's not a task, a piece of work, I can't do.

"Now, then, as for Callista," he went on, drawing up stools for Lucian and himself while Fronto thrust his head over Lucian's shoulder, "let's do a little reckoning. I'll have to lay in provisions, water, extra gear. Some few chores to finish. Aye, all told, we'll set sail in, say, five or six days."

"What?" burst out Fronto. "We can't possibly wait that long."

"You're not only a jackass, you're a landlubber as well," Oudeis retorted. "Go off ill-fitted? Do you suppose I'll risk my neck and my ship? Not counting your necks—which, I'll tell you frankly, don't weigh heavy in comparison. No. Out of the question."

"I wouldn't dream of doubting your judgment." Lucian put up his hands in resignation. "You know your trade. A week? A month, if need be," he added as Fronto stared aghast. "We'll have to wait, since that's the best you can manage. I understand now. Calling yourself Clever Oudeis was only a fanciful manner of speaking."

"Fact!" Oudeis slapped a heavy hand on the table. "I tell you there's nothing—" He stopped and cocked an ear, then laid a finger on his lips. He stood and pulled the netting from the beams.

"You're going fishing?" protested Fronto. "We require your undivided attention."

"Be quiet, jackass." The shipmaster went swiftly from the hut. Lucian soon heard scuffling and a few colorful oaths from Oudeis, who was back within moments, the net and its wriggling contents slung over his shoulder.

"Here's a fish for you!" Oudeis tossed his burden to the floor. "I've not seen the like of it. What is it? A creeping, crawling, eavesdropping land-fish?"

The shipmaster untangled the net.

Out popped Catch-a-Tick.

18

The Voyages of Oudeis

W hat are you doing here?" Lucian burst out.

"You know this wretch?" Oudeis glowered at the boy, who was swaggering around as tickled with himself as he could be. "First, a jackass. Now, a goat. Look at him, he's got mud on my floor." The shipmaster made to seize Catch-a-Tick, who stuck out his tongue and ducked behind Lucian.

"I'll deal with this," said Lucian. "How did you find us? More to the point, why did you run off? That's what you did, isn't it? Your mother must be out of her wits. Your father, too. You'll be in for a good tanning from both of them."

"No, I won't," Catch-a-Tick declared. "My mother said I could go with you."

"To Mount Panthea? I doubt that."

"All right," admitted Catch-a-Tick, "I suppose she thought I'd come straight home with the others. By the time I caught up, you'd already gone through the mountains. So, I followed. I wasn't told not to, was I? They'll guess I went with you and the pythoness. Where is she?"

"She's—staying behind. At the sanctuary."

"Well, even so," said Catch-a-Tick, "you'll take care of everything. Yes, I heard about what you did with the Horse Clan. You'd left by the time I got there, but they all talked about you. How you defeated their best warriors and—"

"And now you're going home," Lucian interrupted. "We're getting ready to sail on a journey."

"So much the better. I've never been on a ship."

"You won't be on mine," said Oudeis. "Go back wherever you came from."

Catch-a-Tick folded his arms. "If you try to leave me here, I'll swim after you."

"Please, please," said Fronto. "We'll decide what to do about him later. We have plenty of time to think it over, as we're stuck here for a week."

"Who says?" Oudeis squinted a dark eye at Lucian. "I told you I could do anything that needed doing—if I've a mind to. Well, my lad, I'll prove it to you. We sail with the night tide. I'll make do with what I have and take on the rest at one port or other. So, stir your stumps and lend a hand. The jackass, too. What about the goat-boy?"

Catch-a-Tick began whining, begging, demanding, and carrying on so much that Lucian put his hands over his ears.

"Enough! You'll come with us. Only because I want you where I can keep an eye on you. If I leave you running loose on your own, you'll get in worse trouble."

Oudeis, meantime, set about gathering what food and gear his hut offered, as well as a coarse shirt and cloak for Lucian, a blanket for Catch-a-Tick, and several wide-brimmed straw hats. Loading the cargo required a few trips between the hut and the pier, where a single-masted boat bobbed in the water. It was well after moonrise when Oudeis declared that all was to his satisfaction and ordered his passengers into the vessel.

"Cramped quarters," remarked Fronto, who had clambered unsteadily over the side. "No matter, we'll be more comfortable once we're aboard."

"Ass," retorted Oudeis, "you're aboard right now."

"But—the great ship?" cried Fronto. "We saw it in the cove."

"That's the Lady's," Oudeis said. "Not for the likes of you or me. This little beauty's mine, built with my own pair of hands."

"You didn't leave much room for your crew," said Lucian.

"What crew?" said Oudeis, casting off the mooring lines. "I'm the crew. I work my ship myself. That's not to say you lubbers will sit at ease. Put your back into those oars," he ordered Lucian and Catch-a-Tick. "Do you know what an oar is? You'll find out quick enough. Once clear of the harbor, I'll hoist sail and hope for a breeze."

Under the shipmaster's instruction, Lucian and Catch-a-Tick plied the long wooden sweeps: a labor heavier than Lucian expected. The little ship skipped along on the tide, bobbing and tossing over the gleaming black water. By the time Oudeis called a halt, Lucian's muscles were twitching in protest, and he was glad enough to rest on his oars. Oudeis, with remarkable strength, hauled on a cat's cradle of lines; and, little by little, the sail rose and spread.

"Here's for you, old Earth-Shaker," Oudeis called over the side. He unstoppered his wineskin and spilled some of its contents into the lapping waves. "Oh, I'm devoted to the Lady. But Earth-Shaker's been there long before her, long before the Great Ones. Aye, since the day the world began.

"It's a good thing to stay on the lee side of him; he's not one to trifle with. I've heard the old boy roar like thunder and send up seas high as mountains. I've seen waterspouts taller and thicker than oak trees, and whirlpools that could suck in half a dozen ships and spit them out again."

"Even so," said Lucian, "you still follow the sea."

"And keep promising myself I'll give it up, for all the good it's brought me. Once, my home port was Metara," said Oudeis, an undertow of yearning in his voice. "Those days, I had a fine ship, with a fair business in the cargo trade. And a sweetheart. A plump, lively lass: Mirina was her name. We were betrothed, but I was ever putting off our wedding day. You see, I wanted to wait until my fortunes were better; for I had the notion of buying a little tavern, and the two of us running it happily and handing it down to our young ones when they came along.

"One day, at the docks, a long-jawed, narrow-nosed fellow steps up to me. 'My name is Diomedes,' he says, 'and I'm told there's no better shipmaster in Metara.'

" 'Or anywhere else,' I say. 'You're not from these parts or you'd have known without being told.'

"He gives a dry sort of chuckle and nods his head. 'I'm glad I found you,' says he, 'because I want to make you a rich man.'

" 'I share your ambition for me,' say I. 'Would you care to mention how you'll do that?'

" 'Sheepskin,' says he. 'Hear me out,' he goes on, as I had started laughing in his face, sheepskins being no profitable cargo. 'I'm not talking wool, but gold. Sheepskin of pure gold.'

"That hooked my attention. All the more as he goes on to tell of a land some ways overseas, northeast of Metara; and a mighty river that washes gold down from the mountains. There, the folk lay sheepskins in the riverbed to trap the nuggets, hang the fleece to dry on trees, then comb out a treasure with no more effort than combing your hair. 'I know how to find the place,' he says, pulling out a chart. 'I and my friends propose to go and lay hands on all that fleece. You provide the ship and stores, and you'll come in for your share of the wealth. It's a speculative venture, we win all or lose all together. But,' says he, with a wink, 'I don't expect we'll lose.'

" 'It sounds like speculative robbery to me,' I answer, but he only shrugs and tells me these folk have no end of sheepskins, the river's rich, they'll never miss what's taken.

"Now, I'm no more honest than the next fellow, but I don't much care for bald-faced thievery. And yet, I was starting to think how this might be my best chance for that little tavern, to set up Mirina and me snug for the rest of our days. As those river folk have an endless golden stream, it's no great harm to them and a great good for us.

"And so—to my shame, as I'm first to admit—I agreed, and we clapped hands on the bargain. When I proposed assembling my crew, Diomedes tells me he has his own. 'And a remarkable band they are,' says he. 'Each man's as good a seafarer as you'll find, but most have yet another skill. There's a fellow with eyes keen as a lynx's—he's our lookout. There's another, quick and hard with his fists. For the heavy work, there's one so strong you'd swear he could uproot a tree as easy as you'd pull up a scallion. Have no fear, you'll never see a crew like that again.'

"I studied his chart, calculated the voyage there and back to last most likely three months, which chimed with his own reckoning. So, Diomedes goes off to gather his companions; and I take my leave of Mirina, giving her a few good swacking kisses, vowing I'll be home even before she misses me, with a fortune in my hands and a merry life for us both.

"And so we set sail, and a fair voyage it was. But, little more than halfway on our course, Diomedes sidles up to me, gives me a warm smile and a cold eye, and says, 'You've done so well for us, from here on I think we can forgo your services. What we wanted was your ship. Now we have it, no need for you.'

"I barely had time to curse myself for a gullible fool when Diomedes' bully boy—a thick-headed oaf who carried a cudgel and wore a lion's skin around his shoulders—picks me up like a feather and pitches me over the side. And the ship sails on, leaving me to the mercy of the waves.

"Much later, I heard that most of that motley crew of villains came to bad and bloody ends. Diomedes, I gather, got his sheepskin; but he took up with the daughter of one of the local worthies and there were some nasty doings in consequence. As for that lion-skinned ruffian, that's a tale in itself."

"Who cares about them?" cried Fronto. "Don't keep us hanging while you're floundering in the sea."

"I think he's doing it on purpose," whispered Lucian. "Isn't that what you called 'suspense'?"

"A little goes a long way," said Fronto. "Come on, Oudeis, you didn't drown, since you're here to tell the tale. What happened next?"

"I fought the waves and swam until I was out of strength," Oudeis continued. "Sure my end had come, I turned my last thoughts to Mirina, a widow before she was even a wife, and resigned myself to a watery grave.

"That moment, up swims the biggest dolphin I've ever seen. The Lady sent it out of mercy for me, no question about that. I flung my arms around it and climbed astride, and that blessed creature carried me on its back all day and night until we reached shore. And there it gave me a big smile and left me safe and sound.

"All along that beach, what do I see but tents and piles of gear and cook fires. And men armed to the teeth, a hundred or more, a rough-looking lot, indeed. I step up to the one who seems to be in charge, a beefy, red-faced fellow in helmet and breastplate—Strong-of-Will, as he named himself—tell him my tale, ask where I am and how I can reach Metara.

" 'You're far off your course,' says he, 'and I can't help you. I've more on my mind than a washed-up sailor.'

"He goes on to tell me they're from a kingdom a few days' voyage from here, where the king was about to marry a young maiden. 'But a youth came passing through, he and the wench took a fancy to each other. Next thing you know, they ran off and he brought her here, to his own country. My warriors and I have orders to fetch her back,' he told me.

"He points up the beach to a pretty little town overlooking the sea. 'They're behind those walls. The folk have no warriors to speak of, beyond a few watchmen and constables, and we far outnumber them. But we can't get in. We've tried every way. Storming the ramparts, throwing fire pots, whatever. The walls defeat us, and here we've been sitting for weeks, made to look like a pack of squabbling fools.'

" 'It seems easy enough to me,' I answer. 'Break down the gates, and there you are.'

"At this, he laughs in my face and tells me how they've tried that a dozen times. The gates are too strong, no way to breach them.

" 'In that case,' I answer, 'find a means to make the townsfolk themselves open the gates. Lure them out, then rush in as soon as the gates are ajar.'

" 'Do you think we haven't tried?' says Strong-of-Will. 'Useless. No, the trick's to get a few of my people inside and open the gates for us. And you, young fellow-me-lad, you tell me how to do that and, by heaven, I'll sail you home on one of our ships. We've got a fleet of them moored down there in the cove.'

" 'Consider it done,' say I, my mind running fast as a sea wind. And, after a little thought and calculation, I shaped a plan for him then and there. In sum: Use the timbers from one of his ships to build a great wooden jackass with a hollow belly big enough to hide a couple dozen warriors. First, I thought of a horse, but an ass struck me as being more insulting. Once the contraption's done, Strong-of-Will must proclaim loud enough for all the town to hear that the siege is over, everyone's going home, and here's a little gift expressing our opinion of you. Then, the warriors make a show of leaving, but stay lurking nearby.

" 'I'll miss my guess,' I tell Strong-of-Will, 'if the townsfolk don't haul the thing in as a prize of war and hold a triumphant celebration. At the right moment, your fellows climb out, unbar the gates, and the town's yours.'

"To keep a long tale short," Oudeis went on, "Strong-of-Will agreed. It took a good while, but I built that wooden jackass practically single-handedly. My plan worked exactly as I said it would. I'm sorry it did. That day still gives me nightmares.

"Strong-of-Will and his warriors got through the opened gates. I tagged along and saw it all. They burned that pretty little town to the ground, put every man to the sword; most of the women, too—the lucky ones. They found the runaway couple in the house of the lad's father. No more than half-grown youngsters, scared witless, huddled in a corner, clasping arms around each other. Strong-of-Will killed them both with one blow. He was bloody to the elbows, happy as if he was at a birthday party."

Oudeis waved a hand, as if brushing spiderwebs from his face. There was only the lap-lap of waves for a time, then he spoke again.

"Strong-of-Will was good as his word, I'll say that

much. He gave me a ship and crew. That's the last I saw of him."

"And so," said Lucian, "you got home."

Oudeis shook his head. "The ship foundered in a storm, all hands lost but me. I was washed ashore, who knows where, more dead than alive. From then on, I think I was a man accursed. The harder I tried to reach home, the farther I got from it. Oh, I could tell you how a one-eyed lunatic blacksmith wanted to chop me up for his dinner. And a dozen more disasters. But those are tales for another day."

"Do you believe a word of that?" whispered Fronto. "Dolphins, wooden jackasses, cannibal blacksmiths—"

"It's a great story, true or not." Lucian turned to Oudeis, who was staring into the water. "At the end, though, you must have found your way to Metara."

"Aye, after seven years," said the shipmaster. "As soon as I docked there, I went straight to Mirina's house. In I walk and there she is at her loom, winsome as ever. 'Mirina, my sweet,' I call out, 'I'm home!' She stares as if the eyes would pop out of her head. 'Why, honey-girl,' I say, 'don't you know me?'

" 'You?' she cries. 'Gone for three months, was it? And back seven years later?'

"And she throws a pot at my head, follows it up with other crockery, lays into me with a broom until I had to run for my life. I set sail that instant and never again showed my face in Metara. I took up the cargo trade once more, with hard years of little luck. But, at the end, the Lady of Wild Things gave me safe haven where you found me. Now, here I'm off to sea with a jackass aboard—which no doubt pays me back for building that wooden one."

"I've heard your account," came a voice from astern. "You're perfectly welcome to blame me for your troubles."

"Ops!" burst out Lucian as the scapegoat crawled from a hiding place amid the pile of provisions. "How did you manage—?"

"I brought him with me," said Joy-in-the-Dance.

19

The Voyages of Lucian

That's a harrowing tale, Oudeis." Joy-in-the-Dance untangled herself from the lines and netting. She winked at the shipmaster. "It gets better each time you tell it."

Lucian jumped up, to embrace her; but, while his heart leaped, his feet slipped, and he promptly fell flat on his face as the vessel pitched on the rising waves. Oudeis cocked an eye at the girl, with as much fondness as astonishment.

"Is this the lass I used to bounce on my knee? Eh, little lady, I've not seen you since you went off to be a pythoness. But, here, here, what are you up to? I hadn't counted on two more passengers."

"Ops and I got aboard while you were all traipsing

back and forth loading things. It seemed the best way to save a lot of discussion."

"When your mother sent you away," began Lucian, picking himself up, "I thought I'd never see you again, never have a chance to tell you—"

"You truly are an Aiee-Ouch. You actually imagined I'd sit and twiddle my thumbs while you went sailing off? I told Ops he should stay behind, but he wouldn't hear of it."

"I felt it was my duty to be with all of you," said Ops. "So many things can go amiss on a sea voyage, I knew you'd need my services. Laurel-Crown and I have much to talk about and much to tell each other, but I promised I'd come back to her and she promised to wait for me."

"For you—for a pythoness—to disobey the Lady is bad enough," Lucian began. "Worse, because you did it on my account."

"There are going to be serious consequences," said Joy-in-the-Dance. "I know that. But I made my choice." Her face fell for an instant. "Do you wish I hadn't come?"

"I've heard all I want," broke in Oudeis. "Get those oars in the water," he ordered Lucian and Catch-a-Tick. "You, too, Oops, or whatever your name is. Hop to it."

"My good shipmaster," said Fronto, "you don't intend rowing all the way to Callista, do you?"

"Pull for shore," snapped Oudeis. "You, little lady, are going home."

"No, I'm not," said Joy-in-the-Dance. "Since I'll be punished anyway, I might as well be punished after I get back. And you, Oudeis, you know what it's like to be apart from someone."

Oudeis muttered and rubbed a big hand over his jaw. That instant, a brisk wind rose; the sail caught it and billowed taut. The waves heaved up and the little ship leaped ahead. Oudeis seized the rudder as the vessel sped seaward.

"It seems that Earth-Shaker's made the decision," said Joy-in-the-Dance. "He must have enjoyed that drink of wine."

By dawn, the shore lay far behind and they were in open sea, waves flashing in the early sunlight, the wind never slackening. The craft skimmed along faster than Lucian had imagined. With Joy-in-the-Dance beside him, the salt spray stinging his face, the vessel plunging up and down, he had never been in better spirits.

"Your mother couldn't tell me my best occupation," he said. "But here aboard—it's marvelous, it makes me wonder if—"

He broke off, sprang to his feet, and raced for the side. Fronto was already there, his neck stretched over the rail. Lucian followed the poet's example. The seafaring life, he decided, had its disadvantages.

He did not die. He was sorry about that, for he would have welcomed the relief. The endless tossing of the ship, the horizon tilting every which way, the blinding sun, the stink of pitch in his nostrils turned his stomach inside out and made his head reel. Joy-in-the-Dance, Ops, and even Catch-a-Tick were in fine fettle and hearty appetite, while Lucian spent much of his time hanging his head over the side. Fronto was in worse case. The miserable poet, his white-tipped nose gone pale green, sprawled on the deck, pitifully wheezing and groaning.

"Stop the boat," he wailed. "Heave-ho, or whatever you fellows do. I care no longer what becomes of me. I'll gladly stay a jackass forever. Only put me ashore."

"You'll find your sea legs," said Oudeis, unmoved. "Get up, you lubber, and stir yourself. Keep carrying on like that and, yes, by thunder, I'll maroon you on the first spit of land I come to."

"Don't talk about spit," whimpered Fronto.

Oudeis now handed out the straw hats from the pile of gear. To accommodate Fronto, he cut earholes in the crown of one and set it on the poet's head.

"It's quite becoming," remarked Joy-in-the-Dance. "You look very jaunty."

"Thank you," said Fronto. "I'll be sure to wear it when I jump overboard."

As for Lucian, the shipmaster gave him so many tasks that he had no time to be seasick. More frustrating, he and Joy-in-the-Dance stood separate watches, and he found no right moment for speaking his heart to her. He cheered himself by turning his thoughts to the shipmaster's tale.

"What a storyteller Oudeis is," he said to Fronto, who had recovered enough to sit up on his haunches. Lucian shook his head in admiration. "I hope he'll tell us more of his tales."

"He's one of the best I've heard," said Fronto, "but that wooden jackass could stand a little improvement. I understand why he used an ass. Even so, I'd change it to a horse. Though I hate to admit it, a jackass doesn't have the same elegance, that certain flair. And another thing: Strong-of-Will and his men were a grubby lot of provincials. That doesn't exactly pluck at the imagi- nation."

"You could change that, too," Lucian suggested. "You could make his army bigger, with, say, a thousand ships. And the town bigger, with huge, high walls, topless tow- ers. And have the bravest townsmen come out and do mortal combat with Strong-of-Will's people. You know, slashing each other with swords, the kind of thing you expected from the *lyrikos.* Maybe on horseback—"

"Why, my boy, I believe you're beginning to see how

it's done. Yes, of course. Mighty warriors with plumed helmets, powerful thews, girded loins, and all that. An array of proud and noble heroes—"

"Bilge," said Oudeis, passing by. "I've seen many a brawl and no heroes in any. Unless you count some wretch knifed in the belly, holding his guts in his hands and bawling for his mamma. Nobility? Not a speck."

"Even so," said Lucian, "I'd think you'd need glorious heroes in a tale for people to admire and praise and be inspired to act like them."

"Eh, lad, you may be right." Oudeis shrugged. "Otherwise, who'd ever want to go fighting?"

A few days out, after taking stock of the dwindling stores, Oudeis declared that he would have to make for the nearest port. He had sighted land and what looked like a harbor off the starboard bow.

"I don't know the place. There's more islands in these waters than even I've seen. I wanted to wait and tie up in a snug little place where I'm well known, but I can't risk it. We're too low on supplies. So, I'm putting in as quick as I can."

"By all means!" cried Fronto. "For mercy's sake, let me stand on dry land until my stomach and I are friends again. Don't tell me about getting my sea legs. You forget I have four of them to deal with."

As Oudeis set a landward course, the harbor came into better view. Fishing boats and a long ship, its black sail reefed, were at the wharves. Lucian made out a pleasant-looking, unwalled town, some tree-lined avenues, and a large, stone building overlooking all. Oudeis lowered the sail and ordered his crew to the oars. Fronto clambered to the prow and stood like a long-eared figurehead.

"They've seen us. They're waving," he called. "Some of them have bunches of flowers. A happy welcome, indeed. Faster! Pull hard on those oars."

With Fronto urging more effort, and Oudeis skillfully steering past the harbor bar, the ship glided into port and slid gently to an open pier. Some of the townsfolk ran to catch the line that Oudeis cast over the side. Others set up a gangplank and beckoned the visitors to step ashore.

"Keep your mouth shut. Say nothing," Lucian warned as Fronto, with a joyful hee-haw, clambered onto the dock, Catch-a-Tick at his heels. Having secured his ship, Oudeis strode after Lucian, Joy-in-the-Dance, and Ops. A crowd had gathered, smiling and offering flowers to the newcomers.

"I don't quite catch what they're talking about," said Joy-in-the-Dance. "The language is a little bit of Mother Tongue but mostly something else. The island's Tauros —that's what it sounds like. I'm not sure, but they seem to think we've come to collect some kind of tribute."

"I'll sort it out," said Oudeis. "Seafarers understand each other."

By this time, an escort of warriors in helmets and breastplates had pressed through the crowd and pointed up toward the town. "They want us to see their king," said Joy-in-the-Dance. "So I gather, anyway. His name's Bolynthos."

"I look forward to the opportunity," Fronto said under his breath. "As a poet, I was never invited to meet royalty."

"Nor will you meet any this time," said Oudeis. "You stay with me. A palace is no place for an ass; not the four-legged kind, at any rate. I'll need you to help load provisions."

"The Bull Court?" Joy-in-the-Dance murmured to Lucian as the warriors formed ranks around them. "Is that what they're saying?"

The escort marched them along an avenue lined with onlookers, cheering and tossing flower petals. The building that Lucian had sighted from offshore—the royal palace, he supposed—bulked larger than it had first appeared. Of heavy stone slabs, it was flat roofed, almost windowless. Adjoining it rose a circular structure, a sort of amphitheater with arched entryways. Beyond the palace gates, at the end of a flagstoned passage, attendants flung open bronze portals to an audience chamber. Rows of torches blazed, a sickly sweet aroma of incense hung in the air. On a throne of ornately carved wood, a powerfully built man sprawled lazily. A purple cloak was draped over his shoulders, a gem-studded leather collar circled his thick neck. For a moment, he observed the arrivals with vague interest, then made an offhand gesture for them to approach.

"King Bolynthos?" Joy-in-the-Dance courteously began in Mother Tongue. "We thank you for your welcome and—"

"Not asked to speak," the king interrupted, in a rough version of Mother Tongue. He had the dark brown eyes of an ox and they seemed too large for their sockets. His long black hair had been curled into ringlets around a wide and bulging brow. He turned his massive head toward Lucian. "This man answers."

"This woman answers." Joy-in-the-Dance said in Mother Tongue. "I am the one who speaks for all of us."

"Silence!" The king's eyes suddenly widened to show white all around, and dark blood rushed to his face. Just as quickly, his features relaxed into a crooked smile. "You dance well for me, that is all." He returned to Lucian. "Say on."

Lucian glanced at Joy-in-the-Dance, who shrugged

and translated the king's words. He began slowly, "We come from Arkadia, most of us. We have stopped here to buy—"

Bolynthos scowled and waved a hand laden with bracelets and rings. "Arkadia? I know of Arkadia. Beyond the sea. The rest—I cannot understand your tongue. Let the woman address the Bull King."

"Your Majesty," said Joy-in-the-Dance, holding down her annoyance, "we stopped for food and water. We must keep on our way. We seek no tribute from you."

"From me?" Bolynthos flung back his head and bellowed with laughter. "I do not give. You give."

"There's a misunderstanding," said Joy-in-the-Dance. "We have no tribute."

"You do," said Bolynthos. "All of you. Were you not told? The tribute is—your lives."

"That," said Joy-in-the-Dance, "is a very serious misunderstanding."

20

Asterion

For Lucian, a number of daring possibilities sprang to mind: flinging himself bodily on the king, who had folded his arms and was grimly smiling at his captives; or snatching a sword from one of the guards; or taking hold of Joy-in-the-Dance and dashing headlong from the audience chamber; or signaling Ops to join him in fighting off the warriors while the girl and Catch-a-Tick made their escape. He did, as it turned out, none of these.

In fact, before he could weigh the advantages and disadvantages of his choices, he was already being hauled away by the guards and punched or kicked when he struggled and tried to drag his heels; what he mostly did was to shout indignant protests and colorful threats. It took him a few moments to realize that Joy-in-the-Dance was no longer with him.

By then, he was being frog-marched down one passageway after the other, with so many twists and turns, so many dark galleries, ramps, flights of stone steps going up and down that he entirely lost his bearings. He had not the vaguest notion where he was or, even if he could break loose, how to find his way out.

Ops kept a cautious but alert silence. Catch-a-Tick pranced along, not the least dismayed.

"Aiee-Ouch, that was a clever trick to get us out of the throne room," he whispered. "Who'd have thought of letting them drag us off?" When Lucian only shook his head, Catch-a-Tick gave a knowing wink. "Right. Not a word. They might overhear us."

Lucian, more than half out of his wits over the unknown fate of Joy-in-the-Dance, was too distressed to correct the boy's admiring view. Also, he was dazzled a moment by sudden light after so many dim corridors; for his captors now thrust their prisoners into a large stone chamber, where afternoon sun poured through a long, narrow grating in the far wall. Blinking in the glare, he first made out a huddle of shadows: some dozen men in dirty tunics, in coarse shirts, or stripped to the waist. Catch-a-Tick ran to peer through the bars. Ops, hands on hips, stood observing appraisingly as these captives got to their feet and gathered around the newcomers, talking all at once.

"I don't know what you're saying," Lucian broke in, recognizing only a word here and there. "Does no one speak Arkadian?"

"I do." A tall, reddish-haired young man approached, and the others drew aside to let him pass. "Why are you here? Bolynthos has no claim on Arkadia."

After Lucian explained that they had merely stopped to take on food and water, Asterion, as he named himself, smiled bitterly. "A costly mistake. Alas that you ever set foot on Tauros. This is the time when Bolynthos receives his tribute."

Asterion gestured toward his companions. "Each year, he demands youths and maidens from the king of Naxos. The girl you spoke of is no doubt with our women, penned up as we are. You will surely see her again: tomorrow, at the bull dance. I am sorry."

"I don't understand any of this," replied Lucian. "How could we have known? Everyone seemed friendly. They were throwing flowers at us."

"Of course," said Asterion, "they were overjoyed to see you. On the voyage from our island, two of our company sickened and died; two others, in despair, threw themselves overboard. Thus, the full tribute is lacking. When that happens, Bolynthos is too impatient to await replacements from Naxos. He chooses victims from his own people. Small wonder you were so happily welcomed. Your unlucky arrival spared some Taurians their lives. As long as he has victims enough to satisfy him, Bolynthos cares not where they come from. You are here, you will serve the purpose."

"I've seen goats dance." Catch-a-Tick, all ears, came to join his elders. "But—bulls? They're so stupid and heavy-footed. Dance? What a sight!"

"And one you shall see for yourself," Asterion said. "Those who live through it are, by rule, set free. But no victim has ever survived to claim that right. Yes, it is a dance—a dance of death."

"The king of Tauros is a beast," said Lucian, "and his people no better, if they take pleasure in bloodshed."

"The people are sick of it," Asterion replied. "They come to watch because they fear to do otherwise. Those who show no stomach for the sport could find themselves ordered into the arena. But unless all rise as one against Bolynthos, the killing will go on."

"What about the king of Naxos?" said Lucian. "If he knows what happens to his people, why does he keep sending them?"

"He has little choice," Asterion said. "The yearly tribute began when Bolynthos came to the throne. At that time, he sent an ambassador to us, to discuss trade, treaties, and such affairs of state. There was a quarrel, tempers rose; a rash, ill-considered blow, and the ambassador was slain. This was a blood crime of gravest consequence. The person of an ambassador is sacred, inviolate. As was his right, Bolynthos demanded retribution: not in goods or money, but in lives. He required a group of young men and maidens to be sent him as sacrifice. We could not refuse.

"And so it was done. This should have washed clean our blood guilt, yet Bolynthos remained unsatisfied. Each year, he demanded yet another tribute, and another. He took pleasure in their death. When we protested, he warned that he had ships and warriors enough to invade Naxos and burn it to the ground.

"The king bowed to his will, reckoning the sacrifice of a few would safeguard the lives of many. Every year, victims were chosen by casting lots. But now, in this first season of my manhood, I resolved to end this slaughter. I joined the group ready to set sail, despite my father's pleading. As his son, I was exempt—"

"Wait a moment," said Lucian. "You didn't have to take your chances when the lots were cast?"

"Did I not make it clear? My father is the king. I am Asterion, prince of Naxos."

Ops, listening closely and silently during this, now spoke up. "You chose nobly, Lord Prince," he said, "but if your goal was to save your people and end the tribute, allow me to ask—with all respect—how have you gone about doing it? What plan have you shaped?"

"None," replied Asterion, "because none is possible. When I sailed from Naxos, I had a dozen schemes in mind. Now that I have seen for myself, my plans turned out to be useless fantasies."

Ops frowned. "Lord Prince, you are a leader of your people, are you not? Would you have me believe you've done nothing? Let me point out—again, with all respect—that if nothing is possible, you have nothing to lose. Even the most desperate action is better than none at all."

Ops had spoken in a tone Lucian had never heard before. Looking at the scapegoat now, he realized that Ops had changed since Mount Panthea. His voice was calm but firm, his bearing showed an authority Lucian had not suspected. He suddenly remembered that Ops himself had been a chieftain.

"I said you had done nothing," Ops went on. "I was wrong. You have done something. You have waited to be killed."

Asterion's chin went up. His voice was low and cold. "How dare you rebuke me? As I cannot save my people, the best I can do is die with them. Who are you to tell me otherwise? You know nothing of what happens here. You speak from ignorance."

Asterion took a pace closer to Ops and thrust his face at him. "When you have seen what we have seen, then will you have the right to reproach me. Escape? None, save into the bullring. Beyond this chamber, we would be lost in the passageways. Bolynthos had them built for that purpose. The maze is a better warden than any guard. I know this. Do not take me for a fool, let alone a weakling. I and some of my companions burst out once when the guards came to feed us.

"They made no attempt to stop us. They watched, and laughed; and after we had wandered blindly, they fetched us back at their leisure. In the bullring, there is no way to flee. Only the dead leave it. Each morning, they herd us there and we wait our time to face the bulls.

"On our first day," Asterion went on, his voice faltering an instant, "Bolynthos ordered out three of our maidens, one of them little more than a child. They were nimble. Yes, and clever, too. They did not cling to one another, cowering in fright, but ran in different directions to confuse and distract the bull.

"They were very brave. I was proud of them, and even thought they might live out the day. But their efforts only exhausted them. They tired long before the bull did.

One lost her footing, stumbled, and fell. The creature was upon her within the blink of an eye.

"The other two—it was only a matter of time." Asterion strained to keep his voice under control, but his eyes darted back and forth. "Afterward, the attendants spread fresh sand where it was needed, and raked it smooth. They like to keep the arena tidy.

"And thus it has gone, day after day, always much the same. Now," said Asterion between his teeth, "perhaps you will be kind enough to instruct me in my proper duties, and point out to me what I should do. I will be most interested in your suggestions."

"Indeed, I spoke from ignorance," murmured Ops. "I well understand your fear—"

Asterion gave a bitter laugh. "Fear? We have gone past the limits of fear. Here, we eat and drink it, and finally grow bored with it. I no longer pray for courage. I pray for madness. Sanity becomes too heavy a burden."

"You are still their prince," Ops replied. "It is a burden you must carry."

"I shall gladly lay it down."

Asterion turned away and strode to a corner of the chamber.

"Don't you worry, Asterion," called Catch-a-Tick, swaggering up and down and pointing to Lucian. "Here's the greatest hero in Arkadia. Lucian Aiee-Ouch, mighty warrior, lord of wolves and everything else you'd care to mention. Yes, and I also happen to be the son of a king. I'm Goat Prince Catch-a-Tick, friend of the hero. Everything will be fine. We have a plan—"

"Be quiet," Lucian ordered.

"I forgot. Sorry," said Catch-a-Tick. "You wanted to keep it mum." He closed his mouth tightly and trotted over to Ops, who had gone to Asterion's side.

Lucian went to the grating and stared out at the empty arena. He could not clear his head of Asterion's words. He seemed to hear endlessly echoing screams, to smell fresh blood and the animal reek from the bull pens. He could not guess where Joy-in-the-Dance had been locked up. For all he knew, her cell could be far across the stretch of sand or next to his own. He called out, but no answer came.

He stood some while as the shadow that covered half the arena crept to the farthest tiers of benches and all lay in darkness. He sank down, at last, and put his head in his hands. Catch-a-Tick came and sat beside him, yawning.

"Now you can tell me, just between us," the boy whispered. "You've got it all thought out, haven't you?"

"I don't know what you're talking about."

"The plan! It's working, isn't it? You got us into the same cell as those Naxians. That was the cleverest yet.

Asterion—I hope I didn't make him feel second-rate."
Catch-a-Tick yawned still more widely and leaned heavily against the wall. "He's not much of a prince. And he's no kind of hero at all."

"Neither am I," Lucian said firmly. "I want you to stop this nonsense. Half of what I told you I made up, and you made up the other half. There weren't any meat cleavers. I never led any wolves. Most of the time, I was afraid they'd bite me. Warrior? I got smacked on the head with the flat of a sword. That's all. Nothing but stories and stories and stories. I don't have a plan. I never did. I just want to crawl in a hole somewhere and hide. Do you understand what I'm telling you?"

The boy said nothing. Lucian raised his head and glanced at him. A happy smile on his face, Catch-a-Tick was fast asleep.

21

The Bull Dance

It was a busy morning. Asterion and his companions had been up early, belting tunics, lacing sandals, rubbing arms and legs with oil, as if getting ready for a day of sport. When Lucian asked why they bothered with such careful preparations, Asterion shrugged and said that it gave them something to occupy their minds.

Lucian, in his own way, had been doing much the same, turning his thoughts to Joy-in-the-Dance, Fronto, and Oudeis. He was sure that Oudeis had already learned of their plight. If the shipmaster was as clever as he claimed to be, he would have understood that he could do nothing to help. His only practical choice would be to set sail as quickly as possible. Fronto, at least, would be on his way to Callista.

He still had no idea where Joy-in-the-Dance was being held. Asterion pointed toward a line of shoulder-high wooden barriers on the far side of the arena. Like the men, the women would be taken behind them to wait until ordered into the ring.

"For you and your friends," Asterion added, "there is little advice I can give. Never turn your back on the bull. Stay as far from the beast as you can. Apart from that, it becomes a highly personal matter between you and the bull."

Soon afterward, guards came to lead the victims through a tunnel that opened onto the arena. There was some joking back and forth, and some easy conversation. The guards, good-natured fellows, were trying to keep the business from turning too grim.

Lucian spoke closely with Ops. "Asterion says to keep our distance from the bull. He should know, but I can't help wondering if that's best. I had an idea—"

"I knew it!" cried Catch-a-Tick. "You're working on your plan. Tell me what I do."

"What you do is stay away from us. I don't want you anywhere close to Ops and me."

"I don't think much of that," said Catch-a-Tick.

"Never mind. Just do as I say," Lucian ordered and finished his talk with Ops out of the boy's hearing.

The tunnel ended abruptly at the edge of the arena.

The sudden burst of light, the yellow sand under the glaring sun dazzled him. He shaded his eyes to look across the amphitheater. He thought he saw a hand waving and raised his own in answer. Most of the benches were filled, spectators still picked their way to the upper tiers. On a stone platform at the edge of the ring, Bolynthos sat under a fringed canopy. In full regalia, jewels glittering, he cradled a long-handled, double-headed ax and a scepter topped by golden horns. His eyes were bulging and rolling, his face flushed. He motioned with his head. Trumpets blared, someone began shouting an announcement Lucian could not understand.

"You Arkadians lead off," Asterion explained. "Step out boldly. If you try to hold back, it will only go worse for you. Lucian Aiee-Ouch, whoever you are, I wish you well. I trust you are the hero your young friend believes you to be."

The prince of Naxos turned to Ops. "You were right to rebuke me. For that, I thank you. I had almost forgotten I was a prince. When my turn comes, I hope I shall behave like one. Farewell."

Before Lucian could stop him, Catch-a-Tick darted through the gap between the barriers and trotted to the middle of the arena, where he put his hands on his hips and grinned around impudently. No cheers or shouts came from the spectators, only a long, sighing murmur;

then, silence as the gates at the far end flung open. Bolynthos leaned forward. The bull had come into the
arena.

The creature no doubt had been deliberately goaded
and tormented to liven him up, for he burst out of the
gate at full speed, bellowing, tossing his horns, galloping
around the ring. He was very angry. He was very large.

Lucian stared, rooted to the spot. His plan had been
simple and logical. As he explained it to Ops, instead of
keeping their distance and wasting their strength avoiding the creature, they would go straight at the bull, each
grip one of the horns and hang on to it. Thus, they
needed only keep hold and do nothing more. The bull
would have to tire before they did.

As he had thought about it in the cell, the idea
seemed excellent. He wondered why it had never occurred to Asterion. Now that he was actually in the arena,
he understood. He had never imagined the animal to be
quite so huge and powerful. In fact, he had never seen
a bull face-to-face. He had, he suspected, misjudged the
reality of the situation. All things considered, taking to
his heels seemed the more attractive course. But as in a
nightmare, he could not force his legs to move.

The bull, meantime, had stopped galloping aimlessly
and cast about for some object on which to vent his rage.
Ops glanced at Lucian, motioned with his head, and be-

gan cautiously approaching the animal. Lucian finally ex-
torted some grudging obedience from his legs, but they
felt made of lead as he plodded over the sand. It was
important, he realized, to grasp the horns before the creature charged.

The bull had a different plan in mind. Lucian had
gone less than halfway when the creature drew into himself, gathering his force, then bolted forward, head lowered, faster than Lucian believed possible. Ops leaped to
one side, Lucian to the other, as the bull slewed around
to charge again.

Catch-a-Tick, so far, had obeyed Lucian's orders to
stay away; but now, legs pumping, the boy shot across
the ring straight for the bull. The animal paused a moment, as if considering what to do about this new arrival.
Without breaking stride, whooping and crowing, Catch-
a-Tick vaulted onto the creature's back. The bull did not
like this. He bucked and reared, flinging the boy into the
air. Catch-a-Tick landed with both feet on the massive
shoulders. Turning his attention from Lucian and Ops,
the bull strove to shake off what he must have judged to
be some oversized and exasperating fly, heaving and
twisting, bellowing at the top of his lungs. Each time
Catch-a-Tick was tossed aloft, he nimbly regained his
perch on the bull's back or hindquarters and, once, even
managed to do a somersault in midair.

Seeing the bull preoccupied with Catch-a-Tick, who had begun a jaunty little dance up and down the creature's spine, Lucian and Ops darted ahead, each seizing one of the curved horns. Lucian feared his arms might tear loose from their sockets, but he clung with all his strength. Ops, little by little, was wrestling the shaggy head closer to the sand. From the tail of his eye, Lucian glimpsed a slender shape speeding from the women's barrier.

"Stop that!" cried Joy-in-the-Dance. "You're annoying the poor thing."

She stepped to the bull and laid a hand between the horns, murmuring something Lucian could not understand. The animal left off struggling and blinked at her. "Let go, Aiee-Ouch. You, too, Ops. Catch-a-Tick, come down from there."

The girl stroked the hairy ears, all the while whispering and half singing. This was not only the first time Lucian had seen a bull, it was also the first time he had seen one smile. The crowd was cheering and shouting. The bull trotted to the edge of the arena, folded his legs, and lay down. The crowd started a rhythmic chanting and clapping.

"They want us set free," Joy-in-the-Dance explained while Catch-a-Tick bowed and capered. "Bolynthos won't dare refuse. Oh—now they're saying that—"

She broke off. Ignoring the swelling tide of voices, the king had jumped to his feet. He gestured for a new bull to be sent in. The gate remained shut. The crowd roared all the louder. Bolynthos, cheeks twisting and twitching, sprang from the platform. Brandishing the double ax, he strode toward Joy-in-the-Dance.

The girl calmly pointed her outspread hands at him. "Here, look. Why are you holding that serpent? It's enormous! See, it's coiling around your arm. It's going to strike. Those fangs—look at them, they're deadly poison. Quick, quick, get rid of the horrible thing."

Bolynthos stopped in his tracks, gaping. He stared at the ax, struggled with the handle as if it were indeed coiling around him. With a shriek, he threw down the weapon.

"Run, you three," ordered Joy-in-the-Dance. "I can't hold his mind much longer."

"Bolynthos!"

Asterion had sprinted from behind the barrier, his companions at his heels. Bolynthos shook himself, as if suddenly waking. He thrust aside Joy-in-the-Dance and lurched to recover the ax. Asterion snatched it and sprang away. The king's hand went to the sword at his belt. Asterion swung the ax like a man felling a tree. Bolynthos grunted and dropped to one knee. Asterion struck again.

Lucian did not look back at what Asterion was doing. He could barely keep his heaving stomach where it belonged as he ran with Joy-in-the-Dance to the arcade circling the arena. Before they reached it, the gate of the bull pens opened. Lucian called a warning. Joy-in-the-Dance halted to face another onslaught.

Fronto trotted out. He stopped a moment, blinking in the sunlight. As the cheers rose louder, the poet bent a foreleg and bobbed his head in acknowledgment, then galloped to Lucian's side. Oudeis and a crowd of seafaring men pressed into the arena after him.

"That was a nice round of applause they gave me," said Fronto. "Who's the fellow with the ax?"

"Never mind that now," said Lucian while Oudeis and his comrades hustled them unchallenged past the bull pens and out of the amphitheater.

The streets lay empty; nearly all the townspeople were still at the arena. Lucian hurried to follow the shipmaster toward the waterfront.

"By luck, I ran into some of my old shipmates," Oudeis said. "I found out quick enough what was going on, and they were glad to give me a hand. They're not fond of Bolynthos. Nobody is. I'm sorry it took us so long. We couldn't risk getting lost in those passageways, so we had to wait and follow the crowd into the arena."

Catch-a-Tick, skipping beside Lucian, kept recounting the events to Fronto. "Aiee-Ouch planned the whole thing. He had it all worked out from the first. Oudeis didn't need to bother rescuing us."

"I wish I'd been able to recite a paean of victory," said Fronto. "I don't usually find such a large and enthusiastic audience."

"No more tribute, no more victims," Lucian said to Joy-in-the-Dance. "What a relief for his father and the whole kingdom when Asterion brings home the good news. You saved us all when you made Bolynthos see the snake."

"I didn't make him," the girl corrected. "I only suggested."

"Whatever you did," said Lucian, with a shudder, "it felt like some of it rubbed off on me. For a moment, I thought I really saw the ax coiling around him. But why didn't Bolynthos spare our lives? That's what the crowd wanted. He must have gone mad, if he wasn't mad in the first place."

"I didn't have a chance to explain then," said Joy-in-the-Dance, "but there was something more. The crowd started shouting for him to give up his throne or they'd take it away from him. That was enough to put him in a fine rage. What sent him over the edge—well, you see, they not only wanted to get rid of him, they also wanted me to be queen of Tauros."

22

Earth-Shaker's Chickens

Lad, that's a tale to match any of mine," said Oudeis as the boat sped over calm waters and the island dropped from sight. The shipmaster had been listening with rapt attention, hanging on every word while Lucian gave his account of all that had befallen them—and Catch-a-Tick kept interrupting to add details of his own part in it.

"Well told, my boy," said Fronto, nodding approval. "Satisfyingly bloodcurdling but, perhaps, needing a touch of something to relieve the grimness and lighten it up a bit. Next time you tell it, you might work in some tender moments. To warm the heart and bring a tear to the eye. The only thing more touching than lovers separated is

lovers reunited. You could use those twisting passageways to better effect, as well. What I'd suggest—"

"Stow all that! Take the tiller!" Oudeis shouted to
Ops. The shipmaster had gone pale beneath his tan.
"Blast me for a fool! I've been listening to that yarn spinning as if nothing else mattered in the world." He rummaged in the cargo and pulled out the wineskin. "It
slipped my mind. A drink for Earth-Shaker."

"Come now, Oudeis, be reasonable," said Fronto.
"You did your duty by him when we sailed from Mount
Panthea. Don't waste wine that could be put to other,
some might say more discriminating, use."

"A lot you know, you landlubber." Oudeis, much agitated, upended the wineskin and poured its contents
over the side. "Whenever I've neglected Earth-Shaker—
and it hasn't been often—there's trouble. There, that's
the best I can do. I hope it's not too late."

"I'd say the old fellow's been doing well for us,"
Fronto said confidently. "We couldn't ask for calmer
seas, a better breeze, or a clearer sky."

"What do you call that, eh?" Oudeis pointed upward.
"It wasn't there a moment ago." He squinted at the gray-
ish cloud high overhead, so distant it seemed no bigger
than a fist.

"Hardly worth getting upset," said Fronto.

"You think not?" snapped Oudeis. "Stick to poetry, jackass, and don't teach me about weather." Taking the tiller from Ops, the shipmaster ordered his passengers to lash down the cargo. Sniffing the wind, keeping an eye on the cloud, he held the vessel steadily on course.

"It's my fault," Lucian said to Fronto. "I shouldn't have talked so much. Going on about what happened—I made him forget his gift to Earth-Shaker."

"Oh, you got his attention," said Fronto. "From a yarn spinner like Oudeis, that's a high compliment. It's not often that one storyteller bothers listening to another.

"Here's something that's occurred to me," Fronto went on. "The Lady couldn't tell you what occupation to follow. But I can. I've been observing you, my boy. I have the answer."

"Then you've found it sooner than I have," Lucian said. "What is it?"

"Storytelling, what else?" declared Fronto. "You have the knack for it. Of that, I'm certain. A little practice and you'll come along nicely."

"No, I'm afraid not," Lucian said, with a shadow of regret. "That takes more skill than I'll ever have."

"Nonsense," Fronto insisted. "You're already a story-teller without even knowing it. Indeed, nothing would please me more, and I'd be proud to call you a colleague. You think over what I'm saying—Haw! Haw!"

Fronto choked and rolled his eyes in alarm. "What was that? I didn't mean to say it. That haw-haw slipped out by itself. That's pure jackass, not me at all.

"The Lady warned me," Fronto went on, in mounting panic, "I'd start losing my speech and be more and more a donkey. It's happening already? Dear boy, this is dreadful."

"You're speaking clearly as ever. You're fine," Lucian hastily assured him, trying to hide his own sudden alarm. "Don't upset yourself. It might—it might have been something you ate."

"I haw—I hope—you're right," Fronto said unhappily. "Yes, perhaps only a transitory hiccup."

Putting all thoughts of Fronto's advice out of his mind, Lucian hurried to Joy-in-the-Dance, who had finished knotting a rope around the kegs and jars. The girl frowned when Lucian told her what had so distressed the poet.

"That's not a good sign," she said. "My mother told us he had time enough to get to the island, but she didn't count on our getting thrown into a bullring."

With Lucian, she went to Oudeis, who was glumly scanning the horizon. "How much longer to Callista?"

"Ask Earth-Shaker. It's more up to him now than to me."

"We've a good strong wind," put in Lucian. "That should help."

"Too strong, and it's fishtailing all around. I can barely hold course. I don't like it. And I don't like— them."

Oudeis gestured astern. A flock of birds had appeared, following the wake of the vessel. Lucian shaded his eyes. The birds were sleek and slender, black with a flash of white; their widespread, sharply curved wings bore them swiftly, ever closer.

"Earth-Shaker's chickens, we call them." Oudeis grimaced. "Or wave walkers."

"We call them Lady's hens," said Joy-in-the-Dance. "They're petrels, they won't harm us."

"Storm birds, by any name. The bigger the flock, the bigger the blow."

"They follow storms, they don't cause them."

"It comes to the same. Shoo, shoo!" Oudeis shouted and flailed an arm as if he were, indeed, chasing off invading chickens.

Even as Lucian watched, the waves turned choppy and rose higher. The wind freshened; within moments, the vessel heaved and shuddered. Oudeis laid all his strength of arm on the tiller.

The little fist-shaped cloud had lengthened into a gigantic hand, its twisted fingers clutched the darkening sky. The craft shot ahead like an arrow from a bow, tossed so high that it seemed to fly through the air.

Fronto, knocked off his legs, braying in terror, went skittering across the deck. Catch-a-Tick jumped up and down, gleefully whooping.

Lightning clawed the sky. A thunderclap set Lucian's head ringing. The shock staggered him; he felt as if the air had been sucked out of his lungs. The kegs and jars had begun jolting free of their lashings.

Oudeis bellowed for Ops to lend a hand. "The lines are fouled. I can't lower the sail. It has to come down, or the gale's going to smash us into kindling." He spat furiously. "No use. To the masthead! Cut those lines or we'll all go visiting Earth-Shaker."

Still dazed, Lucian stared around. Oudeis shook his fist at him. "I'm talking to you, idiot. Get aloft. Snap to it."

"Me?"

"Who else, you lubber? I need Ops to help me hold the tiller. I'm your only navigator. The goat-boy and the jackass can't do it. I'll not risk the little lady's neck. That leaves you."

"I appreciate your reasoning," said Lucian.

"Then do, you lump-head!" Oudeis snatched a knife from his belt and tossed it to Lucian, who stumbled toward the mast. Blade clenched between his teeth, he took hold of the rigging and tried to persuade himself it was not much worse than the tree he once climbed.

"There goes Aiee-Ouch!" Catch-a-Tick jigged up and down and clapped his hands. "Who but Aiee-Ouch would dare do that!"

The swaying mast towered above him. Hand over hand, he inched his way upward. The vessel tilted, nearly capsizing. He hung on, dangling from the lines as the craft righted itself. The sky split, rain began sheeting down. His foot caught in one of the lines, he kicked loose and climbed higher. A line had tangled around the yard-arm. He slashed at the wet knots. The line frayed, then parted with a snap. The sail billowed free as the mast shuddered, groaned, and toppled into the web of rigging. Lucian jumped clear. The craft spun around and flung him against the railing. The tiller had shattered. Oudeis was shouting something. With the wind howling in his ears, Lucian heard none of it; nor did he hear the ship scream as the hull ripped apart.

⚶

He knew he was alive because he was choking and coughing. He knew he was on land because he was flat on his stomach with gritty sand on his face and in his eyes. He rolled over and blinked. It was a clear and beautiful morning.

"Hullo, Aiee-Ouch." Joy-in-the-Dance was on one side of him, Ops and Oudeis on the other. "You must have swallowed half the ocean, but we've squeezed most of it out of you."

"I knew my services would be needed," said Ops as Lucian sat up, relieved to find the amulet still around his neck; the pouch, with the sling and firestones, had likewise survived the battering.

"You cut down the sail at just the right time," said Catch-a-Tick, "so the boat smashed on those rocks. Oudeis says if we'd been farther from land, we'd have drowned. Fronto let me ride on his back when he waded ashore."

The poet himself was standing stiff-legged, wheezing and snuffling. "Difficult to express adequate joy that we're all alive," he said in a husky voice. "Either I've caught cold or it's getting harder to talk. Not that it matters. One way or another, I'm doomed."

"Belay that maundering," ordered Oudeis. "Just be grateful we slipped through Earth-Shaker's fingers." He glanced seaward, shaking his head. "My little ship, my brave little ship, gone to splinters, not enough of her left to cobble a raft."

"Farewell, Callista," groaned Fronto. "I'll be a jackass for certain."

"I said I'll take you there," declared Oudeis, "and so I will."

"Perhaps you're thinking of building wings," remarked Fronto, "so we can flap our way off this island."

"What island?" retorted Oudeis. "I've been doing some calculations. As I reckon it, counting from the time we were blown off course, we're not on an island. We're on the south coast of Arkadia."

"Arkadia?" Lucian jumped to his feet. "Last place in the world we want to be!"

"Here we are, no matter," said Oudeis, "and we'll have to make the best of it. So, we're going to walk. No use following the shoreline. There aren't many folk in these parts. Maybe a fishing village or two. But a fishing boat won't do for a voyage to Callista. We need a good seaworthy craft. I know how to get one.

"We head inland," he went on. "It would take too long to go by way of the coast. We go due north awhile, then turn seaward. In less than a week, we'll reach Metara."

"Oudeis, I don't dare set foot in Metara," said Lucian. "If anyone from the palace sees me, if Calchas and Phobos find out I'm there, it's worth my life."

"We have no other choice," Oudeis said. "We won't go into the town. We head straight for the harbor, where the merchant vessels put in. It's a sure thing I'll find some old shipmates to help us. You have the Lady's amulet? Good. There's many a shipmaster owes her a favor. We'll have a deck under our feet and be off to Callista quick as you can whistle. I'll sail with you, to be certain all goes handsomely."

Oudeis ordered them to scavenge among the broken timbers and other flotsam that had washed ashore. The search yielded little: a small keg of dried fish, a cook pot, and Fronto's straw hat. With these, and a couple of cloaks, Oudeis was satisfied, declaring they could add to their provisions along the way.

"I'll tell you right now," said Oudeis, setting off over the sand dunes and up to the bluffs overlooking the coast, "this is my last voyage. Dry land for the rest of my days. No more touch-and-go with Earth-Shaker. Once I'm back from Callista, by thunder, I'll take an oar and walk inland. When someone asks, 'What's that strange-looking piece of wood?'—there's where I'll settle."

Oudeis proved as skillful a pilot on land as on sea; only Joy-in-the-Dance could match him in choosing the easiest paths leading steadily north. Their first day, as they crossed the windswept moorlands beyond the coast, Lucian observed a solitary bird high in the clouds.

"An eagle," said Joy-in-the-Dance as the bird glided closer, hovering on outspread, golden wings. "Did my mother send it to watch over us?"

For all her efforts to lure it down, the eagle came no nearer. Nevertheless, during the following days, it was seldom out of sight.

The moorlands gave way to richer vegetation; the trees became denser, the undergrowth heavier. Catch-a-Tick, proud to show off his skill, taught Lucian how to strike sparks from the firestones. With the boy's instruction, Lucian was soon able to build a cook fire; and Joy-in-the-Dance was always quick to find roots and berries to eke out their scanty meals.

Late one afternoon, when they halted for the day, Lucian spoke apart with her. "Do you remember the night of the dancing? Something your father said to me. And I keep thinking—when your mother sent me away. I've been wanting to tell you—"

"Be quiet, Aiee-Ouch."

"But I want you to know—"

"Hush. Somebody's in the bushes and it isn't one of us."

The girl motioned for Ops and Oudeis. That moment, a bulky figure lurched from the undergrowth. The man's garments hung in tatters, his hair and beard so matted and his face so begrimed that Lucian hardly recognized him.

It was King Bromios.

23

A King in Rags

Lucian jumped to his feet. "Your Majesty—"

"Stand away!" Bromios shoved him aside and lunged for the cook pot. Though the vessel had been simmering over the fire, he snatched it up, paying no mind to his burned fingers, and began scooping out the contents and cramming the morsels into his mouth as fast as he could.

"Here, you, that's our food." Catch-a-Tick started toward Bromios, who held one arm protectively over the pot and fended off the boy with the other.

"Let him be." Joy-in-the-Dance put a restraining hand on Catch-a-Tick's shoulder. "I'm interested to know what the king of Arkadia's doing here."

"That's a king?" said Catch-a-Tick.

"Never. Not me." Bromios sat down heavily and tossed aside the empty cook pot. "Nothing to do with kings. I'm a humble peasant."

"Your Majesty," said Lucian, "I know you're the king. I've seen you a hundred times in the palace."

"What palace? Don't bedevil me, boy. Where's more food?"

"I was one of your clerks," Lucian insisted.

"He's really the king?" put in Catch-a-Tick. "You're face-to-face with your mortal enemy! Go at him, Aiee-Ouch. Hit him with the cook pot. Smite him down!"

"Keep out of this," Lucian said. "I'm not smiting anybody."

"You're showing mercy." Catch-a-Tick nodded. "That's heroic, too. But not as good as smiting."

"I could try my hand at a little smiting." Oudeis stepped up to Bromios and shook a fist. "You miserable specimen of a monarch, you're at the bottom of everyone's troubles, including mine. What you started ended up with me transporting a talking jackass, losing my ship, nearly drowning—"

"That's right," broke in Fronto, too indignant to keep silent. "It's a chain of circumstances, cause and effect. And when we come to the effect of our being here in deplorable circumstances, you're the cause."

"Cause? Of what?" said Bromios. "I have nothing to do with a jackass."

"A poet, actually," corrected Fronto. "You're to blame for what's happened to all of us."

"Poet?" Bromios squinted at him. "I never met one, but you're not what I might have expected."

"I never met a king," returned Fronto, "and I could say the same."

"And don't blame me for your troubles. They're no fault of mine."

"Whose, then?" said Joy-in-the-Dance.

Bromios groaned. "That monstrous Woman-Who-Talks-to-Snakes. I wish I could lay hands on her."

"What would you do?"

"Do?" cried Bromios. "I know just what I'd do. I—" He stopped as if the wind had suddenly leaked out of him, and put his head in his hands. When he finally looked up, he spoke barely above a whisper: "I'd beg forgiveness."

"You'd what?" exclaimed Joy-in-the-Dance.

"Yes, I'd beg forgiveness. Oh, I admit I vowed revenge. Calchas and Phobos couldn't have been happier. But, since then, nothing's gone right. Planting? Not done as it should be. The harvest? Who knows if there'll even be one. Sickness? No wise-women to cure it. The people

are against me, men and women alike, and that's a painful state of affairs. I don't like being hated. A king has
feelings, too, you know."

"You should have thought of that before you wrecked
everything," said Oudeis.

"I'm not good at thinking," protested Bromios. "Calchas and Phobos are supposed to do that sort of thing
for me. But I'm not blind. I saw how badly I'd done. The
Lady's followers were the only ones who knew how to
get us out of the mess. I wanted to take back my decrees.

"Calchas and Phobos wouldn't hear of it. They wanted to crack down even harder. I couldn't understand that.
They knew things were getting worse. But I overheard
them, one night, chuckling about what good fortune it
was, food and everything else starting to be in short supply. That's a puzzler."

"Not to me," said Lucian. "I think I understand it
very well. I kept your palace accounts. I found out that
they were cheating you already. I'll make a good guess
they're buying up everything they can lay hands on to
sell later at ten times the price. Simple as that."

"If you say so," replied Bromios. "Arithmetic's beyond
me. All I know is: The more I wanted to take back the
decrees, the more they talked against it. When I told
them I'd do it no matter what they said, they came out
with a better notion.

"A great honor and privilege is what they had in mind for me," Bromios went on. "The grandest, noblest deed a king could do. The chance of a lifetime: the rite of immolation."

"Right of who?" said Catch-a-Tick. "Moles?"

"Not *r-i-g-h-t*," said Fronto, "but *r-i-t-e*. We poets call that a homonym. It sounds the same, but it's different. Immolation—they were going to sacrifice him."

"They made it out to be a wonderful opportunity," said Bromios. "Not every king was so lucky."

"Bromios," Joy-in-the-Dance said, "didn't you understand? They were going to kill you."

"Not permanently," said Bromios. "They explained it very clearly. In the olden days, when things went badly, to set them right again the king gave his life for his people. But—and here's the best part—after he's sacrificed, he goes to the Great Hall of the Sky Bear; feasting, revelry, merrymaking, all he could want. Then he comes back here, good as new. I'd have a star named for me, too. Even a whole constellation."

"You didn't believe them, did you?" said Lucian.

"Well, yes, I did. At first," said Bromios. "But after I thought it over for a couple of days, I didn't much fancy the idea. I'm a warrior, I've seen dead people. They didn't look in any kind of shape to do anything, let alone come back to life. A king, now, maybe that's different. Or maybe not. Even so, I got to wondering: Suppose something goes wrong? Suppose I lose my way to the Great Hall? Or who knows what? Do I just drift around forever? It's an honor having stars named after you, but cold comfort, when you come right down to it. I thanked them for the opportunity but said I'd decided to pass it up.

"They told me it was too late," Bromios continued. "I was already marked down for sacrifice. They set a guard over me, then. To make sure no harm came to me while they got ready for the ceremony. Well, I didn't want any part of it. I knocked a couple of heads together and slipped out of the palace.

"They sent warriors—my own troops!—after me. Once, they nearly caught me. They're still hunting me, like some sort of animal. I've been running ever since, hiding in bushes and burrows, with hardly a wink of sleep, nor bite of food, nor drop to drink."

The king's burly shoulders sagged. "Where can I go? What can I do? If I could only talk to the pythoness again, plead with her to have mercy and save me. But she's gone. I'm lost. I'll be a constellation, like it or not."

"Bromios," Joy-in-the-Dance said quietly, "I'm Woman-Who-Talks-to-Snakes."

"Don't mock me," Bromios moaned. "That's a cruel joke."

"It takes a while to get used to the idea," said Lucian,

"but it's true. She's also the daughter of the Lady of Wild Things."

"No such person," Bromios said. "She doesn't exist."

"My mother would be surprised to hear that. As for my being the pythoness—listen."

She raised an arm to screen her face with the cloak and began, *"O Bromios, Bromios, your life-threads are spun—"*

"That voice! Those words!" The king's jaw dropped and he clapped his hands to his head. "You? It's you?" As the girl nodded, Bromios gave a cry and threw himself at her feet. "Forgive me! Have mercy!"

"Forgiveness is something you'd have to talk over with my mother," said Joy-in-the-Dance. "Mercy? You're welcome to mine, if it makes you feel better. In a practical sense, it won't much help you."

"Nor will we," put in Oudeis. "Frankly, your pathetic tale doesn't tug at my heart. You've taken our time, eaten our food, and I think you'd best shove off. We're in a hurry. The jackass here has to reach Callista—"

"The island?" Bromios stopped groveling and looked up eagerly. "I'd be safe there. They'd never find me."

"Oudeis," Joy-in-the-Dance began, "talking about practical help, do you suppose we could bring him along—?

"Absolutely not," declared Oudeis. "It's bad enough shipping out with an ass. No runaway kings."

"He's a sorry example of a king, I admit," said Ops. "But he's still a person."

"Noble soul!" cried Bromios, seizing Ops by the hand. "Thank you for those words. What royalty of spirit! I wish I'd had some of it."

"Fronto's the one to decide," put in Lucian. "He's the most concerned. He should say who goes and who doesn't."

"I have to agree with Ops," said Fronto, after some moments. "There's not much king in him, but he is a human being. Which is more than I can say for myself. Yes, take him with us."

"Dearest friend!" Bromios flung his arm around Fronto's neck. "What did you say your name was? Calchas and Phobos never had a good word for poets. Idle, untrustworthy riffraff is what they called them. I see they were wrong about that, too."

If Bromios resembled little of his former self, Oudeis tried to make him even less so. With his knife, the shipmaster hacked at the king's hair and beard, stained his face with berry juice, and set Fronto's straw hat to shadow his brow.

"Best I can do," said Oudeis while Bromios underwent the shipmaster's finishing touches in patient silence.

"There's a lot of him, and I can't change his size. But, if he keeps his trap shut and doesn't call attention to himself, he'll pass well enough for an upcountry lout."

Next morning, they set off again, Bromios striding between Fronto and Ops, his newest and dearest companions. As the king's spirits revived, so did his appetite. The remaining supplies and what Joy-in-the-Dance could gather did nothing to take the edge off it. No sooner had he downed his portion than he looked around, hopefully licking his chops. When Ops thought no one was watching, he handed the king a good share of his own rations. As it turned out, so did Lucian and everyone else.

For the most part, Bromios was pathetically grateful and anxious to be helpful. From time to time, however, he forgot he was a runaway sacrifice. Each time his thoughts turned to Calchas and Phobos, he growled and muttered, threatened awful punishments, kicked tree trunks, and snapped branches as if they were the soothsayers' necks. After offering to tend the fire, he usually let it go out; or neglected to clean the pot, as Oudeis ordered; or made messes, which he regally ignored.

"It's rather like having a tame bear for a pet," Fronto observed. "You can't help being fond of him, but you keep wishing he were a cat."

No one, however, not even Oudeis, suggested abandoning him. The shipmaster, at first, had feared that

Bromios would hinder them. On the contrary, the royal sacrifice set such a pace that they reached the outskirts of Metara two days sooner than Oudeis reckoned. As he promised, Oudeis did not venture into the city. Instead, he turned off and took a roundabout way seaward, following the narrow beach in the shadow of high cliffs. Not long after midday, the harbor opened in front of them.

"The port—just as you told me, Aiee-Ouch!" Catch-a-Tick stared, round-eyed. "The boats—herds of them! And people—I've never seen so many all at once!"

There were, in fact, fewer passersby than Lucian expected. Among the vessels at the landing stages, only one was being offloaded, and none taking on cargo. Many shops stood empty; the stalls of fishmongers and vegetable sellers displayed hardly any wares. Oudeis stopped in front of the first tavern they came to and motioned them to go in.

"Wait for me there," the shipmaster ordered. "I'll be back in no time, with money in my purse and quick passage out. No, not you," he told Fronto, who had started for the tavern. "Stand outside. You're still an ass, so behave like a proper one."

"I'll stay with him," Lucian said as Oudeis hurried down to the waterfront and the others led Bromios through the tavern door.

Fronto had trotted a little way along the street, where he gazed anxiously seaward. "I pray Earth-Shaker gives us a speedy voyage. We'll reach Callista none too soon. Haw! Haw! There—haw!—it goes again. Dear boy, I'm more donkey than ever."

"You're tired, overexcited." Lucian put as much assurance as possible into words he did not entirely believe. He was much aware that Fronto had been snorting and braying more than usual.

"Trust Oudeis," he said, patting Fronto's neck. "If he promised to get you there—"

"Thief!" roared a voice in Lucian's ear.

A heavy hand gripped him by the scruff of the neck. Shaken and buffeted, Lucian was roughly spun around to find himself nose to nose with Cerdo.

24

The Hall of Sacrifice

The donkey robber!" Cerdo shook him until his teeth rattled. "Got you! I'll teach you to steal my beast."

Lucian scuffled free of the merchant's grip. "Not yours! He's mine!"

"Liar! There's my brand on his rump. I'll have him back, and I'll have your hide into the bargain!"

Fronto, horrified to recognize his brutal master, bucked and reared, braying at the top of his lungs. Seeing the enraged merchant start after Lucian again, the poet laid back his ears and snapped his jaws, nipping whatever parts of Cerdo he could reach.

"Help! Help!" bawled the merchant as Fronto's attack from behind rousted him off his feet. "Save me! It's a killer jackass!"

A handful of waterfront idlers had already gathered; passersby, sniffing possible amusement, hurried to watch as Cerdo, scrambling up, seized Fronto's tail while Lucian clung to his neck, and both hauled in opposite directions. The commotion had also caught the attention of a mounted patrol of warriors, who plunged their horses through the crowd.

"Arrest him!" Cerdo stabbed an accusing finger at Lucian. "He stole my property. This ass is from my pack train. There's the rest of them, down there." He waved toward the dock where goods were being unloaded. "You look at the brand on him. And this young villain—he's a runaway from the palace."

"I'm a soldier, not a judge. This is a case for a magistrate—Here, now, just hold on a minute." The captain had been eyeing Lucian. "I've seen this fellow before."

"Not me," blurted Lucian. "I'm somebody else."

"I commandeered his donkey as royal property, then it got stolen from me. This is a murky business," the officer added. "Until it's settled, I'm impounding the ass. You, too, my fine fellow. You'll both come along with me."

"By thunder, no, they won't!"

Bromios had shouldered his way past the onlookers, with Joy-in-the-Dance tugging at his cloak and Ops doing his best to hold him back.

"What's one of my troop captains doing in a wrangle over a jackass?" Bromios put his hands on his hips and thrust out his jaw. "Back off. Get about your duties. Let him be, he's my friend. The lad, too. They all are," he went on while Joy-in-the-Dance kept signaling him to hold his tongue.

The officer squinted and rubbed his eyes. "Your Majesty?"

"Who else?" shouted Bromios. "Are you deaf as well as blind? I gave you an order. Do it, blast you! I'm your king."

The onlookers gasped and drew back. The officer hesitated, shifting uneasily on his mount. "Your Majesty —in this case, your soothsayers are authorities even higher than you. Their command—if you're found, you're to be escorted to the palace."

"Nobody's escorting anybody anywhere," said Joy-in-the-Dance.

"Don't try anything," whispered Lucian. "They'll find out who you are."

The captain had drawn his sword. Bromios strode up to him. "You dare threaten me?"

"Not you, Majesty," said the officer. "You're the royal sacrifice. Your person is sacred. Forgive me, but I have to take you in. If your friends hinder me, I'll have my men cut them down. You come quietly, Majesty, and they go free."

Bromios glared and chewed his lips. At last, he nodded. "So be it." His face wrinkled as he turned to embrace Joy-in-the-Dance, Lucian, and Ops, and he patted Catch-a-Tick on the head. He laid a stubbly cheek on Fronto's nose. "A swift and happy voyage, friend. You did your best for me, all of you.

"Eh, eh, no glooming," he added. "I'll be back good as new. You'll see some changes, then, starting with Calchas and Phobos. If not—well, you look for my star. I'll wink at you, so you'll know it's me."

"My property!" squealed Cerdo as the king swung up behind the captain.

"Find a magistrate." The officer waved him aside. "I've got more important business."

The patrol closed around Bromios and galloped off. Helpless to stop them, Lucian turned to face a closer, louder threat: Cerdo, bawling for watchmen and constables.

"Get him off the street," Lucian ordered, "before he stirs up the whole port."

Between them, Lucian and Ops hauled the sputtering merchant into the tavern and flung him down on a stool.

"I'll deal with this," said Joy-in-the-Dance. "Listen to

me, Cerdo. One peep and I'll do something you won't like."

"Thieves! Villains!" yelled Cerdo. "I'll have the law on all of you."

"Don't say I didn't warn you." Joy-in-the-Dance made quick gestures at the merchant. "Here, look. How awful! See—Oh, this is dreadful! Your beard's on fire. The flames! They're going up your nose."

Cerdo screamed and beat his face with his hands.

"It's all right now. The fire's out. That really must have smarted," said Joy-in-the-Dance. "But you're going to keep your mouth shut, aren't you?" The terrified merchant nodded. "Good. Make sure you do."

Fronto, meantime, had trotted into the tavern. At the sight of a donkey in her establishment, the proprietress snatched up a broom. "No donkeys here! Out, out, shoo!"

That same instant, Oudeis burst through the door. "What's amiss? There's talk that Bromios was taken—" He stopped short and stared at the tavern mistress. "My honey-girl? Mirina?"

The stout, gray-haired woman dropped the broom and stared back. "Oudeis?" With a joyous outcry, she ran to fling her arms around him. "Where have you been? I've waited and waited for you all these years. This is my tavern. My uncle left me money to buy it. I've kept it for us. I'd almost lost hope—"

"Dearest Mirina, more beautiful than ever," exclaimed Oudeis, wiping a tear from his eye. "How I've longed for you. But, my sweet, when last we met I recall you threw a pot at my head, tossed crockery at me, laid into me with a broom—"

"Numbskull!" retorted Mirina. "It didn't mean I wanted you to go away."

"No matter, I'm home to stay," said Oudeis. "Almost." He turned to Fronto. "I have a ship. We sail for Callista on the morning tide."

"What?" Mirina picked up the broom and shook it at Oudeis. "Sail where? You wretch, I've turned down a dozen offers of marriage for your sake. Don't you talk to me about sailing."

"Please, please, my little darling, I'll explain it later." Oudeis turned back to Fronto. "You're in luck. It's the only vessel I could get. Nothing else for weeks. It's your best chance; and, I daresay, your last.

"Sweet one," Oudeis added, "bar the door. No intruders. Now, quick, what's this about Bromios?"

"Don't be alarmed to hear me speak," Fronto whispered to Mirina. "You see, something quite astonishing happened."

"With that here-today-gone-tomorrow Oudeis home when I'd about given him up for dead," replied Mirina, "nothing astonishes me, least of all a talking jackass."

"Oudeis, it's true," Lucian said. "Bromios ran out to help Fronto and me. A patrol recognized him. He gave himself up so they wouldn't arrest us. Cerdo, that scoundrel sitting there, set off the whole thing."

"I'm truly sorry." Oudeis sadly shook his head. "I'd grown fond of the lout. At the last, he did you a good turn. For us, now: We go aboard after nightfall—"

"They're going to kill Bromios," Lucian broke in. "Don't you understand? We can't let them."

"Lad, that's out of our hands," replied Oudeis.

"Not if I can help it," put in Joy-in-the-Dance. "There has to be a way to save him. If we can get to him—"

"What?" cried Oudeis. "Have you lost your wits? You, the pythoness? They'll kill you along with Bromios. And you, too," he added to Lucian. "And you, jackass, you can't risk a delay. And there you have three good reasons not to set foot in the palace even if you could."

"And one best reason why we have to," said Joy-in-the-Dance. "Listen to me, Oudeis. If Bromios is sacrificed, who rules Arkadia? Calchas and Phobos, of course. They'll claim they're just looking after things until Bromios comes back. Which he won't. Meantime, you'll have disaster worse than ever.

"But if we rescue him," she went on, "he'll have learned a good lesson. He'll have sense enough to get rid of that pair. He said he wanted to take back all his decrees. He can't do that if he's dead, can he?"

"I'm not a statesman," said Oudeis. "That's no business of mine."

"Oh, yes it is." Mirina shook the broom at him. "I've heard of new laws in store that won't let women own so much as a stick of property. And there goes my tavern. You want to sail to Callista? All right, I'll wait for you again. But if you won't help this young lady, who seems a lot cleverer than you, I'll do more than throw a pot at you."

"There's still another best reason," put in Fronto. "Bromios called us his friends. Poor fellow, at this point we're the only friends he has."

"Stop, enough!" cried Oudeis. "Yes, I admit it goes against my grain to do nothing for the poor lubber. But what? You tell me that and I'm with you."

"To begin with, we have to get inside the palace," Lucian said. "I know how to do it."

"Of course you do," said Catch-a-Tick.

"Cerdo's a royal purveyor," Lucian went on. "He's in and out all the time. He'll take us along with his pack train. No one will question him."

"Aiee-Ouch," said Joy-in-the-Dance, "for once you have an interesting idea."

Cerdo opened his mouth to protest but closed it rapidly at a look from Joy-in-the-Dance.

"You will do exactly as you're told," she said. "Otherwise, you'll have more than your beard on fire."

"There's a stableman," Lucian continued. "Menyas, an old friend of mine. He'll help us if anyone can."

"Aye, lad, I'll give you credit," Oudeis admitted, after a moment. "You could be on to something that might work. So far, so good. Now, let's say we get ourselves into the palace. What next?"

"After that," said Lucian, "what we do is—yes, well, what we do is"—he paused and shook his head—"I haven't the least idea."

"Oh, a marvelous plan," retorted Oudeis, rolling his eyes.

"Better than nothing," said Joy-in-the-Dance. "We'll do it."

"We will?" said Lucian.

&

With Ops on one side of Cerdo and Joy-in-the-Dance on the other to prod the merchant along, they left the tavern and hurried down the waterfront. Mirina had insisted on joining them to keep an eye on Oudeis. "I've waited this long for the footloose rogue, I'm not letting him out of my sight."

The merchant's pack animals were already laden with bales and baskets. Tethered one behind the other, a couple of mules, a swaybacked horse, and eight or nine scrawny donkeys waited in gloomy resignation.

"I see some of my companions in misery," Fronto murmured. "Yes, there's poor old Lop-Ear. And Spindle-shanks. Ah, my boy, I shudder to think I used to be one of them."

"I'm afraid you'll have to be one of them again," said Lucian. "Just a little while."

"A little while may be all I—haw—have," replied Fronto. "Running into that vile Cerdo again seems to have frightened more speech out of me."

As Lucian instructed, Fronto took his place at the head of the train. Joy-in-the-Dance whispered to Cerdo: "Tell your people you've hired extra hands for this delivery. That's all. Not a peep more. Don't even blink."

Protectively clutching his beard, Cerdo obeyed the girl's orders. Far from being suspicious, his servants appeared glad for the added help. The pack train, with Fronto leading, set off as quickly as their burdens allowed. Catch-a-Tick skipped at the rear, urging stragglers to keep pace.

A little after sundown, they reached the back gate of the palace. So accustomed to the arrival of the merchant and his goods, the sentry waved him and his animals into the yard, only remarking that he was later than usual.

Lucian halted near the storehouses. A chill ran through him. Never had he imagined setting foot in this place again; and he still had no idea what next to do. Ops and Joy-in-the-Dance had started unburdening the animals. Lucian looked around for Menyas.

He saw nothing of him in the stables, then sighted him by one of the granaries. The old stableman's face was gray and careworn, and he seemed older than Lucian remembered.

Lucian ran to him. Menyas blinked, hardly recognizing him, then gave a glad cry. "Lad, is that yourself? Here?" He glanced about hastily. "Get into the stable. It's worth your neck if you're caught—"

"Never mind that. My friends are with me. We want Bromios." Lucian drew him aside. "The sacrifice—we have to stop it."

"Are you out of your head? First, why meddle in such a business? Second, there's naught you can do."

"There must be." As quickly as he could, Lucian stammered out what had happened since meeting Bromios. "Where's the king now?"

"Lad, I don't make sense of half what you're babbling. The king? He's to be offered up when the Bear Star rises." Menyas squinted at the darkening sky. "Any time now.

You won't save him. They've already got him in the Hall of Sacrifice."

Without waiting to hear more, leaving Menyas standing bewildered, Lucian shouted for Joy-in-the-Dance and Ops. The girl threw aside the basket she was unloading and started after him. Cerdo, seizing the chance to escape, bawled for help at the top of his voice and scurried across the yard, Ops at his heels. The pack animals brayed and whinnied, straining at their tethers. From the tail of his eye, Lucian glimpsed guards racing to the stables.

Not daring a backward glance, he dashed down the walkways, past the sheds and chicken run. Footsteps clattered from behind him, and then Catch-a-Tick was racing at his side.

"Aiee-Ouch, I want to see you do the rest of your plan," he called out. "I want to be there when it happens."

"Stay out of this. Go back. Fetch the pythoness. And Ops."

"They're busy. You see, what happened—"

"Then go help."

Catch-a-Tick paid no attention to him. Wasting no more time or breath trying to shake him off, Lucian pressed on. Torches lined the pathway to the Hall of Sacrifice. Two warriors guarded the open portals. Skirting the hall, Lucian cast around for another entry. The lath and plaster building was open-sided, with rows of wooden pillars holding up the roof. Calchas and Phobos ordinarily used it for consulting the oracular chickens. Now it was filled with palace officials come to witness the solemn ceremony. A low wall of boards ran between the pillars. Lucian scrambled to the top of it. Catch-a-Tick climbed up beside him.

"What next, Aiee-Ouch?"

Lucian did not answer. His eyes had gone to the far end of the hall. Crimson draperies hung from the rafters overhead. Tall iron braziers flamed on both sides of the stone altar where Bromios, in a drugged stupor, lay in his bearskin regalia. Calchas held a long, glittering knife. Phobos was gazing beyond the pillars into the night sky. For some long moments he stood watching, then turned and nodded. "The Bear Star has risen." Calchas lifted the blade high above his head.

The throng held its breath. Lucian, frozen, could only stare as Catch-a-Tick nudged him anxiously. Then he burst out with the only words that sprang to his lips.

"No! Stop!"

Calchas hesitated and glared around. "Who dares to speak?"

"The sacrifice is not acceptable," cried Lucian. "These

soothsayers are unworthy to perform it. Their hearts are stained with crime. Thieves and traitors!"

"The tongue of a liar!" Calchas had fixed a furious eye on Lucian, who was standing on the wall. The crowd murmured uneasily. "Seize him. Fetch him here."

Phobos was frantically gesturing for Calchas to strike. "Do it, you fool. Do it."

Lucian's heart sank. The crowd was too thick for him to force his way through and make one desperate attempt to seize the blade from Calchas. Then it flashed into his mind: the gift from Catch-a-Tick. The sling.

He snatched the bag from his tunic, fumbled a stone into the pouch, and whirled the thongs around his head. The missile whirred through the air.

It missed its mark.

He had taken dead aim at Calchas. To his horror, that same instant, Bromios sat up. The stone struck the king squarely on the head. Bromios toppled off the slab.

Catch-a-Tick crowed triumphantly. "You saved him! Marvelous!"

It took a moment for Lucian to understand. The stone had knocked Bromios to the ground just as Calchas brought down the knife. The blade shattered on the empty altar.

Lucian sprang from the wall. Bromios, dazed, stumbled to his feet and lurched into a smoking brazier. The red-hot coals went flying, the crimson draperies burst into flame. Phobos, yelping as sparks showered him, streaked for the open side of the hall.

But Calchas would not be cheated of his victim. Even as the flames licked at the rafters, he snatched up a cleaver from behind the altar and swung it wildly at the reeling Bromios. By then, Lucian was upon him. The soothsayer turned to face his attacker.

"Watch out for that cleaver, Aiee-Ouch!" cried Catch-a-Tick.

Calchas halted in midstroke. Cerdo had dashed into the hall. As the onlookers scattered, the merchant streaked toward Calchas, bawling for help. Behind him, braying and snapping, galloped Fronto and all of Cerdo's donkeys.

Making straight for Calchas, Fronto reared and lashed out with his hooves. Calchas jumped back and flung away the cleaver. The roof had begun blazing like matchwood. A burning rafter fell in a fountain of sparks, striking Bromios across the shoulders and sending him headlong to the ground.

The onlookers, shouting in panic, jostled their way out of the hall. Cerdo dived over the wall. The pursuing donkeys jumped after him. The fire, by now, had spread to the nearby sheds and outbuildings. Catch-a-Tick was dancing with gleeful excitement.

"Aiee-Ouch, you're burning down the whole palace!"

"Get out!" Lucian struggled to lift the king to Fronto's back. The blazing rafters collapsed. The roof fell in on itself. Lucian gave an anguished cry. Fronto lay beneath the crackling timber. Lucian plunged into the flames.

"No use," Fronto gasped. "Save yourself, my boy. Too late for Callista. I can barely speak. Leave me here. Better a dead poet than a live jackass."

Lucian flung up his arms as a curtain of fire swept over Fronto. Choking, blinded by smoke, Lucian groped helplessly. Fronto had vanished.

Strong hands gripped Lucian's shoulders and dragged him clear of the burning wreckage. He tried to fight free of his rescuers. Joy-in-the-Dance was there; beside her were Buckthorn and See-Far-Ahead.

25

A City in Ashes

Nothing was spared. The fire had raged all night, sweeping over sheds and storehouses. Half the palace had been gutted; the rest was smoke-blackened or gnawed by flames. Clouds of ash sifted down on the rooftops, turning the city gray. About dawn, a sour little rain began, the droplets hissing and steaming as they touched the hot embers. Menyas and some household servants had gotten the horses and livestock to safety. Of the palace officials, most had fled; only a handful of warriors stayed at their posts. Some fifty of the Horse Clan who had ridden with See-Far-Ahead kept as much order as possible among the city dwellers. The folk of Metara had never seen the like of these tall, graceful men and women, and stared with wonder at them, as if they were beings from an unknown, marvelous world.

"The Lady of Wild Things had news from the eagle that followed you," See-Far-Ahead later told Lucian. "When Bromios came upon you, she feared for your lives. Though she could not be sure of its nature, she sensed that great peril lay ahead. She urged me to summon warriors and ride with all speed for Metara while she herself made ready to set sail and join us here.

"As we passed through the domain of the Goat Folk, Buckthorn asked to accompany us. There was the matter of a certain disobedient young member of his family," See-Far-Ahead went on. "Only the wind itself could have gone more swiftly than we did. Alas, we came too late. Now my heart aches for your friend and for you."

In the morning, when it was barely light enough to see, with Bromios in the care of Ops and Mirina, Lucian and the others picked their way through the rubble to what had been the Hall of Sacrifice. Joy-in-the-Dance kept his hand clasped in hers. Since Lucian had been pulled from the wreckage, the two had never been out of each other's sight, and rarely out of each other's touch.

The Hall of Sacrifice had burned to the ground. The heaviest rafters still smoldered; the reek of charred wood caught in Lucian's throat; his eyes watered in the haze of smoke. Or so he thought, until he realized he was weeping. See-Far-Ahead and Buckthorn set about heaving aside what remained of the fallen timbers.

"There's naught here, lad," Buckthorn said gently. "All burned beyond a trace. Let be," he added as Lucian searched through the wreckage. "Take no more grief than you can bear."

Catch-a-Tick's face puckered and he leaned his cheek on Lucian's arm as Joy-in-the-Dance led them back to the stable yard. Menyas had found some sheets of canvas and Oudeis began rigging a makeshift awning to keep out most of the rain. Bromios, still in what remained of his bearskin cloak, was sitting up. The drug had worn off and he looked not much the worse for being nearly sacrificed.

"Any sign of our friend?" The king's face fell as Lucian shook his head. "No, I was afraid not. I'm sorry. He'd be on his way to Callista by now if it hadn't been for me. The rest of the prophecy's come true, the city's in ashes; but I didn't think it would cost his life instead of mine."

"I wonder if there's a constellation for jackasses," added Bromios. "If there is, he deserves to have one." He turned to Lucian. "As for constellations, thanks to you I'm not one of them. You saved my hide with that business about an unacceptable sacrifice. I never heard of such a rule."

"Neither did I," said Lucian.

"It was all part of his plan," put in Catch-a-Tick. "Just like hitting you instead of the fat fellow. Who but Aiee-Ouch would have thought of doing it? Or setting loose the donkeys?"

"Listen to me," said Lucian, "none of it was any plan of mine."

"The donkeys were Fronto's idea," said Joy-in-the-Dance. "He was afraid his time was short, he wanted a chance for himself and the others to get some of their own back on Cerdo." She smiled at the recollection. "Fronto called it 'jackass liberation.' What he most wanted, though, was to help Aiee-Ouch."

"He did," said Lucian. "In the nick of time, just as if it had been a tale. Hitting Bromios by mistake—he'd have thought that was a nice touch.

"He did more than save my life," Lucian went on. "He gave me a new one. He told me I should be a storyteller—that I was a storyteller already and didn't know it. I've been turning it over and over in my mind. I'm not sure he was right, but that's what I'll try to be."

"I know he was right," said Joy-in-the-Dance, adding fondly, "do you remember that preposterous tale you told me when we first met? As truth, it was ridiculous. As a story—it wasn't all that bad. You'll learn to do better. If Fronto set you on your occupation, he gave you a great gift."

"I'll find out soon enough if it's true," Lucian said, brightening. "He told me he'd be pleased and proud if I were his colleague. I only wish he knew."

"Perhaps he does," put in Bromios. "I hope so, anyway. But, speaking of gifts, you tell me what I can do for you."

"There's nothing." Lucian shook his head. "I'd only ask you to be a better king."

"No," declared Bromios. "Certainly not. I won't be a better king. I can't," he pressed on despite an indignant outcry from Joy-in-the-Dance. "Because I'm not a king at all. You have a new one. As royal a fellow as ever you'll find. King Ops."

"What's he saying?" exclaimed Lucian, turning to the scapegoat. "Is that true? You're the king of Arkadia?"

"I'm afraid so," admitted Ops. "At first, I told him it was out of the question, but he kept at me. He was very persuasive. He vowed he'd crack my head if I didn't accept."

"That's wonderful!" Lucian clasped the former scape-goat's hand. "Congratulations—Your Majesty!"

"Ops, that's the only wise thing Bromios has ever done," said Joy-in-the-Dance, embracing him. "It makes perfect sense. Your father was of the Bear tribe; your mother, of our people. You're both. If anyone can settle our differences, you can."

"You'll still have your old occupation," added Lucian. "You like taking on people's troubles. Now, you'll have a whole kingdom to serve."

"I hadn't looked at it that way," said Ops. "Yes, it does save wandering about. And I'll set up councils with both men and women."

He stopped as a disheveled figure edged his way into the shelter. The intruder's face was smudged with ashes, his lank hair tangled and matted; his only garment, a length of tattered cloth, with holes burnt in it, which he had wrapped around himself as best he could.

"Here, now, what are you after?" demanded Oudeis. "We're having a serious, private conversation."

"We just got a new king," piped up Catch-a-Tick. "He's King Ops."

"Really?" said the new arrival. "Marvelous news! I'm delighted to hear it. Let me be the first to wish him well, if the rest of you haven't done it already."

From the moment he had begun to speak, Joy-in-the-Dance had fixed her glance on him, studying him intently. Lucian, too, had been watching and listening, all the more bewildered as the stranger, smiling happily, continued.

"It will be my great joy, honor, and privilege to write a coronation ode—"

Lucian jumped to his feet, staring speechless. His ears were playing tricks on him. He dared not believe what they were telling him.

"Dear boy, I'm not a ghost. If I were, I'd hope to be a little less famished."

"Fronto?" Lucian gasped. "You're not. You can't be."

"Can be. And am," replied the poet as Joy-in-the-Dance drew closer, her eyes lighting up. "Yes, beyond question, I'm me. Myself again, altogether in splendid shape—my usual shape, that is. I have a tender spot where Cerdo put his mark on me, but I expect it will fade away in time.

"I hope I didn't cause undue concern," Fronto went on. "I got here as quickly as I could. I do admit I wasn't sure, at first, if I'd get here at all."

"But you were burned up," Lucian stammered. "I know—I saw—"

"Aiee-Ouch, be quiet," said Joy-in-the-Dance. "Let him tell us."

"Yes, well," said Fronto, "if you recall, the Lady of Wild Things mentioned using a blazing pyre to transform me. She didn't recommend it, and I quite understand why. Indeed, I might have been burned to a crisp. In fact, I was. So to speak. My jackass exterior, in any case. Of that, there was nothing left at all.

"Of myself—I can't describe it precisely, I was neither

here nor there, neither one place nor the other. Betwixt and between, you might say. For a while, I had the impression I was turning into a tree. Then a bird. Then a fish, a rabbit, a hedgehog, and half a dozen other creatures one after the other.

"Until my own body came back, I had no idea who was who or which way was which. An unsettling condition, but a very interesting one, as I look back on it. For us poets, a state of confusion is quite ordinary.

"When I did, at last, come to myself, I still had one trivial difficulty. My clothes had vanished along with my hooves, tail, and the rest. I could hardly, out of modesty, go parading around like that. These bits and pieces were all I found, but they'll do for the moment.

"And so, I'm overjoyed to be with you all—Haw! Haw! Ah—don't worry about the occasional hee-haw. Old habits tend to linger."

"Fronto," said Lucian, embracing him, "it's you. It really is."

"Was there ever any doubt?" said Fronto.

26

New Metara

The Lady of Wild Things was in Metara. Watchers at the port had, from a distance, sighted the golden sail and banks of flashing oars; and, by the time the long, slender vessel glided into the harbor, word had spread from one end of the city to the other. See-Far-Ahead and his horsemen galloped to escort her from the landing stage. If the townsfolk had marveled at these splendid riders, they stood speechless in even greater wonder as the procession made its way to the public square. The jeweled diadem shining at her brow, a blue sea-cloak around her shoulders, her leopards padding beside her, the Lady of Wild Things moved with graceful strides at the head of her white-robed Daughters of Morning.

At first, the crowds lining the streets hardly dared

whisper among themselves. Some had never believed that she existed; those who did believe had never dreamed she would set foot in Metara and they would see her with their own eyes. Then, one voice rose, another, and another until it seemed the whole city had joined in a single joyous outcry.

As the Lady of Wild Things entered the stable yard, Joy-in-the-Dance ran to her arms. Lucian felt his heart clench as the Lady's last words to him came back as piercingly as when she had spoken them: *That is her life. You can have no part in it.*

"Lord See-Far-Ahead has told me all that has happened," the Lady of Wild Things said. "I am indebted to him for his help, though I understand it was little needed." Before she could say more, Fronto, unable to restrain himself, eagerly hurried forward.

"Dear Lady, I'm myself again," he began, bowing deeply. "In case you don't recognize me—"

"Poet," the Lady said, "I would recognize you anywhere, jackass or otherwise. I am happy to see you in your own form. That much is settled, but other questions remain."

"Yes, and one of them has to do with me," put in Bromios, who had been shifting uneasily back and forth. He ventured to approach and then knelt at the Lady's feet. "The pythoness showed me more mercy than I deserve. I don't expect forgiveness, but I'll beg it from you anyway."

"King who used to be," replied the Lady, "as I forgave this poet for being an ass, so I forgive you for being a fool. You played your part, however unwittingly, in fulfilling the prophecy."

"Oh, it worked out," Bromios ruefully answered, "exactly as the pythoness foretold."

"But not as you understood it." The Lady of Wild Things turned to Ops. "*Khaire*, Argeus Bright-Face. The prophecy spoke of a king in rags. It was you, not Bromios."

"Dear Bright-Face! What have they gone and done to you?" Laurel-Crown broke away from the other Daughters of Morning to fling her arms around him. "Lay a burden like that on you?"

"I really hadn't much to say about it," said Ops, beaming at her. "I wanted an occupation and that's what it turned out to be. I hope you don't object."

"We'll have to make the best of it," said Laurel-Crown. "I had other things in mind for us, but we'll manage—"

"Return to your place," the Lady ordered. "I have more urgent matters to settle: my daughter and this Lucian Aiee-Ouch."

"Punish me any way you choose." Joy-in-the-Dance

stepped to Lucian's side. "We won't be kept apart."

"Be not too severe, Amaranth Flower-Never-Fading." See-Far-Ahead laid a hand on the Lady's arm. "Think of a young warrior and a certain sanctuary maiden. Against her mother's wishes, did she not ride by night to his camp, where they exchanged marriage vows? Do you remember?"

"I remember well," said the Lady, giving him a smile overflowing with love. "It is not a question of punishment, but of pardon. Not to grant, but to ask it." Her eyes went to Lucian. "And so, Lucian Aiee-Ouch, I ask your pardon."

So taken aback by her words, Lucian was at first convinced he had misunderstood them. Braced for some terrible judgment, he realized his ears had not deceived him only when the Lady had gone on.

"You have been much in my thoughts since last we met. I saw you then only as my enemy, as I believed all Bear tribe men to be. My eyes were blinded by concern for my child. I did not see you as yourself and as you truly were. You spoke a hard truth when you had courage to tell me that, by judging every Bear man alike, I was scarcely different from Bromios. I know what has befallen you, and that your love for my daughter has never faltered.

"She, too, wished friendship between our peoples.

That, now, is my wish; and so it shall be. Yes, she disobeyed me. But her disobedience also showed me the strength of love in her own heart. Punishment? No. You both have my blessing."

"Do you mean—are you telling us—?" stammered Lucian, all the more bewildered as Joy-in-the-Dance clasped his hand.

"Don't babble," she whispered to him. "Think it over. Even an Aiee-Ouch can figure out what she means."

"Here's one who won't get off as happily," declared Buckthorn, tightening his grip on Catch-a-Tick's ear. "Disobedience and running away? I have something to say to you, and I'll say it with the flat of my hand."

"I only wanted to see Aiee-Ouch being a hero," protested Catch-a-Tick. "Now I want to see him get married."

Oudeis, cocking an eye at the rain clouds, urged all to take shelter under his awning. Mirina offered to lodge everyone in the tavern, including the leopards. "There's room enough," she said, "if some of you squeeze together."

"It is not necessary," said the Lady of Wild Things, allowing Oudeis to lead her, and the others, out of the downpour. "I shall not long remain here. But until the king of Arkadia has a better roof over his head, he and his companions are welcome to the hospitality of my ship."

"Give me a day and a few willing hands," said Oude-is, "and I'll put together something neat and snug here for everybody. It will do nicely while I deal with the rest of the palace. I'll plan out a whole new one," he went on, his enthusiasm growing. "Aye, and see it's built as it should be. For that, of course, I'll need a bit more time, and all the carpenters, all the lumber I can get—"

"Oudeis," Lucian broke in, "you're talking about building in wood. Can you build in—marble?"

"Stupid question. I can build with anything."

"Laurel-Crown told us the finest marble comes from the cliffs near Metara. If you could find quarrymen, stonemasons, devise machines to hoist the slabs—"

"Why, lad, that's finally a task to match my skill." Oudeis pursed his lips and a gleam came into his eyes. "Yes, by thunder, so I'll do."

"If you want a quarry master," said Bromios, "that's work more to my liking than being king ever was. And if Calchas and Phobos, and Cerdo, too, are ever caught, I'll set them to breaking rocks for the rest of their days."

"Done!" cried Oudeis. "I'll begin with the palace, but I won't stop there. I can rebuild the whole city, a new Metara. What a dream!"

"Yes, and while you're dreaming up your grand schemes," Mirina said under her breath, "you'll leave me the hard work of running the tavern. Well, play with your building blocks. It's better than having you go off sailing whenever the mood strikes."

"And in the middle of the public square," Oudeis pressed on, "I can see it now. A monument to the Lady! Columns, porticos—"

The Lady of Wild Things raised her hand. "No city could have a finer architect than you, Clever Oudeis, but I wish no empty monument."

"Why empty?" Lucian asked. "Long ago, your great sanctuary was filled with books of lore and learning. These were destroyed, but they can be written down again and put in the new building."

"Written?" The Lady frowned. "No, that is not our way."

"It used to be, once," said Lucian. "Why not now? Yes, writings can be stolen, or changed, or used for evil purposes. But isn't the risk worth taking? The more people who share knowledge, the greater safeguard for it. Isn't there more danger in ignorance than knowledge?"

The Lady did not reply. Lucian quickly went on.

"It can be a place for teaching, too. Whoever wanted

to could come and learn the arts of healing, the secrets of planting, and all such. Oudeis himself could teach architecture, navigation—"

"I'll be delighted to instruct in poetry," Fronto put in. "After I've learned a little something about it myself."

"So be it," said the Lady, after a long moment. "This house of teaching shall be in my daughter's charge. The cave and pool at Mount Lerna cannot be restored. She can best serve here in Metara, along with any Daughters of Morning who wish to remain."

"You'd do well to attend and study a few things yourself, my boy," Fronto said to Lucian. "A little knowledge never harmed a storyteller."

"I'll do that gladly," said Lucian. "Then," he said to the Lady, "all the tales I've heard from Oudeis, Gold-Horse, Buckthorn—someday I want to write them down so they won't be forgotten. Those and everything that's happened to me, as well. Sometimes," he added, "they all get mixed up together in my head, as if the tales were my life and my life was a tale."

"When you asked what shape your life should take, I could not tell you," the Lady said. "I gather you have learned that for yourself."

"Thanks to Fronto," replied Lucian. "I've already told

him what I want to do. He wasn't surprised. He said I was a storyteller without knowing it."

"Indeed so, my dear colleague," said Fronto. "And, should you need assistance in the way of improving, refurbishing, adding a few nice touches here and there, I'll be happy to instruct you."

"I'll go to school with Aiee-Ouch," declared Catch-a-Tick.

"Oh, no you won't," said Buckthorn. "You'll come along—" He stopped and scratched his jaw. "And yet, from what I've heard of your doings in the wide world, goat herding may have turned too narrow for you. I'll have a bushel of explaining to do to your mother—but, yes, you little goat-scut, stay awhile among your friends. You might learn something besides mischief."

"Settled, then. I'll start my work," said Oudeis. "But, Lady, I seek one favor. If you'd perform a marriage ceremony for Mirina and me, as I promised her years ago?"

"So I shall, Clever Oudeis," said the Lady. "But mind you also help her with the pots and pans while you dream of a new Metara."

During this, Laurel-Crown and Ops, heads together, had been whispering to each other. "My dear Laurel-Crown has chosen to stay here," said Ops, beaming.

"We'd be honored if you'd do the same service for us. I realize this comes rather suddenly—"

"Not to me it doesn't," said Laurel-Crown. "I had it in mind from the moment I set eyes on you."

"Remarkable!" said Ops. "So did I."

"And us?" Lucian said to Joy-in-the-Dance. "If I understood what your mother told me—"

"Yes, Aiee-Ouch," said Joy-in-the-Dance. "I think you finally figured it out."

"What a tale all this would make!" exclaimed Fronto. "My boy, be sure to write it down. As for me, I feel the urge to compose a wedding anthem. I do believe the old inspiration's bubbling up again."

"Poet, my heart is glad for you," said the Lady of Wild Things, beckoning to him. "I could not give what you sought in the pool at Mount Lerna. But," she added, gently kissing Fronto's brow, "I give you my grace and my blessing."

The rain had stopped. A bright band of colors arched across the sky.

So ends our tale, more happily than it began. What remains to tell is that three weddings were celebrated, with singing and dancing throughout Metara. When the Lady of

Wild Things departed, all the city came to watch. At the same time, flights of birds soared overhead, cranes and sandpipers danced on the shore, otters frolicked in the shoals while seals clambered to the rocks and clapped their flippers, and dolphins leaped from the waves. As the ship sailed from the harbor, the Daughters of Morning began a song of farewell, and the melody hung shimmering in the air long afterward.

The
Remarkable Journey
of Prince Jen

BOOKS BY LLOYD ALEXANDER

The Prydain Chronicles
The Book of Three
The Black Cauldron
The Castle of Llyr
Taran Wanderer
The High King
The Foundling

The Westmark Trilogy
Westmark
The Kestrel
The Beggar Queen

The Vesper Holly Adventures
The Illyrian Adventure
The El Dorado Adventure
The Drackenberg Adventure
The Jedera Adventure
The Philadelphia Adventure

Other Books for Young People
Gypsy Rizka
The Iron Ring
The House Gobbaleen
The Arkadians
The Fortune-tellers
The First Two Lives of Lukas-Kasha
The Town Cats and Other Tales
The Wizard in the Tree
The Cat Who Wished to Be a Man
The Four Donkeys
The King's Fountain
The Marvelous Misadventures of Sebastian
The Truthful Harp
Coll and His White Pig

Time Cat
The Flagship Hope: Aaron Lopez
Border Hawk: August Bondi
My Five Tigers

Books for Adults

Fifty Years in the Doghouse
Park Avenue Vet (with Dr. Louis J. Camuti)
My Love Affair with Music
Janine Is French
And Let the Credit Go

Translations

Nausea, by Jean-Paul Sartre
The Wall, by Jean-Paul Sartre
The Sea Rose, by Paul Vialar
Uninterrupted Poetry, by Paul Eluard

The
Remarkable Journey
of Prince Jen

LLOYD ALEXANDER

DUTTON CHILDREN'S BOOKS   NEW YORK

Library of Congress Cataloging-in-Publication Data

Alexander, Lloyd.
    The remarkable journey of Prince Jen / Lloyd Alexander.
        p.   cm.
    Summary: Bearing six unusual gifts, young Prince Jen
embarks on a perilous quest and emerges triumphantly into
manhood.
    ISBN 0-525-44826-8
    [1. Adventure and adventurers—Fiction.   2. Princes—
Fiction.   3. Fantasy.]   I. Title.
PZ7.A3774Re   1991   91-13720
[Fic]—dc20   CIP
                                                            AC
Published in the United States by Dutton Children's Books,
a division of Penguin Books USA Inc.
375 Hudson Street, New York, New York 10014

Editor: Ann Durell   Designer: Riki Levinson
Printed in U.S.A.   10 9 8 7 6 5

You must know nothing before
you can learn something,
and be empty
before you can be filled.
—MASTER SHU

· *Contents* ·

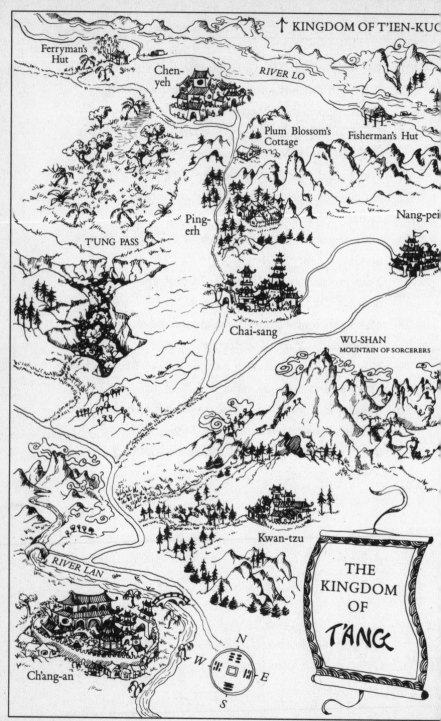

KINGDOM OF T'IEN-KUO

Ferryman's Hut

Chen-yeh

RIVER LO

Plum Blossom's Cottage

Fisherman's Hut

Nang-pei

Ping-erh

T'UNG PASS

Chai-sang

WU-SHAN
MOUNTAIN OF SORCERERS

Kwan-tzu

RIVER LAN

THE KINGDOM OF T'ANG

Ch'ang-an

N
W E
S

Map by Debby L. Carter

1

*   *Arrival of Master Wu*   *
*   *Prince Jen hurries to the Pavilion*
    of Joyful Mornings   *
    *   *Mafoo makes a suggestion*   *

ONE MORNING, A RAGGED OLD MAN came hobbling
to the Jade Gate of the Celestial Palace in Ch'ang-an.
He leaned on a staff, his robe was kilted to his knees,
red dust caked his bare feet. He was not a beggar, since
he asked for no alms. He was not a man of wisdom,
since he did something ridiculous: He demanded an audience with King T'ai.

The guards would have had rough sport with the
foolish old fellow, but the look in his eyes made them
uneasy and uncertain what to do about him. So, they

reported his presence to the Department of Further Study. There, the officials decided that he was merely a wandering lunatic and should receive five blows from the Rod of Correction. However, when the guards returned to administer Benign Chastisement, he had vanished.

Later that day, Young Lord Prince Jen was practicing archery at the far end of Spring Blossom Garden. It was one of his many accomplishments, which included appreciation of the new moon at the Mid-Autumn Festival, riding, fencing, writing poetry, and knowledge of the Six Forms of Polite Address, the Eight Mandarin Ranks, and other essential information.

His servant, a round-faced, bandy-legged fellow named Mafoo, had gone to retrieve an arrow when Prince Jen glimpsed an astonishing sight: an intruder on the palace grounds. At first, Jen thought it was his beloved old teacher, Master Hu, who had instructed him in Princely Virtues, as well as all the other precepts, principles, and analects that a young man of Jen's rank was required to know. Jen and the ancient sage had been devoted to each other. One day, however, Master Hu disappeared from the palace and never returned.

It was not Master Hu. Unhindered by walls, gates, and sentries, a stranger was making his way across the gardens toward the Pavilion of Joyful Mornings, where the ailing King T'ai customarily took the fresh air.

Prince Jen immediately summoned Mafoo, who peered in the direction his master indicated.

"Do you mean that old codger in a red robe?" Mafoo said, squinting one eye, then the other. "Carrying a walking staff? Prosperous, distinguished looking, with a long white beard?"

"Exactly," Jen said.

"I see nothing at all," Mafoo said. "Since it's not allowed, he isn't there. He's a figment of your imagination."

"You see him as well as I do," Jen said, hustling Mafoo toward the pavilion. "Don't play the fool."

"Who's playing?" Mafoo muttered. "This is something out of the ordinary. I've served long enough in the palace to know one thing: What starts by being unusual ends by being troublesome."

Jen's astonishment grew. Outside the pavilion, instead of rushing to protect King T'ai, the royal bodyguards stood about in befuddlement. Some leisurely scratched themselves, others stared blankly at the clouds. A few had gone to sleep on their feet and snored loudly.

Jen hurried into the pavilion. There sat his father conversing with a lean old man whose weathered face was brown and wrinkled as a walnut shell.

"My son, how surprising this is," King T'ai said. "I was about to send for you this very moment. Here is Master Wu. He has journeyed great distances and learned much of interest to me during his travels. I confess he so startled me at first that I feared I must have died without noticing it and he was a spirit come to lead me to my ancestors. I could only wish he had chosen a more conventional way of obtaining an audience."

"With all honor and respect, Your Highness," replied Master Wu, "had I done so, would it have been granted? I understand an old man of the streets sought a hearing but was sentenced to a beating."

"If so, I regret it," said King T'ai. "I know nothing of him. My councillors decide who is admitted into my presence. As for yourself, Master Wu, you seem a person of substance and rank. Your request would surely have been given every consideration."

"Perhaps, or perhaps not," Master Wu said. "Yet, as the poet Lo Yih-tsi wrote:

> Whether it comes wrapped
> In fresh leaves or old straw,
> The discerning cook smiles and says,
> 'What an excellent fish!' "

Master Wu now turned his attention to Prince Jen. The wayfarer did not fling himself to his knees and knock his head on the ground, as the law required. After a calculating glance, he nodded briefly.

"I was speaking to His Majesty," Master Wu said, "of a happy, harmonious realm."

"Clearly," Mafoo said under his breath to Jen, "the old geezer doesn't mean our Kingdom of T'ang."

"The old geezer," said Master Wu, whose ears must

have been as sharp as his eyes, "was referring to the Kingdom of T'ien-kuo."

"Is there truly such a place?" asked Prince Jen. Long ago, Master Hu had spoken of T'ien-kuo, but the old sage himself was not certain whether it existed or was only a fairy tale.

"So I gather, from all I have heard and read," Master Wu said. "It is a remarkable kingdom. Far north of here, in its great capital, Ch'ung-chao, reigns the noblest and most generous of rulers: Yuan-ming. His subjects thrive and prosper, the land yields harvests in abundance, the arts flourish as richly as the orchards. The laws are just, but seldom enforced, since the inhabitants deal with each other as they themselves would wish to be dealt with. Thus, few officials are needed, but they serve their monarch and the people well."

"If true," Jen said, "it must be the Sphere of Heavenly Perfection itself."

Master Wu chuckled like a dry branch scraping a roof. "Indeed not. How could it be? Even in T'ien-kuo, none can escape living or dying, the pains of rheumatism or the pangs of a broken heart. There, simply, a reasonable amount of happiness is a definite possibility."

"I would be glad for half as much in my own kingdom," said King T'ai. "I wish to consult Yuan-ming and learn how he governs his people. I have little strength for a long journey, but I must make it nevertheless."

Prince Jen was about to speak, but Mafoo dropped

to his knees before the king. "Divine Majesty, I offer a humble suggestion. The journey will be difficult, uncomfortable to say the least, with who knows what dangers. Send someone else to observe Yuan-ming's methods and principles. Give the task to the lowest-ranking official in the palace. If something fatal happens to him, he won't be missed. Better yet, send a high official, who will be missed even less."

"Would they report the truth to me?" replied the king. "I doubt it. They would tell me what they wished me to hear, for their own benefit. Who goes in my place must be one I trust beyond question."

"Honored Father," Prince Jen began, "hear my own thought."

"Young Lord, be careful," Mafoo whispered. "I know you're good-hearted, well-meaning, kindly, with a sweet and innocent nature. Therefore, you're about to do something stupid."

"Honored Father," Jen continued, "let me make the journey."

"I knew it!" groaned Mafoo. "Young Lord, you've never set foot outside the palace grounds. You've never put on your clothes for yourself, or even washed your own feet. For your own good, avoid such a journey."

Prince Jen, despite Mafoo tugging at his sleeve, went on so eagerly and persuasively that King T'ai nodded agreement.

"Go, then. Study and learn all that is possible. If Yuan-ming is as generous as Master Wu tells us, he will surely welcome you and share his wisdom. I will anxiously await your return."

"Young Lord," whispered Mafoo, "will you give your groveling servant permission to speak?"

"Mafoo," said Prince Jen, "first, when have you ever groveled? Second, when have you ever asked permission for anything?"

"Young Lord," said Mafoo, "I haven't told you this before, but I have to tell you now. No one could hope for a better master than your noble self. Since your revered mother passed away, I have served you with admiration and affection growing greater every day. The thought of your leaving on such a journey is more than I can bear. Therefore, I beg you: Stay in the palace. Find someone else to undertake the hardships."

"Good Mafoo!" cried Prince Jen. "Faithful Mafoo! What you have said touches me deeply. I had no idea you would be so grieved by my absence. I cannot bring myself to put such a painful burden on your loyal heart."

"Blessings on you," exclaimed Mafoo. "I knew I could count on your kindness and compassion."

"You can," said Prince Jen. "Therefore, I have decided to take you with me."

"What?" Mafoo clapped his hands to his head. "Young Lord, do you realize—?"

"So be it," said King T'ai. "What better companion than one who declares such deep devotion?"

"Your Highness," Mafoo said hastily, "there has

been a small misunderstanding. I only wanted to protect the Young Lord."

"So you shall," said King T'ai. "I count on your affection and obedience. I have every confidence you will not let Prince Jen come to harm. See to his comfort as you would your own."

"Of that," answered Mafoo, "you can be absolutely certain."

"Make preparations now," declared King T'ai. "I will order an escort of my finest troops, and write a royal warrant, stamped with my vermilion seal, commanding every subject, every official throughout the land to provide all that Prince Jen may require."

"Wait." Master Wu raised a hand. "There is one difficulty."

◆　◆　◆　◆　◆

Our young hero is eager to start his journey, but Master Wu seems to be casting a dark shadow on a bright prospect. What can be the difficulty? To find out, read the next chapter.

2

• Seeking worthy offerings •
• Six valuable objects •
• One inconvenience •

JEN'S FACE FELL. He stared in dismay at Master Wu.
"But—all is settled. What difficulty can there be?"

"Finding suitable gifts," replied Master Wu. "All
who seek an audience with Yuan-ming must bring him
worthy offerings. Not to do so would be a most profound discourtesy, a mortal affront. Yuan-ming is a
kindly, reasonable monarch, but on this point I understand he is unshakable. Without acceptable tokens of es-
teem, Young Lord, you would surely be turned away."

"That difficulty is easily overcome," said King T'ai.

"I will open the Hall of Priceless Treasures and hold back nothing that may please Yuan-ming."

Jen's concern vanished. "Only a matter of costly presents? Master Wu, you'll find more than enough."

"Perhaps," Master Wu said. "We shall see." He turned to the king. "I must be allowed to choose the gifts, without question or objection to what I select."

King T'ai nodded. "I put all my possessions at your disposal."

The guards by now had recovered from their befuddlement and rushed into the pavilion. King T'ai gestured for them to lower their swords and lances. He ordered their captain to carry word to General Li Kwang, the king's commander of palace troops. Li Kwang was to attend him later in the Chamber of Private Discourses; meantime, he was to assemble a princely escort of horsemen and foot soldiers, holding them ready to depart for the Kingdom of T'ien-kuo at the earliest moment.

From the Pavilion of Joyful Mornings, the king led Master Wu, Prince Jen, and Mafoo to the Hall of Priceless Treasures. The surprised First Custodian unlocked the teakwood cabinets, opened huge golden coffers, and drew back the silken drapes from the alcoves. Master Wu glanced around him as the Second and Third Custodians scurried ahead to unbar other chambers.

Even as Master Wu began peering at the store of treasures, news of the king's intention spread from one department to the next.

The highest officials urged King T'ai to give up his ill-considered, ill-advised, and impossible plan. For once, the king refused to heed them. If they thwarted his wishes, he warned them, every official in the palace would be demoted by two grades. They fell silent instantly.

Meanwhile, Master Wu continued inspecting the royal treasures. For three days, he paced the chambers and galleries. Each day, Prince Jen grew more dismayed. Master Wu shrugged at the priceless figurines of rare jade. He wrinkled his nose at the exquisite porcelain ware and waved a scornful hand at the intricate objects of pure gold.

When King T'ai came to learn the reason for the delay, Master Wu shook his head.

"Among all these treasures," he declared, as Prince Jen's heart sank, "I find none worthy of offering to Yuan-ming."

One chamber remained unexamined. The First Custodian assured the king that it held items of little value or interest. They had not been sorted, listed, or classified and hardly merited even counting as part of the royal collection.

"Let me look at them nevertheless," Master Wu said.

Following him into this last chamber, Prince Jen glimpsed only a hodgepodge of dust-covered articles. He was about to turn away, disappointed, when Master Wu's eyes brightened.

"Here—yes, here is one acceptable gift." He pointed

to a curved sword leaning in a corner. The First Custodian hastened to fetch it. Master Wu stepped toward a
pile of harness leathers, stirrups, and other gear.

"There is a saddle," he said. "I choose it as well."

From then on, Master Wu unhesitatingly selected
one item after the other, though his choices struck
Prince Jen as being of much less value than the treasures
in the other chambers. In addition to the first two,
Master Wu rummaged out four more. He bobbed his
head and pronounced himself satisfied. The First Custodian begged to mention that a list must be made of any
objects removed. He produced a tablet of paper and
wrote according to Master Wu's direction:

Item: one sword, iron, with scabbard likewise, including tassels and attaching rings.

Item: a saddle, of tooled leather, with stirrups and bridle.

Item: a flute, of painted wood.

Item: a bowl, bronze, one handspan in circumference.

Item: a box, of sandalwood, containing one paintbrush, one
ink stick, and one ink stone for grinding same.

Item: one kite, paper, bird-shaped, with wooden rods and
struts (disassembled), including one ball of string.

"A child's toy?" Prince Jen, hearing this last object
named, whispered to Mafoo. "What value does this
have for Yuan-ming? Can Master Wu be serious?"

Mafoo shrugged. "At least it's easy to carry. What
if the old bird had picked a pair of ten-foot vases?"

General Li Kwang had done his king's bidding perfectly. Assembled in the palace courtyard the next morning, a splendid escort of cavalry and foot soldiers stood ready while Prince Jen knelt to take leave of his father. He had expected Master Wu to be on hand to offer parting words of advice, but the old man was nowhere to be found.

The six chosen objects had been wrapped in silk and set beside Prince Jen in a carriage canopied in yellow brocade. Mafoo had appointed himself driver of the pair of white horses. The Jade Gate was flung open. Tall banners fluttering, tassels swinging at the necks of the steeds, horsehair plumes waving at the crests of glittering helmets, the procession crossed the Great Square of Tranquil Harmony. Word of Prince Jen's purpose had been cried throughout Ch'ang-an. As the carriage passed, the townspeople dropped to their knees and called down ten thousand blessings on the journey.

As for Prince Jen, his long hair bound up under a tall cap stiff with gold embroidery, his robes wrapped around him and tied with a sash at his waist, he composed his features in a look of calm dignity, as he had always been instructed to do. However, with the cheers of the townsfolk ringing in his ears, he found this attitude more and more difficult.

"Has there ever been a day like this?" he cried. "Has the sky ever been so blue? Or the sun so bright? The air has a fragrance I never smelled in the palace. What is this spicy perfume?"

"Let me analyze it." Mafoo sniffed loudly. "Ah. Yes. I can identify the subtle ingredients. One part fried cabbage. One part wandering livestock. Two parts old rags. Four parts sweat. The rest, a concentrated absence of cash. Mixed with the correct proportions of thievery, beggary, and a generous pinch of greedy officials, it is called 'Sublime Essence of Wretchedness.'"

"You make sport of my ignorance," Prince Jen said reproachfully.

"No, no," Mafoo protested. "Ignorance is a common ailment. In time, it goes away. Unless it proves fatal."

Passing through the outskirts of Ch'ang-an, Prince Jen was appalled to observe the ramshackle dwellings, patched together with paper, straw, and plaster, none of them as spacious as the palace kennels or pigeon coops. Street urchins picked through heaps of rubbish, a bent-backed old woman and a dog lean as a skeleton disputed over a bone in the gutter.

"One of our nicer neighborhoods," Mafoo remarked.

"Can there be worse?" Jen burst out. "I never realized—Mafoo, I must learn all I can from Yuan-ming, and come back as soon as possible to help these folk."

"Agreed." Mafoo slapped the reins. "Especially the part about 'as soon as possible.'"

Passing the Happy Phoenix Gardens and crossing the Lotus Bridge, they left the capital well behind them. Prince Jen's earnest concern for what he had seen strengthened his resolution. At the same time, he could not imagine a pleasanter way to accomplish a noble purpose. Halting at the end of their first day on the road, Mafoo pitched a silk tent and set up comfortable couches; from the supply wagons, he obtained chairs, taborets, flowered screens, and a cooking brazier.

As courtesy required, Prince Jen invited Li Kwang to share the excellent meal Mafoo himself had prepared. After the obligatory expressions of gratitude, the gray-headed, battle-scarred warrior addressed Prince Jen.

"His Divine Majesty entrusted your life to my care," Li Kwang said. "I gave him my solemn vow that I and my men would guard you with our lives. Young Lord Prince, I repeat that vow to you."

"Honorable Li Kwang," Prince Jen graciously replied, "between you and my good servant, what harm can come to me?"

Next day, Prince Jen wondered if he had spoken too soon. The royal retinue had been following the River Lan, which Li Kwang intended crossing, thus gaining the easier roads through the western province. A disturbance at the head of the column caused Mafoo to rein in the horses. Moments later, Li Kwang galloped up, dripping wet.

"My outriders saw an old man struggling in the river," he reported. "They halted to pull him out."

"They did well," Prince Jen said. "Aiding the elderly is, as Master Hu taught me, one of the Fourteen Excellent Deeds."

"They failed," Li Kwang replied. "For all their efforts, my men could not remove him." Li Kwang added that he himself had plunged into the river and failed equally. Even at this moment, the hapless victim still struggled, his strength ebbing.

Puzzled as to why a simple matter had proved so difficult, Prince Jen impatiently jumped from the carriage and beckoned Mafoo to accompany him. At the banks of the Lan, he hurried down the grassy slope. Half a dozen of Li Kwang's soldiers continued striving vainly to haul ashore a frail, white-bearded figure. Prince Jen quickly realized that the soldiers were hindered by their armor and the quilted skirts of their tunics.

"Mafoo," Prince Jen ordered, "go yourself and pull him out."

Casting an uneasy eye at the swift current, Mafoo scrambled down to seize the old man by the scruff of the neck. Soon, however, Mafoo stumbled back to the side of Prince Jen.

"He's slippery as an eel!" Mafoo cried. "I can't keep hold of him. I must believe he prefers not to be rescued."

"Then why is he shouting for help?" Surprised at the inability of Mafoo, and seeing that no further moments could be wasted, Prince Jen strode to the water's edge. There, the aged man sputtered and blubbered, desperately begging for someone to save him.

Prince Jen rolled up the sleeves of his robe and took

a firm grip on the skinny hand reaching out to him. Next moment, Prince Jen's arm was clutched with astonishing vigor. Before he could dig in his heels, he found himself pulled headlong into the stream, seized around the neck, and so buffeted by flailing legs that he went spinning and choking to the riverbed.

◆　◆　◆　◆　◆

Prince Jen's praiseworthy attempt has only put him in danger of being drowned. The outcome is told in the next chapter.

3

· *Prince Jen's patience is severely tried* ·
· *A meddlesome passenger* ·
· *A muddy road* ·

·

PRINCE JEN HAD NEVER IMAGINED anyone would be
so stubborn about being rescued. Thrashing around in
panic, the victim grappled with his would-be benefactor, and his struggles only hindered Prince Jen's efforts
to save him. Mafoo and Li Kwang, seeing their master
vanish below the surface, were after him instantly. By
the time Prince Jen succeeded in getting a firm hold on
the old man and bringing him to the water's edge, servant and warrior were on hand to haul him ashore. The
object of Prince Jen's good deed at last released his grip
and fell in a heap on the grassy slope.

"Young Lord," said Li Kwang, "I beg you: Never again put your noble person at such risk."

"Being helpful is one thing," Mafoo added. "Getting drowned is something else."

Prince Jen had no breath to answer. His robes were sopping, the tide had carried off his gold cap, and he felt that he had swallowed a good portion of the Lan. He gratefully allowed Mafoo to peel away the duckweed entwining him.

As for the old man, strings of white hair clung to his half-bald cranium and his robe had dredged up mud from the river bottom, but he seemed no worse for his harrowing experience. He shook himself like a wet dog, scuttled over, and knocked his head at the Young Lord's feet, showering him with gratitude and water. It took a few moments for Prince Jen to realize that Master Fu, as he identified himself, had addressed him by name.

"You and your most excellent and honorable mission are everywhere known," Master Fu replied when Prince Jen asked how he had been recognized. Master Fu explained further, without being asked, that he was a poor wandering scholar, that he had been so absorbed in a treatise on how to travel safely that he had paid more attention to his reading than to his feet and had unwittingly strayed from his path.

"All has ended well," Prince Jen said, impatient to get into dry clothing and set off again. "Go your way safely."

Master Fu clasped his hands. "Young Lord, my poor

strength is gone. Allow me a little while to regain it. Let me ride with your escort, only a short distance along the road. It would be one of the Eighty-seven Acts of Kindness."

"There should be an eighty-eighth," put in Mafoo, cocking a sharp eye at the scholar. "Don't impose on someone's good nature."

Master Fu clapped a hand to his brow. "Forgive me, Young Lord. How did I dare—what could I have been thinking of? I should never dream of delaying you by so much as an instant. What possessed me? To save my wretched self a few steps? No, no, better I should perish ignominiously, shrivel up like a husk on the highway, rather than put Your Lordship to even a moment of inconvenience. Ten thousand blessings on you for saving my ignoble, despicable existence—no matter what becomes of it later."

Master Fu picked up the staff he had dropped in the process of falling into the river. Snuffling, moaning, holding first his head, then the small of his back, he tottered away.

"Wait." Prince Jen beckoned him. "Ride with my escort. Go and find yourself a place."

The old scholar burst out with another ten thousand blessings and made his way up the bank with more agility than he had shown before.

"For the sake of mercy, what else could I have done?" Prince Jen asked Mafoo, who had come back with dry clothing. "Pitiful creature, I had no heart to deny him. A modest favor—"

"Which he accepted nimbly enough," Mafoo said as they hurried back to the roadside. There, Prince Jen found Master Fu sprawled comfortably in the carriage.

"Forgive me once more," Master Fu said. "I only wished to rest my aching bones before submitting them to the jolting of the baggage cart, the proper place for this unworthy individual. I shall remove my humble self from your radiant presence, even though I am so weak from hunger my head is spinning. Absorbed in study, I forgot to eat. My sack of food is nourishing the fish in the Lan. No matter, I shall scrape something from a refuse pit and hope to keep body and soul together."

Master Fu looked so woebegone and truly so close to starvation that Prince Jen ordered Mafoo to fetch food and drink.

"Only a sip of water," Master Fu insisted. "A handful of millet. Unless there might be a few drops of stale beer. Or a tiny morsel of carp. And if, in your compassionate generosity, you saw fit to add a chicken wing—"

Mafoo, at Prince Jen's instruction, brought back victuals from the kitchen wagon. By the time the escort set off again, Master Fu, protesting all the while, had downed four pots of beer, two fish, and a whole chicken, along with eight rice cakes. His ability to consume large quantities of food was matched only by his endless chatter. Belching loudly, scratching himself, dripping water over the upholstery, Master Fu never stopped talking. From the moment the procession began wending its way along the road, he rambled on about his cosmological theories, mixing them in the same breath with complaints about his bunions, his poor digestion, and the palpitations of his liver.

Master Fu suddenly broke off his catalog of ailments and stared around him. "But—but we travel in the wrong direction," he cried. "We are going west!"

"Indeed so," Mafoo replied.

Master Fu's jaw dropped. "Did I neglect to mention that my path lies eastward?"

"Tiresome old crock!" exclaimed Mafoo, whose patience had been shrinking with each moment in the scholar's company. "You should have spoken up sooner."

Master Fu turned to Prince Jen. "I have only myself to blame. Through no fault of your own, your munificent kindness has put me in a worse state than before. However, it is the intention, not the result, that gains you merit. No matter that my toes are swollen, my knees trembling. Set me down here, I shall retrace the steps your benevolence made me lose."

"Excellent idea," said Mafoo.

"Leave him on the road?" Prince Jen said. "I meant to do him a small kindness, not a great disservice. We will take him where he wishes."

Prince Jen ordered the retinue to turn east. The grateful Master Fu assured him that the delay would be no more than half an hour's time. Yet, whenever Prince Jen suggested they had gone far enough, Master Fu begged him to keep on a few moments longer.

Throughout, Master Fu never left off his constant chatter. And, despite his accidental bath in the Lan, he generated an assortment of odors as distressing as they were various.

"This Master Fu is a pitiful, needy creature," Jen told himself. "Surely, he deserves assistance. Even so, it would have been pleasanter to do a kindness for someone who talked a little less and smelled a little better."

Master Hu would have judged this thought as uncharitable, so Jen made every effort to tolerate the old scholar. This grew more difficult, for Master Fu proved to be as meddlesome as a monkey. He examined the appointments of the carriage, fingered the upholstery, and peered under the seats. His eyes inevitably fell on the silk-wrapped gifts. Before Prince Jen could stop him, Master Fu seized upon them. He pulled away the covering from the saddle and studied it inquisitively.

"It is not my lowly place to question the Young Lord," Master Fu said, "but would this be a gift for Yuan-ming? It is a handsome saddle. Yet, allow me to make a humble observation. It puzzles me that the great Yuan-ming should be offered something less than perfect. See here, the cinch belt is broken and has come loose. If Yuan-ming were to use this gift, he might suffer a serious, even fatal, fall."

Prince Jen was equally puzzled. As far as he knew, the saddle had been undamaged when they had left Ch'ang-an. Now, clearly, the cinch was broken. As he wondered about this, Li Kwang rode up.

"It is not practical for us to go farther," he said,

gesturing toward brambles and dense shrubbery. Only the narrowest of lanes led where Master Fu had begged to be taken. "Even my foot soldiers would have difficulty following such a path, and many more hours of delay."

"The difficulty isn't the path, it's the passenger," Mafoo told Prince Jen. "Enough is enough. You saved his life, filled his belly, put up with his yammering, and eased his journey past anything that ancient crackpot could expect. We have two choices: Take him by the scruff of the neck and throw him out, or take him by the seat of his pants and throw him out."

"I shall burden you no more," put in Master Fu. "I am so close to my destination, barely another half hour. Let me go now on my poor, tottering legs. What difference if my weak old heart fails me and I die in the bushes? Young Lord, with my last breath I shall bless you for your kind intention."

With Master Fu wheezing, moaning, and already going blue in the face, Prince Jen could not bring himself to follow Mafoo's advice. "We've carried him this far," he said to Li Kwang. "It would shame me not to go the rest of such a little way. The lane is wide enough for my carriage. Mafoo and I shall drive him where he wishes. You and your men wait here."

Li Kwang, uncomfortable at letting his prince out of his sight, offered to ride with him.

"There is no need," Prince Jen said. "I would rather you attend to another task." He showed Li Kwang the damaged saddle. "Have one of your men repair this."

Li Kwang examined the saddle. "It is easily mended. The leather is not broken, it has merely come loose. I myself will see to it, and have it ready by the time you return."

Mafoo, grumbling, turned the carriage into the rutted lane. "The only good part of this," he muttered, "is that we'll soon be rid of the old geezer once and for all."

The lane, however, became rougher and rougher. Despite Mafoo's capable hands on the reins, the horses could barely make their way. Lurching and jolting, the carriage went at a snail's pace. Master Fu kept insisting that his destination, the village of Kwan-tzu, lay only moments away.

Two hours had already passed when, as if out of sheer spitefulness, the bright sky suddenly clouded. Rain bucketed down in such blinding sheets that Mafoo could only let the horses stumble ahead at their own slow gait.

The lane, difficult enough to begin with, turned quickly into a river of mud. The horses nearly foundered; the carriage slewed from side to side and, with a bone-shattering jolt, stopped altogether. Mafoo shouted and slapped the reins, the horses strained, but the wheels only sank deeper in the mire.

Cursing under his breath, Mafoo climbed down and put his shoulder to one of the rear wheels, hoping to dislodge it. As the work proved too hard for him alone, he ordered Master Fu to lend a hand and make himself useful.

"Gladly," Master Fu replied. "No matter that the weather has touched off my rheumatism."

"Then hold the reins." Prince Jen, frankly wishing he had never laid eyes on the scholar, sprang from the carriage to join Mafoo.

While Master Fu, sitting dry and comfortable under the canopy, called out words of encouragement, Prince Jen and Mafoo hauled and heaved as best they could. The rain fell harder and the mud deepened.

"Give it up," Mafoo panted. "We're stuck. There's only one thing to do."

◆　◆　◆　◆　◆

Having already been over his head in water, our hero is up to his ears in mud, a situation hardly befitting his rank. What happens next is told in the following chapter.

4

· *The yamen of Cha-wei* ·
· *Voyaging Moon solves one problem* ·
· *Another arises* ·

"I SUGGEST THE FOLLOWING," Mafoo said. "I take one of Master Fu's ankles. You take the other. Then we turn him upside down and stick his miserable head in this mud as deep as we can."

"How will that move the carriage?" Prince Jen said.

"It won't," Mafoo said, "but it will cheer me up considerably."

"Why blame him?" Prince Jen said, bending all his strength against the sunken wheel. "None of this is his fault."

"Isn't it?" Mafoo retorted. "If he hadn't fallen into the river, you wouldn't have pulled him out. If you hadn't pulled him out, he wouldn't have begged a ride. If he hadn't begged a ride, we wouldn't have gone out of our way. If we hadn't gone out of our way, we wouldn't be wallowing in muck up to our ears."

Prince Jen gritted his teeth. Contrary to the instructions of Master Hu concerning respect for the elderly and the Eighty-seven Acts of Kindness, at this moment he would have been delighted to follow Mafoo's suggestion. His fingers itched to seize Master Fu not by the ankles but by the exasperating wretch's skinny neck. Instead, he flung himself against the wheel and strained and heaved beside Mafoo.

The carriage moved, rolled back a little, and finally lurched free. Mafoo's shout of triumph turned to a groan of dismay.

"We're no better off," he cried. "Look here. Half the spokes are cracked. The wheel won't hold." Hands on hips, he glumly regarded the disabled vehicle. "We have two choices. We can unhitch both horses and ride back to the main road. Or I take one horse, and you stay in the carriage and wait until Li Kwang sends help."

"What is the difficulty?" Master Fu had climbed onto the backseat, where he had been observing with great interest the efforts of Prince Jen and Mafoo. "The wheel will hold for a little distance. In Kwan-tzu, it can be repaired while you find shelter. Only a few moments more."

Prince Jen hesitated. As the rain pelted down, apart from throttling Master Fu, the one thing he most wished for was a roof over his head. Wet and exhausted, he would have been grateful for the roughest comfort.

"One instant longer than those few moments," he said, "and you will have a heavy account to settle with me."

"Allow me to disagree," Mafoo said. "I'll be the one to settle his account."

Master Fu, for once, proved accurate in his claims. The wheel wobbled but did not break. As twilight gathered, Prince Jen saw lights glowing ahead, sooner even than Master Fu promised. An added relief, the downpour stopped as suddenly as it had begun.

Entering the village of Kwan-tzu, Mafoo trotted the horses across a little public square, its ground dry and hard-packed, as if there had never been a rainstorm. He had no need to ask the location of the yamen. The headquarters of the local official was the biggest building in Kwan-tzu, surrounded by high walls, the only entry an iron gate.

The watchman's jaw dropped in astonishment when Mafoo announced the arrival of the Young Lord Prince. He hurried to fling open the gate and call for attendants to receive the royal visitor. Within moments, a handful of bewildered servants came scrambling out, stunned and mystified by Jen's presence in the village. Mafoo drove the carriage into the courtyard. Stepping down, Prince Jen glanced over his shoulder. He saw nothing of the old scholar. Master Fu, for reasons of his own, must have clambered from the other side of the vehicle and scurried off into one of the alleys. Prince Jen heaved a thankful sigh, not in any way unhappy over Master Fu's disappearance without a word of gratitude.

The village administrator now came forward. Cha-wei by name, this Official of the Third Rank looked as mystified as his servants.

"Young Lord Prince! What a joyful surprise!" Cha-wei bowed and made every effort to twist his long-jawed face into an expression of pleasure. "Still more amazing, you are unharmed. Ferocious bandits—the Yellow Scarves—have been attacking all travelers in these parts. How did you escape such danger?"

"I saw no bandits," Jen replied. "The only dangers were being soaked to the skin by the rainstorm and my carriage foundering in the mud. A wheel is damaged. Have it repaired. Meantime, I and my servant will change into dry clothing."

"Yes, yes, Young Lord, as you command. Only forgive me for not offering hospitality at once." Cha-wei wrung his hands and blinked his close-set eyes. "My astonishment, my relief at your safety, made me forget proper courtesy. Alas, this wretched yamen is ill-prepared to offer a fitting welcome. Even so, I beg you to avail yourself of my humble and most unworthy facilities."

"They will be sufficient for our needs," Prince Jen

replied. "See to my carriage immediately. I wish to leave as soon as possible."

"Your visitation will be short? I am filled with unbearably painful regret," returned Cha-wei, brightening. He clapped his hands, ordering attendants to conduct Prince Jen and Mafoo to the best available chambers.

"Hardly the Celestial Palace," observed Mafoo, after servants had brought fresh robes, "but not too bad for the provinces. I'd guess that Cha-wei treats himself well enough. What official doesn't?"

Mafoo was correct, as Prince Jen discovered when they were led to Cha-wei's private apartments. There, tables had been spread with quite acceptable refreshments. In addition, Cha-wei had summoned his household musicians. With the melodies of zither and flute, the chiming of bells, the tuneful sounds mixing with incense from iron braziers, Prince Jen felt reasonably at ease for the first time in a trying day. He briefly explained the events that had brought him to the village.

Cha-wei gave him a puzzled look. "How interesting that Your Lordship mentions a downpour. Highly localized atmospheric disturbances, of course, are not impossible. Nevertheless, here we have not had a drop of rain for five days."

"You saw our clothing," Jen curtly replied, "wet and muddy. Honorable Cha-wei, I know when I've been rained on."

Cha-wei tactfully let the matter drop and begged his royal guest to speak more of the purpose of his journey. Prince Jen's fatigue, however, must have weighed on him more heavily than he realized, for he found his thoughts drifting away, floating with the music, soaring with the shimmering tones of the flute. Only when Mafoo nudged him did he abruptly raise his head and open his eyes.

"Whatever Your Lordship requires . . ." Cha-wei was saying.

"Oh? Yes—" Prince Jen blinked. He had, for the moment, been happily elsewhere. The voice of the flute had led him spinning like a leaf in a silver stream, past waterfalls that turned into rainbows and rainbows that turned into bright-plumaged birds. Cha-wei's yamen was a dull, boring place in comparison.

"What His Lordship requires," put in Mafoo helpfully, seeing his master look around absently, "is an armed escort. With dangerous bandits in the vicinity, the Young Lord must not travel unguarded."

"Mafoo is right," Prince Jen said. "Yes, we wish an escort. Assemble them, have them ready with their weapons. A dozen mounted men should suffice."

"It should, if only I had them to offer," Cha-wei replied. "Lord Prince, I beg your gracious indulgence. There is not one able-bodied man in Kwan-tzu. They are all in the countryside, seeking to capture the bandits."

"The Young Lord must have a suitable escort nonetheless," Mafoo said. "Lacking anyone else, that leaves yourself and your attendants."

"That would be an honor beyond what I deserve," replied Cha-wei. "My servants—mere cooks, clerks, low-ranking deputies and their assistants—are entirely unworthy of such a noble task."

"Then," demanded Mafoo, "what do you suggest?"

"Ah—yes, what I suggest," Cha-wei answered, "is another joyful possibility." Cha-wei looked as if he had swallowed a bowl of scalding tea as he continued. "I urge His Lordship to accept my hospitality, wretched and despicable though it is, for a week, ten days perhaps, until the village men return."

"I cannot be delayed that long," said Prince Jen.

"Out of the question," agreed Mafoo. "There's nothing else for it," he added, as Cha-wei's features grew more and more pained, "you and your servants will have to do. So, put on your armor if you have any. You'll need swords, lances, bows and arrows."

"What bliss," Cha-wei murmured in a strangled voice, "to die in the service of the Young Lord."

"If His Lordship permits me to address him, I know a better way."

These words came from one of the musicians, a girl who set aside her flute and came forward to approach Prince Jen.

"Forgive such impertinence," Cha-wei hastily put in. "This pitiful creature is Voyaging Moon, a bond-maid who has shown some small ability in music. I have taken a slight degree of—of benign interest in her well-being. Ignorant, ill-favored though she is, her thoughts might conceivably be of value. Your Lordship may deign to favor her by listening to them."

"Let her speak," said Prince Jen. Until now, he had taken little notice of the individual musicians. The flute girl, however, had caught his full attention. Compared with the noble ladies in the Celestial Palace, Voyaging Moon could hardly count as beautiful. Far from an oval perfection, her face had the sharp, high cheekbones of eastern province peasants. Instead of being arranged in a lacquered tower, the girl's black hair hung loose over her shoulders and was held only by a white headband. He motioned for her to continue.

"An armed escort might offer some protection," Voyaging Moon said in a voice that Jen found as melodious as her instrument. "At the same time, it would attract unwanted attention. These bandits will stop at nothing. Their leader calls himself Natha Yellow Scarf. He's worse than the rest of them put together. He'd be more than happy to cut your throat. So, the best thing would be to go quickly, quietly, and not be seen at all."

"Exactly as I was about to say," exclaimed Cha-wei. "Much as I yearn to give my life defending the Young Lord, I reluctantly admit that her idea has merit."

"In other words, I'm to travel secretly? Furtively?" said Prince Jen. "Do you think it honorable for me to skulk like a coward through my own kingdom?"

"I'd have supposed that skulking was part of a princely education," Voyaging Moon said.

"Certainly not," retorted Jen.

"Then here's a chance to learn," said Voyaging Moon.

"She's right," Mafoo whispered. "Better to be unnoticed than dead. A little skulking never harmed anyone."

"I was born and raised in this district," the girl continued. "I know pathways that will keep you clear of Natha and his gang. They'll never catch a glimpse of you. Now, I can see Your Lordship's about to suggest taking me as a guide. A brilliant idea. For my ignoble self, it would be the honor of a lifetime, enshrined forever in my memory. Naturally, my esteemed master would have to agree to do without my worthless presence for a short time."

"Oh, I agree, I agree," burst out Cha-wei.

"Yes, well then—" Jen began. The girl was looking straight at him. She had used all the proper terms of self-deprecation, but he had the uneasy feeling she meant not a word of them. "Now that you've suggested—or I was going to suggest," he stammered, "your presence with us would be a pleasure. That is, useful. Very acceptable."

Cha-wei, sighing with happy relief, eagerly offered to provide a horse on which the flute girl could return to the village. It was decided that all would be ready by daybreak, and Prince Jen and Mafoo were again installed in their sleeping chamber.

"About that flute girl," Jen said as he stretched on the couch, "I'm glad for her help. But—did you find her somehow irreverent? Impertinent, even?"

"No more than I am." Mafoo yawned. "You'll manage to put up with her."

Prince Jen did not reply, and soon fell asleep. But the voice of the flute echoed in his ears. The features of the girl filled his dreams. He awoke feeling vaguely un-settled and too distracted to observe and properly ad-mire the rising sun.

The artisans had repaired the wheel. The girl, in coarse cotton trousers and jacket, waited at the carriage. Because of her knowledge of the countryside, Mafoo allowed her to take the reins. Cha-wei, at the yamen gate, did his best to look heartbroken by the early de-parture of his royal guest.

Prince Jen would gladly have conversed with the flute girl, but each time he tried, he grew strangely tongue-tied. At last, he gave up his attempts. His glances, nevertheless, continually went to Voyaging Moon.

For her part, the girl was as good as her word. She followed practically invisible paths and trails, driving quickly and efficiently. Prince Jen, in fact, felt a twinge of regret at reaching the road so soon.

His regret turned to alarm when Voyaging Moon drew up at the spot where he had left his escort. He sprang from the carriage. Looking in every direction, he saw nothing of Li Kwang or a single one of his men. The road lay empty.

•   •   •   •   •

Has our hero begun to develop some affection for a flute girl? A more urgent question: What has become of Li Kwang and his warriors? The answer is given in the next chapter.

5

· *The Tale of the Warrior's Saddle* ·

HONORABLE GENERAL LI KWANG had never lacked in courage or failed in duty. Among themselves, his men called him "Broken Face" because of all the battle scars crisscrossing his cheeks and brow. They were devoted to him, though, and would have followed him to the ends of the earth.

Now, on this journey to T'ien-kuo, Li Kwang had vowed to guard his prince with his life. Uncomfortable at the Young Lord's decision to part from his escort even for an hour, Li Kwang watched, frowning, as the carriage turned off into the narrow lane. Li Kwang thought, first, of galloping after him; but Prince Jen had ordered Li Kwang to wait, and so he did.

Telling himself that his unease was groundless, that no harm could befall the prince in such a brief period of time, Li Kwang ordered his men to stand to their arms while he turned his attention to the saddle he had undertaken to mend.

As he worked, Li Kwang marveled at the craftsmanship given to the making of the saddle. Intricate patterns had been tooled into the leather, itself soft and smooth as silk. The stirrups and the bit were of burnished gold.

"This truly is a gift fit for a king," Li Kwang said. "Never have I seen anything to match it."

Most astonishing to Li Kwang, however, was not its excellence but its lightness. Finishing his task easily and quickly, he now found the saddle and all its harness weighed next to nothing.

"No more than a butterfly!" he exclaimed. "Less than a feather!"

The more he marveled, the more he yearned to try it out for himself.

"Such a saddle will never again come into my hands," Li Kwang thought. "Still, it would be improper for me to use what is meant as an offering to a mighty monarch."

While he stood, chin in hand, admiring the saddle, his roan mare, Autumn Dew, trotted to his side. She was the most faithful and obedient of steeds, answering to Li Kwang's lightest touch on the reins, to his smallest gesture or softest word of command.

"And you," said Li Kwang, stroking her high-arching neck, "you have long gone heavily burdened and carried me, my weapons, and my armor without complaint. Would it not be a pleasure for you to feel the comfort of such a fine harness?"

Autumn Dew nuzzled the saddle, then whickered and tossed her head.

"You admire it as much as I do," Li Kwang said, smiling wistfully, "but it is destined for the great Yuan-ming, and too magnificent for any of lower station."

About to put it carefully aside, Li Kwang hesitated a moment.

"This is a piece of ancient workmanship," he said. "Who made it and for whom, I do not know. But, in all those years, many must have ridden on it, and they could not have been every one a king. What difference could one more rider make?"

Nevertheless, he told himself that as long as it was in his charge he would not meddle with it. Still, he could not keep from running a hand over the saddle, which grew more beautiful the more he looked at it.

"Once given to Yuan-ming, what then?" Li Kwang said. "No doubt it will be locked in his treasure house. Yuan-ming may well have a dozen others more splendid than this, and it would mean nothing to him. What a waste if it were merely stored away to gather dust."

But that, Li Kwang told himself, did not concern him. What Yuan-ming chose to do with the gift was a matter for the king's own judgment.

He turned away, hoping that Prince Jen would soon come back so they could set off again and Li Kwang could rid his mind of tempting thoughts.

"One thing troubles me," Li Kwang said. "Suppose Yuan-ming does not store it away but makes use of it. How can I be sure it is well mended? How do I know the repairs will hold?

"Suppose, for example," Li Kwang went on, "Yuan-ming rides to the hunt. What if the saddle gives way and he falls? If he falls, he might break a limb, or even be killed. That would be my fault."

Satisfied that he understood his responsibility and obligation, he unharnessed Autumn Dew and replaced her saddle with the gift for Yuan-ming. The mare pranced and curvetted with pleasure, and it gladdened Li Kwang's heart to see how handsome his beloved steed looked. All the harness leathers seemed firmly in place.

"Even so," Li Kwang said, "nothing is proved without practice. If there is any risk, I must be the one to take it. I must seat myself and ride a few moments. Only then will I be certain. That is my duty. Afterward, I will put it away and explain to Prince Jen what I did, and why, and how thoroughly I completed my task."

Hesitating no longer, Li Kwang mounted. No sooner was he astride than Autumn Dew reared, whinnied, and shook her mane. Then she laid back her ears and bolted like an arrow down the road. The startled Li Kwang pulled back on the reins. The usually obedient Autumn Dew only stretched into a faster gallop.

Li Kwang was a skilled horseman, but he could do nothing to curb Autumn Dew. He called out to her, coaxing with every endearment, soothing, commanding, all in vain. He thought, then, to risk leaping from her back. He could not kick his feet free of the stirrups or lift himself out of the saddle. He waved his arms and shouted for his men to help.

Li Kwang's cavalry troopers, seeing their commander's gestures, believed he was ordering them to follow. They leaped astride their horses and galloped after him. The foot soldiers likewise misunderstood. They seized their weapons and set off running as fast as their legs could carry them to catch up with their comrades. The drivers of the baggage carts and supply wagons whipped up their animals. In moments, all the train of warriors and retainers was streaming down the road. The wagoners caught their breath in astonishment at the speed of their usually slow-paced horses. The pack mules sped over the ground as if their burdens weighed nothing. The foot soldiers found themselves racing without effort, their boots barely skimming the road.

The wind whistled in Li Kwang's ears as Autumn Dew galloped ever more swiftly. After a little while, the mare veered sharply eastward off the road and plunged into the undergrowth. Twisted branches sprang out at Li Kwang. He flung up his arms, expecting to be swept from Autumn Dew's back. Suddenly the branches drew aside, the brambles and bushes opened before him, the undergrowth parted, and a clear pathway rose toward high mountains ahead.

Li Kwang glanced back. Behind him, his warriors never slackened their pace. Still they climbed, higher and higher. The time must have sped as quickly as Autumn Dew, for Li Kwang grew aware of the sun setting—or so he supposed, for the mountaintops, gray and bare, blazed red as rubies.

Autumn Dew galloped on. The mare made straight for a rocky mass towering above the neighboring peaks. At the foot of the mountain, she still kept her wild course. Li Kwang saw the black mouth of a cavern. Autumn Dew sped into it.

Here, Li Kwang was sure she must halt. A wall of stone rose just ahead. At the approach of Autumn Dew, it split in two and the huge slabs of stone fell open. Li Kwang was borne past these massive portals into the mountain's heart.

His men followed, riders and foot soldiers alike. Once they had entered, Li Kwang heard an earthshaking rumble as the giant slabs swung shut behind him and all his troops.

Li Kwang was a brave warrior, but seeing himself and his men so trapped, his courage almost faltered. Autumn Dew trotted on, picking her way delicately over loose stones rattling beneath her hooves. Li Kwang could see nothing in the darkness that had swallowed him. He dropped the reins and let Autumn Dew go where she pleased. The mare, unhesitating, continued down long galleries and corridors.

A burst of light dazzled Li Kwang. Autumn Dew, he thought as his heart leaped, had found a passage outward. When his vision cleared, he knew he was still deep within the mountain. He rubbed his eyes but still did not believe them. Stretching to a horizon wide as the world spread rich green fields, woodlands, and terraces. Rivers and streams sparkled under a cloudless sky. As he looked, his amazement gave way to a sense of peace and harmony. Li Kwang's delight grew as the mare carried him down a well-paved street into a large town.

Here, he saw busy marketplaces, open-fronted shops, weavers at their looms, potters at their wheels, passersby, men and women in bright costumes, children at their games. At the sight of the train of warriors, the townsfolk ran to wave and smile, as if Li Kwang and his men had been long awaited.

There now approached Li Kwang a tall woman clad in robes of silver spun as fine as silk. Long silver tresses fell from beneath a headdress set with every kind of precious gem. Li Kwang at last found himself able to swing down from the saddle as the woman drew closer.

"I am the Lady of Fearful Awakenings," she said, making a graceful gesture of welcome. Smiling, she gazed at him with eyes the color of burnished copper. "And you are the one called 'Broken Face Kwang.'"

"How do you know this?" Li Kwang murmured. "Where have I come?"

"Where you have often wished to be."

She beckoned for him to accompany her, indicating an unwalled building a little distance ahead. The structure was more palatial than Li Kwang had ever seen, with high-peaked, sharply curved roofs set one on top of the other, tall towers, and ornamental bridges. All around were gardens filled with blossoms and orchards laden with golden fruit. Li Kwang heard bird songs and the chiming of wind bells.

Li Kwang held back for a moment. "What of my men and horses? And my own steed, Autumn Dew? We have ridden hard and far."

"They will be as well attended as yourself."

The Lady of Fearful Awakenings spoke so reassuringly that Li Kwang went happily with her. As they walked side by side, hand in hand, Li Kwang gathered from her words that she already knew of Prince Jen's journey and its purpose and the happenings that had brought Li Kwang into the mountain. How was this possible, wondered Li Kwang, and why should one so beautiful be so unfortunately named?

These questions vanished from his mind as the Lady of Fearful Awakenings led him up a broad flight of steps and into a spacious chamber. The ceilings rose so high that he could not see where they ended. Shafts of sunlight filled the room and the hallways beyond. Yet he barely glanced at the handsome furnishings, for a heavy weariness had come to settle over him. His eyes began closing despite himself, his legs felt leaden, and he gladly allowed the Lady of Fearful Awakenings to draw him to a couch that seemed in readiness for him.

"Rest a while," the Lady of Fearful Awakenings said as Li Kwang sank into the deep cushions. She covered his face with her hands. Li Kwang gratefully closed his eyes.

The fatigue that overwhelmed him did not come entirely from his ride through the countryside. It was, rather, as if all battles he had ever fought now pressed upon him. Every step marched, every league ridden compressed into a single massive burden.

For a time, he dreamed of those past combats, of hissing arrows, bloody swords, riders clashing, horses shrieking and striking out with their hooves. Cries of the wounded and dying filled his ears, the reek of old battlefields choked his nostrils.

The nightmares faded. In their place arose mineral visions: sharp-edged stars of crystals, geometric shapes shifting and combining, growing like frost patterns; mountains cleaved to reveal dark inner veins; snowflakes of garnet; the dreams a stone might dream.

He awoke. The chamber had vanished.

Li Kwang sat astride Autumn Dew. They were in the cavern once again. Unable to move arms or legs, he could open his eyes no more than a crack. Crystalline growths jutted like fangs around him and gave a dim greenish glow. Glancing down with difficulty, as if his eyes had frozen in their sockets, he glimpsed his hands on the reins. A cry like rocks grinding together caught in his throat.

Li Kwang had turned to stone.

So had Autumn Dew. Li Kwang could not see them, but knew with cold certainty that his warriors shared the same fate.

He tried to fathom how this had come about, hoping that by doing so he might devise a way to free his warriors from this horrible captivity. But his thoughts moved as slowly as a glacier. Time itself seemed turned to stone—he could not calculate how long he had slept or how long he had been in the cavern. He only understood how well named had been the Lady of Fearful Awakenings.

Despite all, deep within his shell of stone he sensed a constant throbbing, and he envisioned a crimson spark pulsing faintly but steadily. As long as his heart beat, he knew himself to be a living man.

A tall form took shape in front of him. Li Kwang's eyes had become crystal prisms and he saw a dozen images of an old man in a red robe.

"I have been waiting for you," Master Wu said. "You have slept, now you must wake."

"You? Here?" murmured Li Kwang. "Was it you who caused this?"

"I cause nothing," Master Wu replied, "though

from time to time I make arrangements. Had you not tried the saddle, things would have gone otherwise. Now, they are what they are and what they must be. You are in Wu-shan, Mountain of Sorcerers."

"What of Prince Jen?" Li Kwang said. "If I failed him, if I did not guard him as I vowed, let me not fail him again. How can I rejoin him?"

"Prince Jen follows his own road," Master Wu said, "and must go wherever it may lead him. Your path has taken a different turning."

"I accept my punishment," Li Kwang said. "The blame is mine alone. Therefore, I ask you to free my warriors. They followed me, but this was their duty, not their fault. I ask you as well to free Autumn Dew. Her place is not here. Allow her, at least, to return to the fields and forests and the open sky."

"Broken Face Kwang," Master Wu said, "your words do you credit. You will gain merit for them. Whatever else," he added with half a smile, "you do not have a heart of stone.

"I cannot grant your wish entirely," Master Wu continued. "That is not in my power, but in yours."

"How?" Li Kwang replied. "I can no more move from this spot than could a rock or a boulder."

"Have you the will to do it?" Master Wu said. "Try."

Summoning all his strength of spirit, Li Kwang discovered that indeed he could move a little, and Autumn Dew likewise; but so grindingly and agonizingly that all effort seemed doomed to fail. Nevertheless, whatever the painful cost, he resolved to guide his faithful horse and warriors into the sunlit world of living beings.

Master Wu nodded, satisfied by Li Kwang's determination, and gave him certain instructions. "Only if you are able to follow them," he added, "only then can there be any shred of hope."

"Given that much," Li Kwang said, "I ask no more."

· · · · ·

Leaving Li Kwang and his stone warriors to whatever the future holds for them, we now return to Prince Jen, Voyaging Moon, and Mafoo. How they deal with their own plight is told in the following chapter.

6

· *Prince Jen follows the flute girl* ·
· *What they find in the cavern* ·
· *What finds them* ·

THE ONLY TRACE OF THE WARRIORS was a saddle by the roadside. Prince Jen knelt to examine it.

"This is Li Kwang's." He glanced anxiously at Mafoo. "Where is the one I gave him to mend?"

"Forgive this unspeakably ignorant flute girl for even daring to say this," put in Voyaging Moon, "but when all of your people seem to have disappeared, and you're far from your palace, alone in the middle of nowhere, very likely without provisions, one saddle more or less is the least of your worries."

"The least?" Prince Jen cried. "It was in my charge. A gift for Yuan-ming. Master Wu chose it." He stammered out a quick account of his journey and its purpose.

"I understand why you'd want it back," Voyaging Moon said. "Of course, you've already considered the possibility that your officer left his own saddle here and put the other on his horse."

"He could have," Prince Jen said. "But why? And why isn't he here? He was ordered to wait for me."

"First, find him," Voyaging Moon said, "then you'll find what happened."

"Oh, brilliant!" Mafoo snorted. "And how to do that?"

"But surely you know." Voyaging Moon smiled at Mafoo. "By now, you've looked at the roadway. And very cleverly observed the hoofprints and wagon tracks."

"Eh?" said Mafoo. "Oh. Yes, I was just about to do that."

"Not that a shrewd, quick-witted fellow like you needs any help," Voyaging Moon added, "but if I were asked, I might agree to come along. In case—a remote possibility, but just in case—you missed some tiny detail."

"There's a slight odor of rat somewhere in this," Mafoo murmured to Prince Jen. "She has something else in mind."

"Would you help us?" Prince Jen asked eagerly,

paying no attention to Mafoo. "Cha-wei will commend you for a good deed."

"I doubt it," Voyaging Moon said. "He won't have the chance. I'm not setting foot in Kwan-tzu again. I've run off."

"There's the rat!" cried Mafoo. "I knew I smelled one."

"The Honorable Cha-wei thinks I'm with you," Voyaging Moon said to Prince Jen. "By the time it occurs to him that I'm permanently missing, and he searches for me, I'll be out of reach. If he does happen to catch up with me—why, I'm simply doing the Young Lord a service."

"You left your master without permission?" said Prince Jen, taken aback. "You've committed a serious crime."

"I certainly have," Voyaging Moon happily agreed. "Cha-wei plans to bestow a great honor on me."

"Then why run away? You should be grateful."

"Do you think so?" said Voyaging Moon. "First, let me tell you this. My father was a peasant; he could barely feed himself, let alone a family. When my mother died, he sold me to a spice merchant in Kwan-tzu. The merchant raised me as a handmaiden for his wife. I was taught to read and write, play the flute, prepare tea correctly, and all such accomplishments. In time, the merchant wanted an important favor from Cha-wei. I was offered as a gift, which Cha-wei was pleased to accept. The merchant got his favor. Cha-wei got a flute girl.

"Now," she went on, "he wants to honor me by installing me in his bedchamber. That's an honor I decided to do without."

"I'm glad—I mean, that is, I can understand," Jen replied. "Yes, but—regrettably, the law is clear. It requires me to send you back immediately. I don't want to, but—"

"Young Lord," Mafoo whispered, drawing Jen aside, "just between the two of us, I'm not quite as clever as this flute girl thinks I am. Tracks? I can't even see them, let alone follow them. The law's already broken. What's the harm in breaking it a little more? In any case, you're the prince. The law's what you decide it is."

Prince Jen grinned. "As I was just about to say."

With Mafoo jogging behind in the carriage, Prince Jen tried to keep pace with the girl's long strides. After a time, Voyaging Moon halted and pointed toward the hills. From the torn undergrowth and trampled ground, she judged that the warriors had gone straight into the uplands. However, no sooner did Mafoo try to turn off the road than the mended wheel shattered again. The vehicle lurched and sent him tumbling into the bushes. Crawling out, shaking his fist, Mafoo laid this new misfortune on the head of Master Fu.

"We've had bad luck ever since we laid eyes on him!" cried Mafoo. "He plagues us even when he isn't here!"

"Leave the carriage, it's useless," Voyaging Moon

said. "We can bring the horses—as you were about to suggest."

Mafoo unhitched the animals. Prince Jen took the bundle of gifts. Having endangered, perhaps even lost, one of them, he chose to carry the rest himself. They pressed through the undergrowth, following the sure-footed Voyaging Moon. For well into the afternoon, they continued upward, walking their mounts where the woods grew too dense. A little before dusk, the girl halted at the foot of a towering mass of gray rock, dotted with patches of scrubby vegetation. The tracks led to the mouth of a cave.

"They've taken shelter there," Prince Jen said. He ran ahead into the cavern. He could see nothing in the deep shadows. He called out Li Kwang's name. Only echoes came back. Tethering the horses, Voyaging Moon and Mafoo brought in torches they had made from dead branches. The flickering light showed an earthen floor marked by boots and hooves.

"Your men stopped here," Voyaging Moon said. "That's plain enough."

"Then what?" Mafoo demanded. "Vanished into thin air?"

The girl shrugged. "I see what I see."

"Are there other chambers?" Prince Jen took a torch and paced the length and breadth of the cave. The few recesses and passages were all too shallow and led nowhere.

"I know exactly what happened," Mafoo declared.

"Very simple and logical. They came in. They stopped at the wall. Obviously, they couldn't have gone through it. So, they turned around and left."

"If they did," Voyaging Moon said to Prince Jen, "you'll no doubt ask me to pick up their trail again. All right, as you insist. It's too dark to see anything now. Best stay where we are. In the morning, I'll do what I can."

At her instruction, Mafoo built a fire to keep off the chill of the cavern. From her saddlebag, Voyaging Moon shared some of the food she had extracted from Cha-wei's larder. Prince Jen ate with excellent appetite, feeling in better spirits now than when first setting out. Though he reproached himself for his misjudgment in letting the saddle out of his hands—for all that it had seemed right and sensible at the time—he was confident of finding Li Kwang and seeing the matter finally settled.

Despite his complaining at the hard ground and sharp stones, Mafoo curled up and immediately began snoring. Voyaging Moon stretched out, her jacket rolled up under her head. Prince Jen, who had never reposed on anything harsher than silk, propped his back against the stone wall and found it not unbearable. For a while, he happily observed the sleeping flute girl, and, at last, his eyes closed.

Voices roused him. Voyaging Moon had already leaped to her feet. Prince Jen scrambled up. The torches had burned low; gray morning light filtered through crevices in the ceiling. A tall figure stood in the mouth of the cave. Tied around his head was a bloodstained yellow scarf.

◆　◆　◆　◆　◆

Though Prince Jen is unaware of it, we already know what has happened to Li Kwang. But now is a new disaster about to overtake our three travelers? For the answer, read the following chapter.

7

· *Natha Yellow Scarf* ·
· *Two good reasons for sparing Jen's life* ·
· *A third is needed* ·

"BRING LIGHTS HERE." The man, big, rawboned, was dressed in a rag of a shirt and a pair of tattered trousers. A sword hung at his side. Two quick paces and he was inside the cavern. Prince Jen flung a protecting arm around Voyaging Moon. Mafoo, rubbing sleep from his eyes, hurried to join them.

The tall man set his fists on his hips. His face was chalked a deathly white and streaked with crimson; across his brow, a smear of bright yellow. Some half-dozen companions, as roughly garbed and fiercely daubed as their leader, drifted in behind him.

"What have we found?" The man's eyes glittered as one of his comrades held up a lantern. "A farm girl: peasant stock, from the look of her. But these two are a different breed. Town rats, I'd say. That one with a belt too short for his belly has spent some time in dumpling houses. The other's no pauper, not in those fancy clothes. A young idler from a rich family. Father's pride, mother's joy."

"I know of you." Prince Jen looked squarely at him. "Natha Yellow Scarf. The law will deal with you, not I. You are not our concern. Either leave us or let us leave."

"What, you order me?" Natha's eyes blazed. He thrust his face close to Prince Jen's. "Oh, my lad, you say you know of me, but you know me not at all. You have a glib tongue. Mind how it wags. You may lose it."

"What he means to say," Mafoo hastily put in, "is that we're only passing through. Harmless travelers, as you see."

"We, too, are only passing through. The horses outside made me wonder who might be inside. Idle curiosity. We won't inconvenience you more than we need."

"Yes, well, in that case," Mafoo said, "we'll go quietly on our way and about our business. There's nothing you could want—"

"But there is. Indeed, there is. What do I want? Let me think." Natha paced back and forth, chin in hand. He stopped in front of Prince Jen. "Yes. What I need, first, is three good reasons why I shouldn't cut all your throats.

"It should be easy," Natha went on, before Prince Jen could reply. "A moment's thought and you'll have dozens. I ask only three. Nothing comes quickly to mind? Let me start you off."

Natha raised a finger. "One. You'll tell me I'm a kindhearted, easygoing sort of fellow. That's good. I'll accept that.

"Two." He raised another finger. "Why not say, 'It would be a shame to spoil a sunny morning'? All right, I'm in good spirits. We had a little scuffle with some yokels from Kwan-tzu. To celebrate our victory? That's another good reason.

"Two, so far. Now we must seek a third. What can it be?" Natha frowned and shook his head. "Harder than I thought. Yet you must find it.

"Yes, here it is!" He turned to Voyaging Moon. "Third. The farm girl's going to bargain for your lives."

"Stand away from her," Prince Jen burst out. Voyaging Moon made a quick gesture for him to be silent.

"Another order?" Natha snapped. "Why, lad, she may offer me the best reason of all. I've seen prettier, but she may turn out to have a charm all her own."

Voyaging Moon's chin went up. Natha reached out and held her face in a tight grip. "As I take a better look at her, I think we may come to an agreement."

"Let her be." Prince Jen tore Natha's hand away. "Do you want another reason? I'll give you one."

Natha's eyes widened for a moment, then he grinned like a sword pulled from a sheath. In one sudden movement, he struck Prince Jen full in the face.

The blow sent Prince Jen reeling against the cavern wall. Natha's henchmen sprang to surround Voyaging Moon and Mafoo. Stunned, bewildered, Prince Jen put his fingertips to his mouth and stared at the blood staining them. It was not the pain of the blow that shocked him, but that it had been struck at all. He could scarcely comprehend something so monstrous, unthinkable. He drew himself up to his full height.

"How dare you?" He spoke barely above a whisper, but the tone made Natha stop short. "How dare you defile my royal person?"

Prince Jen's voice rose. It rang through the cavern. "Kowtow! To the ground. All. Obey. I am the son of His Divine Majesty. I am Jen Shao-yeh. The Young Lord Prince."

Natha started a moment. Mafoo rolled up his eyes and held his head in dismay. Voyaging Moon broke the sudden silence.

"Don't play the clown," she cried out to Prince Jen. "At a time like this? Silly fool, you'll have us all killed. No more jokes. Be serious for once."

Natha glanced from Prince Jen to Voyaging Moon and back again. He clapped his hands and burst into laughter.

"Why, you truly are a fool! Think yourself clever? Is that your third reason? Oh, no, no, lad. Son of King T'ai? That would be the best reason—to slit your gullet here and now." Natha spat scornfully. "King? As much king as a bundle of straw. The officials are his masters. And ours. And strip us to the bone. Ask the peasant girl."

"And you?" Voyaging Moon said. "You're treating us as badly as any official. We've done you no harm, but you talk of cutting our throats."

"Not yours," Natha said, after a moment, as Voyaging Moon looked steadily at him. She had spoken lightly, but her voice had an edge to it. He turned away, unable to meet her gaze. "To the devil with you." He grimaced. "I had half a mind to take you with me. You'll go free. I think you'd be more trouble than you're worth.

"Even so," Natha went on, "I want my third reason from that pair. Since they can't seem to find one, I'll have to find it for them. Let's consider gold and silver."

"None," said one of his companions. "We've already searched the fat one. Not a purse, not a coin."

"I'll have something for my trouble," Natha cried angrily. His eyes lit on the bundle of gifts by the wall. "What's that?"

"Of no value to you." Prince Jen went to stand in front of the gifts.

"I'll see that for myself." Natha strode after him. He pushed Prince Jen aside and tore away the wrappings.

"What rubbish is this? A paint box? A kite? Are those your playthings?"

That instant, before Natha caught sight of it, Prince Jen snatched up the sword and tore it from the scabbard. Natha halted abruptly. "Ah. Now that's a little more interesting. Hand it over."

Prince Jen's blood had been aboil from the moment Natha had dared to strike him. The sight of the grinning, garishly daubed face, the hand outstretched and fingers twitching, swept away every shred of caution. He had already parted with one gift. He would not part with another.

"No need to shed blood," Natha said soothingly, "neither yours nor mine. You've shown a bold face, you've made the noble gesture. Enough. I need a sword more than you do. Throw it down and there's an end. I won't kill you or the dumpling eater unless I have to. My word on it."

Prince Jen raised the sword point. Seeing their chief threatened, a couple of Natha's companions started forward. Natha waved them away. "We have a fighting cricket here. I can deal with him."

Natha's hand went to his own sword hilt. Prince Jen crouched, ready for the attack. Natha drew out only the jagged stump of a blade.

"I broke this against those Kwan-tzu yokels." Natha tossed aside the shattered weapon. "I must have another. You can't expect me to go unarmed"—Natha spread his empty hands—"not in my trade. We can settle the matter reasonably between us."

Prince Jen had been well instructed in swordplay, but Natha suddenly leaped faster than his eyes could follow. He swung the blade wildly, borne back against the cavern wall. In the instant, Natha seized him by the hair with one hand and by the throat with the other.

"Here's the nub of it," Natha said through clenched teeth. "You try a stab at me. If you can. The question: Will you do it before I snap your neck? Think it over. Quickly. You manage to put that blade in my belly? Do you suppose my people would let you or your friends out of here alive?"

Prince Jen gave a stifled cry as Natha tightened his grip. His stomach heaved, a sickening tide welled into his throat; he was drowning in it. His world had become suddenly very small: only a black whirlpool and his death at the bottom of it. He could not tell whether he was screaming or weeping.

He made a last effort to break free. His head swam, his eyes dimmed. He opened his hand. The sword fell to the ground.

Natha grunted in satisfaction. He threw Prince Jen aside and picked up sword and scabbard. He hefted the weapon, swung it around, then nodded.

"It will serve." Natha motioned toward Mafoo and the half-conscious Prince Jen. "We can use their boots. Take them. The fancy robes, too."

Prince Jen was hardly aware of his robe being stripped away or the boots wrenched from his feet. He crouched against the wall, his head bowed. Natha stared down coldly at him.

"I'd have killed you, had I wished. Like that." Natha snapped his fingers. "You knew it. Death. You smelled it, didn't you? And didn't like the stink of it. Cheer up. None of us does. Be glad I kept my word."

He made an exaggerated bow to Voyaging Moon. "Not for his sake. A small courtesy to you. I hope our paths cross again in pleasanter ways. Meantime, send the boy home to his doting parents."

Natha turned on his heels. His comrades followed him out of the cavern. Voyaging Moon knelt beside Prince Jen and put a hand on his arm.

"Forget the sword. It's gone, and that's that," she said. "You're lucky he didn't break your neck for sheer amusement. You did the only sensible, reasonable thing."

"No." Prince Jen's face burned. "Master Hu would have been ashamed of me. Reason! Sense! It was fear. Only fear."

"Still a good reason," Voyaging Moon said, "and a very common emotion. Your subjects know it well."

"I am not one of my subjects."

"Oh, that's right. I forgot." Voyaging Moon smiled. "Then, count yourself even luckier."

• • • • •

We must now, for the time being, leave Jen unhappy and ashamed so that we can follow Natha Yellow Scarf and the sword he gained. That story is told in the next chapter.

8

· *The Tale of the Thirsty Sword* ·

THE BANDIT NATHA YELLOW SCARF had once been a
peasant with a small farm of his own. Bad times fell
upon him and he borrowed money from a more prosperous neighbor. This man, however, secretly coveted
the land and wanted to add it to his holdings; and so,
when the time came to repay, he falsified accounts to
make the debt appear triple the sum. Natha pleaded his
case in the law court, but the magistrate had been
bribed to judge against him. Stripped of house, land,
and livestock and left with little more than the shirt on

his back, Natha turned to banditry. Others who had suffered like injustices came soon to join him.

From then on, great landowners, high officials, and traveling merchants trembled when the Yellow Scarves, as they called themselves, prowled the countryside. Ruthless though they were, they often shared their plunder with the needy. As a result, the Yellow Scarves were coming to be admired by the poor while feared by the rich.

Now, having taken robes, sword, and horses from the travelers in the cave, the Yellow Scarves galloped off in haste; for the men of Kwan-tzu, regrouping after the earlier skirmish, were still on their heels. Natha intended leading his men into hiding, but a scheme took shape in his mind. He ordered a halt. Leaving his companions to divide the loot, he went off to ponder his idea.

Natha sat down on a boulder. Chewing over questions about his plan, he drew the sword and toyed with it. The hilt fit his hand as if made for it. The keen edge shimmered.

"Fine prize. Better than I thought," he said. He stood and made a few passes in the air. His eye lit on a young pine tree. Thinking to test the blade against it, he swung the sword lightly and easily. It cut through the trunk so swiftly and cleanly that the tree remained standing. Natha stared, hardly believing what he had done.

Their nest disturbed, hornets swarmed out. Natha

waved the sword to fend them off. In a twinkling, the
blade sliced them to bits. One angry insect flew at him.
The blade seemed to leap instantly and cut it in two.

"This sword grows interesting," Natha said. He
laughed and brandished the weapon. "I think we'll get
on well together."

He rejoined his companions to find them grumbling
and scowling. One, a narrow-faced, hardmouthed fellow called Feng, had decked himself out in Prince Jen's
robe.

"We've been well tricked," Feng called out, handing Natha a document that had been tucked away in
the garment. "That young fop told the truth."

Natha squinted at the official calligraphy and vermilion seal. He understood it was a royal warrant, its
bearer indeed the Young Lord Prince. Some of the Yellow Scarves clamored to go back and lay hands on him,
kill him outright, or hold him for ransom.

"Be silent, all of you," burst out Natha, swallowing
his anger at being duped. "Go back after him? He's
long gone by now. Kill him? No, let him slink home
with his tail between his legs. He can tell King T'ai
that here, in these mountains, I'm a ruler better than he
can ever be. Ransom? What I took is worth as much as
any ransom."

Natha tore the warrant to bits and threw the shreds
to the ground. He strode some dozen paces away and
ordered Feng to shoot an arrow at him.

"Let it fly as near to me as you can. Mind your

aim," Natha said. "Nick me and you'll get a nick from this blade."

Feng, puzzled, did as Natha bade him. He drew his bow and sent a shaft hissing toward his chief. In a trice, Natha swung up the sword and with a quick stroke cut the arrow in two as it sped by him. He did likewise with two more shafts aimed still closer. Now confident, he commanded Feng to loose a third arrow straight at his breast. This, as well, Natha cut to bits with a single stroke before the arrow came near its mark.

The Yellow Scarves gaped in wonder. The astonished Feng, shaking his head, stepped up to Natha.

"What's the trick? How's it done?" Feng reached out. "Give it here. Let me try."

Natha struck Feng's hand away. "Paws off! All of you. This is mine, no other's."

He then called his followers around him and told them his plan, for the sword had given him a resource better than he could have devised. Natha had first intended to make a hasty raid on Kwan-tzu before the village men returned. Now a bolder thought had come to him. The sword seemed to have filled him with such strength and determination that he knew he could not fail.

So, instead of eluding the villagers, Natha and his companions turned and sought them out, soon coming upon them in a clearing where they had stopped to rest. The villagers sprang up and would have beset the Yellow Scarves; but Natha strode to face them, holding aloft the sword and demanding for them to hear him.

His tone and bearing stopped them in their tracks. His voice rang as he addressed them, calling them brothers, reminding them they had never suffered at his hands and many had benefited.

"Now you want to capture and kill us," Natha cried. "Only tell me one thing: What will you gain? Will your wives and children be better fed? Will the merchants and moneylenders be generous to you? Will Cha-wei listen closer to your grievances? Will he give you even grudging thanks?"

"And you?" one of the villagers called out. "What will you give us?"

Natha would have been a commanding figure in any circumstances, but now, sword flashing and his words stirring the villagers' hearts, he seemed to stand even taller. His eyes blazed, his voice thundered:

"What will I give you? Why, brothers, no less than what you deserve. I'll give you Kwan-tzu!"

The villagers roared agreement, shouted allegiance to Natha when they heard what else he promised. And so, joining forces, the Yellow Scarves and their would-be captors galloped back to the village.

There, following Natha's orders, before Cha-wei or any local dignitary understood what was afoot, the villagers broke into the granaries and the storehouses of food and clothing, smashing and burning the shops of any who stood against them. The richest merchants and moneylenders were dragged from their houses, cash boxes pried open, and all their valuables heaped in the public square. Under Natha's instructions, the Yellow Scarves shared out the plunder among the rejoicing villagers, laughing and dancing as if at a festival.

The yamen officials and servants, wailing, weeping, eyes rolling in terror, were also herded into the square. Natha strode back and forth, spitting curses at them for their greed and dishonesty, arrogance and laziness. He declared himself chief of Kwan-tzu and demanded their sworn obedience. If any hesitated for so much as a moment, he turned them over to the rough justice of the crowd.

Those who vowed to serve faithfully and dutifully were set free. Two men remained: Official of the Third Rank Cha-wei, blubbering and kowtowing; and a spice merchant begging for his life, moaning louder than Cha-wei.

"Look at me!" Natha shouted. "Do you know who I am?"

The two stared up at him. Their pleading words shriveled in their throats. They could only nod. For, indeed, Cha-wei was the magistrate who had connived against Natha. The other was the man who had cheated Natha of his landholdings and, profiting from them, had set himself up and made a fortune as a spice merchant.

Natha smiled. "I will be merciful."

With one blow of the sword, he struck off their heads.

That night, Natha lodged in Cha-wei's yamen, in

Cha-wei's apartments, and slept in Cha-wei's bed. Toward dawn, he was roused by a faint voice crying:

"Give me to drink."

Thinking it was one of the servants, wakeful and restless, Natha paid no heed, rolled over, and slept again.

Next day, with the Yellow Scarves in attendance upon him, Natha summoned all villagers with grievances to declare them and have them redressed. Some who came complained of having been cheated in business transactions, others of being given short weight from dishonest scales, still others whose petitions had been ignored. Natha heard each one and decided each case fairly.

The last man appeared uneasy and reluctant to speak. Finally, at Natha's urging, he drew himself up and stated:

"Honorable Sir, when the goods were shared out, someone laid hands on much more than his proper portion. Also, he forced others to give him many strings of cash."

Several witnesses came forward to bear out this testimony. Natha replied angrily that such conduct called for severe punishment and demanded the name of the criminal.

"Honorable Sir," the villager stammered, "it was a Yellow Scarf—one of your own men." He pointed toward Feng, standing by Natha in the Chamber of Audience.

Natha turned to Feng. "True?"

Feng shrugged. "What do villagers need with all that cash? Without us, they'd have had nothing. We deserve the greater share."

"You acted no better than Cha-wei or any greedy official," Natha retorted. "This is my judgment."

He leaped to his feet, drew the sword, and, before Feng could speak further, cut him down on the spot. The Yellow Scarves, outraged, started toward Natha; but he threatened them with the sword and declared he had done only simple justice. In the end, fearing his wrath, they agreed it was so. Natha ordered Feng's head hung at the yamen gate as a warning to all who dealt unjustly with their fellows.

Again that night, Natha was awakened by the same voice crying:

"Give me to drink."

Natha sprang up. The voice seemed to be in the chamber. He lit a lamp and, suspecting some treachery, peered into every corner and cabinet. The voice called out once more. Natha stopped short. He turned his gaze upon the sword, for the words had come from it.

Frightened at first, Natha raised a hand to ward off any ghost or demon. But the sword whispered and murmured so cajolingly and with such plaintive insistence that his fear quickly vanished. He sat down on the bed, the sword across his knees.

"What are you?" he asked, in wonder. "Why do you speak? What do you want of me?"

The sword only replied, "Give me to drink."

Natha questioned it no further. He felt sure now that some marvelous thing had come into his hands.

"And why?" he asked himself. "Clearly, because I alone deserve to wield it."

Natha said nothing of this to any of his companions. In the days following, however, he kept himself a little apart from them, the sword ever at hand. The Yellow Scarves wondered about this behavior but dared not question him, for the forbidding look on Natha's face warned them off. Nevertheless, Natha governed more justly than Cha-wei or any official had.

At this time, word reached Natha that the prefect of the district, learning of the happenings in Kwan-tzu, had sent a strong force of warriors to recapture the village. That night, Natha pondered what best to do, and if he should withdraw and lead his Yellow Scarves to a safe hiding place in the uplands. Deep in thought, turning questions over in his mind, Natha was roused by the insistent voice:

"Give me to drink."

"Yes!" cried Natha. "So I will!"

Next day, Natha ordered his Yellow Scarves and all the men he could muster out of Kwan-tzu. Instead of retreating at the approach of the warriors, Natha struck first. He himself galloped foremost into the fray, and laid about him ferociously with the sword, cutting down so many of his opponents that the rest, in terror and despair, flung away their weapons and surrendered to him. As he had done before with the villagers, Natha offered to spare their lives if they would swear allegiance to him. This they gladly did, and Natha led them all triumphantly to Kwan-tzu.

But now, with such a number of new followers, Natha was hard-pressed for provisions to feed them. Though he required the villagers to give up much of their own small stores of food, it was not enough. Villagers and warriors alike grew hungry and restless, and some began muttering doubts about Natha's wisdom.

"Give me to drink," the sword whispered.

And Natha called a party of warriors to him and led them into the countryside, demanding victuals from the peasant farmers and tribute from the smallest hamlets. Where Natha once shared his takings, he demanded these folk to empty most of their larders. Some did so, but many refused. From them, Natha carried off all they had, burned their farmhouses as an example to the others; and, if any raised hand or voice against him, he slew them.

The poorest found their only hope in joining his growing forces, but this in turn obliged him to plunder still farther afield.

Always, the sword murmured, "Give me to drink."

The provincial governor, alarmed to learn that Natha Yellow Scarf had come to hold sway over much of the region, determined to settle the matter once and for all. He ordered every warrior at his disposal to ad-

vance on Kwan-tzu, crush this challenge to his authority, and take Natha dead or alive.

Reports of the heavily armed force soon came to
Natha. For the first time, his resolution faltered. He
knew his followers were greatly outnumbered; he
doubted that even he could convince such an army to
join him. Prudence dictated retreat. About to give that
order, he heard the voice of the sword:

"Give me to drink."

And so, once more, he led out his men. They fell
upon the governor's warriors as Natha plunged into the
thick of the fight like a maddened tiger. Those who
saw him that day believed he had grown gigantic in
stature and his horse had become a dragon. Foam
flecked Natha's lips, his frenzied roars drowned out the
din of battle as the sword flashed in lightning bolts,
hewing and slashing, cutting down all before him, pursuing and killing even those who fled in terror.

Before the day was out, the provincial troops broke
in panic and scattered, leaving their dead and wounded
behind them.

Natha, spattered with the blood of his enemies, galloped to the crest of a little hill, where he threw back
his head and laughed in jubilation at the sight of the
shattered army.

"Who can stand against me?" he cried. He started
to signal a return to Kwan-tzu, then halted and spat
scornfully.

"One wretched village?" he said. "A handful of

miserable peasants? Is that to be my realm? Pitiful! Shall I choose to be so small? Why not choose to be great?"

The sword whispered:

"Give me to drink."

. . . . .

What becomes of Natha Yellow Scarf lies hidden in the future. For now, we go back to Prince Jen and his friends where we left them in the cavern. Robbed and terrorized by bandits, they are worse off than ever. What can they possibly do? That is told in the next chapter.

9

· *When is a prince not a prince?* ·
· *Mafoo comforts his toes* ·
· *Voyaging Moon plays the flute* ·

"MY WARRANT'S GONE!" Only now did Prince Jen realize that more than the sword had been taken. Stripping him of his robe, the bandits had also made off with his royal identification and authority.

"Never mind that. You can't ride a scrap of paper." Mafoo shook his fist at the Yellow Scarves, who had already galloped out of sight. "Sons of turtles! They stole our horses!"

In the course of what had at first promised to be a pleasantly interesting journey, Prince Jen, so far, had been half drowned, mired in mud, and imposed on by a disgusting old crackpot; and now robbed, terrorized, and forced to gulp down shame enough to last a lifetime. Even a gentle-natured prince has a limited store of tolerance, and Prince Jen, blood in his eye and ferocious thoughts in his head, was set on personally throttling Natha and all his band as well. He jumped to his feet and started for the mouth of the cavern.

"Jen!"

He was partway down the path when this call from Voyaging Moon brought him up short. Somehow it pleased him that she had overlooked the royal title.

"Young Lord Prince—" Voyaging Moon corrected herself.

"No. Only call me 'prince' when I get back my warrant. And the saddle. And the sword."

"If you like," Voyaging Moon said. "It does save time. Now that you've calmed down a little and started thinking sensibly, you've already figured it out. Find Li Kwang and you'll have that saddle you say is so important. Then, with him and his troops, you'll have a better chance of following the Yellow Scarves and getting the sword from Natha."

"I want more than that from him," Jen muttered between his teeth. He went back and bundled up the remaining gifts. He hurried from the cavern and, with Voyaging Moon, set about finding the warriors' tracks.

"Ai-yah! Ai-yah!" Trying to keep up with his master and the flute girl, Mafoo hopped as if he were crossing a bed of hot coals. "My feet aren't used to this torture. I wish those devils had taken my trousers instead of my boots."

Jen, for his part, paid no heed to the stones that bruised and bloodied his own unshod feet. While Voyaging Moon searched in one direction, he pressed farther ahead in another, with no success. Though it was now full daylight, the girl's quick eyes caught no trace of the vanished escort.

"Mafoo thought they doubled back," Jen called. "Could they have gone all the way down again?"

No longer content to let the flute girl take the lead, Jen ordered Voyaging Moon to quarter one side of the path and Mafoo the other, then set off practically racing downhill.

"He's acting more like a prince without that warrant than he did when he had it," Mafoo groaned, trying to rub his feet and walk at the same time. "Life was less strenuous before he decided to take charge of things."

Late in the day, when the travelers came back to the roadside, they found no sign that Li Kwang and his men had ever returned. Mafoo hunkered down in the bushes and comforted his toes. Jen and Voyaging Moon gave one last, fruitless search. The girl's spirits had not flagged until now, when she wearily admitted she could do no more.

"Not a footprint. Not a hoofprint," she said. "We've lost them for good."

"Then what?" Jen's vision of courageously regaining the sword was rapidly fading. Li Kwang might as well have disappeared from the face of the earth. What grew clear, instead, was that he had little chance of recovering the saddle or the sword. "We can't stand here in the middle of the road."

"Yes, we can," Mafoo said, "until my blisters heal."

"Is there a village nearby? A farmhouse?" Jen asked Voyaging Moon. "Anyplace at all we can shelter?"

"I'm out of my district," the girl said. "I don't know this part of the province."

"We'll keep on until we find something."

"And when you do?" Voyaging Moon said. "You'll make a grand procession with your band of retainers, all two of them. And the royal prince himself—I'm sure you'll forgive me for pointing this out—looking like the king of scarecrows. You can explain everything, of course; and why you haven't a scrap of evidence to prove it. Also, it's going to be dark. Do you mean to go hacking through the countryside all night?"

"I admire your line of reasoning," Mafoo said, beaming. "The most practical thing at the moment is the simplest: sit down."

Jen bristled. The girl nettled him, as did Mafoo for agreeing with her. Nevertheless, he had no ready answer. He reluctantly followed Mafoo a little way off the road. Like a dog making its bed, Mafoo flattened a space in the undergrowth and curled up in one corner. Resigned to spending the night, Jen dropped the bundle of gifts, much lighter than before, and sat cross-legged beside it.

"Mafoo warned me," Jen said, as Voyaging Moon settled next to him. "He didn't want to go to T'ien-kuo, and he didn't want me to do it either. I should have listened to him. What do I know of learning to govern? Or taking charge of Yuan-ming's gifts? I've already lost two of them. Someone else should have gone in my place. Who, I don't know. I think anyone would have done better."

"You can still make your way back to Ch'ang-an," Voyaging Moon said.

"Yes. In disgrace," Jen said. "Shall I tell my father I failed before I barely started? He trusted me to do what he wasn't able to do. Shall I tell him how frightened I was? A sorry sort of courage for a prince."

"A prince isn't required to be a fool," Voyaging Moon said. "Anyone would have done the same. Show courage by letting some hulking ruffian snap your neck? Brave? I'd call it plainly stupid. Anyhow, what you do next has to be up to you."

"Suppose I went to Kwan-tzu?" Jen said, after a time. "Cha-wei knows he's obliged to give me provisions, horses, everything we need. Don't worry about him," he added. "I'll tell him you're under my protection. Like it or not, he won't dare do anything."

"He's tricky," Voyaging Moon said. "I don't like the idea of being anywhere near him."

"What else then? We need food, water, clothing.

Now we have nothing." Jen glanced at the small bundle. "Only these, and they're no help to us. Valuable gifts? Natha called them playthings."

He undid the wrappings. "I wonder why Master Wu chose them. Worthy offerings for a great king?" He picked up the flute and smiled at Voyaging Moon. "This makes me think of that night in Cha-wei's yamen. You played beautifully. I'd never heard anything like it. Please play again."

Voyaging Moon put the flute to her lips. Instantly, the notes rose and hovered gently in the air. She stopped, surprised. "It hardly needs a breath. I don't know about the other gifts, but this one—Master Wu chose it well."

The girl began once more. At the first floating strands of melody, Jen felt his heart lighten. Within moments, his humiliation at the hands of Natha, his dismay at Li Kwang's disappearance, his failure to guard the offerings all turned weightless, borne away by the song of the flute.

As for Voyaging Moon, he could scarcely believe this was the same girl, barefoot, in coarse garments, with her high-cheeked peasant features. Her face shone with a golden light in the rays of the setting sun. Watching her, he felt she might vanish at any moment, carried off on the stream of music. He hardly dared to breathe. He sat motionless, hands folded, eyes lowered.

Mafoo stirred and raised himself on an elbow. "Marvelous!" He sighed. "It made me dream of dumplings."

Voyaging Moon laughed. The spell was broken. She put down the flute. Jen urged her to keep on. She shook her head sadly.

"This is not mine to play."

"It must be given to Yuan-ming, if ever I reach him," Jen said, his voice heavy with regret. "It is not mine, either. Until I have to part with it, I leave it in your hands, to play as you will. This gift, at least, is worthy—"

Voyaging Moon put a finger to her lips. "Quiet. Careful," she whispered. "Don't move suddenly. Something's behind us in the bushes."

* * * * *

What now? Does yet another danger threaten our hero and his friends? To find out, go quickly to the next chapter.

10

· The Mad Robber ·
· The Ear of Continual Attentiveness,
the Nose of Thoughtful Inhalations ·
· Moxa begs forgiveness ·

JEN SPRANG TO HIS FEET. For an instant, he feared
one of the Yellow Scarves had come back. He threw
himself at the black-garbed figure. Voyaging Moon and
Mafoo instantly followed, wrestling the intruder to the
ground.

Finding himself so briskly set upon, the man produced a number of bloodcurdling yells. Eyes rolling in
terror, his long, ropy hair swinging wildly, he turned
and twisted in every effort to shake free. By then,
Mafoo had clutched him by the ears, and Voyaging
Moon had gripped the collar of his long-tailed shirt;

their opponent, all the while, bawled indignantly: "Be calm! Be calm! I only want to rob you!"

"That," burst out Jen, "is all I need to hear!"

"Turtle!" Mafoo shouted. "Son of a turtle! You'll get something you didn't bargain for."

"Leave us alone," Voyaging Moon ordered. "We've been robbed already."

"Oh? You have?" The man stopped struggling. "Never mind, then. My humblest apologies."

"Let him up," Jen told Mafoo, who had taken a seat on the would-be robber's chest. "Whatever he is, he's no Yellow Scarf."

"Certainly not," the man replied, in a wounded tone. "Honorable sirs and lady, you do me a grave injustice if you think I have any part of them. That gang of lawless ruffians? No, no, I go about my business according to the highest standards of conduct, the Precepts of Honorable Robbery. Ask anybody. You'll hear nothing but favorable reports of Moxa. Or, if you prefer, the Mad Robber."

"I never knew of a robber apologizing, that's true enough," Voyaging Moon remarked.

"I made an unfortunate error. But how could I have guessed?" Moxa sat up and rubbed his ears. In the tattered black shirt that hung below his knees, the ropes of hair drooping below his shoulders, the self-styled Mad Robber appeared more poverty-stricken than mad. He was thin as a rail, with lanky legs, bony arms, and sharp elbows. His attempt at growing a mustache had clearly failed; he had sprouted only a few reluctant hairs, giving his face the look of a starved cat with a very large spider sitting on its head.

"I'm happy to advise you," Moxa continued, "you qualify under the Precepts, which I consider inviolable. In all my career, I have never broken one of them."

"What are you telling us?" Jen asked. "Robbers have precepts?"

"Hardly any. That is, none at all. Not in these times. They have no respect for decency and tradition. Except my humble self. Centuries ago, the Great Robber Kwen-louen laid down the Precepts, which I follow as a matter of moral principle. The one that applies to you is: Never rob someone who has already been robbed; as they are already distraught, it would be heartless to make them feel worse.

"As for the others," Moxa added, "never rob the poor, for that would only add to their misery. Never rob someone you know, for that would be treacherous. Never rob the happy, celebrating some good fortune, say a birthday or a wedding, for that would spoil their moment of joy. By the same token, never rob the unhappy, which would make them lose hope altogether."

"That leaves only rich strangers?" said Jen, who had been listening with curiosity to Moxa's explanation.

"Exactly. Unless, of course, the other Precepts apply. A rich stranger may be as unhappy as a poor acquaintance; or have just been robbed; and so on."

"You don't look as though your Precepts are any help to you," Voyaging Moon observed.

"It's difficult to find suitable candidates," Moxa

agreed. "When you come down to it, most of them are exempt for one reason or another. No matter. I scrupulously obey the Precepts. Otherwise—why, I'd be no more than a common thief.

"But the fact is I didn't mean to rob you. Not at first. No, it was the flute. I was merely passing by when I heard it. Skulking and lurking as befits a robber, you understand. And what strikes my Ear of Continual Attentiveness?" Moxa tugged at one of his remarkably large appendages. "Music! Marvelous! Irresistible! It seized hold of me, pulled me along. I had to hear more.

"You were the one playing," Moxa said, with an adoring glance at Voyaging Moon. He jumped to his feet, eyes alight. "Amazing sensation! It made me think of home and loved ones. Not that I ever had any, but I thought of them, even so. And all manner of joyful things that never happened to me but seemed as if they should have. When you stopped playing," he added, "I thought: Ah, well, I'll practice my profession since I'm here. Nothing malicious, we all have to live as best we can. You didn't have to kick me. Or sit on me. Not necessary."

Moxa broke off suddenly. "Have you eaten?"

"We can't feed you," Jen said. "You'll have to find someone better provisioned than we are."

"I didn't mean that," Moxa said. "I meant that if you haven't eaten within recent memory—as my Eye of Discerning Perception tells me may be the case—I'll be happy to share what I have."

With that, the robber pulled out a sack he had

dropped in the bushes. He rummaged in it, dredging up knotted cords, iron hooks, strips of wood, and a jumble of objects that Jen could not begin to identify. At last, he retrieved a handful of dry morsels and eagerly passed them around. With the efficiency of long practice, he scooped up twigs and dry branches and, within moments, lit a cheerful fire; all the while, like a host at a feast, he urged his guests to enjoy their food.

Biting into the leathery substance, Jen could not decide whether it was fish that had been too long in company with a chicken or the other way round. His hunger, nevertheless, had grown sharp, and he gnawed away gratefully.

"This won't keep us long from starvation," he murmured to Mafoo, who had downed his portion in one gulp. "I don't see any better course. We'll have to go to Kwan-tzu."

"What? What? Where?" Moxa exclaimed, cupping his Ear of Continual Attentiveness. "Kwan-tzu, did you say? Not the best of places. Not now."

"If you don't mind," Mafoo said, with a hard glance at the robber, "this is a private discussion. It doesn't concern you."

"Of course not, of course not, if you say so," Moxa replied. "But I can tell you this: While I was skulking and lurking, I came across those Yellow Scarves. And a band of villagers. I hid and listened to them. Trouble in the wind. The Nose of Thoughtful Inhalations sniffed it instantly. The Voice of Solemn Warning"—Moxa lowered his tone—"says: Keep away."

"The Yellow Scarves are the ones who robbed us," Jen said. "They took something from me. I want it back."

"Whatever it is, you won't get it," Moxa replied. "My Ear of Continual Attentiveness told me they're going to capture the town and kill the officials, the merchants—anybody who isn't with them. Go there and you won't come out again.

"On the other hand," Moxa continued, his eyes brightening and his cat's whiskers twitching, "the Voice of Daring Enterprise says: Why not?" Moxa waved his arms. "We dash in, take them by surprise, fight our way out, hacking right and left—do you have anything to hack with?—then, triumphant celebration! Do it! Risk all! Magnificent!"

"Lunatic!" snapped Mafoo. "I have a voice, too. I call it the Voice of Plain Common Sense. It tells me: Don't look for trouble, we've had enough already."

"Mafoo's right," Jen said, after some moments of thought. Moxa, deflated, went back to munching his food. "Very well," Jen added, "we won't go there. But then what?"

"Young Lord," Mafoo began, "it seems to me—"

"What was that?" Moxa stopped in midmunch. "What did you say? You called him—"

"Keep your Ear of Continual Attentiveness to yourself," Mafoo retorted, "and your Nose of Whatever out of other people's business."

"Young Lord? Young Lord?" Moxa's agitation grew. "There were rumors of—Prince Jen! You're the son of King T'ai? The prince himself? In this condition?"

Jen nodded.

"What have I done?" Moxa clapped his hands to his head. "Assaulted a Royal Person! Monstrous! Horrible! A capital crime! Oh, misery! Oh, death! Sliced to bits, cut to pieces!

"Worse, I've broken a Precept!" Moxa wailed. "There's yet another: Never assault the Divine King or his offspring, it shows lack of respect. I'd put it out of my mind, almost forgotten. No likelihood of its happening. But it has happened. Unpardonable! Unforgivable!"

"Don't upset yourself," Jen said, trying to calm the despairing robber, whose howls grew louder with each breath. "I was the one who assaulted you. So, you aren't the one who broke a Precept. In any case, it doesn't matter. Because I officially forgive you."

"You do?" Moxa left off his wailing to stare open-mouthed. "You really do?" He flung himself at Jen's feet. "No one's ever forgiven me for anything! My life is yours!"

"Not necessary—" Jen began.

"I insist!" cried Moxa. "Wherever you go, whatever you wish, the Hand of Enthusiastic Obedience, the Heart of Eternal Devotion will serve you."

"Don't think me ungrateful," Jen replied, "but there's no way you can help us. For one thing, I don't even know where we're going. We started out for T'ien-kuo—"

"T'ien-kuo?" cried Moxa. "That marvelous kingdom? I've heard of it since I was a child—at least, I think I did. The tales said it was far to the north. If it exists in the first place. You're going there? Lord Prince, why would you undertake such a journey?"

Despite Mafoo's disapproving frown, Jen explained his mission and told the robber what had befallen them since leaving Ch'ang-an.

"All the more reason for me to serve you," Moxa declared. "I can guide you partway. It's not for the likes of me to set foot in such a place. No robbers allowed, I'm sure. But I'll take you as far as I can. The Eye of Perpetual Vigilance will watch over you. Starting this moment."

Before Jen could answer one way or the other, Moxa loped to the fringe of the bushes, folded his skinny arms, and stationed himself as motionless as a statue, peering into the rapidly gathering darkness.

"It's not such a bad idea, having him along," Voyaging Moon said. "If we need protection, a robber's as good as anyone."

"He's a maniac," Mafoo retorted. "Eye of Perpetual Vigilance, is it? Yes, well, I'll want to keep my own eye on that fellow."

"I think he's going with us whether we like it or not," Jen said. "Maniac he may be, I'm glad for any help, as things stand now. Let him stay."

Since there seemed to be no alternative, Jen resigned himself to spending the night outdoors. Voyaging Moon, wakeful, sat watching the embers; but Jen, to his surprise, found himself drifting off to sleep as soon as his head touched the ground.

It was daylight when he opened his eyes again. Voyaging Moon, up and about, pointed to the pair of figures.

"Moxa hasn't moved from the spot," she said. "He's watched over us, as he said he would. And Mafoo's been watching over *him*. Between the two, we've been well guarded."

Seeing his master awake, Mafoo came to join him. Moxa, about to do the same, halted and cupped his ear.

"Hark!" he cried. "Does the Ear of Continual Attentiveness hear the sound of horses? What can that mean? I'll find out."

"Wait," Jen called, "what are you going to do?"

"If they're travelers," Moxa said, with a snaggletoothed grin of happy anticipation, "I'll rob them, of course. But—no, no, I won't rob them. You will."

⋄　⋄　⋄　⋄　⋄

Will our hero, already a victim of bandits, turn bandit himself? Will the Mad Robber lead our friends into still more trouble? The answers are found in the following chapter.

11

"YOU'LL DO THE ACTUAL ROBBING," Moxa went on. "As a precaution, you understand. Since it's not your profession, you aren't bound by the Precepts. Whereas if I do it, there's always a chance the candidate may qualify for exemption and I'd have to let him go."

"Moxa," Jen said, "I'm not robbing anybody. There's no way I can do that."

"A dozen ways," Moxa said. "Don't worry. Nothing to it, you'll see. As an amateur, you needn't concern yourself with refinements and niceties. I'll be there, of course. Not in a professional capacity, only to give small pointers when required."

Before Voyaging Moon and Mafoo could offer their own opinions, Moxa seized Jen by the arm and eagerly hurried him into the underbrush. The robber flung himself onto the ground and peered through the tall grass. Moxa's Ear of Continual Attentiveness had not deceived him. Within a few moments, Jen glimpsed a procession of some dozen attendants on foot, a supply cart, and a couple of pack mules. At the head rolled a boxy, two-wheeled carriage, its curtains drawn.

"All we really want is food. Anything else would be a nice little extra," Moxa said. "But, this being your first time out, don't bother about money, trinkets, that sort of thing. People get too upset when it comes to losing their valuables. The main thing is to halt the carriage. I'll do the rest. Any pretext will serve. Tell them your grandmother has colic, tell them—whatever comes to mind. Or do you prefer armed assault?"

"Lunatic!" Mafoo cried. "You'll get us deeper in a mess. Go rob them yourself. Better yet, just go."

"We need food, no question about it," Voyaging Moon told Jen, "but the simplest thing would be to ask."

"You say 'ask'?" Moxa exclaimed. "The Ear of Continual Attentiveness hears 'beg.' What, the Young Lord Prince turns beggar? Please maintain dignity. Propriety. Begging, indeed!"

"Safer than robbing," Voyaging Moon replied.

"If it weren't for the Precepts, I'd do the work myself," said Moxa, whose face had lit up and whose Nose of Thoughtful Inhalations had begun trembling with excitement. "What's to go wrong? Here you have the most elementary type of robbery. The great Kwen-louen named it Bee Approaches Tiger Lily. Simple. Straightforward. Compared with breaking and entering—"

By this time, the procession had drawn close enough for Jen to read the calligraphy on the fluttering red banners proclaiming this to be the entourage of Official of the First Rank Fat-choy. With a cry of relief, Jen sprang to his feet.

"Now, once you're there," Moxa went on, "the first thing to do—"

Jen had already started through the bushes. He motioned for Voyaging Moon and Mafoo to stay back. "Keep Moxa out of sight," he called, hastening toward the road. "This could be a palace official. I'll deal with him myself."

He ran down the slope and broke through the undergrowth, hurrying to overtake the procession. Waving his arms, shouting at them to halt, he headed for Fat-choy's carriage. A pair of attendants blocked his path, angrily warning him away. Jen pressed on, calling out to Fat-choy, demanding assistance in the name of King T'ai.

With the attendants gabbling and clutching at him, Jen shouldered his way to the carriage. As the surprised driver reined up, the curtains shot open and Official of the First Rank Fat-choy himself popped out his head.

"Why stop?" Fat-choy's head, bald as a lemon, took up most of the window. His jowls overflowed his high-necked collar, his eyes bulged out at the sight of Jen, and he began puffing and wheezing with indignation. "What does this mean? Disgusting individual, how dare you approach me?"

"Do you come from Ch'ang-an?" Jen demanded. "The Celestial Palace? You know me, then. I require your help. I am the Young Lord Prince."

Fat-choy pursed his lips. As he looked Jen up and down, his indignation turned to amusement. "What good fortune is mine, to meet such an exalted person-age. No doubt you are in disguise, for reasons best known to your royal self."

"Thank heaven you recognize me." Jen heaved a sigh of relief. "When did you leave Ch'ang-an? How is my father?"

"For one thing," Fat-choy replied, "I am not at-tached to the Celestial Palace. Since you are gracious enough to inquire, allow me to inform you that I have been transferred from Feng-sia to be chief magistrate of Chai-sang.

"For another," Fat-choy continued, "you must admit that it is highly unusual to find the Young Lord suddenly appearing out of nowhere. Forgive me if I restrain my joy until I first beg to inquire how this has come about."

Fat-choy spread a fan and waved it lazily while Jen explained what had brought him to such a state.

"Naturally," Fat-choy said when Jen finished his account, "you can offer some small proof of these most remarkable statements."

"I told you my warrant was stolen," Jen said, with some impatience. "What proof? I have my servant—"

"Enough." Fat-choy gave Jen an oily smile and snapped the fan shut. "As a magistrate, it is my profession and my skill to distinguish between truth and falsehood. I have listened with undivided attention and the highest degree of interest in your testimony and have reached the only proper and correct conclusion. You shall be granted what you require, what you clearly deserve and to which you are fully entitled.

"You asked if I recognized you," Fat-choy went on, beckoning to his attendants. "Although I have not seen you before, I know you very well indeed. That is to say, I know you for a barefaced, insolent liar." Fat-choy turned to one of the servants. "Take this dog and beat him thoroughly."

Before Jen could make a move, one of the retainers seized him by the hair and flung him to his knees while the other belabored him with a bamboo rod. Shouting with pain and outrage, Jen fought to break free. Fat-choy's retainer doubled the blows. Struggling, gasping for breath, Jen ground his teeth in useless fury.

"Lay on, lay on," Fat-choy urged, watching with a critical eye. "Diligence is a virtue. He thought to take advantage of my good nature. He should be grateful his punishment is not worse."

All that kept Jen from howling like an animal was his refusal to give Fat-choy added satisfaction. As the blows continued to rain relentlessly, Jen bit his lips, spat out blood and curses, while Fat-choy smiled and nodded, ordering his retainer to apply the rod more vigorously.

Jen felt himself spinning into unconsciousness when explosions ripped the air. The horses reared in alarm. Fat-choy dropped his fan, his chin collapsed into his neck. As the explosions continued, a gaunt figure bounded into the roadway. Shrieking horribly, shirt flapping, his ropy hair whirling about his head, Moxa leaped and spun like an acrobat, kicking out his legs, flinging himself against the terrified retainers.

Fat-choy regained his wits long enough to consider his immediate well-being. He bellowed for his driver to speed for their lives, popped his head back into the carriage, and snapped the curtain shut. The horses plunged ahead, the retainers took to their heels, and the disarrayed procession went scrambling down the road in a cloud of red dust.

Next thing Jen knew, Voyaging Moon's arms were around him. Dizzy and breathless, his back feeling as if it had been rolled in hot coals, he tried to sit up while Moxa cavorted triumphantly, making impudent gestures at the departing carriage.

"Magnificent!" The gleeful robber turned his attention to Jen. "Never anything so splendid!"

"Are you out of your mind?" retorted Voyaging Moon, who had begun peeling off Jen's shirt to examine his injuries. "Look what they've done."

"Yes, marvelous, isn't it?" Moxa wobbled his head in admiration. "The Young Lord's brilliant inspiration! Who would have thought of getting yourself beaten to distract the candidate? A completely new technique. I must add it to my list. Call it Butterfly Dares Lightning."

"What exploded?" asked Jen as Voyaging Moon dabbed at his back. "It kept Fat-choy from taking off the rest of my skin, whatever it was."

"Firecrackers," Moxa said happily. "I always carry them in my sack. Part of my stock in trade. They do produce a lively effect, don't they?"

Mafoo, clucking anxiously like a bandy-legged hen, had meantime hustled to his master's side. He and Voyaging Moon helped Jen off the road while Moxa retrieved his sack and rummaged out a jar of ointment.

"I keep it on hand for scrapes and bruises," the robber said. "I gather a number in my profession."

"No doubt," Jen said glumly as Voyaging Moon gently rubbed the salve over his shoulders. "I've gathered a number, too, with nothing else to show for it."

"I wouldn't say that," put in Mafoo. "While our flute girl was setting off those firecrackers, and that madman was jumping up and down, I made off with the provisions." Mafoo's lumpy face broke into a proud grin as he motioned toward a horse and a cart full of victuals. "Fat-choy won't eat much today. But we will."

Instead of continuing immediately on their way, Voyaging Moon urged waiting until next day, and Jen was glad to agree. Despite Moxa's ointment, his back still throbbed, and he had turned a little feverish. He ate nothing of the meal Mafoo prepared, but slept fitfully, with Voyaging Moon at his side to calm him when he started up from a troubled dream. At nightfall, the girl took the flute from the bundle of gifts. As she played, the voice of the flute seemed to ease his injuries better than Moxa's ointment. He no longer reproached himself for having lost two of the valuable objects, and as his strength came back, he was eager to begin afresh. He felt confident of reaching the end of his journey, but his thoughts turned more to Voyaging Moon than to T'ien-kuo.

Next day, with Moxa striding out ahead, Mafoo and the cart bringing up the rear, Jen and Voyaging Moon walked along easily, side by side, hand in hand. After a time, however, Voyaging Moon began glancing at the sun and frowning with some perplexity. She called out to Moxa, who came loping back, cheerfully grinning.

"Explain something to me," Voyaging Moon said. "T'ien-kuo's north, isn't it? Why are you taking us west?"

Moxa blinked at her as if astonished by such a question. "Because the road's better, of course."

"Wait a minute," put in Jen, alarmed. "You're taking us in the wrong direction just because of a good road?"

"Naturally," Moxa said. "I'd be a fool to follow a bad one, wouldn't I? It's the nature of roads to turn, as this one's bound to do. I'm not in the least worried about it."

Mafoo by this time had come up to them. When he heard the robber's explanation, he dropped the horse's halter and seized Moxa by the shirtfront.

"Come straight out with it, you idiot!" cried Mafoo. "You don't have any idea where you're going."

"I do, I do!" Moxa protested. "We'll find our way, you'll see."

The two would have kept on squabbling, but Jen ordered both to silence. Hobbling down the road came an old man barely able to support himself on the staff he carried.

Jen stared, taken aback at the sight; for the man's head, covered with long white hair, matted and befouled, thrust out from a hole in a heavy square of wood wider than his frail shoulders.

"Avoid him!" Moxa turned his eyes away. "Don't go near. He wears the cangue, the Collar of Punishment."

Jen and Voyaging Moon, however, had already started down the road. "What punishment is this?" Jen murmured, appalled. "The cangue? I've never heard of it."

"Not likely you would," Voyaging Moon said. "A prince isn't expected to concern himself with small legal details."

As they drew nearer, Jen cried out in dismay. Despite the old man's blistered, sun-blackened face, Jen thought for an instant that he recognized him.

"Master Wu? No—it can't be. Master Fu?" Jen stopped short and looked again. His eyes had deceived him; it was neither.

For his part, the haggard old man peered sharply at Jen. "Why do you thus address me? I am Master Shu. And you? Are you the one I seek?"

"Who's done this to you? Why?" Jen bent closer. "Never mind that now. We'll get that collar off, to begin with."

"Beware." Master Shu raised a hand in warning. "My cangue is bolted, sealed with a magistrate's seal. It means a death sentence for the one who tampers with it. You know the law."

"I don't know it, but it won't be a law any longer, not if I have any say about it," Jen replied. "Whatever you've done, you'll be free of this collar. By my royal command. I'm Jen Shao-yeh, the Young Lord Prince."

"Are you, indeed? So much the better." Master Shu narrowed his eyes. He studied Jen for a moment, then spat in his face.

◆ ◆ ◆ ◆ ◆

What ingratitude is this? By now, our hero should have learned caution in identifying himself to strangers. But who is Master Shu? What crime deserves such horrible punishment? Who is Master Shu seeking? The answers to these and other questions are found in the next chapter.

12

"THERE," SAID MASTER SHU. "I hope you are sufficiently insulted and infuriated. If not, I shall find some other way to anger you. Have you suggestions?"

Jen, too shocked to reply, had stepped back. Despite his reminding himself that this was a feeble old man, his chin shot up and his eyes flashed. Having recently been beaten with a stick, he was not in a frame of mind to be spat upon, least of all when he intended a kindness.

"Excellent," said Master Shu. "I perceive definite evidence of irritation. By all means, nourish it. When it grows ripe enough, you might care to pick up one of those large rocks over there. Or do you own some weapon? I would prefer it to be sharp-edged and quick."

"Don't let him bait you," Voyaging Moon murmured to Jen, who was still making an effort to keep his temper. "I know what he wants you to do."

"You seem to have grasped my purpose quicker than your companion," Master Shu said. "If he will not oblige me, perhaps you will."

"What purpose?" Jen demanded. "To begin, why insult me? You have no reason."

"Indeed, I do," Master Shu said. "First, if you are the Young Lord Prince, as you claim, you deserve to be insulted for allowing such atrocities as this"—he indicated his wooden collar—"to exist in your kingdom."

"Not my doing," Jen protested. "Palace officials deal with laws. I know nothing of them."

"My point exactly," Master Shu said. "Second, no matter who you are, I hoped you would be furious enough to put me out of my misery. I will beg no one to release me from this cangue; that would set his own life at risk. Therefore, my alternative has been to seek someone who will do me the inestimable favor of dispatching me as rapidly as possible. Now, before your temper cools, please get on with it."

"I have the authority to free you," Jen said. "I'm the Young Lord Prince, whether you believe me or not."

"Oh, I believe you," Master Shu said. "What sane

person would claim to be prince of such a kingdom as ours? Since you appear more or less in possession of your faculties, I conclude you have told the truth."

As Jen wondered whether to take Master Shu's logic as yet another insult, Voyaging Moon beckoned to Moxa, who had been cautiously keeping his distance.

"The Voice of Prudent Obedience tells me not to meddle with the law, no more than I've already done," said Moxa, when Voyaging Moon asked if he had means of breaking the bolts holding the collar shut. "However, the Whisper of Sympathetic Consideration tells me: 'Set the old boy loose and let the law look after itself.'"

From his apparently depthless sack, the Mad Robber produced a couple of iron bars and a wedge. He and Jen succeeded in cracking the seal and prying open the cangue. Mafoo, observing their efforts, threw up his hands.

"Not another old crock!" he moaned as Jen ordered him to bring food and drink for Master Shu, who had sat down in the middle of the road. "Remember that bird of ill omen, that wretched Fu! Please, no more stray geezers! Feed this one, yes, but send him on his way."

Master Shu evidently had no intention of moving from the spot. He wolfed down the victuals that Mafoo brought and seemed to regain a little strength even as Jen watched.

"I feel light as a feather." Master Shu licked his

cracked lips and stretched his neck, which had been rubbed raw. "I had almost forgotten what it was like to be without this collar. How long did I wear it? A year? More? I have lost track of time. Magistrate Fat-choy sentenced me to the cangue for the rest of my life. Surely, he never expected me to survive this long."

"Fat-choy condemned you?" Jen broke in. "That overblown toad?"

"Yes, the magistrate of Feng-sia," Master Shu said. "I am a poet by occupation, and some of my verses offended Honorable Fat-choy—as, indeed, I hoped they would. Nevertheless, I must admit that he chose a most emphatic way of expressing his critical opinion. Your reference to an overblown toad leads me to believe you know him."

Mention of Fat-choy made Jen's back smart again. He ruefully told Master Shu what the official had done, as well as everything else that had happened since leaving the palace.

"An admirable undertaking marred by regrettable incidents," Master Shu said sympathetically. "However, if you wish to reach T'ien-kuo, you must not continue on this road."

"Just as I thought." Mafoo beetled his brow at Moxa. "This idiot's taken us in the wrong direction."

"T'ien-kuo lies beyond the River Lo," Master Shu went on. "This road will eventually lead you to it, but it is long and very roundabout. From here, there is a much more direct way; also, much more difficult.

However, if you have strength to follow it, you will arrive sooner at your destination."

"I'm sure you'll be kind enough to explain how we find that path," Voyaging Moon said.

"I was about to do so," Master Shu said. "It is somewhat complicated, but if you listen carefully—"

"The Ear of Continual Attentiveness—" Moxa began.

"Never mind that." Mafoo then quickly whispered to Jen, "Be sensible. How can we be sure he knows what he's talking about? He's a poet, isn't he?"

"You are quite right in raising such a question," said Master Shu, whose long punishment in the cangue had not damaged his hearing. "However, I assure you I am competent to speak of T'ien-kuo."

"You've been there?" said Voyaging Moon.

"Indeed, I have," Master Shu said. "It is a remarkable kingdom. I have seen it for myself. In a manner of speaking. That is to say, I have dreamed of it."

"What?" cried Mafoo. "Idiot! You've only been there in your dreams and you expect us to believe—"

"Poets are seldom believed," Master Shu said, "but I can tell you that my dreams are very clear, precise, and exact. You can rely on them far more than on maps and geographical treatises."

Mafoo clapped his hands to his head. "Young Lord, send him off. He's worse than Moxa."

"Do we have better information?" Jen said. "Master Hu told me once that a dream can be as useful as a fact."

"Yes, especially in the case of T'ien-kuo," Master Shu said.

"If you're sure you know the way," Jen said, after some long moments of thought, "will you guide us?"

"I am not at all certain I have the strength to venture so far," Master Shu said. "On the other hand, if you insist, how can I refuse?"

"You can if you try," Mafoo said to him. To Jen, he muttered, "First, you put yourself in the hands of a lunatic robber; now, another old crock, and a poet on top of it. Your trusting nature will be your ruination. And," he added, "mine as well."

◆ ◆ ◆ ◆ ◆

Is Mafoo right? Has our hero made yet another mistake? How reliable is Master Shu? These questions require time to find their answers, so it will be necessary to go on to the next chapter.

13

· *Guidance of Master Shu* ·
· *Affairs of the feet and stomach* ·
· *Affairs of the heart* ·

MAFOO EYED MASTER SHU with the same enthusiasm he would have given a ten-day-old carp. Jen had no misgivings. He willingly followed the poet's instructions, turning off the road and onto a track leading across open countryside. Voyaging Moon urged Master Shu to ride in the cart. He shook his head, declaring that he had been tramping so long he would be uncomfortable doing otherwise.

"My feet will outlast any horse's hooves." Master Shu displayed his soles, covered with thick, scarred calluses, tougher than leather. "By the time we reach the River Lo," he added, "yours will be the same."

"Now, there's something to look forward to. I can hardly wait," Mafoo remarked. However, seeing no choice in the matter, he trudged beside Moxa, who continued insisting that he had not misguided them.

Despite his rising spirits, three questions troubled Jen. As the day wore on, he ventured to speak of them to Master Shu.

"About the gifts for Yuan-ming," Jen said. "As I told you, Master Wu chose six and I've lost two. Dare I now present only four? It seems a small number for such a great king."

"For one thing," Master Shu replied, "as you described the circumstances, I would not say that you lost them. You did what seemed altogether reasonable. Certainly, as far as the sword is concerned, had you not let that ruffian take it you would not be alive at this moment to make the journey.

"For another, will Yuan-ming know or care how many gifts you started out with? The important thing is that you will not arrive empty-handed. Besides, along the way, you may find other gifts even more valuable."

Master Shu's words reassured Jen to some extent. He was satisfied that he still had sufficient offerings. Now he brought up another question troubling him as much.

"My royal warrant is gone. How can I prove who I am? You believed me, but Fat-choy didn't. Why should Yuan-ming take my word? I'll be a stranger to him—not a very princely looking one, at that. Will he even admit me to his presence?

"Once we reach the capital," Jen continued, "should I first write him a petition explaining what happened?"

"That's a reasonable thought," Voyaging Moon said. "It might be wiser than just walking up to the palace and trying to persuade the guards to let you in."

"Do you believe so?" Master Shu said. "Let me tell you the tale of Foolish Yang and the shoes.

"Deciding to buy a new pair of shoes, Foolish Yang measured his feet and wrote the figures on a piece of paper. Hurrying to the seller of shoes, he requested a pair matching the dimensions he had noted down. The merchant found such a pair and, offering them to Yang, urged him to try them on.

"Yang did so, then burst out unhappily: 'They pinch my toes! They rub my heels! Too short in length, too narrow in width. They fit me not at all!'

" 'Let me see that paper,' said the shoe seller. 'Now, look here, Honorable Yang, they tally exactly with these measurements.'

"Yang scratched his head and pondered a while. 'You are right,' he said at last. 'Obviously, I made a mistake when I wrote out the figures. Very well, there is nothing else for it. I must go back home and measure my feet again.'

"By the same token," Master Shu said, "to which will Yuan-ming give more belief: a scrap of paper, or the individual who wrote it? My dear young man, Yuan-ming is wise enough. He will know you for what you are."

Again, Jen felt reassured. One last question troubled him, and most deeply of all.

"My honored father wishes me to learn how Yuan-ming governs his kingdom," Jen said. "It did not occur to me at the time, but now I realize it means I'll have to study every one of his laws and precepts, his regulations, ordinances, decrees, analects—how shall I do this? I wasn't educated to be a scholar or official. I understand nothing of these things."

"You must know nothing before you can learn something, and be empty before you can be filled. Is not the emptiness of the bowl what makes it useful? As for laws, a parrot can repeat them word for word. Their spirit is something else again. As for governing, one must first be lowest before being highest. The pot must be broken before it can be mended—"

Master Shu left off, for Mafoo was calling to them. In the course of their conversation, Jen and the old poet had lagged behind. Running to catch up, Jen saw that Mafoo had halted at the edge of a steep cliff.

"Fine guide!" Mafoo exclaimed as Master Shu approached. "If I hadn't my wits about me, I'd have gone tumbling over, horse, cart, and all."

"Dear me, dear me," Master Shu said, "that would have been regrettable, especially for the horse. Very well, unhitch him and let him go his way."

"What?" cried Mafoo. "What are you saying?"

"We can hardly take a horse and cart," Master Shu replied. "We shall have difficulty enough climbing down with sacks of provisions on our backs."

"He's right," said Voyaging Moon, looking into the valley. "Too steep. There's no path at all."

"Master Shu," Jen demanded, alarmed. "Where have you led us?"

"Where you must go," said Master Shu.

Now followed a conversation between Mafoo and Master Shu. It consisted, for the most part, of Master Shu saying nothing, while Mafoo vigorously suggested that Master Shu was a greater lunatic than Moxa if he expected them to give up their only transportation and much of their food.

"He is very persuasive," Master Shu said to Jen when Mafoo ran out of breath, "and he has your best interests at heart. The problem is: Either you trust me or you do not."

Jen stepped to the girl's side and studied the downward slope. As Voyaging Moon had told him, it was not possible to take the horse and cart.

"I have to trust him," Jen said finally. "I don't know what else to do." He took Voyaging Moon's hand. "If I follow him, will you come with me?"

"Did you think I wouldn't?" Voyaging Moon said.

Jen turned to Moxa. "I'm going with Master Shu. I can't ask you to do the same. You'd do better to go back to robbery—if you can ever find a likely candidate, that is."

"Never!" cried Moxa, flinging himself at Jen's feet. "The Heart of Eternal Devotion, the Hand of Enthusiastic Obedience—"

"Mafoo," Jen said, disentangling himself from the devoted clutches of the Mad Robber, "my good Mafoo, best of faithful servants, you are wiser than I am, but I can only do what seems good to me. Go safely to Ch'ang-an. Tell my father I ordered you to do so."

"Young Lord," Mafoo said, "if you're set on doing something as foolish as this, all the more reason for me to keep an eye on you."

With that, Mafoo stumped to the cart and set about unhitching the horse. Master Shu trotted after him as the animal, glad to be relieved of its burden, tossed its head and kicked up its heels. The old man patted the horse's neck.

"Get along with you," Master Shu said. "You are free. Go about your business."

"Oh, no!" Mafoo puffed out his cheeks. "The old boy talks to horses?"

Shouldering as many sacks of food as they could, the travelers followed Master Shu, who had begun scrambling down as nimbly as a monkey. The old man was quicker and more surefooted than Jen could have imagined; nevertheless, it was late afternoon by the time they reached the floor of the dry gorge. Jen glanced at the cliffs towering high above.

"I'm wondering," he said to Master Shu, "how we're going to climb up on the way back."

"Do not concern yourself," Master Shu said

brightly, turning a sharp eye on Jen. An odd note came into his voice as he added, "You will not set foot here again."

In the days and weeks that followed, Jen wondered if he had, in fact, done well to follow Master Shu. The old poet had warned of difficulties and had not exaggerated. This stretch of the valley, he explained, had long ago been the bed of a mighty river. The earth had rumbled and shattered, the river vanished; boulders greater than the whole Celestial Palace had been flung up as if no more than pebbles. Astonishingly, Master Shu easily clambered up them while Jen and the others strained and sweated to keep pace with him. Sometimes they lost sight of the old man, only to find him perched on the highest peak of a stone slab, waving his staff and beckoning to them.

In time, however, they grew hardened to the rugged course Master Shu had set, and the old man no longer outdistanced them. In the matter of their feet, Master Shu's prediction had been correct. Jen ceased to be aware of the sharp stones; Voyaging Moon, though accustomed to going unshod, saw that her soles had toughened still more. Moxa's boots had long since been torn to shreds, but he loped along, agile as a cat, making long-legged leaps from one rocky outcrop to another.

The summer sun blistered their faces and parched their throats. Yet, when their mouths had so dried that even Mafoo could barely grumble, Master Shu found some rivulet or trickle of water. As for food, by Jen's calculations it should have long since run out. Nevertheless, the apparently empty sacks of provisions always held yet another handful of rice or millet cakes. What disappeared was Mafoo's paunch.

"Look at me," he groaned. "Now my belt's too long by half. Keep on like this and I'll be thinner than a shadow."

"I don't think he minds all that much," Voyaging Moon whispered to Jen, glimpsing Mafoo furtively admiring his new leanness. "Even so, I have to agree with him."

Soon after, an eagle flew overhead, gripping a wriggling fish in its talons. Next moment, it let go of the fish, which dropped at the feet of Master Shu.

"Marvelous!" cried Mafoo. "Here's our dinner falling from the sky! Hold on there, old fellow, what are you doing?" he added as Master Shu bent down to put his ear close to the fish and seemed to strike up an earnest conversation.

"Begging his forgiveness and asking if he objects to our eating him," replied Master Shu. "That is only common courtesy. He agrees this time, but tells me not to make a habit of it."

Mafoo threw up his hands. "First he talks to horses, now he talks to fish." He cocked an eye at Master Shu. "Enough of your nonsense. How do you know what he says? You're not a fish."

"Nor are you Master Shu," replied the poet, smiling. "How do you know that I do not know?"

With Mafoo trying to puzzle out Master Shu's logic, the travelers enjoyed their best meal since entering the gorge.

That night, as she had always done, Voyaging Moon played the flute. Its music, in these bleak surroundings, had never sounded sweeter. When she finished and the last echoes died away, Master Shu happily announced that the most difficult part of their journey now lay behind them; within a day, they would reach the T'ung Pass, and from there he foresaw less than a week of easy travel to the banks of the Lo.

The old man's news should have cheered Jen as much as it did Moxa and Mafoo. Strangely, the closer he drew to his destination the more reluctant he became to end his journey. Even if Yuan-ming accepted him, Jen could not guess how long he might be obliged to remain. Weeks, probably months of study lay ahead before he started homeward again. Another question concerned him still more. While the others settled into sleep, he spoke of it to Voyaging Moon.

"If the end of my journey also means parting from you," Jen said, "I—then I think I will have journeyed uselessly. Whatever else I might gain, I will have lost something greater. Will you stay with me in T'ien-kuo? Yuan-ming surely will make a place for all of us."

"If I do?" Voyaging Moon quietly replied. "And afterward?"

"Come back with me to Ch'ang-an," Jen said, taking her hand.

"Does the Celestial Palace require a flute girl?" Her voice was light as her teasing laughter.

"No, it doesn't." Jen smiled at her. "I do."

"Aren't there enough musicians in the Celestial Palace?" Voyaging Moon said. "Why should the Young Lord Prince wish another?"

"There's no Young Lord Prince," Jen said. "Between us, there's no Jen Shao-yeh. Only myself. And yourself."

"That's easy to say, sitting on a pile of rocks in the middle of nowhere," Voyaging Moon replied. "Once you're in the palace again—"

"You have my promise as well as my heart," Jen said. "I have no betrothal token. What I would offer you is a gift that must be given up: this flute. Even so, carry it now as if it were your own. If Yuan-ming is as gracious as Master Wu claimed, he'll understand that it is yours more truly than it can be his."

Voyaging Moon nodded and picked up the instrument she had set aside. "Whether I must part with it or not, you, too, have my promise—"

A cry from Master Shu made Voyaging Moon break off. The old man suddenly sat bolt upright, muttering wildly. As Jen and Voyaging Moon hurried to his side, he rubbed his eyes and blinked around.

"Dear me, dear me," he murmured, "have I been dreaming? I hope so. Sometimes it is difficult to be sure. There was another poet, once, who dreamed he was a butterfly. When he woke, he could not decide whether he was a poet dreaming he was a butterfly or a butterfly dreaming he was a poet. No matter, either way it is only a dream."

Master Shu would say no more of what had disturbed him, and he beamed with delight when Jen and Voyaging Moon told him of their promises to one another. By this time, Mafoo and Moxa had awakened, and the news had to be repeated; it was met with so many joyous congratulations and blessings from the two of them that Master Shu at last had to urge them to leave off.

"That should be ample happiness for one day," he said. "Keep a little stored away. It might be needed."

◆　◆　◆　◆　◆

Marvelous turn of events! What could be happier? Those who are content to end the tale here with two young lovers need go no further. Those curious to learn more of the journey must read the next chapter.

14

· Happiness of Jen ·
· Sadness of Master Shu ·
· Ferryboat at the River Lo ·

MASTER SHU, NEXT DAY, led the travelers through the T'ung Pass. Here, the rock-strewn course veered away. Jen found himself in the greenest woodlands and meadows he had ever seen. Along the forest track, yellow and crimson wildflowers turned the air fragrant. Birds of every color flew overhead or perched, singing, amid the trees. Monkeys skittered along the branches and chattered at the human intruders. Voyaging Moon laughed in delight as a gazelle daintily trotted across the path and halted a moment to glance at her before vanishing into the foliage.

Jen would have gladly lingered. He had never been happier. Hand in hand with Voyaging Moon, smiling whenever their eyes met, his loss of the sword and saddle and his beating by Fat-choy's retainers no longer seemed important.

"Mafoo once complained about Master Fu," Jen said to her. "If he hadn't fallen into the river, I wouldn't have fished him out and taken him with us. If I hadn't done that, I wouldn't have gone to Kwan-tzu. If I hadn't gone to Kwan-tzu, we wouldn't have met. Blame Master Fu? I should thank him."

As for Mafoo's usual complaints, they stopped altogether. Even more surprising, he no longer grumbled about Moxa and in fact had come to be on friendly terms with the Mad Robber. One day, when the travelers were obliged to ford a deep stream, Mafoo unhappily eyed the swift current and admitted he could not swim.

"Hop on the Shoulders of Reliable Support," Moxa said. "You're lighter than you used to be."

With Mafoo clinging uneasily to his back, Moxa plunged into the water up to his nose. Once across, when Mafoo thanked him, Moxa shook his ropy hair and grinned happily.

"Glad to oblige," Moxa said, adding, "I needed your weight to keep me from floating away. I forgot to mention: I can't swim, either."

Instead of berating him, Moxa burst out laughing; and the two of them raced on ahead, capering like a pair of schoolboys.

Only Master Shu seemed low-spirited. His steps had slowed, he leaned more heavily on his staff. Often, as they made their way through the woodlands, Voyaging Moon played the flute she now carried, but its music brought only shadows to the old poet's furrowed face.

Two days later, they left the forest track to follow a hard-packed roadway. Here, they saw other travelers, merchants in carriages or sedan chairs, farmers with ox carts and wheelbarrows of produce on their way to Chen-yeh, the district capital close to the banks of the Lo. Mafoo licked his lips at the prospect of dumpling houses, but Master Shu announced that they would turn away from the town and go farther upriver, where they would attract less attention. He recalled a ferryman there who would row them across.

The old man urged them to make haste. For some while, Master Shu had been sniffing the air and casting uneasy glances at the gathering clouds. The closer they drew to the river, the darker grew the sky. Late that afternoon, by the time they sighted the ferryman's hut, the first raindrops had begun to fall.

Of the ferryman himself, there was no sign. Mafoo and Moxa went off to find him, while Jen and Voyaging Moon made their way to the water's edge. The river was broader than Jen had envisioned, and he could barely make out the green banks of the farther shore.

Master Shu pointed with his staff. "Once across, you must yet go many leagues to Ch'ung-chao. I had hoped I might guide you all the way."

"What do you mean?" Jen replied. "Of course you will. Why wouldn't you?"

Master Shu did not answer. Before Jen could question him further, Mafoo and Moxa were back; with them was the ferryman, shaking his head and pointing at the lowering sky.

"He's worried about a storm. Once the rain starts, the fellow claims it could last for days," Mafoo said. He added brightly, "Nothing else for it. We'll have to go to Chen-yeh and put up with the hardships of an inn, with all those hot meals and soft beds."

"I'm bound to find a client or two there," Moxa said. "We'll manage nicely."

"A few more days won't matter," Voyaging Moon said, while Master Shu remained silent, offering no opinion.

Jen hesitated. Delay would make little difference. Yet, with the river before him, his impatience grew. He wished to be across and on the way to T'ien-kuo. He questioned the ferryman, who admitted he could likely reach the farther shore before the storm broke. The return was what troubled him. He might, he protested, be stranded on the opposite bank who knew how long, away from wife and children, soaked to the skin, catching a cold into the bargain.

"Aha!" cried Moxa. "The Nose of Thoughtful Inhalations smells a question of money. Well, then, cash cures all complaints." Delving into his sack, he produced a handful of silver coins and a string of coppers, and the sum, indeed, outweighed the ferryman's reluctance.

"Settled, then," said Jen. "We'll cross now."

The ferryman urged the travelers to board immediately. Voyaging Moon, tucking the flute in her jacket, sprang lightly into the boat. Jen helped Master Shu to a place astern, between Mafoo and Moxa. The ferryman bent to his oars, the craft slid into the current.

The wind had freshened; the waters of the Lo turned choppy. Well before the boat reached midstream, the waves began snatching at it. Despite his efforts, the ferryman could not hold to his course. The current bore the craft farther downriver, well away from the little dock on the opposite shore.

Now the sky had turned black, and the rain began in earnest, pouring down in blinding sheets. The wind rose to a screaming gale. The boat pitched and spun like a leaf on the tide.

"Row back! Row back!" Mafoo cried, gripping the side of the boat, while Moxa crouched beside Master Shu.

"No!" Jen shouted, throwing his arms around Voyaging Moon. "That's as dangerous. Keep on. If the wind slackens—"

The ferryman could obey neither command. As he hauled with all his might at the oars, one of them snapped, and he tumbled backward. The helpless craft slewed around in the clutches of tide and gale.

The boat plunged into the trough of the waves,

then suddenly flung upward, lurched sideways, and shuddered an instant before it capsized.

The shock tore Voyaging Moon from Jen's arms. Water closed over his head. He fought his way to the surface again. Lightning like clawing fingers ripped the sky. In flash after flash, he glimpsed Mafoo and Moxa floundering in the tide, the ferryman trying desperately to keep afloat. Master Shu had vanished, his staff tossed like a straw on the waves.

Jen, in that moment, saw Voyaging Moon struggling against the current. He shouted to her, but the wind bore away his words. Then she caught sight of him and stretched out her hands. He swam toward her. The shattered boat spun between them. A broken timber struck him full force. Her face was the last thing he would remember.

◆ ◆ ◆ ◆ ◆

Jen is snatched from his beloved, his friends swept away in the tide and scattered to the winds. However, before returning to our hero and his fate, we must now follow along with Voyaging Moon. The tale of her own journey is told in the next chapter.

15

· *The Tale of the Singing Flute* ·

A MAN CALLED HONG was innkeeper of the Golden Grasshopper in the town of Chen-yeh. This fellow Hong had a quick eye for profit and a deaf ear for whatever did not work to his advantage. He gave nothing without getting more in return. No one ever bettered him in a bargain. When a terrible storm forced travelers to seek refuge at his inn, Hong doubled his prices for food and lodging, delighted that the misfortunes of others turned into a benefit for himself.

It was at this time, some days after the storm had

passed, that a young girl came to the kitchen door and politely asked for food. Her face was bruised, her garments were torn and weather-stained. Even so, she did not have the air of one accustomed to begging. The cook would gladly have given her a handful of leftovers, but Hong happened to come into the kitchen at that moment. When he saw what the cook was about to do, Hong shouted angrily at him and pushed him aside.

"Do you mean to bankrupt me?" he cried. "Your business is cooking food, not giving it away." He turned to the girl. "Be off. You'll get nothing for nothing here."

The girl did not move, but looked squarely at Hong. She was none other than Voyaging Moon. The gale that had swept away Jen and the others had flung her amid the reeds and cattails of a little backwater. Battered, half-drowned, she opened her eyes to find herself alone, the flute clutched tightly in her hand. For days afterward, she searched along the riverbank from dawn to dusk, even through most of the nights. She questioned children playing along the shore, women washing clothes in the shallows, and everyone who crossed her path. No one, they told her sadly, could have survived such a tempest on the river. What kept her heart from breaking then and there was her certainty that since she was alive, so must the others be.

At last, driven by hunger and exhaustion, she came to Chen-yeh and the Golden Grasshopper. Once she had eaten a little and regained strength, she determined to search yet again, to comb both banks of the Lo from source to mouth if need be. The innkeeper's refusal did not discourage her in the least.

"Nothing for nothing?" Voyaging Moon said. "That's a fair exchange. What of something for something? My work for your food."

Hong thought this over for a few moments. His inn was crowded, his servants hardly able to keep up with their tasks, his guests already complaining and threatening to leave if conditions did not get better. He badly needed another pair of willing hands, and he quickly calculated the girl's labor would be worth far more than what she ate. Of that, he would make sure.

"Agreed," Hong said, with a show of reluctance, "but only because I have a generous heart. You can have what you scrape out of those pots and pans and not a mouthful more. For the rest, you'll do as you're told, no shirking, no laziness. Even at that, I'm cheating myself. But I can't help it, that's how I am."

"Generosity must be a painful affliction," Voyaging Moon sympathized. "I hope you don't suffer too much from it."

All that day, Voyaging Moon did every task that Hong demanded, scrubbing, sweeping, fetching water, hauling charcoal, with never a word of complaint. The cook secretly made sure the girl was fed with more than pot scrapings, and he prepared her a pallet of straw in the kitchen corner.

At nightfall, when Voyaging Moon finished her work, she did not rest. A hopeful thought had come to her mind. She left the kitchen and climbed to the roof of the inn.

There, perched cross-legged on the tiles, she put the flute to her lips and played a soaring melody, praying that somehow Jen would hear it wherever he might be and that the music would bring him to her.

As she played, her heart followed the notes shimmering like stars in the dark sky. The voice of the flute sang of love, longing, and hope. Indeed, the instrument seemed to have its own spirit that spoke wordlessly but clearly, as if playing of itself, its tone more beautiful than it had ever been.

Voyaging Moon stopped. She was not alone. The music, meant for Jen, had drawn other listeners. Guests had come out of their chambers, tradesmen from their shops, passersby had halted in the street below. As Voyaging Moon put aside her instrument, cries of disappointment rose from the crowd, and they pleaded for her to continue.

The innkeeper had hurried from his counting room to learn the cause of the commotion outside.

"Come down," he shouted when he saw Voyaging Moon and her flute. "You should be scrubbing pots for your keep, not amusing yourself on my valuable time. You'd best put a broom in your hand instead of that wooden whistle."

At this, the crowd around Hong protested loudly,

insisting on the girl playing again. A few even threatened to give Hong a good beating if he forbade her to do so. Many more, however, pressed money into his hands, urging him to reward such a marvelous musician and induce her to keep on. The bewildered innkeeper had wits enough to pop the cash into his purse. Though he had no ear for music, he heard coins clinking merrily enough; and, by the time Voyaging Moon climbed from the roof, Hong's vinegar frown was transformed into a honeyed smile.

"My dear young lady," Hong said, "if I spoke harshly it was only because I feared for your safety. You could have fallen and harmed yourself. Step inside, night air is bad for the lungs. If only you had told me you had such a valuable skill! Have you eaten well today? Come along, come along," he added, taking Voyaging Moon's arm and drawing her inside.

The guests, along with a number of passersby, followed. All begged to hear more of her music. Hong made a place for Voyaging Moon in the middle of the eating room, called for food and drink to be served to her; then, rubbing his hands, he asked her to take up the flute again.

"Surely you won't deny these good folk the pleasure of your music," Hong said. "Look around you, lovely lady, and see how many have come to hear."

Though Voyaging Moon's grief had burdened her heart, it had not dulled her wits. She saw that Hong had gone to each one in the room, demanding more cash. His purse was already full to bursting. It came quickly to her mind that a share of Hong's profit would allow her to hire a riverboat, buy provisions, and employ helpers in her search for Jen.

"I won't deny anyone the pleasure of my music," she replied sweetly, "and you, Master Hong, won't deny me payment for it. As you yourself told me: nothing for nothing."

Hong sputtered and protested, but the guests had grown impatient, threatening to leave and demanding their money back. So, Hong fished into his purse and produced a couple of coins.

"Why, Master Hong, what of your generous heart?" Voyaging Moon said. "Not to mention the weight of your purse. It seems to me we can strike a better bargain. Equal portions should be a reasonable division. No, no, you're right, that won't do at all," she added, as Hong squealed indignantly. "Much better to make it three coins out of ten. That is, three for you and seven for me."

Hong shook his fists and tore his hair, claiming that Voyaging Moon would ruin him.

"How can that be?" Voyaging Moon said. "Since it cost you nothing to begin with, what you gain is pure profit. Furthermore, if I refuse to play, you'll gain nothing at all."

No matter how the innkeeper groaned and wrung his hands, Voyaging Moon held to her offer. Finally, Hong grudgingly accepted. Voyaging Moon then played for the assembled audience, so charmingly and graciously that Hong was able to extract still more cash from them as well as from new arrivals. At the end of the evening, Voyaging Moon required the innkeeper to spread all the coins on a table, holding nothing back, and she herself made the division. Even with his three coins out of ten, Hong reckoned on fat profits in his future.

"I should also mention," Voyaging Moon said, "that I'd play much better if I slept in my own chamber instead of a straw mat in the kitchen."

Hong ground his teeth but finally had to agree. Voyaging Moon tucked her earnings into her jacket and retired to the room Hong reluctantly provided. Next evening, she played again before an even larger audience, to the increasing joy of the innkeeper. She did likewise the following evening. Nevertheless, when she had finished performing, she still climbed to the roof and poured out her music to the night sky, ever hopeful it would reach the ears of her beloved.

By the end of the week, Voyaging Moon calculated that she had earned enough to continue her search better outfitted than before. She announced to the innkeeper that she would depart the following morning. Hong was furious at the thought of losing future profits. Voyaging Moon, however, told him flatly that she would play no longer and in no way could he force her to do so.

"If you try," she warned, "I'll play so badly it will

drive every guest from your inn and you'll be worse off than ever."

Hong could not browbeat her into changing her mind. Realizing she was no longer of use to him, he quickly shaped a plan. "The wench thinks she's had the better of me? That remains to be seen."

Hong set his plan in motion without an instant's delay. That very night, he struck up a conversation with a merchant who had just arrived and planned to leave early next morning.

"One of my bondmaids has taken advantage of my good nature," Hong told the merchant. "She's turned slack and impudent and I'd like to be rid of her. I haven't the heart to throw her out into the street. I'll sell her to you at a bargain price if I'm sure you'll give her a good home. She may need a stricter hand than mine. I've been too soft with her; that's my nature. But, if you pay no heed to the lies and wild tales she tells, and let her know who's master, she'll be obedient enough. She can even tootle a few notes on the flute, but I won't ask extra for that. One thing I do want," he added, "is that jacket she wears. I loaned it to her and must have it back."

Considering that his wife had been plaguing him to buy a bondmaid, the merchant gladly paid out the low price Hong demanded. Before dawn the next day, they went to Voyaging Moon's chamber. Hong had forewarned the merchant that the girl was so devoted to him that she would resist every effort to take her away;

therefore, the innkeeper provided some lengths of rope at no added charge.

Voyaging Moon was already awake and dressed when the two burst in. Though taken unawares, she kicked and bit and fought with all her strength. But they overpowered her. Hong tore away the jacket, where she had hidden her money. Voyaging Moon found herself bound and gagged, hauled down to the stable, and thrown into the merchant's carriage along with her flute. Captive, robbed of her earnings, she was borne southward, far from the River Lo where she had planned to search.

For all that, she kept a brave heart. Her determination only strengthened. Therefore, during the days that followed, instead of raging and struggling, she cleverly made a show of docility. The merchant felt confident enough to remove her gag. She told him she was glad to be free of Hong—which was quite true. She gathered that the merchant lived in Chai-sang, the capital of the northern province. She resolved to escape before they reached that city.

During the journey, the merchant lodged Voyaging Moon in stables of roadside inns where they halted at each day's end. Before retiring, he made sure the girl was securely tied for the night. One evening, as he was about to leave the stable for his chamber, Voyaging Moon called him back.

"Now that we're far from Master Hong," she said, "I can tell you this. He cheated you. You brought my flute along, didn't you? Yes, well, what he didn't tell you is that it's a remarkable instrument. When played, you'd be amazed at what it does."

Voyaging Moon would explain no further. The merchant, his curiosity roused, took the flute from the carriage. He examined it, finding nothing extraordinary. Voyaging Moon urged him to blow into it. When he did so, however, he produced nothing but squeaks and whistles.

"Let me show you how," Voyaging Moon said. "Untie my hands so I can hold it properly."

The merchant did as she asked, then sat down in a corner of the stable and watched her closely. Hoping and praying her plan would succeed, Voyaging Moon put the flute to her lips. Hardly breathing, she played the softest, gentlest melody. The flute whispered and murmured as if its spirit answered her wishes.

"Remarkable, indeed," the merchant said in a hushed voice. "Why, it seems the same lullaby my mother sang to me when I was an infant. I've heard nothing like it these many years." He brushed away a tear. "Keep on, keep on, I beg you."

The merchant closed his eyes and blissfully smiled. Within moments, his head nodded and dropped to his breast. Blowing out his lips, toying with his fingers, he soon snored and gurgled happily away.

Voyaging Moon tucked the flute into her shirt. "You don't mind if I borrow your horse, do you?" Receiving no contrary answer, she quickly unhitched the animal. Before climbing astride, she patted the slumbering merchant on the head.

"Sweet dreams," said Voyaging Moon.

Though it was not the largest of towns, Nang-pei boasted the finest theater in the province. Traveling companies of tumblers, jugglers, singers, and dancers went out of their way to stop there. The folk of Nang-pei always welcomed these performers. That autumn, however, the one who drew their warmest applause, their loudest cheers, and their delighted devotion was a girl who charmed them with the music of her flute. She could not set foot in the streets without admirers crowding around her. Young swains, love-smitten, sent her jewels, necklaces, and bracelets, along with flowers and heartrending notes begging her hand in marriage. But the girl graciously declined all such offerings. Rumor had it that she was richer than any of her would-be suitors.

When not performing, she kept mainly to herself in chambers above the theater. Unlike her colleagues, she did not bedeck herself in bright robes, fanciful headdresses, and other garish finery. On stage, she wore a coarse cotton shirt and trousers. This peasant simplicity endeared her all the more to her devoted audiences. Also, she had the strange custom, each night, of climbing to the rooftop and, alone, playing melodies still more beautiful than those she played in public. This odd habit only enraptured her listeners.

Because of a certain air of mystery about her, and because she was never seen in public eating rooms, tea-houses, or taverns, the townsfolk affectionately called her Lady Shadow Behind a Screen.

She was, in fact, Voyaging Moon. All this had come about after she had galloped off leaving the merchant sleeping soundly. Heading northward again, she happened to fall in with a troupe of dancers and jugglers on their way to Nang-pei. Seeing that she carried a flute, they persuaded her to play and were so enchanted they urged her to join them. At first, she refused. She intended to continue to the River Lo. This, she was told, would be extremely dangerous, if not altogether impossible.

As one of the jugglers explained, a powerful warlord was ravaging the countryside, defeating every army sent against him. He already held sway in many districts. His troops showed no regard or mercy for innocent folk caught between the lines of these fierce battles. It was said he had once been a bandit. Now, he called himself the Yellow Scarf King.

Voyaging Moon remembered all too well the brutality of Natha. Impatient though she was to continue northward, she could not risk falling into his clutches again. For the moment, she reluctantly had to admit, the sensible course was to heed the troupe's warning and follow their advice. And so she went with them to Nang-pei.

There, the theater director was as openhanded as

Hong had been tightfisted. Hearing her play, he promised a handsome share of his profits and was better than his word. Her fame and fortune grew. Voyaging Moon—or, Lady Shadow Behind a Screen—was able to commission the best craftsmen to build her a carriage, so spacious and well-appointed that she could live in it as comfortably as in a chamber. She bought six fine horses and began to lay in a store of provisions, hoping the fighting would subside and she might leave Nang-pei before winter.

Meantime, she played her flute alone each night on the rooftop, her thoughts ever turning to Jen. Had he continued to T'ien-kuo? Had he found Mafoo or Moxa? Was he still alive? Of that, she never permitted herself to doubt.

"If he has gone," she told herself, "he will come back. If he is searching for me, he will find me."

* * * * *

Are Voyaging Moon's hopes justified? While she, by accident, has gained fame and fortune, what has become of her beloved Jen? To find out, leave Voyaging Moon in Nang-pei and read the next chapter.

16

· What is fished out of the river ·
· What is told to Jen ·
· What is to be decided ·

HE LAY ON A PILE OF STRAW. Sunlight streamed through a narrow doorway. A gray-haired woman bent over him. A man's weathered face peered down.

"Where are they?" Jen tried to sit up. He was in the corner of a hut. Nets hung from the low ceiling. His head pounded as if the storm filled it. He could scarcely bring his eyes to focus. "Where—?"

"Safe." The woman smiled. "I'll fetch them."

"Fished out along with you," the man added. "Wet, but undamaged."

Jen gave a joyous cry. His last memory was the face of Voyaging Moon, her hands outstretched, struggling in the tide. The storm was over. They had lived through it.

The woman was back. She held out a bundle. "See. We kept your goods carefully."

"No!" Jen burst out. "Not these! My friends—"

"No others," the fisherman said. "You were alone. More than half-drowned, and with a broken head, too."

"They must be nearby. Washed ashore with me." The hut spun before Jen's eyes. "We were all together, crossing the river yesterday. The boat foundered—"

The fisherman and his wife exchanged glances. The woman spoke gently. "The storm passed a week and more ago. You've lain here since then. We feared you'd never come back to your senses. Rest. Take food now."

"A week?" Jen stared around wildly. "Where is this? We crossed above Chen-yeh—"

"Chen-yeh?" The fisherman raised his eyebrows. "You're leagues from there. The river carried you far downstream. Be glad you're alive."

"My friends are alive, too. They must be."

The fisherman was about to speak. His wife gestured to him. "Let him believe so, if that will help him," she murmured.

"I'll find them." Jen lurched to his feet. His legs buckled under him. He fell back onto the straw. He had heard the woman's words. "Yes, they are alive," he said. "I believe it. I know it." He wondered if he was telling himself the truth.

Two days passed before Jen could stand unaided, and another day before he could walk. Even then, he was light-headed, his steps uncertain. The fisherman and his wife urged him to wait until he had his full strength again.

"Young man," the fisherman said, "who you are and what your business may be is no affair of ours. You don't strike me as a murderer or a thief. If you've run afoul of the law in some way—there's plenty like you in the kingdom, for His Majesty's officials deal out more injustice than otherwise. No matter, you stay with us, if you want, as long as you want."

Only then did Jen realize the couple had never asked his name, but tended him nonetheless. "I've not run afoul of any laws," he said. "I'm seeking to learn better ones."

"So I hope you do," the fisherman said, questioning him no further.

When Jen thanked the couple, telling them he must seek his friends, the fisherman and his wife shared what food they could spare to help him on his journey. Taking grateful leave of them, Jen set out following the river upstream. He thought to find the ferryman's hut. If the man had lived out the storm, he might know something of Voyaging Moon, Mafoo, Moxa, and Master Shu.

Meantime, trudging along the Lo, he questioned all

who lived near the riverbank. They treated him kindly, gave food when his supply ran out, and let him sleep under their roofs at night. But they could tell him nothing.

Despite that, his hope did not lessen. For there were times, when he lay restless and wakeful, half in a dream, it seemed that the voice of Voyaging Moon called out to him. He even imagined hearing the shimmering notes of the flute. This, he knew, was only a memory that both saddened and lifted his heart.

He came in sight of Chen-yeh by week's end. He did not skirt the town as he had planned. Rather, he found his steps drawn to crooked streets of dwellings and shops, hawkers of rags, of sweetmeats, of fighting crickets. A seller of birds, with bamboo cages stacked high beside him, cried his wares.

"Buy! Buy! All sweet singers. Sweet as the flute girl's melodies."

Jen stopped short. He had heard correctly, his ears had not deceived him. He ran to the bird seller. "What flute girl? What melodies?"

The man blinked at him. "You're a stranger in Chen-yeh, that's easy to guess. Flute girl? We've all heard and won't forget her. She used to play at the Golden Grasshopper, the inn of Master Hong."

"Where?" Jen's heart raced. The bird seller pointed up the street.

"A stranger for sure, if you don't know the Golden Grasshopper. There, to the right, past Phoenix Lane."

Jen set off running where the bird seller had indicated. In the courtyard of the inn, a man with the look of the proprietor was berating a servant maid for laziness. Jen strode up to him.

"A girl who played the flute. She was here. I was told so. Where is she now?"

"What's that to you?" Hong looked him up and down. "Get out. I don't lodge beggars."

Jen took Hong by the shirt collar. "What it is to me," he said between his teeth, "is this: I asked you a question. I'll have an answer."

Hong choked, his eyes bulged as he tried to shake free of Jen's grip. "Madman! Hands off! I'll call the law on you. All right, let go," he gasped. "She's gone. Long gone."

Jen set the innkeeper down hard on his heels. Puffing and scowling, Hong rubbed his neck. "Lunatic devil," he muttered. He cocked an eye at Jen. "Yes. She was here and she left. Good riddance to her."

"Her name?"

"How should I know? She worked in my kitchen. I don't concern myself with scullery maids. Peasant girl, from the look of her," he quickly added, backing away as Jen stepped closer. "Yes, she played the flute a few times. I paid her well for it, the ungrateful wench."

"Then?"

"Gone, I told you," Hong flung at him. "Who the devil are you? What do you care? Aha—your little sweetheart, eh?" A look of sly malice crept into the innkeeper's eyes. "So that's your interest, is it? Well, my handsome fellow, I can tell you a little something else about her. Oh, she's gone, yes," Hong added. He grinned at Jen. "But not alone—if you take my meaning."

"What are you saying?" Jen demanded. "Who was with her?"

"Not a wretch like you," Hong said. "I'm a tender-hearted man, I wanted to spare your feelings. But why should I? She had eyes for one of my guests, with more in his purse than you have. The pair of them ran off together. And there you have it. The way of the world."

Hong gave Jen a scornful glance, turned on his heel, and hurried away, leaving Jen staring after him.

By the time Jen found words, Hong had disappeared. Jen stood, head reeling as if he had been struck in the face. He started after the innkeeper. As he did, one of the grooms loitering close by beckoned to him. Still trying to swallow what Hong had said, Jen stepped toward the man.

"Too bad you didn't choke that son of a turtle," the groom said under his breath. "I saw it all. Listen to me, lad. Hong's a liar as well as a cheat. The girl was here a while, true. How did she leave? I was in an empty stall that night. There was scuffling that woke me up. I saw Hong and one of his lodgers, the girl bound and gagged between them. A merchant of some sort, I don't know his name. They packed her into his carriage, and he drove off as fast as he could. Later, I heard the merchant went south, to Chai-sang. That's all I can tell, for what good it may do you."

Jen blurted his thanks and ran from the courtyard. Voyaging Moon lived. Nothing else mattered. He would search and find her at all cost.

He halted. To break off his journey now, having come so far? Chai-sang lay in the opposite direction. What if he could not find her? How long would he dare to delay? What of Mafoo and Moxa? Too many questions. He could not gather his wits to think clearly. Then he remembered Master Hu's long lecturing on royal virtues. The old sage would have advised him to press on to T'ien-kuo. To do otherwise—Jen could see Master Hu's frown of disapproval. A prince worthy of his title would not even consider forsaking his duty.

"Yes, that is true," Jen admitted. "Then, as it is true, I am a prince no longer."

He turned south, toward Chai-sang.

* * * * *

An ignoble, unworthy decision. Yet, how can we not forgive a loving heart? Before judging Jen too harshly, continue to the next chapter.

17

*· Jen turns his back on one journey
and his face toward another ·
· Fragrance of Orchid and her grandmother ·*

THERE WAS FIGHTING in the southern districts. As often as local governors ordered out warriors, as often they met with defeat. Some troops deserted, throwing in their lot with a former bandit now arrogantly calling himself the Yellow Scarf King. Peasants whose fields had been trampled, villagers whose dwellings had been ravaged first by one side and then the other, took to the roads and fled northward. They loaded their few possessions into ox carts and barrows, or bore their goods in bundles on their backs.

It was from one of these trains of men and women,

old and young, that Jen heard a name he had forgotten. It came about one evening. Having turned away from T'ien-kuo and set his path for Chai-sang, Jen fell in with a ragged band of folk heading in the opposite direction. Jen himself had been many footsore days on the road when he found them camped for the night in a stubble field, huddled around cook fires. They took him, first, for a straggler from some burned hamlet. When he told them his destination, they took him for a fool.

"Stay clear of Chai-sang," one of the men, a villager, warned. "The Yellow Scarf King's on the march around there."

"No stopping him," put in a rice farmer. "His army gets bigger every day. If he keeps on, he'll be master of the whole country." The farmer shook his head. "You'd think he had a charmed life. I saw him once. He was right in the thick of it, slashing about him with that sword of his. A dozen warriors set on him—he cut them down like grass."

"I heard it told," said the villager, "he rides a dragon instead of a horse. His sword flashes lightning. A magic blade is what they say, big as a tree. Nobody stands against it."

"Dragon? Nonsense." The farmer spat scornfully. "A horse like any other. And he's a man like any other, his real name's Natha. Sword big as a tree? More nonsense. And yet," he added, "there's something strange about that blade. I've seen it slice through a helmet, armor and all. You could almost believe it's magical."

Jen turned away and put down the bowl of food they had given him. For a while, his love of Voyaging Moon had washed away his memory of the cavern. As he squatted by the fire, listening to the farmer talk, it came blazing into his mind.

"It was I," Jen murmured to himself. "I gave him the sword. Because I feared him. Because I feared for my life. I put it in his hands. This is what has come of it."

He tried to reason, telling himself that if he had let Natha kill him the bandit would have taken the sword in any case. Reason did not speak as clearly as shame suddenly did. With that burden, heavier than his bundle of offerings, he set off again the next morning.

"What you can do," one of the men told him, as Jen took his leave, "if you're set on going to Chai-sang, you can try the long way round. Go cross-country to Nang-pei and approach from the east. It's a good bit off your road, but a lot safer."

Jen thought this over. Following that advice would cost him as much as a week. On the other hand, with less risk, he could also manage to find food and shelter in Nang-pei. At last he decided. Weighing possible danger against certain loss of time, he chose to head straight for Chai-sang. He saw no use in turning aside.

And so he did not go to Nang-pei.

During the next couple of days, he grew all the more satisfied that he had chosen well. From others he met on the road, he gathered that Natha and his warriors had fallen back a little, there was a lull in the fighting, and his chances of reaching Chai-sang unhindered were better than before.

This knowledge quickened his steps and brightened his hopes. In Chai-sang, he told himself, he would surely find Voyaging Moon. Together, they would search for Moxa and Mafoo. Even Master Shu might have lived through the storm.

As for T'ien-kuo, he knew he had chosen ignobly. Worse, he did not regret his decision. Someday, he vowed, he would set it right. Reunited with Voyaging Moon, they would cross the Lo and continue their journey. He would not be altogether empty-handed. Three offerings remained. Yuan-ming would grant him an audience. Though Jen had forfeited the right to call himself prince, the words of Master Shu came back to him: Yuan-ming would know him for what he was.

"And yet," he added, "if I am not Jen Shao-yeh, the Young Lord Prince—what am I?"

To this question, he doubted that Master Hu himself could give an answer.

His concerns, in any case, were more immediate: food and a roof. One chilly evening, he stopped at a small farmhouse, having learned that the folk of this district were hospitable to travelers poorer than themselves.

A sturdy, open-faced old woman in cotton skirt and straw sandals greeted him politely. Out of courtesy, she asked nothing of his destination or purposes. Her name, she told him, was Plum Blossom. Jen at first thought she lived here alone. But when his eyes grew accustomed to the dimness of the room, he noticed a low cot. A child was curled on it.

"My granddaughter, Fragrance of Orchid," the woman said as Jen begged pardon for disturbing her sleep. "No, she does not sleep. Nor does she wake. She's lain thus from the day the Yellow Scarves burned our village. Her mother and father were killed. I carried her in my arms to this little property of mine. Here, I thought she would recover. But she neither eats nor drinks, only what I force between her lips. She does not speak, she does not move."

"Is there no way to rouse her?" Jen asked. "Can nothing be done?"

"What have I not done?" replied Plum Blossom. "I've talked to her, sung to her, whispered, pleaded, scolded. I walked miles to find a healer, a herbalist, and brought him here. She is beyond his skill. If she continues unchanged, I am told she will die." Plum Blossom glanced at Jen with fierce determination. "So, I must find some other means."

"Her eyes are open." Jen had stepped quietly to the cot. He bent over the motionless figure, a girl of perhaps ten years. "She sees. She follows the motions of my hand."

"The spirit is lacking," Plum Blossom said. "Without that, can she be called living? Even so, I'll not cease trying to make her live."

"What of toys?" Jen asked. "Her favorite playthings? A doll she loved?"

"Toys? She seldom played with them. Birds were her greatest joy," Plum Blossom said. "She loved to see them fly. She would wave and call to them. Now the birds in these parts are gone, their nests are empty. Fighting and destruction have driven them away."

Jen stood some silent moments watching Fragrance of Orchid. He turned to the old woman. "I have a bird."

Plum Blossom looked at him, puzzled, as Jen undid his bundle. "Not a real bird," he said. "But it can fly."

He took out the kite.

While Plum Blossom, curious, held a lamp for him, he spread the rods and struts on the earthen floor. Working deftly, he put the pieces together. The kite grew to the shape of a bird, its beautifully painted wings wider than Jen's outstretched arms.

He carried the finished kite to Fragrance of Orchid and held it in front of her, moving it back and forth. The girl did not stir. Jen sadly shook his head. He would have turned away, but Plum Blossom snatched his arm.

"Wait! She raises her head."

Indeed, Fragrance of Orchid was struggling to sit up. Her eyes fixed on the kite. She smiled.

Plum Blossom threw her arms around the girl. "Does she live again?"

Jen put down the kite to help the old woman lift the child from her cot. Fragrance of Orchid reached out, murmuring. She bobbed her head happily when Jen brought the plaything to her once more.

All that night, Plum Blossom and Jen stayed at the bedside. Plum Blossom fed the girl, caressed her, and whispered to her. Each time Fragrance of Orchid showed signs of dropping back into her strange sleep, Jen had only to set the kite before her and she would rouse again, all the stronger.

By morning, Fragrance of Orchid was able to stand unaided though unsteady. Beyond a few murmured words, she had not spoken. But her eyes sparkled as Jen led her outside into the farmyard.

There, he flung up the great kite to the freshening breeze. Fragrance of Orchid clapped her hands and laughed with delight to see it soar aloft at the end of its cord. It swooped and swerved, its colors dazzling in the sunlight.

Jen started to haul it back to earth. Fragrance of Orchid shook her head and pointed upward, clearly entreating him to keep it in the air.

"No, I won't fly it anymore," Jen said quietly to her. "You'll do it." He took her hand and curled her fingers around the cord. "Keep this. It is yours."

· · · · ·

A gift meant for Yuan-ming has found its way into the hands of a child. But who could wish Jen to have done otherwise? To learn more about the kite and Fragrance of Orchid, leave Jen for the time being and read the next chapter.

18

· The Tale of the Soaring Kite ·

THE MOMENT FRAGRANCE OF ORCHID felt the tug of the kite as it flew aloft, her strength began returning. Her eyes brightened, and she laughed to see it dip and veer in the breeze.

"My tame bird!" cried Fragrance of Orchid. "See, it will do whatever I ask."

"You are a little bird yourself," replied Grandmother Plum Blossom, beaming to see the girl happy and high-spirited again. "A marvelous gift! What a shame the young man left so quickly. We had no time to thank him enough. Even so, we must always remember him."

"I will," Fragrance of Orchid said. She could, in fact, recall his every feature, for the stranger's face was one of the first things she saw after the kite roused her. "But why did he have a kite with him in the first place?"

"Who can tell?" replied Plum Blossom. "We can only be glad he did. Come now, bring down your new plaything before you tire yourself."

Fragrance of Orchid obeyed, although reluctantly. No sooner did the kite touch ground than her face clouded and her eyes lost their sparkle. Plum Blossom could see her granddaughter's heart grow heavy when, moments before, it had been so light.

That evening, while she did not fall back into her trancelike sleep, Fragrance of Orchid sat motionless and silent, gazing wistfully at the kite.

"If the toy so cheers her," Plum Blossom thought, "then let her play with it as often as she likes."

Next morning, therefore, Plum Blossom did not burden the girl with household tasks, but allowed her to fly the kite to her heart's content.

Each day thereafter, Fragrance of Orchid sprang out of bed at the crack of dawn, ran outdoors, and flung the kite into the breeze. And, each day, her strength and spirits grew better.

Also, the more she played with the kite the more skill she gained in flying it. The slightest movement of her fingers on the string made the bright wings dip and dance, pitch and plunge as if alive.

"Almost a real bird!" Fragrance of Orchid cried. "It flies of itself!"

So, indeed, it seemed. At first, to let it catch the wind, Fragrance of Orchid raced across the farmyard and outlying fields, paying out the line as she sped lightly over the ground. But soon she realized that she need only toss it a little above her head, and the kite would soar immediately skyward.

One day, Fragrance of Orchid went as usual into the fields. Before she could raise the kite, suddenly it leaped from her hands and went circling upward.

The string whipped through her fingers so rapidly it burned them. Fragrance of Orchid nevertheless did not let go. She bent all her strength to hold on to the taut line. She tugged and strained, doing her best to haul the kite earthward, but it climbed ever higher. Though she dug her heels into the ground, the kite soon pulled her along on her tiptoes, sweeping her across the dry grass.

Within moments, the kite flew so high that it went to the full length of its string. Fragrance of Orchid, however, clung to the end of the line. Otherwise, she would have to let the kite fly away; and this she was determined not to do.

"Sail high as you like," Fragrance of Orchid cried. "If you won't come down, I'll come up after you."

Fragrance of Orchid tried to climb up the kite

string. Even as she did, she felt herself lifted from the earth. Her toes no longer touched the ground. Still clutching the string, she skimmed over the field. The kite bore her higher and higher, above the tallest trees in the fringe of woodland.

Hearing her granddaughter's voice, Plum Blossom ran from the farmhouse. In a quick downward glance, Fragrance of Orchid saw the old woman wave her arms, then set off to follow as fast as her legs could carry her.

"Grandmother Plum Blossom will find me once I come down," Fragrance of Orchid told herself. And so she clung bravely to the string even as the kite rose far above hills and forests. Those first moments, as the ground fell away beneath her, she shut her eyes tightly, not daring to look down. As the kite sped along, she ventured to open them again. She found herself above a shoreless ocean of clouds under a bright blue sky stretching farther than she could see. Sunlight poured over her, the wind sang songs in her ears. Instead of being frightened, she laughed with joy as she soared higher than birds had ever flown.

How long, how far the kite carried her, Fragrance of Orchid could not guess. But now the kite began dipping slowly downward. She passed through towers and castles of clouds and saw, just below, the high peaks of mountains. The kite dropped toward the rocky face of the tallest, and the girl braced herself, expecting to be dashed against the crags. The kite, however, lowered her gently into a huge nest of branches, twigs, and leaves.

The line slackened without her weight on it, and the kite glided down to land beside her.

"So," Fragrance of Orchid said, "you've decided to come back, have you? Very well, you flew me here and you can fly me out again."

She held the kite up, as she had often done before. It did not rise again.

"Then," said Fragrance of Orchid, "I'll have to find my own way down."

First, she thought of tying the kite string around one of the jagged rocks and lowering herself on it. She quickly calculated the string was too short to reach anywhere near the ground. Before she could devise some other means, she glimpsed a bird flying rapidly toward her.

As it drew closer, she saw it was an enormous eagle. Its feathers glittered like burnished gold, its eyes flashed like diamonds, and its outspread wings beat so power-fully that wind whistled through the crags.

Fragrance of Orchid forgot her own predicament to marvel at the sight. Never had she seen so magnificent a bird; nor was she frightened in the least when the eagle sped to the nest and landed at her side.

Folding its wings, the eagle turned its eyes on Fra-grance of Orchid, who gazed back in fascination.

"What is this?" the eagle said. "A new chick in my nest?"

Fragrance of Orchid was hardly surprised to hear the eagle speak, for she had always believed that birds could talk. So it seemed only natural, and no stranger than being carried away by a kite.

"I am Niang-niang, she-eagle of Mount Wu-shan," the great bird continued. "And you are the fledgling Fragrance of Orchid."

This surprised the girl more than anything else. "Yes, I am," she said, "but how is it that you know my name?"

"I know many things," replied Niang-niang. "I have observed you often during my flights here and there. What I have not seen for myself, my fellow creatures of the air have told me. I know, for example, you shared your food with the winter birds when they found nothing to eat. I also know that once, in the bird market, you opened the cages. Oh, yes, and were punished for it, too."

Fragrance of Orchid nodded, for all this was true. "Niang-niang," she replied courteously, "as you know so much, do you know one thing more? How shall I climb down from here and find my way home?"

Niang-niang shook her golden head. "Little fledgling, I may not tell you. Nor am I certain you shall do so. Had you let go the kite string and let it fly free instead of clutching it, things would have gone otherwise. Now they are what they are and what they must be."

Fragrance of Orchid had so far kept courage in the face of all that had happened. Hearing these words, however, she felt her heart must break, as now she feared she had lost kindred and home past recovery.

"What is lost may, with hope, be found again," said Niang-niang, as if reading her thoughts. "Were I permitted, I would carry you where you wish. That is forbidden to me. I cannot change the path you follow, though it may or may not lead you back to earth."

"Stay with me," the eagle urged. "The sky is vaster than the earth, as you will see. You, who have so loved and befriended all birds, would you not care to be one of us?"

"How is that possible?" Fragrance of Orchid said. "Even if I wanted, I can't fly."

"You can," said Niang-niang. The eagle then instructed the girl to untie the kite string and take firm hold of the wooden rods and struts that made the frame of the silken wings.

"Now what shall I do?" asked Fragrance of Orchid, having followed Niang-niang's directions.

"Very simple," Niang-niang said. "Climb from the nest. Dive into the air as if into a pool of water."

Fragrance of Orchid hesitated. A glance at the ground so far below made her head spin.

"Do as every fledgling must," Niang-niang said. "If you trust what I tell you, no harm will come to you."

Fragrance of Orchid was fearful despite the eagle's reassurance. Nevertheless, plucking up her courage, she climbed over the rim of the nest, took a deep breath, and resolutely sprang into empty air.

At first, she plummeted downward, gripping the spinning kite as she sped past the crags to the forest floor. Within moments, however, she felt the kite lift and begin to soar into the clouds. Her fear vanished and she laughed with joy as she swooped and circled, sailing on the air tides with Niang-niang flying beside.

"Enough now, little fledgling," the eagle called. "You have begun well. There is much more to learn."

Fragrance of Orchid reluctantly followed the eagle back to the nest, sorry to leave the air and eager to fly again. Niang-niang promised they would venture farther next time. And so Fragrance of Orchid curled up in the nest and slept that night under the soft warmth of the eagle's wing.

Each day thereafter, Niang-niang brought the girl food and cared for her as if Fragrance of Orchid were an eaglet. And, each day, they flew still greater distances. Sometimes they joined flocks of sparrows, swallows, or ravens, who dipped their wings in recognition and called out fondly to the girl, delighted to see her among them in the sky.

"You fly well," Niang-niang said. "Now you must learn to see, farther and clearer than you have ever done before."

"Gladly," said Fragrance of Orchid, "but how shall I do so?"

"Again, very simple," Niang-niang said. "To begin to see, you must first begin to look."

Fragrance of Orchid puzzled over what Niang-niang told her. Nevertheless, during their flights, she tried her best to look carefully at the fields, hills, and woodlands that spread beneath her. Little by little, her vision sharpened. One day, as they swooped through a bank of clouds, Fragrance of Orchid cried out in amazement:

"I see fish swimming in the river! And there, a woman feeding chickens in a farmyard. And there, a town," she called, as they flew onward. "The houses, the streets. I see children racing. Ah, one of them tripped and skinned her knees! And there, a fruit seller giving change to a customer. I can count the coins in his hand." Fragrance of Orchid laughed. "It's not the right change, either. There's the buyer arguing. Now they've settled it."

"Your eyes have grown almost as sharp as mine," said Niang-niang. "Having learned to see, now you must learn to understand."

Girl and eagle continued their flights, farther and farther, sometimes resting on a mountain peak, sometimes flying all night long under moon and stars.

"Are we still in the Kingdom of T'ang?" Fragrance of Orchid said. "Have we left it and crossed into some other kingdom?"

"The first thing to understand," Niang-niang said, "is that there is no Kingdom of T'ang, nor any other realm. Do you see borders? Is one countryside so different from another? Is not a mountain a mountain, a tree a tree, wherever it may be? Kingdoms? They are pitiful inventions of humankind. They mean nothing to us. We see there is only the world itself, nothing more, nothing less."

Fragrance of Orchid saw this, too, with her own eyes. Also, she saw much more. She saw the earth turn, from sunrise to sunset. She saw many mountains, and learned they sprang from the same root. She saw many rivers, and learned they were only arms of the same river; and that the greatest oceans merged with all other oceans.

And so, Fragrance of Orchid, with the great eagle always at her side, lived her days aloft, sleeping in tree-tops or mountain peaks, setting foot on ground only to find food and drink.

Each new sight and each new discovery delighted her. Happy though she was, her thoughts turned ever homeward. She wondered if, during her flights, she might someday catch sight of Grandmother Plum Blossom, and if they would be together again.

"Even my keen eyes cannot see so far ahead," Niang-niang replied.

Nevertheless, Fragrance of Orchid stayed watchful for any sign of Grandmother Plum Blossom.

"If I look hard enough, and see clearly enough," said Fragrance of Orchid, "sooner or later I must find her."

"If that is where your path leads you in the end," replied Niang-niang, "then you surely will."

* * * * *

Leaving Fragrance of Orchid high in the air, we now return to the ground, where we left Jen on his way to Chai-sang. Whether he reaches there or not, and what happens to him in the meanwhile, is told in the following chapter.

19

• Jen holds an umbrella •
• Chen-cho paints a picture •
• An invitation to dinner •

FOR SOME DAYS AFTER LEAVING Grandmother Plum
Blossom and Fragrance of Orchid, Jen pressed on toward Chai-sang. Sometimes he slept in the encamp-
ments of fleeing peasants and villagers, but as often as
not, he bedded down in the underbrush amid the fallen
leaves of autumn. Someone had given him a length of
quilt. Nights, he rolled up in it; days, he wrapped it
around his shoulders and belted it with a rope at his
waist. A raw north wind had risen, nipping at him as
he struck cross-country over fields crackling with
morning frost under heavy purple clouds.

The first snow showers began as he made his way through a narrow valley, past low brown hills and bare trees. Until now, after leaving the roads, he had come upon no other travelers. But here, beside a shallow stream, he stopped short. For all his discomfort, he could not help laughing.

A young man in quilted jacket and felt cap with earflaps jutting like wings squatted on the turf. With one hand, he tried to keep a sheaf of papers from blowing away; with the other, he attempted to put up an umbrella. He was not succeeding at either task.

"Don't stand there gawking and grinning, fool! Lend a hand," the stranger called, just before the umbrella collapsed over his head and he disappeared into the folds.

Jen hurried toward him, helping to keep the papers from flying off and to disentangle its owner from the octopus clutches of the umbrella.

"Excellent. That should do it." Having crawled out, the youth securely raised his portable canopy and settled his cap on his head. "Untrustworthy contraption. It attacks me out of sheer malice. When I paint, I use it to keep the sun out of my eyes, you understand."

"I'd understand better," Jen said, laughing, "if the sun were shining. It pleased you to call me a fool, but I wonder which of us is the greater."

"I meant it only in a friendly sense. Since there are more fools than wise men, I assumed it more likely you were one of the former. But, you're right. No sun, of course not. I should have said snow. Let us now scrutinize and determine if my latest effort is completely ruined."

Chen-cho, as he named himself, took up the scroll he had been working on. Jen saw the beginnings of a landscape painting, done with a few bold strokes and, here and there, splashes of muted earth colors. Unfinished, Jen recognized it was nonetheless beautifully done and complimented the artist on his work.

"You like it? Tell me, then, what shall it be called?" Chen-cho was about Jen's age and stature, with a good-natured face and quick, wry smile. The deep lines at the corners of his eyes may have resulted from squinting far into the distance or peering closely at his handiwork. "Ten Thousand Blotches? The snow drops have melted all over it. But—no, not ruined at all. Better than I could have done on purpose. Now, if your honorable self would favor me by holding this accursed umbrella over my head—"

Jen did as Chen-cho asked. The artist worked quickly, making the wet spots and stains a part of the picture. Jen shook his head in admiration. Chen-cho merely shrugged, declaring that someday he would do a better one. With that, he packed up his materials, balanced the umbrella on his shoulder like a spear, and invited Jen to come with him to the nearby village of Ping-erh.

"You look as if you could stand a good meal," Chen-cho said as they walked along. "I'm staying at a reasonably acceptable inn. That is, the food won't poison you. The landlord will put you up for the night, if you want. He still owes me for the work I did for him."

From this, Jen assumed that Chen-cho had bargained one of his pictures for food and lodging. The artist chuckled when Jen asked him if such was the case.

"No, no, better than that," Chen-cho replied. "I painted his door. Not a picture of it. I mean that I painted it with red lacquer. Also, I wrote out a piece of calligraphy for him, a magical charm: 'Protect this dwelling from dragons.' The fellow's quite happy with it, he's convinced it works. In fact, it does," Chen-cho added, with a wink. "There's not a single dragon anywhere in the neighborhood.

"And you, Honorable Ragbag—your name's Jen, you said?" the painter went on. "What's your occupation? A prosperous merchant in disguise? No. A government official? Hardly. You look seedy enough to be an honest fellow."

Jen laughed. "I have no occupation. No longer. I'm searching for someone. A flute girl. And my friends."

"Search away, good luck to you," Chen-cho said. "I also search. In my case, for landscapes to paint. This one's interesting. Bleak, at first; but, if you look at it the right way, quite marvelous. Someday, I'd like to do the Lotus Bridge in Ch'ang-an, or the Happy Phoenix Gardens near the river. I've heard they're very fine."

"Yes, so they are." Jen's heart turned suddenly heavy at the recollection. "I'd almost forgotten."

"You've been there?" Chen-cho said, impressed. "You've seen them? You'll tell me more of them later. A merry dinner will jog your memory."

Chen-cho rambled on, gossiping, telling tales and jokes. His contagious high spirits lifted Jen's own. The two travelers had become good companions by the time they reached Ping-erh.

At the inn, however, they found no merry dinner, nor cheer of any kind. Villagers filled the little square, scurrying in all directions. Some had grimly begun loading household goods into carts and barrows.

"Closed! Closed!" The landlord waved his arms as Jen and Chen-cho stepped into the eating room. "Out! Be off while you can!"

* * * * *

Jen has struck up a pleasant friendship with the good-natured Chen-cho, but it seems both will have to go without their dinner. Why such alarm? To find out, read the next chapter.

20

* *Pebble and avalanche* *
* *Meeting with an old enemy* *
* *Parting from a new friend* *

"BE OFF?" CRIED CHEN-CHO. "Off nowhere till we have our dinner."

The landlord paid no further attention and went back to tearing his hair and yelling at his servants to pack up all they could carry. Some local men and women had come into the eating room, where they stood talking urgently among themselves. While Chen-cho still protested at missing his dinner, Jen hurried to ask them the cause of such alarm.

"Where have you been all day? Living on the

moon?" retorted a big-framed peasant whose name, Jen learned, was Chang. "My elder brother brought me word this morning. The Yellow Scarf King's riding with his advance guard, so the rest of his army isn't far behind. I'd reckon he'll be here in two day's time at most."

Jen questioned Chang more closely, gathering from his account that Natha meant to take Ping-erh for a winter headquarters.

"I say let him have it," put in one of the villagers. "Our officials didn't waste time scuttling off, so neither will I. That Yellow Scarf devil won't find me here."

"I'm sure he won't, you turtle," one of the peasant women flung at him. "Turn tail, the lot of you. Don't stand up to him. No, don't give that a thought."

"Here, now, he doesn't speak for all of us," Chang said. "I'd stand up to him, if any stand with me."

"Against a natural man, I would," said a farmer. "He's no human being, he's all devil. That's what I've heard. And that sword of his! He got it from the king of devils himself."

"He's a man, no more nor less than you are," Jen broke in. He turned to Chang. "Any to stand with you? I will."

"Hear that?" exclaimed the woman. "This fellow's a stranger, but he puts our own men to shame."

"You're only one," Chang said to Jen. "That's—"

"That's two, counting you," Jen said.

"That's three," put in the woman, "counting me."

"There's enough of you, Mourning Dove, to make three by yourself," a villager called out to her. "Best go back and tend your chickens. What do you know about any of this?"

"I know enough to guard the henhouse door when the fox is on the prowl," said Mourning Dove.

At this, a handful of locals began disputing among themselves. Chen-cho, giving up all hope of a meal, had been eavesdropping on the conversation. He drew Jen aside.

"What are you up to?" he muttered. "You're not a fool, you're an idiot. Natha Yellow Scarf? You don't know who you're dealing with."

"I know," Jen said. "I bought my life from him. I think I might have paid too high a price."

Leaving the artist to puzzle over that, Jen went to the villagers. Mourning Dove and Chang had already persuaded most of those present to stand against Natha.

"The others?" Jen asked. "Will they stay, too?"

"If they believe there's a chance of holding him off," Mourning Dove said.

"It also works the other way round," Jen said. "There's no chance of holding him off if they don't stay. Go into the square. Tell them there's a way they might save the village."

"Is there?" asked Chang.

"There could be," Jen said, "if enough of them help."

"I'll see they do," Mourning Dove declared. She

strode out to the square, Chang and Jen following. They pressed through the crowd. Mourning Dove climbed atop an ox cart and tried to make herself heard above the commotion. At first, the villagers paid little heed, but as the peasant woman's voice rose, more and more paused to listen. Chen-cho had come out to observe, and the painter shook his head in surprised admiration.

"You're the one who put her up to this, but she's doing well on her own." The artist chuckled. "Had I any taste for this kind of thing—which, luckily, I don't—I'd be tempted to lend her a hand."

"You will," Jen said. "I have a thought, and I need you and your brush to put it on paper."

Jen led the painter to the inn. Mourning Dove, Chang, and half a dozen others, who had formed a makeshift council of war, soon hurried back with news: Most of the villagers had chosen to stay. By this time, following Jen's instructions, Chen-cho had sketched out in workable details what had been only vague ideas in Jen's mind.

"I had an old teacher once," Jen said, as the artist tucked his box of brushes and pigments back into his jacket. "He taught me the history of T'ang. I was a slow student, but I remember his tale of the warriors long ago who defended Ch'ang-an against invaders when the city was no more than a village like this. It could help us now. We'll need carpenters, woodcutters, rope-makers."

"You'll have them," said Mourning Dove, examining the sketches and nodding approval. She sent Chang to rally as many artisans as he could find, then turned her attention to matters Jen had not considered.

He listened to her, astonished. Mourning Dove, as she frankly admitted, could neither read nor write. At first glance, she would have been taken as no more than a farm wife who only knew to count eggs. But she had already calculated the strength of the villagers and planned out their positioning, how best they should be divided, and how the outlying forests and streams could be used to their advantage. She had guessed at the number of Natha's advance guard and the path they would most likely follow.

"I know a general," Jen remarked to Chen-cho. "The best of warriors. I doubt that he'd have done better."

"First, you say you know the Yellow Scarf King," replied Chen-cho. "Now, a general. Honorable Ragbag, allow me to ask: Who the devil are you?"

"If I knew for certain," Jen said, "I'd tell you."

Jen sat astride the horse he had asked for. Mourning Dove had given him the best in the village. In the first raw light of dawn, he huddled the quilt around his shoulders. He had asked for a weapon as well, and Chang had found a blade from the abandoned yamen. It would serve. He had put Yuan-ming's sword in Natha's hands. He would have it back again.

The horse whickered and blew white smoke from its nostrils. Chen-cho and a party of villagers stamped their feet and beat their arms against the chill. All day and all night, the artisans of Ping-erh had worked to build wooden frameworks bristling with long, sharpened poles wrapped in oil-soaked straw. Dozens of such barriers had been hidden along the forest fringe, at every pathway leading toward the village. At other gaps, the folk of Ping-erh had hewed down trees, piling trunks and branches into dense barricades.

Mourning Dove, in a heavy jacket, a cloth knotted around her head, had given a last sharp scrutiny to the frames. She stood, hands on hips, beside Jen.

"We've done all as you showed us, young scholar," Mourning Dove said, having decided for herself that such was Jen's occupation. "I'm not rash enough to think we can battle Yellow Scarf's warriors hand to hand."

"No, but you can turn them away," Jen said. "Make Natha see Ping-erh's too much trouble, not worth his effort."

"Oh, we'll show him how troublesome we can be." Mourning Dove grinned, pushed up her sleeves, and went to talk quietly with each one of the grim-faced, restless villagers. Jen strained his ears for the sound of horsemen. A pebble may stop an avalanche, Master Hu once told him. The folk of Ping-erh were small pebbles, but here the avalanche must either halt or crush them. This portion of the forest was the last easy access to the village. Beyond, a line of rugged hills barred the way.

Jen stiffened in the saddle. The notes of a bugle pierced the air. That would be from Chang, at the opposite end of the woodland, where Mourning Dove had expected Natha's first approach. Moments later, Jen heard distant shouting. Black trails of smoke rose above the treetops. Chang and his people had set their barrier ablaze. If the plan worked, each party of villagers, one after the other, would set their own frameworks alight. Each entry would be barred by a wall of fire whenever Natha and his warriors sought to turn and make their way through some other woodland path. They would find gate after flaming gate flung shut against them.

Mourning Dove raised her arm. By now, Jen heard hoofbeats. The warriors would be galloping along the fringe of woods. Now, at Mourning Dove's signal, the villagers brought torches to their barricades. The wrappings, soaked with oil and pitch, burst into flames. Natha and his men were clearly in sight. Jen saw the leading horsemen rein up their mounts. The animals reared, heads tossing, eyes rolling in terror of the fire. The riders kicked vainly at their steeds' flanks; the horses shied away. He glimpsed Natha, his face scowling under his gleaming helmet of lacquered leather. He halted an instant, glaring at the barrier. Then he spat scornfully and signaled his warriors to fall back.

The villagers roared in triumph. Mourning Dove, calling out joyfully, ran toward Jen. He did not wait.

Another moment and Natha would be amid his retreating warriors. Jen galloped from the fringe of trees.

"Natha! Natha Yellow Scarf!"

Natha wheeled and pulled up his mount, staring curiously at the lone horseman bearing down on him. He grinned with amusement, as if observing the progress of some audacious bug, but gave not the faintest sign of recognition as Jen galloped closer.

Gripping his blade, Jen pressed on. With a movement almost leisurely, Natha drew his sword. Jen plunged headlong, only at the last moment wheeling his horse broadside of Natha as he swung the blade with all his might.

Natha's sword flashed quicker than Jen's eyes could follow. There was a grating clash of blade on blade. Jen cried out as the shock numbed his arm. His weapon had been cut in two. He stared at the useless hilt in his hand. Natha raised his sword again.

Jen heard hoofbeats behind him and someone shouting at the top of his voice. A rider drew up beside him: Chen-cho.

"Get back, Ragbag!" The painter snatched at Jen's bridle.

Natha, surprised for an instant, hesitated, then swung up the sword again. Chen-cho's hand darted into his jacket. He snatched out his paint box and flung it straight at Natha's face. The Yellow Scarf King's head jerked back, his sword stroke wavered the fraction of a moment; then he slashed at this makeshift missile, his blade moving so swiftly the wooden container scattered in a blur of splinters.

Chen-cho had by then kicked his own horse and Jen's into a gallop, and they sped for the safety of the woodlands. Without so much as a backward glance at this pair of annoying gnats, Natha turned his steed and cantered to rejoin his departing warriors.

"Ragbag, you are a true simpleton," Chen-cho remarked as they gained the skirt of trees. "I take it you had a score to settle. It must have been a large one, but you're an idiot if you thought you'd take him on by yourself."

"I did, once," Jen said. "And failed. Now, failed again." He flung away the shattered sword. "No matter, I should thank you for saving my life, whatever that may be worth."

"There's enthusiastic gratitude," Chen-cho said. "All right, then: You're welcome."

They rode back to Ping-erh with Mourning Dove and the villagers rejoicing that Natha had turned away to seek a less troublesome target. Jen paid little heed to the festive crowd in the square. He retrieved his bundle while Chen-cho gathered up his papers and umbrella. When he asked where the painter would go next, Chen-cho shrugged.

"I'd have stayed here a while," said the artist. "There were a few more scenes I wanted to do. Your Yellow Scarf friend has more or less put me out of my occupation. That sword of his turned my brushes into matchwood. But, I'll find others."

"You already have." Jen undid the bundle, which had grown small and light by now. Unhesitating, though with a half smile of sadness, he put the sandal-wood box into the painter's hands.

"Here, what's this?" Chen-cho exclaimed. "What's a fellow like you doing with such a thing? Are you also a painter and never let on?"

Jen shook his head. "I had it for another purpose. I think you can make better use of it."

Chen-cho had opened the box to examine the brush, ink stick, and ink stone. "Honorable Ragbag, I can tell you're no artist, or you'd never have parted with this. Wonderful! Look here, have you the least idea what these are?"

By then, Jen had waved a farewell and was gone from the inn, setting off on his way again.

• • • • •

Leaving our hero to continue his search, with one gift fewer than before, we turn our attention to Chen-cho and the sandalwood box. What has the artist seen that so pleases him? To find out, read the next chapter.

21

· *The Tale of the Tiger's Paintbrush* ·

CHEN-CHO THE PAINTER was a good-natured, easy-going sort. He liked his food and drink, though as often as not he did without either. Not because he suffered any lack of customers. He was, in fact, a most excellent artist, and many who saw his pictures wished eagerly to buy them. To Chen-cho, however, parting with one of his landscapes was like having a tooth pulled. Sometimes, of course, he was obliged to do so, when he needed a few strings of cash to keep body and soul together—although usually he spent the money on paper and paint. On the other hand, out of sudden impulse or foolish whim, he was just as likely to give away one of his pictures to a passerby who wistfully admired but could ill afford to purchase it.

For the rest, he was a little absentminded, his head so filled with colors and shapes that he lost track of time, forgot to wash his face or change his clothes. With his collapsing umbrella, his felt cap, his bespattered trousers flapping around his ankles, he became a familiar sight in towns and villages where he stopped in the course of his wanderings. Children tagged after him, fascinated to peer over his shoulder as he worked. Local officials, however, felt more comfortable after he left.

Now, with the sandalwood box on the table in front of him, paying no attention to the rejoicing villagers crowding the inn, Chen-cho gleefully scrutinized his gift. As an artist, he had immediately recognized the excellence of the materials, but he studied them again to confirm his first opinion.

He picked up the stick of black ink and rolled it around in his fingers. He sniffed at it, even tasted it, and licked his lips as if it were some delicious morsel.

"Marvelous!" Chen-cho said to himself. "Perfect! No question, this ink's made from the ashes of pine trees on the south slope of Mount Lu, the very best."

Next, he turned his attention to the ink stone, with its shallow little basin for water at one end and its flat surface for grinding the solid ink at the other. The stone was fine-grained, flawless; and, in color, an unusual reddish gray. Chen-cho rubbed his thumb over it lovingly and shook his head in amazement.

"Here's a treasure in itself! I've heard of stones like this. They come only from one place: a grotto in Mount Wu-shan. I never believed they were more than legend. Yet, I have one right in my hand."

Chuckling over his good fortune, blessing the stranger he had fondly nicknamed Honorable Ragbag, the painter picked up the last object in the box: a paintbrush with a long bamboo handle.

"This is odd." Chen-cho squinted at the brush hairs, tested them on the palm of his hand and the tip of his nose. "Soft? Firm? Both at once? What's it made of? Not rabbit fur, not wolf hair, not mouse whiskers."

The painter could not restrain himself another moment. He called the landlord for a cup of water, poured a little into the basin of the ink stone, then carefully rubbed the tip of the ink stick against the grinding surface. No matter how much he rubbed, the stick showed no trace of wear.

"At this rate," he said to himself, "it will last forever. One stick, and ink enough for the rest of my life. There's frugality for you!"

He pulled out a sheet of paper. Moistening the brush, rolling the tip in the ink he had ground, he made a couple of trial strokes. As he did, a thrill began at the tip of his toes, raced to his arm, his hand, his fingers. The sensation turned him giddy. He glanced at the paper. His jaw dropped. The brush strokes were not black. They were bright vermilion.

"I'd have sworn that ink was black," Chen-cho murmured. "Was I mistaken? Yes, no doubt. The light's dim here."

He made a few more brush strokes. They were no longer vermilion, but jade green. Chen-cho put down the brush and rubbed his chin.

"What's happening here? That ink stick's black as night, through and through. What's doing it? The stone? The brush? No matter, let's have another go."

Chen-cho daubed at the paper, which was soon covered with streaks of bright orange, red, and blue. Anyone else might have grown alarmed or frightened at such an uncanny happening. But Chen-cho enjoyed surprises, mysteries, and extraordinary events. And so he laughed with delight to find himself owner of these remarkable materials.

"Well, old fellow," he said to himself, "you've come onto something you never expected and probably better than you deserve. Let's try something else. Those are marvelous colors, but what if I wanted a sort of lilac purple-green with a reddish cast?"

No sooner did Chen-cho imagine such a hue than it flowed from his brush. He quickly discovered that he need only envision whatever shade he wanted, and there it was, from brush to paper.

"That's what I call convenient and efficient," exclaimed the joyous Chen-cho. "No more paint pots and a dozen different pigments. Here's everything all at once."

With that, he clapped his felt hat firmly on his head, seized a handful of papers, packed up the box, and hurried out of the inn. He ran all the way to the stream where he had first met Ragbag. There he settled himself, ignoring the weather, forgetting to put up his umbrella, and worked away happily, letting the brush go as it wished, hardly glancing at what he was doing.

It was dusk and the light had faded before he could make himself leave off. But the picture was finished, better than anything he had ever painted. Chen-cho laughed and slapped his leg. "Old boy," he told himself, "keep on like this and you might even do something worthwhile."

He went back to his room at the inn. Excited by his wonderful new possessions, he forgot to eat his dinner. He barely slept that night, eager to start another picture.

Next morning and for several days thereafter, Chen-cho went into the countryside looking for scenes to paint. Each landscape that took shape under his hand delighted him more than the one before.

It snowed heavily on a certain morning. Chen-cho usually paid no mind to bad weather. That day, the wind blew so sharply and the snow piled up so deeply that he decided to stay in his room. Nevertheless, his fingers itched to take up the brush. Ordinarily, he painted outdoors, according to whatever vista caught his eye. This time, he thought to do something else.

"Why not make up my own landscape? I'll paint whatever pops into my head and strikes my fancy."

Taking one of his largest sheets of paper, he set about painting hills and valleys, forests and streams, adding glens and lakes wherever it pleased him. He painted rolling meadows he had never seen; and bright banks of flowers he invented as he went along; and clouds of fantastic shapes, all drenched in sunlight, with a couple of rainbows added for good measure.

"What this may be, I've no idea," Chen-cho said when he finished. He blinked happily at the picture. "All I know is: I've astonished myself. That's something that never happened before."

Chen-cho could not take his eyes from his handiwork. He peered at it from every angle, first from a distance, then so close he bumped his nose.

"If I didn't know better," he said, "I'd swear I could smell those flowers. In fact, if I hadn't painted them, I'd believe I could pick one."

He reached out, pretending to pluck a blossom. Next thing he knew, the flower lay in his hand.

Chen-cho gaped at it. He swallowed hard, then grinned and shook his head. "What you've done, you foolish fellow, is go to sleep on your feet. You're having a dream. A marvelous one, but that's all it is."

He pinched himself, rubbed his eyes, soaked his head in a basin of water, paced back and forth. The flower was still where he had set it on the table. Fragrance filled the room.

"I'm wide-awake, no question about it," he finally

admitted. He went again to the picture. "That being the case, let's examine this reasonably. It seems I've put my hand into it. What, for example, if I did—this?"

Chen-cho poked his head into the painted landscape. Indeed, he could look around him at the trees and lakes. The sunshine dazzled and warmed him. He sniffed the fragrant air. He heard the rush of a waterfall somewhere in the distance.

"This is definitely out of the ordinary," Chen-cho murmured, pulling back his head. "Dare I explore a little farther?"

With that, Chen-cho plucked up his courage and stepped all the way into the picture.

He was not certain how he did it. The painting was large, but far from as large as the artist himself. Yet, it must have grown spacious enough to take him in, for there he was, standing knee-deep in the soft grass of a meadow.

"So far so good," he said. "But now I've gone in— how do I get out?"

He answered his own question by easily stepping back into the room. His first apprehension gave way to delight as he discovered that he could walk in and out of the painting as often as he pleased.

With each venture into the landscape, Chen-cho found himself becoming all the more comfortable and confident.

"It's quite amazing, hard to believe," Chen-cho remarked. "But I suppose one can get used to anything, including miracles."

A fascinating thought sprang to mind. What, he wondered, lay beyond the fields and forests and across the valleys?

"I've no idea what's there," he said, "which is the best reason to go and find out."

Chen-cho picked up the sandalwood box and a sheaf of paper in case he found some especially attractive scene. Stepping into the landscape, he set off eagerly along a gentle path that opened at his feet. He soon came to a high-arched bridge over a stream lined with willows. The view so charmed him that he spread his paper and began to paint.

He stopped in the middle of a brush stroke. He had the impression of being watched. When he turned around, he saw that his impression was correct.

Sitting on its haunches, observing him through a pair of orange eyes, was an enormous tiger.

"Hello there, Chen-cho." The tiger padded toward him, stripes rippling at every fluid pace. "My name is Lao-hu. I've been expecting you."

"A pleasure to make your acquaintance," replied Chen-cho. Having by now grown accustomed to marvelous happenings, the arrival of a tiger did not unsettle him too much, especially since the big animal had addressed him in a friendly tone. "However, I can't truthfully say I was expecting you."

"You must have, whether you knew it or not," Lao-hu said. "Otherwise, I wouldn't be here. Ah. I see you've been using my brush."

"Yours?"

"My hairs," Lao-hu said. "From the tip of my tail. I hope it pleases you."

"A remarkable brush," Chen-cho said. "I'd go so far as to call it miraculous. From the tip of your tail? Yes, but in that case, I'm a little puzzled. I hope you don't mind my asking, but if you weren't here until I painted this picture, where were you before I painted it? If you were someplace else, how did you get here? And who plucked out those hairs in the first place?"

"Why concern yourself with details?" Lao-hu yawned enormously. "It's a tedious, boring matter you wouldn't understand to begin with. Let me just say this: You're not the first to paint such a picture, nor the last. Many have done still finer work. And you're certainly not the first to use my brush."

"Tell me, then," Chen-cho said, "can others find their way into my picture? A question of privacy, you understand."

"Of course they can," replied Lao-hu. "It's your painting, but now that you've done it, it's open to anybody who cares to enter. But leave that idle speculation and nit-picking to scholars who enjoy such occupation. You've hardly seen the smallest part of all this"—Lao-hu motioned around him with his long tail—"so let me show you a little, for a start. Climb on my back."

Chen-cho gladly accepted the tiger's invitation. Lao-hu sprang across the stream in one mighty leap. Chen-cho clamped his legs around the tiger's flanks and his arms around Lao-hu's powerful neck. The tiger sped across meadows, through forests, up and down hills. Chen-cho glimpsed garden pavilions, farmhouses, towns and villages, sailboats on rivers, birds in the air, fish leaping in brooks, animals of every kind. Some of what he saw looked vaguely familiar; the rest, altogether strange and fascinating. Lao-hu promised they would continue their explorations and carried the painter back to where they had started.

As easily as he had stepped into the painting, Chen-cho stepped into the room. Lao-hu followed, much to the surprise and delight of the painter, who was reluctant to part from his new companion.

"I can go wherever I please," Lao-hu replied when Chen-cho asked about this, "just as you can."

"Can other people see you?" asked Chen-cho, wondering what his landlord might say if he came into the room and found a tiger.

"Of course they can," Lao-hu said. "I may be a magical tiger, but I'm not an invisible one."

With that, Lao-hu curled up at the foot of Chen-cho's bed. The tired but happy painter flung himself down and went to sleep, thinking that, all in all, it had been an interesting day.

Next morning, when the storm had passed, Chen-cho packed his belongings and set off on his way again. Lao-hu had jumped back into the picture, which the artist had rolled up and carried under his arm. Once away from the village, Chen-cho unrolled the painting. He saw no sign of Lao-hu. Dismayed, the artist anxiously called for him. The tiger appeared an instant later, sprang out, and padded along beside Chen-cho.

From then on, whenever he was sure they were unobserved, Chen-cho summoned Lao-hu, and the two of them wandered together, the fondest companions. When Chen-cho stopped to paint some scene or other, the tiger would stretch out next to him or disappear into the picture on some business of his own. Nevertheless, Chen-cho had only to call his name and Lao-hu would reappear immediately; and Chen-cho always kept the painting beside him when he worked.

As for his other paintings, thanks to the tiger's brush, the marvelous ink stick, and the grinding stone they became better and better, as did Chen-cho's reputation. Whenever he lodged in a town or city, he could expect any number of customers to come clamoring for his pictures. However, as always, he parted with few. Nor would he even consider selling his marvelous landscape, no matter what price was offered. So, more often than not, would-be purchasers left disappointed at being refused.

Only once did Chen-cho have a disagreeable encounter. In one town, a merchant came to inspect Chen-cho's paintings, but as soon as he saw them, he shook his head in distaste.

"What dreadful daubs are these?" he exclaimed. "Not one suitable to put in my house! And this"—he pointed at the landscape, where Lao-hu had prudently hidden himself out of sight—"worst of all! An ugly, blotchy, ill-conceived scrawl! I've had nightmares prettier than this."

Chen-cho, glad to see the merchant stamp off, flung a few tart words after him. He was, nonetheless, puzzled. He called Lao-hu, who popped out instantly.

"Easily understood," Lao-hu said, when Chen-cho told him the merchant's opinion. "As a painter, you should know this better than anyone. We see with eyes in our head, but see clearer with eyes of the heart. Some see beauty, some see ugliness. In both cases, what they see is a reflection of their own nature."

"Even so," replied Chen-cho, "a painting's a painting. Colors and shapes don't change, no matter who looks at them."

"True enough," said Lao-hu. "Very well, then, let me put it this way: You can't please everybody."

"That, I suppose," Chen-cho said, "is a blessing."

* * * * *

While Chen-cho happily paints away with Lao-hu at his side, Jen is arriving at Chai-sang. To learn what he finds there, accompany him into the next chapter.

22

THERE WERE SEVERAL THINGS Jen did not know. For one, that word had spread throughout the northern province. Following Ping-erh's example, other villages stood against Natha Yellow Scarf like so many gnats and mosquitoes that he wasted no more time and effort swatting them. He turned south again, his eye on greater prizes. Jen had failed to settle accounts with his old enemy but otherwise had succeeded better than he realized.

Another thing he did not know was how, in a practical way, to find Voyaging Moon. Late one afternoon, he at last trudged into Chai-sang. He might as well have stumbled into an anthill. The streets of the provincial capital swarmed with carriages, sedan chairs, carts, barrows, and jostling passersby. It was all he could do to break free of the crowd and find a quiet spot where he could make plans, of which he had none.

Of immediate concern was still another thing he did not know: how to stay alive. He had eaten up his small store of provisions two days before. A wet snow had begun, the heavy sky threatened more, a rising wind was sharp enough to bite through the quilt around his shoulders. Following his first thought, he entered the nearest inn. No sooner did the innkeeper catch sight of this clearly unprosperous new arrival than he berated him for dripping on the clean floor. He threatened to call the watchmen if the wretch did not take himself off instantly. Jen tried to explain that he wished to work in exchange for food. The innkeeper would hear none of that. He hustled Jen into the street and promised him a number of disagreeable things if he ever again set foot inside his establishment.

Jen tried several other inns and eating houses with the same result. By this time, he could barely keep his thoughts straight. Master Hu had firmly lectured him on the virtues of honesty, but the notion floated into Jen's head that a little robbery might be unvirtuous but appropriate, and he wished he had paid more attention to Moxa.

So far, his belly had been clamoring wildly for food. Now it spoke to him calmly and reasonably.

"What could be simpler?" it said. "You have the answer in your bundle."

"The bowl?" Jen said.

"Of course," his belly replied. "Master Wu chose it as a suitable gift. Therefore, it must have value. What has value can be sold."

"The last of my offerings?" Jen protested. "I can't. Then I'd be truly empty-handed."

"Come now," said his belly, "be reasonable. When you find Voyaging Moon, as you surely will, she'll no doubt have the flute. So, you'll offer that to Yuan-ming. Assuming you reach T'ien-kuo in the first place. If you don't, then what difference will it make? Therefore, you'd be foolish to hold on to something worth a few strings of cash. More, for all you know."

Jen hesitated. His belly went on in a wheedling vein, suggesting tasty dishes and a warm bed. Jen began to suspect that his belly was very clever and subtle, with its own purposes, and not to be trusted. By now, his head was going around in circles and his knees had turned unreliable. He stumbled out of the crowd and sat down with his back against a wall.

He unwrapped the bowl and stared at it. If he chose to sell it, as his belly recommended, where could he do so? He pondered this, eyes half-closed. A voice shouted in his ear. Jen blinked up at a furious face attached to a rag-covered body.

"My corner!" the face shouted. "Get on with you. Find your own place to beg."

The man shook a heavy stick and seemed perfectly willing to crack Jen's skull with it. Instead of offering explanation or apology, Jen thought it wiser to follow the man's suggestion. He clambered up and set off down the street. Along the way, he stopped a passerby.

The man eyed the bowl in Jen's hand. "Be off! If I gave to every impudent beggar, I'd soon be one myself."

"No, no," Jen said, "to sell this—who'd buy it? Where would I go?"

"Do you take me for a pawnbroker? Well, then, go to Green Sparrow Street." The man waved impatiently and doled out directions as grudgingly as if he were handing over coins.

Jen set off accordingly. Either he had been misinformed or had misunderstood, for he found himself in a maze of alleyways. His belly continued to mutter complaints. Also, his teeth began chattering; he felt hot and cold at the same time. He picked his way through heaps of litter. He no longer remembered exactly where he had been directed. Just ahead, he caught sight of a bent figure hobbling along, leaning on a staff. Jen gave a joyful cry and ran to him.

"Master Shu!"

The old man turned. "Shu? Honorable young sir, you mistake yourself."

Jen rubbed his eyes. The man was as ragged and

grimy as Master Shu had ever been. But, indeed, he was not the old poet.

"Shu?" The aged beggar shook his head. "Not I. Chu. You seek a Master Shu but find a Master Chu. And you? Whoever you may be, I am happy to make your acquaintance. It is always a pleasure to meet a colleague.

"New to the profession, as well, if you've come to this neighborhood looking for alms." Master Chu peered into Jen's bowl. "Empty. Empty as your belly, I might guess."

"Not looking for alms," Jen said. "I want to sell this bowl. Where can I—"

"Sell your bowl?" Master Chu broke in. "Young man, a beggar without a bowl is no proper beggar at all. Why, it's your stock in trade, your trusty friend, your faithful servant. Beg well and you'll fill it with food, or a coin or two. In the course of time, what it brings you will be worth more than the little cash you'd get for it."

"Master Chu, I'm not here to beg," Jen said. "I was told that a young woman has been taken to Chai-sang. I must find her."

"Ah? That's a different matter. But, most assuredly, you will not find her. Not in your present state. You look hardly able to find your nose in the dark. Have you eaten? No? Come along, then."

Too confused and shaky to ask questions, Jen allowed Master Chu to lead him to something resembling a small shed or a large dog kennel patched together from matting and bamboo poles. Helping him inside, Master Chu rummaged through a pile of rags and torn quilts.

"I was not expecting to be honored by a guest for dinner." Master Chu unearthed a broken millet cake. He handed it to Jen. "Humblest apologies. My larder has not been overflowing these days. Eat, eat," he insisted, when Jen refused what certainly was the last of the old man's store. "By no means enough for two, but perhaps enough for one."

By this time, Jen's belly had surrendered to the assault of chills and fever. Master Chu eyed him with concern. He piled the quilts around Jen and obliged him to stretch out. "You need more than I have here," Master Chu said. "Never fear. I shall set that right."

He took the bowl from Jen's hand. "Empty, at the moment. But the usefulness of the bowl lies in its emptiness; it must be empty before it can be filled."

"Someone else said that—" Jen stared at him. "Is that you, Master Shu? Don't you know me?"

The beggar shook his head. "It is your fever speaking."

Yet, as Jen watched, for an instant the beggar's features blurred into those of the old poet. Or was it the face of Master Fu? Master Wu? All at the same time? Jen's head fell back on the pile of rags. The faces whirled before his eyes, then he saw none.

Master Chu was gone when Jen opened his eyes

again. He groped for the bowl. It, too, was gone. He cried out in dismay. He heard someone chuckle as he tried to sit up.

"Did you think I had stolen it? No, as a beggar I observe a rule of meticulous honesty." Master Chu bent over him and held out the bowl.

"As I told you," the old man said, "it must be empty before it can be filled. As it is now. Thanks to leftovers from an eating house, enough for both of us. If I have done you a service, you have done one for me.

"Unlike most of my colleagues in Chai-sang," he added, as he continued feeding Jen from the bowl, "I am not a resident beggar, but a wandering member of the profession. As for my bowl, you may well ask: Where is it? Broken, alas. Some while ago, I made a regrettable mistake in judgment. I begged alms from the one who calls himself Yellow Scarf King. As I held out my bowl to him, he struck it from my hands and smashed it under his heel. For which I was grateful, since he might have done likewise to my head. Since then, I have not been able to replace it. My takings, in consequence, have suffered—I have eaten only what my bare hands could carry. Therefore, I am glad for the use of your bowl as you, I hope, are pleased with its contents."

"Natha," Jen murmured. "Yes, Master Chu, I know his ways. He takes from prince and beggar alike."

His words went unnoticed as Master Chu kept filling Jen's mouth with food. Or, if the old man did reply, Jen did not hear, having drifted back into fevered sleep.

For several days he lay half in stupor. And each day, Master Chu went out with the bowl and came back with it refilled, feeding Jen and himself from it. When Master Chu finally allowed him to sit up, Jen spoke more of Voyaging Moon and his search.

The old man shook his head. "A needle in a haystack, I fear. Chai-sang has many merchants and many young women. A flute girl? That would narrow it down a little. Difficult, nevertheless. Let me see what I can do."

"One thing more," Jen said. He had made his decision some days before, but now he put the bowl in the hands of Master Chu. "Keep this. For the sake of your kindness and your own need. If I find the one I seek, I'll have no use for it. If I do not find her, then it will make no difference to me."

Master Chu's eyes brightened. The old beggar was as delighted as if Jen had given him a dozen taels of gold, his pleasure so great that Jen felt no regret at parting from this last of his offerings. On the contrary, he felt free and lightened of the burden he had carried since leaving Ch'ang-an so long ago.

As for Master Chu, while Jen regained his strength, the old man set his plan in motion.

"I have spoken with all my colleagues," Master Chu later told him. "They know more of the goings and comings here than anyone in Chai-sang. So far, they have told me nothing of a flute girl, but they will keep eyes and ears open. They will know whom to ask and where to look. If she is here, they will find her."

Jen's hope rose. Days passed, however, with no success. Despite the efforts of the Chai-sang beggars, it was Jen himself who had word of Voyaging Moon.

It came about by accident. In addition to help from the beggars, Jen roamed the streets every day, too restless to sit and wait in Master Chu's lean-to. He hoped he might hear the sound of the flute, or perhaps be lucky enough to glimpse her at a window or passing in a carriage.

Crossing the central square one morning, he found himself jostled into a band of jugglers. Overhearing their grumbling, he gathered they had received cold welcome and were leaving the city.

"Had the flute girl been with us," one said, "it would have gone better. There was none like Voyaging Moon to fill the theater, and all our pockets."

"The name you spoke—" Jen seized the juggler's arm. The performer stared as if Jen were a maniac. "You said 'Voyaging Moon'—"

"What if I did?" The juggler tried to step aside. Jen held him fast. As he hastily poured out his account of being separated from her, the man's face softened. "Your sweetheart, eh? You're a lucky lad, then. Yes, your girl's in Nang-pei, when last I saw her, and making a fine fortune for herself."

Jen took hardly an instant to thank the juggler. He ran from one street to the next looking for Master Chu, eager to tell the news and bid him fond farewell. Jen cursed himself for not going to Nang-pei in the first place. He resolved not to lose another instant in Chai-sang. He saw nothing of the old beggar. He ran to the lean-to. It was empty. He started back toward the square. Before he reached it, he came upon one of Master Chu's colleagues, hobbling along with a crutch under his arm.

"Where's Master Chu?" Jen demanded. "I must find him quickly. There's news. Have you seen him?"

"Yes." The man's face fell. "Yes, I was there. I saw everything."

"Saw what?" Jen burst out. "What are you telling me?"

"In custody." The beggar grimaced. "He's been arrested. A grave offense."

*   *   *   *   *

Generous, kindhearted Master Chu arrested? How can this be? What crime could he possibly have committed? Jen will find this out in the next chapter.

23

"BAD ENOUGH TO COST HIM HIS HEAD," the beggar added. "Illegal possession of royal property: a valuable bowl. He stole it, they say. Who'd have thought it of old Chu?"

Jen had heard enough. He turned and raced back to the square. He was breathless by the time he reached the Hall of Sublime Justice. Guards blocked his way at the portals. He blurted that he had important information in the matter of one Master Chu, that he must speak to the officials in charge.

"Witness?" a guard said. "Not that one's needed. Go in, then, for whatever it is you have to testify."

Jen flung himself past the guards and into the Chamber of Truthful Testimonies, fearing he might be too late or that Master Chu had been taken elsewhere. He cried out in relief. The hearing was still in progress. Master Chu, with two burly attendants flanking him, was on his knees before the magistrate's heavily carved desk.

Heads turned as Jen pushed through clerks and court officers. At the sight of him, Master Chu's face wrinkled in dismay and his lips tried to shape a silent warning.

"Never fear," Jen murmured. He halted beside the old beggar and faced the official he took to be the prosecutor, firmly declaring, "The accusation is false. I swear to that. There is injustice—"

"Hold your tongue." The official looked Jen up and down coldly. "You have just come into this honorable court. What do you know of the accusation to call it false? Justice has not been delivered. Therefore, how dare you call it unjust?"

"An accusation of theft—" Jen began.

"A charge I myself laid against this criminal," the prosecutor snapped. "I passed him in the street not two hours ago. I observed the bowl he held out. With a trained eye for such rare objects of art, I recognized it as valuable. Too valuable to be in a beggar's hands. When I examined it, I saw the dragon emblem on the bottom. Only royal property bears that mark. Thus the correct conclusion is that it is stolen. What possible testimony can you add?"

"I can add that he didn't steal it—"

"Let him speak, first, in his own defense," broke in the official. "Why does he refuse, as the record shows?"

At a sign from the prosecutor, the court scribe read aloud from a page of notes:

"Questioned as to possession of stolen object, accused states he was given it by a friend. Asked to name that individual, he stated that he refused to do so."

The prosecutor shrugged. "The reason is obvious. He refuses to say who gave it to him because he himself stole it. A pitiful attempt to trick the court. The accusation stands. The case is clear."

"It is, indeed. I am quite satisfied," said the magistrate. Until now, he had been bent over the bowl, studying it closely. He set it down in front of him and raised his head. "There is no possibility that a beggar has come by this honestly."

Jen stifled a gasp. He found himself looking into a heavy-jowled, toadlike face. Suddenly the memory flashed into his mind—the official who had ordered him beaten, who had arrogantly declared his rank and destination: Official of the First Rank, Chief Magistrate of Chai-sang, Honorable Fat-choy.

For his part, Fat-choy gave no sign of recognition. He yawned, tapped his fan, and gestured impatiently. "What further testimony? You come as witness?

To this thief's good character? One villain to praise another?"

Fat-choy glanced around. The court officials giggled dutifully at his show of wit. He nodded and went on. "The law requires me to hear you. It does not require me to hear you in perpetuity. Speak up quickly. Waste no more of the court's precious time, or mine."

"This man told the truth," Jen replied. "He did not steal the bowl. I gave it to him."

"Ah? Did you?" Fat-choy raised his eyebrows. "I compliment you on such magnificent generosity, one of the Eleven Principal Virtues. Logic now compels me to inquire where, in turn, you obtained it. Perhaps from some other mysterious, unnameable friend?"

Master Chu wrung his hands. "Fool, fool," he whispered. "I tried to warn you to keep silent. Do you mean to dig your own grave? I am so close to mine it hardly matters. Oh, you should have let well enough alone."

"It will be easily settled." Jen gave him a reassuring smile. He looked squarely at Fat-choy. "The bowl is, in fact, royal property from King T'ai's Hall of Priceless Treasures. It was put in my charge. You shall prove the truth of this by sending word to the Celestial Palace in Ch'ang-an.

"Until you receive a message confirming what I have told you," Jen continued, "I accept being kept in custody here, wherever you choose to confine me.

"One thing more." For the first time in many

months, Jen spoke aloud and clearly his rank and name. "I am the Young Lord Prince. I am Jen Shao-yeh."

The prosecutor's jaw dropped. "But—but this is hardly credible. You? As you claim—yes, that can be proved. Be certain that an inquiry will be dispatched immediately to the Celestial Palace. Until then—"

"No need," broke in Fat-choy. From the moment that Jen named himself, the official's eyes lit up in sudden recollection.

"I know this man," Fat-choy declared. "Prince? Yes. Prince of Robbers. He and his band assaulted me on my way here. They stole horses, carts, provisions. Even then, to confuse me and distract my attention, he pretended to be the Young Lord. Now he offers new trickery. Put himself in custody? Live at public expense to further some devious plan of his own?"

Jen's eyes flashed. "Have a care, Official of the First Rank Fat-choy. You deal with a royal personage. Your conduct will be noted—"

"Silence!" shouted Fat-choy. "Impudent liar! You dare to speak of my conduct? Insolence on top of insolence! Do you think you can employ some clever ruse and brazen your way out of punishment?" Fat-choy struck his fist on the desk. "Another word, villain, and you shall be bound and gagged." He turned to Master Chu, who was staring openmouthed at Jen.

"As for you," Fat-choy declared, "there is no longer a case against you. This wretch has confessed to possessing and transmitting stolen property. Knowing him as I do, I willingly believe he gave you the bowl, no doubt to rid himself of incriminating evidence. Since you are innocent, I shall only have you flogged out of Chai-sang. Set foot here again and you will pay with your head."

Fat-choy motioned to the attendants, who dragged the bewildered and protesting Master Chu from the Hall of Sublime Justice. Two guards came forward to lay hands on Jen.

"Your case is more difficult," said Fat-choy, fixing a bulging eye on Jen, "but you shall have justice nonetheless, impartial, guided by the law, which is more than you deserve.

"First," he continued, "in the matter of your robbery and attack on an official, I would gladly punish you to the full extent. However, your vicious assault took place beyond my present jurisdiction. It cannot figure here and, regretfully, I must set it aside.

"In the matter of the bowl, you have condemned yourself out of your own mouth. This is a capital crime. The punishment is beheading.

"And yet," Fat-choy went on, as Jen stared horrified, "much as you merit the extreme penalty, the law forbids it. Because you have made voluntary confession, I am required by statute to mitigate your sentence and to show you clemency. Which I now do. Your life is mercifully spared."

Jen heaved a sigh of relief. Then his blood froze as the official continued. "Instead of a death sentence, by the benevolence and compassion of the law, you shall wear the Collar of Punishment."

Fat-choy motioned to the guards. "Take him to the public square immediately. Set the cangue around his neck."

"Chief Magistrate." Jen looked straight at Fat-choy. Whatever else, he would give the chief magistrate no further satisfaction. With the princely bearing he had learned from Master Hu, he said, "Your judgment is incorrect. It is also incomplete. You have not specified the length of sentence."

Fat-choy smiled. "It is not given to mortals, or to this court, to know precisely how many years one may live. For you, what that number may be, such will be the duration."

•   •   •   •   •

Gross injustice! Will Jen escape the dreadful punishment of the cangue? Before that is answered, we leave him being dragged to the public square and turn our attention to Fat-choy in the next chapter.

24

· *The Tale of the Bronze Bowl* ·

HONORABLE CHIEF MAGISTRATE, Official of the First Rank Fat-choy admired himself as a personage of refined taste and delicate sensibilities. He wore robes of exquisite materials richly embroidered. If he judged his meals to be less than perfect, he flung the dishes to the floor and ordered his cook beaten to perfection. His chambers were filled with superb antiques, pieces of jade, porcelain, gold, and silver, and he sought always to add rare items to his collection.

When a bronze bowl was presented as evidence in a

case of theft, Honorable Fat-choy's eyes popped and his fingers itched. To one of less perception, it would have seemed a common object. Honorable Fat-choy, however, saw its subtle decorations, graceful proportions, and excellent craftsmanship. He was more than a little vexed that Honorable Prosecutor Ch'iang-to had seen it first. The conceited fellow thought himself also a connoisseur. Fat-choy thought him a fool.

"Had it been me," Fat-choy muttered, "I'd have simply taken it away from the beggar who was holding it—the wretch wouldn't have dared to complain—or given him a few coins and said no more. But no, this idiot makes a court case of the matter. Now the thing turns out to be royal property. By law, it must be sent back to the Celestial Palace."

Fat-choy pondered the situation and soon found an answer.

"True, the law requires me to return the bowl. On the other hand, it does not specify how quickly this must be done. That leaves it to the discretion, honesty, and efficiency of the chief magistrate, who, fortunately, is myself. A heavy responsibility, but I am capable of bearing it."

Fat-choy, therefore, ordered the bowl placed in his chambers along with his other prized possessions.

Honorable Prosecutor Ch'iang-to ventured to raise a question. "Most worthy and excellent Chief Magistrate, since the bowl figured as evidence in a criminal trial, until it can be sent back to its rightful owner, in my considered opinion it should remain in custody of the Department of Legal Technicalities."

"Of which you, most admirably diligent Honorable Prosecutor, are the head," replied Fat-choy. "However, since the case has been judged and closed, the bowl comes under the purview of the Department of Vigilant Administration."

"Of which you, Honorable Fat-choy, are the head," answered the prosecutor.

"Correct," replied Fat-choy, "and, may I point out, your superior in rank. In my considered opinion, the times are too unsettled to return the bowl immediately. Harm might come to it in transport over bandit-infested roads. What safer place, for the moment, than my private chambers, where I may constantly keep an eye on it?"

Honorable Ch'iang-to could only bow agreement. Fat-choy waddled off to his quarters. He had, that day, ordered an old beggar whipped out of town, condemned a thieving impostor to the Collar of Punishment, imprisoned half a dozen rogues to prevent them from committing offenses they might have contemplated in the future, and decided in favor of litigants who had impressed him with the righteousness of their purses and their generosity in sharing the contents with him, and he was altogether fatigued by dispensing so much justice.

He enjoyed a delicious dinner, allowed a servant to anoint him with fragrant essence of rose petals, and spent the rest of the evening fondling his collection of treasures.

He set the bowl in a place of honor on a teakwood stand. The more he studied his new acquisition, the more he admired it, and the more he congratulated himself on his dealing with Honorable Ch'iang-to.

"What a distasteful example of greed," Fat-choy said. "He had the notion of dishonestly keeping it for himself. Well, here it is, here it stays. Sooner or later, one of these years, I shall return it. If I remember to do so."

Fat-choy went happily to sleep. Next morning, like a child with a new toy, he hurried over to inspect this latest item in his collection. He had to look three times before he believed his eyes.

The bowl held a gold coin.

"Well, well, well," said Fat-choy, picking up the coin. He squinted at it, rubbed it between his fingers, bit it, rapped it on the tabletop. It was genuine, of purest gold. "I don't remember dropping this into the bowl last night. Yet so I must have done without thinking about it."

Fat-choy slipped the coin into the purse at his belt and went about his daily duties. That evening, returning to his chambers, he went to admire the bowl again.

Two gold coins lay in the bottom.

Fat-choy rubbed his jowls and blinked his eyes. This time, he was sure he had not absentmindedly dropped money into the bowl.

"Ah, now I understand," he said. "My servants found these on the floor while cleaning my room. Yes, I must have dropped the coins. They rolled into some corner, my servants discovered them and put them where I would be sure to see."

Satisfied by his analysis, he attacked his dinner with a keen appetite and went to sleep.

In the morning, the bowl held four gold coins.

This bewildered Fat-choy and made him a little uneasy. Someone must have come into his chamber while he slept. Again, he turned his mind to solving the mystery, which now seemed a highly profitable one.

"Of course," he finally said to himself, "now it becomes clear. Someone, plaintiff or defendant, has a case coming up for judgment. These coins are tokens of his respect and good will. They indicate justice is on his side. In the course of time, this righteous individual will make himself known. Meanwhile, he has asked one of my servants to bestow this money on me discreetly."

To prove this, he called in his servants. All replied they knew nothing of such a petitioner. Fat-choy sent them away and went back to unraveling the mystery.

"Simple explanation," he said. "They are lying. All in a good cause, and I forgive them. This unknown personage has ordered them to keep the matter secret. All will be revealed in proper time."

That evening, when Fat-choy returned to his chambers, he saw the bowl held eight coins.

"Now at last I understand," he cried in delight. "At

first, I thought it must be some litigant or favor-seeker. But they would be bolder and blunter and take up the matter with me directly. No, this is a graceful, elegant, feminine way of going at things.

"Yes, a lady is involved," he went on, preening himself, "a lady of wealth. Beauty, surely, to go with it. She has observed me about town or in the Hall of Sublime Justice and has quite lost her heart. She wishes, naturally, to remain unknown for a while, to see what I shall do. Perhaps it is a little humorous game to find out if I can discover who she is. That might be difficult, for there must be countless rich and beautiful ladies filled with tender emotions for me."

Next morning, the bowl held sixteen gold coins.

Fat-choy hugged himself gleefully. "Ah, flirtatious minx! How she must enjoy the riddle she sets me!

"If this is a little game," he continued, "two can play at it. I have already established that someone is tiptoeing in during the night. A servant or, perhaps, the lady herself, who has bribed her way into the yamen. Very well, I shall go to bed as usual, but only pretend to be sleeping. At the sound of someone entering, I shall spring up and surprise whoever it is."

Despite his efforts, he could not keep himself awake all night.

When he opened his eyes, he saw thirty-two gold coins in the bowl.

"How did she do it?" he cried. "To creep in so quietly, with never a sound?"

The following night, Fat-choy bolted his door, thinking this might cause the unknown admirer to change her method and make herself known.

Next morning, he found sixty-four gold pieces.

The following days, each time Fat-choy left his chambers he returned to find double the previous amount. He tried sitting up all night watching the bowl. However, when he glanced away even for a moment, still more coins had appeared when he looked back.

"Finally, I understand!" he joyfully exclaimed. "Why did I not realize it from the beginning? This fortune is no gift from favor-seeker or admirer.

"Celestial providence is showering me with gold! A reward for my honesty and diligence, for my generosity and nobility of spirit, for my wise dispensation of justice.

"Yes, I have read tales of kindly spirits rewarding mortals worthy of such benevolence. And who could be worthier than I? I never believed those tales, but here is proof."

With the amount continually doubling, the gold coins soon overflowed the capacity of the bowl, covered the table, and spilled onto the floor. Fat-choy piled the coins into his cabinet and locked the bowl there as well.

But the cabinet itself became filled. Fat-choy began wondering where else he could store this multiplying treasure.

"No telling when it will stop," he said to himself. "Perhaps it never will! Indeed, why should it?"

He needed no abacus to calculate he would shortly become rich beyond imagination. His head spun at the prospect of dozens of gorgeous carriages and teams of horses, of thousands of new robes, luxurious furnishings, priceless objects of art, residences to house them all; as well as gardens, orchards, pavilions. Each day, he could hardly wait to return to his chambers and peep into the overflowing cabinet.

At this time, there arrived in Chai-sang Honorable Inspector General Tso-tsang. It was the duty of this high official to examine account books and ledgers, to conduct investigations, perform inventories, and verify all expenses connected with yamens throughout the kingdom.

Fat-choy was too preoccupied with counting his growing treasure to give more than briefly formal welcome to this visiting official and paid no heed to his doings. Later, when Fat-choy opened his chamber door to insistent knocking, he saw Inspector General Tso-tsang in company with Honorable Prosecutor Ch'iang-to.

"Forgive this intrusion, Honorable Chief Magistrate," said the Inspector General as the impatient Fat-choy ushered them in, "but a question has arisen in regard to certain accounts and inventories."

"It is your worthy function to deal with it," replied Fat-choy. "I am concerned with duties more important than counting bushels of rice and adding up kitchen expenses."

"It is a little more serious than that," the Inspector General said. "As required, I personally examined the strong room where reserves of currency are kept."

"Excellent," said Fat-choy. "I am happy to know that you are carrying out your duties so meticulously. Now, if you will excuse me."

"Honorable Fat-choy," said the Inspector General, "I discovered something highly troubling. In fact, disastrous. Every sack of gold coins stored there is empty."

"What?" cried Fat-choy. "How can that be? Quite impossible. Honorable Tso-tsang, you must get to the bottom of this incredible situation immediately."

"As I have been doing," replied Tso-tsang. "It is obviously the work of a most audacious robber, one within the yamen itself. No other could have access to the strong room."

"Of course it is," replied Fat-choy. "Every servant, every official, from lowest to highest, must be closely questioned." He glanced sharply at Ch'iang-to. "Including the Honorable Prosecutor himself."

"I am happy that you agree," said the Inspector General. "I have already conducted such an investigation, to no avail."

"Then probe deeper," said Fat-choy. "I urge you to do so without delay."

"Your encouragement is commendable," said the Inspector General. "That is exactly why I have come to you. So far, all officials, including the Honorable Prosecutor, have allowed me to search their chambers. I have no doubt that you, Honorable Chief Magistrate, will do likewise. Purely as a gesture of good faith and token of enthusiastic cooperation.

"The sooner we begin," Tso-tsang went on, "the sooner this inconvenient formality will be ended. Shall we, then, start with . . . oh, let us say, with your cabinet? A handsome piece of furniture, I hasten to add. I offer compliments on your taste."

"But—but this is unseemly! It impugns my dignity! It—it is outrageous!" Fat-choy had broken into a cold sweat. He scowled and glared, with as bold a face as he could put on. He blustered, protested, and, finally, folding his arms, refused to submit to such humiliation.

"In that case," replied the Inspector General, "I must take other measures."

He clapped his hands and a number of clerks and scribes entered. At his bidding, while Fat-choy gasped and sputtered, they broke open the cabinet.

Coins flooded out in a golden stream. Fat-choy collapsed on a chair. The Inspector General turned a severe eye on the Chief Magistrate.

"With utmost courtesy, allow me to inquire how you came by such bounty?"

"Gifts! Gifts!" cried Fat-choy. "Gifts from kindly spirits!"

The Inspector General and the Honorable Prosecutor exchanged glances. The clerks and scribes set about counting the coins. When they finished, the sum tallied exactly with the amount of missing treasure.

"Honorable Chief Magistrate, Official of the First Rank Fat-choy," said Prosecutor Ch'iang-to, smiling blissfully, "it is my painful duty to place you under arrest."

Fat-choy, thereupon, was put under guard and hustled into the Hall of Sublime Justice. He was forced to kneel before his own desk and his own chair, occupied now by the Inspector General, legally empowered to sit as judge in such extreme cases.

"The bowl!" blurted Fat-choy, when permitted to speak in his defense. "The kindly spirits put coins into it each day! The bowl filled more and more with gold. I had nothing whatever to do with it. Prove it for yourself. Take the bowl. Put it in your chamber. Go to sleep. See what it holds next morning."

"The bowl in question," said the Inspector General, "an item of royal property, which should have been immediately returned to the Celestial Palace, was in your custody. It cannot be found. This is yet another breach of your responsibilities."

"Gone?" burst out Fat-choy. "The kindly spirits have taken it away!"

"My reply," said the Honorable Prosecutor, "is a simple one. Never in all my career have I heard such a pitiful and ridiculous explanation, and the most barefaced, preposterous lie that any arrant criminal has ever invented. Even more preposterous than the thief who recently claimed to be the Young Lord Prince."

"I have heard enough," said the Inspector General. "Under the law, I have authority to condemn you to death. But the law is merciful as well as just. I must take into account the fact that every coin has been retrieved. The bowl alone is missing, but I charitably presume it will eventually be found. Also, I must consider that you are—or were—a colleague, and professional courtesy has certain obligations. Therefore, I pronounce a compassionate and lenient sentence upon you."

Accordingly, Fat-choy was stripped of his rank, his position, and his belongings, including his collection of antiques, and was flung out the gates of his former yamen. All his rich garments had been forfeited, but he was permitted to keep one cotton undershirt.

Fat-choy, reduced to being a beggar, proved a most unpopular one. He constantly whined, moaned, and ranted about his former wealth and his cruel betrayal by malicious spirits. Some good-hearted soul had given him an earthen pot as a begging bowl, but he seldom filled it, for passersby paid him little heed and for the most part brushed him aside.

As for the bronze bowl, a thorough search of the yamen failed to discover it. As far as could be determined, it had vanished beyond recovery and the case was closed.

One morning, however, an old beggar hobbled to a riverbank near Chai-sang. Amid the reeds and cattails, he glimpsed an object half sunk in the mud.

"Ah, so there you are," said Master Chu.

He bent and picked up the bronze bowl, examined it carefully and nodded with satisfaction. Then, clutching his find, he tottered off as quickly as his frail legs could carry him.

◆ ◆ ◆ ◆ ◆

Leaving the miserable Fat-choy in the streets of Chai-sang, and Master Chu holding the last of Jen's gifts, we now return to Jen himself and what happens to him in the next chapter.

25

MASTER HU HAD ONCE REMARKED that everything was interesting if looked at carefully. Jen applied this observation to his present circumstances. First, he put Chai-sang out of his thoughts. He admitted that he had not entirely behaved with the dignity and noble fortitude Master Hu would have liked. In fact, when the Administrator of Benevolent Correction bolted and sealed the wooden collar, Jen was raging and kicking and had to be held down. Sent stumbling through the streets, goaded past the outskirts of town, he gladly

took refuge in the empty countryside. He hoped somehow to meet Master Chu. The old beggar might be
hiding in the underbrush, waiting for a safe moment to
appear. This did not happen. Jen, therefore, set about
finding a way to free himself and to calmly analyze
what he had to deal with. Master Hu had been correct.
Considered as object—aside from being fastened around
his neck—the cangue, in its own way, was interesting.

At first glance, it was only a simple piece of wood
with a hole in it. On one side, hinges allowed the device to swing open like jaws, and then snap shut around
the victim's neck. But, as he discovered, it was heavy.
The muscles of his shoulders already ached a little. The
weight of the cangue slowed his steps and caused him
to walk with a stoop. This posture strained his back and
tired his legs. If he tried to walk quickly, his breath
grew shallow and labored. When he sat down to rest, if
he bowed his head the collar pressed against his upper
legs. To lie flat was difficult, for his neck was forced to
bend awkwardly. It was interesting that a mere plank
could be so uncomfortable.

Its size and proportions were also interesting. The
collar was quite wide. His arms, no matter how he
stretched them, could not encompass it. His hands could
not touch his head. His mouth lay beyond the reach of
his fingers. He put aside the problem of how to feed
himself. He had, in any case, nothing to eat. He turned
his attention to breaking free.

Master Hu had always urged him, in his studies, to

go to the heart of the problem. Here, the heart of the problem was a thick iron rod. Clamped on the unhinged edge of the collar, it served as a bolt to keep the device firmly closed. If he could pry loose this bolt or somehow shatter it, the collar would swing open. How to accomplish this would require careful analysis.

"Master Cangue," Jen said, "whoever devised you did it cleverly and neatly." He had once held a conversation with his belly, so it seemed not too extraordinary to hold a conversation with a piece of wood. "To undo you, I must be equally clever."

The cangue did not answer.

"Very well," Jen said. "To business."

Thus began his war with the cangue.

He scuffed through dry leaves. His foot soon struck what he wanted: a rock large enough to serve his purpose, but not so heavy that he could not handle it. He knelt and groped to pry it from the frozen ground. He had to apply some effort, but at last it came out like a loose tooth. He hefted it, satisfied.

With all his might, he struck at the bolt. The rock glanced off the bar. Unable to see his target, he had not struck it squarely. He recalculated and hammered at the bolt again. The iron rang dully. The impact of the blow jarred his head and neck. He continued, nevertheless. He heard a crack. Something had broken. It was not the bolt. The rock had split in his hand. He threw the fragments aside.

"You are stubborn," he said.

The cangue said nothing.

It took him some time to find another suitable hammer. He set about pounding at the bolt again. With the weight of the cangue and the difficulty of striking at something he could not see, he was quickly out of breath, sweating despite the cold. His arm grew weary, his muscles lost their strength.

He understood. The cangue, in its own sly way, was trying to exhaust him. He could not allow that.

He sat on the ground until his strength came back. He began again. Sometimes he struck heavy blows, sometimes he tapped and chipped at the bolt. He believed that if he hit at the proper angle he would find its weak spot.

His persistence was rewarded. Another blow and the iron rod dropped at his feet. Jen gave a cry of triumph.

The cangue did not open.

This puzzled him. Then, from the corner of his eye he glimpsed what he had overlooked. The cangue was cleverer than he had supposed.

There were two more iron rods. They were affixed to the front of the collar on either side of the hole. He could not reach them.

He forced himself to stay calm. The cangue had lured him into believing it was a simple matter of breaking a single bolt. He had worn himself out uselessly. He would have to reconsider his situation.

He clung to reason and logic. He could not break all the bolts. Therefore, he must break the collar.

He set off through the woodlands, casting around until he saw what he required. Two trees had grown close together, the slender trunks nearly touching. There was room enough; he could wedge the cangue between them. This would give him the leverage he needed. If he applied enough force, the collar would split. Accordingly, he thrust one side of the cangue into the angle where the trunks nearly joined. He twisted back and forth and pressed all his weight against the collar.

The cangue did not yield. He fell back, gasping from his exertions. His strength was working against itself. His neck would snap instead of the collar.

He began to tremble. His head spun, his thoughts tumbled over each other. Throwing aside reason and logic, he desperately battered the cangue against the trees. He stumbled back, then ran headlong, plunging between the forking trunks. He cried out in pain as the cangue bit into his collarbone and wrenched his shoulder.

Somewhere in his mind, a little frightened animal began to scurry back and forth. Its name was panic. He threw himself blindly against the tree trunks until his whole body screamed with pain. He seized the edges of the cangue. By sheer strength he tried to rip the thing from his neck. The cangue tore his skin and turned it slippery with blood.

For the first time, he had to consider the one possibility he had refused to admit: that he could not free himself. Little by little, the full horror of his plight dawned on him. It was as if the cangue had foreseen his every effort and had known in advance each attempt he would make. It had patiently waited, allowing him to match wits and strength against it, to fling himself back and forth, to roll on the ground, twisting and turning. And it was still there.

The cangue had been silent, as though observing Jen's struggles with amusement. Now it spoke close to his ear:

"Did you not suppose every prisoner has done likewise? How foolish to think you might succeed where others failed. Understand one thing. There is no escape from me. I am Master Cangue."

The cangue said no more. If it did, Jen did not hear. He had thrown back his head and was howling like a wolf.

* * * * *

What hope is left? In the grip of the cangue, what can Jen do? Is there any possibility of ridding himself of this monstrous device? These questions, as well as other matters, are taken up in the next chapter.

26

· Stern teacher ·
· Marvelous dreams ·
· Reflections in a puddle ·

IT SNOWED THAT NIGHT. By morning, black branches
turned sparkling white. Bare hillsides were dazzlingly
blanketed. Snow collected in dry, rocky valleys that
now looked like so many gleaming lakes. The sky
cleared to rich blue, dabbed here and there with pink.
An orange sun floated low on the horizon. A landscape
worthy of the painter Chen-cho.

The prisoner of the cangue had spent the night
crouched in a bush. He had not slept well. He had not,
in fact, slept at all, except for the occasional moment

when his head dropped and his chin rested on the wooden collar. The skin of his neck, where the collar gripped, had been torn in the course of his struggles. The blood had clotted, or frozen; the collar fretted away the scabby crust, biting into exposed flesh. The prisoner of the cangue ignored this discomfort. The animal panic of the day before had gone into its burrow, having worn itself out. The prisoner of the cangue was reasonably calm. He had much to do.

He crawled out. He could not stand upright. His spine and his knees seemed to have bent and frozen stiff. He limped from the woodlands and crossed snowy fields, trying to kick away the cramps in his legs. He bore northward, away from Chai-sang. Later in the morning, he struck what he was looking for: a fairly good road that would lead him in the general direction of Nang-pei. He had given up the prospect of reaching T'ien-kuo. Not entirely given it up. It hung somewhere in the shadows of his mind. It simply no longer had any great importance. He concentrated on finding a flute girl and, meantime, getting free of the cangue.

Country folk were on the road. Some trudged beside ox carts or pushed barrows. They were on their way to market in Chai-sang or some neighboring village. The bright morning had put them in good spirits. Children frolicked beside their elders, shouting and tossing snowballs. The sudden appearance of the prisoner caused uneasiness. The straggling procession of carts and barrows veered aside, giving him wide berth.

Several of the folk stared curiously. Most kept their eyes fixed straight ahead.

The prisoner of the cangue had given further thought to his condition. He accepted one fact: He had no means of breaking himself from the collar. He must find means. The prisoner observed the passersby. He singled out a bluff, hearty-looking fellow who laughed and joked with his companions.

The prisoner of the cangue approached him, making friendly gestures. The banter stopped. The man's friends, silent, glanced at each other and edged away.

The prisoner asked for something to pry open the cangue.

"I do anything like that," the man retorted, "I'll end up with one of those on my own neck. I'm sorry for you, but that's as far as it goes. Be on your way."

The prisoner wondered if he should identify himself. He decided it would be useless. Instead, he repeated his request for tools.

"None here," the man said. "Be off, I told you."

"You have an ax." The prisoner pointed at a heap of oddments in the cart.

"There is no ax."

"I see one. Give it here."

"There is no ax."

The man turned away. The prisoner followed, insistent. The man warned him to keep his distance. The prisoner pushed past him and tried to lay hands on the implement. Alarmed, the man cursed and shoved him aside. The prisoner was stubborn. He lunged toward the cart, swinging the edge of his collar against the man, who was now frightened. He stepped ahead of the prisoner and seized an ox goad. He brandished the iron-tipped pole.

"Enough of that. Get away."

The prisoner would not be denied. He started once more for the cart. The man struck him with the ox goad. The prisoner reeled back, regained his balance, and tried to snatch the pole. The man understood that he was dealing with a dangerous criminal. He brought the ox goad down on the prisoner's head. The prisoner fell. The man pondered whether to strike again. He judged it unnecessary. He set off with his cart as quickly as the ox could go.

The prisoner had been thoroughly stunned. By the time he got his wits back, the country folk were too far down the road to be overtaken. He started north again. He did not feel kindly disposed toward those folk. He halted. By the roadside, someone had set a pile of broken victuals. The prisoner flung himself on the bits of food. He could not put them into his mouth. On all fours, he devoured them where they lay.

At this point, the prisoner had worn the cangue less than two days.

It snowed often that winter. Bad weather forced the prisoner to go at a snail's pace. Sometimes he lost his bearings amid the whirlwind of white flakes. Once, in the weeks that followed, he went in a large circle, ending where he had begun.

The cangue did not speak to him again. It was, nevertheless, an excellent teacher—stern and demanding, but always fair. As long as the prisoner did what the cangue required, they got on well enough. The cangue taught him many useful things: how to lap water like an animal; how to sleep sitting up; how to walk half bent—the prisoner found a staff to help him do so.

The cangue also taught him to avoid towns and villages when possible, to enter them only if absolutely necessary. The prisoner was not welcome there; his presence made the inhabitants uncomfortable and they sometimes drove him off with sticks. So the cangue taught him to shelter in peasants' outbuildings and to be quiet about it and not approach the dwellings. With the same instinct that told them a fox or wolf roamed their fields, the farm folk knew he was there. Some chased him away, but most ignored his presence. As often as not, they set out food for him. The cangue taught him to crouch over it and gulp it down before other stray creatures snatched it from him.

The cangue rewarded him for learning such lessons. It granted him marvelous dreams. Asleep, the prisoner was deliriously happy, his dreams so bright, so real that he was often confused when he woke. He could not be certain whether he was a prisoner dreaming of happiness, or a happy man dreaming he was a prisoner. Someone had once told him something like that. He could not remember who or when.

The cangue rewarded him, as well, by allowing him to lose track of time. The prisoner at first counted the days. So many accumulated that they became as heavy as the wooden collar. The cangue permitted him to forget such details. It was either dark or light, snowing or not snowing, he had either eaten or had not. This relieved him of painfully calculating how long he had been on the roads.

One day, he grew vaguely aware of a greenish cast to the landscape, a green thickening among trees and hedges, rain instead of snow, mud instead of frozen turf. This pleased him.

The sun had grown noticeably warmer by the time he reached Nang-pei. He had been ill and feverish, but his spirits lifted and he felt a joyful excitement until now confined to his dreams. He made his way cautiously into the town, to the thieves' and beggars' quarter, which the cangue had taught him to sniff out unerringly.

He singled out a possible source of information: a street urchin, a ragged boy with a shrewd look on his narrow face. The prisoner beckoned. The boy swaggered over, grinning, studying the collar around the prisoner's neck as if he himself expected to wear one someday and wished a close look at what lay in store.

The prisoner inquired if he knew of a certain flute girl, a performer at the theater.

"Who doesn't?" The boy put his hands on his hips. "Lady Shadow Behind a Screen."

The prisoner did not recognize that name. From the

boy's added description, he knew who it must be. He asked how to send her a message.

"You and a hundred others." The boy chuckled. "Can't be done."

The prisoner replied that it must be done.

"Can't," the urchin repeated. "One good reason: She's gone. That's right. In a great carriage. We lined the streets to wave. We were sorry to see her go. Where? No idea. North? South? East? West? It would have to be one of them, wouldn't it?

"Here, now, old uncle," the boy added, rapping sharply on the front of the cangue, "don't go to sleep."

The prisoner had not gone to sleep. He had merely shut his eyes and let his head drop forward. He could barely absorb what the urchin told him. The boy waited a few moments. The prisoner did not move. The boy wondered if he had died. He shrugged and went off whistling down the street.

The prisoner dimly understood he would have to think what next to do. To begin, he must leave Nang-pei. He hoped some thoughts would come to him by the time he reached the outskirts. None did. He sat down by the roadside. A strange new creature had roused inside his head; he glimpsed it lurking in the shadows.

Children played nearby, splashing in the puddles. They sidled up to the prisoner. He wished to tell them that their parents would be distressed and angry to see them loitering around him. But his tongue had grown thick and unmanageable, and he could not shape his words. He gestured them away. The children were not afraid. They observed him with interest. One cheerfully asked what crime he had committed. A girl held up a rice cake she had been munching. Did he want it? She stepped closer and put the cake into his mouth, grinning proudly, as if she had dared something highly dangerous.

Since the prisoner only sat motionless and showed no sign of doing anything exciting, the children grew bored and drifted away. The prisoner, actually, was very busy with the new animal. It was not panic, not love, fear, anger, hatred, or anything he had known. It had sharp claws and sharp teeth.

The prisoner had developed a raging thirst. Leaving the beast crouching in his mind, he lurched to one of the puddles and bent over it. He did not drink. A face stared up at him. The hair was long and matted, the nose and brow almost black, the skin flaked and peeling. It reminded him of someone. He racked his memory. Finally, it struck him.

"Where have you been?" he cried. "Master Shu!"

He reached out to embrace the old man. The animal, despair, took advantage of this moment of inattention. It leaped and sank its teeth.

◆ ◆ ◆ ◆ ◆

Must a journey that began so brightly come to such an end? Jen has lost hope; will he survive without it? For the answer, turn to the next chapter.

27

· Two prosperous merchants ·
· Fortune changes for the better ·
· Or for the worse? ·

THIS DREAM WAS DIFFERENT. It was not as marvelous as the others. It kept breaking into bits and disappearing. People he did not know floated in and out. He felt as if he had been wrapped up, unable to move. Sometimes his mouth was opened and things put into it, which he chewed and swallowed instinctively. Most of the timeless time, he drifted through lightless corridors. As always, in his dreams, he wore no wooden collar. That was good. Otherwise, disappointing. He had hoped for something brighter. He had hoped to meet Voyaging Moon, as he so often did.

Eventually, he could see more clearly. Here were two gentlemen, both well-dressed. They could have been prosperous merchants. They looked vaguely familiar. One had a round, lumpy face; the other was lean, with long, ropy hair. It took him a while to recognize them.

"Mafoo? Moxa?" Jen said. "In handsome new clothes? What a fine dream this is turning out to be."

"Call me a dream, eh?" Mafoo slapped his large and solid belly. "Here's reality, well-stuffed. I got back better than I lost. You're awake, be sure of that."

Moxa came to the bedside. "If you think you're dreaming, what do you say to this?" He held up something in front of Jen. "Go on, touch it. See for yourself."

It was the cangue, shattered.

"I cracked it open," Moxa said proudly. "Good thing no one saw me, or we'd all have been in trouble."

Jen took the collar in his hands. He passed his fingers over the splintered wood and broken bolts. He looked up at Mafoo and Moxa.

"No dream," Jen murmured. "I'm free of it." For the first time since he had worn the collar, he wept with joy.

"You'll tell us later how you got yourself into such a plight." Mafoo gently put a hand on Jen's shoulder. "The main thing is that you're out. Give that monstrosity here. I'll get rid of it now."

"I'll keep it," Jen said. "If I ever wonder if this is

still a dream, all I need to do is look at it. And at the two of you. My dear friends, how did you find me? And where am I?"

"Specifically," the Mad Robber said, "we found you in a mud puddle. Generally, you're in Nang-pei— at the best inn available, you'll be pleased to know. You've been sick a good while. We've had doctors coming and going, stuffing pills and potions down your gullet, and servants feeding you between times. You were far gone; we feared you mightn't come back."

"We've been trying to catch up with you for months," added Mafoo. "We lost track of you at the beginning of winter. Moxa picked up your trail again a few weeks ago."

"By the Ear of Continual Attentiveness!" exclaimed the Mad Robber. "It never fails. Talk, rumors, gossip. Some grateful villagers in a backwater called Ping-erh remembered you well. Ah, if only we'd found you before this."

"We did the best we could," Mafoo said. "I and this skinny madman," he added, with an affectionate grin at Moxa, "got swept beyond the mouth of the Lo, almost out to sea. We hung on for dear life to what was left of the boat. It took some doing to paddle back. We must have saved each other's life half a dozen times. We made shore at last and started upriver on foot. We sheltered in a fisherman's hut. He told us about a young fellow—we guessed it was you—who might have headed for Chen-yeh."

"No sign of you there," Moxa put in, "but the Ear of Continual Attentiveness heard of a flute girl who'd been at the Golden Grasshopper long before. We talked to the proprietor, a disagreeable creature."

"And got nothing from him," Jen said bitterly.

"On the contrary," Moxa said. "We got a great deal. On the Feet of Stealthy Silence, I went back that night and robbed him. At last, a perfect client! Not one of the Precepts of Honorable Robbery applied to him; I had no compunction whatever. In fact, I enjoyed it. Better yet, that villain's cash was the foundation of our fortune. Of course, if you look closely enough, most fortunes have robbery of one sort or another at the bottom."

"With Master Hong's money, we bought a carriage and pair of horses," Mafoo said. "We thought that would be quicker than tramping through the country-side. We bought new clothes, too. No use rousing suspicion that we were vagrants. In fact, we looked so prosperous and substantial that I was able to do a little business here and there. For a while, we had a finger in the dumpling trade, with a handsome return on the investment. Trying to follow you from one place to another, we bought bolts of cloth, pots, pans, and such and sold them at an excellent profit. Had we kept on, we'd have made our fortunes a couple times over.

"It's mostly thanks to this long-legged lunatic," Mafoo continued. "He turned out to be a better businessman than he ever was a robber."

"It's the Eye of Discerning Perception," Moxa said, beaming proudly. "And the Nose of Thoughtful Inhalations. They served me well in ferreting out lucrative enterprises. I'm thinking seriously of giving up robbery and becoming a merchant. In business, there are no Precepts whatever to inconvenience you."

"You pair of rascals!" Jen burst out laughing. "To think I was ready to give you up for drowned! I wish I'd done as well as the two of you.

"As for me," Jen said, after telling what had befallen him, "the gifts for Yuan-ming are gone. Voyaging Moon may still have the flute. Whether she does or doesn't makes no difference. All I want is to find her. With the three of us together now, we can surely do that."

"Don't think we haven't tried," Mafoo said. "We searched for her as hard as we searched for you. She was here in Nang-pei until winter. We talked to the theater director. He couldn't help us. He had no idea where she went."

"Then we'll keep looking," Jen said. "I'll need clothes, to begin with. You have a carriage and horses? We can start off today."

"That won't be possible," Mafoo said.

"Why not?" returned Jen. "What's to stop us?"

"We'll not give up searching," Mafoo said, "but it must be put off a while. Before that, you must go to Ch'ang-an. As quickly as possible."

"What?" exclaimed Jen. "No, no, I see no use—"

"My plump friend is correct," put in Moxa. "The Heart of Sentimental Sympathy grieves for you. The Voice of Stern Practicality tells me you must do as he says."

Jen looked from Moxa to Mafoo. "I don't understand."

Mafoo's face was grave. "We heard of this a short while ago. Your honored father fell ill soon after you left the Celestial Palace. At the end of last week, the worthy man joined his honorable ancestors."

"My father—dead?" Jen gave an anguished cry. "And I not with him! No, not true."

"Alas, it is," Mafoo said quietly. "You are no longer Young Lord Prince. You are King of T'ang."

• • • • •

From wretched prisoner to King of T'ang! What will Jen do in these new circumstances? What of his beloved Voyaging Moon? This, and more, is told in the following chapter.

28

THREE MERCHANTS LEFT NANG-PEI at dawn. The innkeeper felt sorry to see them go. They had paid handsomely for services required. One had been ill but was now recovered, and all had set off south on business. What their business was, the innkeeper neither knew nor cared.

He did wonder, idly and briefly, why these gentlemen traveled without servants or carriage driver. The stubby, paunchy one took the reins himself and seemed quite skilled at it. The innkeeper did not inquire why he performed a task more befitting a groom or household servant. The long-legged one struck the innkeeper as a trifle eccentric, ever muttering about his nose and ears. But, wealthy guests were entitled to be eccentric.

As for the youngest, he said little, appearing withdrawn; the result, no doubt, of illness. A junior colleague, the innkeeper assumed, not having been informed that the young man happened to be the new king of T'ang.

This secrecy had been Jen's choice. As he told Mafoo and Moxa, the last thing in the world he wanted was to proclaim his identity.

"Without proof?" Jen said. "Whenever I tell anybody who I am, either they take me for a madman or I end up in trouble. Can you see us walking into an official's yamen and trying to convince him? He'd throw us all in prison, or worse."

Mafoo disagreed. "The palace has to know you're alive and on your way back. Otherwise, the ministers and councillors will be flapping around, making a mess of things. No telling what those fools will be up to. We'll send word. Privately."

Jen finally consented. At their first halt after leaving Nang-pei, he wrote a message in accordance with Mafoo's suggestion. Mafoo picked out a sturdy, reliable-looking fellow among the servants at the village inn, bought him a horse, handed him a purse of money, and ordered him to ride for Ch'ang-an as fast as he could.

"He'll be there well ahead of us," Mafoo said. "Since he can't read or write, he has no idea what he's carrying and won't gossip about it along the way. He'll do as he's told, he won't make off with the horse and money because he knows he'll be paid again doubly once he reaches the palace."

"Excellent plan," put in Moxa. "Greed will keep him honest."

Jen was satisfied with that. And not satisfied at all.

"Do I return as a king? No, I return as a failure," Jen said, in bitter self-reproach. "My father depended on me, but I turned away from my journey. The gifts he entrusted to me are lost, every one. I've even lost Voyaging Moon."

"You'll find your flute girl," Mafoo insisted. "You have royal power now. Once home, you can order searches in every corner of T'ang. Notify every official in every yamen. She's bound to turn up somewhere sooner or later."

"We might even come across her on the way," added Moxa. "The Nose, the Ear, the Eye are devoted to your service. In short, I'll keep on the lookout for her."

Jen had to admit that Mafoo was right. As king, Jen commanded more resources than before. The sooner in Ch'ang-an, the sooner he could use them.

In all haste to reach the capital, Jen urged Mafoo to continue on the roads past nightfall and to set off again before daybreak, with fresh horses wherever they could be found. Sometimes they galloped long stretches without a halt, one taking the reins while the other two slept. Near the end of their longest day, the weary travelers came in sight of the Lotus Bridge and the city's outskirts.

"Our messenger got there safely." Mafoo pulled up the horses. "We're expected. Look, they've sent an escort to welcome us. Out with you, Divine Majesty, and submit to the formal greetings."

Moxa had leaped from the carriage and was eagerly beckoning to the escort by the time Jen climbed down. With Mafoo beside him, Jen stood, hands in sleeves, while the warriors galloped toward them.

"Are you Jen Shao-yeh?" The troop captain reined up his mount. "The Young Lord Prince?"

Before Jen could answer, Mafoo stepped forward.

"No, he is not," Mafoo indignantly retorted. "What discourtesy is this? Dismount, captain. Pay respect properly. He is no longer Young Lord Prince, but His Divine Majesty Jen."

The troop captain seemed familiar. Jen had seen him before. Among the palace guard? Li Kwang's warriors? The memory teased and eluded him.

"There is no such ruler," the officer replied.

Jen suddenly recalled the cavern, the bandits. The man had been one of the Yellow Scarves. Jen cried a warning to Mafoo and Moxa. Too late. The troop had surrounded them.

"There is only one king of T'ang." The warrior drew his sword. "King Natha."

The prisoners were to be granted indulgence by the grace and generosity of Natha, King of T'ang. The troop captain informed them of this as they were herded under guard into the Celestial Palace, down corridors usually bustling with officials but now empty and echoing.

"Indulgence?" muttered Mafoo. "Grace and generosity? We're prisoners no matter how you look at it."

"He's doing us the favor of keeping us alive, I suppose," Jen said. "He could have had us killed out of hand."

"Then," Mafoo remarked, "be sure he's saving us for something equally nasty."

"The Nose of Suspicion failed," Moxa groaned. "I should have smelled a trap."

"Natha would have caught us sooner or later," Jen consoled the dismayed robber. "As we're alive, we may still have a chance."

They halted at a heavy door where two warriors stood guard. The troop captain unbolted it and gestured for them to enter. The portal swung shut behind them. The lamplight showed chambers sparsely furnished. The room held another occupant.

"Young Lord! Why did you not tell me who you were?"

An old woman hobbled toward Jen, who stared a moment before recognizing her. "Plum Blossom?"

"You brought my Fragrance of Orchid to life again." Plum Blossom would have kowtowed, but Jen took her hands in his own.

"The child is well, then?"

"Your gift restored her," Plum Blossom said, "and she flew away with it. Even so, I must believe she lives, happy wherever she may be."

The old woman's words puzzled him as much as her presence here. Jen asked no further explanation. His eyes had gone to the slender figure who had stepped from the adjoining chamber.

He cried out as Voyaging Moon ran to him. His months in the cangue, his hopeless searching, his failed journey all vanished from his mind. Mafoo's eyes popped, Moxa grinned all over his face.

"The Heart of Devotion swells!" exclaimed the Mad Robber. "The Eye of Tender Affection sheds a tear of joy—but if your sweetheart's in the palace, Your Majesty, it occurs to me she's a captive as much as we are."

"I couldn't warn you," Voyaging Moon said. "Natha told me you were on your way. The message you sent fell into his hands. He and his warriors had already captured the palace. They attacked Ch'ang-an when your father died. Plum Blossom and I had no chance to escape.

"Natha had secret dealings with some of the officials, so I heard," Voyaging Moon went on. "They practically invited him in. As for you, they thought they were well rid of you. They knew you were supposed to learn how Yuan-ming governed his kingdom and do likewise in T'ang. A king who knew how to rule was the last thing they wanted. They were afraid you'd be wise enough to kick them all out. Natha promised them—"

"That makes no difference now," Jen broke in. "We have to find a way out. We're together. That's all that matters. I lost you once. I won't lose you again. For the rest, for the palace, for Ch'ang-an, for the Kingdom of T'ang, I don't care—"

"You have to care," Voyaging Moon said. "You're king, not Natha. You know what he is. A brute and a killer. He forced you to give up the sword. Will you let him take your people, too?"

"Can I stop him?" Jen returned. "Any more than I stopped him from taking Yuan-ming's gift?"

"I don't know," Voyaging Moon said, "but you'd better start thinking about it. And about your father. He never lost hope that you'd come back. He counted on you to rule wisely in his place. I told him I knew you would. He was happy with that, and at peace—"

"You saw my father? You were here, then—?"

"I was with him when he died," Voyaging Moon said quietly. "I told him about our betrothal. He was glad. He gave us his blessing. Yes, I came to Ch'ang-an," she went on. "I'd been looking everywhere for you. Finally, I knew I couldn't find you on my own. I needed more help. I thought your father could give it. And so he'd have done, had there been time."

"I'm surprised they let you into the palace," Mafoo put in. "You've no idea how hard it is to gain an audience."

"Not for Lady Shadow Behind a Screen." Voyaging Moon grinned immodestly. "Her reputation traveled as fast as she did. The famous, mysterious flute girl? With news of the Young Lord Prince? They fell all over themselves opening the gates.

"And you, dearest Jen," Voyaging Moon continued, turning to him, "I played for you wherever I went, hoping you'd hear. Now I wish I hadn't. Because all it did was draw Natha's attention. He knew of Lady Shadow Behind a Screen. To find her in the palace— what an unexpected prize for him! All the more since he remembered me from the cavern. He remembered me all too well. Pig! He really gloated over finding me again. He's been keeping me under lock and key. Plum Blossom, too."

Voyaging Moon put a hand on the old woman's arm. "Poor soul, I saw her limping along the road, in the midst of a snowstorm. I took her into my carriage. She told me about her granddaughter. And the young stranger who gave her a kite. So I knew at least you hadn't drowned in the Lo. I meant to do Plum Blossom a service, taking her with me to Ch'ang-an, to get help from your father. Now she's in the same pickle as we are."

"Natha has no grievance against her," Jen said. "Why should he do her any harm? For myself, that's a different matter. He'll have to get rid of me. I'm surprised he hasn't done it already. I'm surprised he even let me see you. He's not one to do favors."

"That," said Voyaging Moon, "was my idea. I struck a bargain with him. He agreed to give me a few hours with you. Royally generous! He thinks himself quite the king, but he's still the same arrogant ruffian. Worse. He's gone a little mad on top of everything else. I've heard he talks to his sword. He struts and preens enough to turn your stomach. He wanted an ornament for the palace, something to flaunt and boast about. In this case: Lady Shadow Behind a Screen.

"That's my part of the bargain," Voyaging Moon added. "I told him I'd marry him."

◆ ◆ ◆ ◆ ◆

Noble sacrifice! Terrible bargain! Has Jen found Voyaging Moon only to lose her, along with his life? What hope at all for him? Can a desperate situation turn worse? It can and does. To learn how, go on to the next chapter.

29

"HUSH, HUSH. IT WON'T HAPPEN." Voyaging Moon put a hand on Jen's lips. "Do you think I'd keep a bargain like that? Natha gave me what I wanted. He'll get nothing back for it.

"I wanted you with me, and so you are," Voyaging Moon went on. "I wanted time. We have some. Not much. But if I can stretch it out, we might have a chance. The longer you stay alive, the better chance we'll have."

"How can there be any chance at all?" Jen said. "Time? Time for what?"

"Natha calls himself King of T'ang," Voyaging Moon said. "He isn't. I've heard things since I've been here. The northern province is rallying against him. It started last winter. One village held him off. That heartened other villages. Now, half the districts are up in arms. He's had to send most of his warriors north. They put down one uprising, another starts. He's bitten off more than he can chew. King? Yes, in Ch'ang-an and some of the outlying towns. Even there, he's stretched too thin."

"That's all as may be," Mafoo put in. "What's happening someplace else doesn't do anything for us here. That turtle has the palace. Worse, he has us inside it."

"So, the more delay the better," Voyaging Moon said. She turned back to Jen. "You have more friends than you think. Not all the officials took up with Natha. Some turned out surprisingly honest and spoke against him. It cost their lives. A lot of others are on your side, but they're too terrified to say anything. Once word spreads that you're here, they could try to help you. The palace troops have been disarmed. If they can get their weapons back—"

"If?" Jen said, with a bleak smile. "So many 'if's. If I hadn't fished Master Fu out of the river? If we hadn't gone searching for Li Kwang? And still another 'if.' If you can't put off Natha? If he forces the marriage?"

"I've thought of that, too," Voyaging Moon said. "He's let me have serving women. I talked one of them into giving me this."

The girl reached into her jacket and brought out a dagger. "At the ceremony, as soon as I'm close enough to him—"

"No," Jen said. "His guards would kill you an instant later. No. I can't let you try."

"Dear Jen," Voyaging Moon answered, "you may not be in a position to say much about it."

"It's a fine scheme!" exclaimed Moxa. "I see it now! The wedding ritual cut short—for Natha, in every sense of the word. But the unwilling bride won't be our lovely flute girl. It will be: myself!

"I'll be robed and veiled," Moxa hurried on. "Your serving women will help with that, won't they? I'll have the dagger ready to hand. Then, I step up to embrace that villain—"

Voyaging Moon smiled and shook her head. "Moxa, you're a lunatic. A courageous one, and we love you. But, for one thing, you can't pass yourself off as me, no matter how you dress up. For another, you'll end up dead. For still another, your arithmetic's bad. One captive missing? What will I be doing in the meantime? What does Natha have in store for the rest of you?"

"Correct," said Mafoo. "That scheme's ridiculous on the very face of it. If we try anything, we try to get ourselves out of here. I've been calculating exactly where we are."

"We aren't near the royal apartments," Jen said. "I don't know this wing of the palace."

"I do," Mafoo said. "Inner chambers. At ground level. Beyond that wall should be arcades, the Gardens of Tranquil Delight—"

"Utterly simple!" cried Moxa. "Why didn't you say that before? You forget I was a professional robber before I took up an easier trade. Here, let me have that dagger."

Voyaging Moon handed him the blade. At Moxa's instruction, Jen and Mafoo tore down the draperies covering the wall. Mafoo eyed the heavy stones.

"Robber or not, you can't dig your way through that."

"Of course I can." Moxa rolled up his sleeves. "There's always a weak spot somewhere. If I chip away the mortar, get one stone loose—"

Jen watched doubtfully as the robber scraped and scratched at the unyielding wall. Mafoo glanced at Jen and shook his head. Undaunted, Moxa kept on.

"The Hand of Consummate Skill," declared the robber. "The Spirit of Patient Determination—"

The blade snapped.

Moxa stared, crestfallen. "Ah—yes, the Hand might have gone at it a little too vigorously."

"Let it be," Jen said. "We can't do anything from inside. We'll need help from outside. You have serving women?" he asked Voyaging Moon. "Could they get word to an official we trust?"

"Possibly," Voyaging Moon said. "They come in the mornings. I don't know if we dare wait that long."

"No choice," Mafoo said. "Keep thinking, mean-time. Even Moxa might come up with a workable plan."

In the lamp-lit chamber, Jen could not tell night from day. As they settled themselves, Voyaging Moon brought out the flute and quietly played. Jen closed his eyes and listened gratefully, but his heart was heavy, scarcely open to the melody. For the few moments that he drowsed, he dreamed the wooden collar hung once again around his neck.

He started up. The lamps guttered. The door had flung open. Armed warriors were upon them, seizing Jen, surrounding Voyaging Moon and the others.

"Stand away. Let him face me."

Natha swaggered into the chamber. The bandit glittered in full armor. At his side hung the sword destined for Yuan-ming.

Natha put his hands on his hips and looked Jen up and down. His eyes glittered like his breastplate. "You told the truth when last we met. If I'd known you were a royal whelp, you wouldn't be alive at this moment. For all that, you served me well. The sword you gave me—unwillingly, but you gave it nonetheless— that sword and I are close comrades." Natha glanced at the weapon. "Aren't we, my thirsty friend? Together, we rule."

"Bandit then, bandit now," Jen replied. "Your kingdom's narrow as the edge of your blade."

"Is it?" Natha grinned. "I don't think so. Oh, no,

my lad, I don't think so at all. Your gift turned out more interesting than you might have known. I spared your life in exchange for it. That was a mistake. No matter, it will be corrected. You'll soon count yourself among your ancestors."

The terror which had threatened to drown Jen in the cavern began rising. Yet, as he raised his head to meet Natha's eyes, the tide ebbed and drained away. He could see the man before him as no more than a grotesque, posturing shadow, weightless, without substance. Jen looked at him with contempt and with a strange pity. "You have already lost. You have lost without knowing it.

"Do you remember Ping-erh? I thought I failed. Perhaps I did. But others did not. Pebbles stopped the avalanche. In the end, they will break you, and you will break yourself on them."

Natha's hand went to his sword. Foam flecks came to his lips. Jen thought the man would strike him down where he stood. Natha ground his teeth and drew a great breath. His glance wavered. He turned away to fix on Voyaging Moon.

"Lady Shadow Behind a Screen. You and I have a bargain."

"Broken," Voyaging Moon said. "Broken even as I made it."

"You'll keep it," Natha said, with a cold smile. "Willing or not." He turned to Mafoo and Moxa. "You'll follow your master."

Mafoo shrugged. "As I've always done."

"The Sinews of Courage!" cried Moxa. "The Heart of Devotion will not falter!"

"You think not?" Natha said. "Poor fools, both of you. Have you seen a man killed? A head roll in the dirt? Oh, you will. You'll smell real blood. Then find out how long your bravery lasts. I'll hear you scream for mercy."

"Let the old woman go," Jen said. "She has no part in this."

"She does," Natha said. "I want her alive, a hostage to guarantee the flute girl's good behavior." He motioned to the warriors. "Take them. The headsman waits."

Before Jen could embrace his beloved for the last time, he was marched from the chamber. Mafoo and Moxa, Plum Blossom and Voyaging Moon were prodded along behind him, out of the palace and through the Jade Gate.

Men at arms hedged the square. In the pale morning light, a crowd had gathered, held back by spearmen and archers. Many there had seen the Young Lord Prince depart happily from the city, and they had cheered him. Now they stood mute with despair. Two of Natha's guards seized Jen, led him a little distance from the gate, and halted him before the executioner.

The headsman gestured for the guards to stand aside. He seized the condemned man by the hair and forced him to his knees, then brought up a long-bladed sword.

Weapon poised, he tightened his grip on the hilt. Outcries rose from the crowd. The executioner hesitated.

"Strike!" Natha's voice rang out.

Sword raised, the executioner stood as if frozen. His eyes had turned from his victim to the far fringe of the crowd. The cries spread, swelling to wild screams. Low rumbling filled the air. The executioner's mouth fell open. He stared in terror and disbelief.

The crowd parted. Onlookers flung themselves aside, scattering to make way for a column of horsemen and foot soldiers. The ground shook beneath the tread of the approaching warriors. Unswerving, step by step, they moved across the square: not men, but statues sprung to life.

The warriors were of solid stone.

Leading them, his granite features set in grim determination, eyes blazing with the cold brilliance of diamonds, rode Li Kwang. Having struggled from the cavern, obeying the instructions of Master Wu, he and his troop had borne steadily toward Ch'ang-an. Day after day, month after month, in summer sun and winter snow, they held their slow and agonizing course. Through mountain passes, trackless forests, every inch seeming a mile, Autumn Dew had never faltered, nor had Li Kwang lost hope. Now, at last, Li Kwang had reached his goal.

He and his troop pressed forward. At sight of them, Natha's guards attempted to hold them off, raining volley after volley of arrows on the cavalcade. The shafts rattled and glanced off; the warriors never halted their inexorable advance. On they came, while spears shattered against their stone breasts. Horses' hooves and booted feet pounded a relentless rhythm. Threatening to crush all who stood in their path, the warriors drew ever closer. No beings of mere flesh and blood could resist this massive onslaught, like a glacier on the march. Seeing attack was hopeless and defense impossible, Natha's guards broke ranks and fled.

"Strike!" Natha roared again. "Strike now!"

But the executioner had already raced away in panic. Spitting curses, Natha snatched his sword from its scabbard. Glimpsing Li Kwang, Jen sprang to his feet. By then, Natha was upon him, kicking him to the ground, raising the sword high in both hands to sweep it downward.

* * * * *

Has Li Kwang come too late? Will nothing save Jen? Those who care to know what happens should go quickly to the following chapter.

30

THEY FOLLOWED THE RISING SUN. With Niang-niang, the great eagle, at her side, Fragrance of Orchid sailed amid shafts of light. The kite bore the girl on the wind tides, up the slopes and down the valleys of air currents. She had learned to guide the kite, to fly as skillfully and swiftly as Niang-niang. Laughing, she plunged down through the clouds. Niang-niang beat her powerful wings to catch up with the child.

They swooped lower. Fragrance of Orchid glimpsed rooftops, streets, and bridges. Tall towers, flashing golden, caught her eye. She veered to hover above them.

"The Celestial Palace in Ch'ang-an," the eagle told her.

"How beautiful!" exclaimed Fragrance of Orchid. "We've never been here before. Oh, Niang-niang, I must have a closer look!"

Fragrance of Orchid dropped earthward. "See all the people in the square," she called to Niang-niang. "Is it a festival? But why are soldiers holding them back? And there, what are those? Can they be statues?" She caught her breath in astonishment. "Yes, warriors of stone," she gasped, "but they're marching! Marching into the square!

"And there's a man holding a big sword. And someone's being dragged in front of him. What's happening?" Fragrance of Orchid narrowed her eyes and sharpened her vision. "Niang-niang, I know who he is! He gave me this kite!"

Fragrance of Orchid's gaze fell on other figures. "I see Grandmother Plum Blossom! How has she come here? Why are soldiers around her? No matter, I've found her. You said I would, if that's where my path led. Come, fly down with me."

"I am not permitted," said Niang-niang. "You, yes. Fly, if you wish, as fast as you can. Your grandmother is being held captive. The stranger who gave you the kite is the rightful King of T'ang. He has been condemned to death."

"We have to save them both," cried Fragrance of Orchid. "Please, Niang-niang, please help me. I need you more than ever."

"I cannot do as you ask," replied the eagle. "You have come to the end of your journey, if indeed you choose to end it. But I must tell you this: If you set foot upon the ground here, then you and I must part forever. And you, child, will never fly aloft, except in dreams."

Though fearing her heart would break, Fragrance of Orchid hesitated less than an instant. "Farewell—farewell, dear Niang-niang."

"Farewell, dear child of air and earth."

Only once did Fragrance of Orchid look back for a last glimpse of Niang-niang. But the great golden eagle had vanished.

Jen thought it was a huge bird swooping from the sky. Then he realized it was a kite with a child clinging to it. That same moment, plummeting at top speed, Fragrance of Orchid flung herself upon Natha before he could swing the sword. The girl's attack threw him off balance, and he staggered back, half-stunned.

Jen sprang up. Believing him safe, the girl gave a cry of joy and ran to the arms of Plum Blossom. Voyaging Moon, Mafoo, and Moxa sped to Jen's side.

But Natha would not be cheated of his victim. Roaring, brandishing the sword, he set straight for Jen.

"To Li Kwang!" Jen shouted, thinking to take refuge amid the ranks of stone warriors.

Natha's guards, however, fearing their chieftain's wrath more than Li Kwang's grim troop, plucked up their courage and regrouped, blocking the path of the escaping prisoners.

"This way!" Mafoo gestured frantically. "Li Kwang will deal with those fellows. Out of here! Out of Natha's reach!"

Mafoo raced from the square. Jen and Voyaging Moon, with Moxa loping beside them, followed. Natha, in hot pursuit, was at their heels, gaining ground as they plunged down a narrow street and swung around a corner.

Had Mafoo sought to escape through the twisting lanes and alleys, his plan failed. Natha, maddened with rage, still followed. Moxa, shouting for his companions to press on, halted and tried to fling himself on their pursuer. Eyes only on Jen, Natha lunged past Moxa, sending him head over heels, and doubled his pace. In moments, he would be within striking distance. Natha tightened his grip on the sword. Ahead, Jen faltered for an instant. Natha shouted in triumph.

It had been a long journey for Master Chu. From the day he picked up the bronze bowl at the riverbank, he had turned his steps southward. All through the winter, he made his way along snow-drifted roads, plodding from village to village, town to town, sleeping in doorways or under bridges. Sleet froze in his beard, wind buffeted him but he continued nevertheless. Though he asked for no alms, many folk felt strangely drawn to him and eager to fill his bowl. Some offered him shelter in their homes. He smiled, thanked them kindly but shook his head and continued on his way.

At last, one morning, Master Chu came to Ch'angan. The streets were nearly empty. Most of the townspeople had gone to the square in front of the Celestial Palace. Master Chu did not join them. Instead, he hobbled down a twisting lane not far from the palace.

Turning a corner, he stopped short. Several people raced toward him. Master Chu stepped aside as Jen and his companions sped past. Close behind them came an armored man wielding a sword.

"Natha Yellow Scarf," Master Chu called out, "you easily broke an earthen bowl. Let us see what you can do to bronze."

He flung the bowl at Natha's feet, tripping him and sending him pitching headlong.

Natha scrambled up almost immediately and resumed the chase, but his victims had for the moment outdistanced him. Master Chu retrieved the bowl and hobbled after them.

In the Happy Phoenix Gardens, an individual wearing a felt cap with earflaps sat at a folding table, an umbrella beside him. Chen-cho had fulfilled one of his ambitions. He had long dreamed of seeing the famous gardens. At last, he had made his way there, arriving just in time to catch the morning light. Next to him, as was his habit now, he had set up the landscape he had painted months before in a village called Ping-erh. Chen-cho had dipped his brush and begun to work. He stopped in midstroke.

"Now, what the devil is this?" Chen-cho had hoped to be undisturbed, but several people were streaking in his direction. Why they were running at such speed and what their purposes might be were none of his business. He started back to his painting. He looked again and set down the brush.

"Why—it's Ragbag! That rascal! Oho, I see what this is all about." Chen-cho chuckled to himself. "He's run off with a girl. And two friends helping them elope. And here comes her angry father. In a fine fury, I'd say. He's got a sword—"

The painter's amusement suddenly vanished when he saw the pursuer was Natha Yellow Scarf.

"Ragbag! Ragbag! Here!" Chen-cho shouted. He turned to the painting beside him. "Quick! Lao-hu!"

Even when he had time to think about it, Jen could not entirely piece together what happened so quickly. First, he heard Chen-cho calling him. He halted and spun around, only to find Natha behind him.

Jen flung up his arms. Teeth bared, eyes blazing, Natha raised the sword for a last killing stroke. That instant, Jen believed he heard a voice cry out:

"Give me no more to drink!"

The blade shuddered and twisted like a living thing and wrested itself from Natha's hands. Despite his bewilderment, Jen snatched up the fallen blade.

At the same time, across the garden paths bounded an enormous tiger.

Natha fell back, lurched away, and sped down one of the paths, the huge animal at his heels.

"Lao-hu!" Chen-cho shouted and waved his arms. "To me!"

With the tiger snarling behind him, Natha was driven toward the artist, who was holding up a painting.

"Hurry, Natha!" cried Chen-cho. "Into the woods! Jump!"

Before Jen could swallow his astonishment at seeing the artist, let alone the sudden appearance of a furious tiger, he was astonished again. For the next thing he saw, though he could not believe his eyes, was Natha plunging into what Jen took for a painted landscape. The tiger leaped after him. Both vanished.

By this time, with Moxa and Mafoo at her side, Voyaging Moon had run to Jen, who stared dumbfounded while Chen-cho laughed and clapped him on the shoulder.

"Never fear, Honorable Ragbag. I don't think that villain will be back."

Jen rubbed his eyes. "Chen-cho? What are you telling me? Where's Natha? For a minute, I'd have sworn I saw him jump into that picture."

"Oh, he did. He did, indeed," replied Chen-cho. "I'll tell you about that later. One thing I can promise you now. He's not where he'd like to be. If he's anywhere at all."

Chen-cho held the painting for the baffled Jen to examine. "Nice, isn't it? Lovely landscape, best I've done. Thanks to the brush and ink stone you gave me. Look closer. You might see a friend of mine." Chen-cho bent and called out, "Lao-hu? Are you busy?"

Jen peered at the beautiful scene of meadows and forests. Voyaging Moon was the first to notice, and she pointed to a thicket of greenery. Gazing out from it, orange eyes aglow, was the head of a tiger contentedly licking his chops.

"No question," said Chen-cho. "Natha won't be back."

Jen had still digested none of this when a horseman cantered up and sprang from the saddle.

"Li Kwang!" Jen stared at him. "In the square—I saw you and your men. As if you were stone statues—"

"Stone once, but no longer," Li Kwang replied. "A promise has been made and kept. Much has happened to us, but for now you need only know this: Master Wu found us trapped in Mount Wu-shan. He told me that if I and my men could reach Ch'ang-an, and you still lived, we would again be flesh and blood. And so it has come to pass. I failed once in my duty toward you. I have not failed again."

Jen, during this, caught sight of an old man limping toward him. "Master Chu?" He would have gone to the beggar, but Li Kwang raised a hand.

"My warriors have armed the household troops. Natha's men have fled, all who lived to do so. Go immediately to the Celestial Palace, Your Majesty."

"What did he say?" murmured Chen-cho. "Your Majesty? King Ragbag?"

"Something like that." Jen grinned. "Come with us. And bring your tiger."

They gathered in the Great Hall of Audience. On the Dragon Throne, Voyaging Moon beside him, with Mafoo and Moxa close by, Jen listened with ever-growing amazement to each account of the objects he had given during his journey.

Li Kwang had brought the saddle with him. He laid it at Jen's feet.

"This is not mine to ride," Li Kwang said, "and so I return it to you."

Master Chu held out the bronze bowl. "This belongs in your Hall of Priceless Treasures, and I have brought it here."

"Your kite let me fly, as I always wished," said Fragrance of Orchid, leaving Plum Blossom's embrace to stand before Jen. "Now it's yours again."

"I'll say likewise for the brush and ink stone," put in Chen-cho. "I painted as I never painted before. Even so, I can manage well enough without them."

"No," Jen said, looking at each in turn. "You must keep them. All that was given has come back to me, but I give them again to each of you. Were they valuable objects when I first set out with them? No, I think not. You have made them so. Gifts? You offered me gifts greater than ever I gave you: friendship, devotion, help when I most needed it. Only the sword will be kept, and locked away, for I do not intend to use it."

"What about the flute?" Voyaging Moon said, with a teasing smile. "Lady Shadow Behind a Screen hasn't offered to give it back. I suppose I should."

"Never." Jen smiled back. "Master Wu said it was a gift for Yuan-ming. I believe he made a mistake. It was yours, always, from the first."

"I think you're right," said Voyaging Moon.

◆　◆　◆　◆　◆

Happy end at last! Not yet. Those who have come this far have read tales of six valuable objects. Now, Jen must have a tale of his own, and it will be found in the next chapter.

31

*· The Tale of King Jen
and the Second Journey ·*

KING JEN AND PRECIOUS CONSORT VOYAGING MOON
governed happily and wisely in the Kingdom of T'ang.
Their chief councillor was a good-natured, practical-
minded fellow named Mafoo, who had served his master from the days when King Jen was still the Young
Lord Prince. First Official of the Treasury was a re-
formed robber, Moxa, who was best able to keep an
eye open for possible thieves.

Once, long before, when he was a young man, Jen
had set out for the marvelous realm of T'ien-kuo. He

had never reached his destination and he regretted it. He still remembered the vow he had made to himself on a bleak road in the northern province to continue his journey with Voyaging Moon. Yet, each time he thought he might keep that promise, he found himself always too occupied with other matters of benefit to his own kingdom.

And so the years passed. Jen and Voyaging Moon raised many sons and daughters. The people of T'ang were as happy as their rulers. They thrived and prospered, the land yielded harvests in abundance, the arts flourished as richly as the orchards. The laws that King Jen devised were just, but seldom enforced, since Jen encouraged his subjects to deal with each other as they themselves would wish to be dealt with. Few officials were needed, but they served their monarch and the people well.

At last, Jen saw that the best moment had come, and he resolved to set out once again for T'ien-kuo.

"From what you once told me," Precious Consort Voyaging Moon said, "we can't go empty-handed to the palace of Yuan-ming."

"True," King Jen said, "but we shall go empty-handed nevertheless. Since I do not know what to offer, I shall carry nothing at all.

"The great Yuan-ming will not grant us audience, nor shall I seek one. I wish only to see his kingdom with my own eyes. In that way, perhaps, I may learn how better to govern T'ang."

Voyaging Moon agreed. So, leaving the Celestial Palace in the good care of Mafoo, Moxa, and the steadfast general, Broken Face Kwang, they traveled northward, as Jen had done so long ago.

Jen and Voyaging Moon drove their carriage themselves, taking no escort or entourage, knowing they would be welcomed and received with affection at every stop along the way.

However, scarcely a full day from Ch'ang-an, they halted. In the road ahead stood an old man, white-haired, barefoot, leaning on a staff.

"Can that be Master Wu?" Jen climbed from the carriage and, with Voyaging Moon, hurried to greet him.

"No, it's not Master Wu," Jen said, drawing nearer. "It's Master Fu. No, it's Master Shu. Or—can that be Master Chu?"

It was none of them. It was Master Hu, his beloved teacher who, years before, had vanished from the palace.

Jen gave a joyful cry and ran to embrace him. "Dear Master! What happy chance to find you. But— here? Of all times and places."

"Time and place are not important," replied Master Hu, beaming. "Indeed, I get myself constantly mixed up in them; I can never be certain which is which, where or when, and so I ignore them. As for chance, my boy, is there such a thing? Do we call 'chance' only what we cannot foresee?

"If we look backward instead of forward," he went on, "might we not discover that one thing set in motion sets all else moving? Tug the edge of a spiderweb and the center moves. But I have no intention of lecturing you. Tell me, rather, why you have left your palace."

Jen recounted what had befallen him during his first journey and explained the purpose of his second.

Master Hu shook his head. "My dear boy, have I failed in your instruction? Have I not taught you to avoid useless pursuits and the pointless waste of time?

"An old tale tells of a traveler who kept walking northward," Master Hu continued. "At last, he returned to the spot where he began. The Kingdom of T'ienkuo? If, indeed, such a realm exists, it is any place you make it to be. Therefore, why seek what you have already found?"

Jen puzzled over this. By the time he grasped what Master Hu meant by it, Voyaging Moon had already understood. Smiling lovingly, she took Jen's arm.

"Come, dear Jen," she said. "Come home. If, that is, we ever truly left it."

And that was exactly what they did.

· · · · ·

The IRON RING

BOOKS BY LLOYD ALEXANDER

The Prydain Chronicles

The Book of Three
The Black Cauldron
The Castle of Llyr
Taran Wanderer
The High King
The Foundling

The Westmark Trilogy

Westmark
The Kestrel
The Beggar Queen

The Vesper Holly Adventures

The Illyrian Adventure
The El Dorado Adventure
The Drackenberg Adventure
The Jedera Adventure
The Philadelphia Adventure

Other Books for Young People

The House Gobbaleen
The Arkadians
The Fortune-tellers
The Remarkable Journey of Prince Jen
The First Two Lives of Lukas-Kasha

The Town Cats and Other Tales
The Wizard in the Tree
The Cat Who Wished to Be a Man
The Four Donkeys
The King's Fountain
The Marvelous Misadventures of Sebastian
The Truthful Harp
Coll and His White Pig
Time Cat
The Flagship Hope: Aaron Lopez
Border Hawk: August Bondi
My Five Tigers

Books for Adults

Fifty Years in the Doghouse
Park Avenue Vet (with Dr. Louis J. Camuti)
My Love Affair with Music
Janine Is French
And Let the Credit Go

Translations

Nausea, by Jean-Paul Sartre
The Wall, by Jean-Paul Sartre
The Sea Rose, by Paul Vialar
Uninterrupted Poetry, by Paul Eluard

The
IRON RING

Lloyd Alexander

DUTTON CHILDREN'S BOOKS

NEW YORK

Library of Congress Cataloging-in-Publication Data

Alexander, Lloyd.
The iron ring / by Lloyd Alexander.—1st ed.
p. cm.
Summary: Driven by his sense of "dharma," or honor, young King
Tamar sets off on a perilous journey, with a significance greater
than he can imagine, during which he meets talking animals,
villainous and noble kings, demons, and the love of his life.
ISBN 0-525-45597-3
[1. Fantasy.] I. Title.
PZ7.A3774Ir 1997
[Fic]—dc21 96-29730 CIP AC

Published in the United States by Dutton Children's Books,
a member of Penguin Putnam Inc.
375 Hudson Street, New York, New York 10014
Designed by Claudia Carlson
Printed in U.S.A.
First Edition
7 9 10 8 6

For promise-keepers
and true dreamers

Author's Note

------◆------

The dazzling mythology of ancient India has always delighted and fascinated me—but, at first, in bits and pieces. Only later in life, when I ventured to explore it more deeply, did I realize, as many other writers have realized, that this marvelous literature is a treasure trove of fairy tales, folktales, animal fables, and teaching-stories. India's great national epics, the *Mahabharata* and the *Ramayana*, are profound, powerful masterpieces that rival the *Iliad* and the Arthurian legend.

Admittedly, this mythology may seem alien, strange, even forbiddingly complex. As in any encounter with a different culture, what appears difficult or incomprehensible quickly grows familiar. The farther we journey through its rich landscape, the more we understand that what lies beneath the brilliant, exotic surface is, in essence, a world we clearly recognize. The warrior's code of honor, for example, is nearly identical with the knightly code of chivalry. Earth-shaking clashes between good and evil, courageous heroines and gallant heroes, steadfast love, daring rescues, loss and recovery—these are elements in our universal heritage of story.

Dharma, the driving force in this present tale, is equally familiar. It encompasses ideals of goodness, conscience, doing what is compassionate and right. These qualities and values lie at the heart of all the world's great literature.

The following pages are not intended as a picture of India some thousands of years ago. While the story evokes the atmosphere, themes, and concerns threading through Indian literature, it is a work of imagination, its author's response to a deeply moving experience, a loving homage to its source. I hope it offers a kind of feast of many flavors: high adventure, poetic romance, moments of wild comedy and dark tragedy, anguish at promises broken, joy at promises kept. I hope especially that readers may find more similarities than differences between cultures, and, between human hearts, no boundaries at all.

Drexel Hill,   LLOYD ALEXANDER
Pennsylvania

Contents

List of Characters and Places

Adi-Kavi (*ah*dee-*kah*vee): journeyer with unusual powers, first met while living in an anthill

Akka (*ah*-kah): adventurous young monkey with a taste for flying

Arvati (ahr-*vah*-tee): mild, gentle elephant, ill-treated in captivity

Ashwara (ahsh-*wahr*-ah): lion-eyed fugitive king of Rana-pura

Bala (*bah*-lah): shrewd, calculating king of Muktara

Chandragar (*chahn*-dra-gahr): kingdom ruled by King Rudra

Danda-Vana (*dahn*da-*vah*nah): ancient, mysterious forest with impassable thornbushes

Darshan (*dahr*-shan): trusted commander of Tamar's army

Garuda (gah-*roo*-dah): eagle fallen on hard times, constantly protesting and complaining, yelling "Shmaa!"

Gayatri (gah-*yah*-tree): Tamar's beloved white mare

Griva (*gree*-vah): a rough, unwelcome intruder

Hashkat (*hash*-kat): king of the monkeys; practical joker punished by a powerful *rishi*

Jagati (jah-*gah*-tee): dapple-gray horse of Rajaswami

Jamba-Van (*jahm*-bah *van*): philosophical bear; calms his quick temper by smashing crockery

Jaya (*jah*-yah): sinister, mysterious king who challenges Tamar to a fateful game

Kana (*kah*-nah): arrogant nobleman, nephew of Nahusha

Kirin (*kee*-rin): devoted younger brother of Ashwara

Kumeru and Sumeru (*koo*-meh-roo, *soo*-meh-roo): twin peaks, the highest in the Snow Mountains

Kurma (*koor*-mah): river, near Mirri's village

Mahapura (*mah*-hah-*poor*-ah): Jaya's stronghold

Mirri (*mee*-ree): beautiful, brave cow-tender who first meets Tamar in the middle of a river

Muktara (mook-*tah*-rah): realm of King Bala

Nahusha (nah-*hoo*-sha): villainous traitor, cruel and murderous cousin of the noble Ashwara

Nanda (*nahn*-dah): village chief, foster father of Mirri

Rajaswami (*rah*-ja-*swah*-mee): Tamar's old teacher, unfailingly cheerful, who always urges him to look on the bright side

Rana (*rah*-nah): river and valley west of Ranapura

Ranapura (*rah*-nah-*poor*-ah): Ashwara's kingdom and fortified city

Rasha (*rah*-shah): one of Ashwara's treacherous troop captains

Rudra (*roo*-drah): king of Chandragar; staunch ally of Ashwara

Sabla (*sah*-blah): river with headwaters in the Snow Mountains

Sala (*sah*-lah): cruel elephant master

Shesha (*sheh*-shah): prince of the Serpent Realm, wears a brilliant sapphire on his head; wrestles Tamar

Shila Rani (*shee*-lah *rah*-nee): queen of the Serpent Realm

Skanda (*skahn*-dah): Ashwara's adoring youngest brother

Snow Mountains: high range north of Ranapura

Soma–Nandi (*so*-mah *nahn*-dee): tiger trapped while seeking her lost mate

Sunda (*soon*-dah): Soma-Nandi's lost mate

Sundari (soon-*dah*-ree): Tamar's small kingdom

Surabi (soo-*rah*-bee): Mirri's favorite white cow, named after mythical cow who could grant all wishes

Takshaka (tahk-*shah*-kah): the Naga Raja, ancient king of the Serpent Realm, who offers Tamar a choice of jewels

Tamar (*tah*-mahr): noble-hearted young king of Sundari, honor-bound to keep a dreadful promise

Vati (*vah*-tee): little girl from Mirri's village who sings song explaining the Choosing festival

Yashoda (yah-*show*-dah): wife of village chief Nanda; foster mother of Mirri

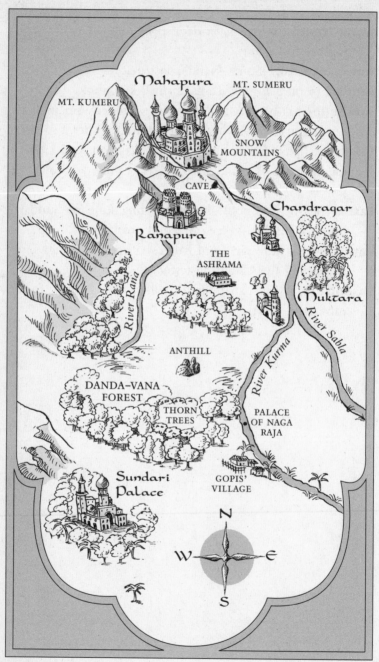

Map by Claudia Carlson

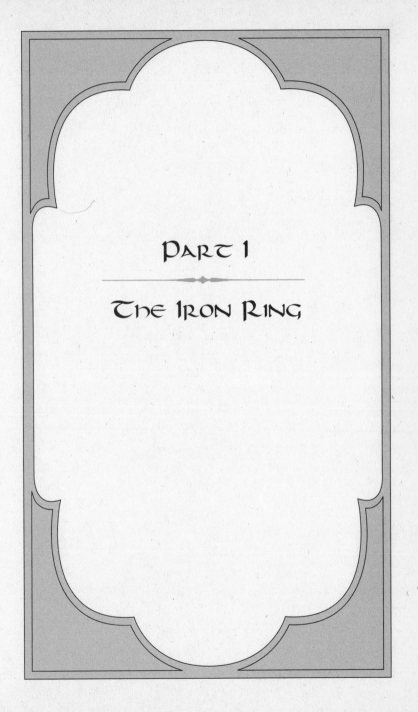

PART 1

THE IRON RING

1. A Friendly Game of Aksha

Elephants were in Sundari Palace courtyard, half a dozen or more, torchlight flickering on tusks ornamented with gold bands and ropes of pearls; horses with jeweled saddles; chariots flying flags and banners; and a dark figure striding through the gates. Servants ran to wake the young king, Tamar, already up and watching from his balcony. Curious, naturally. Not altogether pleased. No more than anyone would be, jolted out of a sound sleep by unexpected elephants.

Lamps were being lit throughout the palace when Rajaswami bustled in, beard sleep-tangled, robe kilted askew. Usually, Tamar's old tutor serenely smiled on all around him like a benevolent baby. At the moment, he twittered.

"Dress quickly, my boy. I'm told someone calling himself King Jaya has arrived. Most remarkable! I've never seen the like—clearly, a great monarch. A veritable maharajah. A little too much display and ostentation," Rajaswami added, "but overdoing things is in the nature of maharajahs."

"Revered teacher," Tamar said, "remarkable it may be —but does anyone know who he is? What he wants? And whatever he wants, why does he want it from me?"

"I haven't the slightest idea. We may assume he comes in peace. Neither he nor his retainers bear arms, not a weapon to be seen. He seeks hospitality. By custom, you must grant it."

"Which I do. Have refreshment and lodging ordered for him and his people," Tamar told a servant, "and see his animals well tended."

"One thing more," said Rajaswami. "He demands an audience."

"I'd have liked it better if he'd said 'requests.' Even so, I must receive him. Honor requires it."

"There's yet another thing," said Rajaswami. "He insists on seeing you immediately."

"Demands? Insists? Immediately? Maharajah or not, he could still show common courtesy. Well, to the devil with him. He can wait. Morning will do. He'll have time to mend his manners."

"Tut, tut, my boy. You're entitled to be prickly on occasion. That's quite as it should be. You're a king, after all. But never answer discourtesy with discourtesy. Surely, I've taught you better than that."

Rajaswami had indeed been his instructor from earliest childhood. Tamar's army commander, Darshan, had trained him in the skills of a noble warrior, a *kshatriya*. But it was Rajaswami who had taught him reading and writing; schooled him in proper behavior; and, above all, taught him the principles of dharma—the code of honor, conscience, the obligation to do what was right and royally virtuous. Tamar, sitting at Rajaswami's feet, had always listened eagerly and lovingly to the kindly old sage's teachings and would have rather given up his life than lose his honor or break his dharma.

"Always look on the bright side," Rajaswami added.

"Being gracious to the ungracious is all the more to your credit. Besides, nobility does have its obligations:

A king must ever be polite,
Even in the middle of the night.

"I may run short of patience, but you'll never run short of verses," Tamar said. He laughed fondly. "This king obviously hasn't enjoyed the benefit of a Rajaswami. So be it. I'll receive him now and have done with it."

So, he beckoned for the servants to replace his night linen with formal robes and bind up his hair. When one offered him the royal sword, Tamar shook his head.

"Since this maharajah carries no weapons, neither will I. Come, let's be polite hosts to an impolite guest."

By the time they reached the durbar hall, the great audience chamber, all the courtiers had gathered at the canopied throne. Darshan, shrewd old warrior, suspicious of unknown newcomers, stood alert and none too happy; nor were the ministers of state overjoyed to be summoned from their beds.

Tamar turned to the unexpected guest waiting alone in the middle of the hall: a big, dark-bearded man, head and shoulders taller than Tamar; a hard-muscled frame under soft, silken robes. Around his neck, jewels hung from gold chains; bracelets gleamed on his wrists and forearms. His heavy-lidded eyes seemed to have looked at the world and found it insufficiently amusing.

"Be welcome." Tamar pressed his palms together. "I hope your patience has not been too sorely tried. We are not used to such grand—and urgent—visitations."

"I should think not. Forgive this intrusion," Jaya replied, as if it made no difference to him whether he was forgiven or not. "I am on a long journey. My people and animals are weary. Night fell upon us; I required food and shelter for them.

"I gather your kingdom is small," Jaya went on. "Not unpleasant, from what little I have seen. Sundari? I am not familiar with it."

"Nor I with yours."

"Mahapura. It lies to the north, in the valley between Mount Kumeru and Mount Sumeru, where the Sabla River takes its source. Tucked away in your charming, quiet little realm, it would surprise me had you heard of mine."

"I hope my charming, quiet little realm, as you call it, offers hospitality fitting your needs." Tamar gestured toward a side table set with as many dishes as the palace cooks could prepare at short notice. Inviting Darshan and Rajaswami to join them, Tamar himself served portions to his guest, who only picked at the food. When Darshan tried to draw him out, asking details about Mahapura, the nature of its fortifications and warriors, Jaya shrugged.

"My mountains are defenses better than any I could devise. I need no army and thus am happily spared dealing with inquisitive officers." While Darshan bristled, Jaya glanced at Tamar.

"And you, Majesty, tell me: Is your kingdom a happy one?"

"I hope it is. I wish it could be more so."

Jaya gave a dry laugh. "A little misery is not such a bad thing."

"A curious idea." Tamar frowned. "You'll permit me to disagree."

"What I mean is this," Jaya said. "There are many kings more powerful than you. Like wild dogs on the hunt, they scent ways of adding to their dominions. A thriving, prosperous—and small—realm makes a tempting morsel to gulp down."

"We have not been troubled by these wild dogs," Tamar said, "nor do we expect to be."

"Nevertheless," Jaya replied, "it is always wiser not to draw too much attention upon yourself. Is there not the old tale of a hawk and a sparrow?"

"There is, indeed," put in Rajaswami. "I shall most willingly recite it."

Jaya sighed and looked up at the ceiling as Rajaswami began:

> *A lordly hawk once told a sparrow,*
> *"Dear bird, your nest is far too narrow,*
> *With barely room to hatch your eggs,*
> *To spread your wings or stretch your legs.*
> *You need a home that's far more ample.*
> *Larger chambers, for example."*
>
> *"How true," the smaller bird replied.*
> *And so, with diligence and pride,*
> *She added terraces and bowers,*
> *Balconies all decked with flowers.*
>
> *The hawk observed with envious eye:*
> *"Fit for a king to occupy,*
> *This better suits a bird like me."*
> *He drove her out and said, "You see,*
> *Instead of tearing you apart,*
> *I spared you. I've a tender heart."*

"Instructive little verses," said Rajaswami. "If you would care to hear others—"

"King of Mahapura," Tamar broke in, "do you suggest that I am a sparrow?"

"Put it that I do not see you as a hawk," Jaya answered. "Enough of these matters. Small talk between kings grows rapidly tiresome: military affairs and money, money and military affairs. Such conversation is limited and soon exhausted. May you and I sit privately at our ease?"

"If you wish." As Tamar rose from the table, Darshan plucked at his sleeve.

"Majesty, let me stand at your side," he murmured. "This king troubles me."

"He troubles me as well," Tamar said in passing, "though not for long. Why should he linger and delay his journey? Under my own roof, what danger can there be?"

He led King Jaya to a chamber adjoining the hall. After his guest had settled himself on a couch, Tamar spoke plainly:

"King of Mahapura, what business have you with me, so urgent it could not have waited a few hours?"

"My urgent business at this moment," Jaya said, leaning back amid the cushions, "is to rest in comfort, perhaps with some small distraction to lighten a tedious day."

"Do you wish music? Let me summon my performers to play for us."

"In Mahapura, I keep my own musicians. None rival them in sweetness of sound. They have, regrettably, spoiled my taste for anything less."

"Naturally, they would. Singers, then? Dancers? Not comparable to yours, no doubt, but they may offer modest entertainment."

Jaya stifled a yawn. Tamar, his patience rubbing a little ragged, went on:

"Acrobats? Jugglers? My household, as you have observed, is limited in its diversions."

Jaya glanced around the room. His eyes fell on a dice table with its ebony cup and ivory cubes. "Do you play *aksha?*"

"Only to pass an idle moment. It is more a child's pastime; the game turns neither on strength nor skill, only luck."

"Exactly. That is why it pleases me. A king's commands are obeyed to the letter, his orders carried out to the last jot and tittle. It is amusing and refreshing, from time to time, for a king—whose word is law—to subject himself to the vagaries of the dice and bow to a law greater than any of his own: the law of chance. Will you play a while? A friendly little game?"

"If you like." Tamar brought the table and set it between them. Jaya nodded, with the first flicker of interest that Tamar had seen from him.

"As your guest," Jaya said, "it is I who set the stakes and first roll the dice. Agreed?"

"Of course. That is the rule."

"The wager. What shall it be?" Jaya toyed with his beard. "Something of no consequence, a mere token for the sake of the game."

From his neck, Jaya took one of the chains, which he dropped offhandedly on the table. "For you, King of Sundari, to match."

Tamar stiffened. The links were heavy, of solid gold, worth more than enough to keep all his household fed and clothed for many months. What made him catch his breath was not the chain alone. Twice the size of a dove's egg, the diamond flashing at the end was a fortune in itself.

"Does this inconvenience you?" Jaya glimpsed the look on Tamar's face. "We are kings, not children playing for sweetmeats. Once laid down, the wager cannot be changed. But, in our harmless amusement, the rules may bend a little. I gladly withdraw it for something less, better fitting your circumstances."

"No. It stands." Tamar's chin went up. "We play by the rules, as they are. I have no single jewel like this, but I will have all my finest gems brought. You shall choose as many as needed to equal its value."

"Leave them in your treasury. We shall settle once the game is over. You have pledged them. Your word is sufficient."

Jaya dropped the cubes into the ebony cup, rattled them a moment, and rolled them out. He raised an eyebrow. "A number difficult to surpass. The odds favor me, it would seem. But who knows the subtle ways of chance? You, now, King of Sundari."

Tamar, in his turn, shook the cup and cast the dice onto the board.

2. The Iron Ring

K ing of Sundari"—Jaya half smiled—"I spoke of the vagaries of the dice. Here you see proof. The odds were in my favor, yet fortune stood at your side. You have won."

"Yes." Tamar breathed again. He stared at the diamond. Jaya scooped up the dice and once more dropped them into the cup.

"A small loss," he said, "but I shall try to regain it."

"No need." Tamar pushed the diamond and chain across the board. His hands shook, as if he had just been pulled back from the edge of a cliff. "Enough. I have no desire to play again. A friendly game—friends do not keep each other's possessions. Take back your wager. I shall find you some better distraction, if it pleases you."

"It does not please me. You dishonor me by scorning what you rightfully won."

"Call it a gift. Call it whatever you choose. I play no more."

"That is not for you to say," Jaya returned. "By rule, it is I who declare the game over. No. I set the stakes again. Double what they were."

Tamar's face tightened. What Jaya proposed would have put most of Sundari's treasure at risk. Tamar shook his head. "A king serves his people as well as himself, and answers to

them for his actions. For me, it would be reckless steward-
ship."

"Will you be reckless with your honor? You agreed to
the rules of *aksha,* did you not? Obey them."

"Lower the stakes, then, as you first offered to do."

"At first, yes. You did not accept. I no longer offer."
Jaya leaned over the table. "The game continues; we will
play it out. A childish pastime? Also a question of dharma.
We are both bound by dharma, King of Sundari.

"I do not break dharma," Jaya went on. "But you, if
you choose to break yours by refusing, so be it. End the
game—and shame yourself."

Tamar's blood rose. "Take up the dice."

Jaya rattled the cup and casually spilled out its contents.
"How interesting. Once more, the odds favor me. Once
more, will fortune favor you?"

The dice danced on the board as Tamar threw in turn.
Jaya's smile was thin as a thread.

"You have won again, King of Sundari. Now, to me.
At triple the stakes."

Without awaiting a reply, Jaya cast the dice. When
Tamar played in turn, his head spun like the ivory cubes.
He dimly grasped that his score was higher than his
opponent's.

"Truly, you are fortune's darling," Jaya said. "We play
on. Triple what I have lost."

How long even a maharajah might continue so rashly,
Tamar could not guess. Winning the next turn yet again,
Tamar gave up trying to calculate what he had gained. King
though he was, he had never imagined such wealth within
his reach. His thoughts raced over all the plans he had, until

now, only dreamed: waterways from the outlying hills to the public squares, parks and gardens throughout the city, wide streets, shining new buildings, houses for even the poorest of his subjects. He seized the dice cup eagerly, threw—and won again. He was giddy, flushed with wild joy and soaked in cold sweat.

The king of Mahapura yawned. "The game grows boring. One final throw for each of us. But, to play for meaningless trinkets—surely there are more exciting wagers. Something to add a touch of spice, a little stimulation."

"Wager what you please," Tamar said impatiently. The game had caught him up and held him in its arms like a lover, whispering in his ear.

"Honor binds you to accept it."

"As I do. Lay down the stakes."

"Life against life."

Tamar's head went back as if he had been struck. He was suddenly cold. "I do not understand."

"Very simple." Jaya folded his arms and looked impassively at Tamar. "Win, my life is yours to do with as you please. Lose, your life is forfeit to me."

"I cannot—"

"Can. And must." With a lazy movement, Jaya scattered the dice over the board. He pursed his lips. "Fortune still favors you. My score is small, easily surpassed."

Tamar's fingers had gone numb, scarcely able to hold the cup. The dice seemed to leap out by their own will.

"King of Sundari," Jaya said, "you have lost."

For long moments, Tamar did not speak. Then, in a voice he barely recognized as his own, he murmured, "This is folly. Madness."

"No. It is honor," Jaya said. "And you, so proud of keeping it, learn what it truly is. Have you ever tested it? I think not."

"I lost a wager. I still keep my honor."

"Then obey dharma." Jaya rose, taller than he had first appeared. "Hear me; understand me well. I leave you now; I have other matters to deal with. But, from this moment, you are at my command. You will go to my palace in Mahapura and there make good on your debt. Vow to do so without fail."

Tamar stood and looked squarely at Jaya. "You have my word as king and *kshatriya.*"

"I accept it." Jaya nodded. He gripped Tamar's wrist in one hand with such strength that Tamar clenched his teeth to keep from crying out; and, with the other, set a ring of black iron on his finger.

"The emblem of your pledge," Jaya said. "Your life is my property."

"So, King of Mahapura," Tamar flung back, "what will you do with it?"

"How dare you question me?" Jaya answered in a voice of cold stones grinding against each other. "Do I explain myself to a dog if I choose to kill him?" He dropped Tamar's wrist and turned away.

"I am not your dog!" Tamar lunged after him. Jaya was already through the doorway. Tamar would have followed, but a roar like breaking surf filled his ears. His legs gave way; he stumbled and fell to the floor. The ring felt as if it had been bound tight around his heart.

"I am not your dog!" he shouted again. And again. Until he drowned in the echoes.

3. Questions in the Palace

he woke sprawled on the carpet. The gaming table had been knocked over, dice and cup scattered. The iron ring circled his finger. Shuddering, he turned his face away. Then Rajaswami was there, and Darshan. Counselors and attendants crowded behind them. He could not understand why all were in night-robes.

"Are you ill, my boy?" Rajaswami knelt beside him. "Why aren't you in your bedchamber? Whatever happened? We heard you shouting. You roused the whole palace."

"Jaya. The king of Mahapura." Tamar sat up. "Where has he gone?"

Darshan put a hand on Tamar's shoulder. "What king, lad? No one's been here."

"He was. He came with horses, chariots, elephants. I saw them. You yourself warned me against him." Tamar turned to Rajaswami. "And you—you recited verses. The hawk and the sparrow."

"Recited? Dear boy, I haven't left my bed all night. Ah, of course. You've had a dream. Not a pleasant one, I should guess."

"And this?" Tamar thrust out his hand. "Look at it. Touch it. King Jaya put it on my finger." He blurted out all that had happened during the night. "We gambled," he said finally. "At the end, I wagered my life against his. I lost.

15

I gave my word of honor; I swore to surrender myself at Mahapura. And so I must."

"Surely you must not," Darshan said bluntly. "You dreamed. A dream binds you to nothing. No strange king has been in the palace. That is fact. How the ring comes to be on your finger, I cannot say. For the rest, put it from your thoughts. I tell you plainly and simply: It did not happen."

Darshan had spoken with so much certainty that Tamar almost believed him, and longed to believe him. He shook his head. "It happened," he murmured, "exactly as I said. I wish it had not. But it did. The debt is to be paid. Have I any other honorable choice?"

He turned to Rajaswami who, so far, had stayed silent and thoughtful. "*Acharya,* dear teacher," Tamar said, addressing the old man as he had done when a child, "guide me in this. What should I do?"

"A question not easily answered," Rajaswami replied. "Word given, word kept. Yes, that is dharma. But it does not apply to a vow made in a dream. The more difficult problem: Was it indeed a dream? How can you, or I, be certain we are not dreaming this very moment? Are you merely part of my dream? Am I merely part of yours? Was your game of *aksha* real, and what seems here-and-now is illusion?"

"How, then, can I know?" Tamar asked, in an anguished voice. "Tell me, *acharya.* My life depends on it."

"Alas, there is no way that you can be certain." Rajaswami sighed heavily. "This is beyond my guidance."

Tamar bowed his head. For some while, he said nothing. When at last he spoke, his voice was low and questioning:

"Perhaps there is some simple explanation for the ring.

As for the king of Mahapura, none of you saw him, his retainers, or his animals. I believe you. There is no sign he was ever here. And so it may well have been only a dream.

"Yes, I doubt that it happened—and yet, at the same time, I believe that it did. There is a way, and one way only, to be sure: I go to Mahapura."

"No!" Darshan burst out. "There's more in this than your own honor. You owe a debt? What do you owe to your kingdom? Your people?"

"Can I be a worthy king unless I'm first an honorable man?"

"Can you be a worthy king if you're dead? Throw your life away? If you think that's honorable—then, lad, you know nothing of the world and its ways.

"Do not do this," Darshan pressed. "No realm could hope for a finer king. Lad, when you first came to the throne, some of your own counselors spoke against you; you were too young; they doubted you could rule wisely. But I and your *acharya* knew your heart; we were sure of your worth. Your people love you. Do not abandon them for the sake of a foolish dream. All your hopes and plans for Sundari—will you leave them in the hands of self-serving courtiers?"

"I leave Sundari in the best of hands," Tamar said. "Yours."

"Not mine," Darshan returned. "I'm no courtier. I'm a soldier."

"Then obey your king," Tamar said. "I start for Mahapura now. To linger would only grieve me all the more."

"Are you sure that is what you wish to do?" said Rajaswami. "To undertake such a journey when you are filled with doubts and uncertainties?"

Tamar smiled at him. "I'll have to take my doubts and uncertainties with me."

"At least go in strength," Darshan urged. "Lead your army there. Make a show of force. The king of Mahapura —if such there be—will not dare to harm you."

"Will an army follow an uncertain leader on what may be a pointless quest?" replied Tamar. "A dream? Or not? I ask no one else to follow it."

"Not alone," said Rajaswami. "I shall go with you."

Tamar shook his head. "No. Dear *acharya,* I can't let you. Leave your studies and meditations for a long journey? The hardships will be more than you can bear."

"I shall bear them nevertheless," Rajaswami said. "I must. I swore to your parents I would be always at your side. Dear boy, I was there when you were born. I shall be there when you die, if it comes to that. It is my dharma."

"I can't order you to break it." Tamar smiled and embraced the old teacher. "Nor do I wish to."

They set off later that morning. Tamar had agreed that Darshan and a cavalry troop would escort them to the outlying Danda-Vana forest. Astride Gayatri, his beloved white mare, Tamar had exchanged royal silks for hunter's buckskins, his only weapons a sword and hunting knife, a bow and quiver of arrows. Rajaswami, in his usual white robe and scarf, perched uncomfortably on the dapple-gray Jagati.

Throughout the city, word had spread of the king's departure and the fate likely in store for him. Tamar could barely bring himself to look into the eyes of the townspeople crowding the streets. Some wept; some called out, begging him to stay; some watched in silent grief. He feared he might weaken and gladly turn back.

At the forest fringe, Darshan again pleaded to ride with Tamar; and again, Tamar refused.

"Stay as I ordered. If I live, I promise to return. If not, Rajaswami will bring you word. Until then, old friend, care for my people as I would do."

"I have laid your sandals on your throne," Darshan replied. "They will stay there as token that you are still king of Sundari and, to me, will always be."

Darshan and his warriors turned their mounts and rode from the forest. Tamar watched until they were out of sight. His heart was heavier than ever it had been. The light was fading. He tethered the horses and spread blankets from the saddle packs.

"I'm sorry, *acharya*," he said. "This is the best hospitality we can expect."

"For the moment, perhaps," Rajaswami said cheerfully, all the while rubbing his stiff legs. "We may find shelter in the occasional hermitage. Forests have always been a refuge for sages who prefer to shun the world's distractions. They dwell in their cottages and *ashrama*s and pursue their contemplations. I suspect they enjoy a visitation now and again, a welcome relief from their rigorous mental exertions."

"For your sake, I hope so," Tamar said. "Rough living and cold comfort—I don't have an easy mind about your well-being."

"I shall manage, never fear," said Rajaswami. "You, my boy, are trained to endure hardship. You are a *kshatriya,* born to the caste of warriors, highest and noblest—except, of course, for the *brahmana,* my own caste; whereas we *brah-*

*mana*s are devoted to matters of the spirit—high thinking, not earthly physicalities. But I shall accommodate myself, even to this fearsome place."

"Why fearsome? One forest is like another."

"Not this. It was old when much of the world was young. It was full-grown even in the Golden Age, those ancient days when gods and goddesses walked the earth, as the tales tell, and forest creatures could speak with human-kind.

"It's only for you, dear boy, that I'm here now. I've read of too many strange happenings; I'd prefer to leave this forest to itself. Furthermore, if a creature addressed me— why, I should hardly know what to answer."

With that, Rajaswami curled up on the grass. Tamar sat awhile. Darshan's words still troubled him. He was doing what honor demanded; but was it honor only for himself, not his kingdom? He had chosen duty to his warrior's code over duty to his people. A misjudgment? A false step on the path of what Rajaswami called "karma"—actions good or bad, all combining to shape a destiny, each deed sending ripples, like a stone dropped into a pond. Had his fate already encircled him in an iron ring of its own? No answer came, and he was too wearied to seek further.

To his surprise, next morning he woke lighthearted. *"Acharya,* I had a marvelous dream. I was here, in the forest. And all the trees turned bright gold. It was dazzling, wonderful—"

"Oh, my poor boy, I'm sorry to hear that." Rajaswami's face fell. "Not a happy dream. To see trees turn to gold— a bad omen. It foretells death."

Tamar's good spirits chilled. "Mine. A fitting dream."

"Not necessarily," Rajaswami hastened to assure him.

"Yours—perhaps. Or, indeed, mine. Or someone else al-together. Put it from your thoughts. The dream is done; you can't change it."

They ate quickly and in silence, neither one with ap-petite, then set off, walking their horses through the denser stretches of forest. Recalling Jaya's description of Mahapura, Tamar planned to bear east to the Sabla River and follow it to its headwaters. The sun was high as the forest thinned a little and a hard-packed trail opened. Tamar halted in mid-stride.

A man had stepped into the path. His face was scarred and weather-beaten. He wore hunting garments much like Tamar's, with a stained rag knotted around his head. Tamar quickly motioned for Rajaswami to back away.

The hunter had drawn a heavy bow to full stretch. Notched and ready on the string, a barbed arrow pointed at Tamar's throat.

4. Questions in the Forest

oosen your bow." Tamar spread his empty hands. "You have no quarrel with us."

"For me to say." The hunter's eyes narrowed. "I have a quarrel with all who come to poach in my forest."

"Yours?" Tamar said lightly. He glanced around. "Do you claim all this as your realm? A mighty kingdom."

"My hunting grounds. Will you dispute it?"

"Where you hunt is no interest to me," Tamar said. "We are not here to steal your game. We only pass through. We have other business."

"If you could direct us to a nearby *ashrama*," put in Rajaswami, "we would be greatly obliged. I find the lack of even rudimentary means of cleanliness unsettling, which you"—Rajaswami cast a disapproving eye on the hunter's grimy face and tangled, greasy hair—"apparently do not."

The hunter squinted. "What kind of old loon is this?"

"My good fellow, I am a *brahmana*." Rajaswami drew himself up in dignity. "As you should realize from my costume. My person is inviolate, not to be threatened with insults and arrows."

"Well, *brahmana*, you ask directions. I'll give them. I direct you to turn around and go back where you came from. You keep your life. I keep your horses. A fair exchange."

While the hunter's glare was on Rajaswami, Tamar un-shouldered his bow. In one swift motion, he snatched an arrow from the quiver and had it notched and aimed at the man.

"What you keep," said Tamar, "is your distance."

"Clever. Well done." The hunter gave a barking laugh. "Where did you learn that trick? Now, the question is: Can you loose your shaft faster than I can loose mine? Or have you the stomach to do so?"

"Find out for yourself."

The hunter stood awhile, holding his aim. He shrugged and lowered his bow. "I have no time for games of bravado. Go where you please. Wait!" he called, as Tamar stepped ahead. "Who are you?"

"Not your concern."

"Call it my curiosity. I let you live. You owe me an answer."

"I let you live. We are even. I owe you nothing."

"Tell me this, at least: What do you judge to be most valuable?"

"What is that to you?"

"Very little. Tell me, even so."

"An easy question, an easy answer," said Tamar. "Honor."

"What is the most dangerous battle?"

"With a stronger, better-armed enemy."

"And the best end to a battle?"

"When the enemy is defeated," Tamar said. "What else could it be?"

"Those are warrior's answers," the hunter said. "You are no poacher of rabbits."

"As I told you."

"One thing more. For amusement. To see if you can hit a mark as easily as you drew your bow." The hunter unstrung his own bow and threw it to the ground. "No fear. See, I am disarmed.

"Look there." The hunter pointed at a gnarled tree, almost out of bowshot down the path. "Do you see the knot in the trunk? Can you hit it?"

"Like you," replied Tamar, "I have no time for games."

"Or is the game too difficult? Would a closer target suit you better?"

"You chose it," Tamar said. "It will serve."

He drew the bowstring full and loosed the arrow. The shaft hissed through the air, straight to the tree and the center of the knot. The arrow strike had roused a hulking, ungainly bird, which flapped up from the branches, beat its ragged wings, and sped off in a lopsided flight, squawking indignantly.

"I left room for your own arrow." Tamar stepped back a pace. The hunter, along with his bow, had vanished. The forest was silent except for the fading screeches of the bird.

"Gone so fast?" Tamar looked around. "Where?"

"I didn't notice," said Rajaswami. "I was watching your arrow. Obviously, he slunk away ashamed, as well he ought to be."

Puzzled, Tamar whistled for the horses. With Rajaswami trotting at his heels, he strode toward the tree, but stopped short. From close at hand rose shrieks and howls, and desperate shouts for help. On the instant, beckoning to Rajaswami, he set off through the brush, scrambling over tangles of roots, plunging into the high grass and foliage lining a riverbank. At first, he thought he saw a man, half in half out of the water, clutching at the ground.

It was a monkey, nearly the size of Tamar himself, with arms longer than his own. A huge serpent had wrapped its coils around the creature, who yelled and squealed, struggling to keep from being dragged into the current.

"For mercy! Save me!" the monkey burst out, seeing Tamar. "Set me free of this overgrown worm. He'll drown me—if he doesn't first squeeze me to death."

"Hold on." Tamar sprang to the side of the monkey, whose face puckered and whose eyes rolled as his grip weakened. "I'll get you loose."

"You have my undying gratitude," the monkey gasped. "Undying, that is, if you'll be quicker about it."

Tamar sought to unwind the enormous reptile; but its coils were as big around as his waist and, for all his strength, he could not budge them. He drew his sword.

"That's good. Cut him to pieces," urged the monkey. "Chop him in two. Or three or four. The more the better. Only mind you don't slice my tail."

As Tamar raised his sword and was about to swing it down, the serpent lifted its head and hissed a warning:

"Stay your hand. You do ill to take my life. You have no right to interfere. It is a matter between this sneaking simian and myself."

"No longer," Tamar replied. "He begged me for help; I said I would give it, and so I must. Now it is a matter between you and me."

"You spoke too quickly," said the serpent, "in ignorance of my grievance against him."

Rajaswami, meantime, had clambered down the bank. "He has a point," he murmured to Tamar. "You've put yourself in a difficult situation without knowing the facts."

"I do no more than execute simple justice," the serpent said.

"A simple lie!" bawled the monkey. "Pay no attention. I'm the innocent victim of this armless, legless, hairless slug. He's a snake; he's likely to tell you anything. Ignore him. Chop away. I didn't do any harm."

Tamar looked from one to the other. "I'll judge the truth of that. As for you," he added to the serpent, "set him loose. He's in my charge while I hear your accusations."

"So be it." The great snake uncoiled. The monkey scrambled out of the water and flung himself to the bank, muttering insults and stretching the cramps from his arms and legs.

"I am Shesha, prince of the Naga-loka, the Serpent Realm," the snake began, raising himself partly upright. His scales glistened in rainbow colors; his tongue darted in and out like forked lightning. He spread his wide hood and Tamar saw that he bore on his head a sapphire, the gem as blue as the sky and even brighter.

"The facts are clear," Shesha went on, fixing Tamar with an unblinking eye. "I wished only to take my rest in the sun, here on this riverbank. While I slept, this insolent ape—"

"I'm not an ape, you scaly piece of rope," put in the monkey. "There's a difference—"

"Not to me," replied Shesha. "You are insolent, whatever you may be, and a thief as well." He returned his gaze to Tamar. "This jabbering creature came to steal my jewel. And would have done so, had I not awakened in time."

"You'd still be snoring away," said the monkey, "if some frowsy bird hadn't flown by, screeching its head off. That's what roused you. There's the real cause of the trouble. Otherwise—"

"Otherwise, you would have snatched my gem and made off with it. Yes, the bird woke me, for which I am grateful."

"And then?" said Tamar.

"There is no more than that," replied Shesha. "Because the bird luckily disturbed my repose, I was able to catch a thief red-handed. Now, King of Sundari, judge whether I have the right to punish him."

Tamar, taken aback at hearing himself so addressed, had no time to ask how Shesha knew this, for the monkey bounced up with a gleeful cry.

"We are fellow kings! I, Hashkat, am ruler of the Bandar-loka, the Monkey Realm." He lowered his voice and spoke hastily in Tamar's ear. "Between kings, one helps the other. A matter of professional courtesy."

"A matter of justice, even between kings," replied Tamar. "I have heard Prince Shesha. Now, King Hashkat, I will hear you."

"Nothing of what this prince of wigglers has told you is true," declared Hashkat. "The bird, yes, that much is correct. But I didn't come here with malice aforethought; I happened to pass this way by accident. One of my people is missing. No one can find him."

"What does this matter to me?" The Naga prince eyed Hashkat. "It is your concern, not mine."

"Tie a knot in that forked tongue of yours," retorted Hashkat. "As I was trying to explain, I myself was looking for little Akka. My search brought me here. I had no intention of stealing this reptile's jewel. It caught my eye; I stopped to admire. What harm in that? Even had I taken the jewel, I swear on my honor—"

"A monkey's honor?" Shesha hissed scornfully. "There is no such thing."

"There certainly is," Hashkat flung back. "I follow my dharma as faithfully as anyone."

"Do monkeys have dharma?" Tamar asked Rajaswami.

"Of course," the *acharya* replied. "All creatures do. Theirs, however, may be altogether different from yours."

"That's right," agreed Hashkat. "In this case, what someone else might call stealing is, among the Bandar-loka, a matter of highest principle. We devoutly believe that if something isn't nailed down, it's free for the taking; and if it can be pried loose—it isn't nailed down.

"Apart from that," Hashkat went on, "as far as the jewel is concerned, I'd have surely given it back. Probably. Maybe. If I'd been asked politely."

"Enough!" broke in Shesha. "You have heard us both. There can be no question in your mind. Justice must be executed."

"Yes, so long as it is justice," Tamar said. "For the sake of a jewel, I see no cause to take a life, even a monkey's. Prince Shesha, I cannot allow you to do so."

"And I do not abide by your judgment," replied Shesha. "You have a sword to enforce it," the Naga prince added. "With it, you can easily kill me if you choose, whereas I have no such weapon. If you wish to dispute me, do so without your blade. Unarmed, strength against strength. This monkey's miserable life? I challenge you to wrestle me for it."

5. Naga Raja

No, no, that won't do at all." Rajaswami raised a protesting hand. "My dear Prince Shesha, you complained of being at a disadvantage. What you propose is entirely to your own advantage. The match is grossly unfair."

"There, you see how he is," put in Hashkat, who left off grooming his long and luxuriantly furry tail. "Sneaky and slippery. Of course he'd choose wrestling. With those wriggling, writhing coils, he'd have it all his way. I suggest a footrace."

"Be silent," ordered Shesha. "You have no say in this."

"And you, my boy," Rajaswami added to Tamar, "I'm not certain it would be proper for you to take the risk. After all, you have a previous engagement, so to speak."

"By the code of honor, a warrior doesn't refuse a challenge," replied Tamar.

"Perhaps I can think of some exception to that rule," said Rajaswami.

"No discussions," the Naga prince hissed. "No hairsplitting excuses."

"A fine one to talk of hair," muttered Hashkat, curling a long upper lip. "Bald from head to tail."

"These are my terms," Shesha went on, ignoring the monkey. "We wrestle in the water—"

"Really, prince, you go too far," Rajaswami interrupted. "There you are even more at home than on land."

"Let him continue," Tamar said, "and make his challenge clear."

"If, even for an instant, you bring any part of me to dry ground," said the Naga prince, "I withdraw my claim. If you fail, or if you choose to give up the contest, his life is forfeit."

"Agreed and accepted. And you, king of monkeys," Tamar said, "stay here until the match is decided."

"What?" cried Hashkat. "I sit and cool my heels, my life in the balance, while you two flop around in a river? Majesty, with all respect, suppose you lose? I'm expected to give myself into his hands—hah, what hands?—and be swallowed up or squeezed into a pulp?"

"You'll wait with Rajaswami," Tamar ordered. "I want your solemn vow as a king."

"Of course, of course." Hashkat grumbled, "I know all about kings' solemn vows."

"See that you keep yours." Tamar stripped off his buckskins and shed his sandals while Hashkat hunkered down on the bank.

The Naga prince had already slithered into the river, leaving barely a ripple in his wake. Tamar plunged after him. No sooner was he in the water than he realized his mistake. He had misjudged the swiftness of the current, and had to fight against it even before grappling with Shesha.

He shook his dripping hair from his eyes. At first, he saw nothing of the serpent. When he did glimpse Shesha's head surfacing for a moment, he understood that he had made yet another miscalculation. The Naga prince intended staying in the middle of the river, making it all the more difficult for Tamar to force him to either shore.

Strong swimmer though he was, by the time he reached the spot where he had seen Shesha, Tamar's muscles ached with the strain of battling the current. The Naga prince had vanished. Treading water, Tamar cast around for Shesha.

Suddenly the river churned into foam. Shesha's tail lashed around Tamar's waist. Next instant, he was being dragged toward the river bottom. The Naga prince, Tamar realized, had chosen to fight not *in* the water but under it.

Before Shesha could throw another coil around him, Tamar squeezed free and shot to the surface, filling his lungs with air as the serpent turned and attacked. His best hope, he calculated, was to swim for shore, staying always a little out of reach, luring the Naga prince into the shallows.

Kicking his legs, sweeping his arms, Tamar struck out for the green line of the riverbank. Shesha writhed ahead of him, swung around to block his way, then lunged to seize him. Tamar flung himself aside as water roiled around him, and once more made for the river's edge. Shesha, however, gripped him by a leg and plunged downward.

Mud and gravel from the river bottom swirled in a yellow-brown cloud. Tamar, blinded, could not tell whether he was grasping Shesha's head or tail, but threw himself astride the scaly body and clung as to a bucking horse. The Naga prince heaved up and down, thrashing first one way then another, to dislodge his rider.

Their struggle brought them to the surface, but Tamar had only a moment of breath before Shesha dove again, straight to the riverbed; and there rolled over, slithering through weeds and water plants, across jagged rocks, seeking to scrape Tamar loose. Here, Shesha made his own miscalculation. The serpent lunged through a tangle of dead branches that clawed Tamar away, but left the Naga prince trapped amid the limbs as if caught in a net.

Tamar floated free. He glimpsed Shesha flailing vainly in the mesh of branches. The Naga prince halted a moment, swung his head around, and stared coldly. Tamar hesitated; he had only to swim upward into air and sunlight, leaving Shesha below in a death trap. The serpent was watching him without a sign of surrender or plea for help, only the flat, steady gaze.

A few strokes brought Tamar to the imprisoning branches. Holding what breath he had left, he threw all his strength against the underwater thicket, while Shesha heaved and strained until the limbs gave way. Tamar kicked clear of them and headed for the surface.

The Naga prince seized him. For all his outraged struggles, his fury at betrayal instead of gratitude, Tamar could not escape. Shesha bore him farther along the riverbed. Lungs ready to burst, Tamar found himself dragged into a black tunnel.

The passageway curved downward, turned up sharply first one way then another. Tamar could breathe again. The water had fallen away. Shesha wriggled onto the wide shelf of what seemed the mouth of a cavern. Still gripping Tamar, the serpent slid through the arching entrance and unwound his coils. Panting, Tamar stumbled to his feet and turned, angry and questioning, on Shesha.

"You have broken off our contest, Prince Shesha. Do you dare claim to have won?"

"Our combat is unfinished," Shesha declared, "but, since you saved my life, I fight no more against you. As there is no clear victor, I leave it to my father to say in his wisdom where justice lies."

Shesha motioned with his head. At the far end of the cavern, two huge serpents lay on thrones of carved crystal. Both wore crowns encrusted with jewels. The chamber itself blazed with gems set into the walls and heaped high in every corner.

Tamar stared at the dazzling stones. "Where have you brought me?"

"To the heart of the Naga-loka," replied Shesha. "This is the palace of my father and mother."

The elder serpent stretched up and spread his hood. His ancient scales were thick, heavy as armor, gleaming and twinkling as he swayed erect. His tongue flickered in and out while his voice came as a long, sighing whisper.

"Approach, King of Sundari. I am Takshaka, the Naga Raja; and, here, my revered wife, Shila Rani."

"How do you know me?" Tamar stepped closer to the thrones. On either side, he saw other serpents, the Naga courtiers and attendants, coiled and looking at him in silent curiosity.

"You have been observed many times," Takshaka replied. "The domain of the Naga-loka reaches through all waterways, through all rivers and lakes. We see you here and there in Sundari when you take your ease at a woodland pool or ramble along a stream."

"The doings of a small king of a small kingdom should hardly interest the Naga folk," Tamar said.

"The deeds of kings are always of interest," said Takshaka, "to others, if not to themselves. The actions of the powerful have bearing on all around them."

"This is true," Shila Rani said. "Listen."

One day, beside a brook,
A half-grown boy
Played in the grass
And laughed with joy
To see a Naga
Hatching from its shell.

The lad was strong and fearless
And could well
Have crushed the feeble snake
Beneath his heel
Without a second thought
Or need to feel
Remorse or grief. But, no,
He turned aside

And let the Naga live
That might have died.

"The new-hatched Naga was Prince Shesha," explained Shila Rani, "and you were that half-grown boy."

"If I left him unharmed, I'm glad," replied Tamar, "but I remember nothing of that day."

"We remember," said Takshaka. "We Naga are an ancient folk. We have seen much. Little happens in your human realm that escapes our notice. And we forget nothing."

"Even so," said Shila, "we are puzzled to find you in our kingdom."

"I begin a long journey," Tamar said. "Allow me to continue it."

"Not yet," said Shesha. "We wrestled over the life of Hashkat, the one who calls himself king of the Bandar-loka," he added to Takshaka, "and now ask you to judge us."

"Why concern yourself with foolish monkey folk?" asked the Naga Raja.

"I am concerned when anyone dares to steal what is mine," said Shesha, beginning his account of what happened at the riverside. When he had finished, Tamar offered his own.

"All that Prince Shesha tells is true," he concluded. "Whether Hashkat would have stolen the gem or given it back, I do not know. I cannot guess his intentions. In any case, the gem was not stolen. Prince Shesha has it still, and has lost nothing. Should Hashkat be punished for what he might have intended, but did not do? Perhaps, perhaps not. Either way, it should not cost him his life. I say no more than that."

"Prince Shesha acted correctly," the Naga Raja declared. "He was gravely offended. It was his right—indeed, his dharma required it. Correct—yes, but only up to a point. The punishment would have gone beyond that point."

The Naga Raja turned to Shesha. "You allowed your wrath to overwhelm you. That was an offense against reason. You would have used power against the powerless. That, my son, was an offense against compassion. In the light of those considerations, hear my judgment: The monkey's life is to be spared."

"I am reprimanded." Shesha bowed his head. "You have spoken in your wisdom. Let it be as you have decided."

"And you, King of Sundari," put in Shila Rani, "we are curious to know what led you to this encounter. A journey, you said? What is the nature of it?"

"A dream," Tamar said, after describing his night in the

palace. "Sometimes I think it is nothing more. Yet, when I see the ring on my finger I must believe it happened, then only doubt and wonder again.

"Can you help me?" he went on. "Your domain reaches far and wide. Do you know of King Jaya? Of Mahapura? That would assure me there is such a person, at least."

"Only vague rumors, nothing more," answered Takshaka. "I am saddened I cannot ease your heart."

"I, too," Tamar said. "Now let me join my *acharya* and Hashkat. The monkey will be glad to hear your judgment."

"You have my leave," the Naga Raja said. "Prince Shesha will guide you through the passageways. First, as token of our goodwill, choose gems from any that you see here."

"Thank you," replied Tamar, "but your goodwill needs no token. Where I go, I have no need of jewels."

"Will you dishonor us by refusing an offered gift?" said Shila Rani. "Take as many as you please, King of Sundari."

Takshaka likewise insisted. So obliged, Tamar went to the heaps of precious stones, scanning one after the other. Among them glittered diamonds bigger even than Jaya's. Any one of them would have made his kingdom rich, if he broke off his journey and brought this treasure back to Sundari. He wondered if it was his karma to do so, and if this was the purpose of his dream. Ruefully, he shook his head. His eye fell on the smallest of the gems: a ruby that fit easily into the palm of his hand as he bent and picked it up.

"I choose this one," he said, "though your generosity is greater than any of your jewels."

The Naga courtiers whispered among themselves. Takshaka nodded approval.

"You have chosen modestly, without greed," the Naga

Raja said. "I commend you. Your choice is more interesting than you know. We call it 'Fire Flower.' See the lotus carved on it. This is the most curious of our treasures. One of my people found it by chance in a lake bed and bore it to me. How or why it came to be there is a mystery."

"And may always be," added Shila. "Now it is yours."

As Tamar pressed his palms together in the gesture of *namaste,* to thank and honor the Nagas, Prince Shesha declared:

"I will take you back to the river. Tell the monkey he is fortunate that my father was more lenient than I."

Tamar followed Shesha from the cavern and took firm hold of his tail as they slid through the tunnels. Once gaining the shallows, Shesha twisted away, leaving Tamar to find his footing amid the pebbles and flat stones of the riverbed.

The Naga prince vanished. Tamar stood, pulling off the strands of weeds clinging to his face. Before he could wipe the water from his eyes and clamber ashore, laughter burst from the riverbank.

6. A Beautiful Gopi

———————◆———————

Some dozen dark-skinned and bold-eyed girls knelt by the shallows where they had been doing their laundry. By the time Tamar, taken by the sight, realized he had left his buckskins with Rajaswami, the girls burst into greater fits of laughter. Stepping back into deeper water, he slipped and went floundering head over heels, making them laugh all the more. He came up choking; and, even for a king, found it as difficult to keep his dignity as it was to keep his footing. He wondered if he was blushing royally.

The girls, meantime, giggled among themselves. Some frankly stared; others made a show of covering their faces with the ends of their saris, or whispered behind their hands, all of them finding his predicament marvelously entertaining.

In better circumstances, Tamar would not have objected to the attentions of winsome young women; by now, however, he had had his fill of being soaked and chilled, let alone being giggled at, and he called out to them to throw him one of the garments they had been scrubbing.

This set off a new chorus of laughter as the maidens waved pieces of laundry at him, urging him to come ashore and fetch them for himself.

"Never fear, we won't harm you," cried a girl. "We're only bashful *gopis*—cow-tenders, village milkmaids. You see how shy we are."

One of the *gopi*s at last had mercy on him. She picked up a length of cloth and waded knee-deep into the current. Some of her companions egged her on; others teased her as much as they had Tamar.

"Look at Mirri, the shameless creature," clucked one. "How does she dare? A stranger! Who knows what sort he is?"

"A handsome sort," replied her neighbor. "You're only vexed you didn't think of it first."

Instead of wrapping himself in the linen that the *gopi* named Mirri held out to him, Tamar only gaped like a smitten idiot. Of darker complexion than her companions, her skin glowed richly; her shining black hair fell to her waist. The ruby was clutched safely in his hand, but his heart was leaping every which way like a fish on a line. Paying no attention to the *gopi*s whooping merrily along the shore, his gaze never leaving Mirri, who stood with the current swirling around her, he began:

> *A stranger, lost, from riverbed I rise*
> *To lose myself once more in lotus eyes*
> *And dark-hued grace no king has ever seen.*
> *What realm is this, so blest with such a queen?*

To which Mirri lightly answered:

> *A queen am I, with all I could desire.*
> *My palace is the pasture and the byre.*
> *My royal robe, a cowgirl's rough attire.*

Tamar went on:

> *If made of flowers, as the poets tell,*
> *How do love's arrows fly so well?*

Swift to my breast they go and there strike deep
A heart no longer mine, a gopi's now to keep.

Mirri, with the trace of a smile, replied:

Fresh in their colorful array,
Flowers that blossom in a day
May by evening fade away.

On lotus, dew soon turns to frost.
Gopis discover, at their cost,
A heart can be too quickly lost.

With that, Mirri turned and waded to the riverbank. Tamar hastily wrapped the length of cloth about his waist and tucked away the ruby. As he climbed ashore, the *gopis* surrounded him, chattering questions and casting appraising glances, until Mirri at last had to shoo them off.

"Thank you for these elegant garments." Tamar grinned and pressed his palms together. "I never knew that *gopis* had this custom of welcoming strangers."

"Perhaps because we see so few of them." The girl's black eyes looked steadily at Tamar. She stood as tall as Tamar himself, with a slender neck and narrow shoulders. From her bearing, Tamar judged that she had considerable authority among her companions. "Let alone strangers who claim to lose their hearts while up to their ears in a river," Mirri added. "I could also ask if it's the custom, wherever you're from, to try to turn the head of a humble village cowgirl?"

"If that's what you please to call yourself," replied Tamar. "I've seen princesses less royal."

"If you say so," Mirri answered. "No doubt you've seen more princesses than I have."

"Did you come for the Choosing?" piped up one of the smaller girls.

"Hush, Vati," Mirri said to her. "If he did, you'll find out soon enough. Let him first tell us who he is."

However, when Tamar gave his name, Mirri shrugged. "I don't know any more of you than I did before. A name says nothing of the one who carries it. I think there may even be a king called Tamar, in the realm of Sundari."

"There used to be," Tamar said. "No longer. And your village? To what kingdom does it belong?"

"To none," Mirri said proudly. "Ours is a free village, and so it has always been. We grow enough to feed ourselves, we tend our cattle, we don't steal our neighbors' herds or land, and our doings are of no interest to anyone but ourselves."

"The Choosing! The Choosing!" The girl called Vati interrupted, poking at Tamar. "Is that why you're here?"

"Small *gopi*," Tamar said, "if I knew what it was, I could answer you better."

"Everybody knows," Vati insisted. "The song tells it."

> *Village lads and cowherds vie,*
> *Striving to catch a gopi's eye.*

> *Gopis raise melodious voices*
> *And declare their loving choices.*

> *A wreath of flowers is the token*
> *Of a pledge that's never broken.*

Handsome youth and maiden fair
Join to make a happy pair.

Feasts are set, musicians play
To mark this joyful wedding day.

"It's our betrothal festival," Mirri explained. "When the girls turn the age to wed, our young men show off their strength and skill—running, wrestling, shooting arrows, and all such. Each girl chooses the one who best pleases her and sets a wreath of flowers 'round his neck."

"And you," Tamar said to Mirri, "of course, you have your eye on some strapping village lad, and your mind already made up."

"No. I'll take no part in it."

"Why not? You'll break the heart of some adoring, hopeful cowherd."

"Because I care to make no choice."

"I've never seen such a festival. I'd like to be on hand for the happy occasion."

Mirri looked away and did not answer. Tamar went on:

"First, I need to find my companion. We were separated, I don't know what's become of him, and he knows nothing of what's become of me."

During this, he had been anxiously glancing up and down the riverbank. As best he could reckon, the current had borne him downstream. He would have to retrace his steps to where he had left Rajaswami and Hashkat. He shuddered at the thought of the *acharya* on his own in the wilds with only a monkey—and a feckless one, at that.

When he asked Mirri if he might borrow some better

clothing and a pair of sandals, she nodded, tight-lipped, and gestured toward the nearby village.

With the *gopi*s trailing behind, chattering among themselves, he followed Mirri to a cluster of flat-roofed, open-fronted buildings. A handful of youngsters was sweeping and sprinkling the market square to keep down the dust; banners had already been hoisted on long poles, with garlands slung between. Beyond lay cattle pens and fenced pastures of sweet grass.

Mirri led him across the veranda of the largest house and into a cool, shaded common room. The thickset man who came to greet them, his bronze skin darkened still more by sun and wind, was Nanda, the village chief. He had, as Mirri explained, adopted her when her parents died. His wife, Yashoda, a gray-haired, vigorous woman in a neatly wrapped sari, hurried to offer a tray of fruit, then spoke apart with Mirri.

As Tamar sat on a bench at the wooden table, the two women disappeared, while Nanda eased into a place beside him and eyed the unexpected guest with curiosity. Unwilling to break hospitality by too closely questioning Tamar's business, Nanda took the countryman's way of sniffing around the edges of the subject. Tamar, however, told only of encountering the maidens on his way to the Sabla.

"Well, you're on the right path," Nanda said, "though you've a good long ways to go. This river here is the Kurma. Just you follow it upstream. You'll find where it branches from the Sabla.

"As for our village girls, pay no heed to their antics. Before the Choosing, they all go light-headed."

"Not all," replied Tamar. "There's one who tells me she won't take part."

"Mirri. Yes." Nanda sighed. "It's time for her to wed, and expected of her. And there's not a lad who wouldn't be overjoyed if she chose him. Even if I put my foot down and insisted—eh, she'd still do as she pleases. We love her as dearly as if she'd been born to us, but she's willful, with a mind of her own. Always was. A real marvel with our animals, though. The cows even give better when she's the one to milk them, as if they know what she wants and are happy to oblige.

"No, I'll not force her to marry. Even when she was tiny, there were times when she seemed to be waiting, looking for something no one else could see. So, best leave her to decide matters for herself.

"You, now." He cocked an eye at Tamar. "You're a high-caste sort of fellow, plain as day to see, and a good many cuts above us folk here. You'd not be much interested in our doings, would you?"

Before Tamar could answer, Yashoda came with sandals, tunic, and cowherd's leggings. Tamar went to a corner of the room and put on the coarse garments. Through the open back door, he caught sight of Mirri by the pasture fence, where a white cow nuzzled her hand. He stepped outside and went to her.

She started as he drew closer, then said, "You're better dressed than you were, but no one would mistake you for a cowherd. I thought you'd go looking for your friend."

"I will. I wanted to thank you. I hope I didn't interrupt your conversation."

"With Surabi? I've named her after the magical cow in the old tales, the one who could grant any wish."

"So you were wishing? What for?"

"If I could wish"—Mirri hesitated, then turned her eyes full on Tamar—"I might wish you'd never come here."

Tamar bridled. "I hadn't planned on it. What does it matter to you, in any case?"

"Because you've set my life topsy-turvy. I was happily going about my business—until you came. I hadn't expected someone popping out of a river. My heart was my own, before that. As I wanted it to be."

"And now?"

"I don't know. It's all changed. I don't know what to do about you. I don't even know who you are."

"I told you all that was needed."

"You told me nothing." She seized his hand as Tamar reached out to her. "What are these?" She touched the thin white scars deeply bitten into his wrist. "The marks of a bowstring. Warrior's marks?"

"And if they are?" He broke off. Yashoda was calling him. Mirri turned away. Tamar hurried into the house. From the veranda Yashoda beckoned urgently, saying that someone had come asking for him.

There was great excitement in the square. Nanda and a crowd of villagers had gathered to admire the pair of fine horses and to murmur over the splendid quality of the sword, bow, and quiver tied to Gayatri's saddle pack.

"Rajaswami!" Tamar pressed through the circle of onlookers to embrace the old *acharya*.

"Ah, here you are, safe and sound." Rajaswami's face lit up at the sight of Tamar. "Excellent. And what a pleasant little spot for a rest. My bunions need some consolation after scrambling along that riverbank."

"How did you find me?" Tamar, much relieved, drew

him apart. "Where's Hashkat? His life is spared. He'll be glad to know."

"I'm sure he would be, if he'd waited to find out. But, you see, he ran off—"

"Broke his word? Wretch! He promised, he swore—"

"Don't think too harshly of him," said Rajaswami. "A monkey's dharma no doubt encourages that sort of behavior. Otherwise, he was most helpful. He went up and down the river, watching for you. When he saw you come out, he ran back to tell me. So, here I am. And you, my boy, where did you get those clothes? They have a distinct odor of cow."

Yashoda, meantime, had come to welcome this second visitor. Tamar signaled Rajaswami to say nothing of their quest. Yashoda, in any case, asked no explanation and invited the grateful *acharya* to wash and tidy himself. She ordered some of the village youngsters to fetch buckets of water; and, in a quiet corner behind the house, Rajaswami scrubbed away the dust and grime while Tamar replaced the cowherd's garments with his own buckskins.

As the *acharya* wrung water from his beard and soaked his tender toes, Tamar quickly told him of Shesha, Naga Raja, and the gift of the ruby; and finally, of the *gopis* and his meeting with Mirri.

"Ah—yes, one thing more," Tamar admitted after some hesitation. "You see, what's happened—*acharya,* I'm in love with her."

Instead of showing surprise or disapproval, Rajaswami only smiled cheerfully and shook his head. "Oh, my boy, I doubt that very much. You may believe so at the moment —you're a young man, after all. But, no. Let me point this out:

What seems to be love beyond any question
Is usually a case of simple indigestion.

"I'm quite sure she's a perfectly splendid young lady," Rajaswami went on, "but I needn't remind you there's a question of caste. Plainly put, you're of the nobility, whereas, dear boy, she's a *shudra,* the lowest caste of all— except, of course, for the *chandala*s, so low they count as nothing whatever.

"That in itself presents a serious difficulty," he warned. "Even apart from the difference in caste, you're hardly in proper circumstances for affairs of the heart. But, cheer up. By tomorrow, when we're on our way again, it will all be forgotten."

"No, it won't—" Tamar began.

Yashoda was calling them for the evening meal. Rajaswami eagerly took a place at table beside Nanda. Tamar, without appetite, barely touched the food that Mirri silently brought. The girl, in fact, never spoke or looked at him, but stayed with Yashoda, talking in whispers.

Only after all had eaten, and Yashoda was laying down mats for the visitors to sleep on the veranda, did Mirri step forward. She stood a moment, gave Tamar a quick glance, then turned to Nanda.

"I've changed my mind," she said, as if in challenge. "Tomorrow, I'll take part in the Choosing."

7. Thorns

---◆---

ajaswami had been too well fed to be very much
awake. Tamar was too happy to sleep at all. Sitting
cross-legged on the dark veranda while the *acharya* drowsed,
he kept up a long, one-sided conversation, going over every
word he and Mirri had exchanged as if he were admiring
precious jewels.

"She'll be at the Choosing," he said, for the third or
fourth time. "You know what that means."

Rajaswami opened one eye. "It means, as you've already
told me, she'll choose her future husband. As will the other
village girls. It should be an enjoyable rustic festival. We
might spare a few moments to observe it from a distance."

"What distance? *Acharya,* she's going to choose me; I'm
sure she will."

"Or is that what you want to believe?" Rajaswami,
yawning, sat up. "I've only been half asleep, so I heard half
of what you told me the first time, and the other half the
second time. And didn't you say she wished you hadn't
come here? That you'd upset everything?

"Besides, dear boy, you can't take part. You? No, no,
out of the question."

"Why not? These games—running, wrestling, archery
—how can I lose? Against cowherds? I'm a warrior, with
better skill than any—"

48

"That's precisely why you must stay out of it. You, a trained warrior, a king, set yourself against village lads? Absolutely improper! By the warrior's code, you may never challenge a lesser opponent. To do otherwise would be dishonor past mending.

"As for marriage between high caste and low," continued Rajaswami, "that could possibly be overlooked in a special case. But, my boy, the young lady may well choose some village youth merely to keep her life from being turned upside down by an unknown wanderer. And your own life? It is yours no longer. You pledged it to King Jaya—if he exists. You have no business giving your heart to anyone, let alone accepting Mirri's, even if she offers it."

"*Acharya,* do you tell me I have no right to love?"

"Ah, my boy, at your age grand passions come and go. There's always another. It may sting and smart at the moment, and you have my sympathy; but, keep looking on the bright side.

"Apart from that," Rajaswami added, "you have all your journey ahead of you. The promise you made—"

"But if it was only a dream? *Acharya,* what do you expect of me?"

"The proper question is: What do you expect of yourself? Will you break your dharma? My heart aches for you, whatever you decide; but it's altogether up to you."

Tamar stood and leaned over the veranda railing. The little square was empty in the moonlight. By morning, he well imagined, it would be alive with eager suitors, *gopis* and their wreaths of flowers, Mirri among them. He clenched his hand so tightly that the iron ring bit into the flesh of his palm.

"Come, *acharya,*" he said at last, in a flat voice. "I'll fetch the horses."

"Now?" Rajaswami frowned. "Leave in the middle of the night, without a word of thanks for hospitality? A farewell to the young lady?"

"Don't ask me to do more than I can bear. Get your things ready."

Gayatri whickered fondly as Tamar patted her neck and swung astride. With Rajaswami trotting behind him, they rode silently across the square and toward the river. Only once did Tamar allow himself to look back. By then, the village was lost to sight.

—◆—

"Majesty!"

Tamar reined up. In the pink traces of dawn, he glimpsed a long-tailed, slope-shouldered figure scuttling from the bushes. As Tamar dismounted, Hashkat, in a bowlegged, lurching gait, came to a halt in front of him.

"Forgive me." Hashkat wrinkled his brow and pressed his palms together. "It's not my fault."

"Forgive you for what?" Tamar eyed the monkey severely. "For being dishonorable? For breaking your word to me? For running off when I told you to wait? Or whatever else? You've been pardoned by the Naga Raja himself. Why ask forgiveness?"

"Well, I don't. Not really, not for any of that," Hashkat replied, with no sign of being any way ashamed of himself. "Considering the possibility of being gobbled up and digested by some ill-tempered reptile, I did what any decent, right-thinking monkey would have done: left the premises

immediately. Among us Bandar-loka, one of the highest virtues is: Don't get eaten."

"I rather suspected that was the case," said Rajaswami.
"My boy, you can't blame him for adhering to his principles."

"I only ask forgiveness for not joining you sooner," said
Hashkat. "I gather you won the wrestling match and I simply wanted to thank you. I may be a monkey, but I'm not
an ingrate. I saw you go into the village. I didn't dare follow.
I'm too well known. I couldn't risk it."

"Of course not. An upcountry little village of cowherds
and farmers is surely a dangerous place."

"For me it is," said Hashkat. "Oh, I used to venture in
from time to time, lurking about here and there. Once,
when the *gopis* were bathing in the river"—at this, Hashkat
gave a toothy grin, wagged his head, and chuckled gleefully—"I crept up and stole away their clothes. They came
after me like a swarm of hornets, but I was too quick for
them. They spent the day plucking their saris off tree limbs.
I can't say that endeared me to them.

"Naturally," he went on, "I'd sometimes pop into one
house or another and make off with a nice lump of butter
or some tasty victuals."

"You're a thief on top of everything else?" Tamar exclaimed. "A shameless robber?"

"Of course. Completely shameless," agreed Hashkat.
"You have to understand. That's what we monkeys do. Our
business, so to speak, is—monkey business. What else? But
now, in any case, I won't set foot in the village. One night,
you see, I was a bit thirsty and sneaked into a cowshed. One
of the *gopis* caught me milking her cow.

" 'Milk do you want?' she cried. 'Milk you'll have!' So she poured it all over my head. And swore if I ever came back she'd tie so many knots in my tail I'd never unravel them.

"That was warning enough." Hashkat protectively curled his tail around him. "She'd have done it, for sure. A handsome, buxom *gopi,* but a tiger when she's roused. 'I'm king of the monkeys,' I tell her. 'Then here's your crown,' says she, and bangs the bucket down on my head—it took me half an hour to pull it off. No, I won't risk crossing that one's path again.

"So, I waited until you left the village. But, indeed, I'm in your debt. You wrestled that overweening angleworm for my sake. You saved my life—a small matter to a king like you, but of intense personal interest to me. Another essential rule in a monkey's dharma: Stay alive."

Rajaswami, meantime, had been clearing his throat and making hungry noises. Tamar, without much interest, lit a cook fire and laid out a meal from the saddle packs. Food being the furthest thing from Tamar's mind, Hashkat helpfully downed his benefactor's portion, smacking his lips, sucking his long fingers, and scooping up any leftovers.

"Now," said Hashkat, leaning back on his haunches, "I've told you I'm searching for little Akka—a promising young fellow, I hope he's come to no harm—dare I ask what brings you from Sundari?"

"I should think His Majesty's purposes are no concern of yours," said Rajaswami.

"Of course, they aren't," said Hashkat. "But that's another rule among the Bandar-loka: If it's none of your business, be sure to stick your nose in it."

Tamar's heart still weighed so heavily that he was glad

to unburden it even to a monkey, and he explained the circumstances that had set him on his journey.

"You obey a stern dharma," Hashkat remarked, when Tamar finished. "Very noble, honorable, commendable, and all that. I admire and revere you for it, but—well, it's just not my style."

"You follow your own rules," said Tamar. "A monkey would hardly understand a warrior's code of honor."

"Oh, but I do," protested Hashkat. "I used to have one. I was born into the warrior caste—"

"What?" exclaimed Tamar. "What are you telling us? A monkey—and a *kshatriya?* Impossible!"

"Majesty, it's true," Hashkat insisted. "You see, I wasn't always a monkey. I was born a human being of noble family in the kingdom of Muktara. I confess I never took to being a warrior, to the disappointment of my parents. They chided me for being idle and frivolous, which I certainly was. When my classmates were diligently studying matters of dharma, or exercising with weapons, I preferred swimming in the river or climbing trees in the forest.

"When I was grown, they expected me to go off shooting arrows and chucking spears every time the king squabbled with his neighbors. The more I thought about that, the more I wondered: Why should I do harm to total strangers? And, for that matter, why should total strangers do harm to me? So I quit the warrior trade and took to the road, free as the breeze, living by my wits. Ignoble cowardice, according to the code of honor; to me, plain common sense."

"That tells us nothing about your being a monkey," said Tamar.

"I'm coming to it," said Hashkat. "Yes, well, I was walking along the road one afternoon and there's a *brahmana* sound asleep under a tree. This old geezer had the longest beard I'd ever seen. I couldn't resist. I took the end of his beard and tied it around his ankles. Then I tickled his nose with a blade of grass until he woke, scrambled up the tree as fast as I could, and sat on a limb to watch the fun.

"Oh, you should have seen him stumbling, tripping over his feet, getting himself knotted worse than ever. I laughed so hard I nearly fell out of the tree. When he finally untangled his beard, he shook his fist at me, calling me a disrespectful, impudent ne'er-do-well.

" 'Make sport of a *brahmana?*' he cries, his eyes like a pair of hot coals. 'Come down immediately, you wretch, and accept the punishment you deserve.'

" 'I don't think so,' I say, safe on my perch. 'If you mean to punish me, you'll have to catch me first.'

" 'Insolent rogue,' the old coot says, pointing a skinny finger at me, 'you'll get your comeuppance no matter how high you climb. Hear me well:

> *Monkey see, monkey do.*
> *Monkey's just the same as you.*
> *Do like a monkey, be a monkey too.'*

"Next thing I know," said Hashkat, "I'm a monkey, tail and all. The *brahmana* vanished, I don't know how or where. I was too busy wondering what had happened to me. Plainly and simply, I've been a monkey ever since."

"He transformed you? Then and there? Unbelievable!" Tamar turned to Rajaswami. "Can this be so? Can such a thing happen?"

"Oh, yes," Rajaswami said. "There have been many similar cases. I've read about them in the old lore. But this can be done only by a great sage, a most mighty *rishi* who studied long, hard years to gain the secret of such power. The one who transformed Hashkat was no ordinary *brahmana.*"

"A terrible punishment." Tamar put a hand on Hashkat's hairy shoulder. "I'm sorry for what happened to you."

"No need," said Hashkat. "Once I got used to being a monkey, I was grateful to that *rishi*. It's a relaxing life, without much to do except look for mischief. Easier than when I was expected to behave like a warrior. Besides, since I was bigger and stronger than your average monkey, in no time at all the Bandar-loka chose me as their king—which made things even pleasanter."

"You never miss being a human?" asked Tamar.

"A little bit from time to time," said Hashkat, happily scratching himself. "A monkey's life has its limitations, but a monkey's dharma suits me very well. What it comes down to is: If it tastes good, eat it; if it feels good, do it. I recommend your trying it. Why go on a journey when you expect to be killed at the end of it? No sensible monkey would consider such a thing.

"I'll tell you what I'll gladly do," Hashkat went on. "The realm of the Bandar-loka is large. Actually, it's anywhere and everywhere we happen to be. Stay with me and I'll share my kingship with you. For one thing, you saved my life, so I'm obliged to you; for another, you're a real king and know more about that business than I do. We'll divide the responsibilities—there aren't many. Nobody can really govern monkeys. Who would want to?"

"That's a generous offer." Tamar smiled and shook his head. "But I mean to keep on with my journey."

"Your dharma must pinch you something awful,"

replied Hashkat. "You'd find a little elbow room a lot more comfortable. As I said, I admire you, but I don't envy you. In any case, let me do you a service by warning you: Don't follow the river, not at this point. You'll come up against a heavy thorn forest just ahead. You can't get past. Turn off, circle around. Then you double back to the Kurma."

"Turn aside only because of thorns?" Tamar said. "I have an advantage." He pointed at his sword. "I'll cut a passage through them."

"A warrior's way of doing," said Hashkat. "Straight ahead, hacking and hewing. I should have expected that of you. Well then, let me come along and save myself some time."

To this, Tamar willingly agreed; and they set off, leading the horses, with Hashkat scuttling ahead. As the monkey king had warned, a tall curtain of tangled vines soon rose in front of them, stretching in both directions as far as Tamar could see. There were, at least, fewer thorns than he expected.

He hesitated, wondering if there were some better way past the barrier. But since he had already declared his decision, he drew his sword and took a powerful swing at the prickly obstacle. The blade bit deeply into the vines. However, when he tried to pull it loose and launch another stroke, the sword would not come free. He gripped the hilt in both hands and, for better leverage, set a foot against the vines. For all his strength, the sword still would not budge. Nor would his foot.

With a cry of annoyance and impatience, he tried to struggle free. Hoping by sheer force to part the thorny curtain, he grasped the vines, only to find his hands caught as tightly as his foot. Now alarmed as well as vexed, he heaved himself back and forth, thrashing up and down, side to side, which made his predicament all the worse.

The vines had captured him.

8. A Miserable Bird

At first, he believed the thorns had trapped him; but Tamar quickly understood otherwise. What held him fast was a sticky juice, a thick resin oozing from the vines. Hashkat scurried to help. Before Tamar could warn him, the monkey was firmly glued and in an even worse plight. His long tail was caught, and his struggles only succeeded in turning him head over heels, dangling upside down.

Rajaswami trotted up. "Good heavens, whatever are you doing?"

"Keep back," Tamar called over his shoulder. "Or you'll be stuck along with us." The sap from the vines was hardening and he saw it was urgent to break free; yet each movement embedded him deeper.

"*Acharya,* listen to me carefully," Tamar ordered. "We'll need the horses to haul us loose. Fetch ropes from the saddle packs."

"Step lively, too," put in Hashkat, flailing back and forth. "Do you think I enjoy hanging here like a bat?"

"Hashkat first," Tamar said, when Rajaswami hobbled back with the coils of rope. "You'll need to make a harness for him; then hitch the line to Gayatri."

The more the *acharya* attempted to heed Tamar's directions, the more he fumbled vainly with the cords, and almost tangled himself into them. At last, despairing, he threw up his hands.

"Forgive me, I can't do it," he moaned. "There has to be a better way. Let me contemplate. Something will come to mind." He plumped himself down on the ground, crossed his legs, and folded his arms. "An idea's bound to seize me."

"I'll seize you, if I ever get loose!" yelled Hashkat.

"*Acharya,* there's no time." Tamar renewed his struggling. The sap had begun to glaze and turn nearly solid.

"There's a sight," declared a familiar voice. "One sound asleep, the other—"

"I'm not asleep," Rajaswami broke in. "I'm contemplating."

Tamar twisted his head around to stare into the shining black eyes of Mirri. Her long hair had been bound up and she wore the jacket and leggings of a cowherd.

"The other stuck in brambles," she went on, "and still another—"

"It's the *gopi!*" squealed Hashkat. "The one who crowned me with a bucket."

"And—what, the king of the monkeys again?" Mirri set her hands on her hips and cocked an eye at Hashkat. "Well, Your Monkeyship, you've got yourself in a new pickle."

"How did you find us?" Tamar broke in. "What are you doing here?"

"Nanda told me you were heading north along the river," Mirri said, all the while taking stock of Tamar's situation. "You were easy to follow."

With no need for instruction, Mirri looped the rope around Tamar's waist and under his arms, tying the knots deftly and securely, then did the same for Hashkat. Hitching up the horses, she urged them to start pulling. Tamar felt his harness tighten, biting into his chest and almost cutting off his breath. The sap refused to give up its grip; until, at last, one of Tamar's feet came free, then the other. His hands suddenly tore loose and he tumbled to the ground. Hashkat rolled onto the grass beside him. Mirri undid the ropes and lashed them around the hilt of Tamar's sword, and the horses hauled it clear as well. Tamar's hands smarted where shreds of skin had been ripped away. Hashkat had fared worse. Patches of his fur clung to the vines, and a good length of his tail was stripped raw.

"What I don't understand," said Mirri, while Tamar sheathed his sword and Hashkat ruefully eyed the damage to his tail, "is how you got in such a mess to begin with. You should have seen right away you couldn't get through."

"We have to get through." Tamar glared at the brambles as if they were an enemy who had bested him. "I said I would."

"That's how he is," put in Hashkat. "With him, it's a point of honor."

"Honor's one thing, stubbornness is another," returned Mirri.

"Tut, tut," Hashkat snapped, "that's no way to speak to the king of Sundari."

"The what of what?" Mirri rounded on Tamar. "King? You lied to me at the river—"

"I didn't lie," Tamar protested. "I'm not the king of Sundari. I gave it up. I turned the kingdom over to my army commander."

"You're splitting hairs," Mirri retorted, eyes flashing.

"Leave that sort of niggling to the *brahmanas*. I guessed you were at least a warrior, and you said nothing. And what about those fine words you were spouting when you were up to your neck in water? I want to know more about this king who isn't a king."

Tamar nodded. "Yes. You have every right."

"My boy," Rajaswami interrupted, "this is hardly the moment for amatory confessions. If you don't wish to delay, you'll have to turn aside and circle around these brambles."

"You could go to the river's edge and swim past," said Mirri.

"Goodness, no," cried Rajaswami. "I can't swim. That won't do at all."

"We could pull you along by your beard," suggested Hashkat. "It looks pretty well stuck to your chin."

"Certainly not," sniffed Rajaswami. "As a *brahmana*, I insist on maintaining a measure of dignity."

"If you knew as much about country life as you do about your honor," Mirri said to Tamar, "you might have figured how to go at it." She led him to the thorny barrier. "That sticky sap—we have bushes near our village that put out something like it; not as strong, but much the same kind of resin. We collect it and use it in our lamps. It burns brighter than oil. What I'm wondering—"

"Set fire to the vines?"

"We can try. See what happens." Mirri strode to a chestnut mare grazing beside Gayatri and Jagati. "Nanda let me borrow a horse," she called back, adding, with a glance at Hashkat: "I'm not a monkey—I didn't steal it."

The girl rummaged through her saddle pack and drew out a flintstone and steel fire-striker. Warning Hashkat and

Rajaswami to keep their distance, she knelt at the roots of the vine. Tamar watched closely while she struck a spark that went dancing into the brambles.

The sticky resin hissed and flared. A yellow flame spurted, small at first, then soon rose crackling and licking at the vines, blossoming in all directions. Another moment and the fire was roaring, burning faster than Tamar could have imagined. He flung up his arms to shield his face from the sudden burst of heat.

Mirri, instead of drawing back, seized a dead branch and began thrusting at the blaze, stirring and spreading it deeper into the brambles. She struck away the charred vines and plunged into the gap, driving the fire ahead of her until she had hacked out a flaming tunnel.

"It's burned through to the other side," she called, beckoning to Tamar. "Get the *brahmana* and the monkey. Blindfold the horses, or they won't go near the fire."

"Gayatri will do whatever I ask," Tamar called back. "The others will follow her."

While Mirri continued to clear away the smoldering vines, Tamar sent Rajaswami stumbling headlong through the passage, then shoved Hashkat after him. He ran back to fetch the horses, who whinnied fearfully but nevertheless heaved their way through the dense, black smoke and showering sparks. At the same time, Tamar heard loud squawks and screeches from somewhere above. Paying no heed, he hastily led Gayatri and the other two steeds into the open air beyond the brambles.

There, Rajaswami was coughing and rubbing his eyes. Hashkat, brushing cinders from his fur, protested that he could have had his tail burnt to a crisp. Mirri, her face smudged still darker by soot, closely observed the smoldering passageway.

"Bravely done." Tamar went quickly to her. "You have the heart of a warrior."

"I hope not," Mirri said. She pointed at the brambles. "Look, the flames are dying down. Good. Otherwise, I'd have to find a way to keep them from spreading too far."

"What does it matter? You got us through it."

"Burn down a whole forest for the sake of convenience? That might be a warrior's way, but it's not mine. Strange, though. The vines are growing again."

Even as Tamar watched, new tendrils sprouted, fresh and green, beginning to entwine and fill the burned-out gap. He called over Rajaswami, who peered at the thicket, which had grown almost as dense as it had been.

"Most peculiar," murmured the *acharya,* as puzzled as Tamar. "Not at all to be expected from ordinary vegetation." He frowned uneasily. "Very odd, indeed. Even magical."

"The door's closed behind us, so to speak," said Hashkat. He glanced at his scorched tail. "That's all right. I don't intend going back. I admit the *gopi* did us a service, but I might have ended up roasted."

That same instant, before Tamar was aware what was happening, a large and lopsided bundle of ragged feathers came swooping straight at him, beating its widespread wings, buffeting him about the head and shoulders, screeching furiously.

"*Shmaa! Shmaa!*" squawked the bird. "Enough is enough. I'll stand for no more of your persecution and harassment. You've gone too far."

While Tamar fended off the assault, the bird kept up its cries of outrage and indignation until, suddenly, it flopped to the ground, rolled onto its back, and shut its eyes tightly.

"What is this creature?" exclaimed Tamar, still bewildered by the attack. Mirri and Rajaswami drew closer, to stare curiously at the motionless form. Hashkat squatted down and poked it with a finger.

"It looks like a cross between a buzzard and a trash heap," said the monkey, "whatever it's called."

The bird opened one red-rimmed eye. "Garuda is what it's called. Not that it matters. Who cares? It's just poor, helpless Garuda. Call him a buzzard, call him trash, whatever you please. Go ahead, you grinning idiot, aren't you going to kick me when I'm down? You might as well. You've done your worst already."

"What are you talking about?" Tamar knelt beside the disheveled bird, who rolled over and stood up on a pair of scabby legs. "We've done nothing to you."

"Nothing?" Garuda snapped his hooked beak. "Of course not. Nothing to make you lose a wink of sleep, nothing to weigh on your conscience for even an instant. No, you've only burned up my nest, destroyed my home—Well, this time I've lost patience. You've driven me past endurance."

"I'm sorry," Mirri began, reaching out a hand to calm the bird. "I didn't know you had a nest there."

"A likely story," Garuda flung back. "I should believe that? Why do you think I built it in the thorniest place I could find, and avoiding that horrible goo? To get a little peace and quiet. Don't tell me you—and he, and the *brahmana,* and the scruffy-tailed banana-gobbler didn't plan the whole thing. What's to do for sport this morning? Why, let's go burn Garuda's home to cinders.

"You aren't the only ones after me," Garuda pressed on. "Just the other day, I'm perched on a tree, minding my own business, when some malicious fool shoots an arrow at me. Missed me by a hair. I flew off as fast as I could before the numbskull tried again."

"So, he's the one who woke up the snake and got me in trouble," said Hashkat.

"I shot the arrow," Tamar said. "I was aiming at the tree; I saw no bird."

"Aha!" cried Garuda. "You're all in it together, just as I thought."

"He's quite mad," Hashkat muttered to Tamar. "Leave him. Let's be on our way."

"Oh, no, you don't!" cried Garuda. "You wrecked my home. You owe me. You owe me plenty for all the pain and misery you've caused."

"I regret to say," Rajaswami told Tamar, "accident though it was, the young lady acted for your benefit, so you must bear some responsibility. And you were the one who disturbed him in the first place. As he claims, you owe him something:

A king never forgets
To pay his debts.

"He's not a king anymore," Hashkat protested. "Let this moth-eaten sack of feathers build another nest. What else does he have to do with his time? Or, he can go roost with his fellow vultures."

"First, you call me a buzzard—now, a vulture!" cried Garuda, so furious that he was quacking like a duck. "You don't know who you're dealing with. I'm an eagle!"

9. Lost and Found

────────◆────────

Eagle?" Hashkat slapped his knees and hooted with laughter. "What, did a wandering *rishi* lay a curse on you, as one did to me when I was a human?"

"So that's what happened to His Monkeyship," Mirri said apart to Tamar. "Somehow, I'm not surprised."

"Whatever you did, I'm sure you deserved to be cursed for it," snapped Garuda. "I'm an eagle now and always have been." The bird shook his wings and looked down his beak at Hashkat. "I'll have you know, in my better days—ah, ah, better days they were—I served a mighty king."

"As what?" Hashkat stuck out his tongue. "A feather duster?"

"His trusted messenger," Garuda retorted, with an air of shabby dignity. "No errand was too difficult or dangerous. One day, His Majesty sent me on a most important mission.

"A treacherous servant had stolen an extremely valuable gem and given it to a *rakshasa,* an evil demon, in exchange for the gift of eternal life. You can see how precious the jewel was, to be worth that sort of bargain. The *rakshasa* didn't keep his word."

"They never do," put in Rajaswami. "When will people realize there's simply no dealing with them?"

"Feel free to interrupt whenever you please." Garuda

glared at the *acharya*. "I'm only telling you the story of my life.

"As I was saying— Eh? Where was I?" Garuda blinked and wagged his head. "Ah. Yes. The servant came to a messy end. The *rakshasa* and the jewel vanished.

"In time, my royal master learned the *rakshasa* had hidden the gem in a mountain cavern, protected by a ring of fire. Who had strength even to reach that cavern? Or, once there, courage to risk the flames?"

Garuda paused and glanced around. "I just asked a civil question. It's too much, I suppose, to hope for a civil answer."

"You were the one," Mirri said, with an encouraging smile. "The king sent you, of course. Then what?"

"Thank you for your interest," said Garuda. "Yes, I went. Oh, my wings—they ache when I think of it. How long I flew over peaks poking up at me like daggers, through rain and hail, sleet, snowstorms—"

"All right," said Hashkat. "How long?"

Garuda rolled his eyes. "I can't remember. But, at last, I found the cavern.

"And there was the gem in the midst of a circle of flames. Not for an instant did I hesitate. I plunged through —oh, the pain, the pain!—I could smell my feathers burning, my talons shriveling, but I snatched up the gem in my beak. Hard to believe such a small ruby could be worth so much. For a moment, I wondered if it was the right one. No mistake. As I'd been told, it had a lotus flower carved on it—"

Tamar stiffened. He was about to interrupt, but Mirri put a finger to her lips. Garuda went on:

"I flew from the cavern. The fire had scorched and blackened my golden plumage, my tail feathers were little more than a charred stump. No matter. I had served my king well, proved worthy of his trust, done as he commanded."

Garuda shuddered and bowed his head. "I had nearly reached the palace when another bird flew by—an ill-favored, ungainly creature who had the gall to mock me. 'What's this?' he called. 'A plucked chicken ready for the oven?' He kept up his taunts and jeers until I could stand no more. Goaded by pride and anger, forgetting the prize I carried, I opened my beak to answer insult with insult.

"I dropped the ruby," Garuda said in a choked voice. "It fell into a mountain lake. I swooped down, dove into the icy water, again and again. Soaked and freezing, I searched until I could search no more. I had lost the gem, past finding.

"I was too ashamed to face my master. So I never went back. I hid myself deep in this forest—" Garuda broke off his account and gave way to sighs and moans.

"Poor bird," Mirri said. "No wonder he's in such a state."

"I can help him set things right," Tamar said, while Mirri stroked Garuda's ruffled feathers.

Tamar reached into his jacket. "Garuda, I have something to show you."

"What, something else to aggravate me?" Garuda snapped. "Let me be. I don't want to see it."

"I think you do." Tamar drew out the ruby and held it glittering in his palm. "Do you recognize this? Is it the one you lost?"

Garuda stared at the gem. For a moment, his beak

opened and shut silently; then he burst into furious squawks:

"Shmaa! That's it! How did you get your hands on it? Where? Stolen, I'm sure. You're keeping it for yourself, just to torment me."

"A gift I didn't ask for and didn't want," Tamar said, ignoring Garuda's reproaches. "It has followed a strange path back to you, but here it is. Carry it to your master. Your dharma will be whole again. Take it. That pays my debt to you."

"Oh, no, it doesn't," Garuda retorted.

"Miserable creature!" Hashkat burst out. "It's worth more than some frowsy nest."

"Correct," agreed Rajaswami. "A most generous settlement."

"No." Garuda snapped his beak. "What, in my condition? Look at me! I hardly know what I'm doing from one day to the next. Sometimes I even forget how to flap my wings. Shmaa! I'm not the eagle I used to be."

"For certain," muttered Hashkat.

"I'd lose the jewel again before I was halfway to Mahapura," Garuda rattled on. "Can you see me in those mountains? Me? Alone, friendless, scorned—"

"Mahapura?" Tamar broke in, shaken to hear the name. "Between the mountains Kumeru and Sumeru?"

"Where else would it be?" said Garuda.

"Who is king there?"

"As I said—or did I say?" Garuda replied. "I think of him often. Sometimes I dream about him, and see his kindly, wrinkled old face, his snow-white beard. I wish I could forget; the memory pains me too much. The king? Oh, yes. A great ruler: King Jaya."

Tamar caught his breath. He glanced at Rajaswami.

"That's not the same one I diced with. Yet, one calling himself Jaya commanded me to his palace in Mahapura." He drew closer to Garuda. "What more can you tell me of this king? I journey to see him."

"You can first explain to me what you're talking about," said Mirri. As Tamar began his account, she listened more and more intently. When he finished, she said quietly, "You told me none of this before."

"Who cares what he told or didn't tell? Who cares how or why a bunch of snakes got the ruby?" squawked Garuda. "What about it right now? You carry it for me; you're going to Mahapura anyway. That's the least you can do. You owe me that much, and a lot more besides."

"You'd trust me with it?" said Tamar.

"Of course not," Garuda snapped back. "I'll be keeping an eye on you every step of the way."

"There's a joyful prospect," said Hashkat.

When Tamar agreed to hold the gem in safekeeping, Garuda seemed grudgingly satisfied. Mirri did not. She beckoned for Tamar to follow her a little way across the clearing.

"I don't want His Monkeyship eavesdropping on us," she said, leading him to the side of a huge anthill, its peaks and pinnacles head and shoulders taller than Tamar himself. "You and I have something to settle."

"Yes, we do." Tamar sat down at the foot of the ant castle. "One thing, first: Why did you leave the Choosing?"

"Why did you?"

"It was for the best."

"You could have asked my opinion about that."

"What would you have said?"

"Had you waited," replied Mirri, "you'd have found out."

Tamar shook his head. "I had no right to stay in the village. Do you think I didn't want to? I had no right to ask or offer anything. How could I? My life isn't my own. Do you understand that now?"

"I understand you pledged your life to someone who might not even exist. Yes, I understand that very well, and it makes no sense to me."

"To me, it does," Tamar insisted. "At first I doubted. I thought it could have been a dream. Now, Garuda talks about a realm called Mahapura and a king named Jaya."

"A king nothing like the one who came to you in Sundari."

"That puzzles me," said Tamar. "I don't know what to make of it. I'm still not sure; but sure enough to keep on with my journey. If I'm right—"

"If you're right"—Mirri bit her lips and looked away—"you'll find your death waiting for you at the end of it."

"You forget I'm a warrior. We learn how to die." Tamar took Mirri's face between his hands. "I promised only my life to Jaya. Not my heart."

Before Mirri could answer, Hashkat scuttled up. "You two, come! Better not stay here."

"Let us alone, will you?" Mirri burst out. "Can't you see we're talking?"

"I'll go away." Hashkat shrugged his shoulders. "I don't think *they* will."

The monkey drew Tamar from the wall of the anthill and pointed across the clearing. From the distant fringe of trees, four riders galloped toward them. "Quick! They've seen us, but if we run for those woods—"

"Why should we do that?" asked Tamar.

"They have swords."

"So do I."

"We don't know who they are."

"Then I'll find out. Stay by Rajaswami. Mirri will go with you." Tamar stepped away from the hill and waited for the horsemen to come closer. Though Hashkat had scurried off, the girl was still there. "Go with the monkey. As I said."

"Are you king of Sundari again? A royal command?"

"They're warriors. I know how to deal with them."

"They're men. I know how to deal with them."

By now the horsemen had reined up and dismounted some paces away. One beckoned and called out:

"You, huntsman! Here. Lord Kana wants to see you."

"He sees me." Tamar folded his arms.

The man scowled and muttered something to the tallest of the riders, who was richly dressed in embroidered vest and kilt, a silk scarf draped casually over his shoulders. With long, fair hair held by a gold headband, an arrogant arch to his high-bridged nose, he was, Tamar recognized, not only a warrior but a noble of highest station.

Lord Kana, as Tamar knew he must be, stood for a moment studying him with an air of amused contempt; then, his attendants following, he took a few strides forward.

"Ashwara is in sorry state," remarked Kana, looking Tamar up and down, "if he seeks help from a common huntsman, let alone a *shudra* herd boy.

"What have you to do with him?" Kana's voice hardened. "Are you to meet him here? Is that why you signaled? We saw the smoke, as could anyone for miles around. That was not clever of you."

"We signaled no one," Tamar coldly replied. "I have never heard of this Ashwara, whoever he is or whatever state he may be in."

"He's lying," muttered one of the attendants.

"Perhaps," said Kana. "Perhaps not. These folk are too simpleminded to be good liars. Or, they might be excellent ones."

Tamar's face flushed. "I told you the truth. Now, you tell me who you are. I hear accusation in your words and I have been called a liar, which I do not accept."

"Temper your own words, huntsman." Kana's chin went up. "You speak above your caste. Respect your betters."

"I do," replied Tamar, paying no heed to Mirri nudging him to hold his tongue. "When I meet them."

"We were only burning some vines," Mirri hastily put in, as Kana's face tightened. "We have no idea what you're talking about. We're on our way north, in company with a devout *brahmana.*"

Kana, turning closer attention to Mirri, clapped his hands and gave a drawling laugh. "Herd boy? No, by heaven, a *gopi!* Let's have a better look at the creature. If it were properly groomed, and rid of the cow-barn stink, even I would make room for it in my kennel."

"Your kennel is no doubt already crowded," Mirri answered, tightening her grip on Tamar's arm as he angrily tried to lunge forward. "I prefer cows to dog-fanciers, in any case."

"A quick tongue! All the better." Kana hesitated, then sighed and shook his head. "Unfortunately, I have no time for pleasure."

"Your loss," Mirri said. "Not mine."

"I seek a traitor, not a passing amusement." Kana stood for some moments studying Mirri and Tamar, then waved a hand. "These are not Ashwara's people," he told an attendant. "They interest me no longer. Come."

"Hold." Tamar flung free of Mirri's grasp. "We are not finished, you and I."

"Idiot!" Mirri whispered. "What are you doing?"

"What I must."

"Let be, you fool. Walk away."

"I have been thought a liar, accused falsely of what I know nothing." Tamar's hand went to his sword as he faced Kana. "You have spoken ill to a woman. No affront goes unanswered, and so I answer yours now. *Kshatriya,* arm yourself."

"A ferocious fellow, indeed." Kana raised his eyebrows in mock terror. "And a vexing one. Let me teach you better conduct."

Kana suddenly swung up his arm and with the back of his hand struck Tamar full in the face. "There, boy. Study that lesson."

Tamar snatched out his sword, unmindful of the blood streaming from his mouth. "Your men will stand away," he said, between clenched teeth. "You and I only. In single combat. By the warrior's code."

"You challenge me? I accept no challenge from inferiors. I do not fight them." Kana drew his blade. "I slaughter them."

10. Ashwara

Tamar flung Mirri behind him. Kana's men had drawn their blades. Tamar crouched, his glance darting from one warrior to another, his sword point flickering. "Which of you?" he cried. "Come!"

Kana himself was first to spring forward. His sword hissed in a long, slicing stroke. Tamar caught its edge on the hilt of his blade, then threw himself against the *kshatriya,* jolting him back. One of the warriors leaped past Kana to thrust at Tamar's face, while the others attacked his open flank. Tamar spun around, whirling his blade in a flashing circle.

Rajaswami clapped his hands to his head and stammered unheeded protests. Hashkat, meantime, went bounding toward the anthill. Teeth bared, he pummeled one of Kana's retainers about the head and shoulders. The warrior, more astonished than hurt by this onslaught from a monkey nearly as big as himself, swung his blade, missed widely, then kicked out to send Hashkat to the ground.

Garuda, screeching at the top of his voice, flew back and forth, beating his wings and pecking at the assailants. Kana had stepped into the fray again, but Mirri scooped up a handful of loose dirt and gravel and threw it with all her strength into his face.

Darshan had taught him well, but Tamar's opponents

were more seasoned, craftier *kshatriyas*; nor had he reckoned on them breaking the warrior's code by setting upon him all at once. His skill counted little against sheer weight of numbers, and he was growing arm-weary fending off attacks from every side. Against all honor, one of Kana's men launched a blow at Mirri. Raging, forgetting the others, Tamar leaped in front of her and furiously beat the blade aside.

Another of Kana's retainers seized the chance to spring at Tamar, but the man stiffened as though frozen in mid-stroke. Eyes staring, mouth agape, he dropped the blade and plucked at the *chakra,* the sharp-edged iron discus thrown with all force to lodge in his chest.

"Kana! Kana! Face me!" From the edge of the clearing ran the man who had flung this deadly missile. He was tall, big-framed, in deerskin vest and kilt. His tawny hair hung about his shoulders; his golden eyes blazed. Sword raised, he strode past the fallen warrior, making straight for Kana. Leaving Tamar where he stood, the remaining attendants sprang to challenge the stranger. Before Tamar could help him, the newcomer swung a deep-cutting blow at one and, in the same instant, sent the other sprawling.

Kana raced to mount his horse. The attendants, one bleeding heavily, stumbled to their own horses and galloped after him. The stranger made no attempt at pursuit and was about to turn away when Tamar approached him.

"I thank you for your help." Tamar pressed his palms together. "Who are you, to have risked your life for us? I think," he added, "you are called Ashwara."

The man's lion eyes glittered. "Yes."

"Also called a traitor."

Ashwara smiled bitterly. "When a man does a crime

against another, what better than to cry treachery? It is a balm for his conscience."

"Kana accused us of signaling you," Tamar said. "Why? It was not us but you that he was seeking."

"And found me," said Ashwara. "He knows where I am, which is more than he knew yesterday. I regret that. It makes my task more difficult.

"I too saw the smoke and wondered what caused it," Ashwara went on. "You and your friends seemed no threat to me, and I would have gone my way. When Kana and his people set upon you, in all honor I could not have let him kill you. He would have spared none of you, not even the *brahmana*."

"We are all in your debt," Tamar said. "You did us a service, traitor or not."

"Judge what I am when you know more," Ashwara said.

"I already know you're very quick at killing people," said Mirri.

"Only my enemies," Ashwara replied. "As for that, one duty remains." He glanced at the warrior on the ground. "I took his life. I will not disgrace his death."

The tawny-haired man bent and lifted the figure as if it weighed nothing and carried it beyond the trees. Mirri watched until he disappeared into the overgrowth.

"He frightens me a little," she said in a low voice. "I don't know what to make of him. He kills a man without batting an eye, then he's tenderly concerned for his body. I have a feeling he draws trouble like a honeypot draws flies."

"He's in worse trouble now," Tamar said. "He put himself at risk because of us. If he hadn't stopped to help—"

"And if you hadn't challenged Kana—"

"Be that as it may, my dear *gopi*," Rajaswami said.

"We must look on the bright side. We are missing no bodily parts or essential organs and have survived undamaged."

"Speak for yourself, you silly *brahmana,*" cackled Garuda. "What about me? Harassed, aggravated, put upon—"

"We're grateful to you," Tamar began. "You did your best for us."

"For you lot?" snapped the bird. "For my ruby! Suppose you'd been chopped to pieces? Where would that leave me? Suppose they'd taken the ruby from your horribly mangled cadaver? A fine fix I'd be in!"

"So would we all." Mirri turned to Tamar. "That's one thing. The other is: We shouldn't have been in a fix to begin with. If only you'd kept your mouth shut—"

"How could I? He offended you, insulted me, struck me. By the warrior's code—"

"Yes, well, my code is: Use common sense. You should have just walked away. Your warrior's honor might have got us all killed. As it is, there's one man dead."

"Two, in fact," put in Ashwara, who had come back to join them. "The second has his death wound. He will not live out the day. It is my fault. I am sorry."

"And should be," said Mirri.

"Sorry I did not slay them all," Ashwara continued, to Mirri's dismay. "Kana dishonored himself when he did not stand against me. I would have pursued him, but I have already been too long delayed. No matter. He counts little, and there will be another time.

"But now let me see closer who has turned me off my path." Ashwara folded his arms and looked around with curiosity. "A bird of some sort—"

"Eagle," said Garuda.

"—and a remarkably large monkey. A charming young

gopi disguised as a herd boy. A huntsman who fights like a warrior—"

"We already know who we are," put in Mirri, "which is more than we can say about you."

"It is no secret." Ashwara pressed his palms together and inclined his head toward Mirri. "I am the king of Rana-pura."

"Amazing!" Hashkat clapped his hands. "Yet another king!"

"Be quiet, Your Royal Monkeyship," Mirri said. "I want to know why this one's hiding in a forest."

"For much of it, I blame myself." Ashwara bent his long legs and set his back against the anthill. "For some time, there had been whispers that my kinsman, Lord Nahusha, was scheming to seize my kingdom for himself. I turned a deaf ear, refusing to believe them.

"Nahusha was of my blood, he had sworn allegiance to me," Ashwara went on. "That he would break dharma, forfeit sacred honor by treachery? Impossible. Yet, as I found out only later, he had promised lands and riches to neighboring princes if they would support his plot; he turned many high officers and ministers against me as well. At the end, he sought to slay my two brothers and myself."

"He dared even that?" Tamar said. "A *kshatriya* and your own kinsman?"

"Even that." Ashwara nodded grimly. "Nahusha, all smiles and loving concern, offered us a pleasure-cottage on his estate. He urged us to take our ease there, hunt in his park, boat on his lake, and enjoy his openhanded hospitality a little while. Unwitting, my brothers and I accepted this poisoned generosity."

Ashwara's golden eyes flashed as he continued. "Nahusha had made the house a firetrap, soaked the roof, walls, and rafters with oil and wax.

"Kana, Nahusha's nephew, willingly agreed to set it ablaze while we slept. A loyal servant warned us in time. The cottage burned to ashes, but we escaped. We went into hiding, knowing that Nahusha would murder us if we were found.

"He crowned himself king of Ranapura and occupied my city with his troops. Since then, he has ruled by terror and torture. Those who so much as murmur protest are imprisoned or slain. Of his own officers, the ones who urged even some small measure of moderation were put to a slow death. I have heard that Nahusha himself watches with pleasure as they die in agony. I have heard, as well, that he seeks to spread his rule beyond Ranapura. No kingdom may call itself truly safe."

"This is evil on top of evil," Tamar said. "No man of honor can allow it."

"Nor will I," Ashwara said. "My brothers and I rallied what troops we could. Also, we journeyed seeking help from other kings. When Nahusha learned of this, he proclaimed me a traitor." Ashwara smiled bitterly. "Having stolen my throne and tried to burn me to death, he accused me of plotting against him."

"A *kshatriya*'s sacred honor?" Mirri said under her breath. "It seems more a matter of convenience."

"Nahusha sent searchers to find and kill us," Ashwara went on. "We have eluded them. Until now. Kana has seen me. He will carry word to Nahusha. Meantime, I have my own task."

Ashwara stood and softly whistled. A black stallion

trotted from the woods and came to nuzzle his master's shoulder.

"I ride to Muktara, a few days north," Ashwara said. "I must treat with King Bala and persuade him to join forces with me. I have already spent too long following roundabout ways to keep Nahusha's warriors off my trail. I can delay no more."

"You hindered yourself by helping us," Tamar said. "No debt may go unpaid. Ask of me what you will."

"Your intention is honorable," Ashwara said, "but how shall a lone huntsman aid my cause?"

"No huntsman!" exclaimed Hashkat. "He's the king of Sundari!"

Ashwara narrowed his eyes at Tamar. "Truth? How can this be?"

Ashwara listened closely while Tamar explained his circumstances. "A strange tale and not a happy one. What to make of it?"

"I'll give you my own opinion," said a muffled voice.

The anthill's high earthen rampart stirred and cracked. From the breach, a pair of sharp, gray eyes peered out; then, a broad face, wide-browed, stubble-bearded, clotted with dirt and sand. The man broke a larger opening, thrust out his head, shook his burly shoulders, and stepped clear of the hill.

11. The Choosing

O ne moment." The heavyset man scooped up earth and
gravel to patch the broken side of the hill. "There. It's
hardly good manners for a guest to leave someone's home
in ruins. As I was saying—"

"Guest?" Tamar, like the others, had been staring in
astonishment. "You—inside? How? Doing what?"

"A guest of the ants." The big man dusted off his thread-
bare vest and wiped his hands on the grimy cloth wrapped
around his middle. "Doing? Living with them, naturally."

"I wouldn't call it natural," put in Hashkat, as Ashwara,
having drawn his sword, slid it back into its sheath. "Trees
are for monkeys, hills for ants. You're neither. What I want
to know is why you were there in the first place."

"My name is Adi-Kavi," the man replied. "I came to
be there by happy accident. I had sat down, one morning,
to meditate—so deeply that time went by faster than I realized. When I opened my eyes, the ants had built their
castle around me. They invited me to stay, which I did.
Excellent folk, as I've learned to know them. Busy, hard-
working. Very earnest. A little too single-minded, if you ask
me. But, that's their way, and it suits them.

"The commotion outside disturbed my observations,"
Adi-Kavi went on. "I've been listening—eavesdropping,
if you like, which is something I do at every opportunity.

Finally, I had to come out and see for myself. You have to understand: I'm cursed."

"What, something like Hashkat?" said Tamar.

"No," said Adi-Kavi. "Cursed with curiosity. I was born that way. And so, I was irresistibly curious to have a look at all of you.

"Here, of course, is Mirri," continued Adi-Kavi, putting his palms together. "Just as I imagined her. Lovely face, shining eyes: and, plain to see, a *gopi* of great spirit.

"And this must be the young king of Sundari." Adi-Kavi nodded to Tamar. "A strange journey you've set out on, the strangest I've ever heard of. You've started my curiosity itching ferociously. The only way I can scratch it is to find out what happens to you in Mahapura. Allow me to join you."

"I'm turning aside from my journey for a few days," Tamar said. He faced Ashwara. "I may be able to pay a little of my debt to you. I ask to be with you when you meet King Bala.

"Let Bala know that the king of Sundari supports your cause," Tamar urged. "My commander Darshan rules in my stead; but, if I wish him to do so, he will put Sundari's army at your disposal."

"Nobly offered, gladly accepted," Ashwara answered. "Beyond doubt, it would add weight to my words; enough, perhaps, to sway Bala in my favor. If so, the tables turn, and it is I who will be in debt to you."

"My curiosity itches me again," said Adi-Kavi. "Present company excepted, but kings bargaining are like thieves trying to rob each other, and much less straightforward. Still, I can't resist knowing the outcome.

"Young Tamar here puts himself at your service," Adi-

Kavi said to Ashwara. "So do I. From time to time, I've been a *suta*—a royal crier."

"A crier?" Mirri asked Tamar. "What kind of work is that?"

"A palace attendant," Tamar said. "He's paid to declaim a king's merits, his courage, wisdom, generosity—"

"Whether he has those virtues or not," put in Adi-Kavi. "In any case, it's beneath royal dignity for a king to praise himself. So, with a *suta* to put matters in their best light, a lovely *gopi* to lend an air of charm, and a *brahmana* an air of piety, King Ashwara will at least have some sort of retinue. That's always impressive. A solitary beggar may have a grudging coin flung at him. A king with retainers looks strong and prosperous and is showered with favors. Appearance counts. The less you seem to need, the more you get."

"You speak some truth, observer of ants." Ashwara smiled wryly. "I shall decide that later. Meantime, if you wish to ride with the king of Sundari and me, I shall not refuse."

"I lived in Muktara before I was turned into a monkey," said Hashkat. "I know the lay of the land and all the shorter paths. I'll guide you there and keep an eye out for little Akka on the way."

Ashwara agreed that all would go with him, and offered Adi-Kavi the horse of the slain warrior. Hashkat, about to climb up behind Ashwara, saw Garuda already perched on Tamar's saddle.

"What are you doing there?" Hashkat called to him. "You're a bird, aren't you? Why don't you fly?"

"You're a monkey, aren't you?" Garuda retorted. "Why don't you swing from tree to tree? My wings are tired. Shmaa! You expect me to walk?"

Rajaswami, before mounting, plucked Tamar's sleeve. "I must know more about this Adi-Kavi," he whispered. "If, indeed, the ants built their hill around him while he sat meditating—my goodness, do you realize how long that must have taken? And living inside? Without food or air? This is most unusual, the sort of thing you'd only expect from a *rishi,* and a powerful one. But he looks like no *rishi* I've seen."

"Whatever he is," Tamar said, "if he can do Ashwara a service, so much the better."

"Yes, yes, of course," said Rajaswami. "Still, it would be more proper, before we meet King Bala, if he might see fit to launder his clothes."

With Hashkat directing him along one forest track after another, Ashwara pressed on with rarely a halt, despite the groans from Rajaswami. If Mirri suffered fatigue, she gave no sign; but even Tamar, long trained to the saddle, felt his joints and muscles protest the strain. Nevertheless, to lag behind would have disgraced his caste. Ashwara sat easily, head high. The shafts of sunlight through the archway of tangled branches turned his face as golden as his eyes. With his noble bearing and air of kingly command, Ashwara could as well have been leading a proud army of warriors instead of this mismatched handful. Despite Adi-Kavi's assurance, Tamar had to wonder if such a retinue would make any great impression on the king of Muktara. Even so, urging Gayatri to hold pace, he kept that question to himself.

Hashkat, not Ashwara, was the one to cry a halt. The light was rapidly fading, and the monkey declared he could no longer be certain of the pathways. They dismounted in a little grove and tethered the horses near a stream. No longer fearing pursuit, Ashwara himself gathered twigs and lit a small cook fire and shared out provisions from his saddle pack. Garuda swooped down, snapped up the morsels as if they might be snatched from him at any moment, and flapped to roost on a high branch. Ashwara touched nothing until sure the others had their fill; even then, he ate and drank sparingly.

Adi-Kavi, unwilted by the hard ride, waved aside his portion. "I had a good dinner before I joined the ants. No point overloading my stomach."

"Nothing else? In all that time?" Rajaswami, settling closer to Adi-Kavi, eyed him with growing wonder.

"Only to sample a few bits and pieces of what the ants carried in," said Adi-Kavi. "Out of politeness. Not much to my taste, I admit."

"Do you do that often?" Mirri asked.

"Live with ants? No, little *gopi*. Once is enough. One anthill is much like another. But I've swum with any number of fish. Some of my fond friends are crocodiles. I've helped a few birds build their nests, and brooded a clutch of eggs until they hatched. What a mess those broken shells are."

"I thought you were a royal crier," Tamar said.

"Used to be," said Adi-Kavi. "You see, my mother was of high *brahmana* family; my father, a *kshatriya*. I claim neither caste. The *kshatriya*s disapproved, the *brahmana*s likewise, and the other castes wanted no part of me. Astonishing how you can vex so many people all at once by simply being what you are.

"I had a glib tongue. Too glib for my own good, some said. So, what better than hire out as a *suta*? An unwise

choice, given the disposition of kings. Ashwara—he's something else again. I know his reputation. I've heard it told
he's the best of them, a truly noble *kshatriya*," Adi-Kavi
went on, lowering his voice and glancing in the direction
of Ashwara, sitting apart, silent and deep in his own
thoughts. "That must make life difficult for him.

"The others—an unpleasant lot, those I've seen. As for
you," he added, "you're too young at the trade to be despicable."

Tamar laughed. "You don't mince words."

"No. I respect them—when they tell the truth. Any
wonder I did badly as a *suta*? What king pays good money
for plain truth? Oh, I've tried my hand at all sorts of work.
But when you come down to it, I'm a journeyer. I calculate,
if I journey long enough and far enough, I might find out
what makes the world go 'round."

"Allow me to inquire," said Rajaswami, "how you came
by your highly unusual abilities. You must have been instructed by some great *rishi*."

"I had a better teacher," said Adi-Kavi. "Curiosity.
Amazing what you can learn if you're curious enough."

"If you're neither *brahmana* nor *kshatriya*," Rajaswami
pressed, "what is your dharma?"

Adi-Kavi chuckled. "I suppose my dharma's to see the
world as it is."

The *suta* was interrupted by long moans, wails, and gargling noises from Garuda on the branch. Hashkat, who had
been listening to Adi-Kavi with interest, shook a fist:

"Can't you be still, you dreadful bird?"

"Shmaa! Shmaa!" retorted Garuda. "I'm singing myself
to sleep. It consoles me. Do you mind?"

Hashkat put his hands over his ears. Adi-Kavi fell silent.

Though Rajaswami was eager to pursue further questions, the *suta* fixed his eyes on the fire, his thoughts elsewhere. Tamar was about to speak aside with Mirri when Ashwara beckoned to him.

"I shall stand watch the first half of the night; you, the second," Ashwara ordered, then added, "I am glad for the *suta*'s good opinion." He smiled at Tamar's surprise. "A king overhears much, most of which is usually less than agreeable."

"He wishes you well," Tamar said. "All of us do. You have justice in your cause; and honor, as well."

Ashwara did not immediately reply. When he did, he spoke in a pained voice. Shadows, darker than the night around him, drifted across his face. "This is true, I know it beyond question. For all that, none can tell how matters will turn. Whichever way, one thing is certain: At the end, bloodshed. Death for friend and foe alike. I grieve for all of them, even now."

"I, too," Tamar said. "I have never sought a man's death, and never wished it. My kingdom has always been at peace, no battle ever forced upon me. But you, how can you do otherwise? You are a king and a *kshatriya,* doubly bound by your honor and your dharma. You have no different course."

Ashwara nodded slowly. "I see none. And yet—a throne, a kingdom, what are these worth in blood? Is it honor that demands such a price? Or arrogance? Is it truly dharma that compels me? Or wrath? Can a warrior's virtue lead to evil ends? Have I misunderstood what I thought I knew?"

"Are you saying," Tamar answered, hardly believing Ashwara's words, "that a king such as you has doubts?"

"Have you none? I think you do," Ashwara replied, "but you are young and bear your doubts more lightly. In time, they grow heavier." He stopped abruptly and waved a dismissing hand. "What happens, happens as it must. Go, now. See to the horses, then sleep."

Leaving the king of Ranapura standing silent, Tamar went back to the dying fire. Only Mirri was still awake. She held out her hand and walked with him to the horse lines, where Gayatri whinnied a fond greeting.

"My question still waits for an answer," Tamar said. "Why did you leave the Choosing?"

"Need you ask?" Mirri turned her face toward his. "I listened to my heart. And yours. Why should I have stayed? There was no reason to, since I'd already chosen."

From the pile of gear and harness, she opened her pack and took out a garland of white blossoms. "Do you remember little Vati's song when you and I first met? *A wreath of flowers is the token of a pledge that's never broken*. I give you mine."

As Mirri was about to put the garland around his neck, Tamar raised a hand. He could barely speak above a whisper:

"No. Go back to your village. This is a pledge that can't be kept. My journey lies between us. Would you have me give it up? Bring you to Sundari? A king shamed by breaking his dharma? Or stay with your people, knowing I'd lost all honor?

"If I could be sure my dream was nothing more than that, I'd do it gladly. I still question it. Even Ashwara questions what he must do, but will do it nevertheless. So will I."

Mirri drew away. "And so, king of Sundari, you tell me to leave you?"

"Yes. Live out your life happily, not with one who has no life to give you. Follow your own dharma."

"My dharma tells me it's better to look for a way to live instead of a way to die. It also tells me to stay with the one I love."

She threw aside the garland, turned on her heel, and strode back to the others. Tamar stood a long time by the horse lines. When at last he went to her, she was asleep, her head resting in the crook of her arm. He touched his lips to her hair, with its fragrance of clove and cinnamon. Mirri stirred but did not wake. In the forest, the only sound was Garuda's moaning.

PART 11

IN THE FOREST

12. Bala's Durbar

———◆———

Next morning, Mirri announced her decision. Once they had done what they could to help Ashwara, she would ride with Tamar to Mahapura. "And that," she declared, "settles that." With only a token show of reluctance, Tamar agreed. He was, in fact, overjoyed. Rajaswami was not.

"I'm sorry, I can't approve." The *acharya* shook his head. "Expose this young lady to who-knows-what perils? No, no, no, it's simply not the correct way of things."

"*Acharya,*" replied Tamar, "do you mean to forbid—"

"I didn't say that," Rajaswami corrected. "I said I can't approve. You and your *gopi* must do as you see fit. Though I firmly disagree—dear boy, I haven't the heart to separate you two. Did you think I would?"

"I didn't." Mirri smiled at him. "You needn't worry about me."

"But I will, even so," said Rajaswami.

The *acharya,* in any case, had other difficulties to occupy him: particularly, his bald spot. In the course of the following days, as Hashkat led the retinue closer to Muktara, the forest thinned; dusty, open stretches gave little shade. Rajaswami's scalp turned bright pink, then deep red, and finally blistered. Though he draped his scarf over his smarting pate, he found no relief.

"I wouldn't want your brain to roast," said Adi-Kavi, giving him a good-natured slap on the back. "I'll take care of this."

The *suta* disappeared into the scrub, returning with handfuls of what seemed to be prickly blades of grass. With strong fingers, he squeezed out the juice and dripped it on Rajaswami's head.

Mirri came closer to watch the procedure. "I've never seen a plant like that."

"There are plants and herbs even you country folk don't know about," said Adi-Kavi. "They can do astonishing things you couldn't begin to imagine. If you're curious, I'll tell you about them. Too bad the *brahmana* didn't think cooling thoughts, to begin with. He'd have spared himself blistering."

"Thoughts can cool?" Mirri said.

"In a certain way," Adi-Kavi said. "Do it right, you can turn yourself cold or hot, forget you're hungry or tired— and a lot more besides. There's a special way, a sort of knack. My guess is," he added, with an appraising look, "you might already have the knack without knowing it. We'll find out, when things are more settled."

"This is quite remarkable," said Rajaswami, fingering his bald spot. "The sting's gone. I'm entirely comfortable."

Garuda did not fare as well. In addition to his usual daily lamentations and nightly singing, he endlessly complained of being jolted, knocked about, given indigestible food and not enough of it in the first place.

"I have a nervous stomach," he whined, as they camped for the night. "I'm not used to being flung gobs of who-knows-what. It brings on colic and makes my pinfeathers twitch."

"By the time we reach Mahapura," Tamar assured him, "you'll be better than ever."

"I should wait so long? Shmaa! There'll be nothing left of me."

"There's too much of him already," said Hashkat, as Garuda flapped to a branch. "He's putting it on; he's a malingering sack of feathers."

"I'm not so sure." Mirri glanced up. In the fading light, Garuda had tucked his head under a hunched wing. "He isn't singing himself to sleep."

"A small mercy," said Hashkat.

———◆———

Next morning, Garuda was lying on the ground, head drooping, eyes half closed. When Mirri went to him, the bird gave only a feeble squawk.

"If he were a cow," Mirri said, as Tamar and the others joined her, "I'd know what to do."

"Not as bad as it looks." Adi-Kavi carefully probed the bird's midsection and blew gently into Garuda's open beak. "He'll come around. Mash his food with a little water and make a paste of it. A pinch of gravel wouldn't hurt, either."

"Oh, no," Garuda croaked, as Tamar began following the *suta*'s advice. "How do I know you aren't trying to poison me? That would suit all of you. No more Garuda. Keep the ruby for yourselves."

"Let me deal with him," said Hashkat. "I'll make sure he gets what he needs. Count on it."

"No," snapped Garuda. "I want the *gopi* to feed me."

"You scalded chicken," Hashkat retorted, "you're lucky anybody feeds you at all."

Garuda clamped his beak shut and would let no one but

Mirri spoon the mixture down his gullet. By the time the girl finished, the bird was making happy rattling and purring noises, and casting adoring glances at her.

Though Ashwara was impatient to set off, Garuda flatly declared that he could neither fly nor cling to Tamar's saddle.

"Stuff him in one of the bags," Hashkat suggested. "Then we won't have to listen to his yammering."

Mirri found a better answer. Borrowing Rajaswami's scarf, she knotted it and hung it over her neck, with Garuda slung inside. As they set off, the bird poked out his head, looking around with smug satisfaction. After another day, when he had recovered, he flapped to the girl's shoulder and had little to do with anyone else.

Late that afternoon, when they came in sight of the city, Ashwara ordered a halt, deciding it best to seek an audience with King Bala next morning.

"I've been thinking about that," said Hashkat. "If I'm to go with you, I can't go as I am. A naked monkey doesn't set the right tone. For that matter, we could all spruce up."

"You have a point," said Adi-Kavi. "Appearance, that's what counts. Ashwara and young Tamar here have weapons enough to look like they mean business, not to be trifled with. The rest of us? Nothing to be done, I'm afraid."

"I'll see about that." Hashkat pursed his lips and made hooting and barking noises.

For some while, Tamar had been aware of small shapes scuttling along amid the foliage. Now, at Hashkat's signal, half a dozen monkeys clambered from the trees to crouch a little distance away.

"Some of your subjects, Your Monkeyship?" said Mirri. "Invite them over. I'd like to meet them."

"They don't much care to associate with humans," said

Hashkat. "All things considered, that's understandable. I'll go have a few words with them. They can help. I have something in mind. Stay right here till I get back."

The monkey king went to join his subjects. Moments later, they all faded silently into the undergrowth. Garuda raised his head as they disappeared.

"It's good-bye, monkey. That's the last we'll see of him," Garuda croaked. "Once he's off cavorting with his cronies, do you imagine he'll give a thought to any troubles of mine?"

Recalling that Hashkat had run off once before, Tamar waited with a touch of uneasiness; and, as the night wore on, standing watch to relieve Ashwara, he wondered if Garuda could be right. By the first streaks of dawn, however, Hashkat reappeared. The smaller monkeys stayed in the shadows as he triumphantly threw down the bundle on his shoulder.

"Here, *suta,* a nice mantle for you. Once you're washed and scrubbed, you'll look quite impressive." Hashkat held up a length of embroidered drapery and tossed it to Adi-Kavi. "A new sari, all fine silk, for the *gopi.* A few little things for me." He produced a warrior's studded vest and leather kilt, a somewhat rusty sword, and a crested iron helmet. "And for the *brahmana—*" Hashkat proudly unfurled a large white umbrella.

"A most useful assortment," said Rajaswami, as Mirri went to change her cowherd's garb for the sari. "Especially the umbrella. My rank entitles me to carry it, and it will certainly keep my head from blistering again." He hesitated, and his happy expression turned to one of concern. "But— how did you come by them? Not, I trust, by dishonest means."

"That depends on how you look at it," said Hashkat. "The way I look at it, since they weren't nailed down—"

"You purloined them?" Rajaswami dropped the umbrella he had been admiring as if it were about to bite him. "Good heavens, you should know I can't accept stolen property. It goes against all standards of correct behavior."

"Not so fast, to talk about purloining," said Hashkat. "For one thing, the sword and armor belong to me. I buried them in my garden the day I quit the warrior business. I sneaked back there; the monkeys helped me dig them up.

"As for the clothes and umbrella," Hashkat added, "they were provided by a rich goldsmith and his wife living in my old house. I gather the two of them moved in and took it for themselves, with never a coin in payment. I consider it a matter of collecting a little overdue rent. Since they were both asleep, it was a painless transaction."

"Ah, yes, in that case there may be a measure of justice in what you did," said Rajaswami. "I'm sure if they'd been awake they'd have been happy to settle accounts. And I assume these items weren't actually nailed down. In those circumstances, yes, it might be permissible—"

"*Brahmana,*" said Hashkat, "are you starting to think like a monkey?"

"Goodness me, I certainly hope not," said Rajaswami. "It is quite a handsome umbrella. I wouldn't want to offend you by refusing it."

By daybreak, they were ready to enter Muktara. Garuda railed bitterly at being left behind to wait. Only Mirri's promise to come back without delay pacified the bird. "You'll stay on your branch," Mirri said, scratching his neck.

"You'll be a good bird, behave yourself, and act like a brave eagle." Garuda muttered a few "Waas" and "Shmaas," but finally nodded his head.

They soon came to a well-paved road along the river-bank. Suddenly, Rajaswami urged Jagati to a gallop.

"Quickly, my boy! Let us get past this dreadful place," Rajaswami called out, as Tamar rode abreast of him and asked what had alarmed him.

"It's a *shmashana.*" Rajaswami shuddered and pointed toward a stretch of barren ground by the river. Here and there rose wisps of smoke. Tamar glimpsed a few half-naked figures carrying what seemed bundles of rags.

"Don't look," Rajaswami whispered. "It's the public burning ground. They're cremating paupers' bodies."

Tamar shivered in spite of himself, but could not turn his eyes away. "I've never seen the one in Sundari."

"Of course you haven't. Nor should you see one now. Did you suppose I'd ever take you to visit such a hellish spot? Good heavens, have you forgotten what I taught you? Those men doing the burning—they're *chandala*s. It's work forbidden to higher castes. Who'd want to do it in the first place? The *chandala*s are already the lowest of the low, so it makes no difference to them.

"As I warned you long ago, I remind you now," Rajaswami added. "Don't go near them. If a *chandala*'s shadow falls on your food—dear boy, you must throw it away, it's polluted instantly. Should a *chandala* touch you, even accidentally lay so much as a finger on you, your caste is broken. Worse yet, you become a *chandala* yourself, and better off dead."

Still trembling, Rajaswami turned his umbrella to screen the sight of the burning ground and galloped ahead, never

slowing until the *shmashana* lay far behind and they were
inside Muktara.

—◆—

The little procession wended its way through the bustling
streets. Adi-Kavi, dismounted, strode ahead, shouting for the
passersby to make room. Hashkat marched beside him, clad
in his old fighting gear. The monkey had coiled his tail
under the leather kilt and set his helmet, with its jutting
visor, low on his head, shadowing most of his face. Tamar
and Ashwara rode side by side. After them, wrapped in her
silken sari, Mirri held her head as proudly as a maharani.
Rajaswami, mostly recovered from the shock of seeing the
burning ground, brought up the rear, carrying his white umbrella with befitting dignity.

Though Tamar had hoped this escort would make an
impressive showing, it was Ashwara's regal bearing that
opened the gates. For all Adi-Kavi's declaiming and Hashkat's bold posture, Ashwara's air of authority, despite his
rough garments, was enough to make the palace guards step
back and bow him into the courtyard. Servants hurried to
care for the horses; officers were summoned to lead him and
his retinue to the audience hall.

At the far end of the cool, high-ceilinged room, King
Bala was already holding his morning durbar. Courtiers and
attendants drew aside as Ashwara and Tamar approached the
powerfully built figure clad richly in robes of state. Gold
bracelets circled his muscular arms; at his side, a jeweled
sword. The warriors who stood close by the throne were
grim-faced *kshatriya*s, glittering in polished helmets and gem-
studded breastplates. Bala leaned forward to observe his
visitors; his pale eyes seemed to weigh and calculate. The

king of Muktara, Tamar understood, was a man to be reckoned with—a man much aware that he was to be reckoned
with.

Adi-Kavi had only begun his praises of Ashwara and
Tamar when Bala waved him to silence, and motioned for
the *suta* to stand away.

"*Namaste,* Lion-Eyed Ashwara." Bala stood and pressed
his palms together. "I am not surprised to see you, only
surprised that you did not come sooner."

"So I would have done, Majesty," replied Ashwara, "but
certain small inconveniences hindered me. Time presses
now, and I must speak straight out, to make clear to you—"

"There is no need." Bala settled back on his throne. "I
know why you are here. I have followed all the happenings
in Ranapura with concern. It grieves me deeply to learn
what befell you and your brothers."

"Then we understand each other," said Ashwara.
"Good. I count on your troops to help me defeat Nahusha.
Your forces are strong, well equipped. When they join those
of other kings who have pledged support—"

"Do you say 'when'?" Bala interrupted. "I say 'if.' Our
kingdoms have always been linked in friendship. For you
yourself, I have the highest personal regard and affection. I
must, however, put aside my private feelings. You ask much
of me. As king of Muktara, it is my duty to ask no less of
you. What do you offer me in exchange?"

"Majesty," Tamar broke in, "you know Nahusha has
done great evil. It is your duty to side against him. You have
the opportunity to serve justice, for the sake of your honor
as a king and a *kshatriya*. What more could you ask?"

"I hear the voice of noble innocence." Bala smiled sadly.
"Yes, King of Sundari, there is merit in allegiance to a wor-

thy cause. There is also a hard question—as you may understand when you have ruled as long as I. Justice? Honor? Admirable virtues, of course. What are they worth in blood? A wise king does not spend lives for nothing.

"Why, then, should I?" Bala faced Ashwara. "I have no quarrel with you, nor with your kinsman. What difference to me who sits on the throne at Ranapura? A kingdom is a kingdom, whoever rules it."

With that, Bala signaled an attendant to open the door of an alcove behind the throne. A man royally garbed strode out and halted in front of Ashwara.

"You come later than I foresaw," said Nahusha.

13. Nahusha

"Y̶ou look well, cousin." Nahusha stood as tall as Ashwara; his smooth-shaven face was pale, the skin stretched tight over sharp cheekbones, his lips thin and bloodless. "The life of an outlaw skulking in the forest appears to suit you."

Ashwara's chin went up, but he did not deign to answer. Tamar, not only shocked to find Nahusha at the durbar, was taken aback, as well, to realize that this noble *kshatriya,* so splendidly robed and elegantly groomed, had sought to murder his own kinsmen and tortured to death countless others.

"It is always a pleasure to greet you," Nahusha went on. "I would not have deprived myself of this satisfaction. I was already on my way to Muktara when Kana found me. I gather you killed two of my people," he continued, as if commenting on the weather; then said, with a cold smile, "I shall have blood in exchange for that."

"Your warriors attacked us for no reason!" Tamar burst out. "They dishonored me and my companions. Ashwara was within his rights to defend us."

"Is this the king of Sundari? A realm so great, its name has never reached my ears?" replied Nahusha. "Nothing here concerns you, boy. Hold your tongue or I shall have Kana bloody your nose again."

"Do you need a servant's hand? Why not try your

own?" Tamar reached for his sword, but Mirri pulled back his arm.

Nahusha waved his long white fingers as if brushing away a gnat, and turned his eyes again on Ashwara. "And now you come like a beggar to Muktara," he said. "Where is your little wooden bowl? King Bala, in his generosity, may fling you a handful of rice and send you on your way."

"That is for him to decide," answered Ashwara. "Do you speak of begging? Why else are you here?"

"I do not beg, I negotiate," said Nahusha. "There lies the difference. His Majesty and I speak as king to king. You speak as nothing.

"These are your followers?" Nahusha let an amused glance drift over Tamar and the others. "One warrior—the ugliest, most ill-favored *kshatriya* I have ever seen. A hired crier in a red curtain. A stripling with the arrogance to call himself a king. A spindle-shanked *brahmana* with an umbrella—indeed, a terrifying weapon. Oh, cousin, it grieves me to see you fallen so low."

"I really must protest in the most vigorous terms," declared Rajaswami:

> *Respect is a* brahmana's *due.*
> *His wisdom merits reverence, too.*

"It would be wisdom to take yourself off to a quiet *ashrama,* and far safer than consorting with my enemies. Grow vegetables, old fool," said Nahusha, "and share your sermonizing with them."

"This fellow's very good." Adi-Kavi chuckled under his breath. "He manages to exasperate people with no effort at all. A real aristocrat."

"In one thing, Kana misled me," Nahusha continued, "and I shall take him to task for it." He inclined his head toward Mirri. "He spoke of a beautiful *gopi*. He told less than the truth."

"Lord Kana offered me room in his kennel," Mirri said. "He was too generous. Those accommodations would be more worthy of his king."

"And for you, gracious *gopi,* only the palace of a maharani would be worthy. Kana was correct when he said you had a quick tongue. And, no doubt, a temper to match. I should hope so. It pleases me to tame wild creatures. Breaking them to my will presents an exhilarating challenge; in the case of a *gopi,* a delightful one."

Mirri said nothing, but her tightening grip on Tamar's arm made him wince. Ready to fling fighting words at Nahusha, this time he forced himself to swallow them.

"This is unseemly of you, Lord Nahusha." King Bala held up a reproving hand. "Your opinions of a *gopi* are no subject for expression in my durbar. We have a grave question to settle.

"I welcomed Ashwara as I welcomed you, for I hope to find some way of reconciling you. Whatever has happened in the past, there are ties of blood between you."

"Strong ties," said Nahusha, "of bad blood."

"Still no reason to spill it needlessly," said Bala. "I ask each of you: What are you willing to do to end this quarrel?"

"I have no desire to shed blood or spend lives," Ashwara began. "That is a cruel choice; I would turn from it if I could."

"Say, rather," put in Nahusha, "that you have no stomach for it."

"True, I have neither stomach nor taste for it," replied Ashwara. "I take no pleasure in killing. It is an evil karma and puts both our souls in peril. I have thought deeply, and here is my offer.

"At first, I sought revenge," Ashwara went on, "but this was blind rage; the wrath of a man, not a king. It is against dharma. A king protects and cherishes his people. He does not lead them to destruction.

"I give up my desire for revenge. I purge my heart of it. As for you: You sit on the throne by treachery and murder, not by rightful claim. What I say to you is this: I give up my desire for revenge, but I still seek justice. So shall you, in justice, give up a throne that was never yours."

"Possession is its own justice," Nahusha said. "That you lost your throne is excellent proof you were not worthy to keep it."

"I mean to have it back," said Ashwara. "Ranapura must be free of you. But this I pledge: Leave peacefully, and I will do no harm to you or any of your followers. Depart from Ranapura. Go where you please in safety, under my protection. I will not raise a hand against you.

"Such is my offer. Refuse it and I make another pledge: I will fight you to the death. Now the choice is no longer mine, but yours."

"Your generosity overwhelms me, cousin," replied Nahusha. "A beggar promises to spare my life? A truly noble gesture. I can offer nothing to match it. Nevertheless, I make one suggestion."

Nahusha turned to Bala. "I came seeking your alliance —on terms, I must add, highly advantageous and profitable to you. Those benefits remain the same. They will be yours if you agree to my small proposal. First, I ask no support from your troops."

Bala frowned. "I do not understand. You wish nothing from me?"

"I do not wish danger for my warriors or yours," Nahusha said. "A battle, even against a beggar, has its confusions, its mishaps. Why risk lives? I request only one: Ashwara. His brothers do not trouble me; they are nothing without him.

"Ashwara is here at your mercy," Nahusha continued. "So, simple. Kill him. Oh—kill the others, too. They displease me. Except the *gopi*. I shall take her to Ranapura and allow her to enjoy my favors."

"How dare you!" Bala stiffened on his throne. "How dare you ask me to break the law of hospitality? Under my roof, under my protection? No. I will not commit such an abomination."

"Ashwara's life is mine, one way or another," said Nahusha. "I intended only to save a little time and inconvenience. Well, so be it. I shall deal with him myself.

"You, cousin," added Nahusha, "are more a laughing-stock than a threat. Do you care to see my opinion of you?"

Nahusha clapped his hands. From the alcove, a servant came to give Nahusha a long chain. At the end of it, attached by a leather collar, was a monkey.

The small creature had been decked out in mockery of a king's regalia: a silk robe, belted around the waist; at his side, a wooden sword; and, on his head, a gilt paper crown.

Hashkat clenched his fists. "Nahusha's got him," he muttered between his teeth. "It's little Akka."

"I have named him 'King Ashwara,' " Nahusha said, as

the courtiers burst into laughter. "See how he struts and capers, and rattles his little sword. All in vain. I do with him as I please. Here, you jabbering beast." Nahusha gave a sharp tug at the chain. "Down. Lick my boots."

Little Akka shrieked and tried to pull away. Glimpsing Hashkat, he flung himself around and clawed at his collar. Nahusha stepped closer to the frantic animal.

"Watch, cousin, how I discipline your namesake," Nahusha said. "With you, I shall be more severe."

Nahusha raised a hand and struck the monkey across the face. Little Akka screamed and went skidding over the flagstones.

Nahusha tossed the chain to his servant. "Take the vicious brute away. Whip him diligently until he learns who is master."

Growling, teeth bared, Hashkat snatched out his sword. Tamar seized his arm, while Mirri and Adi-Kavi shouldered the struggling monkey king aside.

Murmurs of shock rose from the courtiers, for Ashwara and Nahusha had likewise drawn their blades. Eyes locked, they crouched in fighting posture. Bala sprang to his feet.

"Sheathe your swords!" The king of Muktara's command rang with anger and indignation. "There are no weapons drawn in durbar. Shame! Shame on each of you. You disgrace yourselves and dishonor me, as well."

It was all Tamar could do to force Hashkat to put away the rusty blade; and, even then, he tried to break free of Mirri and the *suta*. "Stop it, you fool," Tamar hissed in his ear. "We can't do anything right now."

"I have seen and heard enough," declared Bala, holding his voice in tight rein. "I will abide no more outbursts and reproaches. I have come to my decision."

14. Bala's Decision

ear me well." Bala's stern glance went from Ashwara to Nahusha. "Enemies you may be; kinsmen, even so. You share blood and lineage. Therefore, the quarrel is within your family. It is improper for one outside that family to interfere in its disputes. Set your own house in order. I give my support to neither of you."

Ashwara bowed his tawny head. "If that is your thoughtful decision, so be it."

"A thoughtful decision indeed, but a costly one," said Nahusha. "I must, of course, withdraw those benefits I discussed with you. Apart from that, is it a wise decision? When families throw stones at one another, an onlooker may get his own head broken. However, you have chosen to make no choice." Nahusha shrugged. "I abide by it."

"Go from here, Ashwara. I urge you to go quickly," said Bala. "Nahusha, I remind you: My hospitality reaches beyond these palace walls. As long as he is within my borders, Ashwara remains under my protection. Make no attempt to harm or hinder him."

"Would I disrespect your royal will?" replied Nahusha. "I only hope my noble cousin and I soon meet on other grounds.

"I cherish the same hope for this ravishing *gopi.*" Nahusha's eyes rested on Mirri. "May the path of her karma and mine one day cross."

"That," said Mirri, "would be a day you'd never forget."

"And you," Nahusha added to Tamar, "trot back to your vast kingdom. The world is a dangerous place for a mighty monarch like you. As you shall find out if ever you come within sword's length of me. Bark all you please, puppy. I bite."

Tamar's face burned. It took all his strength to choke back the challenge he would have flung at Nahusha. He was trembling with fury. Ashwara motioned for him and the others to follow as he strode from the hall. The crowd parted to make way. Hashkat, still agitated, kept looking back. Akka had not reappeared.

Only in the courtyard, waiting for their horses to be brought, and beyond earshot of unwanted listeners, did Tamar speak.

"We failed you," he said bitterly to Ashwara. "Our help meant nothing. How was I fool enough to think otherwise? Impressive escort? A pitiful band."

"Our *gopi* made an impression," put in Adi-Kavi. "You have to admit that much."

"So did you," Mirri said to Tamar. "The dangerous kind. You don't need an enemy like Nahusha. But—I'm proud of you. It must have rattled your warrior's code, but at least you had sense enough to keep your mouth shut. Most of the time.

"Besides," she went on, turning to Ashwara, "I don't think it was all that much of a failure. Something good came of it. Am I right?"

"You are," said Ashwara. "Yes, I was disappointed when

Bala refused me. But he also refused Nahusha. Had Bala sided with him, it would have tipped the balance against me. With the king of Muktara standing apart, I am well satisfied.

"Keep on your journey and take my friendship with you," Ashwara said to Tamar. "Should need arise, I shall find you. However," he added, "be cautious. Ranapura is well to the north of here, where the Snow Mountains begin to rise. That is the direction you should take, but it will bring you into lands that Nahusha controls. Avoid them. Turn east before you come to Ranapura's borders. They straddle the Sabla River, so you must cross and make a long circle back to the mountains. I dare not try to guide you, much as I wish to do."

"You have your own task," Tamar said. "Bala warned you to go quickly. You are under his protection here, but I think he knows Nahusha will not honor it."

Hashkat, during this, had been impatiently nudging Tamar, reminding him Akka was still a prisoner. "I have to get him free, the sooner the better. The way that villain treats him, he won't last long."

"What help can I give?" said Ashwara.

"None that I can ask," said Hashkat. "You need to look out for yourself. You can't risk tangling with Nahusha. Akka's one of my Bandar-loka. He's my responsibility; it's up to me to answer for his safety."

"O king of monkeys," said Ashwara, smiling and touching his palms together, "you are less a monkey and more a king than I supposed. *Namaste.* I revere the spirit in you.

"I can help by telling you this much," Ashwara went on. "Nahusha has surely traveled with a grand escort: chariots, horses, perhaps elephants. So, they must follow the only good road along the Sabla. Whatever plan you shape, set it in motion there. And soon, before he passes into his own territory."

Servants now came, leading their horses. Ashwara turned to Tamar. "King of Sundari, what can I wish for you? That you go well and swiftly to Mahapura, knowing what awaits you? If I read your heart aright, there is some nobility in it. Whether you dreamed or not: Whatever the outcome, may it be to your honor.

"And this *gopi?*" Ashwara looked fondly at Mirri. "What shall I wish for you? That is not for me to say, since you may be wiser than any of us. Trust what your heart and your dharma bid you. To you both: *Namaste.*"

Ashwara embraced all, including Rajaswami, who reminded him to keep looking on the bright side. No sooner had he galloped from the courtyard than Hashkat rounded ferociously on the grooms.

"Where's my horse?" he shouted, shaking his fist. "Idiots, why haven't you brought it? How dare you keep a *kshatriya* waiting! What are you up to? Are you trying to switch mounts and fob off some other? What crooked scheme are you hatching? I'll have all your heads for that."

The confused and terrified grooms, pleading innocence, offered to go immediately and find the missing animal. Hashkat pushed them aside.

"Out of my way, fools! I don't trust you to recognize my steed or even lay a finger on it. I'll go myself."

The trembling grooms, only too happy to escape with their lives, scurried away. Hashkat stamped arrogantly into the stables, while Mirri and Tamar exchanged puzzled glances. He was back within moments, leading a prancing bay mare.

"I needed a horse of my own," explained Hashkat. "So many to choose from, I picked the one who insisted on following me—after I untied her."

Rajaswami sighed. "Since she insisted, I suppose you couldn't have done otherwise. Even so, there are times when I fear for the state of your dharma."

"I fear for the state of my rear end," said Hashkat. "I didn't take time to borrow a saddle."

Galloping from the city, they left the road for the cover of the forest, where Mirri was impatient to change her sari for her cowherd's garments. She had scarcely done so when, shedding clouds of feathers, Garuda swooped down to land with a thud on the turf.

"What, you?" Mirri shook a finger at the bird. "I told you to stay and wait."

"You didn't say how long," whined Garuda. "Shmaa! I should sit in a tree forever? You told me to behave like a brave eagle. I did. I thought you might be in trouble and I'd better look for you. Just to make sure you didn't all decide to go off and leave me."

"We have trouble enough," Tamar said. "Be quiet. If you can. Akka's been caught. We're going to free him." He beckoned to Hashkat and Adi-Kavi. "Ashwara warned us to act quickly. We'll do it as soon as we see Nahusha's escort turn onto the road.

"Hashkat and I have swords," he went on. "*Suta,* can you draw a bow?"

"As well as any, better than some," said Adi-Kavi. "If you're thinking of my fighting anybody—no. By rule, it's strictly forbidden to *suta*s, as it is to *brahmana*s. Were I allowed to put an arrow into someone, it would be Nahusha. But I can't. I'm sorry."

"I understand. I respect your rule," Tamar said. "I'll make do. So, counting two warriors—"

"Which all adds up to one warrior and a monkey," Mirri put in. "You'll attack Nahusha's whole train? I can tell you how far you'll get."

"Do you think I'm that foolish? We'll attack them piecemeal, strike quickly, fall back, strike again. If I must, I'll challenge Nahusha to single combat. He knows I'm a king, so he can't refuse. That's the code."

"I'm sure he'll observe it," Mirri tartly replied.

"Be careful. They're here," interrupted Hashkat, who had been peering through the foliage at the roadside. Tamar hurried to see for himself. Ashwara had been right. The retinue was splendid: half a dozen horse-drawn chariots, each holding a driver and an armored warrior, Nahusha himself in the lead with his banner-bearer; an elephant, covered with embroidered draperies, its mahout perched on its back, carrying a sharp, hooked goad; the pack animals bringing up the rear.

"Let them go by," Mirri said. "Give them a good long head start. We'll have more time to work out something. They'll have to camp at nightfall. By then, we'll know better what we're dealing with."

"By then, we can do nothing," Tamar said impatiently. "The rules of war forbid a night battle. An unbreakable law—"

"Who said 'battle'?" Mirri countered. "We're not battling. We're quietly rescuing one of His Monkeyship's subjects."

"Quietly?" Tamar said. "That's more like 'cowardly.' "

"All the better," said Hashkat. "Not a *kshatriya*'s way, but it suits a monkey. The *gopi*'s right. Sneaky and stealthy."

"Akka's one of your folk. You decide," Tamar said. "First, we have to find out where he is. How?"

"Easily," Mirri said. She turned to Garuda, hunched on the ground beside her. "Fly over Nahusha's escort. They won't pay attention to a bird. You'll see what they've done with Akka and come right back."

"Me do what?" Garuda burst out. "Waa! My nerves won't stand it. I don't have the wings—look, I'm shedding, I'm molting."

"You're an eagle." Mirri smoothed his feathers. "I know you can do it."

"Can't. Won't." Garuda made gargling noises and snapped his beak shut. After a moment, he turned a red-rimmed eye on Mirri and bobbed his head. "All right. But you'll owe me for this, all of you. Shmaa! You'll owe me plenty."

—◆—

The sky was barely lightening when they left their horses by the roadside, with Rajaswami on watch. Much of the night they had waited, sleeping fitfully. Garuda, for all his wails of complaint, had done better than promised. Akka, the bird reported, was with the baggage and pack animals, cramped in a light wicker cage; Garuda had also been able to tell where the chariots had been drawn up, where the horses had been tethered, and how the tents had been arranged.

"What a fine eagle," Mirri had told him, while Garuda preened himself and clucked proudly, all the while turning adoring glances toward the girl. "You knew you could do it."

Now, as they approached the encampment on foot, stepping carefully through the dry weeds, Tamar admitted to himself that Mirri's cautious plan had been best. The warriors' tents had been pitched near the riverbank, with Nahusha's high silken pavilion in their midst. Nahusha, confident, had not troubled to post sentries. The cooks, first to rise, had not yet wakened; the night fires had burned to ashes.

Tamar stationed Adi-Kavi a little way behind them while he and Hashkat moved soundlessly toward the wagons. Mirri followed, keeping an eye on the tents and the servants stretched asleep on the ground, ready to give warning at any sign of Nahusha's people stirring.

Tamar put one hand on Hashkat's arm and, with the other, pointed to a wagon. On top of a pile of bundles sat the cage. Hashkat grinned and bobbed his head; then, as Tamar stood alert, scuttled to the wagon and swung over the side. The small figure curled within the cage whimpered. Hashkat made soft, chirping noises of reassurance. The dawn sky was brightening with bands of pink and gold. Tamar gestured for him to make haste. Hashkat picked up the cage and started to clamber down.

They had not reckoned with the elephant. Sensing strangers, the big animal flapped her ears, raised her trunk, and trumpeted in alarm.

Tamar snatched out his sword. Clutching the cage, Hashkat raced past him. The elephant, meantime, had uprooted the stake that secured her leg rope, and charged blindly through the camp, trampling whatever stood in her way. Bewildered warriors stumbled and scattered out of her path.

Mirri headed for the road, pulling Tamar along with her. Adi-Kavi urgently beckoned for them to follow him. Rajaswami frantically waved his umbrella.

Hashkat, with his burden, had nearly reached the waiting horses. Leaping over a hillock, he misstepped, his foot caught in a tangle of weeds. The monkey king tumbled head over heels and sprawled on the ground. The cage went spinning from his hand.

15. Little Akka

———◆———

Little Akka squealed and flung his arms around his head as the cage rolled beyond Hashkat's grasp, bouncing down the slope back toward the wagons.

Tamar sprang past Hashkat, lurching to his feet, and ran to seize the wicker cage. He halted. Some of the warriors, blades drawn, were rapidly bearing down on him. Mirri turned back to join him, Adi-Kavi close behind.

That same instant, squawking and beating his wings, down swooped Garuda, feathers flying, beady eyes alight. The bird locked his talons around the bars and soared skyward, bearing the cage and its screeching contents high into the clouds and out of sight.

"He'll find us." Tamar jumped astride Gayatri. Mirri, already mounted, plunged into the forest. Hashkat and Adi-Kavi followed, with Rajaswami, brandishing his umbrella, galloping after them.

When at last they halted, well away from Nahusha's camp, Hashkat flung off his warrior's gear and clambered into the treetops. Rajaswami collapsed on the ground, murmuring "Oh, my goodness! Oh, my goodness!" while Tamar ran to the edge of the clearing, listening for any sounds of pursuit.

"Nahusha has enough to keep him busy," Adi-Kavi said. "He won't worry about a monkey."

"But I will," said Hashkat, who had climbed down without catching a glimpse of Garuda. "Akka's worse off than ever. Poor little fellow, he's in the clutches of a lunatic bird, and who knows what that maniac mophead's likely to do? Drop him in the river? That's how he lost the ruby."

While Mirri tried to calm the agitated monkey, Tamar began to calculate how long they dared to wait. He was about to raise that question when Adi-Kavi, peering upward, called out and waved his arms.

Moments later, Garuda plummeted into the clearing, letting go of the cage as he flopped heavily on his belly and skidded to a stop.

"There's my brave eagle!" Mirri cried, as Hashkat ran to break open the locked door. Adi-Kavi and Tamar hurried to help him snap the wicker bars.

Garuda, ignoring even Mirri, had begun a pigeon-toed sort of triumphal dance, treading around and around in a circle, beating his wings, fanning out his ragged tail feathers, gargling, chuckling, practically crowing like a rooster.

"I'm the one who got him!" Garuda warbled. "All you incompetent dimwits fumbling about! Shmaa! What a pack of idiots! And who saved him? Oh, no, don't bother to take time to thank me. But I'll tell you this: You owe me more than ever—all of you—especially that grinning, gibbering baboon."

"We do owe you," Mirri said, while Garuda kept on with his prancing. "That was a great deed."

"Yes," declared Garuda, sniffing haughtily, "it certainly was."

Hashkat, meantime, had reached inside the cage to lift out Akka and hold the young monkey in his arms. Akka's mouth opened and shut wordlessly. He no longer wore the mock-royal costume; the weals and bruises from the whipping Nahusha had ordered showed on his hunched back and spindly legs; and his curling tail, nearly as long as himself, had lost patches of hair.

"Terrible, terrible!" clucked Rajaswami, coming to peer anxiously at the rescued prisoner. "Poor chap! Locked up, tormented—and, on top of it all, swept into the sky."

"That was the best part; it made up for everything else," Akka chattered, regaining breath and voice. "I want to do that again! Where's the bird? Next time, I'll go higher."

"My goodness, I hope not," said Rajaswami. "Let me remind you—and this applies to small monkeys as well as large persons:

A piece of advice that is always sound:
If you have no wings, keep near the ground.

"You just be glad you're in one piece," Hashkat said with some severity, now assured that Akka was largely undamaged. "I've been looking all over for you. What happened? How did you get in such a mess?"

"I didn't do anything," protested Akka, unwinding himself from Hashkat's embrace and hopping to the ground. "Well, all I did was—I only slipped into a village one night, to have a look 'round. And here's a pile of nuts at one of the doorsills. They might as well have been begging me, 'Please take us, don't let us sit here all by ourselves.' So, I grabbed as many as I could."

"Naturally," said Hashkat, "as any right-thinking monkey would have done."

"But then, as soon I did, a noose goes tight around my wrist. A trap!"

"Tricky! Sneaky!" Hashkat burst out. "Present company excepted, but that's humans for you. You never know what crookery they're up to."

"That's been more or less my own observation," Adi-Kavi said. "Even so, young fellow, a clever little monkey like you should easily have got out of a trap."

"I didn't have a chance," Akka said. "Those villagers were quicker than I thought. They tied me up in a sack, enough to stifle me. They kept me awhile; then a trader came passing through and they sold me to him.

"Next thing I know," Akka went on, "I'm in Nahusha's palace. He bought me, you see, for his amusement. I wasn't the only one caged up. He's got a whole collection—birds, beasts—even a tiger."

"That's what he meant," said Mirri, "when he talked about taming wild creatures."

"How he tames them—you don't want to know." Akka shuddered. "They don't last long. He's always in the market for new ones. From what the parrots told me, he doesn't treat his people any better. They hate him, but there's not much they can do. They say Ashwara's coming back someday to save them. Nahusha laughs at that; it doesn't bother him."

"Why so?" Tamar asked. "Does he have that strong an army? How many warriors? War chariots?"

Akka shrugged. "I don't know. He kept me in the palace; I never saw any of that. One thing: He's got a plan of some sort. I overheard him talking with his officers."

"No details? Anything that might help Ashwara?"

"I only know what the parrots told me."

"It seems to me," said Mirri, "Nahusha doesn't have all that many troops. Why would he want help from Bala? He's up to something, and it sounds like trouble for Ashwara."

"I'm afraid you're right, and nothing we can do about it." Tamar turned to Hashkat. "And you? Now that you've found Akka?"

"By and large, I'd just as soon stay clear of humans. We should say farewell and I'll go back to my Bandar-loka—" Hashkat's brow puckered. He chewed at his lips a moment, then quickly went on. "No. It's not in my heart to leave you or even the *gopi,* though she did crown me with a bucket."

Hashkat put his palms together. "Let me go with you. I owe you my life; I haven't forgotten. Besides, you never know when a monkey might be useful."

"Ashwara said you were more a king than he supposed," Tamar answered. "I'd say: Better than a king, a friend. Yes, be at my side when my journey ends."

"I'll be there, as well," Adi-Kavi said. "As I told you, I'm curious to know what happens to you in Mahapura. You may turn out to be a fool, a dreamer, or both. In any case, I've taken a liking to you."

"Be welcome, then—" Tamar broke off and motioned all to keep silent. Beyond the edge of the clearing, faint sounds grew louder. He glanced at Mirri. "Nahusha's warriors?"

The horses had begun whinnying and stamping. Raja-swami defensively gripped his umbrella. Akka had already scrambled up a tree, with Garuda flapping after.

The vines and overgrowth ripped apart. Still dragging the stake roped to her leg, the elephant burst into the clearing. Seeing Tamar draw his sword, she trumpeted a shrill scream. Eyes rolling, ears standing out from the gray dome of her head, she lunged with speed surprising for her bulk. The blade spun from Tamar's hand as she lashed her trunk around his waist and swung him into the air.

16. Elephant Hunters

Tamar twisted back and forth, struggling to get free of the trunk coiled around him. Mirri started forward. Adi-Kavi stepped ahead of her, arms outstretched. Seeing what she took to be a new attacker, the elephant flung Tamar to the ground and, bellowing, swung her head toward the *suta* and made ready to charge.

Before she could launch herself against him, Adi-Kavi strode deliberately to the distraught animal. Tamar shouted a warning. Paying no heed, the *suta* laid his hands on the creature's trunk, all the while murmuring sounds that Tamar could not understand. The elephant reared up on her massive legs. Tamar ran to pick up his blade.

"Stay away!" the *suta* called over his shoulder. "Don't come near her. Drop the sword."

The tone of command in Adi-Kavi's voice made Tamar, still alarmed, do instantly as the *suta* ordered. The elephant hesitated, as if uncertain whether or not to resume her charge. Adi-Kavi fixed his eyes on her and seemed to hold her with his gaze. The big animal drew back, panting and snuffling. As Tamar watched in astonishment, she gradually sank to her hindquarters. Adi-Kavi continued his murmuring. At last, the elephant lowered her head. The *suta* nodded and turned away.

"She's terrified," Adi-Kavi said. "Let her rest. She's more afraid of us than we of her."

"I'm sure she is," Mirri said, going to the elephant's side and gently stroking her trunk. "Poor thing, we don't mean to harm you."

The elephant heaved a huge sigh and fanned herself with her ears. "I'm sorry," she said. "Whatever came over me— forgive me; it's never happened before."

"You can speak?" Tamar stared at her.

"Not usually," said the elephant. "Never, in fact, since I've been in captivity. If Nahusha knew I could talk, who knows what more he'd make me do."

"He won't do anything to you now," Mirri said.

"I hope not." The elephant snuffled. "My name is Arvati," she added. "Nahusha brought me with him so I could show off the tricks I'd learned."

"We're not fond of Nahusha," Mirri said. "I hope you trampled him a little before you ran off."

"Oh, no, I'd never do anything like that," Arvati replied. "I've been well trained. As for running off, I don't know what possessed me. I suppose I lost my head for a moment. It just seemed to happen. I didn't mean to." Arvati's whole bulk shuddered. "They'll punish me, of course, once they get me back."

"Get you back?" Mirri exclaimed. "How? You're a grown elephant; you're more than a match for them. You've made a good start. Keep going. Find your herd."

"If only I could." Arvati sighed. "This forest has been my ancestors' home since the Golden Age. Naturally, I inherited their power to speak—if I choose to.

"I've always dreamed of being with my herd again," she

went on. "But it's too late. I don't know how to make my way in the wilds anymore. I'm sure to be recaptured."

"Yes, if you sit and wait," Tamar said. "Do as Mirri tells you."

"No," said Arvati. "Now I've calmed down and can think more clearly, I'll go back on my own. That way, they'll see I was simply confused and they won't punish me too badly."

"Don't count on it," said Mirri. "You're better off in the forest. Here's your chance to be free of them."

"You don't understand. I'm afraid to do anything else. Nahusha's hunters captured me when I was a calf. I had a gentle nature; so, instead of training me to be a war elephant, they taught me to do tricks. I'm used to that now."

"You see what they've done," Mirri said to Tamar. "She's been so beaten and cowed, she hardly knows anything else."

"Nahusha won't get his hands on her again," Tamar said. "We can't leave her. We'll keep her with us until she can look after herself. But Nahusha won't let her get away that easily. My guess is he's already sent his people to track her down."

"Then," said Mirri, "we can't stand around waiting for them."

"That's just what we're going to do," Tamar said. "We have to deal with them. If we don't, they'll stay on her trail—which means they'll be on our trail as well."

"Right," said Hashkat, judging Arvati safe enough to approach. "She'll leave a path even a blind man could follow."

"Take her deeper into the forest," Tamar told Mirri. "I'll wait behind with Hashkat. We'll take the hunters by surprise, and that's the end of them."

"The warrior's way again," said Mirri.

"The only way I know. But—yes, I should have listened to you before. I'd be glad to listen to you now, if you have a better plan."

"Let me suggest what should settle the matter," put in Adi-Kavi. "I, for one, would relish it—it's the sort of thing that suits me more than bloodshed."

"Nor am I eager for bloodshed," Tamar said after the *suta* explained his scheme. "But—can you make the trackers believe you?"

Adi-Kavi chuckled. "Don't forget I was a royal crier. If I can make a dimwitted lummox think himself a wise and noble king, I don't see any difficulty."

Following the *suta*'s instructions, they tethered the horses out of sight and led Arvati into the screen of underbrush a little way down the forest track. In a small clearing, they set about their other preparations while Adi-Kavi turned back and, staying within eyeshot of them, hunkered down on the ground.

From his perch in the fork of a tree, Tamar watched uneasily as the hunting party made its way through the bushes: the elephant master himself, carrying a long pole with a sharp iron point and hook at the end; three of his fellows bearing coils of rope; a packhorse laden with a net, shackles, and chains.

At sight of them, Adi-Kavi leaped up and ran toward the elephant master, wringing his hands and begging for help.

"Be off, whoever you are." The elephant master roughly pushed Adi-Kavi aside. "We've no help to give, you scruffy lout. There's serious work at hand. Our king's elephant ran away. She's not long gone; her tracks are fresh."

That moment, at a signal from Tamar, Arvati trumpeted loudly enough to rattle the leaves.

"Out of my way," ordered the elephant master. "She's here under our noses."

"Wait! Wait!" cried Adi-Kavi. "Stay back. It's worth your life. She's dangerous."

"She won't be, not when she has a look at this." The elephant master grinned and held up the pole. "She knows what it means. A little taste of the hook, she'll be gentle as a lamb."

With Adi-Kavi tugging at their garments and stammering out warnings, the hunters pressed on to the clearing. The elephant master stopped short:

"What the devil is this?"

At the farther edge of the clearing—one end of the rope tied to the wooden stake set in the ground, the other knotted around his ankle—stood Hashkat.

17. The Rakshasa

———◆———

Hashkat's face and body were striped with yellow clay. His hair bushed out to make him look nearly twice his size. Leaves and vines twined around his head and waist. He slapped his chest, shrieked, hooted, and flung himself about at the end of the rope.

"Devil, indeed," wailed Adi-Kavi. "A *rakshasa!* A demon! Keep away. That fiend can tear you apart," he warned, as Hashkat dropped to all fours, gnashing his teeth while he bounced up and down, sticking out his tongue and wagging it horribly.

"I confess," blurted Adi-Kavi, as the elephant master gaped. "I found your elephant wandering in the forest. I meant to steal her. I knew she'd be worth a fortune.

"No sooner do I tie her down than she turns into a *rakshasa.* I was lucky to get away with my life."

"You're out of your wits." The elephant master nevertheless drew back uneasily. "Arvati changed into a demon? What lunacy are you telling me?"

"I've heard tales like that." One of the trackers exchanged frightened glances with his fellows. "No question, it happens."

"It's this forest," Adi-Kavi whispered fearfully. "It's always been full of demons. One of them pounced out and took possession of her. Well, you deal with her. I'm not risking life and limb. I won't even ask a reward for finding her.

"Best do your work quickly," he urged. "The longer that demon stays there, the bigger it'll grow. Then you'll have no chance at all."

"You seem to know a lot about demons," the elephant master began.

"More than I like. I've seen a few in my day and lived to regret it. At least I lived—which is better than some can say."

"What do you think?" the elephant master said, with mounting discomfort. "Will she ever change back again?"

"Oh, yes. Once you've got that demon tied hand and foot. If it sees it can't move, it'll be gone in a flash—poof! —and there's your elephant again."

"Here's your dear little Arvati," Hashkat called out in a hoarse growl. He rolled his eyes and snapped his teeth. "Come closer. I missed breakfast; I've been hungry all morning." He beckoned to the elephant master. "You first, Sala."

"She speaks?" gasped the elephant master. "Before, she never said a word."

"She wasn't a *rakshasa* then." Adi-Kavi turned to leave. "Well, good-bye, all. I wish you the best of luck. By that, I mean I hope you won't be too badly chewed up."

"Hold on." Sala seized Adi-Kavi by the tail of his vest. "You're not going anywhere. You know the ways of these demons. You give us a hand."

"Oh, no, I'm too fond of being alive," Adi-Kavi protested. "Ah—if you insist," he added, as the elephant master shook the goad at him. "All right, unload the packhorse.

Get those shackles ready. Is that a net I see? Excellent.
We'll use it for a start."

The trackers, by this time, were trembling so violently
they could hardly follow the *suta*'s directions. When at last
they unrolled the net, Adi-Kavi nodded approval.

"Stay close together, shoulder to shoulder," he ordered.
"Hold up that net as high as you can. Wait, I'll take one
end. Easy, now. No sudden moves. Walk toward her. Get
ready to throw it."

As the trackers approached, Hashkat strained menacingly
at his tether. They shrank back, but Adi-Kavi urged them
on.

"Never fear, you'll soon have your elephant again. Oh
—one thing I forgot to mention. Don't look. Turn your
heads away. Keep watching and that demon could change
you all into *rakshasa*s. Better yet, close your eyes. I'll tell you
the moment to open them."

The trackers, ever more frightened, squeezed their eyes
shut. Adi-Kavi guided them toward Hashkat; but, as they
stumbled closer, the *suta* led them past him to the edge of
the clearing. Hashkat, at the same time, untied himself,
pulled up the stake, and sprang silently behind them, taking
hold of one end of the net. Glancing at him, Adi-Kavi nodded and suddenly shouted:

"Help! Help! The *rakshasa*'s loose!"

Tamar and Mirri, meanwhile, sped to help Adi-Kavi and
Hashkat. By the time the trackers realized they were being
set upon—not by demons, but by human beings and an
oversized monkey—it was too late; the net was wrapped
around them. Tamar ran to fetch the chains and bound Arvati's pursuers all the more securely. The packhorse had al-

ready bolted in alarm. Rajaswami trotted from his hiding place to lend a hand hauling Sala and his fellows into the brush.

Certain that Arvati's would-be captors were well tangled in their own chains and net, Tamar signaled Mirri and the others to retrieve the horses. Arvati, with Akka crouched on her head and Garuda on her haunches, plunged through the forest. The trackers' cries of rage had long since faded in the distance when Arvati's rescuers halted.

Tears of joy rolled from the elephant's eyes. "Am I really free? No more hooks and goads? It feels so strange; I don't quite know what to do."

"You'll stay with us as long as you want," Tamar said. "Hashkat, you made a fine demon. You almost frightened me. And you, *suta,* I'm ready to believe you can convince anybody of anything."

"I'm the one who scared the wits out of them," crowed Hashkat. "They won't come after us now. If they get loose, what will they do? Slink back to Nahusha? They lost his elephant; he'll have their heads for it. If they're wise, they'll quietly make themselves scarce."

"No bloodshed, in any case," Tamar said to Mirri, as Hashkat went to scrub off the streaks of clay.

"I found it entirely satisfactory," said Rajaswami. "Indeed, rather stimulating. Goodness me, I was tempted to give those ruffians a good whacking with my umbrella."

"Is this my old *acharya* speaking?" Tamar grinned at him. "Talking about whacking people?"

"An impulse is one thing; doing it is something else," Rajaswami said. "Fortunately, I resisted.

"Sooner or later, someone's bound to find them," he assured Tamar. "They may be uncomfortable for a time; but, looking on the bright side, it will be beneficial and instructive for them to reflect, while they're waiting:

> Let patience ever be your goal.
> It helps to fortify the soul.

◆

So as to stay well away from Nahusha and his warriors, Tamar had chosen to avoid the river road and keep to the forest, in spite of the heavy undergrowth and dense woodlands. He could not have asked for better help from Arvati.

Lumbering ahead, the elephant was able to clear a good path, trampling down thick brush and flinging aside dead branches. For all her bulk and strength, she was a gentle, sweet-natured creature. She willingly let Akka perch on her brow, where he chattered with delight at this new means of transportation. When Rajaswami grew saddle-weary, he ventured to ride on her back, holding his umbrella over his head and beaming happily. Arvati's kindly disposition even had a calming effect on Garuda, who moaned and wailed somewhat less than usual.

"I never reckoned on an elephant for a traveling companion," Tamar said with a bemused laugh, when they halted at nightfall. "Even so, I'm glad we have one." Mirri had come to sit close beside him, while Hashkat and Akka curled by the small fire and Rajaswami nodded drowsily.

The big *suta* stretched out his legs and clasped his hands behind his head. "A good deed, King of Sundari, which gains merit for all of you."

"Merit gained by accident?" Tamar said. "We hadn't planned on rescuing an elephant."

"Does it matter?" Adi-Kavi shrugged his burly shoulders.

"Merit is merit, however it's gained. Intention? That's one thing. What you end up doing? That's another. As happened with the thief and the spider. Let me tell you:

"Late one night, a thief crept into a wealthy merchant's house. Oh—first, you should know he was a young thief, without experience. He had fallen on lean times and decided that burglary was a more straightforward career than law or politics, and an occupation immediately at hand. In fact, this was his first professional appearance.

"And so he had planned everything carefully. He closely observed the merchant's house and the merchant's habits: what time he went to bed; which doors or windows would be most easily opened. Once inside the house, while the merchant was safely snoring away, the thief calculated he could search the place at his leisure and find where the valuables were hidden.

"All went marvelously well at first. He found, as he expected, an unlatched window and wriggled easily and silently through it into the merchant's storeroom. From the bedchamber, he could hear the merchant snorting and snuffling happily in dreamland. But, groping his way through the dark room, he stubbed his bare toe against a table leg.

"Choking back a yelp of pain, terrified of waking the merchant, he smacked himself on the forehead and cursed himself for a fool. He was, as I told you, a mere beginner; and, for all his planning, he had neglected to bring a light.

"In the dimness, however, he was able to make out an oil lamp on the table. He fumbled in his garments, pulled out flint and steel, and struck a spark. The wick flared brightly, and he gave a sigh of relief. As he picked up the lamp, a small spider scuttled out from under its base.

" 'Thank you for saving my life,' said the spider. 'Before

he went to bed, the merchant set this lamp down on top of me so I couldn't escape. If you hadn't come along, I wouldn't have lasted the night; indeed, I'd have perished miserably, far from my web and my brood of little ones.

" 'You have saved a life and shown compassion,' the spider went on, although the impatient thief protested he had no such intention. 'Better yet, you have done so without the least thought or hope of reward. You have gained more merit than you could possibly imagine.'

" 'But you're only a spider,' said the thief.

" 'And you're only a man,' said the spider. 'My dear thief, when you understand that life is life, whether on eight legs or two, you will have understood much. Your deed, in any case, has cleansed all evil from your heart. Go from here with a fresh spirit. And good luck to you.'

"The thief did so," Adi-Kavi concluded, "and never thought to steal again. There, King of Sundari, you have a case of doing good accidentally, even though the intention was evil to begin with. In short, you never know how things may turn out.

"The tale is true, by the way," the *suta* added. "You see, I was that thief."

"You've clearly mended your ways, which is most commendable and meritorious," said Rajaswami. "Nevertheless, let me remind you:

> *Wrong is wrong, right is right,*
> *Clear as the difference between day and night.*

"Between day and night, yes, clear enough," put in Mirri. "But, O wise *brahmana,* what if it's twilight?"

—◆—

Adi-Kavi's tale and Mirri's comment lingered in Tamar's mind and niggled at him for the next several days, until finally, while the others pressed on, Tamar hung back a little and beckoned for Mirri to stay with him.

"Something troubles me," he began, as they dismounted and walked their horses. "If an evil intention can turn to good, can a good intention turn to evil?"

"I'm sure it happens all the time," said Mirri.

"And can doing right lead to something wrong?" Tamar went on. "I did right, leaving Sundari. I had given my word—"

"Or so you imagined," Mirri said. "You still don't know for sure if it was only a dream."

Tamar nodded. "That makes it all the worse. If it was only a dream—I've done a terrible wrong in following it. Darshan warned me of that, but I paid no mind. I've abandoned my people for the sake of it. Who knows what that may lead to? I've put Rajaswami's life in danger, more than he ever bargained for. And you. I even tried to send you away."

"You didn't succeed," replied Mirri, with a loving smile. "Of course, I had something to say about that."

"But suppose the dream was real?" Tamar turned his gaze to the iron ring on his finger. "It's not clear to me anymore. The twilight, you said. In between right and wrong. Is everything twilight? What if Jaya cheated when we played at dice? Does my word still bind me? And Jaya himself? Garuda loves him; he'd have given his life for him. That's not the same king of Mahapura who came to me. He was brutal, heartless. Could he have tricked me with some kind of illusion? Or is everything illusion?"

"I'm not. As you'll find out—" Mirri broke off as Adi-Kavi cantered up.

"We're moving well ahead," the *suta* called out. "Arvati's cleared a new path. We can cover a good bit of ground before sunset."

"Yes, of course," Tamar said absently, remounting Gayatri. "Even so, no need to hurry."

Arvati, indeed, had trampled a good path; nearly half the day still lay ahead. Tamar nevertheless ordered a halt for the night. Hashkat gave a curious glance, but did not question him. Tamar stayed apart for the rest of the afternoon.

Next day, Rajaswami vanished.

18. Soma-Nandi

Tamar, throughout that morning, had set a leisurely pace, ordering all to walk their horses even when the forest was clear enough to let them ride swiftly. He had not shaken off an uncomfortable reluctance to reach Mahapura; a reluctance that slowed his stride and dragged at his feet. Nahusha, by now, would be well ahead. Tamar calculated no risk of running afoul of him and his warriors; so, by rights, he should have turned and followed the quicker way along the riverside. Instead, he kept to the slower paths of the forest. Caught up in his own confused thoughts, he did not notice that Rajaswami had lagged behind. Suddenly, he heard the *acharya* cry out.

Rajaswami had vanished from sight but not from sound. The old teacher, invisible, was yelling at the top of his voice. His white umbrella lay on the ground. Jagati was tossing her head and fearfully whinnying. Tamar ran to the spot, Mirri, Hashkat, and Adi-Kavi at his heels. Akka streaked ahead, chattering and beckoning. Tamar dropped to his knees at the edge of a deep pit. Below, out of reach, the *brahmana* was clinging by his finger ends to the rough earthen wall.

At the bottom of the pit crouched a huge she-tiger. Growling, teeth bared, the great striped animal leaped up, clawing at Rajaswami's feet dangling just beyond her clutches.

At sight of Tamar, Rajaswami left off his shouting. "I'm perfectly fine—as long as she can't get at me. Now, if you'd oblige me by hauling me out."

"Tiger trap," muttered Adi-Kavi. "Leave it to the *brahmana* to fall into it."

"Quite unintentionally, I assure you," said Rajaswami. "I was contemplating a difficult philosophical proposition; next thing I knew, there I was with a tiger nipping at me. The bright side is, I nearly had it solved. The question was—"

"Never mind what the question was," Hashkat burst out. "Stay quiet or you'll fall down and end up a tiger's breakfast. Then where's your philosophical proposition?"

Tamar, meantime, had thrown himself flat on the ground at the rim of the pit and was trying to stretch his arms far enough to reach the *acharya*.

Arvati had lumbered up, with Garuda fluttering beside her. "Here, allow me," the elephant said, seeing Tamar vainly trying to get hold of Rajaswami's hands.

With that, Arvati lowered her trunk, wrapped it around the *acharya,* and lifted him out in an effortless instant. From the bottom of the pit, the tiger glowered up with feverish yellow eyes.

"Help me," said the tiger, in a broken voice. "Hunters set this trap for me. They will return when they know I shall be too weak from hunger and thirst to defend myself. Help me out. Let me go my way. I promise no harm will come to any of you."

"She's hardly more than skin and bones already," Mirri said to Tamar. "She's starving to death. We can't leave her there."

"You promised not to harm us," Tamar said, while the

tiger sank back on her haunches and watched him intently. "How do I know you'll keep your word?"

"You do not know. Nor can you know until you find out for yourself."

"Then so I must," replied Tamar. "Leaving any creature to suffer would be against dharma." He glanced at Mirri, who nodded agreement, as did Adi-Kavi.

"That's correct, my boy," said Rajaswami. "You can't do otherwise—except hope for the best."

"Yes," put in Hashkat, "and we'll be ready to run for our lives."

Tamar, at first, had thought to have Arvati lower her trunk and lift out the tiger as she had done with Rajaswami. Willing though she was, the elephant could not stretch far enough; nor could the tiger spring up to grasp the trunk with her paws.

Finally, Tamar ordered the *suta* to fetch a rope from the saddle packs. With Arvati holding one end, Tamar threw the other into the trap and started to climb down.

"No, no!" Garuda wailed. "You'll be torn to bits, eaten alive, your bones crunched up. Waa! Horrible! Don't go. Send the monkey."

Tamar, meantime, had slid down the rope. The bottom of the pit was narrower than the top, and he found himself barely an arm's length from the crouching animal; close enough to see that the tiger's eyes were sunken in their sockets, her striped coat matted and spiky. Her parched tongue lolled from between her fangs as she swung her head toward him. He drew back and flattened himself against the wall of the trap.

"My name is Soma-Nandi," said the tiger. "*Namaste,*

King of Sundari. Yes, I know of you. Word has been spread by the Naga-loka, the Bandar-loka, by watchers and listeners in the forest.

"It is told that you journey to the mountains of the north, seeking your death," Soma-Nandi went on. "Do you fear that you have already found it in this pit with me?"

"You made a promise," replied Tamar. "I wish to believe you will keep it."

"Why should I? Why should any forest-dweller keep faith with your human kind?" said Soma-Nandi. "Come closer. Look into my eyes."

Tamar could not turn away as Soma-Nandi's eyes widened until they seemed to fill the pit. His mouth went dry, as the tiger's must have been, and he could barely swallow. His lips felt cracked and swollen; pangs of starvation stabbed at him as if he himself had been trapped for endless days.

"Tell me what you see," said Soma-Nandi.

Tamar peered deeper. "I see horsemen riding to the hunt. Trackers and fowlers. I see myself fleeing from them." As he watched, his heart pounded to bursting with terror. The death-cries of all forest creatures burst from his throat, as they fell pierced by arrows or struggled in nets and snares.

"This is *maya;* this is illusion," Tamar murmured.

"No," said Soma-Nandi. "It is truth. My world's truth. I wished to show you, for a moment, lives different from your own. You have seen into me, and I have seen into you. Your heart is good, King of Sundari. Remember what you have been shown.

"Now loop the rope around me," the tiger said. "My word is my law. I will not harm you."

Still trembling, Tamar fashioned a harness for Soma-

Nandi, then called to Arvati, who easily hoisted up the tiger and Tamar along with her.

One glimpse of the tiger's head rising above the edge of the pit sent Garuda squawking into the high branches. Hashkat and Akka kept a wary distance. Soma-Nandi, however, rested calmly on her haunches while Tamar undid the harness and Mirri hurried to set food and water in front of her.

"You have my gratitude and the protection of all the Tiger Clan," Soma-Nandi said, after eating and drinking her fill. "You did more than save my life."

"That's for certain, old girl." Hashkat, reassured by her words, made bold to swagger up and cock an eye at her. "I've seen stray cats in happier shape. The king of Sundari kept you from being a rug on somebody's floor."

"He did far better," said Soma-Nandi. "We can be worth more alive than dead. Had the trappers taken me, they might well have broken my teeth, torn out my claws, and sold me for the amusement of some king or other. I fear this may have happened to my mate. He has disappeared and I have been seeking him."

"Seek on! Seek on!" Garuda called from his branch. "Don't delay another moment. Monkeys! Elephants! Now this! Shmaa! My nerves won't stand it."

"She'll stay until she has her strength back," Mirri said. She put a comforting arm around the tiger's neck. "Akka was lost, then found. You might find your mate again."

"So I must always hope," said Soma-Nandi.

Tamar, meantime, went to speak with Rajaswami and Adi-Kavi, telling them of the illusion that had come over him in the pit. "How could this have happened? How could she have worked *maya* on me?"

"Ah, that I can't say," replied the *suta,* while Rajaswami, admittedly puzzled, shook his head. "*Maya* or whatever, you seem to have understood something you never much thought about before. I'll put it this way: I had my spider; you had your tiger."

19. The Hermit

He had never imagined an elephant could be light-hearted, let alone light-footed. Yet, in the days that followed, Tamar noticed how Arvati's eyes had brightened since her rescue from the trackers. Even when trampling a path, she seemed to dance more than plod. From time to time, she would flap her ears, lift up her trunk, and trumpet exuberantly.

"No more hooks, no more chains," said Mirri, who had also observed Arvati's high spirits. "I think she finally got used to the idea that she's free of Nahusha for good and all."

As Tamar learned, however, Arvati had an added reason. The heavy undergrowth and oppressive shadows of the forest had given way to sunny stretches of rolling grassland. Early one morning, as Tamar saddled Gayatri, Arvati lumbered up to him.

"I've suspected it for a little while," she said. "Now I'm sure. What I'd always dreamed—" Arvati snuffled through her trunk. "I can smell it. I can feel it. My herd isn't far from here."

"That's wonderful." Mirri laid a hand on Arvati's flank. "We'll miss you, but I know how much you want to join them."

"I can't." Arvati sadly shook her head. "For one thing,

I'm in your debt. You gave me my freedom. I have yet to repay you."

"You owe us nothing," Tamar said. "Your freedom belongs to you. We only returned what was yours to begin with."

"There's another thing." Arvati heaved an enormous sigh. "You see, I'm—I'm afraid to go. I haven't the courage—I've been so long in captivity, I don't know how to manage on my own. To make my way alone? No. I'd be too frightened."

"Allow me to help." Soma-Nandi had padded up to listen. "I, too, owe a debt to the king of Sundari. But, with his permission, I shall stay with you until you are safe among your folk. You have nothing to fear, not while there is a tiger at your side to protect you."

"Go together, both of you," said Tamar. "It saddens me to part from you, but you have your own paths to follow."

"So I must," Arvati said at last, with tears brimming in her eyes. She gently touched the tip of her trunk to Tamar's forehead, to Mirri's and the others, even giving Garuda a fond tap on his beak. "*Namaste,* befriender of elephants. We have long memories, and you shall always be in mine."

"*Namaste,* befriender of tigers," said Soma-Nandi, stretching her forelegs and lowering her head in a graceful bow. "Speak my name to any of the Tiger Clan you should encounter. They will do as well for you as you did for me."

"Find your mate soon." Mirri put her arms around the tiger's neck and pressed her lips to Soma-Nandi's brow. "That's our best wish for you."

As Tamar urged them to start without delay, Arvati and Soma-Nandi set off across the meadow, heading for the distant woodlands. They went slowly at first, pausing for many backward glances. Their pace quickened after a time, until the elephant was galloping at top speed, the tiger bounding along beside her. At the line of trees, they halted a moment while Arvati raised her trunk in farewell, then vanished into the woods.

———◆———

Akka, ranging ahead of the others, had been the first to find it, and ran back chattering of his discovery, beckoning the journeyers to the rocky ridge. Below, nestling amid green-gold foliage, the *ashrama* was a rambling sort of cottage. Its flat roof of woven vines had been chinked with earth; wild-flowers bloomed in the crevices. A wide veranda ran along the front; at the rear, a vegetable garden, with melons ripening between the cultivated rows; a little orchard just beyond. Nearby, a wide stream flowed around islands of tall ferns and outcroppings of boulders. Tamar looked down on the hermitage with a measure of wistfulness, uncertain if they should intrude on its occupant. For Rajaswami, there was no question. He was in rapture.

"My boy, you can't imagine how I've longed to find such a resting place. I've been hoping ever since we left Sundari." The *acharya*'s hands so trembled with joyous excitement he could scarcely hold his umbrella. "The resident sage will be delighted to welcome us. What a comfort it will be! Quickly, my boy. Goodness me, I can hardly wait."

"At this point," remarked Mirri, "I think I could stand a little comfort. I won't object to eating at a table and sleeping on a bed."

"Oh, dear girl, I meant far more comfort than that," said Rajaswami, his face alight. "I'm eager for the opportunity to share philosophical speculations and stimulating discus-

sions with the sage, no doubt a wise and learned *rishi* who
has spent years in thought and study."

"I'd be interested in meeting the old fellow," said
Adi-Kavi. "A matter of simple curiosity. As for comfort,
once you've lived in an anthill, you can be comfortable
anywhere."

Rajaswami was bouncing up and down like an impatient
child. Tamar smiled and nodded, and they picked their way
down the slope to the dooryard of hard-packed, neatly swept
clay. Garuda flapped to the roof while Hashkat and the *suta*
led the horses to water at the stream.

Rajaswami clambered onto the veranda and poked his
head through the open door. "I had hoped for someone to
greet us. If not the sage himself, perhaps one of his students.
No matter, we shall wait quietly and respectfully for him.

"On the other hand," he went on, "we should make
our presence known." He stepped across the threshold.
Mirri and Tamar followed him into a pleasant, airy
room, sparsely furnished with a plank table and a few stools.
Shelves of earthen pots and cookware stretched along one
wall. Beaded strands hung across the doorway to a rear
chamber.

Rajaswami pushed aside the beads with his umbrella and
peered in, then put a finger to his lips.

"There he is," he whispered. "Deep in contemplation,
as I might have expected."

In white robes, a scarf draped over his head, a broad-
backed figure sat motionless on a straw mat. Rajaswami was
about to turn and tiptoe away when Akka, chirping inquisitively, scampered between his feet.

At the sound, the figure roused, sprang up, and whirled
around, eyes blazing. Head and shoulders taller than Tamar,

stouter and heavier than the *suta,* what Rajaswami had taken for a meditating sage was a huge black bear.

Akka, jabbering in terror, streaked from the chamber. Rajaswami stumbled backward, brandishing his umbrella. Tamar and Mirri seized the bewildered *acharya* between them and hauled him through the door, out of the *ashrama* and into the yard, the bear snarling and roaring at their heels.

The commotion had brought Adi-Kavi and Hashkat racing from the stream. Sending Rajaswami and Mirri pitching into their arms, Tamar faced the furious animal, who shook his paws like clawed fists at the intruders.

Instead of pursuing the attack, however, the bear halted on the veranda, choked back his growls, and swung his head from side to side, blinking at the journeyers in the dooryard. On the roof, Garuda squawked and beat his wings.

"Shmaa! Fools!" screeched the bird. "Don't stand there. Run for it!"

The bear, meantime, set his robes in better order and, with great courtesy, bowed his head and pressed his big paws together:

"Revered *brahmana,* accept my humblest apologies. I was startled and quite forgot myself. It happens from time to time when things unsettle me. I urge you to overlook this failing and forgive my regrettable outburst."

"Ah—why, yes, of course," said Rajaswami, regaining his composure, pleased at being so respectfully addressed. "Now, be so good as to inform us: Where is the hermit?"

"I know where he is," muttered Hashkat. "That shaggy-haired, slew-footed monster ate him."

"Most assuredly, I did not," retorted the bear, with a reproachful glance at Hashkat. "It would be a physical impossibility as well as a logical fallacy. I am the hermit."

20. The Ashrama

———— ◆ ————

My name is Jamba-Van." The bear motioned toward the door of the *ashrama*. "Come, all, and be
welcome. Allow me to offer whatever rest and refreshment
you desire."

So saying, Jamba-Van led his visitors into the main room
of the hermitage, where he bustled about, finding more
stools and benches, setting out bowls of fruit and pitchers of
cool juices, as eagerly attentive as any human host to the
comfort of his guests. When Tamar identified himself and
his companions, the bear politely nodded to each in turn.

"Few travelers seek shelter here," Jamba-Van said.
"More precisely, none at all. I am thus especially honored
that my first guests include not only a king but, as well, a
learned *brahmana*."

"Your hermitage is lovely," said Mirri. "Are you the one
who built it?"

"No," said Jamba-Van, modestly shaking his head,
"merely small improvements here and there. Nor is the
ashrama mine. I am only its custodian. Naturally, I profit
from the opportunity to read, study, and reflect on cosmic
matters."

"Most remarkable!" Rajaswami exclaimed. "To think
that a savage creature of the forest should devote himself to
such noble endeavors. Most remarkable, indeed."

The bear's muzzle twitched. "*Brahmana,* are you imply-
ing that what you call a savage creature lacks the intelligence
and sensitivity to pursue those subjects? Would you find it
more appropriate"—a low growl began rising in his throat
—"for one to pass his days lurking in the woods? Benighted,
uninstructed, unaware of the finer things in life?"

"Not at all," Rajaswami protested. "I only observed that
it was extraordinary."

"Extraordinary?" Jamba-Van burst out. "Why so? Is a
bear less capable than a *brahmana?* Unfit for subtle reasoning?"

Jamba-Van reared up to his full height, gnashing his
teeth, roaring at the top of his voice. Rajaswami nearly tumbled off the stool while the bear stamped his feet and flailed
his arms; then, before Tamar could decide what to do,
Jamba-Van went lurching toward the shelves, where he
seized half a dozen pots and dashed them one after the other
to the ground.

"Ah. That's better." Jamba-Van blew out his breath. "I
beg your pardon. These moments do come upon me. Pay
no heed."

"That's the trouble with bears," Adi-Kavi whispered to
Mirri and Tamar. "They're moody folk, but you never
know what mood they'll be in from one moment to the
next."

"I find it beneficial and soothing, when I'm unsettled,
to break a few pieces of crockery," Jamba-Van went on. "It
never fails to have a calming effect."

"Glad to hear that, old boy," said Hashkat, while the
bear fetched a broom and swept up the shattered pots, "but
you must run through a lot of kitchenware."

"I fashion more," replied Jamba-Van, seating himself at

the table. "I find that pot making, like tending my garden, frees the mind for philosophical speculation." The bear, now altogether composed, turned a benign glance on Rajaswami. "Before I was—ah, carried away, I was about to agree. My circumstances are somewhat unusual, yet quite logical and plausible. Would you be pleased to hear an illuminating anecdote?"

"Of course, honored colleague, if I may call you that," said Rajaswami. "We shall find it most instructive."

The bear folded his paws and relaxed on the stool. "Unfathomable are the ways of karma," he began. "Consider this example:

"Once, in the forest, a wild bear caught sight of a wandering *brahmana:* long-bearded, wrinkle-browed, with an air of such wisdom that he must surely be a sage or great *rishi.*

"Instead of letting him go by in peace, the bear sprang from the bushes, snarling and rattling his claws. The *rishi,* in no way alarmed, pressed his palms together and bowed courteously.

" '*Namaste,* O worthy bear,' said the *rishi.* 'You appear disturbed in spirit. How may I be of service to you?'

" 'You can start,' growled the bear, 'by providing my dinner.'

" 'I travel lightly, as you see,' answered the *rishi,* 'and carry no edibles with me. However, I'm sure I can find something to satisfy you.'

" 'I've already found something,' retorted the bear. 'You. I intend to eat you up.'

" 'All creatures must have nourishment,' said the *rishi,* unperturbed, 'you as well as I. All right, then, go ahead and eat me up. Where do you wish to begin? Since I'm mostly skin and bones, you must be hungry indeed.'

" 'Eh?' The bear scowled at him. 'I'm not at all hungry.'

" 'In that case,' said the *rishi,* 'why do you want to eat me?'

"The bear hesitated a moment, frowning. 'Because—because I'm a bear. It's my profession. That's what I do.'

" 'Have you never contemplated doing something else?' the sage inquired. 'Perhaps you wish to become a *rishi?*'

" 'Certainly not,' snapped the bear. 'Bear I am, bear I'll be.'

" 'If you devour me, you'll surely be a *rishi,*' the sage replied. 'Once you gobble me up and digest me, will I not turn into your flesh and blood? There I'll be, in your muscles and sinews, heart, brain, and nerves, and you'll never get rid of me.

" 'Consider this logically,' the sage continued. 'You're not hungry. You don't want to be a *rishi.* I haven't offended you. Therefore, why do you choose to harm me? Furthermore, you didn't get up this morning expecting to find me; and just think, suppose you'd taken another path, or I'd taken another path, we'd never have met in the first place.'

" 'Stop! Stop!' roared the bear, who was not in the habit of thinking about anything at all. 'You're making my head hurt. My brain feels like it caught rheumatism: It smarts and twinges; it's going to explode at any moment.'

" 'Yes, thinking is a bit uncomfortable,' said the *rishi,* 'but you'll get used to it. A matter of time and practice.'

" 'I'm sorry I ever laid eyes on you!' howled the bear. 'Go away, let me be.'

" 'No, I won't,' the *rishi* answered. 'You started this business, you'll have to finish it. Calm yourself. Come, walk along with me awhile.'

"The bewildered bear finally agreed. For many days, as

they strolled through the forest, the *rishi* discoursed on stars and planets, suns and moons beyond the sight of the sharpest-eyed eagle; of creatures so tiny their universe fit on the head of a pin; of paradoxes, riddles, anomalies, speculations. The bear, in time, began feeling that a bearish existence was an extremely small and boring one; and, at last, he begged the *rishi* to instruct him.

"I was that bear," said Jamba-Van. "The *rishi* became my teacher and led me to this, his *ashrama,* where he taught me to read and write. He allowed me to remain and study while he continued his wanderings, promising one day to return. Here I have waited ever since. I regret that my bearish disposition gets the better of me on occasion; but, when it does, I can always smash a few pots."

—◆—

Tamar had never seen his *acharya* so happy. Rajaswami seemed to have taken root there, spending hours in philosophical discussions with the bear. When Rajaswami declared that infinity was a straight line, the bear maintained it was a circle—and grew so unsettled that he nearly ran out of cookware to break. Hashkat, during these sunny days, drowsed under the fruit trees. Garuda, in the balmy air of the hermitage, complained less than usual. The bird had lost none of his adoration for Mirri, but had, in turn, gained his own admirer: Akka, who constantly stayed close to him, groomed his feathers, and wheedled Garuda into carrying him aloft for short flights.

Each night, Tamar made up his mind that they would leave the next day. Each morning, he had no heart to order a departure. He told himself he was delaying for the sake of Rajaswami, to let the *acharya* enjoy a few more hours of pleasure, then admitted this was his own reluctance, so strong he could not overcome it. After a while, he understood. Simply, he was happy here.

Mirri—he had never felt closer to her. They were seldom apart, except for her lessons from Adi-Kavi. As promised, the *suta* taught her some of his skills.

"I try to see the world as it is," he began, "but you can see it in different ways. Our learned *brahmana* looks at it with his logic; but it's not always a tidy place, the world. It's full of odd cracks and crevices, and spaces in between; and more's possible than you might imagine. First thing is to have an open heart and a peaceful mind."

To Adi-Kavi's delight, Mirri soon caught the knack of putting herself into deepest slumber, scarcely breathing; to turn her body fiery hot or icy cold; to stay motionless, without the least twitch of a finger or blink of an eye.

When Tamar asked to learn, Adi-Kavi sighed. "If I read your heart aright, it's divided every which way; and too many things rattling around in your head, all arguing with each other. Later, perhaps, when you sort them out."

Regretfully, he knew the *suta* was right. While Mirri kept on with her lessons, he went off to find the bear, who was tidying up the kitchen.

"My learned colleague and I have paused in our discussions," Jamba-Van said cordially. "We are reconsidering our positions on the nature of infinity."

"A vast subject." Tamar smiled. "Between you two sages, you'll get to the truth of it."

"Surely not," said the bear. "Behind one truth, there is always yet another. As you may find when you reach Mahapura. Yes, your *acharya* told me of your journey and how it might end."

"If it ends," Tamar said. "Tell me, O learned bear: Suppose travelers wished to stop and live here. Would it be permitted?"

"Contemplating the hypothetical situation you propose, the answer is: yes. Of course. What is the reason for your inquiry?"

"Merely to know," Tamar said.

During the next several days, Tamar and Mirri rambled through the woods or picked fruit in the orchard. Exploring upstream, they found a waterfall and waded, soaking wet in the spray and foaming current. As if by silent agreement, neither spoke of Mahapura and when Tamar planned to leave the *ashrama*.

One evening, they swam to the biggest of the islands. In a circle of tall ferns, Mirri paced light, dancing steps, moving from one graceful attitude to another.

Beckoning to Tamar, she murmured:

> *Once, long ago, we danced like this*
> *In a forest, by old stones of*
> *Ruined temples. Do you remember?*

Tamar answered:

> *That night, we heard a flute play.*
> *The notes were trembling and shy.*
> *Who was the player? Who were we?*

Mirri continued the verse:

King and queen, or god and goddess,
As we had been forever.
What interrupted our eternity?

Tamar replied:

Time stopped and held its breath,
Waiting for us to rejoin each other.
Now it begins anew.
Forever then,
Forever
Once again.

In the *ashrama* that night, he dreamed of trees turning to gold. A death.

He said nothing of this omen to Mirri; nor had he the heart to tell Rajaswami, who woke bubbling with good spirits, eager to expound a new theory to the bear. Instead, he sought out Adi-Kavi and found him eating a melon in the garden. It was a pleasant, sunny morning. They talked awhile. Tamar later asked Mirri to walk in the orchard.

"I asked Adi-Kavi to carry the ruby," he began. "He said he would. I trust him. I haven't given it to him yet, but I soon will. That much is settled."

"And something else is unsettled. Why are you doing this?"

"He promised," Tamar went on, "whatever else happens, he'll find his way to Jaya."

Mirri took him by the shoulders. "You're going at this sideways. Tell me straight out. What's wrong?"

"Nothing's wrong. Everything's right." He looked squarely at her. "Have you been happy here?"

"You know I have."

"Will you stay with me?"

"Yes."

"I mean, in the hermitage. Jamba-Van will let us live here. He told me so.

"I'm not going to Mahapura," he said abruptly. "I must have known that when we first met. I kept pushing it out of my mind. I was ashamed even to think of breaking the warrior's code. Live by it. Die for it. I can't. Not now. Are love's arrows made of flowers, as poets say? No, they're stronger than that, and they've grown stronger every day.

"Keep my word to give up my life? To someone who may not exist? Once, I'd have accepted that. Promise made, promise kept. A king's dharma. No, that's over with."

He was speaking defiantly, as if to Jaya himself as much as to Mirri. "Was it real? Was it a dream? It makes no difference. I won't lose you for the sake of it. My promise to Jaya? I break it."

He pulled off the ring and threw it away.

PART III

RANAPURA

21. Garuda Does a Service

———◆———

C ome. That's a burden lifted." Tamar smiled and held
out his hands to her. For a king and *kshatriya* who had
broken his sworn word, his code of honor, and his dharma
all within the moment, he felt, on the whole, pleased with
himself, unexpectedly lighthearted. He motioned toward the
hermitage:

"Let's go and tell them. Hashkat should be glad. He'll
go back to ruling his Bandar-loka. As for Rajaswami—that's
going to be hard. My dear old *acharya*. I'm afraid he'll be
shocked. At first. But he'll see the bright side: He can stay
here, philosophizing with Jamba-Van. I think that's what he
secretly wishes."

Instead of smiling back at him, Mirri stood staring, her
dark features frozen, her eyes wide.

"What have you done?" she said in a fearful whisper.

"Done?" Tamar was puzzled. "I did what you saw. I set
myself free. I put an end to a fool's journey."

"You believe so?" she cried. "You broke dharma—"

"Yes. For you. It's what you wanted, isn't it? From the
start—"

"Not like this."

"How, then?" he burst out. "What more? I'm rid of
Jaya. I'm not bound to him. I'm bound to no one. Only to
you."

"That's not true."

"Why? Because I broke one promise, you think I'll break another?"

"No. You don't understand—"

"I understand I've thrown everything away and now you tell me it was wrong."

Without hearing her answer, he turned on his heel and strode from the orchard.

He did not go to the *ashrama*. He went, rather, to the stream. He sat on the grassy bank and looked across at the island where they had danced. He put his head in his hands. Half his heart rejoiced at what he had done; the other half was horrified. Beyond that, he was shocked, bitterly disappointed by Mirri's words.

Her hand touched his arm.

He looked up. "You say I don't understand. There's something you don't understand. I didn't tell you."

"Tell me now." She sat next to him.

"It's been in my mind for us to stay here. I couldn't decide. Then, last night, after we came back, I dreamed the trees turned to gold. Twice now I've had that dream. This time, it tipped the balance. Do you know what it means? It foretells a death. Yours? Mine? If we keep on with this journey? I can't let that happen. It won't, now I'm free of Jaya."

"You're not free of him," Mirri said quietly. "You're truly a fool if you think so."

"I put down that burden. I'd be a bigger fool to pick it up again. You, of all people, want me to do it? No. I won't."

"If you don't, you'll carry a worse burden. Your broken dharma, for one thing. For another: You'll never be sure of the truth. You'll always wonder and question, and chew it over and over: Was it a dream? Or wasn't it? You'll never be rid of Jaya until you know for certain. I've understood that since the night I offered you the garland."

"What does it matter whether I'm sure or not?"

"Because he'll always be a shadow between us. Unless you find out one way or the other, he'll haunt you every day of your life. He'll poison you. In time, it will kill you as if he used a sword. Do you call that being free?"

"If that's my karma, so be it. I can't take back what I've done."

He stood and walked up the path to the hermitage, Mirri silent beside him.

Rajaswami and the bear were at the table in the common room. Adi-Kavi sat cross-legged by the hearth.

"Revered *acharya*." Tamar formally pressed his hands together and bowed his head. "I have something important I must say to you."

"Indeed, my boy? What a coincidence! I have something important to say to you. My learned colleague and I have engaged in many discussions on the shape of infinity. Is it straight? Is it a circle?"

"Please, *acharya*—"

"It is neither," Rajaswami continued. "It is, in effect, rather like a figure eight. A remarkable conception—"

"*Acharya*—"

"Eh? Oh. Yes. What was it, dear boy, that you wished to tell me?"

"The journey to Mahapura—"

"Ah. That. Of course." Rajaswami's face fell. "I understand. The impatience of youth. Yes, well, it has been most pleasant here."

"We aren't leaving." Tamar glanced at Mirri, who was watching him with a look half anguished, half fearful. "You see—"

"Shmaa! Shmaa! Incompetent nitwit!"

Garuda tumbled through an open window to land in a heap on the floor. He picked himself up and strutted back and forth in front of Tamar.

"You'll owe me plenty for this," Garuda crowed. "I won't forget. Don't you forget, either. I'll remind you from time to time. I've done you yet another service. A big one. Careless idiot, you must have lost this in the orchard. Lucky I found it."

Garuda opened his talons and dropped the ring at Tamar's feet.

"Good heavens, my boy, that was careless indeed," Rajaswami exclaimed. "How did you do that? And never notice? But, the bright side is: You have it back, thanks to our sharp-eyed eagle."

Tamar stared at the ring as if it had been a viper coiled to strike. Mirri's words beside the stream rang in his ears, all the more tormenting because, he admitted, they were true.

As though Mirri alone could hear, he said:

> *Not for the warrior's code,*
> *Not for honor's sake,*
> *But for your heart and mine,*
> *Though at the end they break.*

Mirri answered:

> *Though at the end they break,*
> *Death will not keep them apart.*

No ring can bind us closer
Than your heart that holds my heart.

He bent and picked up the ring, which seemed so heavy he could barely lift it. He forced the cold iron circlet on his finger.

"I wish to be gone from here," he said. "*Suta,* fetch the horses."

"But, my boy, what were you saying?" asked Raja-swami. "Not going to Mahapura?"

"Not going—not until I found the ring." Tamar faltered. "No. I haven't lost so much honor that I can lie to my *acharya.* I threw it away."

"Goodness me!" cried Rajaswami. "Why ever would you do a thing like that?"

Before Tamar could explain, the bear pricked up his ears. There was the sound of hoofbeats. By instinct, Tamar reached for his sword. It was not at his side; he had borne no weapon since he had been at the hermitage.

"Still more travelers? How curious to have so many all at once." Jamba-Van lumbered out to the veranda. Tamar, uneasy, stepped after him. Hashkat and Akka came running from behind the stable.

Two men had dismounted in the dooryard. Their horses had been hard-ridden, legs and flanks streaked with mud. The riders were dressed much alike in stained cloaks, long-skirted tunics, and leather leggings. They carried swords at their sides and curved knives in their belts. One seemed Tamar's age; the other, a few years older. Both were fair-haired, fine-featured, with gray-blue eyes. Their faces were as weather-beaten as huntsmen's; but, by their bearing, they were clearly *kshatriyas* despite their coarse garments.

The elder, with a short, reddish-yellow beard, moved in confident strides to Tamar. "*Namaste,* King of Sundari. I am Kirin. This is my brother, Skanda. Your trail led us to this *ashrama.*"

"Lucky to find you still here," added Skanda. "We expected you'd have left by now. This shortens our search."

"Why seek me?" Tamar demanded. "Who are you? Speak quickly. I make ready to leave without delay."

"Allow us to delay your journey a little longer," replied Kirin. "You are a friend to our eldest brother, and so we are friends to you. You know his name: Ashwara."

Tamar brightened, surprised that he had not seen the family resemblance immediately. "Is he well? Safe?"

"He is well." Kirin gave a hard smile. "Safe? Ashwara is never safe. He sends all of you his greetings; and, to you, a message."

"Rest yourselves and your horses. I'm sure that Jamba-Van"—Tamar nodded to the bear—"will gladly offer you hospitality while I gladly hear Ashwara's words."

Kirin shook his head. "Time presses on us, as it presses on you. Ashwara says only this: 'Come to me in Chandragar.' "

22. Kirin and Skanda

<img... A shwara spoke to us of your journey," Skanda said.
"You'll not be much off your path. Chandragar is by
the Sabla River, the course you should follow in any case."

"Did he say no more?" Tamar asked. "Why does he
wish me to go there?"

"He told us little," replied Kirin. "His thoughts are his
own, and it is best that he himself explain them."

"Ashwara is my friend," Tamar said. "For the sake of
friendship, I will do as he bids me."

Mirri glanced uneasily at Tamar, but said nothing against
his decision and set about packing her saddlebags. For Hashkat and Adi-Kavi, there was no question. They would ride
to Chandragar, and Akka insisted on doing likewise. Rajaswami accepted the plan with resignation. Garuda took no
pains to hide his own opinion:

"I thought we'd seen the last of that lion-headed, big-
toothed forest-lurker. Now he's pounced on us again! Just
when I was getting a little of my strength back. Shmaa! Some
people have no consideration."

Tamar again urged the brothers to come inside, whispering that Jamba-Van was more learned than most *brahmana*s but not one to be lightly crossed. So, in spite of the
delay, Skanda and Kirin accepted the refreshments the bear
set out for them.

When they could stay no longer, Jamba-Van ransacked his larder for provisions enough to fill all their saddle packs. He embraced his parting visitors and waved a paw at Garuda.

"Your *ashrama* suits me better than my palace," Tamar said. "I'll remember it dearly—and its hermit."

"Remember, as well," said Jamba-Van, "to look for truth behind truth."

"I hope I know it if I see it," Tamar said.

"Honored colleague," said Rajaswami, as the bear hugged him enough to make the *acharya*'s bones crack, "I am confident that karma, one day, will lead our paths to cross. We still have an infinity of theories to discuss."

"Whatever shape infinity may be," replied the bear, "it offers not enough time for your edifying discourses."

"Nor for your own." Rajaswami dabbed an eye with his scarf. Regaining his usual cheeriness, he added, "We must, however, look on the bright side:

> *Friends who part in deepest sadness*
> *Meet again in greatest gladness.*

Tamar rode out from the *ashrama* as if leaving home for the second time.

◆

They adored their brother. Tamar understood that from the moment they set off for Chandragar. As they made their way toward the Sabla, Kirin and Skanda talked of little else. Skanda's boyish features lit up whenever he spoke of Ashwara. Of the two, he was the more eager: bright-faced and high-spirited, laughing easily, shrugging off the dangers and hardships they had suffered as hunted fugitives; Kirin, the more intense, with lightning flashes in his eyes when he recalled Nahusha's treachery and the blazing trap set for them. Skanda told happily of his boyhood, of Ashwara teaching him swordplay and archery; Kirin, of Ashwara's nobility and wisdom as king of Ranapura. Yet, for all their differences in temperament, they worshiped him equally.

"He saved our lives twice," Skanda said, when Tamar asked to know more of their escape from the pleasure-cottage where Nahusha was sure they would burn to death. "First, when Kana set the torch to the oil-soaked timbers. We had been warned by a loyal retainer, but almost too late, for the doors had been bolted from the outside. Ashwara, even with flames bursting all around us, made us wait calmly until one of the walls had nearly burned away. Then, by sheer strength, he broke a passage through it. Kirin and I were choking and blinded by the smoke. Ashwara dragged both of us to open air and hid us amid the foliage."

"The second time," Kirin added, "was when we sought a way of eluding Nahusha's warriors. Knowing we still lived, Nahusha set his men on watch, to slay us before we could escape into the forest."

"Had they caught us, they'd have killed us out of hand," put in Skanda. "But Ashwara struck on a bold plan. He disguised the three of us as holy beggars. Not difficult. We were already half naked. We streaked our faces with ashes and covered our heads in rags, and trudged barefoot from Ranapura. None hindered us; such saintly wanderers were a common sight. They deserved reverence and their persons were inviolate."

"And so we made our way quietly, almost to the edge

of the forest," Kirin said. "But there, in our path, stood a handful of warriors on the alert, casting hard eyes on all who passed.

"We could not turn aside, for they had already seen us. To flee—that surely would have betrayed us. To fight—we were weaponless and outnumbered. And so Ashwara whispered to us to keep on our way and be silent. Indeed, as we came up to the warriors, they looked at us not with suspicion but with scorn. To their discredit, they showed neither respect nor reverence, and had only mocking laughter and coarse words for our tattered garments and humble bearing."

"Ashwara made no reply to their taunting," Skanda said, "but I can tell you my blood was boiling. Ashwara had warned us not to speak, but I could scarcely hold my tongue. It was all I could do to keep from cursing them and throwing myself at their throats. Because, you see, we knew these men and had trusted them. Now they were among the ones Nahusha had corrupted to turn against us. Standing there was a warrior named Rasha, who had been one of Ashwara's own troop captains.

"Instead of trying to pass by, Ashwara went up to them. Head bowed, eyes to the ground, he held out his hands and silently begged for alms.

"What must it have cost his warrior's pride?" Skanda shook his head. "Abasing himself to those traitors? I couldn't have forced myself to do it."

"He had to," Kirin explained. "Otherwise—a beggar who doesn't beg? It would surely have roused their suspicions. This was our most dangerous moment. No man has ever judged me coward, but I confess my heart was in my mouth. It raced through my mind that, if recognized, we could only sell our lives dearly.

"Rasha barely gave us a glance, but reproached his comrades for mocking us. Then he reached into his purse and took out a coin.

"One of his fellows burst out laughing. 'The smallest coin of the realm! Are you sure you can spare it?'

"Rasha only shrugged, and threw it to the ground. Ashwara, ever silent, bent and picked it up from the dust, and bowed his gratitude. The warriors motioned for us to be gone. And we passed by.

"As we did, Ashwara said under his breath:

" 'O Rasha, you betrayed me. Even so, for the sake of the coin you flung me, when I come again into my kingdom I vow to spare your life.' "

23. At the Gates of Ranapura

A few days later, they reached the woodlands at the outskirts of Chandragar. Gayatri suddenly reared. As if out of thin air, two warriors sprang across their path, bows drawn. Recognizing the brothers, who spoke briefly to them, the sentries saluted Tamar and waved him on, with Mirri and the others trotting after. Only little by little, as he glanced around, did Tamar notice chariots hidden by foliage, stacks of weapons and gear set amid the brush so as to be nearly invisible. Warriors sat in the shadows along the forest track, sharpening swords and knives, waxing bowstrings, trimming the feathers of arrows.

When Tamar spoke admiringly of how cleverly the camp had been disposed, and how Darshan himself would have been impressed, Adi-Kavi nodded agreement, then sniffed the air and grimaced.

"Better than any I've seen," remarked the *suta*. "It's the smell I don't like: trouble. Something bloody's in the wind."

A little farther on, Ashwara awaited them. No tent had been pitched, only a sort of lean-to covered with branches. Ashwara went to embrace them as they dismounted. His lion eyes brightened with pleasure. "I see you have gained another companion." He nodded his tawny head at Akka. "I wish to hear how you rescued him. First, I thank you for turning from your journey. You will not be long delayed. To speak straight out:

"My brothers and I have done well, but not quite as well as I hoped," Ashwara said, beckoning all to sit around him in the shelter. "The king of Chandragar supports my cause with troops and equipment. Skanda and Kirin have convinced other smaller kings to join us. Since Bala chose to take neither side, as you remember, my forces nearly equal Nahusha's. Some you see here." He gestured toward the warriors scattered throughout the woods. "Still more are gathering closer to Ranapura."

"Then you have enough strength to challenge Nahusha and defeat him," Tamar said. "I could not wish better news."

"I said my forces were nearly equal," Ashwara replied, "which means they are not sufficient. Until they are, it would be rash to challenge him. My strength here is at its limit. I must seek more elsewhere. With added troops, my plan will be set, the last gap filled. Without them, if I am forced to give battle, I risk losing all. In either case, this is my only chance. This is my karma. Opportunity will not be given again.

"I do not speak to you now as friend to friend," Ashwara continued, "but as king to king. I ask you one question: Will Sundari join me and give the troops I need?"

"And I, no king, speak to you as friend to friend," Tamar answered. "Before Bala's durbar, I told you my commander, Darshan, would put Sundari's army at your orders if I wished him to do so. That was my pledge then, and my pledge now."

"My question is answered," said Ashwara. As Tamar listened closely, Ashwara detailed his need for light cavalry, foot soldiers, archers, spearmen, and warriors skilled in fighting from chariots. They would, he explained, be his strong reserves, joining his own people only out of necessity. "If all goes as I intend, they will not be ordered into the fray; but I must have them armed and ready. In the heat of battle, even the best-laid plans go adrift. Sundari's warriors will be my firm anchor. Without them, the tide may turn either way.

"Let them come in all haste," Ashwara went on. "They should follow the Rana River. The valley lands are gentle. Your troops can move swiftly through them, and join Skanda in the plains east of Ranapura. He will see to their deployment, and report their arrival to me."

"I will write that order in my own hand to Darshan. He will recognize that it comes from me," Tamar replied. "Choose your fastest galloper to carry it."

"The time it takes a horseman to reach Sundari is empty time," put in Mirri. "Days spent in his travel added to days for the army to reach you."

"You calculate as shrewdly as a moneylender or a general," Ashwara said fondly, "but, clever *gopi,* you tell me nothing I do not know. I am a miser of time; I hoard it and begrudge every wasted moment; yet, I spend it as I must."

"If you're a miser," Mirri replied, "you'd rather save it, wouldn't you? You can send your message a dozen days faster."

Ashwara laughed. "What do you propose? Have you some magical chariot, as the old tales tell?"

"No," Mirri said. "We have an eagle."

All eyes turned on Garuda, who had come to roost in

the lean-to. The bird gaped in horrified disbelief, then burst out:

"Waa! Don't look at me. I have my own troubles. Me? Go sailing across the country? I'm surely not such a fool."

"You're an eagle nonetheless," Mirri said. "You're stronger now than when you were nesting in that thornbush. Your tail feathers are growing back beautifully."

"You really think so?" Garuda said, with a melting glance at Mirri, then hurriedly added, "No, no. Stronger's got nothing to do with it. My nerves are unraveled; my head's addled as a year-old egg. Shmaa! You're all quick at finding ways to unsettle me."

"You did bravely at Nahusha's camp," Mirri reminded him.

"A mistake," Garuda snapped. "I've regretted it ever since."

"No, you didn't," Mirri said. "You were proud of yourself. I was proud of you, too."

"That was different. From here to Sundari and back? Alone? The empty sky? The cold? The wind? The silence? Not a word of cheer? You've no idea how that can tie knots in a bird's mind." Garuda rolled his eyes. "No. Oh, no. Wheedle, wheedle, wheedle. I'm not up to it."

"You won't be by yourself," Akka suddenly broke in. "I'll go with you."

"Eh?" Garuda blinked. "You would?"

"You'll carry me on your back," Akka pressed, "the way we flew around the *ashrama*. We had grand times, didn't we?"

"We might have." Garuda hunched his wings. "So, all right, there was the odd moment of enjoyment." He clacked his beak thoughtfully. "That could put a different light on the matter."

"You'll let me, won't you?" Akka turned an eager face to Hashkat. "You know it's important. Fun, besides."

"We didn't save you so you could go careening through the air on a flying dust mop," Hashkat said. "On the other hand, what I let or don't let hasn't much weight with the Bandar-loka. I won't call it a good idea, but it's not a completely bad idea. Very well. Go with the old buzzard. Have a care. You'll be looking out for him as well as yourself."

While Akka capered gleefully, Garuda flew to Mirri's lap and bent his head to be scratched. Tamar said to Ashwara:

"I'll write the order to Darshan; and, to be doubly sure, another for a horseman to carry. Garuda can leave as soon as I've done."

"It's nearly sundown," squawked Garuda. "I'm an eagle. Shmaa! You think I'm an owl?"

Mirri urged him to make the most of what light remained. Garuda finally muttered agreement. Tamar, finishing his message, rolled up the page and tied it securely to Garuda's leg. Rajaswami came to beam his blessings while Mirri, for a last time, stroked the bird's wings.

"If I were smaller and lighter," said Adi-Kavi, clapping a hand on Akka's shoulder, "I'd be curious to take an air voyage. That's one of the few things I haven't done."

"Something I want to tell you," Garuda said to Tamar, as the monkey climbed astride the bird's back. "You keep this in mind—"

"I know." Tamar grinned at him. "I owe you."

All watched as Garuda and his passenger took flight, soaring above the treetops into the crimson streaks of sunset.

That night, there was no sound of Garuda singing himself to sleep.

———◆———

Ashwara, next morning, ordered his warriors to break camp and take up positions closer to Ranapura, and thus be battle-ready as soon as Tamar's troops arrived. Tamar ventured to ask the reason for Ashwara's decision.

"You're well hidden here," he said. "Will you risk letting Nahusha's scouts see your people on the march? And yourself as well?"

"Nahusha knows exactly where I am," said Ashwara. "I am safer now than I have been. He will wait until he and I come face to face. Kill me? He will prefer to take me alive.

"And you," Ashwara went on, "I thank you and wish you well. Your eagle will find you easily before you have gone far."

"Gone far? How so?" Tamar said. "I stay and await my troops. Did you think otherwise? If I order my warriors into harm's way, how can I not be with them?"

"There is no need," said Ashwara.

"There is every need," replied Tamar. "I abandoned my people once. I will not do so again when they are in danger. I start for Mahapura when your cause is won, not before."

Ashwara glanced around at Mirri and the others. "Leave us. The king of Sundari and I have hard truths to speak."

"There are no truths that cannot be spoken in front of us all." Tamar took Mirri's hand. "Say what you wish."

"Then understand this," Ashwara began. "It is agreed: I do not commit your troops to battle unless I have no other choice; but, if I must, I will not hesitate, cost what it may."

"As you have said. In any event, I lead my own men. This is as it should be."

"Is it?" returned Ashwara. "Tell me one thing: How often have you commanded warriors in battle?"

"Never." Tamar flushed. "Why ask? Do you question my courage to do so?"

"I question your knowledge. I will not have officers around me who are untried and unseasoned. The stakes are too high, the danger too great. For me. And for you."

"I question your opinion of me, but not my duty to my people. I lead them. My right. My obligation as a *kshatriya*. You will not deny me."

The two men had been standing face to face. Tamar's blood ran hot and cold. He could not believe he had dared to gainsay Ashwara as a military commander, or to show anger to him as a friend. For an instant, he half expected the lion-eyed warrior to draw sword and challenge him. His hands trembled. His gaze did not waver. Ashwara's golden features hardened. He said nothing for many moments. When he answered, his voice was icy:

"Lead your troops, King of Sundari. As you demand. Only hear me well. You will command them, but you will obey my orders. Precisely. To the letter. No question. No complaint. You have spoken. I have spoken. So be it."

Ashwara turned on his heel and strode to the horse lines, calling for Kirin and Skanda.

"What have you done?" Mirri rounded on Tamar. "You made him go against his better judgment—"

"And what of my own judgment? This is a matter between warriors. It's settled now."

◆

He saw little of Ashwara in the following days. As the columns of foot troops and chariots moved closer to Ranapura, Ashwara was busy with a hundred things and seemed to be in a hundred places at once. When they did meet, Tamar was not sure if he sensed a deep sadness, or a cold formality, or if Ashwara was simply preoccupied.

Mirri said nothing more on the subject, which made it worse. He could not understand why it gnawed at him. He had acted properly, according to dharma. His right, his obligation, as he had told Ashwara. If he had done right, why did it feel wrong? He finally reasoned it out: If Ashwara mistrusted his skill, the tawny-haired warrior might hold back Sundari's troops even when most needed. A fatal error that might well cost Ashwara the battle.

After another sleepless night, Tamar sought him out. With Kirin beside him, Ashwara was tracing lines in the ground, marking positions his army would take up.

Tamar began by talking about something else. "When Akka was in Nahusha's chambers, he heard there was a plan of some sort. That's all he knows, but Nahusha must be sure of the scheme, so he wasn't troubled when Bala wouldn't join him. Yet Mirri thinks he doesn't have that many troops if he asked Bala's help in the first place."

"She may be right," Ashwara said. "I must try to learn more of Nahusha's plan. Is that all you came to tell me?"

"No. My troops . . ." Tamar hesitated; his words were sticking in his throat.

"What about them?"

"When they're here . . ." Tamar began again. He looked away for a moment. Ashwara waited in silence.

"It's for the best," Tamar went on painfully, "if—if I don't command them. Darshan will."

"As you choose," Ashwara said quietly. He nodded. "A wise decision."

Later, Tamar went back to the shelter. Mirri was relieved when he told her what he had done. He did not tell her his shame at judging himself unworthy. He did not tell her that he had just given up his pride as a king and his honor as a *kshatriya,* and he had nothing left.

❖

Ashwara had attached Tamar to his personal staff, giving him a chariot and a promise that he might command a small detachment. Tamar made himself satisfied with that. But there was no sign of Garuda and Akka. Ashwara's columns had by now reached the edge of the woodlands, halting at the open ground before Ranapura. The eight-sided fortress, with massive walls of golden-brown stone, overlooked a rolling plain dotted with copses of slender trees and, here and there, a rocky knoll. Tall watchtowers rose at each angle of the fortress; Tamar could clearly see the lookouts in the turrets. Beyond Ranapura, jagged white peaks of the Snow Mountains soared into the clouds. Tamar constantly scanned the sweep of sky for a glimpse of a winged shape. None. Even by generous reckoning, Garuda should have found the camp days ago.

Neither the bird nor Akka could have failed to notice the massing of warriors, ranks of chariots, horse lines, and stacks of provisions. Ashwara made no attempt at conceal- ment. He allowed tents to be pitched, cook fires lit. Nahusha had chosen to set his battle lines well in front of the fortress. Warriors moved, unhurried, among the pavilions. Tamar did not see Nahusha, but once caught sight of Kana strolling with a group of officers. It all seemed very leisurely.

At dusk, Tamar went to the tent Ashwara had assigned them. Rajaswami sat cross-legged, deep in contemplation. By the light of an oil lamp, Hashkat sorted out harness leathers, for the monkey had insisted on being Tamar's chariot driver.

Adi-Kavi and Mirri were setting out food. Seeing Tamar's worried frown, the *suta* laid a hand on his arm:

"Put your mind at rest. They'll be here, and your troops soon after. Nothing will happen meantime. Ashwara won't issue his challenge until your people are well in position. Nahusha won't fight until he's formally challenged. You're a king, you know how these things are done."

"I don't," said Mirri. "Ashwara's here, armed to the teeth. Nahusha sees him. What more challenge?"

"Formalities," Adi-Kavi said. "Above all, the formalities must be properly observed. What will happen, when Ashwara's ready, is that he and his brothers will ride up to Nahusha's lines with a flag of truce. Ashwara will declare his grievances and why he intends to fight. He'll demand Nahusha's surrender. Nahusha won't do it, of course. They'll trade some elegantly polished insults; each will declare right and justice on their side. Ashwara will ride back. And so it begins.

"Every game has its rules," Adi-Kavi continued. "This is a game for *kshatriya*s. There are rules about surrendering, carrying away the wounded, breaking off a combat— Oh, it's all neatly planned out.

"Naturally, there's always some hotheaded, battle-mad fool who goes rampaging. It's contagious. His comrades join in, rules to the wind. Then it's butchery, plain and simple: Kill, kill, no matter how. They call it *sankula.*" Adi-Kavi grimaced. "*Sankula?* Bloody lunacy, as I see it."

"How do you know all this?" Mirri asked. "You're a *suta;* you're forbidden to fight."

"True," Adi-Kavi said. *"Suta*s don't bear arms, but I still had to learn. As a royal crier, my duty was to be with my king; and, when the battle ended, make a show of praising his great valor and dauntless courage. I can tell you, though, when you see a king in full regalia leaning over his chariot to puke out his poor terrified guts—praising his valor takes a certain amount of inventiveness.

"At sundown, they leave off slaughtering each other. The warriors go back to their tents, eat, drink, and tell dazzling lies about their heroic deeds. No one fights at night, you see. That's one rule never broken. Unthinkable. Simply not done. At dawn, they go at it again.

"Rules, sweet *gopi,"* said Adi-Kavi. "Absolutely necessary when disemboweling your enemies. Otherwise, we'd be no better than barbarians."

Late morning of the next day, Nahusha attacked.

24. "Sankula! Sankula!"

———◆———

S kanda, flushed and furious, was shouting for him. Tamar stepped out of the tent; he could not believe what he was hearing. He told Skanda it was not possible.

"Not possible?" Skanda retorted. "You think not? Yes, well, Nahusha's done it. No challenge. No warning. Ashwara just found out. All officers report to him."

Kirin and other commanders were already there when Tamar, still disbelieving, hurried into the headquarters tent. The *kshatriya*s were muttering angrily among themselves. Ashwara silenced them with a gesture. He motioned with his head toward a warrior, begrimed with sweat and dust, standing, arms folded and face tight-set.

"A rider from the king of Chandragar," Ashwara said quickly to Tamar. "King Rudra. First to support my cause. A strong warrior, my firm ally from the beginning. His army holds my left flank, close by the Rana." He turned to the message bearer. "Speak further."

"I have spoken all I know," the rider said, "and all that Rudra himself can tell you. A little before midday, Nahusha's warriors attacked us in force. They took us by surprise. No challenge had been given—against honor and the rules of war. How could Rudra have foreseen such a deed?

"They fell on us as if out of nowhere: spearmen, bowmen, hurlers of *chakra*s. We took heavy losses, many slain

183

before Rudra could rally his people and strike back. But when he struck," the man added with grim satisfaction, "he shattered them. They fled, leaving their dead behind. Rudra holds his position. One thing more." The warrior grinned. "Rudra sends these words: 'Say this to Ashwara: If Nahusha thinks to defeat me, he must swallow me whole. If he tries to bite me, he will break his teeth.' "

"Rudra has done nobly," Ashwara said. "Tell him we shall strive to match his courage."

Ashwara ordered his commanders to reinforce all battle lines and stand ready to answer any action by Nahusha. Skanda and Kirin hurried to assemble their troops. Tamar held back a moment, to ask Ashwara:

"How did Nahusha send warriors against Rudra without our knowing? We've watched his camp every day. There was no sign of movement. Even if his columns left by the rear gates, we'd have seen them on the march."

"One answer," Ashwara said. "They did not march from Ranapura. They were already in position, lying in ambush, long before now."

"That's what I'd have guessed." Mirri had been standing unnoticed in a corner of the pavilion. She stepped closer to Ashwara. "I have another idea about it too."

"Speak your mind," Ashwara said. "By rule, women have no part in warriors' concerns." His face softened. "Even so, no rule forbids me hearing a *gopi*'s thoughts."

"Nahusha never intended waiting to be challenged," Mirri said. As Ashwara nodded, she went on, "And you? Did you believe he would?"

Ashwara's golden eyes darkened. "No. I suspected he would not wait; yet, I could not bring myself to strike first and break my dharma. In my heart, I still hoped that he might redeem his own dharma and meet my terms. I had to allow him that chance. King Rudra has paid dearly for my hope. His warriors' blood is on my hands, as surely as if I myself had slain them.

"Now there is no turning back. I do what I must. At Bala's court, I vowed I would fight for justice, not revenge. The moment is upon me, but I question: Can I fight without rage? Without pride in battle? Without joy in victory? Can any man kill and keep his heart pure? If not, then is all slaughter alike, good cause or bad, and the same death for all at the end? Once, I believed that death is the warrior's final truth. Is it only his last illusion?

"Until I understand this," Ashwara continued, "I will not raise my own hand in battle. I will take no part in mortal combat—except against Nahusha himself; he and I, face to face. The path of my karma will cross his for one last time.

"Stay awhile," he said to Mirri. "A *gopi*'s thoughts may be clearer than a *kshatriya*'s. You, King of Sundari, go to Skanda. Put yourself at his orders."

Word of the treacherous attack on Rudra had blazed through the camp. Trumpet calls rang out along the lanes of tents. Warriors ran to assemble, still buckling leather breastplates. Field officers shouted for their companies to form ranks. Without waiting to be told, Hashkat had hitched Gayatri and Jagati to Tamar's light, four-wheeled chariot. At its high, shieldlike prow, the monkey had filled the weapons rack with Tamar's sword, bow, a full quiver of arrows, and set long, slender lances within hand's reach.

Even before Hashkat could rein up, Tamar vaulted over the side rails to gain his footing on the flat bed of planks that served as a fighting platform. He sighted Skanda's own chariot and motioned for Hashkat to catch up to it.

"Nahusha's warriors are in line of battle," Skanda called out as Hashkat drew alongside. His face was flushed; his blue-gray eyes danced and sparkled. He looked like a happy boy. "Kirin's people are going to engage them. I'm in support. We'll have to go at them smartly. Too bad there's not much daylight left.

"Orders?" he said, when Tamar repeated Ashwara's command. "I really don't have any for you. Later, perhaps. Meantime, you'll want friend Hashkat to keep your chariot in a little better trim."

With a wave of his hand, he sped off.

It teetered on the fine edge of insult. Ashwara's army was in high spirits; they had won almost every engagement; Tamar had not been in so much as a skirmish. He had handed over the ruby to Adi-Kavi. Risk of losing it in battle? He could as well have kept it. Ashwara had not given him a company. When Tamar questioned this, Ashwara, too busy to discuss it, urged patience. He wondered if the lion-eyed warrior was deliberately shielding him and if Mirri had anything to do with it.

He did not face her with his suspicion. They saw little of each other. He awoke each dawn, armed quickly, tumbled out Hashkat, and rode to the warriors' assembly. He waited. Neither Kirin nor Skanda had need of him. He was fuming. Also, he was relieved.

His shameful secret: fear. It was like some kind of small, pale worm hiding unnoticed until now. It had raised its head the first day he had seen the dead and wounded carted off the field. The dead, at least, were quiet; he could turn his eyes away. Some of the wounded were very loud. Worse, they were still alive. The worm thrived and fattened, feeding on him. Tamar understood: Before it grew bigger, he would have to kill the worm.

He calculated how to do it. One morning, leaving Hashkat asleep, he rode Gayatri to the assembly. He knew Ashwara's battle plan was to hold Nahusha's troops in check with foot soldiers and chariots while King Rudra swung his lines across the open side of the plain to cramp Nahusha's movement. Skanda's light cavalry harassed Nahusha's flank whenever and wherever least expected. That afternoon, when Skanda's horsemen took the field, Tamar galloped after them.

They skirted the main body of clashing warriors and wheeling chariots, the knots of foot soldiers striking out with spears and heavy clubs, then veered toward the fortress. Skanda was heading behind Nahusha's battle line, attacking the supply tents and stores of weapons.

Except for the first moments, when Tamar thought his heart would leap into his throat, it was marvelous. Everything was suddenly bright and sharp, sparkling clear. He was light-headed, swept up in a wave of wild freedom. He could do anything he wanted. Sword out, he slashed tent ropes, trampling any warriors trapped inside. Everyone was shouting enough to burst their lungs. Skanda's horsemen were torching the provisions and smashing the stacks of arms. Tamar jumped Gayatri over a flaming heap, and pressed on. The worm was definitely dead.

Nahusha's troops fought back as best they could; but they were rear area foot soldiers, not *kshatriyas*. Skanda's riders cut most of them down with least expense of effort and wasted motion; the rest fled—slowly, for it seemed that time had become sticky and sluggish, barely moving. A man

stumbled and flopped awkwardly across Tamar's path, got to
his knees and raised his hands. Tamar could have taken the
soldier's head off in one easy, looping stroke. The man
stared, openmouthed; he was gray-faced, with bad teeth, and
did not want to die. Tamar stared back. As once he had
looked into a tiger's eyes and felt the fear and pain of a
trapped animal, he felt his blade cutting flesh and bone of
his own neck. He pondered this for a seemingly long while.
He turned Gayatri aside. The man got up and went away.

Skanda was whistling for the riders to withdraw. The
raid had wrought satisfactory havoc. Tamar thought it had
lasted all afternoon. It had only been a few minutes. The
sun was still high when Tamar, trailing the horsemen, galloped to Ashwara's lines.

After sundown, Ashwara's field officers gathered in one
of the pavilions. Tamar joined them. Kirin and Skanda were
there amid a crowd of cavalrymen, laughing and tossing
rough jokes back and forth. Skanda caught sight of him:

"Why, here's the king of Sundari." He grinned at
Tamar. "Don't think I didn't see you tagging along with us.
Against orders?" Skanda winked. "Never mind. I know
you're keen to be in the thick of it. I like that in an officer.
Oh—by the way, did you kill your man?"

"Yes. Of course."

Skanda clapped him on the shoulder. "Good fellow.
Good fellow."

Tamar left the tent and did not go back.

◆◆◆

They were killing the horses.

For a moment, Tamar thought he was having a nightmare. He came full awake. Horses were shrieking in agony at the far edge of the camp. He flung on whatever garments lay at hand, snatched his sword, and plunged out of the tent. The sky was as pink as dawn. It took him another instant to understand it was still night. Flames billowed from the pavilions. A fist of hot wind struck him in the face.

He turned back. Mirri and Adi-Kavi were on their feet. Hashkat, blade in hand, started off to hitch up Gayatri and Jagati.

"Let be," Tamar ordered. "Mirri. Adi-Kavi. Take the horses and chariot. Get Rajaswami away. Ride into the woods. Stay there."

Rajaswami rubbed his bleary eyes. "What's the commotion? Good heavens, don't they realize people are trying to sleep?"

Tamar shook him. "Go with Mirri. We're attacked."

"Oh, I shouldn't think so." Rajaswami yawned. "It can't be morning—"

Tamar hauled up the *acharya* and sent him stumbling into Adi-Kavi's arms.

"How will I find you?" Mirri called.

"I don't know. Hashkat—with me." He ran from the tent, the monkey humping along beside him. Rajaswami, fussing and fretting like a child, was demanding his umbrella.

Nahusha's horsemen, brandishing torches, were galloping through the camp, behind them spearmen and sword fighters. When Tamar finally grasped that Nahusha had done the unthinkable and launched a night attack, he also realized it was even worse. Not a sudden raid, a quick and savage foray. Nahusha was throwing most of his forces against them all along the line. Tamar headed toward Ashwara's pavilion. The camp had turned rosy red and orange, bright as day.

The little worm of fear stirred. It was still alive. It had only been sleeping. Tamar shuddered so violently he could scarcely grip his blade. Ashwara's warriors were grappling hand to hand with their attackers. There were no ranks, no formations, only swarms of figures that broke apart and clashed together again. Someone had begun shouting *"Sankula! Sankula!"* The cry spread: one voice, then another. The whole camp seemed to heave like a single, convulsing body.

"Sankula!" Roaring, cursing, warriors flung aside broken weapons or ripped at opponents' faces with jagged ends of shattered blades, clawing, kicking, gouging—it was all *sankula*. Tamar ran blindly on. Hashkat at his heels, he lunged through a thicket of flailing arms and legs, struggling to reach Ashwara's tent. Free from the press of warriors, he sped across a patch of empty ground, lost his footing in a slick of mud, and pitched headlong. When he realized it was not mud, he promptly threw up and continued doing so until his stomach turned inside out. Hashkat crouched beside him.

"A royal sight you are, King of Sundari." The monkey grinned all over his face. "We'll get Adi-Kavi to spout some heroic praises for you."

They both began laughing like a pair of fools.

A yellow-bearded *kshatriya* ran past. Kirin. Tamar scrambled to catch up with him. "Where's Ashwara?"

Kirin had to squint a moment before recognizing him. "In the field." He gestured toward Ranapura. "He's ordered a counterattack."

Tamar looked at him dumbly.

"Are you deaf? Or stupid?" Kirin snapped. "Nahusha's got nearly all his troops here. Who's left? A rear guard with no support. We strike them now. Ashwara thinks we could even take the fortress. So do I."

Kirin ran on. Beckoning to Hashkat, Tamar headed from the blazing camp toward the plain. The *sankula* still raged. Nahusha's troops showed no sign of breaking off their attack. There were no orderly formations, no commands given, only shapeless clumps of men killing each other. From one moment to the next, Tamar could not even be certain which direction he was going. He flung himself into a thicket of struggling warriors. Pulling Hashkat along, he fought clear only to find himself caught up in a stream of carts and supply wagons, the rear area cooks and quartermasters fleeing for their lives into the fringe of woods.

To keep from being borne away by this tide, Tamar wrestled his way free. All around him, the ground was littered with discarded pieces of gear and clothing cast aside in panic, forlorn and ownerless. Hashkat, panting, dropped to one knee. Someone—it might have been Kirin—was shouting for the warriors to disengage and regroup in the field.

Chariots had begun rolling out of the devastated camp, with some foot soldiers running beside them. Hoisting the monkey to his feet, Tamar was about to follow. He stopped abruptly. He stared more closely at one of the chariots. Mirri was driving, Adi-Kavi beside her. Rajaswami, a glazed look in his eyes, was sitting at the rear of the platform, holding his umbrella over his head.

Tamar was furious. He ran to the chariot. "I told you to keep away. Are you out of your mind? What are you doing here?"

"Looking for you." Mirri hauled on the reins. "Get in."

"You should have stayed in the forest—"

"It's full of troops."

"Darshan!" Tamar cried. "He's here at last!"

"No. Bala. He broke his word. He's joined Nahusha."

25. "See the Trees Turn Gold . . ."

———————◆———————

Bala's army—they're spread all through the woods," Mirri hurried on, as Tamar sprang over the railing. "And moving this way, fast."

"What's it cost to buy a king?" Adi-Kavi put in. "Nahusha must have sweetened his offer, enough to make Bala change his mind."

Hashkat had vaulted onto the platform. Mirri threw the reins to Tamar, who sent the chariot rolling into the field. Rajaswami blinked and brightened:

"Is that you, dear boy?" the *acharya* called out in a small voice. "I'm so glad to see you. But, good heavens, you look dreadful. Whatever have you been doing? Are you taking us home now?"

Adi-Kavi glanced at Tamar. "He's got no idea what's happening. He's somewhere else. A blessing for him."

Tamar tightened his grip on the reins. Gayatri and Jagati plunged over the rutted ground. The chariot lurched and nearly overturned. Rajaswami sat smiling calmly.

Tamar urged more speed from the straining horses. "I'll find Ashwara," he shouted to Mirri over the rattle of the wheels. "He doesn't know Bala's attacking."

The sky had turned a delicate pink. Rags of smoke drifted over the plain. Tamar thought, first, that flames were streaking from the camp; then realized it was morning.

Ahead, he could make out lines of racing spearmen. He had
no idea whose people they were. Chariots sped crazily
among the ranks. Tamar drove faster, hoping for a glimpse
of Ashwara. The sun was up, the sky a deep blue. For the
first time, he could see bodies sprawled on the field.

The gates of Ranapura had flung open. Chariots poured
out of the fortress. Nahusha's reserves were greater than
anyone had calculated. The din had become earsplitting.
Tamar feared his head would burst from the endless yelling
and screaming, war cries, roars of rage and pain.

"There!" Mirri seized his arm. "There he is."

Tamar turned where she pointed. Ashwara was on foot
with half a dozen of his *kshatriya*s about him. Some of Nahusha's warriors had set upon them. Ashwara, however, had
not drawn his sword. Tamar, in dismay, remembered the
lion-eyed man had sworn to fight only Nahusha.

With a shout of fury, Tamar sent the horses galloping
into the knot of struggling *kshatriya*s. Nahusha's soldiers scattered, the *kshatriya*s in pursuit. Before Tamar could halt the
chariot, Ashwara strode alongside and swung himself over
the railing.

"Go there." Ashwara gestured toward a rocky knoll.
When Tamar blurted that Bala had broken his vow and was
attacking in strength, the tall man only nodded curtly.

"The camp will be overrun by now." Ashwara's face
was as grim as his voice. "Rudra's lines are adrift, too."

"We disengage, then," Tamar said.

"No," Ashwara said between clenched teeth. "Too late
for that. We still have some chance. Withdraw, we have
none at all. Leave me by the knoll. Find my brothers and
bring them to me."

As Tamar hurried to obey, one of Nahusha's chariots

wheeled to head straight for Tamar's car. The warrior, sword raised, was leaning over the railing. Tamar flung the reins to Hashkat and snatched his blade from the weapons rack.

Mirri seized one of the lances. She braced to fend off the onrushing chariot. At the last moment, Hashkat veered. The attacking car raked Tamar's vehicle along its length, breaking one of the shafts, shearing away the railing, then galloped on. The shock set Tamar back on his heels. The chariot shuddered to a halt. A wheel had shattered. The disabled car listed sharply to one side, its axle furrowing the ground. Gayatri and Jagati sank to their haunches.

"Unhitch!" Tamar threw aside his blade. With Hashkat and Mirri, he ran to free the horses from the tangled harness.

He did not notice until he heard Adi-Kavi call out. He turned to see Rajaswami, jolted into sudden awareness, staring openmouthed at the scene around him. Another moment and the *acharya* jumped to his feet, scrambled from the chariot, and went off at a determined trot, indignantly brandishing his umbrella.

"A *brahmana* commands you!" he burst out in his sternest voice. "Cease and desist immediately, all of you. Disobey at your soul's peril!"

Tamar started after him. The *acharya* was hobbling resolutely into the fray. Taken aback at the sight of him and his umbrella, a few of the fighters halted. Then the press of warriors swirled around the old man. Tamar, with a cry of anguish, tried to force his way through. Rajaswami had vanished in the crowd. Tamar had only a glimpse of the white umbrella before that too disappeared.

Mirri and Ashwara had come to join him. Tamar had no idea where Hashkat was. A handful of Nahusha's warriors raced across their path. The officer, sighting Tamar, broke stride and, brandishing a bloody sword, made straight for him.

Then the officer halted and stared, only now realizing he had come face to face with Ashwara. Even as Tamar sought to grapple with him, in one powerful sweep of his arm he threw Tamar to the ground.

"Ashwara! To me!" The *kshatriya* swung up his blade.

Tamar staggered to his feet. Ashwara stood motionless, his gaze fixed on his attacker. It was Adi-Kavi who sprang forward. Tamar had never seen him move so quickly. Suddenly the *kshatriya*'s blade was in the *suta*'s hand, the man's arm wrenched behind him, legs kicked from under him. Adi-Kavi's boot was on his chest and sword point at his throat.

"Stand away!" Ashwara's voice rooted Adi-Kavi to the spot. "Do as I order you, *suta*. Put down the sword. Weapons are forbidden to you."

Adi-Kavi, bewildered, threw aside the blade and peered uncomprehending at Ashwara, who had come to stand, arms folded, looking down at the *kshatriya*.

"Rasha. So. It is you," Ashwara said.

The warrior bared his teeth. His face was bloody and smoke-blackened. He sat up. Cold lights flickered in his eyes.

"So it is." Rasha blew a short, hissing breath. "Strike, then, Ashwara."

"You threw a coin to a beggar, once." Ashwara raised outspread hands. "For the sake of it, I vowed to spare your life. Go."

"I remember no beggar. I remember no coin," Rasha said. "You vowed to spare my life? I made no vow to spare yours."

It was so quick, faster than Tamar's eyes could follow. Ashwara had started to turn away. Rasha was on his feet. Tamar barely saw the flash of the knife that Rasha seized from his belt. In the instant, he plunged it to the hilt in Ashwara's breast, ripped it free, and made to stab again.

Ashwara put out a hand as if to steady himself, then sank to one knee. Tamar sprang at Rasha. Adi-Kavi had already leaped ahead. Roaring with fury, the *suta* gripped Rasha in his burly arms and heaved him off his feet. Rasha's men were running to him. Adi-Kavi lifted the struggling *kshatriya* above his head. With all his strength he flung Rasha into the midst of the oncoming attackers.

The warriors staggered back. Rasha lay motionless, crumpled on the ground. Adi-Kavi picked up the sword. Whirling it around his head, he started toward them. At sight of the *suta* and his whistling blade, they turned and fled.

Tamar and Mirri had taken Ashwara between them and were carrying him to the shelter of the mound. Adi-Kavi dropped the sword, waved them aside, and picked up the silent form in his arms. Just behind the rocks, he set Ashwara at length on the ground. Mirri cradled the tawny head in her arms while Tamar undid the leather breastplate.

"Get him off the field," Tamar said, still disbelieving what he had seen. "Find a chariot—"

Adi-Kavi had torn open Ashwara's shirt front. He glanced at Tamar. "No use trying to move him. Let him rest. He has his death on him."

"He is right." Ashwara raised his head. "Leave me to it." He turned his eyes on Adi-Kavi. "*Suta,* you did what was forbidden you."

"And would do so again," Adi-Kavi said. "Does it matter, at the end?"

Ashwara smiled. "I think not." He put out a hand to Tamar. "Go on your journey. I follow my own. Mirri? Where is the *gopi?*"

"Here." Mirri bent toward him. "Are you in pain?"

"No. It comes easily enough." Ashwara's lion eyes widened. He looked around at the bare rocks. His face was suddenly shining. "The trees," he said in a voice hushed with wonder. "See the trees turn gold. All the leaves, the branches. How beautiful they are."

"Yes, they are very beautiful," Mirri said.

Ashwara did not speak again. He died soon after.

"I dreamed of golden trees," Tamar said in a torn whisper. "Omen of death. But it was his. Why not mine?"

Drums had begun a frantic pounding. Trumpet calls rang over the plain; warriors were shouting. Tamar sprang to his feet. Rage burned away his grief. Red mist blurred his eyes. He did not hear Mirri cry out to him as he ran beyond the knoll.

A troop of Nahusha's horsemen galloped past, bellowing at the top of their voices. Tamar heard no sound. He snatched up the sword Adi-Kavi had thrown aside. He raced to them eagerly, as if he had something extremely interesting to tell them, and began striking blindly. Arm upraised, one of the riders leaned from the saddle. The last thing Tamar saw was warrior's iron mace sweeping down on him.

26. The Burning Ground

———————◆———————

It was all very puzzling. He was in a tent, but he had the dim recollection of leaving the camp in flames. Also, he was lying on his back and could not move. The war drums were still beating in frenzy. It took him a little while to grasp that the pounding was inside his head. Everything was swimming. Splinters of memory floated by. When, bit by bit, they finally came together, he gave a terrible cry. Then his stomach began churning violently. People seemed to be talking among themselves, making comments about this.

"Stand him up," somebody said.

His legs buckled a little when he was hauled upright. He discovered why he could not move his arms. They were tied behind him. A circle of officers watched with idle interest. One of them was Nahusha.

"It's over, you know." Nahusha had taken off his breastplate and helmet; his sword, as well. They lay in a pile nearby. He was wrapped in a handsome white silk robe, the sash loosely knotted around his waist. "Do you understand? Over. Done with."

Tamar said nothing. Nahusha fluttered his fingers. "Flown off. Scattered to the wind. Gone to lick their wounds or whatever one does when thrashed. Ah, my unfortunate cousins. I should make some effort to feel sorry for them. One must always pity fools.

"But do set your mind at ease. It's all been taken care of," Nahusha went on smoothly. "The noble Ashwara—by the way, is it true, as I've heard? He vowed to fight no one but me? I regret the lost opportunity. In any case, he's been properly dealt with—as a piece of carrion. Your friends will no doubt turn up when we clear away the bodies.

"Oh—the *brahmana*. He's quite well. He's in the palace now. Someone found him wandering around the field and kindly took him in. I commend that. It would be immoral to harm a *brahmana*.

"Forgive me, I almost forgot the most delicious news of all. My beautiful *gopi*. A charming, delightful little thing, and so energetic. Have no fear. She's safe and comfortable, lodging in the women's quarters for the moment, until I can make other arrangements, so to speak. I think, in the long run, she'll do nicely."

Tamar spat in his face.

Nahusha started. His cheeks went dead white. He sucked in a long breath and snapped his fingers. A servant quickly brought a handkerchief. Nahusha carefully wiped his lips.

"That was discourteous of you," he said. "You really should not have done that. You've spoiled things for yourself."

Nahusha looked with distaste at the cloth and threw it away. As an afterthought, he drove a fist into Tamar's face.

Tamar felt something crack. Blood began pouring out of his nose. He would have lunged at Nahusha, but the men on either side of him held fast. He kicked and bucked, trying to wrestle free. Nahusha calmly observed his efforts.

"Little king," he said, "I warned you to keep out of my way."

"Fight me!" Tamar shouted, raging. "Fight, Nahusha! I

challenge you. In front of your officers. They hear me. Accept! You must. Dare refuse? Let them see you shamed."

"What challenge?" Nahusha said. "How can there be a challenge from a dead man? As you are, for all practical purposes. It is merely a question of technical detail. You understand that, surely.

"Only, now, what to do with you?" Nahusha frowned thoughtfully. "You've made me change my plans. I intended killing you, of course. That goes without saying. But, you see, you behaved so badly. You were crude and insulting: conduct unbefitting even your own rustic dignity. In view of that, have you the arrogance, or stupidity, to expect an honorable death? There are limits even to my indulgence."

Nahusha stepped away and called his officers around him. Tamar caught nothing of their conversation, only murmurs back and forth; and someone gave a sour laugh. Then, with barely a glance at him, Nahusha strode from the tent; his *kshatriya*s followed.

Tamar stood waiting. In a little while, when no one came back, he sat down. His shirt was damp and sticky. The two guards, bored, shifted from one foot to the other. They finally sat down too. Tamar's head throbbed; his face had swollen, his eyes puffed. All in all, he did not feel very well. When he asked the guards how long he would be kept there, they shrugged.

Eventually, two foot soldiers came into the tent. He was almost glad to see them. They got him up and took him outside. The bright sun hurt his eyes. It was hot, probably only afternoon, but the morning seemed long ago in some different world.

Nahusha's warriors were striking the last of the tents, loading gear, trundling carts through the open gates. A chariot and driver waited. When Tamar was unable to climb aboard, the soldiers hoisted him onto the platform and clambered in beside him. The charioteer set off at an easy pace, heading from the encampment and skirting the western walls of the city. Tamar saw a wide river sparkling in the sun. He assumed it was the Rana. He wondered, with only passing, objective interest where they were taking him; he did not wish to speculate much on the meaning of Nahusha's parting words. Whatever Nahusha had in mind for him, past a certain point it would not matter.

Closer to the Rana, with the city some way behind, he began to notice a rank odor. Faint at first, it soon grew stronger. The chariot halted at the edge of a barren field. Wisps of smoke rose from nondescript heaps here and there. The stench had become intense. It filled his nose and throat. He could taste it. He gagged uncontrollably. He had, by now, fully understood what it was. He could not hold back a cry of horror. He stumbled to his feet and tried to pitch out of the chariot.

It was the paupers' burning ground. The *shmashana.*

They were expecting him. A few more soldiers and a *nayka,* a low-grade officer, stood in front of a ramshackle hut. They looked impatient, uncomfortable, not at all happy to be there.

The *nayka* beckoned. "Bring him. Get this over with."

Tamar had a flash of memory: of Rajaswami, before Muktara, shuddering at even a passing glimpse of the *shmashana.* He turned and twisted, scuffed his feet on the stony ground. They finally had to drag him.

The *nayka* had something in his hands. Tamar could not see what it was. It was of no great interest. His immediate concern was to be away from this place. He counted his life lost. Worse, his caste was threatened. Whatever else, he was a *kshatriya*. Let them kill him on the road, the riverbank, anywhere but this polluted ground. He had been terrified during the night attack; that already had been shame enough. But now he was on the brink of panic.

He tried to run. They kicked his legs. He stumbled to his knees. The *nayka* stepped behind him, took him by the hair, and pulled his head back. He assumed the man was going to cut his throat.

Instead, something like a thick leather dog collar was quickly set around his neck. He heard the snap of a lock. The *nayka* attached the collar to a heavy length of chain, paid it out, and bolted the end into an iron ring set on a wooden stake. The *nayka* hastily moved away. Tamar lunged to the full length of the chain. The force of his effort jerked him back. He fell down.

The *nayka* paid no further attention. He was talking with his men. "Where's he gone?" he asked the soldiers. "Curse him, he was here just before the chariot came."

"Who knows?" one of the soldiers said. "Doing whatever he does. He'll be back."

"Damned if I wait for him. He's been told. He understands."

The soldiers, relieved to be on their way, trotted toward the road. A figure had come shambling from somewhere behind the hut. Without breaking stride, the *nayka* hurriedly called over his shoulder:

"That's him. Get on with your business."

Tamar could barely keep from screaming. He had never seen one before; but he had been well bred, carefully and thoroughly instructed. He knew instantly what the creature was; and the mere sight was an offense to his eyes. The lowest of the low, as Rajaswami told him. Even too low to have any caste at all.

A *chandala*.

Tamar flung himself as far as the chain allowed. The *chandala* stood looking at him. He was short and stocky, bandy-legged, with long, muscular arms, naked except for the dirty rags roped about his waist. His dark skin was further blackened by streaks and smudges. The tangled, greasy hair fell below his shoulders. The *chandala* studied him a few moments, then said:

"So, you're here. Did they tell you why?"

Tamar did not answer. He was choking on his bile. The *chandala* was actually approaching him. Tamar heaved at the stake, trying to uproot it. Failing, he scuttled crablike out of reach. The chain limited the distance.

The man moved quickly upon him. Tamar glimpsed the knife in his hand.

The *chandala,* with remarkable strength, easily threw him facedown and set a foot on the small of his back. He bent and gripped Tamar's arms. The man had a ferocious stench about him.

"Lie still or I'll cut you."

Tamar realized the *chandala* was slicing through the ropes tying his hands. As soon as he felt the bonds part, he began clawing at the dog collar.

"Leave off," the man ordered. "A waste of time. It's a good strong lock. I know. I have the key."

Tamar stopped short. "Set me loose. They've gone. Who'll know? What difference can it make to—someone like you?"

"A big difference."

"You're going to kill me. Have done with it."

The *chandala* laughed. It was a wheezing, rattling sound. "Do you take me for a fool?"

"What, then?"

The *chandala* squatted down beside Tamar, who shrank back as the man thrust his face closer. "You don't know?" He peered at Tamar with bloodshot eyes. "They didn't tell you?"

Tamar shook his head.

"Why, you've been given to me. Here you are, here you stay. You're mine. My property." The man gave a broken-toothed grin. "See the joke? A *chandala* owning a slave."

Tamar saw the joke. It was too horrible not to be seen. The ground lurched under him. He finally realized what Nahusha intended. He had to be reasonable or go mad. "No, no, this can't be. I'm a *kshatriya*. King of Sundari—"

"You're in my kingdom now," the *chandala* said.

"There's been a terrible misunderstanding," Tamar pressed on. "I'm supposed to be killed. Please. I ask you. I beg you." Tamar could not believe his own words. A *kshatriya* was begging a *chandala*. "For the sake of mercy."

"I'll keep you alive. That's all the mercy I can afford. You'll work for me. Once you're settled in and see how things go, you'll have plenty to do. It's always busy, days after a battle."

The *chandala* stood up. The sun was beginning to set. Wisps of smoke from the burning ground merged with the gathering dusk. "The chain's long enough. You can sleep inside the doorway."

When Tamar said nothing, the man shrugged. "Suit yourself." He started toward the hut. "Oh—watch out for the pye-dogs. They come scavenging around this time. They don't much care if their pickings are alive or dead. Change your mind, the door's open."

He disappeared inside. Tamar sat, face in his hands. He had been touched by a *chandala*. Caste broken. Himself a *chandala*. This was not acceptable. Therefore, the immediate thing was to convince himself the *chandala* had not really touched him.

Given this urgent task, he set about rearranging his memory. He had not even been near the *chandala*. It had worked out in some other way. His caste was unbroken. That was a lie. He knew it. Even so, he had to bury the fact—if he could not erase it—somewhere deep inside his head and let it shrivel there, forgotten. He did not succeed.

The *chandala* came out of the hut. He set an earthen bowl in front of Tamar, who stared at the broken bits of food as if they were scorpions. The man waited a moment or two. Seeing Tamar had no intention of eating, he shrugged and went back inside, leaving the bowl on the ground.

The moon was up, stars clotted around it. Tamar sat motionless, telling himself over and over that he was not a *chandala*. From the tail of his eye, he glimpsed vague shapes, like smears of ashes, darting furtively.

A pye-dog, scenting the food, slunk up, tail between its legs. It was more a skeleton of a dog, ribs jutting from sunken flanks, fur spiky, with bald spots and open sores. It crept forward, belly scraping the ground.

The pye-dog stopped in front of Tamar. Its hackles went up. The creature bared its teeth: half snarling, half whimpering. Tamar still did not move. The pye-dog inched ahead, then halted again. When, at last, it understood there would be no quarrel over the food, it stuck its muzzle in the bowl and gulped down the contents, then drifted off like a puff of smoke.

From across the burning ground, they began to howl: first one pye-dog, then another, until the whole pack was in full cry, baying and wailing. Tamar clamped his hands to his ears. When the pye-dogs finally stopped, he still heard the howling.

27. The Chandala

<hr/>

O nce, long ago, there was a tiger named Soma-Nandi; and there was a young king who climbed down into the pit where she had been trapped. Soma-Nandi was a big, powerful animal. With her sharp teeth and claws, she could have torn apart any hunter who came near. However, as she explained, the hunters knew this. So, they would merely stay away until she grew too weak to defend herself.

Also, somewhere in all this, there was a *gopi* called Mirri; but that was another, different story. He preferred concentrating his thoughts on the tiger. There was a point to be understood. After a couple of days, chained outside the hut, refusing to enter, Tamar at first believed he had grasped it.

Originally, the man had said he would put Tamar to work. He had not done so. Tamar was disappointed. He had reckoned otherwise. If the *chandala* made him work, he would have to unlock the collar; or, at least, the end of the chain attached to the stake and hold him like a dog on a leash. When that moment came, Tamar would rip the chain from the man's hands—always being careful not to touch him—possibly hit him with it, or whatever was needed to make him give up the key, and be gone.

Nothing simpler—until Tamar realized the *chandala*'s cunning. Like the hunters with the tiger, the man was patiently waiting for Tamar to be broken by starvation.

One thing puzzled him: Why did the man keep putting out bowls of food? The man must know that everything he touched was polluted and Tamar would never eat it. He would have to change his plan a little.

Next time the man brought food, Tamar kicked the bowl away and upset it. The man picked up the morsels, dirt and all, and put them back in the bowl.

"I'm not wasting good victuals," the *chandala* told him. "You want; you ask."

After that, he brought no more.

Tamar was pleased. He gleefully calculated how he would cheat his captor, and Nahusha as well, by starving to death as soon as possible. He failed. Hunger did not defeat him. It was thirst.

The *chandala* left the hut each morning and came back late in the afternoon. That day, Tamar was stretched on the ground. His tongue felt as if it had been roasted, and his mouth full of sand. He would have been screaming in agony if his throat had not been parched shut.

As usual, the *chandala* stopped in passing to have a quick, appraising look at him. Tamar could barely raise his head. His tongue, which felt much too big for his mouth, lolled out between split and blackened lips.

"Drink?" said the *chandala*.

Had there been any moisture in his eyes, Tamar would have wept with rage at his weakness. He gave a small nod.

The man had a flask slung over his shoulder. He unstoppered it, knelt, lifted Tamar's head, and carefully poured the tepid water into Tamar's mouth. Tamar drank every drop.

His caste was broken.

There was no way he could lie to himself or pretend

otherwise. He had drunk a *chandala*'s water from a *chandala*'s hands. He had become a *chandala*. However, once his disgust and horror damped down a little, he realized there was an advantage. He had nothing more to lose.

His mind was still working. From then on, he ate every scrap and asked for more. His strength came back; he was actually feeling quite well. This was as it should be; because the next time the *chandala* brought his meal, Tamar set his new plan in motion.

He jumped up, seized the *chandala* by the neck, and began throttling him.

The man stared at him with bulging eyes, his face turning blacker than it was. He made no attempt to break away.

"Key," Tamar said, between clenched teeth.

The *chandala* made gurgling noises. He fumbled in his garment and brought out the key.

"Unlock." Tamar loosened his grip enough to let the man breathe. "Then stand clear."

The *chandala* obeyed. Collar and chain fell to the ground. He stepped away, rubbing his neck.

"Why didn't you just ask?"

"And you'd have given it?" retorted Tamar. "Of course. I'm sure you would. Out of my way."

"You'd have figured some trick, sooner or later," the man said. "You might even have killed me. So, avoid inconvenience. You've killed me anyway.

"You really don't understand, do you?" he went on, as Tamar hesitated. "Nahusha put you on a chain. He put me on one, as well. That's something else they didn't explain to you.

"If you, my lad, escape—they'll kill *me*. They'll look in from time to time to make sure you're here. If you're not, they'll have my life for it. They were clear and detailed along the lines of torture, too. Nahusha can be imaginative when it comes to torture. I'd die, at the end; but it would take a good while."

"You're lying." Tamar knew the man was telling the truth.

"Why should I? It's not your concern, in any case. Go."

"Do you think I won't? You'll do the same, if you have any sense."

The *chandala* shook his head. "I've got my work. Has to be done. It's important."

"To you, not to me. Don't hang your life on mine."

"I don't. Nahusha did that. You stay, I live. That's all there is to it."

"I owe you nothing."

"Did I ask?"

Tamar had begun pacing, agitated. The *chandala* watched, neither pleading nor threatening, saying nothing. Tamar wished the man would attack him, try to force the chain on him again. It would give him excellent reason to fight him to the death. Whose? He knew the man's strength; it had surprised him how easily he had surrendered the key. The *chandala* could likely break him in half without too much effort. That, at least, would settle it. The *chandala* waited, arms folded. The man even looked sorry for him. Tamar hated him for that.

"What will you do?" the *chandala* said at last. "Go or stay? Make up your mind. I'm getting hungry."

It had never occurred to him that a *chandala* might be hungry. It also occurred to Tamar that he was hungry likewise. "I warn you," he said, "I make no promise. If I leave, I leave. What you do about it is up to you."

"Fair enough." The *chandala* jerked a thumb toward the hut. "Go in. Eat."

———◆———

The pye-dogs' howling kept him awake. Worse, after he stretched out on the thin mat the *chandala* gave him, he was terrified of closing his eyes. The nightmare came to him: The man would put the collar on him while he slept. He thought of getting up and running as fast as he could—wherever, anywhere. Let the *chandala* look after himself. Tamar had warned him. The howling of the pye-dogs turned into the screams of someone being tortured.

Tamar sat bolt upright, sweating. The *chandala* was snoring peacefully in a corner of the hut. Tamar's thoughts went around in circles. Nahusha had put him on a chain. The *chandala* had put him on a heavier one. He told himself this was not true. He could escape whenever he pleased.

He sank back on the mat as exhaustion washed over him. Tomorrow. He would go tomorrow, while the *chandala* was out of the hut. For some reason, he could not bear the idea of leaving while the man watched him do it.

He did not leave the next day. The *chandala* had plans:

"Get moving. There's work to do. I told you I could use some help."

Tamar had not expected to be quite so horrified; or, at least, to show it.

"What, afraid?" The *chandala* cocked an eye at him. "You were a *kshatriya*. Killing's a *kshatriya*'s trade, isn't it? A potter makes pots, a warrior makes corpses. Who should fear their own handiwork?"

"I'm not afraid."

"No?" The *chandala* snorted. "I can see it in your face. You're sick with it, enough to drive you mad. Well, that's what Nahusha wants. He counted on that. You couldn't stand it. He was right. You'd best get out of here."

"He was wrong. I'll go with you."

Behind the hut was a stack of kindling wood. He and the *chandala* loaded a cart with it. The man tossed in some buckets, then, like a horse, set himself between the shafts. He motioned for Tamar to join him. Together, they hauled the cart across the barren ground toward the river. The bandy-legged man plodded on, back bent against the burden.

It was all Tamar could do to pull his share of the weight. He had begun breathing hard. He was gasping by the time they came in sight of the river. It was not the effort of heaving at the shaft. The reek of the place was choking him.

The *chandala* halted. There were some shapes lying on the ground. They looked like bundles of sticks wrapped in rags. The *chandala* unloaded the kindling.

"They bring them in wagons from the city," he said. "It was busy days after the battle. I've taken care of all that. These are just your ordinary paupers, starvelings, beggars. The usual.

"Set up a pile of kindling. Careful how you do it. Don't waste wood. I'll show you how. Fetch water. They have to be washed."

Tamar turned away. He put his hands to his mouth. He could carry water; he could manage to deal with building a fire. The rest—his stomach heaved. "Not touch them," he whispered. "I can't."

"That's right. You can't. Because I won't let you." The

chandala rounded on him. "How dare you think I would? They've had no kindness, no respect: nothing, nothing, all their lives. I'll give that to them now, at least. You? Even lay a finger on them? They disgust you. They sicken you. You loathe them—as much as they were loathed when they were still alive. You're filled with horror; you can't bear to face them. Ah, my lad, they deserve better than you. Get away from them. Let me do my work."

Despite himself, Tamar shrank back. He had never supposed the truth could shame him.

The *chandala*'s anger passed. The man was looking at him with an infinite pity such as Tamar had never seen. "Empty your heart," the *chandala* said quietly. "No disgust. No fear. Only love for them. Do that, you might earn the privilege."

For the next few mornings, he went with the *chandala* to the burning ground. He had not noticed, until now, the small bunches of faded flowers or sticks of incense that had been left there.

"Why not?" the man answered, when Tamar questioned him. "Do you think a beggar is mourned any less than a *kshatriya*? What caste is grief? Here, my lad, these folk are equal to a maharajah. All end the same."

"If the same at the end," Tamar said, "why should there be caste at the beginning? What does it matter?"

"You tell me," said the *chandala*.

The man still kept him at a distance and gave him only small tasks: fetching water, unloading wood. To Tamar's surprise, the reek that hung over the *shmashana* had vanished as well as the horror that first overwhelmed him. Watching the *chandala*'s gentleness and humility at his work, he remembered the man telling him, "They deserve better than you." He wondered, now, if he better deserved them. Finally, he asked the *chandala* if he might help. The man looked him up and down. Tamar waited.

"Since you ask," the *chandala* said. He nodded briefly and pointed to a small figure. "Try."

As it was only a newborn child, it was easily done and took hardly any time at all. Even so, he felt greatly blessed.

That evening, as they sat in the darkening hut, for the first time Tamar could bring himself to speak his heart. In one burst, he told of his dream and journey, his love for Mirri, his dear *acharya,* his companions lost. For the first time, as well, he could grieve for Ashwara and dare to remember his look of joy at the end.

"He was the best of kings, a king as I'd have wished to be," Tamar said. "Dead. Slain by a traitor. An evil man still lives. Adi-Kavi would have told me that's the way of the world."

"One of its ways." The *chandala* set down his bowl of food. "There are others."

"Not for me. My way leads to Nahusha. I want his death."

"How will that serve you? Ashwara fought for justice, not revenge. Will you be less than he was?"

"I'm already less. A *chandala.* Do you say I should even give up vengeance? No. I eat it. It keeps me strong. Better than meat and drink."

"Beware how much you eat, then. It will poison you."

"Let it."

"If that suits your taste." The *chandala* shrugged. "Only
tell me: How are you different from Nahusha?"

Tamar did not answer. He stretched out on the mat and
went to sleep. The pye-dogs had started baying. He did not
hear them.

❖

Next morning, at the edge of the *shmashana,* Tamar sighted
a figure stumbling over the barren ground. He dropped his
load of kindling.

Rajaswami, arms outstretched, was hobbling as fast as his
spindly legs would carry him.

"*Acharya!*" Heart leaping, Tamar ran toward him, then
stopped short. He stepped back and raised his hands.
"*Acharya*—no, no, keep away. You'll break your caste. I'm
a *chandala*—"

"My dear boy. Oh, my dear boy." Rajaswami did not
halt but, against all warnings, flung his arms around Tamar.
He looked aged even beyond his years, his face gray and
haggard. "It doesn't matter. Let it break." Tears streamed
down the *acharya*'s cheeks. "It makes no difference. I'm with
you again."

Two soldiers were trundling a handcart behind the
acharya. They drew up and, between them, hauled out a
shrouded figure. They roughly threw it to the ground,
turned, and left the *shmashana* in all haste. The *chandala* went
to see what they had brought.

"Stay calm, dear boy," pleaded Rajaswami. "Listen to
me—"

Tamar broke from his embrace. The figure's wrappings
had fallen away.

It was Mirri.

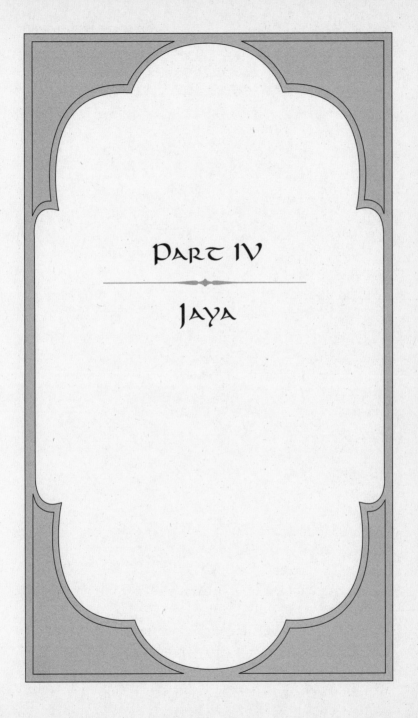

Part IV

Jaya

28. A Life Thread Broken

———◆———

The soldiers had halted by the roadside at the far edge of the burning ground. They stood idly watching. The *chandala* had started toward the shrouded figure. Tamar seized him by the shoulders and pitched him aside so violently, the man lost his footing. Rajaswami was plucking at Tamar's sleeve, stammering something. Tamar struck away the *acharya*'s hand.

"Leave me," he said. "Both of you."

He knelt beside her. Mirri's long, black hair was unbound and draped around her. She had not been in pain. There were no marks on her features. Her eyes were closed, her face peaceful. She was very beautiful. Rajaswami was still babbling.

"I told you. Go away from me," Tamar said. "Do so."

Life had suddenly become quite simple for him. It was so clear and elementary. The first thing he would do was kill the soldiers who were still lounging around. He had no ill feelings toward them, nothing against them personally. He merely wanted their weapons.

Once he got them, he would go and kill Nahusha. No more to it than that.

He stood up and began walking briskly to the roadside. As if reading his thoughts, the *chandala* grappled and held him.

"Dear boy!" Rajaswami was flapping at him. "Dear boy, I beg you. Listen. The bright side, always the bright side—"

"Acharya," Tamar said in a tone like a brutal blow, "you are a fool."

Rajaswami bowed his head. "Yes. I have been foolish in many ways. I taught you my own foolishness. Caste, honor, dharma—it all breaks. Only hear me—"

The *chandala* had been keeping an eye on the road. "I don't like those fellows there."

"Nahusha ordered them," said Rajaswami, "to witness —the burning."

"They won't live to see it. Nor will you," Tamar flung at the *chandala,* "unless you take your hands off me."

"They must," Rajaswami insisted. "They must report to Nahusha. If not, all goes awry. Start the fire."

Tamar, at this, began roaring and struggling with the *chandala.*

"Stop!" commanded Rajaswami. "Be silent!"

The *acharya*'s voice had a snap to it, a teacher to an unruly student, and it set echoes ringing in Tamar's memory; a child at the old man's feet—Tamar obeyed. The *chandala* loosened his grasp.

"It must seem to be done properly." Rajaswami spoke quietly once more. "How, I don't know. A most dangerous business, but all hangs on it. Because—dear boy, the bright side: Mirri is alive."

Tamar stood, mute. Rajaswami was making no sense. The *chandala* moved quickly to bend over the motionless form. He glanced up at Tamar.

"Yes, she lives. Barely."

"How else could we get away from Nahusha?" Raja-swami pressed on. "A desperate measure—"

Tamar heard no more. He dropped to his knees beside Mirri. Even as he stared dumbstruck, her breast began slowly to rise and fall. Her eyes opened. She smiled at him; then grinned broadly; then winked. She was Mirri, with him again.

"Keep your wits about you," she said, making no attempt to get up. "You'll need them. Do as Rajaswami says. If I'm to be burned to a cinder, you'd best be careful about it."

The *chandala* had understood the matter faster than Tamar, still speechless. "Stay there. I see how to deal with this."

"I started planning it out as soon as Nahusha hauled me to the palace," Mirri went on, as the *chandala* hurried away. "I couldn't have done it sooner. It would have looked suspicious. Too convenient. So I waited a little while.

"Nahusha had me locked up in the women's quarters. Once I was there, I pretended to be sick. Horribly, disgustingly sick. I heard Rajaswami was in the palace too; so I insisted on having him come and treat me. When I told him my scheme, he agreed to make a great show of being alarmed. He swore to Nahusha that my life was in danger."

"My *acharya* told a lie? Not Rajaswami."

"Yes. He's not quite the same *brahmana* he used to be. It must have torn the dear old fellow apart, breaking his dharma by lying. But he did it. For your sake and mine.

"The rest—you can thank Adi-Kavi. When we were in the *ashrama,* you remember, he taught me to breathe so little it didn't seem I was breathing at all. He showed me how to make my heart beat so faintly and slowly no one could tell it hadn't stopped altogether. I never thought the knack would come in handy someday.

"From then on, I made believe I was getting worse and worse. Rajaswami played at being more and more in despair. When I knew the time was right—I died.

"Rajaswami claimed I was dead from camp fever or some such fatal illness. Nahusha was in a rage. I'd slipped out of his clutches, so he thought. He raved and cursed, and ordered me carted to the *shmashana*—as I'd counted on.

"He was vicious beyond that. He made Rajaswami go there with me—which I'd also counted on. He expected Rajaswami to be horrified to have his caste threatened, to beg and plead to be let off.

"Rajaswami was very convincing. He wept and wailed, tore his hair. Pretending, yes. But I knew he was in real torment, too. Even so, he went to the last place in the world he wanted to be.

"Your *acharya* loves you, dearest Tamar, and he turned out to be a very brave man. Nahusha didn't care if he came back or not. Caste broken, Rajaswami was good as dead himself.

"And you—Nahusha gloated about having you chained up here. You'd be a *chandala*, a living death. You'd see me on the burning ground, a cruelty on top of cruelty—"

Mirri broke off. The *chandala* was back. Following his instructions, Tamar took the girl in his arms and carried her to a pile of kindling.

"Set her down." The *chandala* pointed to a spot behind the pyre, out of the soldiers' line of sight. He unwound Mirri's shroud and wrapped it around some of the larger branches of wood.

Between them, making sure their watchers could see, Tamar and the *chandala* lifted what they hoped looked like a body and set it amid the kindling. The *chandala* struck a light. The fire blazed.

The soldiers observed the flames awhile. Satisfied, they hurried away. Mirri jumped to her feet. Even after she had thoroughly embraced him, Tamar had some difficulty convincing himself that any of this was happening. It took a few more embraces for him to believe it.

Mirri was urging him to leave the burning ground. He held back. Rajaswami, head lowered, stood apart.

"Acharya—" Tamar went to him and put his hands on the old man's shoulders. "I called you a fool. Forgive me. I didn't know what I was saying."

"You spoke out of grief," Rajaswami answered, "but you spoke truth. Indeed, I have been very much a fool. I thought it better to be cut in pieces than lose caste, and I taught you likewise. Now it's gone, I hardly miss it. In fact, I can't tell the difference."

Rajaswami fumbled in his robe. He took hold of the knotted string he wore across his bony chest. "The sacred emblem of my caste. I treasured it. This was my pride—no, my secret arrogance. I give it up. It means nothing now." He hesitated a moment, then, with a little sigh, snapped the string and tossed it into the embers. "But—there's a bright side. I suddenly feel much lighter."

"Come quickly," Mirri said to Tamar. "There's a lot to do. I thought you'd still be chained up, but you're free."

"Am I?" Tamar turned to the *chandala*. "You knew I'd leave. I must. But I won't put your life in danger. Come with us. I'll make sure you'll be safe."

"I can take care of myself."

"When Nahusha finds out you let me escape, you know what he'll do to you. I can't let that happen."

"It won't," said the *chandala*. "Go. Now."

"If that's what you wish," Tamar said reluctantly. He pressed his palms together. "You taught me much. I thank you."

"Did I teach? Did you learn?" the *chandala* said. "That remains to be seen."

"I never asked your name," Tamar went on. "Forgive me. Tell me now so I may remember it and be grateful."

"Does gratitude need a name? Your chain's gone. That's all you need to know."

"More than a chain binds us," Tamar said. "*Namaste*. I honor you."

"*Namaste,*" the *chandala* said. "I honor what you might become."

Tamar, still unwilling, turned away. Mirri led him across the burning ground, with Rajaswami hobbling after.

"I told you I decided to die when the time was right," Mirri said, as they hurried to the road. "I waited for what I hoped would happen. When it did, I knew the moment had come for me to get away."

"Moment for what?"

"Garuda's back," Mirri said. "He brought your army with him."

29. Garuda's Journey

———◆———

"D arshan comes in time to see us broken," Tamar said
bitterly. "A little sooner— Now, what use? I trusted
Garuda. I never believed he'd fail us."

"He didn't. Not at the end," Mirri said. "You'll see him
soon. Akka, too."

The girl was heading toward a wagon that stood a little
farther down the road. Tamar would have asked for more
news, but something about the horses, befouled and mud-
coated, caught his eye. He quickened his steps, then broke
into a run. The animals whinnied and tossed their heads.

"Gayatri! Jagati! Poor creatures, what have they done to
you?" he cried, as Gayatri nuzzled him and Jagati stamped
the ground. "This is shameful."

"No, it's cautious. They look like cart horses instead of
warhorses." The driver, a heavy man wrapped in a dirty
cloak and headcloth, jumped down and grinned at him. It
was Adi-Kavi.

"Better that none of us look like who we are," the *suta*
explained, giving Tamar a burly bear hug. Mirri and Rajaswami had reached the wagon. Adi-Kavi motioned for them
to climb quickly aboard. "Your message reached me safely,"
he said to Mirri. "Passed yourself off as dead, eh? I'm glad
I taught you that trick."

Adi-Kavi slapped the reins and set off following the river.

225

As much as Tamar rejoiced to see the *suta* alive, there was one question he feared to ask. He asked it:

"What of Hashkat?"

"Mending," said Adi-Kavi. "He managed to crawl off the battlefield. I found him at the edge of the woods. I'd lain quiet among the bodies until dark, you see, and made my way clear of the mess. He'd been badly cut up. I did what I could for him, though I didn't think he'd last the night. He'll be fine. Your horses were wandering loose, no doubt looking for you. Luckily, they came to me."

"Skanda? Kirin?"

"Alive. Heavily wounded, both. They'd fallen back into the Rana valley with what was left of their people. I joined them there.

"King Rudra's dead," Adi-Kavi grimly went on. "His army was pretty well mauled, but Skanda rallied them. The rest of the butcher bill: Nahusha didn't get off free of charge. He lost a lot of troops and half his best officers. Kana: dead. Bala: dead. So, that's how the account stands."

Tamar found no great joy or much satisfaction in Kana's fate or Bala's. His thoughts circled like a hawk around Nahusha, and none other. To no purpose, for he saw no clear way to face him. He had even half forgotten his journey. The iron ring still was on his finger, but it only reminded him vaguely of something that happened long ago or never happened at all. Mirri was talking to him, but his attention kept drifting.

"I learned Nahusha's plan," she was saying. "He told me. He boasted that Ashwara's cause was lost from the start. He'd already decided to attack without warning. The night he stormed the camp—he and Bala agreed on that after we left Muktara. They'd worked it all out ahead of time."

"None of that matters. It's over."

"Is it?" Mirri said. "I might have some ideas of my own. Nahusha had me locked up, but he didn't keep me from knowing what was happening. I had news every day.

"Monkeys," she went on. "Some of the Bandar-loka had been trailing Hashkat. He had a few slip into the city. They found me, and told me how things were going. We sent word back and forth. That's how Adi-Kavi got my message. Then, Akka himself sneaked in. As for Nahusha—"

Mirri broke off as Adi-Kavi turned the wagon off the road. "Some of Hashkat's folk," she said, pointing to shadows scurrying among the trees. "They're always close by him, keeping watch. Hashkat never thought much of himself as a king, but his Bandar-loka are really devoted to him. They're good scouts and sentinels, too. He'll know we're on the way long before we get there."

The light had begun to fade while Adi-Kavi drove deeper into the cover of the woodlands. By the time he rolled to a halt at the edge of the encampment, Hashkat was waiting for them—grinning, waving his arms, overjoyed to see Tamar and Mirri.

Tamar jumped down from the wagon, ran to embrace him, then gasped in dismay. Hashkat's luxuriant tail was gone.

"Not half as bad as what Nahusha did to you," Hashkat said, when Tamar tried to console him. "I lost my tail but kept my life, and that's a good bargain. I miss it; I won't deny that. Still, I'm getting used to being without it."

Little Akka had scurried up, chattering with delight. At the same time, Garuda fluttered awkwardly from a branch and made straight for Mirri. The bird had lost most of his feathers, one wing dragged on the ground, and he looked

more than ever like a half-plucked chicken. Still, he chuckled and croaked happily while Mirri stroked what was left
of his plumage. Deciding he had enough pampering for the
moment, he turned a beady eye on Tamar.

"Irresponsible dimwit! Careless incompetent! Where's
my ruby?"

Tamar had almost forgotten the gem. He paused to collect his thoughts. "I—I gave it to Adi-Kavi before the battle.
For safekeeping—"

"That's right," the *suta* agreed, digging into his garments
and bringing out the stone. "I have it. Here, look. I held
on to it for you. I told you that before."

"I just wanted to bring it to this imbecile's attention,"
retorted Garuda. "Giving it to you showed a glimmer of
intelligence. You weren't supposed to fight, eh? You did
anyway. That was stupid. Shmaa! No consideration for
others!"

Garuda turned back to Tamar. "You should have taken
better care of my property," he rattled on, as Adi-Kavi now
passed the ruby to Tamar. "While I was risking my life, you
were playing fast and loose with a precious gem. You're a
careless lot, all of you."

Tamar took the bird's reproaches in good spirit, only too
glad to see Garuda alive. "The ruby's safe," he said. "But
you? What happened? Your feathers—"

"You noticed? How kind of you to ask," Garuda
snapped. "Well, it's luck Akka and I are here at all. You sent
a horseman with your message, too. Oh, that was clever—
he never got a mile through the valley."

"One of Nahusha's bowmen shot him," Akka put in.
"We flew down to see if we could help the poor fellow.
Nothing to be done—"

"The disgusting ruffian sent an arrow at me, then," Garuda said indignantly. "Out of pure spite and malice. He didn't know me; it was plain, common nastiness. Yes, and he hit me, the villain. I tried to stay aloft as long as I could. Did you ever try to fly with an arrow sticking in you? It's not easy."

"We went crashing to the ground, finally," said Akka. "I didn't remember much for a while after that. Garuda's wing was broken; he'd lost a lot of blood—along with his feathers. My leg was broken, too. We weren't well off, I can tell you."

"My poor friends!" exclaimed Tamar. "Couldn't you find any help? Were none of the Bandar-loka nearby?"

"Monkeys? Shmaa!" Garuda quacked. "There's never a monkey around when you want one. No—nothing, nobody. We holed up for a few days. Akka had gone feverish—and I had my own troubles, too, I'll have you know. I thought if I could rest I'd get my strength back. I still couldn't fly, and we were a long way from Sundari."

"But then," Tamar asked, "what did you do?"

"Shmaa! Idiot! What do you think we did?" retorted Garuda. "Walked."

"That's right," said Akka. "With my bad leg and Garuda's bad wing, we managed to lean on each other. We couldn't go very fast, and it got harder and harder. I thought we were goners for sure. Especially when the hunter saw us."

"And a mean-looking, scruffy fellow he was," Garuda continued. "We tried to get away from him. He grabbed us. I fought him off as best I could. No use. Waa! There, I think, there's the end of poor Garuda."

"It wasn't," said Akka. "Can you imagine? He didn't

harm us. No, he took care of us. Nursed us night and day. We'd never have lasted if it hadn't been for him. He fixed my leg and Garuda's wing, good as new. When Garuda could fly again, the hunter wandered off into the forest. We never saw him after that—never knew his name."

"And so we got to Sundari," Garuda concluded. "A long time. No fault of mine. Oh, now you really owe me plenty. Don't you forget it."

"I owe you more than I can repay," Tamar said fondly. "You can be sure I won't forget."

"Nor will I," said an old familiar voice. "The bird has a braver heart than any warrior. The monkey, too."

Darshan was there. The warrior's eyes brightened and he held out his arms. "Majesty, if only I'd come sooner—"

Tamar drew back. "My caste is broken. Touch me and you risk your own."

"Do you think I care a rap?" Darshan snorted. "I never put stock in that sort of nonsense. I'm a soldier; being alive is the only caste that means anything. And you—I should have disobeyed and never let you leave Sundari without me."

"You're here now, and we need you more than ever," Tamar said. "How many troops with you? What weapons? How soon can they take the field?"

"Hold on, hold on." Darshan raised a hand. "I've been talking with your comrades, Kirin and Skanda. Fine commanders, both. They've regrouped, pulled their people together, and that's a wonder in itself. What chance they have against Nahusha—that's another question."

"I have to talk with them. Where are they?"

Darshan motioned for Tamar and the others to follow

him into the woods. The encampment, Tamar saw, was smaller than Ashwara's had been. The warriors, scattered among the trees, still showed the ravages of battle. Cooking food or mending gear, they were grim and silent. Darshan pointed to a pavilion and Tamar stepped inside.

He barely recognized them. Ashwara's brothers were sitting on the ground, maps spread in front of them. Skanda had lost all of his boyish air; the lamplight deepened the circles under his eyes. Kirin's features were somber and heavily lined. Seeing Tamar, the two got quickly to their feet. As with Darshan, Tamar warned them away; but neither hesitated to embrace and gladly welcome him.

"Doing as he did, Nahusha shamed himself, not you," Kirin said. "Caste brings no honor to a man; a man's worth is what brings honor to his caste."

"So Ashwara would have said," added Skanda, "and I say the same. He was your friend, as we are still."

"I offered Ashwara my help in a just cause," Tamar said. "I offer it again to set his death aright. Now, counting my army and yours, what strength do we have?"

"Strength alone may not be enough." Kirin pointed to the maps, showing Tamar how their troops had been deployed. Skanda, he explained, now commanded Rudra's warriors; Kirin himself, the rest. After their king's death, Bala's troops had withdrawn to Muktara and no longer threatened.

"With your own people," Skanda said, "our numbers match close to Nahusha's."

"What question, then?" Tamar said. "You'll attack, surely. Do as he did to us," he hurried on, his blood rising. "No warning, no challenge. Rules of war? He broke them.

So shall we. *Sankula* from the very start. Give him his fill of *sankula* until he chokes on it. He owes Ashwara a death. I'll see him pay—"

He fell abruptly silent. The rage that swept over him had brought, as well, the nightmare memories: the camp in flames, his terror, Ashwara bleeding his life away. The *chandala* had asked: Who should fear his own handiwork? He feared it. And hated it. Was he still a warrior? Had he ever been? Or had he become simply a washer of corpses?

"Listen to an old campaigner," Darshan said quietly. "Will you let your anger cloud your common sense? Attack Nahusha? Inside the city, he's in a stronger position than any of us outside. He has no need to meet you in battle. Why should he? He'll only wait. What then? Lay siege? How long? We'd wear ourselves out to no purpose."

Tamar nodded. "My words were empty, foolish ones. Yes, I see that."

"Darshan is right," Kirin said. "Nahusha will do nothing but sit behind his walls and let us break our heads on them. If we could take the city by storm—"

"No," Mirri said. "You can't get close enough. There's something you don't know. The front gate's clear, but he's dug trenches all around the walls. Set with spikes and spearheads. Too wide to bridge, too deep to fill. They're death traps."

"He holds us at arm's length," put in Skanda, "with no effort, no cost to himself."

"That's right," Mirri said. "But only as long as he stays inside Ranapura. So, make him come out. There's a way."

30. Mirri's Plan

"Is this a *gopi?*" Darshan laughed good-heartedly and clapped his hands. "Here she sits, cool as you please, ready to tell *kshatriyas* how to go about their business. From the look of her, she knows more than milking cows. Say on, little *gopi*. What makes you think you'll get Nahusha to send out his troops and give us our chance against them?"

"I might do even better than that," said Mirri.

As Kirin and Skanda turned their full attention on her, she quickly told them the shape of her idea, warning it would take some days to set in motion. When she finished, the brothers spoke between themselves, asked her many questions, and, finally, agreed to the attempt.

"I know tactics and order of battle," Darshan declared, "attacks and counterattacks, but never such a plan as this." He rubbed his chin thoughtfully. "And yet, as the *gopi* lays it out, it might well serve. Yes, let her try. Come what may, I'm with her."

Adi-Kavi and Hashkat were both willing. Even though Tamar agreed, he was still troubled. "Too much can go wrong. Too much risk."

"Kirin and Skanda are willing," Mirri reminded him. "Your own commander, as well."

"It's their trade to take risks," Tamar said. "I didn't mean them. I meant *you*. I lost you once. I won't lose you again."

"You never lost me in the first place," Mirri said.

"When it comes to the sort of mischief you have in mind," said Hashkat, impatient to follow Mirri's instructions, "my Bandar-loka won't fail you. I'm only surprised they didn't think of it themselves."

◆─◆

Before the week was out, Akka had done all that Mirri had asked and was back in camp. Darshan, Kirin, and Skanda had already set their troops on the march toward Ranapura. They made no attempt to hide their movements. Instead, they stretched their ranks of warriors and chariots across the plain, in full sight. That alone, Tamar thought, should have been challenge enough, and an insolent dare; but he saw no sign of an answer from Nahusha.

Early that morning, Tamar and Ashwara's brothers, bearing no weapons, mounted their horses and cantered across the plain. Adi-Kavi rode ahead, holding up a flag of truce. It was cool and quiet. The walls of Ranapura were soft pink in the first rays of the sun. The trees had come into rich foliage. There were still a few traces of the ruts left by the wheels of chariots and horses' hooves; but tender blades of new grass had begun to spring up, dew-covered, silvery green. What had been a killing ground looked no more than a pleasant stretch of open countryside. He could not pick out the rocky knoll where Ashwara died. He found that monstrous.

Adi-Kavi, in his loudest royal crier's voice, began shouting for Nahusha to come and meet with them, declaring that someone wished to see him face to face. No answer came from the city. The horses pawed the turf and blew out steaming breath. Skanda glanced, questioning, at Tamar.

They waited. Adi-Kavi was about to turn back, when the gates flung open.

Nahusha stood in the prow of his chariot, flanked by a guard of bowmen. At a leisurely pace, he drew closer, until his driver reined up a few yards distant.

"I heard dogs barking at my gate." Nahusha addressed Kirin, who had trotted forward. "Have you brought your pack for another whipping? What do you seek of me?"

"Since you refuse to give battle, and fear to stand against us," replied Kirin, "I seek nothing else of you."

"I do." Tamar had turned away and hung back a little, unobserved by Nahusha. He now urged Gayatri nearer to the chariot. "I seek your life."

"It speaks?" Nahusha, taken aback for an instant, covered his surprise with a poisonous laugh. He raised an eyebrow and peered curiously at Tamar. "Remarkable. A piece of carrion, a less-than-nothing, actually ventures to say something to me. The animal seems to have slipped its leash. Its master will pay a high price for such inattention."

"You, likewise," Tamar said. "Once, I wished for your death. I yearned to kill you with my own hands. No longer. It is your life, not your death, I seek. I want you to live, Nahusha. As I did. I learned much in the burning ground. For that, I thank you. I hope you too may learn. The chain you put me on waits for you."

"What's this, what's this? Does the creature threaten me?" Nahusha replied. "Put me on a chain, indeed? Bold words. The doing is something else again. If this—this thing—were still a man, I would have it thrashed for its insolence. However, I take no notice of dunghills, let alone converse with them."

Nahusha faced Kirin and Skanda. "Take the cur away.

It offends my sensitivities and befouls my air. Take yourselves
away, as well. It pains me too much to see *kshatriya*s, pitiful
though they are, debase themselves with the company of a
chandala. What sorry times we live in. You have sunk even
lower than your brother.

"You summoned me for this?" Nahusha went on. "Had
you come begging to serve me, I might have been inclined
to listen. You disturb me for no reason, waste my time, and
try my patience. I have occupations more agreeable than the
mouthings of a corpse-washer."

"That is not our purpose," Skanda said. "You have a
right to your trophies of war. We come to give back one
you have lost."

Hashkat, meantime, had driven up in a light, two-
wheeled cart. Seeing this, Nahusha pulled away.

"What trophy?" he cried. "What treachery is this?"

Hashkat reined in Jagati. At the rear of the cart, a heap
of rags stirred. A shrouded figure rose up. The cloth wrappings fell away.

Mirri stood smiling at Nahusha.

"The *gopi!*" Nahusha burst out, his face livid with rage.
"Alive!"

"Am I?" Mirri answered. "How could I be? You saw
me die. Your warriors watched me burn."

For the first time, Nahusha's arrogant bearing was
shaken. He stared at her in fear and revulsion as she held
out her hands, beckoning to him.

"Come," urged Mirri, "I've been impatient for you to
journey with me. You'll see many strange things along the
way."

"Trickery!" Nahusha shouted, horrified nonetheless.
"Illusion!"

"Are you sure?" Mirri said. "If I'm an illusion, why fear me? If I'm alive, claim your prize again. Come, find out for yourself—if you dare."

"Keep away! Don't touch me!" cried Nahusha, recoiling as Mirri made to climb from the cart. "You reek of the *shmashana.*"

"You used to find me attractive," said Mirri. "I'm disappointed in you, Nahusha."

"Ghost or *gopi,* I stomach none of your mockery. Flesh and blood? I'll see that." He motioned to the bowman closest to his chariot. "Shoot!"

The warrior drew his bow and sped the arrow plunging into Mirri's breast.

31. The Bandar-Loka

Mirri looked down calmly at the arrow. She gave a little shrug of unconcern as she pulled out the shaft and threw it aside.

"I thought you'd be glad to see me." Mirri shook her head regretfully. "I'd hardly call this a fond welcome. Come, Nahusha. I'm waiting for you."

"Shoot again!" Nahusha's face twisted in fear and fury. "Dead or living, kill her! Kill them all!"

Mirri made no attempt to move. The bewildered warrior notched another arrow to the string. No sooner did he draw the bow than the stave snapped in his hand.

"Enough of that," said Mirri. "You could hurt someone. Have a care. I might take you with me, too."

The warrior gaped at her, then at his shattered bow. He backed away. His terrified comrades dashed for the gates and he fled after them.

Raging and cursing, Nahusha snatched the reins from his driver, wheeled the chariot, and sent it racing toward the city. Adi-Kavi sought to bar the way, but Nahusha plunged past as if Mirri's vengeful ghost were at his heels. Darshan's horsemen and charioteers had broken from cover to charge across the plain. Troops poured from the city gates. Nahusha's commanders, seeing their king in peril and Ranapura coming under attack, had taken their own decision to meet the oncoming assault.

"That brought them out faster than I hoped," said Mirri. "Hashkat, it's time to leave. We have other things to do."

Tamar's worst moment of fear for Mirri had passed. The breastplate of tough leather, padded with rags hidden beneath her robes, had shielded her. Now all depended on the Bandar-loka.

He clapped his heels against Gayatri's flanks and set off after Nahusha. Kirin and Skanda galloped to join their troops advancing on the city. Nahusha, Tamar saw, was forcing his chariot through his warriors' ranks, trampling and running them over in his haste to reach the gates. Flailing at his men with the flat of his sword, Nahusha shouted at them to withdraw inside the city. It was too late; his commands went unheeded; the battle had gained momentum and a will of its own, as yet more warriors streamed out.

By now, the leading ranks of Darshan's horsemen had clashed with Nahusha's troops. Tamar had only one thought: Nahusha. He galloped clear of the press of foot soldiers and riders. He strained his eyes for a glimpse of him through the rising clouds of dust.

At the same time, one of Nahusha's chariots burst through the ranks of warriors. The driver lashed the horses to greater speed. The *kshatriya* on the fighting platform brandished a spear. Before he could hurl it, the chariot jolted to the ground. A wheel had spun loose from its axle. Kicking and bucking, the horses broke free of the shafts. Trailing their harness, they bolted from the wreckage. Warrior and driver ran for safety within their ranks.

Tamar cried out in triumph. The Bandar-loka! Night

after night, following Mirri's plan, a secret army of monkeys had scaled the front wall of the city. Like silent, long-tailed shadows, they slipped into guard rooms and stores of weapons. They loosened chariot wheels, frayed bowstrings, weakened bowstaves with unseen cuts from thin blades; the bow that shattered in the archer's hand had been the work of their deft fingers. The Bandar-loka had done all they could to cause as much hidden damage as possible.

Akka himself had brazenly stolen into Ranapura a dozen times or more in broad daylight. He perched impudently on rooftops, scuttled among the fruit sellers in the marketplace until he became a familiar sight and harmless amusement. Yet he kept shrewd eyes and ears open, bringing back whatever news he gleaned.

Tamar galloped to snatch up the *kshatriya*'s discarded spear. The Bandar-loka's work had begun taking a heavier toll. Several more of Nahusha's chariots raced into combat, only to overturn as linchpins broke, wheels fell off, and harness leathers parted. For each arrow that flew straight, another was likely to miss its mark or fall from the archer's hand as the bowstring snapped.

Still seeking Nahusha, Tamar urged Gayatri into the fray. Rage swept away fear as he forced his way through the press of warriors. Some thrust at him with their swords or tried to pull him from the saddle. He struck them aside with the spear shaft; their lives were not worth taking. If he was to have blood on his hands it would be Nahusha's alone, as Ashwara himself had vowed.

At first, when so many of their weapons failed them, Nahusha's troops had fallen into disarray. Now, they rallied and fought with the strength of despair. The wreckage of chariots had been turned into barricades; from behind them, warriors hurled *chakra*s, the deadly, sharp-edged iron disks. The lines of battle surged back and forth.

Darshan had galloped up to him. "Fall back! Fall back!"

Tamar could barely hear his shouts over the clash of arms. When he heard, he could not understand. When he understood, his heart sank. Darshan was pointing toward the gates.

Nahusha had sent out his war elephants.

One after another, the immense animals lumbered onto the battlefield. The elephant masters goaded them onward as the *kshatriya*s mounted on their backs flung spears and *chakra*s. Kirin's foot troops, running to support Darshan, wheeled away to escape being trampled under the elephants' feet or gored by their iron-capped tusks. Nahusha's warriors took heart, cheering as the gigantic beasts plowed ahead, scattering all in their path.

Tamar sighted Hashkat astride Jagati and urged Gayatri to his side. "The plan's gone wrong. What happened?"

Hashkat only grinned from ear to ear. That same instant, from the woodlands at the edge of the plain, came a rumbling like the beating of great drums. The ground shook as the pounding grew louder, a rolling thunder over the din of battle.

A huge bull elephant charged onto the field, trunk upraised, trumpeting at the top of his voice. Arvati followed, with Akka perched on her shoulders. Behind her, a herd of elephants bellowed and tossed their heads as the ranks of Darshan's warriors parted to let them pass.

Nahusha's elephants halted in their tracks. First one, then another, then all flapped their ears, waved their trunks, and trumpeted in joyful recognition. The mahouts goaded them mercilessly to attack, but they reared up to shrug off their riders and send them headlong to the ground.

Arvati and her kindred moved steadily across the field. Nahusha's elephants paid no heed to the threats and commands of their masters, but eagerly joined Arvati and their long-lost relatives. Free of their tormentors, they swept away the barricades of wrecked chariots. The warriors scrambled to escape, only to find themselves beset by other foes.

Through the gates rushed wild boars, slashing with curved tusks; wolves, snarling and snapping, followed them; a half-starved tiger and a ragged-maned lion sprang roaring into the midst of the terrified troops.

"More monkey's work!" Hashkat bounced up and down on the saddle. "They've unbolted Nahusha's animal cages!"

Seeing their foe in such confusion, Kirin and Skanda joined forces with Darshan to press a renewed attack. Some of Nahusha's troops had thrown down their weapons and raced in panic from the field. Others tried to make a stand as best they could. The folk of Ranapura had flung shut the gates, leaving the embattled warriors no choice but to fight or fly.

From the tail of his eye, Tamar glimpsed a burly, white-robed figure heaving his way into the midst of Nahusha's ranks. He thought, first, it was a *brahmana* gone mad, then saw the powerful arms and shaggy head.

"Jamba-Van!" Tamar cried, as the bear charged on, dashing to the ground all who stood in his way, as if they were no more than pieces of crockery in his *ashrama*. He turned and saw Mirri.

"Keep back!" Mirri had changed her shroud for hunter's buckskins; and, long hair flying, she sat astride Soma-Nandi.

The tiger, teeth bared and tail lashing, bounded abreast of Tamar. "Stay clear. Leave the rest to Arvati."

As she spoke, Tamar saw the herd of elephants break off their rampage. Arvati was beckoning with her trunk. All her kindred hurried to join her; and, shoulder to shoulder, the elephants formed a massive gray wall to surround the remnants of Nahusha's defeated army.

At the same time, Tamar caught sight of Nahusha's chariot. The driver had jumped out to run for his life. Nahusha, gripping the reins, lashed savagely at the horses. The chariot careened along the wall.

Tamar kicked his heels against Gayatri's flanks. Nahusha had slewed the chariot around the angle of the wall, but Tamar galloped after him through the ranks of retreating warriors. Nahusha was rapidly outdistancing him.

At full stretch, Gayatri checked and nearly stumbled. Ahead, Nahusha's chariot skidded to a halt and tipped sideways. The horses foundered, broke free of the shafts. Gayatri swerved, almost plunging into the wreckage. It took Tamar a moment to understand: Nahusha had driven too close to the edge of the pits encircling the city.

Tamar halted and swung down from Gayatri. Nahusha had clambered out of the disabled chariot.

"Well, well, here's the corpse-washer." Nahusha set his hands on his hips as Tamar leveled the spear. "It seems to have found a pointed stick. Does the creature play at being a warrior?"

Tamar took a pace toward him. "As I told you, Nahusha, I want your life, not your death. Surrender. Face justice honorably and I vow to let you live."

"You bargain with me?" Nahusha glanced scornfully at Tamar. "You want my life? Then come and get it. Throw your little stick at me. I have no weapon. I broke my sword on one of the rabble you sent against me. Are you afraid to kill an unarmed man? You were so eager, once, to challenge me. Now it is I who challenge you. In even combat, hand to hand, by the warrior's code of honor. Have you the stomach to face a real *kshatriya* on equal terms? As I warned you, corpse-washer, I bite very hard."

Tamar gripped the spear shaft and drew back his arm, fury mounting at Nahusha's contempt. In his ears rang Ashwara's question on the eve of battle: Can any man kill and keep his heart pure, or is all slaughter alike? And the *chandala* asking: How are you different from Nahusha?

With an anguished cry, he flung away the spear and sprang to grapple with him.

"No sword, corpse-washer," hissed Nahusha, one hand seizing him by the throat with a strength Tamar had not imagined. "No sword—but this."

Nahusha snatched a dagger from beneath his breastplate. Tamar fought to twist away from the glinting blade. With all his might, he wrestled free of Nahusha's grasp and stumbled back. Before he regained his balance, his legs were suddenly knocked from under him. He fell to the ground as blurred shapes hurtled past. He heard Nahusha cry out, and he flung up his arms against the dagger thrust.

32. To the Snow Mountains

———◆———

It was too late. Tamar could do nothing to stop them. The once-caged animals attacked their tormentor from every side. The wolves flung themselves on Nahusha, one at his throat, the other sinking fangs into his upraised arm. The boar, whose onrush had knocked Tamar to the ground, charged ahead, savaging Nahusha with his tusks. The lion and tiger clawed Nahusha to his knees, while the wolves snarled and set their jaws tighter. The creatures, Tamar saw, all bore marks of the lash or branding iron; half starved though they were, their fury had given them strength to take revenge on their captor.

Nahusha screamed in rage and pain as the animals swarmed over him. For an instant, he kicked free; but, as he tried to stand, he stumbled over the brink of the pit, clutched at empty air, and plummeted onto the piercing spikes at the bottom.

Tamar jumped to his feet. The animals scattered to freedom. The tiger wheeled, fixed glowing eyes a moment on Tamar, then sprang.

The striped body vaulted past him. Mirri had ridden up on Soma-Nandi, and the tiger made straight for them. The girl barely had time to slide off Soma-Nandi's back as the pair of tigers rushed together, rubbing heads, licking each

other's ears, rolling on the ground as playfully as kittens, and
rumbling out loving purrs.

"This is Sunda, my mate." Soma-Nandi paused a moment from the joyful reunion. "I kept searching for him after
I left you. When the Bandar-loka spread word that you
needed help, I came as quickly as I could." She turned melting eyes on Sunda. "I never lost hope of finding you."

"Nor did I," said Sunda. "Even so, without the Bandar-
loka I'd still be in Nahusha's cage."

Mirri had gone to the edge of the pit. She glanced down,
then turned abruptly away. "He'll keep no more prisoners
—animals or anyone else."

Kirin and Skanda had entered Ranapura when Tamar, Mirri,
and the tigers galloped back. The cheering townsfolk had
flung open the gates in welcome. Nahusha's shattered forces
had fled or begged to surrender. Broken chariots and weapons still littered the field; stragglers wandered where the battle lines once stretched. Darshan was shouting for his troops
to form orderly ranks. Arvati and her relatives had already
gone in a triumphant procession through the city, but Tamar
sighted Hashkat in the midst of the commotion. The monkey had tossed aside his warrior's gear and was cavorting
gleefully. Tamar jumped down from Gayatri and made his
way to embrace him. Adi-Kavi elbowed through the crowd,
with Rajaswami and Jamba-Van behind him.

"It was all I could do to hold him back." Adi-Kavi
chuckled. *"Brahmana* or not, he'd have run into the thick
of it."

"I was quite carried away." Rajaswami tried his best to

sound apologetic. "My goodness, I don't know what came over me. And you, dear boy, you're undamaged? Excellent. All went as our dear *gopi* planned. And look who's come to join us," he added, as Jamba-Van laid an affectionate paw on the *acharya*'s shoulder. "What a pleasure to meet again, even in these disruptive circumstances."

"I never foresaw a day when I'd leave my *ashrama*," the bear said, "but when I heard my dear collague was in danger, I had to come here myself. Now that I've learned what happened to all of you"—Jamba-Van bristled and growled at the recollection—"I only wish I'd come sooner."

"Here's someone who wants to thank your Bandar-loka," Mirri said as she brought Sunda to Hashkat's side. "When they unbolted the cages—"

"What, another tiger?" broke in Garuda, who had flapped down to perch on Jagati's back. "Isn't one enough already? Two? Shmaa! You expect me to put up with both of them?"

"Skanda and Kirin were looking for you," Adi-Kavi told Tamar. "How you'll find them in all this lot, I can't imagine. The whole city's turned out to celebrate."

"I have one thing to do first." Tamar swung astride Gayatri; before Mirri could question him, he made his way over the crowded field, heading toward the river.

He went to the *shmashana*.

The burning ground was empty. The door of the hut stood open. He called out. No answer came. He dismounted and walked across the stretch of rubble. The wooden stake and the chain were gone. He stepped across the threshold and peered into the shadows of the room, bare except for a straw mat and a few pieces of earthenware.

Footsteps scraped the gravel behind him. He turned, about to speak. A bent-backed old man, tangled beard falling to his waist, stared at him with surprise and discomfort.

"The *chandala* who lived here," Tamar began. "Where has he gone? I must find him."

The old man shuffled back a few paces and put up his hands to keep Tamar at a distance. "Come no farther," he warned in a cracked voice. "You should not be in this place."

"Yes, I should. The *chandala* was my friend. Grandsire, tell me what became of him."

The man blinked his clouded eyes. "Tell?" He cupped a hand to his ear. "What?"

"All you know. Did warriors come and take him away? Did he escape? Save himself? Where is he now?"

The old man frowned and shook his head. Tamar repeated his questions. "Grandsire, do you understand me? There was a young man, as well. On a chain. Did the *chandala* speak of him?"

"Young man? No. Only me. I know nothing. I mind my own business. I do my work."

"When did you come here?" Tamar pressed. "How long ago?"

"Long?" The man was growing unhappy in Tamar's presence. "Long ago? When? Why do you ask? Go, leave me in peace. This is a place for the dead, not the living."

The old man clamped shut his toothless jaws, shuffled into the hut, and closed the door.

Tamar followed, but stopped at the threshold. He stood some while. Finally, he went back to Ranapura.

❖

The townsfolk had begun decorating the streets with banners and garlands, in memory of Ashwara and in celebration of their freedom. Tamar understood that Kirin had been welcomed and acclaimed king. He made his way quickly to the palace. Mirri was waiting in the courtyard.

"The *chandala* said he'd take care of himself," Mirri replied, when Tamar told what had happened. "I'm sure he's all right. We'll try to find out later. Come, Kirin expects you at his durbar."

She led him, still troubled, to the great audience chamber. He had never seen a durbar such as this. Monkeys perched in every nook and cranny, under the eaves of the high ceiling or on the crossbeams. Arvati and several of her relatives towered over the *kshatriya*s thronging the hall. Beside her crouched Soma-Nandi and Sunda. Garuda and Akka were aloft, amid the Bandar-loka. Paying not much mind to anything else, Rajaswami and the bear were deep in conversation.

Taking on the duties of royal crier, Adi-Kavi called out their names and beckoned Mirri and Tamar to join Hashkat, Skanda, and Darshan flanking Kirin's throne.

"*Namaste.*" Kirin rose and pressed his palms together as Tamar and Mirri approached. His brow was even more deeply furrowed now; his face was heavy with sorrow. "King of Sundari, you have well kept your promise to our brother, and have done far better than your word. And you," he said, turning to Mirri, "with the help of all these forest creatures, you have given us our victory. We thank and honor you.

"Even so, I do not rejoice," Kirin went on. "Ashwara

should be in my place. I take this throne in the shadow of grief for him; and I vow, for all present to witness, that I will rule as he would have done.

"King of Sundari and you, worthy *gopi,* your rewards shall be as great as your service to our cause—"

"Reward? For keeping a promise?" Tamar broke in. "I claim none."

"Neither do I," Mirri added. "We don't ask anything for what we'd have done anyway."

"I offer it nonetheless," Kirin said. "The greatest treasure one kingdom can bestow on another: friendship and peace between my realm and yours."

"I do likewise," said Skanda. "King Rudra gave his life for Ashwara's sake, and I owe a duty to his people. Rudra's *kshatriya*s want me to be king of Chandragar. That's something I never expected, but a high honor"—for a moment there was the trace of his boyish grin—"and, yes, of course, I'll accept. So, I ask that you, in turn, accept my own vow of peace."

"That, gladly," Tamar said.

"I do have one question," Rajaswami put in, when Kirin declared the durbar at an end. "I suppose it's too much to hope, but has anyone noticed an umbrella lying about? No? Ah, well, since everything else turned out so happily, one should be willing to make a small sacrifice."

◆

They rested, for the next several days, in the Ranapura Palace. Skanda then left for Chandragar; and, one after the other, Soma-Nandi and Sunda, Arvati and her kindred, exchanged fond farewells with Tamar and Mirri. Jamba-Van, last to take his leave, did so with reluctance.

"My dear colleague, we part once again," the bear said as Rajaswami embraced him, "but my best hope is that you will someday find your way back to my *ashrama*. I have refined my views on the shape of infinity and would be glad for your opinion."

"I have refined my views on a number of things," said Rajaswami, "and would eagerly discuss them."

❧

"Majesty, when you left Sundari," Darshan later said to Tamar, "I laid your sandals on your throne to betoken that you are still our king—"

"Am I?" Tamar broke in. He had, with Darshan, gone to the rooftop terrace. Beyond Ranapura rose the heights of the Snow Mountains. "Should a king know fear? As I did? In battle, I was terrified—"

"Lad, so was I. Who isn't, if truth be told? You faced it down; no more can be asked. A man who claims to be fearless is an idiot or a liar."

"Even a *kshatriya?* When I rode with Skanda, I spared a man's life and told Skanda I'd killed him. Nahusha—at the end, would it have been my hand that slew him? I'll never know."

"Better a king who holds back from bloodshed than one who relishes it," Darshan said. "Enough, enough, lad. Come home. You see what this dream of yours has cost you already. Give it up; only more ill can come of it."

"Once, I might have done so," Tamar said. "I even tried to throw away my ring. I couldn't." He shook his head. "Tomorrow, we'll go into the mountains. As I must."

"For the sake of a promise you made? Or didn't make?"

Darshan burst out. "That's more than even a king's honor demands."

"This is for my own sake and by my own choice," Tamar said. "You think I only dreamed? That may well be. But I'll never be at peace until I'm sure one way or the other. Mirri understood that better than I did.

"You, old friend, go back to Sundari. Rule well. Love my people; do the best for them. This is my last command to you."

33. The Traveler

◆

Next morning, on the field at Ranapura, Tamar rode through the ranks of his *kshatriyas*, honoring them, saying his thanks and farewells. At the end, he put his arms around Gayatri's neck, taking loving leave of her and Jagati. As Adi-Kavi warned that the high passes would be too difficult and dangerous for the horses, Darshan promised to take the steeds with him.

"They'll be fondly tended," the old warrior said. "They'll wait for you, lad, as I will." With a show of gruffness, he added, "Not happily or patiently."

"You, too, wait for me," Hashkat told Akka. "If I wore sandals, you could put them on my throne—if I had a throne. In any case, you keep an eye on the Bandar-loka while I'm tramping through the mountains."

"Who's tramping?" Garuda squawked. "Shmaa! What about me?"

"Fly, you malingering bird. What else?" Hashkat retorted. "You and Akka did well enough going to Sundari."

"Oh, yes, so I did," Garuda said sourly. "If you don't count being skewered with arrows and lurking in holes in the ground. But I'm not up to flying, let alone tramping."

"Of course you're not." Mirri hid a smile. "You'll stay with me until you get your strength back."

"Faker," muttered Hashkat, while Garuda, cooing happily, flapped to Mirri's shoulder. "Next, he'll want his meals served on a platter."

◆━◆

Kirin had generously outfitted them with warm cloaks and stout boots, as well as stores of food, tents of coarse canvas, and other gear. Rajaswami insisted on carrying as much as his frail bones allowed; the others divided the burdens among themselves. By the time they reached the foothills overlooking Ranapura, Tamar realized why Adi-Kavi had warned against taking the horses. There were no paths, and the rocky outcroppings were too treacherous for even the most surefooted pack animals.

"Something puzzles me," Tamar said, as they gained the first heights. "How did Jaya travel to Sundari?" He pointed toward Kumeru and Sumeru. "No sign of a road, no trail, no footpath. Yet he had elephants, chariots, horses."

"Don't ask me," Garuda said. "I don't recognize any of this. Perhaps I've forgotten; it was so long ago."

"He might have taken a different way," Mirri said. "There could be a dozen roads out of the valley, for all you know, circling around in some other direction."

"If he ever came to Sundari in the first place."

"That's why you're here, isn't it? To find out."

Adi-Kavi was calling them. The *suta* had picked a sheltered spot amid the wind-twisted trees and was lashing together the panels of the tent. Tamar glanced back a moment over the distance they had covered, the stretches of shale and gravel, the stunted vegetation. Black against the setting sun, the bare branches shuddered in the sharp breeze. He blinked and looked again. Far below, a dark shape skirted a ravine, then, within the instant, vanished amid the trees.

Tamar shaded his eyes, waiting to see if the shadow would reappear. Nothing moved. He watched a little longer. It was, he decided, a trick of the light. He went to help pitch the tent and thought no more about it.

Two days later, he saw it again.

They had been following the high ridges overlooking the Sabla. Tamar, at first, hoped to find easier ground along the river itself but, as Adi-Kavi pointed out, the walls of the gorge were too sheer, the iron-dark cliffs falling straight to the water's edge. The *suta* was confident they would soon reach the slopes leading into the valley; and so they pressed on, keeping the winding blue and white current always in sight. That afternoon, Adi-Kavi had chosen to halt in a rocky cavern where wind and weather had eaten away a domed chamber; in the middle, a pool of clear, drinkable water.

They had begun hauling in their gear when Tamar again saw the dark figure appear and disappear behind a distant tumble of boulders. This time, he was sure it was no trick of the light. This time, he was sure it was a man.

He called Mirri and the others and pointed to where he had glimpsed the figure. By then, it was gone. Even the sharp-eyed Adi-Kavi could make out no sign of it.

"You're certain it wasn't a mountain creature of some sort?" Mirri said. "A stray animal? Too bad you didn't have a better look."

"What creature would be fool enough to roam around in this desolation?" said Hashkat. "Not one of the Bandar-loka, I can tell you."

"As long as whoever or whatever it is keeps a polite distance," put in Rajaswami, "I shouldn't be too concerned. He'll go his way, we'll go ours."

Tamar was not satisfied. "If he's following us, I want to know why. Stay in the cave, all of you. I'll go and find out."

"It'll be dark before you get back," Mirri reminded him. She turned to Garuda, perched on a pile of gear. "Can you fly there and see? It's no distance—for an eagle. You'll take a quick glance around and be here again in time for your food."

Garuda grumbled and muttered; but, finally, with a toss of his beak, he flew where Tamar pointed. While Tamar and Mirri hauled gear and provisions into the cave, Rajaswami bustled about laying blankets and lighting lamps. Hashkat and Adi-Kavi had set off to find dry twigs and bits of moss for a cook fire. By the time the monkey and the *suta* were back, the shadows had deepened and pellets of snow whirled over the ridges.

Tamar paced uneasily. Garuda had been gone overlong. Mirri, too, was anxious. They were ready to throw on their cloaks and search for the bird when he swooped into the cave.

"I saw! I saw!" Garuda crowed. His feathers were crusted with sleet, an icicle hung from the tip of his beak, but he squawked jubilantly as he landed on the earthen floor. "It was marvelous!"

"I knew you'd find out." Mirri tried to calm the excited bird, who was clucking with gleeful self-satisfaction. "Tell us—"

"Shmaa! Wonderful. I flew like—like an eagle!" Garuda cackled proudly. "Soaring, diving—"

"Leave off, you puffed-up chicken," Hashkat cried. "What did you see?"

"A man? An animal?" Tamar knelt beside Garuda. "Did you have a clear look?"

"Eh? Oh, that." Garuda shrugged his wings. "No, not a trace of anything or anybody. A waste of my valuable time. I gave up searching. But then, since I was already in the air, I thought: Why not fly just a little farther, toward the valley. And there it was. Mahapura!

"Just as I remembered—or, I'm starting to remember. Beautiful! The tall towers, the eight gates—we're nearly there; I'll finish my errand after all this time. Oh, I hope King Jaya forgives me for taking so long. But I didn't fail him. I'll put the ruby in his hand—"

Garuda broke off and cast a beady eye on Tamar. "The ruby—you've got it safely put away, don't you? Yes? Well, let me see it," he went on, as Tamar took the gem from beneath his garments and held it in front of the bird. "You'll still carry it the rest of the way for me. We've come this far, I'm taking no chances on dropping it again. I just want to look and admire."

"Gloat is what you mean," said Hashkat, as Tamar set down the ruby.

"Call it what you please." Garuda squatted on top of the stone as if about to hatch an egg. "The gem's been tossed around enough. I want it to be with me a little while. I find it very comforting. Do you mind?"

"Enjoy yourself," said Mirri, while Garuda crooned and rocked back and forth. "Sit on it as long as you want. You have a right to be pleased."

"So there truly is a palace," Tamar began, "truly a King Jaya—"

A heavy-set figure was standing in the mouth of the

cave. Tamar got hastily to his feet. The man was wrapped in a cloak of animal skins, a fur cap pressed over a hedge of black hair. Frozen droplets glittered in his beard; snow crusted his heavy boots.

"No harm, no harm," he called out, holding up his hands as Tamar reached for his sword. "I only beg a little warmth, a mouthful of food if you can spare it. My name's Griva."

"I saw you before." Tamar looked closely at him. "In the ravine. Then, by the mound of boulders. Why are you following us?"

"Am I?" Griva stepped all the way into the cave. He seemed to bring the night chill with him. "Following you? We only happen to find ourselves on the same path."

"What path is that?"

"I might ask you likewise. But, your business is your own and no concern of mine—unless we have an interest in common."

"And that would be?" said Mirri.

Griva's eyes darted around the cave. His weather-blackened face folded into a grin. "Stones," he said.

34. The Fire Flower

---

hat's right. Stones. Bright, shiny ones. Gems, eh? You've found a few yourself, I'd not be surprised." He stamped the snow off his boots and started toward the cook fire. Tamar put out an arm to hold him back, but Griva shouldered past, skirted the pool, and hunkered down by the flames. "These mountains are full of them. They hide in all manner of nooks and crannies. Sometimes," he added, with a wink, "where you'd never think of looking. But I sniff them out and pry them loose."

"That's not our business." Tamar drew his sword. "If it's yours, go on about it."

Griva eyed the blade and gave a throaty laugh. "Now, now, no need to get the wind up. I'm no robber, if that's what you fear. Food and drink's all I ask. A little corner to sleep in. You'll not deny me that much, will you?"

"He has a point, my boy," Rajaswami whispered. "Hospitality and courtesy. You can't turn him away."

Griva, meantime, had attacked the food that Mirri handed him, grinding it in his heavy jaws and wiping his mouth on the back of a hairy hand. He squinted an eye at Tamar.

"I'll not intrude on your snug little corner here," he said, settling himself. "I'm not one to stay where I'm not welcome. Oh, yes, you're thinking you'll be glad to see the back of me. Who could blame you? A stranger out of no-where. You'd not expect to have dealings with a rough-and-ready fellow like me.

"But don't be too quick to send me away," Griva added. "There could be a tidy profit for both of us."

"We're not looking for profit," Mirri said.

"What if it jumped out at you?" Griva reached under his cloak and pulled out a leather pouch. He untied it and spilled the contents into his palm: a heap of gems.

"Little twinklers, eh?" Griva licked his lips. "Beauties. You'd almost want to eat them up. I have more, besides. Plenty for all of you."

"Why show us these?" Tamar demanded.

"Whispers. I've heard a few. A word here, a word there. Nothing that means anything by itself. Put them together, you have an interesting tale. How a young lad—very much like yourself—got his hands on something. And what would that be? A stone. A shiny little red stone. Do you follow me so far?"

Tamar did not answer. Griva went on in an amiable tone:

"For the sake of the tale, let's call that little stone a ruby. Now, let's suppose there's a rich man: a gem-fancier, a col-lector, as you might say. He wants a stone like that—not for its value; it's half the size of the ones I've got right here. No, it's just a curio, an odd sort of trinket. But he's made up his mind. You know how these collectors are.

"So he sends a fellow with an eye for such things—a fellow like me, if you will—to track it down and buy it for him. At a good price, that's understood.

"There's a happy ending to the tale," continued Griva. "The young lad's delighted at the chance to reap a fortune;

he trades that little ruby he's carrying for, say, a fistful of diamonds. So, everybody's overjoyed with the bargain; they go their own ways, simple as that. A pleasant story, don't you agree?"

Tamar tightened his grip on the sword. "I don't know who you are or who you serve, and I don't care. Get out."

Griva shrugged and poured the gems back into the pouch. "There's yet another ending to the story, and not such a happy one. That young man and his friends are suddenly dead."

Griva leaped to his feet. Quick as an eye-blink, he wrenched away Tamar's blade and broke it over his knee.

"No more tales, King of Sundari." He gripped Tamar by the front of the jacket and pulled him close, until their faces nearly touched. Griva hissed and bared his teeth. "Play no games with me. I know you've got the ruby. I'll have it now."

Adi-Kavi had sprung up to grapple him from behind, but Griva shook him off and sent him sprawling. "Give. I'll tear you apart, you and all the rest. Look at me. See who you're dealing with."

Griva's face blurred and shifted before Tamar's eyes. The teeth lengthened into fangs, the body swelled and burst from its garments, the fingers clutching Tamar's jacket turned to claws.

"*Rakshasa!*" The *suta* flung himself again on the demon's back and seized him by the hair, holding on with all his strength.

"Garuda, take the ruby!" Mirri shouted. "Fly! Fly to Jaya!"

Seeing the bird snatch the gem from under its feathers, the *rakshasa* tossed Tamar aside and lunged for Garuda.

Wings beating, the eagle streaked from the cave. Hashkat
darted across the ground and wrapped his arms around the
demon's legs. Mirri threw herself on the struggling *rakshasa*.
Rajaswami picked up a burning branch from the cook
fire and shook it at Griva with all the ferocity he could
muster.

Growling, the *rakshasa* seized the branch in his jaws,
snapped it into bits and spat them blazing at Rajaswami.
Griva heaved himself closer to the mouth of the cave.

"Hold fast!" Tamar understood that Griva was not so
much trying to escape his attackers as he was seeking a different victim. "He's after Garuda."

"Let him go," Rajaswami called. "He can't catch an
eagle."

Tamar was about to follow the *acharya*'s urging. It crossed
his mind that Garuda was already aloft and safely in flight to
Mahapura. But, even as he watched, the *rakshasa* hunched
up his shoulders. He spread out his arms: They shuddered
for a moment, then turned into powerful wings. Glossy
feathers like iron scales covered the demon's body. The legs,
with their talons, had become those of a hideous bird of
prey.

Hashkat screamed. The hooked beak now jutting from
what had been the *rakshasa*'s face ripped into the monkey's
arm. Bleeding, Hashkat still clung to the raging bird, but the
creature flung him to the ground. Adi-Kavi, shaken loose,
tumbled backward. As Mirri kicked and pummeled the *rakshasa,* Tamar sprang past the buffeting wings, leaped onto
the demon's back, and locked his hands around its neck.

The *rakshasa* doubled its efforts to gain the mouth of the
cave. Tamar felt his fingers slip as the huge bird twisted its
neck around, trying to savage him with its beak.

That same moment, wings flapping, screeching at the top of his voice, Garuda streaked back into the chamber.

"No! Get out!" Mirri ordered. "Do as I told you. Save your ruby. Save yourself!"

The *rakshasa* whirled to fend off Garuda's attack. Tamar's grip at last gave way; he fell and skidded across the cavern floor. Garuda swooped and circled, striking out with beak and talons. Wind whistled as the *rakshasa*'s wings unfolded to their full breadth, beating Garuda to the ground. The *rakshasa* sprang into the air, ready to plummet onto the stunned eagle.

In the pool, the water roiled and churned into foam. A long shape burst up, scales glistening. The great serpent flung itself at the *rakshasa*.

"Shesha!" Tamar cried.

The Naga prince had lunged to grip the *rakshasa* in his coils. The demon bird flailed its wings, fighting to break free of Shesha's encircling body. The Naga tightened his hold and bore the creature to earth. The *rakshasa* shrieked in fury. Its feathers began glowing red-hot; a tongue of flame shot from its beak. Shesha writhed closer to the edge of the pool; then, with the *rakshasa* locked in his grasp, rolled into the water and vanished in its depths.

The surface of the pool hissed, as if a flaming torch had been quenched. Tamar ran to the edge. He could see nothing of the Naga prince. The water was calm again. Mirri and Adi-Kavi drew him away.

"We were enemies, Shesha and I," Tamar murmured. "We fought once. He would have drowned me. Yet, he came—"

"Yes, King of Sundari, so I did." Shesha's head rose from the water. "For the sake of the mercy you showed me."

The Naga prince slithered all his length from the pool. "The *rakshasa* is destroyed, as he would have destroyed you. His powers were great; only a Naga could have stood against him."

"But you—Prince Shesha, how have you come here?" Tamar pressed his palms together and bowed his head in gratitude. "We owe you our lives. You followed us. Why?"

"We feared for you," answered the Naga. "Some while after you departed our realm, we had word of a *rakshasa* seeking your trail. We could only guess that it had to do with the ruby you chose from our treasure, and that the gem was of even greater value than we had supposed.

"For a time, I lost track of you, and knew only that you wished to go to Mahapura. I could reach you no sooner. The Naga kingdom runs through all waterways and secret springs," Shesha added, "but none of us has dared to venture this far."

Mirri had gone to cradle the motionless Garuda in her arms. Shesha lifted his head, crowned by the glittering sapphire, and cast unblinking eyes around the cave.

"The thieving monkey is still with you." Shesha darted out his forked tongue. "I expected the wretch would have long since deserted you."

"He became a brave friend," Tamar said, "and a worthy king of his people."

"And badly hurt," put in Adi-Kavi, leaving Hashkat's side. "A *rakshasa*'s bite is venomous." He laid a hand on Tamar's arm. "Come to him. I fear he's dying."

35. The Palace of Illusions

Hashkat slumped against the cave wall. The monkey's face was drawn, his eyes sunken. Tamar, with Shesha slithering after, knelt beside him.

"What, the overgrown angleworm?" Hashkat raised his head a little and grinned painfully. "Still after me? I've heard of bearing a grudge, but not so far as this."

"He killed the *rakshasa*," Tamar said quietly. "He came to help us."

"In that case, what took him so long? If that wiggler had a shell, he'd be a snail." Hashkat tried to regain his old impudence, but his voice faltered and he shuddered violently.

Mirri, cradling the stunned Garuda, glanced, questioning, at Adi-Kavi. Rajaswami whimpered in distress. Hashkat curled into himself, his chin sinking to his breast.

"Strong poison," Adi-Kavi said aside to Tamar. "I have no antidote. Nothing I can do for him. This is beyond my skill."

"Not beyond mine." Shesha spread his hood. "I carry the means to heal him. Take the gem I wear. Hold it to his wound. The venom of a *rakshasa* is fatal. It will take all the power of my jewel to work against it. After that, the stone will be worthless. Use it carefully; it will serve this one time only."

"You'd give up the jewel he tried to steal from you?"

Tamar said. "At the riverside, you'd have taken his life on account of it."

"Now I give him his life," replied Shesha. "My father pardoned the foolish creature. Can I do less? The Naga Raja reproached me for letting wrath drive out reason and compassion. His words have weighed on me ever since. As I wish to heal this frivolous monkey, so I wish to heal my own dharma."

Prince Shesha lowered his head. Tamar took the jewel from the Naga's brow; and, as Shesha instructed, set it on Hashkat's arm. Hashkat lay motionless. Tamar feared that the poison had spread too far and had already claimed the monkey's life. The sapphire's blue inner flame dimmed little by little, then winked out.

"It is done," Shesha said. "The stone is useless. Cast it away. If it has failed, I have no more to offer."

Hashkat stirred and opened one eye. "What's that crawler done now?" He sat up and peered at his arm, as whole as if it had never been wounded.

"Saved an impudent monkey is what he's done," Mirri said, smiling.

Hashkat popped his eyes at Shesha. "In spite of all—?" He bowed his head and pressed his palms together. "*Namaste,* Prince of the Naga-loka. I'm grateful. You're a fine fellow." He stuck out his tongue and grinned wickedly. "For a royal wiggler."

"*Namaste,* O flea-ridden tree-climber," Shesha replied, with a fond glint in his eyes. "May your life be as long as your insolence is great."

The Naga folded his hood and turned to Tamar. "King of Sundari, our quarrel is over. Go your way. Guard the ruby well. Its power may be greater than any of us know. I dare stay no longer. Without the protection of my jewel, my own life is at risk. *Namaste.*"

The Naga prince heaved his coils to the edge of the pool. Hashkat scrambled after him:

"Wait, wait! As you saved my life, at least I owe you the truth. I really did mean to give back your gem."

By then, Prince Shesha had slid into the dark waters and vanished.

Garuda, meantime, had begun coughing and wheezing in Mirri's arms. "Set me down, set me down. Shmaa! I can hardly breathe."

"You shouldn't be here in the first place," Mirri said. "I told you to fly off."

"Well, I didn't," Garuda snapped. "Leave my friends in danger? What kind of eagle would I be? I thought—what I wanted to do—" Garuda sniffed and hesitated. He gave Mirri a sidelong glance. "I was going to give that disgusting *rakshasa* the ruby. That's all he wanted; he'd have let you go."

"Oh, I very much doubt it," said Rajaswami. "You can't bargain with those fellows. They never keep their word."

"Even so," Garuda said, "I thought I'd try."

"You'd really have done that for us?" Mirri said.

Garuda ducked his head and shuffled his feet. "Well, yes," he grumbled. "No matter how much aggravation you've caused me—all right, if you must know, I—well, I'm fond of you all, even the monkey. Ruby? Shmaa! A shiny stone. Who cares?"

"You meant to save our lives," Tamar said. "We owe you."

"You can be sure—" Garuda shook his head. "You owe me nothing."

"The ruby's safe?" Mirri said. "Where?"

"There was an accident." Garuda coughed and snorted. "It's stuck in my craw. I swallowed it."

"Ate it?" Hashkat slapped his knees. "You silly rag mop! Come, open your beak. I'll fish it out."

"Get away!" Garuda squawked. "Leave it alone. At least I know where it is."

The world turned green, so green it dazzled him. From the time they left the cave, that next morning, until Adi-Kavi led them on to their final descent, Tamar had seen only grim black outcroppings of bare stones, glaring stretches of empty snowfields, pinnacles of ice. Once, as they inched their way downward, the *suta* had been obliged to chip footholds in what looked like a frozen waterfall. Then the valley burst around them, with sun-swept woodlands and rich meadows; and, ahead, as Garuda had told, the walls and soaring towers of Mahapura.

Hashkat's jaw dropped. Rajaswami stared, eyes full of wonder, and murmured, "Who could have imagined? Yes, this is indeed the realm of a great maharajah."

"And so, at the end, it's true." Tamar took Mirri's hand. "Not a dream, after all. I wish it had been. How Jaya means to deal with me—"

"He'll have to deal with me, too," Mirri said. "He expected a *kshatriya*. I don't think he reckoned on a *gopi*."

Garuda, impatient, had flown ahead. With Mirri beside him, Tamar walked reluctantly through the gates. Before him stretched tree-lined avenues, parks, lakes, and promenades.

"Do you see those crowds?" Hashkat frowned and scratched his head. "Astonishing!"

"I see none," Tamar said, looking where Hashkat gestured.

"That's what's astonishing," said Hashkat. "Nobody. Nowhere. Where are the people? The place is empty. The city of a maharajah? There's not even a monkey."

"Curious, but easily explained," Rajaswami suggested. "They've all gone to—ah, yes, to some local festival."

"Hush." Mirri put a finger to her lips. "I don't see anyone either, but I can hear them."

As Tamar listened, voices rose from all sides: water sellers and hucksters crying their wares, merchants haggling, the laughter of children at play, all the sounds of a busy capital.

"What is this place?" he whispered. "Where have we come?"

A many-towered palace loomed in front of him, the gates open and unguarded. More perplexed than ever, he crossed the wide courtyard, as empty as the rest of the city.

"Where are Jaya's warriors? Chariots? Elephants?" Tamar stepped past the tall portals into a corridor stretching as far as his eyes could see, glittering as if paved and walled with crystal. He took a pace forward, then shouted a warning. The ground had opened in front of him. He stared into a shimmering pool at the bottom of a steep gorge. He stumbled back. Mirri was calling to him. He turned in the direction of her voice, only to collide with a wall.

A dozen figures sprang up, roughly garbed, their faces wind-hardened and sun-blackened. He reached for his sword, forgetting the scabbard was empty. He flung up his arms. The figures did likewise. Only then did he realize he was seeing himself in the surrounding mirrors.

Another corridor opened. He plunged through. Mirri was there. He ran to her. Hashkat and Adi-Kavi had halted farther on, where the passage abruptly ended. Rajaswami, bewildered, turned first one way then another.

"The palace is a trap!" Tamar burst out. "Jaya's caught us in it." He stared around him, raised his clenched fists and shouted, "Show yourself, Jaya! Do you claim my life? Then let me see you: king to king, man to man."

"You waste your breath," said Adi-Kavi, coming to Tamar's side. "If I see the world as it is, I also see the world as it isn't. This is *maya*. Illusion. Nothing more than shadows in our minds. Our eyes are telling us lies and we're believing them."

"We're still caught," Tamar exclaimed. "We can't get out."

"Shadows, only shadows," Adi-Kavi said. "Why fear them? Do as I tell you. Pay them no heed. Don't even look. Close your eyes to them. Walk straight on, wherever it leads you."

Hashkat and Rajaswami had come to join them. With Mirri's hand in his, Tamar stepped blindly ahead, expecting at every moment to lose his footing and topple into a void. When he ventured to open his eyes, he was at the doorway of what was clearly a royal chamber. He glimpsed couches and draperies, richly ornamented silken screens on frames of polished ebony.

"Stay back," he warned Mirri and the rest. "Jaya wants my death, none other. But I mistrust him. He already tried to deceive us. All our lives could be in danger."

Before Mirri could protest, he stepped across the threshold. He glanced hastily around, and took another pace into the chamber. Near a pile of embroidered cushions, he saw a table holding dice, cup, and board for a game of *aksha*.

A figure in white robes and a shawl stood looking out one of the tall casement windows. The man turned and beckoned.

Tamar found himself face to face with the *chandala*.

36. Jaya

"So. You're here, are you?" the *chandala* said. "You found your way after all."

"And you?" Tamar, hands outstretched, had started toward him. He stopped short. The *chandala* was smiling, but something in his voice and bearing puzzled him. "I looked for you at the burning ground. I was afraid you'd come to harm. You'd gone. Here? With Jaya? Where is he?"

"You see him. I am Jaya."

Tamar stared. "This is more illusion. Trickery!" he burst out. "What mockery is this? Who are you? What are you?"

"As I told you."

"Why do you lie to me?" Tamar flung back. "No. The one who came to me in Sundari was a king, a warrior. An arrogant, pitiless *kshatriya*. No man of kindness or compassion. Not you, not you."

"Call me a liar if you will; it is truth nonetheless. Do you doubt me? Shall I repeat the verses your *acharya* recited? The hawk and the sparrow. Not so? Shall I tell you the numbers we threw when we played *aksha?*"

"Tell me what you please. I saw what I saw."

"So you did. Because you yourself were a *kshatriya.* You could not have imagined me as anything else. Would you have welcomed a *chandala* to your palace then?

Would you have agreed to my little game? And given your word, as one warrior to another?"

"Rajaswami and Darshan were there. All my courtiers—"

"You thought so. They were not with you. I caused them to sleep soundly. I laid *maya* on you. There were only the two of us.

"A hunter challenged you in the forest, did he not?" Jaya went on. "And you shot an arrow that set in motion all that followed. I was the hunter, the same who tended Garuda and Akka when their need was greatest—"

Jaya broke off. During this, Mirri and the others—paying no heed to Tamar's warning—had come into the chamber and had been listening, as much taken aback as Tamar himself.

"Namaste, Mirri." Jaya put his palms together. "You have endured much for the sake of your love. Your spirit has only grown more beautiful. And you, *suta,* I am glad to see you safe and well. What a clumsy thief you were. Do you recall a spider whose life you saved? I can tell you now: It was I.

"An insolent youth named Hashkat mocked a wandering *rishi* who turned him into a monkey," Jaya said. "I was that *rishi.* And you, *brahmana,* as for your cherished colleague, I was the sage who offered him knowledge when he intended to eat me.

"I have been all those and many others," Jaya said. "I am as I choose to be."

"I must believe you," Tamar said, after a long moment. "Truth behind truth, as Jamba-Van told me. It wasn't a dream. It happened. We gambled, life against life. I lost.

"Darshan reproached me when I left Sundari. He told me I knew nothing of the world. I know a little more than I did. I've seen kings betray their word, noble *kshatriyas* break their warrior's code, honor meaningless, dharma forgotten. The way of the world. There are other ways—as a *chandala* told me, on the burning ground. He was right. I've seen as much goodness as evil.

"In Sundari, I told a maharajah I was not his dog. Nor am I now. But even a dog's life is as precious as a king's. Death—I've seen my fill. I fear and hate it. I look at my own and see it wears the mask of a friend. Even so, I defy you.

"Once, I'd have accepted death as the price of a game. For the sake of honor. Not now. A fool's wager. A man does not stake his life on a throw of the dice."

Tamar looked squarely at Jaya. "Do you claim my life? You won't take it easily. I'll stand against you with all my strength." Tamar held up his hand. "Your emblem. It binds me no longer. I give it back to you."

In one motion, he tore the iron ring from his finger and flung it on the gaming table. The cup overturned, the dice scattered. In a voice half amused, half pitying, Jaya said:

"Who spoke of taking your life? Is that what you understood? No, I said only that your life was mine. Destroy it? Why should I? You've done as I hoped."

"You hoped? For what?"

"Even I do not know all the paths of karma," Jaya said. "I knew only this: Had Nahusha triumphed, his lust for power would have goaded him to conquer kingdom after kingdom. Yours would not have been spared. I warned you of wild dogs on the hunt. Your *gopi*'s village would have fallen to him as well. Your people, Ashwara's people: all, all, would have been no more than Nahusha's slaves.

"I gambled," Jaya went on, "that you might prevent it. The stakes were higher than any game of *aksha*."

"Are you telling me you foresaw this?" Tamar rounded on him furiously. "Had you no other way to stop him? Only bloodshed and destruction? You caused it? You let it happen—?"

"No." Jaya silenced him with a glance. "You have your dharma as I have mine, and I am bound by it. I set possibilities in motion. They must work themselves out in their own way."

"Why, then, choose me?"

"Choose?" Jaya raised an eyebrow. "Do you suppose you were the only king to play *aksha* with me?

"There were others I visited before you," Jaya continued. "Some declined the game and I went my way. Of those who lost, some refused to honor their pledge. Others tried to keep their word. They lost their lives in the course of their journey, or gave up before it ended. Your kingdom was the last, the least, at which I stopped.

"Take no offense," Jaya added. "You simply happened to be available."

"No more than that?"

"No more than that—at the beginning. At the end, you became a great deal more."

So many questions began jostling into his mind that Tamar was at a loss which to ask first. Meantime, an eagle had glided through the casement. The bird's feathers shone golden, glistening in the sunlight as it flew straight to Mirri's shoulder.

"I'm sorry I couldn't stay with you lot," the bird said. "Did you ever have a ruby stuck in your throat? It hurts. I needed my master's help right away."

"Garuda?" Mirri cried. "Is that you?"

"Shmaa! Who else?"

"It's him," said Hashkat. "I'd know that 'Shmaa' anywhere."

"You're beautiful," said Mirri. "You look—not like yourself at all."

"On the contrary, he looks exactly like himself," Jaya said. "As once he was, so he is again. I admit he was a pitiful sight. I took out the stone—no harm done."

Garuda bobbed his shining head. "I owe you. All of you."

"I, too," Jaya said. "His task was even more important than your own." He opened his hand. The ruby lay like a flame cupped in his palm. "The Fire Flower, as you call it, has come back to me. Had it not, King of Sundari, the consequences would have been far worse than anything Nahusha could have done.

"Even the Naga Raja did not guess its power. The *rakshasa* who stole it from me understood it very well. He had not learned how to make it serve him. In time, he would have done so. Then all would have been lost.

"The Fire Flower is a gem of death—and of life," Jaya went on. "Whoever learns to use it can, within an instant, call down death on anyone he chooses; or, if he so wishes, summon the dead to life. With it, the *rakshasa* would have held the world and all its creatures in bondage."

"And I carried such a gem," Tamar murmured, "never knowing what it was."

"Just as well you did not," Jaya said. "Even to suspect its nature would have been a temptation to use it. Such power is too great for anyone to hold."

"Now you have it again," Mirri said. "It's in safe hands."

"No, it is not," Jaya said. "When it was in my possession, even I found myself drawn to use it. Its flame whispered and beckoned; my heart hungered for it. I told myself I would make it serve only good: Yet, I knew, in time I might not be able to tell good from evil—and do evil, telling myself I was doing good.

"I sent Garuda to regain it for me." Jaya fixed his eyes on the Fire Flower. The man's face, Tamar saw, clouded with regret close to grief. "It draws me, still. I do as I must."

He set the ruby on the flagstone floor and trampled it under his heel.

The gem remained unbroken.

"How can this be?" Jaya murmured. "Have I no strength to shatter it?"

There was fear in the man's voice that Tamar had never heard before. Jaya stared down at the Fire Flower:

"Does a hidden corner of my heart yet wish to keep it? And holds me back, at the end, from destroying it?" Jaya put his palms together and pressed them to his brow. "May I do this in all purity, without misgivings. May this truly be my will, fully and completely."

Jaya drew a long breath and, again, trampled the gem with all his might. Tamar threw up his hands to shield his eyes against the sudden, blinding shaft of crimson flame. It shot upward, whirled in a blazing cloud, then burst and filled the chamber with jagged streaks of scarlet. That same instant,

Tamar felt the ground heave and shudder beneath his feet: a long, sickening tremor as if a crack had opened in the earth.

Wind shrieked in his ears. He flung himself toward Mirri and held her as the chamber seemed to tilt askew. Everything blurred, turned fluid and shapeless. His heart pounded: Each beat took forever, as if time itself had ripped apart.

Then, within the moment, the room was clear and sunlit again. Jaya was standing, head bowed. Of the Fire Flower, there remained only a little heap of red powder.

"It is done." Jaya, after some while, looked up. "I am free of it. Leave me. I wish to be alone with my meditations.

"Our dealings with each other have well ended. Return safely, all of you. I promise your journey will be quicker and gentler than the paths that brought you here.

"Take with you my love and gratitude. You, *suta*, what may I offer you in token? What is your fondest wish?"

Adi-Kavi shrugged. "I've been cursed—and blessed—with curiosity. I'd ask only that I never lose it. Apart from that—as a matter of curiosity—I'd wish to know why Mahapura, so empty of people, is filled with their voices, and your palace with illusions."

"Illusions are made to be seen through, as you did," Jaya said, "and the city is not empty. You have yet to see all that lies beyond your vision. As you will, be sure of it. You see the world as it is; someday you will see it as it might be.

"As for you, Hashkat," Jaya said, hiding a twinkle behind a stern glance, "I suspect you are as impudent now as when first we met. Even so, you have been punished long enough. Monkey, I restore you to your human shape."

"Hold on a minute," Hashkat broke in. "I appreciate

your kindness, but—no, thank you. I've seen enough of humans and their doings. I'm happy as I am. I'll stay a monkey.

"What I might ask, what I've missed more than anything," Hashkat added, "is—my tail. If you could possibly arrange—"

"Your wish is already granted."

Hashkat twisted his head around and whooped with delight to see his tail, longer and more luxuriant than it had ever been.

"And you, King of Sundari? And you, his beloved *gopi,* what are your wishes?"

"For myself?" Mirri said, with loving eyes on Tamar. "All I could wish, I have."

"I, too," said Tamar. "For my kingdom, I wish it to be happy, its people loving and merciful toward each other. I wish there to be an end of caste, a time when *chandala*s will be as honored and cherished as all others."

"I am sorry. I cannot grant that wish," Jaya said. "Only you and your *gopi* bride, and those who come after you, can make it come true.

"But you will not go empty-handed. One thing I give you." Jaya went to a side table and took up a wreath of flowers, still fragrant and unwithered.

"I wove this," Mirri murmured. "I thought it had been long lost."

"Only waiting for you," Jaya said. "Set it now around your beloved's neck. These blossoms that you picked once will never fade."

As Mirri did so, Jaya turned to Rajaswami. *"Brahmana,* what is your own heart's wish?"

"Why—I hadn't really given it much thought," Rajaswami answered. "Since everything's come out on the bright side, I'm quite satisfied. All I would hope is to visit my dear colleague, Jamba-Van, again."

"So you shall," Jaya said. "When the time comes, you will know it is the moment for you to go once more into the forest. You will find the bear's *ashrama*. He will be awaiting you, and there will you stay to your heart's content.

"And so shall you all," Jaya added. "I built the *ashrama* for travelers like yourselves. Your paths will lead you there, if you so desire.

"You, Tamar, and you, Mirri, will find the island where once you danced. You will dance there as you did, and your hearts will ever be those of young lovers. *Forever then, forever once again.*"

"You know the verses we spoke to each other?" said Mirri.

Jaya smiled. "I was the flute player in the shadows." He pressed his palms together. "Go in peace. *Namaste.*"

"Ah—one thing did occur to me," said Rajaswami. "Only a passing thought, a triviality. I wonder—no, no, never mind. It's of no importance."

"On the contrary," said Jaya. "I'd not have let you leave without it."

He went again to the table. "Things that are lost have a way of turning up here. I believe this is yours," he added, putting an object in Rajaswami's hands, as the *acharya* beamed with delight.

It was a white umbrella.

—◆—

Glossary

acharya (ah-*char*-yah): teacher, scholar, spiritual counselor

aksha (*ahk*-shah): gambling game involving dice-throwing

ashrama (ahsh-*rah*-mah): secluded forest retreat for study and meditation, hermitage

Bandar-loka (*ban*-dahr *loh*-kah): kingdom of the monkeys, monkey-folk

brahmana (brah-*mah*-nah): member of highest caste of priests, scholars, philosophers

caste: ancient system of class structure and social order. Of highest rank, the *brahmana*s—scholars, priests, philosophers. Next, the military class of warriors, *kshatriya*s. Third, *vaishya*s, merchants and farm owners. Last and lowest, the *shudra*s, peasants and unskilled laborers. Excluded from the caste structure were the shunned "untouchables," the *panchama*s or *pariah*s, who performed the most menial, undesirable, distasteful work; still lower and most degraded, even criminals, were the *chandala*s.

chakra (*chah*-krah): sharp-edged discus thrown as a weapon

chandala (*chahn*-dah-lah): lowest, most despised, and degraded outcast

dharma (*dahr*-mah): goodness, virtue, righteousness, conscience; a code of proper conduct, a deep and driving sense of obligation to do what is right

durbar (*duhr*-bahr): royal court, assembly, audience

gopi (*goh*-pee): young woman cow-tender, milkmaid, dairy-maid

karma (*kahr*-mah): series of deeds and actions with their consequences; loosely, "fate," or the actions that are the contents of one's fate

kshatriya (kuh-*shah*-tree-yah): warrior, of the high military caste

maharajah (masc.), maharani (fem.) (mah-ha-*rah*-jah, mah-ha-*rah*-nee): great king, great queen; exalted ruler

mahout (mah-*hoot*): elephant driver

maya (*mah*-yah): illusion, spell, enchantment

Naga-loka (*nah*-gah *loh*-kah): serpent kingdom, serpent-folk

namaste (nah-*mah*-stay): expression of respect, honor, reverence; shown by pressing one's palms together

nayka (*nah*-ee-kah): army corporal

pye-dog (pie dog): wild, scavenging dog

raja (masc.), rani (fem.) (*rah*-jah, *rah*-nee): king, queen; powerful ruler

rakshasa (rahk-*shah*-sah): evil demon, able to assume human or animal shape

rishi (*ree*-shee): sage, of great wisdom and spiritual powers

sankula (*sahn*-koo-lah): violent combat; vicious free-for-all fight where no rules of war are observed

shmashana (shmah-*shah*-nah): cremation area where bodies are ceremonially burned

shudra (*shoo*-drah): peasant, unskilled laborer, member of lowest caste or social standing

suta (*soo*-tah): court attendant who declaims praises for a king

Lloyd Alexander's interest in the world's mythology has provided the inspiration for many of his greatest books. The author's numerous honors include a Newbery Medal for *The High King,* a Newbery nomination for *The Black Cauldron*—both in the Prydain Chronicles—and National Book Awards for *The Marvelous Misadventures of Sebastian* and *Westmark.*

His most recent novels, *The Arkadians* and *The Remarkable Journey of Prince Jen,* and his series of books about the heroine Vesper Holly are also beloved. He lives with his wife, Janine, and his cats in Drexel Hill, Pennsylvania.